ABO[UT THE AUTHOR]

Les Daniels wrote [... Frank]enstein and has been [...] since. He is the a[uthor of ... fi]ction studies *Living in Fear: [A Hi]story of Horror in the Mass Media*, *Comix: A History of Comic Books in America*, and the international bestseller *Marvel: Five Fabulous Decades of the World's Greatest Comics*. The editor of *Dying of Fright: Masterpieces of the Macabre* and *Thirteen Tales of Terror* (with Diane Thompson), his short fiction has appeared in many major anthologies on both sides of the Atlantic. The next Don Sebastian novel, *Yellow Fog*, is scheduled for publication by Raven Books in 1995. The author lives in Providence, Rhode Island.

3 COMPLETE NOVELS IN ONE VOLUME

The Don Sebastian Vampire Chronicles

LES DANIELS

RAVEN BOOKS
London

Robinson Publishing Ltd
7 Kensington Church Court
London W8 4SP

This collected edition first published in the UK by Raven Books, an imprint of Robinson Publishing Ltd, 1994

The Black Castle copyright © Les Daniels 1978
The Silver Skull copyright © Les Daniels 1979
Citizen Vampire copyright © Les Daniels 1981

The right of Les Daniels to be identified as the author of this work has been asserted in accordance with the Copyright, Designs and Patents Act 1988.

All rights reserved. This book is sold subject to the condition that it shall not, by way of trade or otherwise, be lent, re-sold, hired out or otherwise circulated in any form of binding or cover other than that in which it is published and without a similar condition including this condition being imposed on the subsequent purchaser.

A copy of the British Library Cataloguing in Publication data is available from the British Library.

ISBN 1-85487-343-1

Printed by HarperCollins, Glasgow

10 9 8 7 6 5 4 3 2 1

The Black Castle

1. Five Gold Coins

FIFTEEN MEN and women, naked to the waist, marched through the streets of the city. Each of them held an unlit green candle. Behind them walked men with whips, their faces hidden by black hoods. The leather thongs flailed at bare and bloody backs, and every stroke was answered by stifled cries and groans, yet the penitents never ceased their mumbled prayers.

Carlos Diaz watched intently as he leaned against a whitewashed wall warmed by the bright morning sun.

"Jews," he muttered, and spat in the hot dust at his feet.

This was his epithet for all heretics, but he knew that the people who passed before him could hardly be guilty of practicing the forbidden religion or they would not have escaped with a punishment as light as the Shame. It had been four years since Torquemada, the Inquisitor General, had persuaded the king and queen to expel the Jews. Those who had not fled Spain had become New Christians, and any sign of backsliding meant not just public humiliation but almost certain death.

Death. Carlos licked his thick lips at the sight of the half-naked women, and thought of the future.

This was Friday; in nine days there would be something really worth seeing. The Inquisition had announced an *auto-da-fé*, an act of faith, and that meant a real spectacle. Not a passing glimpse of pain like this, but a full Sunday of processions and penances climaxed when the worst of the sinners were consigned to the flames.

And some of them, thought Carlos with the satisfaction of a job well done, would be there because of information he had supplied.

The penitents and their tormentors passed him by. Carlos was tempted to follow, to join the crowd that jeered and gaped, but he had other business that was more important. There might be money in it.

He looked across the plaza, but the man he expected was nowhere to be seen. But the Grand Inquisitor would surely cross the square soon, and he would surely be pleased to hear what Carlos had to say. Discovering a dozen heretics would have been enough for Carlos, but he suspected that he had done even more. His foot tapped impatiently.

A fly buzzing overhead dropped and began to crawl across his bald pate. He brushed it away with fat fingers.

Two figures appeared in the entrance of the gray cathedral across the way. They were dressed in the habits of Dominican monks, with black cowls, and white robes tied at the waist with lengths of hemp. As they descended the marble steps to the street, Carlos approached them with studied nonchalance.

The younger of the two monks raised his eyes from their modest contemplation of the ground. Before him stood a short, heavy man of fifty, his face red and his jowls quivering with agitation. His clothes were soiled and he stank of wine.

The young Dominican turned to his superior. So did Carlos Diaz.

"Friar," said Carlos, "I must speak with you. I have seen something."

Diego de Villanueva, Grand Inquisitor, cast a cold eye on the informer.

"Not now," he said. "You should know better than to talk to me like this where anyone might see you. Your own safety is at stake. Come to me this evening, and do not serve yourself so generously with the wine you sell or I may be forced to doubt the tale you tell me."

Carlos opened his mouth to reply, thought better of it, and hurried away, glancing from side to side as though expecting an ambush.

"Not a pleasant fellow, but a useful one," observed the Grand Inquisitor as they continued down the street. "He keeps a small inn and drinks most of the profits, but he has a sharp eye, and sometimes he hears the loose talk his business breeds. Now that you are my vicar, Miguel, you will doubtless see him many times again. His word has sent more than one sinner into the Holy House, and he must be counted a servant of the faith."

The Grand Inquisitor paused. "Yet sometimes I think it is not piety that prompts such service. Carlos Diaz is a good Christian, I suppose, certainly a careful one, and perhaps he seeks to make amends for the small sins that he commits. But he seems to take a strange delight in the suffering that must be the lot of the unrepentant heretic. There is some malice in him, not just the unsullied desire to rid Spain of heresy and save what souls we can. Still, his information has always been accurate, and we cannot expect each man to be a saint. He contributes in his own way to our glorious endeavor."

Miguel Carillo, lately appointed vicar to the Grand Inquisitor, nodded gravely but did not speak. Silence seemed best in the presence of such a man famed for his sanctity and feared for his severity. Miguel himself was still a bit afraid of him, even after almost a month in his service, for Diego de Villanueva was no ordinary Inquisitor. The man who walked beside Miguel had studied under no less a teacher than Tomás de Torquemada, the founder of the Inquisition, and had been received at the court of Ferdinand and Isabella.

In fact, it was remarkable that Diego de Villanueva had sought a post in a district as small and remote as this one. He was of a wealthy and powerful family; his lineage alone was sufficient to guarantee him comfortable employment in one of the great cities of Spain. For a man of his background and ability to be so far from the centers of power was little short of a scandal, yet the choice had been his own. Perhaps a sense of duty had sent him back to the city of his birth, for he watched over its people as surely as did the ancestral castle of the de Villanuevas, which had stood empty since the death of his elder brother.

Such a man was to be Miguel's instructor in the

mysteries of the Inquisition. Miguel glanced at him furtively. The face of the Grand Inquisitor was almost entirely hidden by his black cowl, but Miguel needed hardly a glimpse-to remind him of the expansive brow, long straight nose, and thin lips. The face haunted the young vicar, yet the features themselves did not disturb him. It was their expression, or rather lack of it. The face might have been a mask; only the large, luminous eyes seemed alive.

Miguel kept his eyes on the Grand Inquisitor's long shadow as they walked together toward the Holy House. Diego de Villanueva towered over Miguel as he did over most men; he was tall and strong enough to have been a soldier like his elder brother.

As Miguel thought of the soldier, he wondered whether there might be armor beneath his superior's robe. He had heard of one Inquisitor who had saved himself from assassination with such protection and of others who had died for lack of it. Of course, he could find out easily enough—all he had to do was reach out his hand . . .

No. He could not do that. Besides, there was no need. Miguel believed that the Grand Inquisitor was above such devices, and his belief was sufficient. It was as ridiculous to picture armor beneath that habit as to imagine the silk undergarments that some monks were rumored to wear to protect their skins from the coarse cloth of their robes. Miguel did not need to know what lay beneath those dark folds, or behind that dark mask . . .

Where did such thoughts come from? They could not be his own; they were too close to blasphemy. Miguel felt that he was plagued by demons, yet he hardly had the pride to imagine that agents of the pit would bother with him.

Still, there was no need to consider the source of the attack; it was enough to know the best defense. His lips moved silently. He did not merely chant but prayed with his whole being. The sonorous Latin lines were soothing in themselves, but they served their purpose better when he remembered what they meant, when he spoke to the Savior and the Blessed Virgin, and his doubts drifted back into the darkness from which they had come.

"Miguel!"

The young monk started at the sound of his name. He turned and saw the Grand Inquisitor standing before the Holy House. Miguel's thoughts had carried him past his destination.

"I'm sorry. I was praying, and I didn't realize we were here."

"Such devotion is laudable, no doubt, yet we are here not only to dream of Heaven but to do Heaven's work. There is much to be done. Come."

They passed down a long row of pillars and through a massive door carved with images of sad-eyed saints.

Once out of the sun and in the cool, damp, musty building, Miguel felt more at peace with himself. Something had disturbed him, perhaps the manner of the innkeeper Carlos Diaz, but Miguel would have no time for suspicion or skepticism while he labored over the records of the Inquisition. Work was more than a duty; it was a remedy.

The last rays of the dying sun pressed through the stained-glass window, casting cold colors on the walls of the room where Miguel sat at the end of a large table. His left hand supported his head and the fingers of his ink-stained right hand were cramped around a bedraggled quill pen.

He had been there for hours, and the peace of mind that his efforts brought had gradually given way to dull exhaustion. His day began at dawn, and an afternoon spent poring over transcripts of sin and its punishment had left him feeling numb and stupid. His only desire was that his superior should come to dismiss him.

But when the Grand Inquisitor entered, it was for a different purpose. "The innkeeper, Carlos Diaz, has come to see me," he announced, "and I want you to hear what he says. Your duties involve more than studying and recording what has already been done, and this may well be your first chance to follow a case of heresy from start to finish."

He glanced almost contemptuously at the records

scattered over the long table while Miguel pulled himself to his feet, as if to offer his superior the chair. The Grand Inquisitor remained standing, however, and waited quietly until an anonymously hooded figure ushered Diaz into the room.

"Sit there," said the Grand Inquisitor, and the informer sank into the seat, visibly agitated. He was obliged to look up at the two standing monks, and Miguel wondered whether it might be part of a useful technique to tower above witnesses, thus increasing their sense of inferiority.

"Now speak," said Diego de Villanueva.

Carlos had changed his clothing and appeared to be reasonably sober, but he was hardly composed. He squirmed in his chair and cleared his throat before he began to talk.

"I have heard that you are concerned; that is, I have heard you talk of a special heresy—not just these Jews and freethinkers, but something more dangerous—and more evil. I have tried for months to hear some hint, but there has been nothing. But then last night—it was quite by accident, I assure you!—I came upon this ultimate blasphemy. I tell you, Friar, and may God be my witness, I have seen the Anti-Christ!"

Miguel crossed himself hurriedly and stepped back to lean against the cool wall behind him. He had no wish to know of such a horror. And yet, as he looked at his superior, he noticed a gleam in those dark eyes that he had never seen before.

The room was growing dim and the world outside was silent. Carlos wiped the sweat from his face with a fat hand.

"Continue," said Diego.

"Well, you know I have a weakness for wine. I will not lie to you about it, though I hope to reform. I drank too much last night, and there was a quarrel at home . . . no matter. So I went out, and I was drunk. I wandered through the streets. Thank the saints I was not set upon and robbed. Yet that might have been better than what happened. I had a wineskin with me and I walked clean out of the city. Finally, I fell asleep under a tree somewhere."

"Is this but a drunkard's dream?"

"No, Friar! I swear it! I was asleep, but something woke me. My head ached and my ears rang with the noise, but it was no dream. I wish to the Lord it had been. And yet, if I had slept on just a little longer, I think I might have died for it and been dragged straight to Hell by the fiends I saw. It was horrible.

"Oh, I know you despise me for being drunk. I saw the way you looked at me this morning; but if you had seen what I saw, you would have had a few yourself. I mean, not that you would, but Christ, it was horrible. It's hard enough for a man to be a spy and fight against these fools with their false beliefs, but this was something different. I have seen the witches at worship and I have seen the Devil himself."

Carlos Diaz looked up at the Grand Inquisitor and waited for some reaction, but there was none. Diego de Villanueva stood quite still and simply said, "Go on."

"I think it was the music that woke me. There was a beating of drums and tambourines and I heard shouting and singing, but most of all there was the sound of pipes, loud shrill pipes, playing a wild tune like nothing I had ever heard before.

"I didn't know what it was, I was still half-fuddled with drink, but I peered round the tree and there in a hollow I saw the witches at play. There must have been a dozen of them, dancing naked in the moonlight. And seated before them was a creature with the head of a goat. It had two great horns, and a flame burned between them.

"I just stood and stared for a moment—I couldn't believe what I was seeing. And then I turned and ran back to the inn, and roused the boy to open the door. This morning I came to find you."

"Is that all, man? What else did you see? Where was it?"

"I swear before God I don't know. I came there in a fog and left in a panic. I don't know how I found my way home—some saint must have guided me—but I know that I could never find that place again. It was somewhere in the forest, near your dead brother's castle, rest his soul."

"You need not concern yourself with the soul of my

brother Sebastian," said the Grand Inquisitor. "I want to know about the souls of those involved in these devilish rites. Did you recognize anyone? Can you give me a name?"

"I did see one," Carlos confessed, "otherwise I might not have come. I might have been too frightened or have convinced myself it was only a dream. But I saw her face and knew it was my duty to tell you, even though I have no hope of reward this side of Heaven."

"Our rewards sometimes come sooner than we expect," said the Grand Inquisitor evenly."

Carlos felt his pulse quicken. That might have been a threat, a hint that his life would not be a long one, but it might have been a promise that his tale had some value. In any case, he could hardly expect to hear more. Still, he had known from the beginning that he would have to give the name, and only some delight in his own importance kept him from blurting it out at once.

"They were masked," continued Carlos. "All of them were naked, but their faces were covered. For an instant I took them for monsters, but then I saw that they wore false faces. I'm not sure I realized it till this one took off her mask.

"Most of them were women. There were a few men, but most of them were women, and old hags at that. They danced together strangely, back to back, and thrust their hands between their legs to hold their partners. This one danced alone, though, and she was young, so I noticed her especially.

"She had long black hair streaming out from behind the face of a monster. She ran up to the goat-thing and embraced him, then tore off her mask to give him a kiss. I could see her clearly in the light from the fire between his horns.

"It was Margarita de Mendoza.

"When I saw that, I turned and ran. She was kissing that thing! And that is all I know, Friar."

Carlos Diaz sighed and sat back with the satisfaction of a man who has completed a heroic task. By now the room was almost dark. He was suddenly anxious to be gone, to retreat to the security of his inn and the wine waiting there, but he sensed unhappily that the Grand Inquisitor was not yet ready to dismiss him.

"Margarita de Mendoza," repeated the Grand Inquisitor. "You say you recognized her. How do you know her?"

"Oh, you must know her too, sir. She is a Conversa, a New Christian. Her mother was a Christian but her father was a Jew, and when the king and queen signed the edict outlawing the Jews her parents fled Spain, as did so many others.

"That was in 1492, when this Margarita had just come of age, and she chose to stay here and be baptized into the Church. She was a beauty and had just become betrothed to a young man from a good family. No doubt she thought she had reason to stay, but she was fooled." Carlos laughed and slapped his thigh.

"The young man, or perhaps his family, reconsidered the matter of Margarita's tainted blood and she never became his bride, nor anyone else's, for that matter. Of course, her father's property was confiscated and she was left with nothing."

"I don't know if I remember her family," said the Grand Inquisitor. "So many fled four years ago, and of course those Jews who chose exile are no longer the business of the Inquisition. But with no family and no property, how does this woman live? And how do you know her face so well?"

"Well, as for that, she was saved from the streets by some relative of her Christian mother who gave her a little plot of land. It might have been only to prevent her disgrace from becoming too public. She lives outside the city in a hut and raises sheep. She lives like an animal, though once she thought herself some sort of lady. What made me sick, though, when I saw her face, was the thought that I buy my mutton from her for the inn. God knows what kind of meat I have eaten!"

The Grand Inquisitor regarded Carlos sternly. "You are, then, prepared to testify that this woman has been seen engaged in these obscene rites?"

"I am, yes . . . in secret, of course, that is," mumbled Carlos.

"You know that you have nothing to fear on that account. The Holy Office has no wish to expose its friends to its enemies. Margarita de Mendoza will never learn the name of her accuser."

"But there must be two witnesses, must there not?"

"I will attend to that. If what you say is true—and God help you if it is not—there will be evidence, and the one who finds it will be able to testify. You need not concern yourself further. Miguel!"

The young monk emerged from the shadows by the wall.

"You will prepare a deposition," Miguel's superior said, "setting forth the facts in the proper form; do it this evening. And you, Carlos Diaz," he said, addressing the informer, who had risen from his seat and was moving as imperceptibly as possible toward the door, "you will return here tomorrow to sign it. I need hardly caution you to mention this matter to no one. And beware of the wine."

Carlos was as startled by this last suggestion as if the Grand Inquisitor had read his mind. Perhaps he had. Carlos stood nervously, half bowing and half backing out of the room, until a gesture of dismissal sent him through the door, moving at last with undisguised alacrity.

Outside, a moment later, the pleasure Carlos felt at escaping that penetrating gaze began to give way to another sort of anxiety. He was no longer in the sanctuary of the Inquisition but was alone on a dark street far from home.

A sudden clanging broke through the silence and Carlos jumped, but he realized at once that it was only a bell calling the monks to evening prayers.

The street was full of shadows. It was always unwise to be out at night, but more so, thought Carlos, for a man who bore witness against witches. He pictured again that midnight scene, the horror of it tempered by the vision of a lithe and lovely figure lost in some wicked ecstasy, throwing her arms around a horned monster. He began to wish he had not run so soon. What would he have seen if he had stayed?

Some faint flame of lust gave him courage as he walked. It was not the first time he had felt this way about Margarita de Mendoza, who came often to his inn, but only for business.

A year ago he had tried his luck with her. After all, she was only a peasant dressed in rags, and he would have been generous to her. But she had snatched his fumbling hand from her bosom and buried her strong white teeth in his thumb, almost to the bone.

God, she was strong for a woman! While he had stared astounded at his bleeding hand, she had kicked him twice, then knocked him to the ground with a hindquarter of mutton. She had spat upon him and called him foul names. Carlos had been afraid that she would kill him but more afraid that his wife might hear the commotion.

Still, the whole affair had taken only a minute, and Margarita had stormed away without waiting to be paid for the meat. On the whole, Carlos had come out of it fairly well. His thumb had not become infected, despite his fears, and business with Margarita had continued as before. Her mutton was cheap and she needed his money, but he did not like the look of contempt on her face when they met after that day.

It would be a pleasure to see the slut do her last dance in the flames of the *auto-da-fé*. There were other shepherds.

He hoped that incident would not come out when Margarita was put to the Question. He knew the accused were always asked to name their enemies, and it might mean a bit of trouble if she named him, since it could cast suspicion on his testimony. Did the Grand Inquisitor suspect already? What else could have made him so cold and ungrateful? For this sort of information Carlos expected praise and thanks, and perhaps something more. He would have sworn that Diego de Villanueva wanted a witch, and now he had one.

Carlos Diaz, though, had nothing, and he had put his life in danger. He hoped Margarita would be arrested before he saw her again. He did not know if he could face her. He wondered what kind of magic she possessed. Would he be safe from her spells? He pictured her laughing as she slaughtered sheep, her hands red and reeking.

A huge figure loomed up out of the darkness in front of Carlos and blocked his path.

Carlos gasped and started backward. He tried to speak, to protest his innocence, but no words came. He thought his tongue might be bewitched, and he fell on his knees before the shadowy giant.

Then he saw who it was. Carlos crossed himself in a prayer of thanks for his deliverance and rose unsteadily to his feet.

The man before him was Pedro Rodriguez. This massive old soldier, now a civilian, served the Inquisition and Friar Diego de Villanueva in the war against heretics. He was no stranger to Carlos or his inn.

Carlos started to speak, but Pedro pressed something into the informer's hand and turned away without a word.

Carlos was left alone with his thoughts and five gold coins. He should have known that the Grand Inquisitor would not forget him. It would have been undignified for the holy man himself to reward Carlos, but it was for such purposes, and for less pleasant ones, that civilians like Pedro were employed. These secular servants of the Inquisition were called familiars, Carlos knew—and didn't witches have familiars, too, imps in animal form that were also servants of Satan?

Carlos glanced around as though he expected to see one of the creatures, then cast the idea from his mind and scurried off toward the shelter of his inn.

2. Two Brothers in Black and White

THE CANDLES were lit now in the dark chamber of the Holy House, but they illuminated no more than a small area of the table where the young monk sat again, preparing to write the testimony of Carlos Diaz accusing Margarita de Mendoza of the crime of witchcraft.

Behind Miguel stood the Grand Inquisitor. Miguel bridled inwardly at the thought of being under observation, partly because he realized that he did not really know what to do next. His awe in the presence of his superior was giving way to fatigue and to fear of what he had heard. He did not want to write anymore, particularly about witches. His head ached. He had never transcribed such a deposition before and could not think of the proper form to begin it, though he was certain there must be a good example in the records piled in front of him.

He turned toward the older man. He wanted either to register a protest or ask for advice but was prevented from doing either by the sight of a large leather-bound volume that the Grand Inquisitor held out to him.

"Here," said Diego. "Take this and study it. It will help you to prepare for the work we are about to undertake."

"But the testimony of the witness Diaz . . . you said I should have it ready for tomorrow morning."

"That will be attended to in due course. In truth, the evidence must be given again when Diaz returns tomorrow. I did tell him we would need only his signature, but it is sometimes necessary to veil the truth when dealing with nervous informers. We must adhere to the proper procedure, especially in such an extraordinary case as this. The testimony must be given before assembled officers of the Inquisition, taken down verbatim, and subjected to rigorous cross-examination. There must be no room for error. I am sure that Carlos Diaz knows all this—he has been a witness before—but it reassures him to think that he can escape his responsibilities so easily, and this assures his prompt appearance. There must be no delay."

Miguel took the heavy book in his hands and set it down upon the table. Opening it carefully, he saw that it was printed in Latin, in the black letters of the German presses.

"*Malleus Maleficarum,*" he read. "*The Hammer of Witches?*"

"It was first published ten years ago in Germany. It is sadly lacking in some areas of the greatest interest and importance, but at the present time it is the most complete study on the subject of witchcraft, especially its investigation and suppression. Its authors are two Germans, brothers of our own Dominican order, Heinrich Kramer and Jacob Sprenger.

"Their work has brought them recognition and influence throughout their native land and far beyond. The book has been published in Germany, France, and Italy, and it includes a bull of Pope Innocent VIII commending their efforts and granting them extraordinary jurisdiction to prosecute witches throughout Germany."

"Then are there so many witches?" Miguel asked apprehensively.

"More than any man knows. This most devilish and damnable of heresies rages throughout Europe. Thousands of witches have been detected and destroyed. Yet here in Spain, where our Inquisition is so zealous in protecting the faith, not one witch has been taken."

"Then is this woman the beginning of it here?"

"Who knows? Some say this is a new evil which Satan has unleashed upon our weary world. It must have begun somewhere; perhaps it has not spread far into our land. Yet it infests France, and here in this district we have only a few miles of mountain ranges between ourselves and that bedeviled kingdom. The Pyrenees are hardly high enough to protect us from this spreading infection. I knew the cult would spring up here—it was the reason I requested jurisdiction here—and now it has come. And I am ready. What glory there will be in exposing this evil, and in purging it!"

Miguel viewed the prospect with less enthusiasm. He was glad enough to learn that he would not have to spend the evening transcribing the informer's testimony, but he took no pleasure in the idea of battling black magic. It was one thing to seek out those who were not good Christians and punish those who would not repent, but what sort of business was this? These witches might be more than fools and infidels. Who knew what powers they might possess? The answers, he feared, were in the massive volume that Diego had entrusted to his care.

Sometimes he wished he had not become a monk, or at least that some half-hearted ambition had not led him into the service of the Inquisition. Yet how many choices were there for a younger son who had inherited nothing?

He reflected on the fact that Diego de Villanueva had been in the same position but had nonetheless risen to eminence. Perhaps in this coincidence Miguel could find a topic for conversation, for he was undoubtedly expected to reply to his superior's unwonted enthusiasm but had no wish to talk of witches.

"He said he saw them near your brother's castle," ventured Miguel.

"What? Yes, somewhere in the forest outside the city. Some of them, perhaps, dwell in the mountains nearby."

"They say he was a great soldier, your brother," Miguel persisted.

"Yes," replied the Grand Inquisitor with an air of doubtful pride. "A great soldier and a great scholar, too."

"A scholar? I never heard that said of him."

"There were few who knew him well," said the Grand Inquisitor. "He was much alone. The castle was never a manor house surrounded by the homes of serfs and vassals; it was a true fortress, built to guard the French border. Troops were quartered there years ago but there never was an attack from the north, and the commander, my brother Don Sebastian, spent much time among his books, especially after the death of his young wife. With her died our family, for she bore no sons and Sebastian never wed again. Instead, he shut himself up in the topmost room of the topmost tower and there pondered the mysteries of creation."

"He studied natural philosophy?"

"Among other things. No one really knows. His aim, it seems, was not to add to the wisdom of the world but only to satisfy himself regarding some secrets of his own soul. It was a fruitless quest, and he seems to have realized as much, for when there was a call to arms he answered it. And so he died."

"Fighting the Moors, was it not?"

"At the siege of Malaga in 1487. They say it was a glorious day for Spain, a great defeat for those pagan invaders who had occupied our lands for centuries. It was an even greater day five years later when Granada surrendered without a fight and all of Spain was Christian again, but the reconquest began in earnest at Malaga."

"Malaga," echoed the young monk, filled with vague visions of half-remembered glories.

"You must have been little better than a boy then, Miguel, but the stories of the siege should be familiar even to you: how the king led the soldiers into battle and how the queen, with all the ladies of her court, attended the troops and urged them on to glory. In the front ranks was Don Sebastian de Villanueva, who traveled the length of Spain, from this northeastern corner to the plains of the southwest, there to meet his death."

"But was it not a noble death?" asked Miguel.

"Not, I think, what a true knight might have wished. I have been told, by those who claim to know such things, that this was the first battle in our land where guns and powder were well employed. I know nothing of that, but I do know that one cannon had some flaw in its construction and exploded in my brother's face. Without their leader, his men were easy prey for the Moors, and most of them were slain. Sebastian, with his shattered face, lingered raving for days. He was carried from the siege by the most steadfast of his followers, Pedro Rodriguez, but it was in vain. I never saw my brother alive again."

"Is this the same Pedro . . . ?"

"It is. He now serves me in the army of the Lord, as he once served Sebastian in the army of the king. It was he who brought my brother's body home and entombed him in the crypt beneath the castle."

"But is there no heir?"

"I might have been the heir had I not become a monk. Or the Crown might have confiscated the estate, but that would have been an ill reward for Sebastian's service. As things stand, it is a matter for the courts and magistrates, and their deliberations are rarely speedy. I believe there is a distant cousin somewhere who has a claim, but he has not been easy to find and no one seems to care to seek him out. Until he is discovered, I am caretaker of the castle."

"You mean you visit it?" gasped Miguel.

"From time to time."

"But there may be witches about!"

"All the more reason for me to watch the castle and the countryside around it. Seeking out these wretches is our duty, and we cannot expect much help from the people. If Carlos Diaz told the truth—and I believe he did—there is a cult around us, yet no one has come forward. And someone must have known! They are quick enough to inform on heretics; perhaps they fear some magical revenge from the witches. So we must take this Margarita de Mendoza at once and use her quickly. If she names the others, we shall take them all. If she will not speak, we shall make an example of her and prove to those whose tongues are frozen with fear that the Inquisition is stronger than black magic. Why do you look so pale and stupid, boy?"

"We are stronger, surely?"

"To doubt it would be heresy."

"You spoke of taking them all," said Miguel. "Even the one with the horns? Even a demon, perhaps the Devil himself?"

The Grand Inquisitor reflected on this. "I do not

know," he replied evenly. "But you must not be too credulous. Since there are witches, there may be demons among them, yet I have read that such creatures with the heads of goats are often only men in masquerade, deceiving others for the power it brings them. You need not expect to meet Satan face to face."

Miguel's relief was evident. He had been leaning toward the Grand Inquisitor, twisted tensely in his chair, but now he sat back relaxed and a small sigh escaped his dry lips.

"But we will meet Satan," continued Diego de Villanueva. "We meet him every day, for such is our task. He has no need to walk abroad on earth when there are so many men and women filled with his spirit and eager to obey him. This case is no different than any other.... And yet it is, for we have found the first witch in Spain. There is glory in it, for the Inquisition and for those who serve her.

"Take the book, Miguel. Go to your cell and read, and think on its authors, two humble Dominican brothers like ourselves, who have fought this evil and won fame and power for their work."

Miguel had almost caught his teacher's fever. Clasping the huge book to his chest, he passed through the door and into the gloomy hall beyond, its length composed of a series of vaulted arches. He was too caught up in his own thoughts to notice the dark figure standing in the shadows.

As the sound of Miguel's sandals flapping on the stone floor faded into the distance, Pedro Rodriguez stepped into the dimly lit room. He was a giant of a man with a seamed, sunburned face and streaks of gray in his heavy black beard. He stood filling the doorway like a soldier awaiting orders.

"Pedro," said the Grand Inquisitor. "You found Carlos Diaz?"

Pedro nodded.

"Good. It may be unorthodox to reward him, but he has done me a great service. You heard what he had to say?"

Pedro inclined his massive head again.

"Then you know how important it is. My chance has come at last, and it could hardly have come at a better time. I will be ready soon. What has been done in Germany can be done in Spain."

"Will you go to the castle?" asked Pedro.

"Yes, I must. Tonight. Saddle a horse for me, Pedro, and leave it in front of the Holy House. I will be ready to leave shortly."

"And the witch?"

"That must wait, if only for a day. There will be time enough after the accusation has been formally submitted. It will only be a few hours. Tomorrow night you will take what men you need to arrest Margarita de Mendoza."

"Men? To arrest one woman? Am I a weakling?"

"It is best to be cautious, Pedro. She may not be alone. Surely you know that I have confidence in you!"

"So be it, then I will get the horse."

An hour later, the Grand Inquisitor was riding through the foothills. Around him were the silent shapes of trees dimly illuminated by the distant moon. Beyond were the purple slopes of the Pyrenees and the castle of Don Sebastian.

The old mare knew the way as well as her rider did, and he was grateful for her solid strength beneath him. In other lands a monk might have been expected to show his humility by walking to his destination or at best riding a mule, but here in Spain the breeders of horses were so influential that it was considered unpatriotic to travel without the aid of their art.

Diego de Villanueva, well mounted, contemplated the pleasures of patriotism. It had brought him more than a mount; it had brought him a powerful position, and he was sure that greater rewards lay ahead. In Spain, as in no other country in Christendom, the interests of church and state were inextricably bound together. It was no coincidence that Torquemada, the Inquisitor General, had been Queen Isabella's confessor as well. The monarchs whose marriage had united Spain and whose battles had defeated the Moorish interlopers did not tolerate dissent. In 1492 Ferdinand and Isabella, at Torquemada's urging, had signed an edict outlawing the Jewish religion and there were whispers that the Moors would soon be forced to abandon their faith as well, despite promises made to them when they had surrendered Granada. Then they would be New Christians too, liable to persecution for heresy at the first sign of backsliding.

The queen was pious and wanted Spain united under God; the king was a politician and wanted Spain united under the Crown. Both their ambitions were well served by the Inquisition, and neither monarch had any cause to complain when the royal treasury was enriched, as it continually was, by the confiscated property of convicted heretics. Since there was no conflict between spiritual and temporal authority, as there was in so many areas of Europe, a man serving both masters, as Diego de Villanueva did, could rise to great heights.

He planned to become the greatest witch hunter in the world. With the support of the Inquisition, it seemed to him that he could hardly fail. For years he had studied every available source on the subject of witchcraft, not only books like the *Malleus Maleficarum* but forbidden texts that offered instruction in the practice of black magic. Now his own book was almost ready and he was certain that it would become the definitive work on the subject. He had information no other writer had ever used before, and now he had within his grasp the first member of the cult ever discovered in Spain.

The Grand Inquisitor trusted his mare, hardly troubling to watch the path. If Miguel were with him, he reflected, the boy would surely be peering through the trees, searching for witches lying in wait. Diego de Villanueva knew better. They had held their sabbat just the night before; they would hardly be abroad again the next night. He had nothing to fear from them, he thought, and much reason to be grateful.

He rode out from the shadows of the trees and up a bare slope awash in pale moonlight. At the crest of the slope stood the castle.

This black and forbidding edifice was dominated by a huge, square tower looming above the walls and dwarfing the smaller round towers at each corner of the castle. For centuries the great tower had stood alone, guarding a pass through the mountains. It now served as the keep of the castle, which had been built around it generations later from small stones mixed with clay and mortar. The stones that sheathed the ancient keep, however, were massive boulders buffeted by time. The old tower had frightened Diego de Villanueva when he was a boy, and he had never understood his elder brother's love for it.

A drawbridge guarded the only entrance to the courtyard. The Grand Inquisitor drew his horse up at the edge of the moat and stared down into the foul green water. He saw his own reflection and that of the white moon behind him, both obscured by floating scum. The water did not look deep, but a man who got into this moat would find it difficult to get out again. The castle, though small, had been built to withstand a siege; it was surely safe from trespassers. No crazed peasant women held their revels here.

A groan of wrenching wood sounded above the Grand Inquisitor's head and he heard chains rattling. He looked up to see the massive drawbridge dropping down upon him. The mare danced back skittishly as the wooden planks struck with a muddy thud on the bank of the moat.

Diego de Villanueva watched the gate swing ponderously open and he listened to the creak of heavy hinges. He peered into the shadowed blackness of the courtyard.

"Sebastian?" he called. There was no reply. "Sebastian?"

"Yes, brother," said a low voice, echoing from dark depths beyond the rough gray walls. "It is Sebastian. Who else would it be?"

The Grand Inquisitor gave no answer but urged his mount forward, across the drawbridge and into the castle.

3. Six Black Candles

PEDRO CURSED quietly at the sight of the sheep. They might as well have been watchdogs. There were dozens of them in the rude pen outside the wretched hut, and they had begun to mill around as soon as the men approached. Pedro realized that he and his two companions would have to wade through the nervous animals to get to the entrance to the hut. It would be noisy.

"Well," he said, "we'd better move quickly if we can't move quietly. She may be asleep now, but she'll be awake before we can get past that herd."

"We should be asleep ourselves," said one of the men. "This is no time of night for a man to be out. It looks like rain, too."

"Be quiet," Pedro said. "You're being paid well enough to stand here and grumble, aren't you?"

"I suppose so. Still, I wouldn't mind having one of those lambs. This Mendoza woman won't have much use for them where she's going."

"We're not thieves. We're here working for the Holy Office, and any confiscated property goes to the Inquisition. I don't want to see any stealing. Of course," Pedro continued a little less sternly, "one or two lambs might get lost after we take the prisoner. I have no orders to leave a guard here."

The second man looked happier, but the third continued to finger the hilt of his sword nervously. "Do we have to stand here talking all night? Let's get it done."

"Ready," said Pedro. "There should be just the woman, but watch out for others."

The three men stepped out from the sheltering trees. As they neared the pen they began to run, a futile burst of speed that only served to alarm the animals. The officers of the august Inquisition had to clamber over the rough-hewn wooden fence, then found themselves confronted by a shifting mass of bleating, woolly flesh. There seemed no room to move.

The beasts must be enchanted, thought Pedro, as he kicked at the sheep and beat them back with the flat of his sword. One of the men tripped over a frightened ewe and sprawled, swearing, in a pile of dung. Pedro, still a few yards from the door, was already bawling, "Open! Open in the name of the Inquisition!"

There was no response.

By the time Pedro reached the hut he was furious. He kicked in the ramshackle door without the now-foolish formality of a knock and stood panting on the threshold. His two companions were close behind him.

It was a warm summer night, but there were low flames in the fireplace of rough stones. Something was cooking in a black iron pot. There was not much else in the room: a table, a three-legged stool, and what looked, in the flickering amber light of the fire, like a pile of rags in the corner.

"Christ, it stinks in here," said the man who had fallen.

"You're no rose yourself," Pedro said, but he had to admit that there was something wrong with the smell of the place. It was not an honest odor like that of cooking or animals or unwashed human bodies.

"It's that witch's brew in the pot," said Pedro.

"Witches!" his two companions echoed in chorus, backing instinctively toward the door, and Pedro thought himself a fool for mentioning the word. They need not have known.

"Don't worry, you heroes," he snarled, hoping to stiffen their backbones. "There's nobody here."

He stepped over to the table. Piled on it was a strange assortment of leaves, roots, berries, and fungus, which he gathered up and carried to the fire for a closer look. From the Grand Inquisitor's instructions he recognized one plant, with black, shiny berries and red flowers shaped like bells.

"Belladonna," he said. He had no idea what it was, except that it was evidence. He peered into the pot at the congealed, sticky-looking liquid and nearly gagged at its sickening stench.

He stumbled away into the corner, then realized that the pile of rags there was alive.

"It's a woman," he said, dropping to his knees beside her.

Curiosity overcame fear as the others hurried to him. "Is she dead?"

"No," answered Pedro. "She's breathing. But she can't be asleep, after all the noise we made. . . . Ugh! She's covered with that stuff in the pot! Get me a light!"

One of the men picked up a stick of wood and thrust one end of it into the fire. A moment later he was holding a torch over Pedro's head.

Pedro saw a young woman whose tanned face was framed by a luxuriant mass of tangled black hair. Her lips were full, her cheekbones high, her closed eyes framed by dark brows and thick lashes. She might have been beautiful, but her face was smeared with the thick black slime from the pot.

Her arms and her long legs were similarly smeared; in fact, every inch of her body seemed covered. She wore only a ragged homespun shift of a drab color and lay on her back in a pile of sheepskins. Her breasts rose and fell with rapid, shallow breaths; there was sweat on her brow.

"Well, this must be Margarita de Mendoza," said Pedro. "Bring her along. Let's get out into the air."

The man covered with dung bent down, thrust his hands roughly under her armpits, and pulled her up. "What ails her?" he asked.

"Who knows?" said Pedro. "At least she won't give us any trouble."

As Margarita was dragged to her feet her eyes shot open, glazed and green as a cat's. She looked in dull surprise at her captors.

Pedro stood at the door, the black pot filled with herbs

in one hand. "You are in the hands of the Inquisition," he said.

Her expression did not change, but her right foot flashed out in a well-placed kick that sent the man before her crashing into the table, gasping with shock and pain.

"Bastards!" she screamed, breaking free of the startled man who held her. He fell back heavily into the fire and sat stupidly for a second in the flames. Then he jumped up shouting and cracked his head on the stone fireplace.

"Idiots!" said Pedro. He moved patiently across the floor as Margarita raised her hands above her head and began to chant in some strange tongue.

He knocked her down with a huge fist and hoisted her onto one burly shoulder, still holding the pot in his other hand. "You should have stayed asleep, wench," he said.

At the door he turned for a last look at the two men groaning on the dirt floor. "Go home," he told them. "You've made such fools of yourselves that I doubt you'll talk about this night's work, but if you're tempted, you'll have to deal with me, even before you meet the Grand Inquisitor."

He stepped outside, moved stolidly through the milling sheep, and draped Margarita's limp body over the fence. Once over it himself, he resumed his burden and made for his horse, tethered under nearby trees. He folded the woman across the saddle like a slaughtered sheep and set out for the city.

Diego de Villanueva was waiting at the Holy House for Pedro and his prize. The shepherdess was still unconscious when the Grand Inquisitor's familiar carried her in and dumped her unceremoniously on the floor.

"Here's your witch," said Pedro, "and a pot of stuff she was brewing. She has it all over her. And some of that belladonna. What is it?"

"A foul and dangerous drug," said Diego. He sniffed delicately at the contents of the pot. "She used it in this potion. Too much of it is deadly, but a small amount produces trances and visions. Witches rub themselves with ointments like this to commune with demons."

Pedro held out his great hands in dismay. "I've got some on me! What should I do?"

"Wash it off. And don't worry. A bit like that won't hurt an ox like you. It's most effective when rubbed on parts of the body more sensitive than your rough hands."

Pedro looked at the woman and leered.

"Get that look off your face, Pedro, and get a bucket, too. You should clean some of that poison off her."

Pedro stomped off on yet another errand and the Grand Inquisitor bent over the prisoner lying on the cold stone floor. "Margarita!" He prodded her side delicately with a sandaled foot. "Margarita de Mendoza!" He kicked harder, then sighed and stepped away.

"She sleeps like the dead," he said as Pedro returned with a wooden bucket full of water. "I hoped that the drug might have loosened her tongue, but she seems completely senseless."

She was lively enough a few minutes ago," said Pedro. "Maybe this will rouse her." He emptied the bucket slowly and methodically over Margarita, drenching her from head to toe. She moaned, arched her back, and then sank back into stillness. The wet rag she wore clung to her slender, full-breasted body. Her long, tanned legs sprawled. Pedro liked what he saw.

"It's no use," said Diego. "Take her to the dungeons. I'll talk to her tomorrow."

Again Pedro picked up the unconscious woman, but this time he carried her in his arms, not draped over his broad shoulders as before. He had begun to think of her as something more than a prisoner. She looked much better to him with her face cleaned, and he was conscious of her weight in his arms as something more than a burden to be borne.

In the dark corridor he considered the possibilities of the situation. She seemed less of a witch than a woman to him now, but it might not be wise to risk his soul for a few minutes of fun. Still . . .

He stopped at a heavy door, knocked, and saw a hooded head peer through a barred opening. The door swung back, and Pedro's lust lessened at the sight of the silent figure before him. Another monk, and there would be two more before he reached the dungeons. The Inquisition did not encourage what he had in mind.

He started down a flight of narrow stone steps, realizing all at once how tired he was. It must be very late.

Another door at the bottom of the stairs, and another monk, with keys in one hand and a torch pulled from a wall bracket in the other.

"A prisoner," said Pedro.

The monk did not bother to answer but led Pedro down a damp, chilly tunnel by the wavering light of the torch. Still another monk waited at the end of the tunnel. His hood was not the cowl worn by most Dominicans but a blank black mask that covered his face and rose to a grotesque peak a foot above his head. His eyes were vaguely visible through two small holes. He opened an iron door. Pedro passed through and heard it clang shut behind him, the key grating in the lock.

A ring of still more keys hung from a hook on the wall. Any one of them would admit him to a dungeon where he could have his way with Margarita, but his enthusiasm had waned.

"That faceless one would cool off anyone," he muttered to Margarita, as if she could hear him. "Not much good anyway, with a woman who won't even know I'm there. Besides, Friar Diego said that perfume you were wearing might be dangerous, and I couldn't wash it all off you while he was watching."

He sighed and shifted her weight so she was supported by one of his strong arms. With his other hand he reached out for the keys and dragged Margarita to an empty cell.

A feeble groan issued from a door nearby, but Pedro ignored it and opened the dungeon he had selected for the new prisoner. He could see nothing inside but blackness, although he heard the scampering of rats frightened by the open door.

"At least you won't be living alone anymore," he told Margarita. "And it won't be much worse than your old home at that, not until they put you to the Question."

He let her down gently just inside the cell; his hands

came up foul and muddy from the floor. He wiped them on his doublet and slammed the door behind him.

He was glad to be leaving, to pass through the barriers with their hooded guards, to climb the steep stairs, hurry through the empty corridors, and find himself at last under the open sky, free from confinement, breathing fresh air.

He was more weary from the night's work than he would ever admit. His arms ached. He was growing old.

At least he had not raped the witch, and now he was glad of it. He had done his duty, but no more. This way it would be easier for him to go home and face his daughters. They were not sons, but he loved them both and was proud of their beauty and virtue. They were good girls, Pedro thought, and tonight, at least, he had been a good man. It had not always been easy since his wife had died a dozen years ago.

His house was only a few steps away. It, too, was locked, but that was not to keep the girls imprisoned, only to keep them safe from the dangers lurking outside. He shook his head to clear it of an incongruous image. There was no comparison between his daughters, locked in for their own protection, and Margarita de Mendoza, sealed in a dungeon for unspeakable sins.

He knocked and was answered almost at once by a light voice from within. "Father?"

"Yes, Teresa."

The door was opened by a pale, slight, pretty girl of seventeen. Her eyes were sleepy, but she managed a wan smile.

"You shouldn't be awake, Teresa."

"I'm sorry, father. I can't sleep when you're away at night like this."

Pedro took his daughter in his arms and kissed her cheek. "And the little one?"

"Dolores is in bed. She wanted to stay up with me, but I wouldn't let her."

"Let's go to sleep ourselves, daughter. It's very late."

Margarita leaped to her feet as soon as the dungeon

door slammed shut. She had been conscious for some time, but it had seemed wise to lie still and hope for the best. If her captors thought her drugged or beaten into insensibility, at least the questioning would not begin at once. Now that she was alone she felt safer, but she backed herself into a corner to avoid the rats. It was too dark to see them, or anything else, but she knew they were there. Fortunately, they seemed as frightened of her as she was of them.

The stone walls she leaned against were cold; the air was foul. Her bare feet were ankle deep in an icy slime that smelled worse than mud. Her hair and clothes were drenched and her teeth chattered uncontrollably.

Her whole body was shaking—from the after-effect of the drugs, from a numbing fear, but most of all from hatred. She nursed the small flame of fury within her, for it was the only warmth she had. Margarita watched the flame grow until it enveloped her. It filled the cell with an unearthly light, but she knew that the light was a lie. The flame was a belladonna dream, like the vast head of the goat that floated above her.

The goat was a lie and the goat was her lover, the Prince of Lies. It was he who instructed her, who presided over the ceremonies in the forest. It was the goat who embraced her, the goat who entered her. He was her slave and her master, and he would enter her again.

She stood rigid against the wall, eyes rolling, teeth clenched. She breathed deeply and felt the spirit pass into her lungs. She breathed again and saw the spirit and the flame and the goat flow into her body like a luminous cloud.

Then it was dark again and she sank down into the corner. She sat in the mud, her knees drawn up to her breast, her head bent forward, arms embracing her legs.

She knew she was a dead woman, but she knew that the Inquisition would not break her. She would not confess, would not inform. Her hate was stronger than theirs.

The Inquisition had exiled her parents, lost her a husband, and stolen her home. They had left her nothing but witchcraft, and love for the Lord of Flies. That she would not betray.

After a few hours her mouth grew dry. When thirst became intolerable, she twisted a few drops of water from the hem of her garment and licked the moisture from the palm of her hand.

She had no way of knowing if she would ever be given water or food or if she would ever see light again.

Her mind was still fogged by visions and she had no idea how long she had been in the cell. She was grateful for the drug, though, for it gave her strength. Small smiling imps scurried among the rats, and she spoke with them. They sang songs to cheer her, and they spoke of the goat, the goat with the body of a man, whose great eyes glowed with wisdom.

At last the iron door opened and light spilled into the cell. The dreams disappeared and in their place Margarita saw two men dressed in black robes. Their hands held torches whose sudden brilliance nearly blinded her; their faces were shrouded in the darkness of hideously pointed hoods.

They stood on either side of her, each grasping one of her arms, and they led her down long passageways, up slippery stairs, and through an endless succession of locked doors. They were silent and surprisingly gentle; she would almost have preferred curses and brutality to their grim efficiency.

The last door opened. The scene before her had the vividness of hallucination, but she knew that it was real.

The entire room was draped in black velvet. There was a long table also draped in black. On it were a Bible, a crucifix, and six black candles in silver sticks. Seated behind the six flickering flames was a man whose long, clean-shaven face was partly hidden by a black cowl. Still, she had no trouble recognizing him as Diego de Villanueva, the Grand Inquisitor.

He did not look up as she entered. He held a sheaf of papers in his hand and seemed totally absorbed in them. She wondered if her name was written there.

No one spoke; no one moved. The masked men beside her were as still as statues.

Next to the table was a low pulpit covered with more papers and an ink horn. A young monk stood there with a quill in his hand. His cowl hung back over his narrow shoulders, which seemed to make him more human than the others. He appeared to be nervous, and he looked a bit foolish with his freshly shaven head. He glanced at Margarita but dropped his eyes at once and attempted to busy himself with his papers.

Finally the Grand Inquisitor broke his silence.

"What is your name, young woman?"

Margarita did not answer.

"Come now, surely you will at least confess to your name! You must realize that we know it already."

There seemed no point in resisting on this matter. "Margarita de Mendoza," she said.

At once the young monk began scribbling with his pen.

"What is your father's name?" asked the Grand Inquisitor.

Margarita's resolve was immediately strengthened by the mention of her father. These questions might be a matter of form, but they might be something more. She avoided the bright, icy eyes of the Inquisitor and shook her head. Her long black hair fell into her face.

"What is your mother's name?"

Margarita stared sullenly at the floor.

"My dear young woman, what are we to think of you if you refuse to answer simple questions such as these? Will you speak?"

There was no sound except the scratching of the pen, and then even that stopped. The Grand Inquisitor stood up.

"I fear that your soul is in the gravest jeopardy. We only wish to guide you back into the light. Do you know why you are here? Have you nothing to confess?

"I must tell you that you stand accused of a terrible heresy. Yet we desire to be just and merciful."

Miguel, transcribing the interrogation, recognized the formula as that laid down in the instructions of Torquemada, the Inquisitor General of the kingdom. He knew what the next question would be and began to write it down before it was asked.

"Have you any enemies who might have reason to bear false witness against you?"

Margarita looked up at the Grand Inquisitor and gritted her teeth.

"You are my enemy," she said.

The Grand Inquisitor stood rigidly for a moment, then sighed and sat again behind the six black candles.

"You are terribly misguided," he said. "I am here only to help you, my child, to save you from eternal torment. Will you not speak?"

Miguel looked at Margarita expectantly, but she remained silent.

"Very well," said the Grand Inquisitor. "We will give you time to contemplate your condition, time to be alone and consider the state of your soul. A few days in darkness may make you long for the light."

The masked men on either side of Margarita were suddenly active again. One turned her around; the other opened the black-draped door.

She realized with a sudden contraction of her stomach that they were taking her back to the dark hole again. They might leave her there forever. Panic rushed over her, with an impulse to run back into the velvet room, to confess, or at least to answer the simple questions, to do anything that would keep her for a few minutes more in the feeble glow of the black candles.

It was too late. She was already out in the hall, and the door had slammed behind her, but not in time to shut out the Grand Inquisitor's final instructions: "Put her in chains."

4. The Tower

"WELL, BROTHER, have you captured your witch?" asked Sebastian de Villanueva. It was the first time he had spoken for days.

Diego did not answer at once. He often found his brother's moods disturbing. Tonight Sebastian had met him at the drawbridge as always but had not said a single word. Instead, he had greeted the Grand Inquisitor with an elaborate bow and exaggerated gestures of welcome.

A grotesque parody of a host, tall and gaunt, Sebastian had beckoned his brother across the empty courtyard, always remaining a few paces out of reach. His black velvet clothing made him almost invisible in the night, though the moonlight sometimes flashed from the silver filigree on his doublet or from his bejeweled fingers.

He had led the monk through the dark chambers of the castle, abandoned dusty apartments whose rich furnishings were falling into decay. Here there was no light at all, and Sebastian's presence could be sensed only by the light tread of his Cordova leather boots and the rustle of his red velvet cloak. Diego could not hear even the sound of his brother's breathing, though his own lungs were laboring as he followed Sebastian up the countless narrow steps to the top of the great tower. He kept one hand to the wall, fearing that he might stumble and fall, as he surely would have had he not already known the way.

Gasping for breath at the topmost step, the Grand Inquisitor had been ushered into his brother's study. Here at last was illumination, if only a solitary crimson candle perched atop a yellowed human skull that dripped with red wax. The skull rested on the corner of a small table, its center inlaid with black-and-white squares of onyx and ivory.

Sebastian finally broke his silence as he seated himself behind the table, well out of the light, in a tall and fantastically carved chair that was almost a throne. He spoke again before Diego had a chance to reply.

"I see you are winded, brother. A cup of wine, perhaps?" He reached into the shadows behind his chair and produced a silver goblet studded with rubies. It was already full.

Diego looked at its contents doubtfully. The thought crossed his mind that the wine might be poisoned, but he dismissed the idea almost at once. Sebastian needed him as much as he needed Sebastian. He drank greedily. It was a good vintage.

"No news?" asked Sebastian. "No prisoners? No witches?"

Diego bridled at his older brother's mockery, which he had endured for more than forty years. This was the only man in the world who still made him feel like a fool.

He stared over the rim of the cup at the face of his brother, dead white even in the yellow glow of the lone candle. The expression was sardonic, the eyes lost in shadow. It was a lean face, with a long black mustache that drooped over the emaciated jaw. The hair was long and black, too; parted in the center, it reached to Sebastian's shoulders. An ugly scar, more livid than the ivory skin, ran down the left side of the face, above and below the eye. In the dim light the fine garments were revealed as ragged and worn.

"You look well, brother," said Sebastian. "Of course, there is no need to tell me how I look."

"But who else will tell you, Sebastian? You are not much seen in public of late, and I believe you have no looking glass."

"Yes," Sebastian said. A corner of his mouth turned up slightly. "I am spared at least that one sign of vanity."

"You asked about the witch," said the Grand

Inquisitor. "We have her in a cell beneath the Holy House."

"You seemed so excited two nights ago when you told me you were on her trail. Has she been a disappointment?"

"She has not spoken yet. Of course, she has had only the initial interrogation. A few days in the dungeons alone may loosen her tongue. If not, there is always the rack. I was surprised, though. She refused to answer a single question, even to defend herself. A stubborn woman."

"A bitter woman, perhaps. What else but fury and frustration would drive a soul to embrace its own damnation?"

"A moment ago you mentioned pride, Sebastian."

"One of your seven deadly sins, is it not, Friar? Might it make a monk lust for the secrets of Satan and think that he could gain them all without losing his soul?"

"It might make a man publish a book exposing the ways of witches. Only that. None of us is without sin, though, and I confess to a certain sort of pride. But what do you have to be so superior about? Even now, when the world thinks you dead and I know you for a godless parasite, you still sit on a throne at the top of a tower, decked out in velvet and precious stones, for all the world as if you were still a nobleman."

"I confess, too, brother. Will you absolve me, you, the humble monk, sitting on a bench and dressed in sackcloth?"

"Enough, Sebastian! Why should we bicker? We may not love each other as I have heard that brothers do, but we serve each other's needs. I admit that without your help my book would be nothing. But remember that without my protection, you would be in Hell, where you belong."

"Even so, brother. Let us be sociable. We will speak of the book later. A game of chess?" Sebastian waved a long white hand toward the black-and-white squares on the table.

"I think not, Sebastian. You always win. You toy with

me, and I don't like the way you play."

"Surely you don't object because I give you the white pieces and take the black for myself?"

"I don't like the way you always attack my bishops."

"And you always try to take my castles. I admit, though, that you are less successful. So let us forget chess. Perhaps the cards?"

"The cards?" Diego licked his lips. "Yes, the cards."

"The symbolism bothers you less, does it, when the symbols reveal your own future? Very well, brother, I will read your fortune."

In his right hand Sebastian held a pile of pasteboard cards. "You will insist on using these for vulgar prediction, as the gypsies do? They have a higher purpose. I have told you before that they are not cards, but the pages of a book, a book more full of meaning and mystery than any that you or I will ever write. A book of pictures. But you only listen to what you want to hear."

Sebastian held out the pack to his brother.

"Shall I mix them?" asked Diego.

"Just touch them, brother. No need to trouble yourself."

As Diego reached out and tapped the top card, Sebastian drew the deck back. He opened his right hand and the cards poured from it in a great arc, high above his head. They seemed to float and shimmer in the air for an instant; then they fell, twisting and turning, to form somehow a perfect stack in the center of the table.

As Diego sat staring, the top card detached itself from the pack, flipped gracefully over, and landed face down on the table. The next card did the same, coming to rest beside the first. It happened again and again until there were ten cards dealt out in a neat row. And all the while Sebastian sat quietly with folded hands.

"Tricks with bits of paper," Sebastian said. "Any juggler could do as much."

Diego smiled nervously. "You always were a bit of a mountebank, Sebastian."

"Why do you hesitate, brother? This is your future! Surely the Grand Inquisitor wishes to have his questions answered! Turn over the first card. It is yourself."

Diego did as he was told, then smiled more complacently. "The Hierophant," he said.

The card showed a seated figure wearing a red robe and an ornate triple crown. His hand was raised in a benediction and crossed keys lay at his feet. Kneeling before him were two men with the shaven heads of monks.

The faded drawing on the worn card had been done years ago in black ink, which was now turning brown. The colors, too, had dulled with the passage of time. Diego believed that his brother had designed the cards, but he had never asked. He was more interested in what they had to say.

"What does it mean?" he asked. "Surely I am not to be pope!"

"I think not. This is you as you are now. Be not too ambitious, Diego. You are already in a seat of power. It may mean no more than what you see. This is only the first of ten."

"Are there no hidden meanings?"

"Many. Here, perhaps alliance, or instruction. Or one who seeks the supernatural."

Diego reached impatiently for the second card.

"The Queen of Swords," he announced.

"She crosses you," said Sebastian.

"The Queen?"

"You must not take my little pictures too literally. It might be any woman. A dark woman, and melancholy. She may be given to visions and fond of dancing."

"If this is who I think it is, then I am the one who crosses her. Let me see the next."

He picked up the third card and looked at it in some surprise. "Five Coins," he said.

"A doubtful card, brother. It may mean poverty, but you are already sworn to that. It might represent some sort of bargain."

"I know what it means," said Diego. He reached for the fourth card.

"The Ten of Swords," he said.

"A bad card," said Sebastian. "Cruelty and misfortune.

This lies beneath you, however. It is not your future but the foundation on which you stand."

"So be it," said Diego and reached for the next card.

"Behind you," said Sebastian.

Diego started slightly and turned half around, then stopped. "Oh. You mean the card," he said. "It is the Knight of Cups."

"Perhaps he really is behind you, brother. This signifies the approach of a young man. He is a lover of pleasure, and a dreamer. Do you know him?"

"No."

"Beware of him."

"Why?"

"Because he is a good man."

"Spare me your wit, Sebastian. The next, I believe, shows what is before me?"

At the top of the card was an angel, with wings spread and a trumpet at his lips. Below was the sea and three figures—a man, a woman, and a child. They were naked and their skin was gray. The woman's arms were raised toward the sky; the man's crossed on his chest in the position usually reserved for corpses. Each of the three stood in an open coffin.

"The card of Judgment," said Sebastian.

"What sort of an augury is that? We all face the Last Judgment," said the Grand Inquisitor. Nevertheless, he shivered once, looking at the angel.

"It would be wiser to view it as a smaller judgment," said Sebastian, "a decision of some sort. It might refer, let us say, to the reception the authorities will give to your book on witchcraft and black magic."

"Then let us see the next card," Diego said. He picked it up but kept its back to Sebastian. He studied it skeptically. The drawing showed a hand emerging from a white cloud, holding a long stick.

"The Ace of Wands," Diego said. "What does it mean? No doubt you will try to worry me with it—but I think you have more cause than I to fear a shaft of wood, Sebastian."

Sebastian smiled. The candlelight gleamed on his sharp

white teeth. "The Ace of Wands has great power. It signifies strength in an enterprise, a beginning. Yet it can also mean a disaster of some kind. It is a mystery. Consult the next card."

"Two Swords," said Diego.

"The eighth card represents your surroundings. Another bad card. Strife and sorrow."

"Who cares for my surroundings? What does the ninth card portend?"

"It is your hopes, brother."

Diego turned over the ninth card and placed it on the table. It showed a stone tower shattered by a thunderbolt. The three windows were in flames. A man and a woman fell from the structure toward the rocks below.

"The Tower Struck by Lightning," said Sebastian dryly. "I believe the cards have read your mind."

"Enough of your jokes!" said Diego. "What does it signify?"

"I thought the picture alone would surely satisfy you, but no matter. In general it signifies disaster, an unforeseen calamity."

"And you say that this is my hope?"

"I say nothing, brother. The cards speak to you. I am only their interpreter."

"Are there no other meanings?"

"Each card signifies many things. It might also mean ambition. And it represents the planet Mars. Do you wish for Mars, brother? Come. I will show him to you."

Sebastian grasped Diego by the arm and led him to a wall covered by a Moorish tapestry representing a lion hunt. He drew the tapestry aside to reveal a narrow window. There was no glass, and Diego felt a faint breeze. He looked at the range of misty mountains spread out before him and at the dizzying drop to the ground.

"Look!" said Sebastian, pointing into the clear sky. "The faint red star there, the one that does not glitter. There are your hopes, brother."

The Grand Inquisitor craned his neck. There were thousands of stars. He could not follow the direction of Sebastian's finger. He began to feel a touch of vertigo.

Sebastian's grip was strong and cold, even through the rough cloth of a monk's robe.

The Grand Inquisitor pulled away and walked to the center of the room. "I see nothing," he said. "Astrology, cartomancy, all these things are wicked foolishness. And I am a fool to listen to you."

"Then you do not wish to see the last card? The one showing what will come?"

Diego stepped to the table and leaned on it heavily with both hands. He looked at the nine cards spread before him and the one still face down. Then he looked up at Sebastian, who lounged mockingly against the tapestry.

Diego's fingers reached out for the piece of pasteboard. Still staring at Sebastian, he turned it over. Slowly his eyes lowered. He saw a red sky and a setting sun. A smiling skeleton walked across a fertile field, a scythe in its bony hands, reaping human heads. Its smile was the same as Sebastian's.

"Death!" said Diego in a whisper. Then he began to shout. "It means nothing! This is only a trick! Pieces of paper! You mixed the cards, Sebastian! And you dealt them! This is not my future! It is yours!"

Sebastian smiled in the shadows.

"Calm yourself, brother," he said. "Death is the last card for every man. For every man but me."

Diego stared in silence at the ten cards. A skeleton, a tower in flames, two kneeling monks, a hand with a wand, an angel with a trumpet, a knight, a queen, coins, and swords. The pictures swam before his eyes.

"The card may mean other things," said Sebastian. "Not death, perhaps, but something similar—a transformation."

"It means nothing," Diego repeated.

"You are right, of course. It is only a game. Let us speak of other things. The book! It is coming splendidly. You will astound the world with it. Even the great Torquemada will be surprised!"

Diego had resumed his inscrutable exterior. "You say it is going well?"

"It should be ready in a few weeks. There are still a

number of points that trouble me, but I am working on them. This book will make your fortune!"

"My fortune," said Diego. He looked again at the cards, then shrugged and turned away. "Show me the manuscript," he said.

"Presently," said Sebastian. "I think you are still upset. Have some more wine."

Diego reached for the silver goblet. He would have sworn that he had drained it long before, but when he picked it up he found it was full to the brim.

"And forget the cards," Sebastian said. "You are right: it was a trick; it means nothing."

He gathered up the cards in one pale, cold hand.

And when he opened the hand it was empty.

5. The Question

THE MORE Miguel learned about witches, the less he liked them.

That dark and sullen woman had been in the dungeons for almost a week. Each day the Grand Inquisitor interrogated her, and each day she refused to answer. Miguel was present during all these fruitless exchanges, the ink at the end of his pen drying up as he waited for the confession that never came. Every time he saw her she was thinner and filthier. Her green eyes stared at him strangely. It seemed that she thought him a contemptible creature, and it was small satisfaction to Miguel that he was inclined to agree with her.

It was worse that she had no respect for the Grand Inquisitor. She broke her silence only to swear and spit at him. Miguel was appalled at her effrontery. Didn't she know who Diego de Villanueva was? How could she resist the harsh and honeyed words with which the Grand Inquisitor sought the secrets of her soul?

Such resistance could have only one result, the Question.

Miguel had never seen the Question administered, but he had no desire to be initiated into its mysteries. He knew that it was not just a question—there had been enough of those already—but that it rarely failed to elicit an answer. The answers came between screams, from a long dark room where men masked in black waited beside their cruel machines. Did Margarita de Mendoza know what was waiting for her? Why would she not confess?

He thought sometimes that he should go to her alone

and warn her. It was not that he wished to spare her but that he wished to spare himself from witnessing her torture. He was afraid to see it. Yet he did nothing, for he was more afraid to be alone with her, because she was a witch and he had begun to learn what witches might do.

He had worked and worried his way through half the *Malleus Maleficarum,* which the Grand Inquisitor had ordered him to read, and Miguel found it even more disturbing than he had expected. He had imagined that it would be a catalog of crimes, of the things that witches did. Raising tempests, killing crops, crippling cattle, stealing children, causing enemies to sicken and die—all these he would have been prepared to consider. However, it appeared that the real wickedness of witchcraft lay elsewhere, in activities Miguel found it painful even to contemplate. The details were all too vivid for a young man of his modest nature, but the priniciple was clear enough. One phrase from the book rang through his mind each time he looked on Margarita: "All witchcraft springs from carnal lust."

Miguel learned that it was the greatest joy for witches to copulate with devils. The demons took male or female forms and visited abandoned men and women in the enchanting guises of incubi and succubi. Countless sources were cited for the truth of these allegations, and the points were argued with what seemed to Miguel like irrefutable logic. No particulars were omitted and more than one reason was offered for the devilish enthusiasm with which such seductions were accomplished. They served not only to corrupt the sinful but to increase their number. Miguel wondered how demons could reproduce mortals, but the *Malleus Maleficarum* had the answer. Devils appeared to men as succubi and drew forth from them the seed of life, which could then be delivered to women by the same devils in their roles as incubi. Or the semen could be entrusted to the care of another demon who had a willing woman in his power. In either case, the offspring of these triangular unions were certain to be among the vilest of mortals.

In Miguel's imagination these ideas conjured up

deplorable pictures, which invaded his dreams. Sometimes he saw dim, smoky creatures keeping assignations in the sky and passing things from hand to hand before speeding off upon their rounds. More often, though, came the nightmare of a succubus floating just above his narrow bed, her eyes green, her lips scarlet, her black hair streaming down in cloudy masses to envelop him. The worst of it was that the dreams were exciting. Only his humility kept him from the absolute conviction that some dark power had embarked on a campaign to seduce him. As it was, he tried not to sleep.

While awake, he felt obliged to read further in the book, where he learned that it was the sport of witches to obstruct the act of love for others. There were spells to prevent women from conceiving and, more commonly, to prevent men from performing, thus destroying marriages and luring mortals into adultery.

Even more disturbing was a statement that witches had the power to remove the male organ entirely. There was a separate chapter on this topic, which Miguel encountered with a sinking stomach, even though there were arguments to assure him that the spell was only an illusion, however much it might appear to the victim that he had been utterly emasculated. Miguel read with mounting horror, yet told himself that this sort of curse should not mean much to a monk who had already taken a vow of chastity. Did Miguel need fear that a devil would take away his manhood, when he had already surrendered it to God?

He realized that his left hand was clutching and crumpling the page, which was beginning to tear free of the binding, and he spent the rest of the night trying to smooth it out so that the Grand Inquisitor would not notice. After that night, Miguel's fear of witches began to develop into a positive hatred. He hurried through the book to the third part, where methods were described for detecting witchcraft, capturing it, torturing it, punishing it, and destroying it in flames. Yet still the dreams came.

The six black candles were lit again and the Grand Inquisitor sat behind them. Miguel stood ready with his pen and papers, but his eyes were on the door.

"Will she speak this time?" he asked.

"There is no reason to expect it, but we will take the trouble to inquire once more. If her attitude has not improved, then we will be obliged to try another method."

"The Question?"

The Grand Inquisitor merely nodded.

"At once?" asked Miguel.

"I imagine it will be no more than a few minutes, unless she has unexpectedly seen the light."

"And will it make her speak?"

"I have never known it to fail. Yet this is no ordinary heretic. Some of those are fanatical enough, but there is nothing like a witch for clinging stubbornly to sin. Some of them seem half-possessed and have a strength that will bear almost anything. Others, especially the old women, are reported to collapse at the very sight of the instruments. We can only wait and see. I know this will be your first sight of the Question, Miguel, but bear up and remember that this is also my first witch."

Miguel smiled weakly at the little joke, which he knew was an attempt to reassure him. As such, it was a failure. He could see no grounds for comparing Miguel Carillo to Diego de Villanueva. Still, he tried to respond in the proper spirit.

"It will not be your last witch, I venture," said Miguel. "You will root them all out of the hills, for a certainty you will! And you will become the first witch hunter of Spain and the greatest in Christendom! And your book will be . . ."

"Who spoke of a book?" interrupted the Grand Inquisitor sharply. "Have I mentioned a book?"

"Well, no, that is, not really, but I thought from what you have said that you were working on something . . ."

"All right, Miguel. I had not meant to tell you yet, but it seems I speak too freely. There will be a book. There is much to be learned about witches and their ways, and I hope to cast some light into these dark corners. Perhaps you can help me."

"I? How?"

"With your eyes, and your ears, and your pen. Continue to take down every word the witch utters, and it may be that your transcript will find a place in my work. Stay calm, and do not let the Question disturb you. I know it may seem unnecessary to you, since we have testimony and evidence enough to convict Margarita de Mendoza already. But we may persuade her to name her confederates. And there is another reason: her immortal soul is in the gravest danger. If she confesses and repents she will be saved, but if we condemn her without this final effort, she will be left to an eternity of tortures worse than anything that we can bring to bear upon her corrupted flesh. Do you understand?"

"I do, and I will try not to fail you. I have read about the witches, and I have no pity for her now, though I hope to see her saved."

"Silence! They are coming. Look to your work."

The door opened slowly on well-oiled hinges.

Miguel raised his eyes in spite of his firm resolve to be indifferent. The witch was becoming a horror. Her tanned face had turned pale, except for the purple circles under her sunken eyes. There seemed to be no flesh to smooth the strong line of her jaw, and her sharp cheekbones looked as if they might break through the skin. This face that haunted Miguel's dreams looked to him like a beautiful skull. The emerald eyes turned toward him and one corner of the red mouth lifted. He looked away.

Silence filled the black velvet room. The black candles burned steadily in the stale air and the black-robed jailers stood silently beside their prisoner. Miguel stared at his white paper and nothing happened for a long time.

At last the Grand Inquisitor spoke.

"Margarita de Mendoza," he said. "You know why you are here. You know your crimes, and we know them. We have witnesses and evidence. Yet you have not confessed. If you admit your guilt and name your confederates, then God will forgive you. If you do not, there is no hope for you, in this world or the next. We are weary of waiting for your answers, but I ask you once again to speak.

"And let me tell you this. If you refuse, you will not return to your cell. You will go to another chamber, and there we will persuade you to confess. Believe me when I tell you that you will wish you were back in the dungeons. Consider carefully and accept God's mercy now."

Margarita's heart gave one tremendous thump. She felt suddenly light-headed and there was a ringing in her ears.

"The Devil has more mercy than your God," she heard someone saying far away, then realized that the voice was her own.

"Take her," said the Grand Inquisitor.

Miguel's pulse raced with a kind of sick excitement. He tried to calm himself by remembering the system for administering the Question. There were five parts to the procedure, as outlined in Torquemada's instructions, and the first stage, the threat of torture, had elicited only blasphemy. The woman could burn for that alone, but the point of the Inquisition, he reminded himself, was not to punish her but save her.

Miguel saw her lips moving silently as the guards turned her toward the door, and he wondered if she might be casting a spell. He determined to keep his distance. He had read of a German witch who had breathed into the face of her executioner, and the man had died in three days.

Miguel looked at the Grand Inquisitor, who rose from his seat and gestured for his vicar to follow.

Miguel had never visited the torture chamber and had never even seen the dungeons. As the small procession made its way down dark stairs and through dank passageways, he was amazed at the extent of the Holy House. The rooms above were nothing compared with the secret chambers underground. The walls were wet. The air was cold, but the torches made it smoky, like some icy hell.

A door opened and Miguel knew that it would be the last, for there was no way out of the vaulted stone chamber into which he followed the Grand Inquisitor. The room was unmistakable in any case.

Miguel looked and tried to calm himself with the

knowledge that what he saw was the second stage of the Question. Miguel himself found it more than a little unpleasant, and he thought with resentment that he, like the prisoner, was to be subjected to each stage of the torture; all but the last.

The room was half-illuminated by the ruddy glow from braziers heaped with burning coals, and fitfully brightened by the white flames of candles flickering in the fresher air from the door. The hooded jailers entered with their torches, revealing figures crudely painted on the gray stone walls: gigantic black beasts with horns and claws. Such murals were far from reassuring, but they were only a background for the machines and their attendants. Miguel saw four more men masked by the black, pointed hoods, and he heard the door close behind him with a groan and a thud.

He wished to be gone, but reluctantly he took his seat behind a small table. Behind this was a thronelike chair obviously intended for the Grand Inquisitor, but Diego, not ready for it, instead turned to face the prisoner.

"You see what we have prepared for you, Margarita de Mendoza. Will you speak?"

Margarita did not answer, but Miguel saw that her lips were still moving. Could she be praying? To whom? Her eyes were glassy and seemed to be looking at something not in the room.

"Do you know what these machines are?" asked the Grand Inquisitor. "Let me show you. This is the hoist," he said, and the guards turned Margarita to face it. "You see that it is only a rope, hanging from that pulley in the ceiling. But if your arms were tied behind your back by one end of that rope and someone pulled the other end, you might find it painful. It might dislocate your shoulders. If not, you could be lowered, then raised again. Eventually something would come of it. Or you could be left hanging, with weights on your feet to pull you down. And while you hung, you might be whipped. I am sure you need not be shown the whip to know its uses."

Nevertheless, one of the hooded men stepped forward,

brandishing a whip, lest there be any doubt in Margarita's mind.

"The hoist might stretch your arms a bit," said the Grand Inquisitor, "but we have a better instrument for that. This is the rack." He passed to the next machine with the air of a merchant displaying his wares.

"This is a bed of sorts, but you will not find it very comfortable. It is too hard; but that is not the half of it. If you lie here, these iron bands will be clamped to your wrists and ankles, which look sore enough already. The bands are attached to chains like those in your cell, but these chains are wrapped around wheels. When the wheels are turned, the chains draw tight and something between them must be stretched. The metal is stronger than your flesh. You would not enjoy a rest on the rack. You are already tall for a woman."

This is the third part of the Question, Miguel thought; anyone who was not mad would confess now. Yet he felt that he was more dismayed than Margarita de Mendoza, who glanced at the devices of her destruction as if they were of only passing interest.

"This is the chair," said the Grand Inquisitor, his voice rising as he warmed to his work. He leaned over a mass of glowing coals that threw his features into red relief. Smoky sweat broke out on his brow. "A woman could be locked in that chair with the stocks below it holding her feet. These coals are here to cook those feet. It is not a comfortable chair. . . . Will you speak?"

Miguel shuffled his blank papers but found the sound so loud that he stopped suddenly.

"Let me show you the ladder," the Grand Inquisitor continued quietly. A ladder studded with iron braces slanted slightly toward the ceiling. "You might find yourself locked on this ladder, with your feet above your head and your head held in place by a metal band. This is merely in preparation for the water. Some call this treatment the water, but I prefer to think of it as the ladder, since I have seen so many squirm up it to salvation. There is a clamp here to keep your mouth open, and there are gallons of water in these jugs. There is also a long strip of linen. When we give you the water, this cloth seems to flow down the throat behind it. The result is a choking sensation something like strangling, though we will try not to kill you. But none of this will be necessary if you will speak now."

The tour of the establishment seemed to be over, and Margarita apparently sensed as much. She looked at the Grand Inquisitor as though seeing him for the first time, then shook her head.

"No? Very well," he said. "Prepare her."

This is the fourth stage, thought Miguel, but his mind was no longer on Torquemada's instructions. Instead, his eyes were on the prisoner.

The guard on Margarita's right reached toward her, his white hand reaching out of a black sleeve to grasp the neckline of her bedraggled dress. He pulled at the cloth and yanked her head down with it. The dress tore away, and when Margarita pulled herself up she was naked.

Miguel had never seen a naked woman before. He looked away toward the wall and was confronted by the black silhouette of a painted monster. He turned again toward Margarita and could not look away.

She was gaunt. He could have counted her ribs, but his eyes were drawn almost hypnotically to the full fleshy breasts that seemed incongruous with her haggard frame. He saw the nipples grow hard in the cool air, and the lustrous swirl of black hair curling above her thighs. He stared less in lust than in amazement. She is beautiful, he thought. And then he heard her laughter.

He saw her eyes, staring back at him full of mockery. With her hands on her hips she threw back her head and laughed at him. His face grew hot and he felt naked himself. He wanted to run but could not move.

He saw the hand of the Grand Inquisitor fly toward the woman's face and heard the sharp sound of a slap. The laughter stopped.

"Evil has many disguises," said the Grand Inquisitor, "but none more treacherous than this." He was addressing the ceiling, but Miguel knew that the words were meant for him.

"There is no need for further delay," said the Grand Inquisitor.

"We know what you are," he said to Margarita, "and soon you will be glad to admit it. But how shall we persuade you? The ladder, I think."

Four hooded figures converged on Margarita, each clutching at an arm or a leg. She went limp, her lips still working soundlessly, and was hoisted onto the ladder, her feet above her head. The clamps closed on her ankles, wrists, and forehead.

"I understand that your keepers have been reluctant to provide you with water, Margarita de Mendoza. I promise you that this will be remedied at once. Perhaps when you have had enough water you will be willing to tell me what you know about witchcraft. I see only one problem. You cannot move your hands or feet and will not be able to speak, with the metal in your mouth and linen in your throat. But try to make some sign when you are ready to speak. We wish to be merciful."

This is the fifth stage, thought Miguel, and closed his eyes.

"Begin," said the Grand Inquisitor.

6. The Dream

No, DAMN HER, she won't talk! The ladder, the rack, the chair, the hoist—all useless! Oh, she screams well enough, but nothing more. She must be enchanted. And all the while, that stupid boy Miguel gapes at me, waiting to write down her confession, wondering why his hero is failing. She burns on Sunday, Sebastian—I've had my fill of her!"

Don Sebastian de Villanueva sat in the shadows and said nothing. The Grand Inquisitor saw that his brother had grown thinner, like the witch, that his long black hair fell across his face like hers.

"You are very like her, Sebastian. Must you be silent too? You are both monsters! A wicked woman and a walking corpse. Must my future depend on such as these?"

"I fear that it must, brother. Even monsters have their uses. Without her witchcraft and my wisdom, you will never fulfill your ambition."

"Your wisdom! What has it brought you? You may think that you have cheated death, but you are still a prisoner. You spend your nights in this castle and your days in a coffin. Where is the wisdom in such an empty existence?"

"You may think me a prisoner, brother, but I am not always here."

"What? You leave the castle without me? Would you ruin both of us?"

"Calm yourself, Diego. You misunderstand me. I remain within these walls, but when I lie sleeping in the crypt, I find that part of me is elsewhere."

"Where? In Hell?"

"Not exactly, though I know you are disappointed to hear it. There is no name for such a place. It is not in your theology."

"Tell me of it, Sebastian," said the Grand Inquisitor, leaning forward across the ivory-and-onyx chessboard.

"It may be no more than a dream, Diego. But sometimes I think that it is real, and that this is the dream."

"Tell me your dream, Sebastian."

Sebastian smiled, showing his long teeth. He sprawled in his carved chair and gazed up at the ceiling as if he could see the stars beyond it. "Very well, brother," he said. "I dream that I am in the topmost tower of a castle. It is night. I am surrounded by ancient volumes filled with evil incantations. And there I sit, through all eternity, answering the endless questions of my brother the Grand Inquisitor. And it is Hell for a certainty."

Diego's shoulders slumped. He started to speak again, then clamped his thin lips together and stood up, shaking his head. "I will not play these games with you, Sebastian, and it is not wise for you to toy with me this way. You should be more careful. You are growing old and thin. You are dying. And you need me to quench your thirst."

"You cannot frighten me with death," answered Sebastian. "I have died before, and I will again. I die daily, as one of your saints said. It is especially foolish of you to threaten me, though, when I know that you are here to offer me a feast."

Diego sat again. "True," he said. "We should not argue. This witch, Margarita de Mendoza, must be made to serve us both. You will visit her tomorrow night, the night before she is to die. Take some of her blood. And if you cannot make her speak, the fire may have her."

"I will do my best for you, brother. My visits to the dungeons have helped you before, and not only by giving me the strength to keep to this cursed castle and write your book. I have frightened a few confessions out of your prisoners, but I wonder about this one. If she is really a witch, I may not impress her much. The innocent ones are easier to shock."

Sebastian sat up suddenly. "Tell me, brother," he said, "is it true that in Toledo the monks disguise themselves as demons and creep into the dungeons to terrify the prisoners and force confessions from them?"

"I believe it may be true," the Grand Inquisitor answered judicially.

"Well," said Sebastian, "in the great cities they have more money for such extravagances. But here in the outlying districts you cannot afford to buy expensive costumes, so you are forced to employ real demons. Poor Diego. How can you expect success from such a shoddy substitute as I?"

"You must succeed, Sebastian! It is something to have caught a witch, and I have enough evidence already to convict her, but I want that confession. It would make a splendid chapter for my book on witchcraft, and if she names the other members of her coven, I will have more than a chapter. I will have the greatest *auto-da-fé* in the annals of the Inquisition and even Torquemada will be forced to take notice."

Sebastian sighed and slouched still lower in his chair. He seemed to be boneless. "You amaze me, brother," he said. "Do you really think you can impress that crazed old hypocrite Torquemada? Do you think he will be anxious to promote you? He wants no rivals."

"Torquemada is a great man, Sebastian. He created the Inquisition. But it will outlive him, and I believe he knows it. Someone must succeed him, and I plan to be the one."

"What a day for Spain that will be!"

"I might be more moderate. I understand that our Inquisition is the horror of Europe and that even the pope thinks Torquemada is too zealous. It may be unwise to pursue these petty heretics. But witches! They are hunted everywhere but here. Why should that be? And why should I not be the one to take advantage of the situation?"

"I wish you well, brother," said Sebastian languidly. "And what will become of me when you are Inquisitor General?"

The room in the tower was very still for a moment.

"You are very valuable to me, Sebastian."

"But shall I be when I have finished your book for you?"

"I am sure I will have further uses for you. I believe there is no man in Europe with your knowledge of sorcery and demonology. Trust me, Sebastian. I will never betray you."

"I trust you as you trust me, Diego. For nine years your prisoners have provided me with the blood I need and I have no complaints. But what I see of the future is cold and cloudy. Let it pass, though. Let us take one night at a time."

"I am more concerned about tomorrow night. Will you be able to make her confess?"

"You are asking me if I am more frightening than you are, brother, and I confess I am more afraid of you than I am of myself. Perhaps the witch will look on a creature like me as a friend. Were all your tortures useless?"

"All. We have worked on her for days."

"You must have enjoyed yourself, even if she did not confess. The torture was suspended, of course?"

"Of course. We would not disobey Torquemada's instructions."

"The man's mind amazes me. It might seem unduly cruel to some if monks were to torture their victims more than once, so he declares that the Question is never really stopped but merely suspended. And this gives him a clear conscience."

The Grand Inquisitor was smiling in spite of himself. "I admit that some of the technicalities are preposterous, but they all have their uses. When we condemn a prisoner to death, we do not execute him ourselves but just abandon him to the secular authorities, who do not have such spiritual natures. Our hands are always clean."

"Wonderful," said Sebastian. "And your tortures are such that it can never be said that the Inquisition has spilled a drop of blood. Yet you send a vampire to feed on the condemned."

The Grand Inquisitor laughed. "I see no discrepancy, Sebastian. We are pledged to spill no blood, but I trust you not to spill a drop."

"Indeed," said Sebastian. "And I promise not to waste any of this woman's blood. I will savor it. She must be strong, and courageous. I wish I could have it all."

"Not all, Sebastian. I must have her alive to be burned at the stake."

"Even so," agreed Sebastian, "though it makes me feel a failure. I have been a vampire for nine years, and I have yet to take a life."

"There is safety in moderatior, Sebastian. I provide you with all the blood you need, and you have never left behind a corpse that might betray you."

"It might be a joy to drain her dry," said Sebastian. "Is she beautiful?"

"She was. But her stay in the Holy House has not improved her appearance."

Sebastian frowned.

"Courage," said the Grand Inquisitor. "You will surely find her preferable to the old Jews you have taken before. Yet she herself is half Jewish. I am amazed by your taste. How can you, a high-born nobleman, stand to drink their tainted blood?"

"It is very good blood, I assure you."

"I believe you would drink the blood of a Moor."

"As soon as you are ready to provide it, brother. I imagine it will not be long before Ferdinand and Isabella forget their promise to the Moors and outlaw their religion as well as that of the Jews."

The Grand Inquisitor was disgusted. "I suppose it is possible for a godless monster like you to tolerate the Jews," he said, "but I should think that even you would draw the line at blacks. You died fighting them, Sebastian, and have the scar to prove it."

"The Moors did not kill me. It was that cursed cannon," Sebastian said, fingering the white scar running down the left side of his face. "And it hurt like hell. You will not enjoy dying, Diego. But it was a Spanish cannon, cast by some incompetent workman, and I did not love my country when I found half my face falling off. War is a sure cure for patriotism."

"You should be thankful the cannon exploded. A clean blow from a Moorish lance might have slain you at once and left no time for the rituals that made you one of the living dead."

Sebastian stood up slowly and drew back the tapestry that covered the tower's lone window. A light rain dribbled over the black mountains. "You may be right, brother, but I hate those guns. They will change things. A battery of cannon could crush the walls of this tower in an hour, though it has stood for centuries. Soon there will be no castles. There will be a new world, stranger than the one discovered by that Italian navigator. This is the end of an age, and we are its relics."

"Not I, Sebastian. I am part of the new world you fear."

"Perhaps, Diego. Yet you are my brother, and we are both haunted by the same mysteries, which will have no place in the world to come. You think your Inquisition is the birth of a new light, but I believe it is the death rattle of the old darkness that has nurtured both of us. The persecutions will cease, for no one will care what others believe. And most of them will believe in nothing."

He dropped the tapestry wearily and the window disappeared behind a lion's head. "Yet in one sense I agree with you. Your Torquemada has found something, though it stinks in my nostrils—and I have smelled my own grave. What will survive from your work is the idea of the organization. It is a new sort of evil; beside it witchcraft is nothing."

"What are you talking about, Sebastian?"

"You don't know, do you? That is the beauty of it. A civilization can wreak more havoc than any single man or woman, yet no one is really to blame. It is evil without a sense of sin. Each man will do his duty, Diego, even as you do, and thousands may die for it, but no one will have blood on his hands. I would rather sell my soul outright."

"Sit down, Sebastian, and calm yourself. Sometimes I think that cannon cracked your very brain."

"Just enough to let in the light, brother."

"You fought for Spain yourself, Sebastian," observed the Grand Inquisitor.

"Did I not. A few years ago there was no Spain, only an unruly flock of rival kingdoms. Since my death she has grown into a unified and awesome power, slaughtering her subjects at home and reaching out across the sea to conquer continents we never dreamed of. She is more of a monster than that poor witch in your dungeons, yet every crime committed in the name of Spain is transformed into a virtue. I know not where it will end, but I have no wish to see it. I wish it were morning, so I could sleep."

"You will sleep soon enough, Sebastian, but the sun will not rise for hours. I want to talk with you about the book, and I want to know more about your dreams. You want that woman's blood, but you must work for it."

"Why ask me?" Sebastian sneered. "Doesn't your religion teach you about life after death? Are you still unsatisfied? Have you more questions, Grand Inquisitor? This castle, not the church you swore to serve, provides your catechism."

Diego said nothing but rubbed his hand reflectively across his mouth. "I see you do not deny it," Sebastian continued. "I shall never forget that first night after my death, when you came here thinking you would be alone. How you cried and cursed yourself, standing outside the walls, because you had abandoned your claims to the estate and could never be lord of the castle. And the idiot look on your long face when I came to greet you!"

The Grand Inquisitor bridled. "Of course I was surprised. A man does not expect to meet his brother's ghost. And don't tell me you came to greet me. You came out of the darkness to kill me and you would have, if I had not been wearing a cross."

"Do not depend too much upon the cross, brother. I admit it startled me a bit at first. I don't like the look of the thing, somehow. But I could bear it if I had to."

"Perhaps. And perhaps not. The cross is strong, Sebastian, even in my hands. At least it stopped you long enough so we could talk. The pact we made that night has kept you alive. Without me and the blood I provide you would never have lasted as long as you have."

"True, brother, much as it pains me to admit it. Vampires are fragile creatures. Most that I have heard of were peasants who stumbled from their graves and attacked their own families. They were found out at once, then destroyed. We are so helpless during the daylight that I sometimes think I may be the last of the breed. But at night, Diego—at night! Even now, weakened as I am, I could turn into a beast before your eyes. I could become a glowing mist and pass through a crack in that door. I could sprout great leathery wings and fly out of this window. And you would be left here alone."

"Enough, Sebastian," said the Grand Inquisitor nervously. "I have no wish to see your tricks tonight. Is that all you have learned from your devils? Tricks to frighten children?"

"They might frighten more than children, brother."

Sebastian sat erect, his white hands clutching the arms of the chair. His face went slack and his dead eyes rolled until only the whites were visible.

"Stop it, Sebastian!"

The eyes were gone and the empty sockets filled with smoke that poured over the pale face. Sebastian held up his hands, as though to watch them melting into mist, but he had no eyes, had no face, and then no hands. He was a cloud of smoke, faintly green and pulsing with luminescence as it floated over the empty chair.

"Sebastian! Stop!" The Grand Inquisitor crossed himself and turned away from his brother. He was looking at the door and at the gigantic shadow of himself cast by the candlelight. Smoky shadows rose to envelop it and the flame flickered out. The room was black.

"Sebastian?" whispered the Grand Inquisitor.

Only silence answered him. Even the green glow was gone. He sat very still, afraid to move, and listened to the sound of his heart pounding.

A spark flew from somewhere and the red candle sputtered back to life. Don Sebastian de Villanueva stood in the farthest corner of the room, bent over a shelf of crumbling books. His long black hair streamed over the collar of his crimson cloak. He reached for a dark and dusty tome and turned slowly toward the center of the room.

"What? Still here, brother?" he asked. "I hoped to be rid of you."

"Damn you, Sebastian. I could kill you tomorrow."

"If I thought you dared, then you would die tonight. But you need me to finish the book and to scare your witch into a confession. I was only demonstrating one of my techniques—do you think it might work on her?"

"Well, you are quite a magician, Sebastian," said the Grand Inquisitor with uneasy geniality. "And I know you are capable of more than performances like that one. You practiced sorcery for years, of course, and you should have some skill. I wonder why I never suspected you when you were alive, especially after . . ."

He tried to make the words fade away inconspicuously, but they hung heavily in the air.

"After what, Diego? After the Inquisition took my wife and killed her?"

"Nobody meant her to die," said the Grand Inquisitor hurriedly. "A paltry penance would have been enough. But she wouldn't admit anything. Who would have thought she was so weak? She died before the torture was well begun . . . or so I heard."

"You heard," Sebastian repeated coldly. "You speak as if you were hundreds of miles away, as I was. If I had been there, it would never have happened. But you were there, Diego!"

"Not I, Sebastian! I knew nothing of it. I was a mere novice, little more than a boy like my vicar, Miguel Carillo. How can you suspect me? Do you think I was consulted? And how could I have stopped them, even if I had known? Her beliefs were strange and she did not keep them to herself. And she spoke against the Inquisition!"

"If more had spoken then, your Inquisition might have died aborning. She could not believe that Christians could be so cruel, and she died for it."

"Nobody meant her to die," the Grand Inquisitor said

again. "She should have confessed at once. What was she clinging to?"

"Who knows? But I am sure it was harmless. Gracia believed in a sweet world of saints and spirits. She had visions, but they were not like yours or mine. Apparently, she preferred them to life in your dungeons. I think it might have been very easy for her to die."

"But it was not easy for you, Sebastian?"

"I was not like her. I had no faith. I was not ready to die."

"Will you ever be? What is it like, Sebastian, to be dead? What lies beyond this life? What do you dream?"

"So many questions, Diego! Don't you believe the teachings of your own church? It is very simple, really, what we learned as children. The good boys go to Heaven and the bad boys go to Hell."

"Must you mock me, Sebastian? I believe you know nothing. Anyone can create an air of mystery by keeping silent. What is the color of your wonderful dreams?"

"The color?" Sebastian sank into his chair. "My dreams are silver."

The Grand Inquisitor rose in fury, but his words were cold and calm. "Beware, Sebastian," he said. "Do not depend too much upon my patience. I have not protected you for years because I love your mockery. We have made a bargain, you and I, but it is worthless if you do no more than dream. I want that book. I have waited long enough for it. The time is ripe, and I will not be denied. Deliver it soon and you will find me a grateful man. Delay too long and you will learn what it means to cross the Grand Inquisitor."

7. The Knight of Cups

ANTONIO WORE a new suit of clothes dyed brilliant blue. Together with the horse he rode his outfit had cost him nearly all the money he had, but he was a stranger here and it was necessary to make a good impression. His purse was almost empty, but that hardly mattered now that he had reached his destination. He had not traveled all this way to spend but to be paid. Besides, he reflected, it was unwise for a wayfarer to carry large sums of money. There were thieves everywhere. He had worn ragged garments throughout his long journey but had put them in his saddlebag this morning and donned his new suit, stiff but splendid. He would make a proper entrance.

Antonio was unimpressed with the city. There was not much to it, once past the public square with its cathedral and courts. It was not so much a city as a town, he thought. Compared with Rome or Florence it was nothing. There were a few fine houses, several stories high and built of good stone, but these were all clustered around the plaza. A few moments away there was nothing splendid, only narrow streets that seemed to be made of dust, lined with squat buildings of mud. Some were built of bricks, but they were mud bricks. The homes and shops were equally ugly.

The city was as bad as the country around it, he thought. For days he had ridden through ragged mountains, bare hills, and plains that were nothing but red sand dotted with scrubby bushes. At least there was a river here and a forest leading up into the mountains beyond the city. It was better, but it was not much; this land was bleak. He had heard that the soil of Spain was richer toward the south, but he had no business there. He would have to find his fortune here, in the mud and dust.

He knew that he would have to ask for directions, but he was content to wait a while, to ride aimlessly through the back streets looking for some sign. He had no wish to talk to strangers, since this meant admitting his ignorance of their region and its barbaric tongue. He had studied it for months, but still it stuck uncomfortably to his tongue, as the people he met on the road had been quick to notice. There would be time enough for talk.

His eye caught two girls walking some distance ahead of him. Their backs were to him but he could see that one was little more than a child. The other looked more promising. She was tall and slim, and the hair beneath her red cap was blond. Her coloring was unusual enough to attract his interest; most women he had seen here had black hair and black eyes. Red was common enough, though; it seemed to be the only color these people had ever seen. Everything not red was white or gray or black. Her dress was black.

Antonio urged his horse forward. As he approached the girls, he began to whistle loudly. The tune was nothing special, but it served its purpose. The smaller of the two turned her head at once. She was a pretty little thing, he thought, but his song was not for her. Finally the taller one looked behind her and he saw at once that they were sisters. He was delighted with their appearance and continued to whistle with the diligence of a master musician. Both members of his audience were smiling.

It must be rare, he thought, for them to see such a well-dressed and handsome fellow on these streets. No doubt they would be even more impressed if they knew who he was. He stopped his serenade and grinned at them. The little one laughed and her sister, blushing, turned her around and hurried her forward. Before Antonio could catch up to them, they disappeared into a doorway.

He stopped his horse before the building and looked it over. It was taller than its neighbors, which only made it more of an eyesore, but it looked beautiful to Antonio as soon as he saw the faded wooden sign over the door. Whoever had painted the sign had not been an artist, but its message was clear enough. A hand, inexplicably blue, grasping a lopsided yellow goblet could only be the sign of an inn. Anyone was welcome here, he thought. There was nothing to prevent him from following the girls, and even if he couldn't find them, at least he would be able to wash the dust from his throat. Besides, someone might give him directions. He dismounted rapidly and tied his reins to an iron ring in the wall.

The inn was so much darker than the sun-drenched street that Antonio was blind for a minute. His first impressions of the place were the sour stench of spilled wine and the harsh voice of a man shouting. The words were coming so rapidly that he could understand only a few of them, but he did hear the names "Teresa" and "Dolores." He needed no interpreter to know that the speaker was angry. A low voice answered gently, and Antonio thought he knew its owner.

His eyes adjusted to the dim light and he saw a great bull of a man whose black beard was touched with gray. He sat at a small table in the corner of the whitewashed room with the two girls standing before him. Antonio disliked the man at once, even if only because he was berating the girls, but decided to keep his distance for the moment.

He sat down alone at the only other table in the room, a long slab of oak with two benches and room for twenty men. The other nineteen must know of a better inn, thought Antonio. He stared at the bare wall in front of him as if there were a splendid mural on it, and listened.

"What will people think," roared the man with the black beard, "if the daughters of Pedro Rodriguez walk the streets without a proper chaperone? You are not peasant women! Would you disgrace yourselves? And what are you doing in a low place like this?"

"We came to find our father," said the taller girl quietly. She sat beside the brute and put her arm around him, soothing him as a rider would a troubled horse. "We have not come far, and our reputations are safe. Dolores is too young to have a reputation anyway, and she is my chaperone." She smiled up at her frowning father and continued rapidly, "We had to come. It might have been something important. The Grand Inquisitor wants you. A monk came to the house asking for you. I could have told him where you were, but I thought you might not want them to know where a familiar of the Inquisition was spending the morning."

"All right, Teresa," muttered the man, half-placated. He took a deep drink from a metal cup. "But you must be careful. You are almost old enough to marry now, and you must behave properly. Nothing is more important than honor!"

"Don't worry," said little Dolores. "I was watching her. Anyway, why do we have to stay locked up at home all the time? It's boring. You'd think a touch of the sun would kill us. We're safe enough, father, and you can escort us home. Nobody even saw us."

Antonio smiled at the lie and risked a glance at the little girl. She winked at him. He looked hurriedly down at the tabletop.

"So nobody saw you," repeated Pedro, in a voice just loud enough to be heard. "Not even that bluebird who followed you in?"

Antonio tried not to move. He wanted to jump up and answer this insult with a challenge, but the man was Teresa's father and it would be a shame to kill him. Furthermore, the man was an officer of the Inquisition, and even a foreigner knew enough to beware of men with that sort of friends. So Antonio pretended he had heard nothing, but his hand under the table was on the hilt of his sword.

A man came through the dark doorway in the wall farthest from the entrance to the inn. He was short and fat and bald and his shirt was as filthy as the smoke-stained walls. He leered at Antonio and began to babble inarticulate pleasantries. Half his teeth were missing. He looked to Antonio like a figure from a morality play exemplifying the evils of wine. If he did not discourage his customers, it could only be because his appearance was enough to drive them to drink.

"Wine," said Antonio.

"At once, sir," said the innkeeper. He backed away bowing, casting alternate glances at Antonio and the small table in the corner where Pedro Rodriguez sat with his two daughters. They had lowered their voices at the arrival of their host and their conversation was no longer audible.

The innkeeper shuffled back to Antonio's table with a battered metal cup and set it down with a clumsy flourish. Antonio sipped the wine and grimaced. It tasted like leather. It amazed him that these Spaniards could brag of their wines, yet insisted on storing them in skins that spoiled the flavor. Judging from the look of this place, though, it seemed unlikely that the taste of the skin had done the wine much harm. At least it was wet. He drank again.

The little man hovered over the table. "You are a stranger here?"

"Yes," said Antonio.

"I am Carlos Diaz," said his host. "And this is the Inn of the Golden Cup." Raising his arm in an expansive gesture, he looked around the room as though seeing it for the first time. Something in the sight of it seemed to strike him and he dropped his arm suddenly. "I bid you welcome," he added inconclusively.

Antonio offered up a silent prayer for the swift departure of Carlos Diaz and addressed himself to his drink. He looked warily at Teresa.

She seemed oblivious to him, but Dolores was smiling at him and her father was scowling.

"Begging your pardon, sir," said the persistent proprietor of the Golden Cup, "but might I ask the young gentleman where he has come from? Travelers are so rare in these parts."

Antonio had trouble deciding whether the fellow wanted information or merely wished to be congenial. In either case, Antonio's origin was no secret and could hardly fail to make an impression. He glanced at Teresa again.

"I come from Florence," he said loudly.

Carlos Diaz looked puzzled and his brow furrowed with concentration. "Florence?" he said. "I have never heard of the place. It must be in the south. Am I right?"

Antonio nearly choked on his wine. "What? Never heard of Florence? The finest city in the world! Are you a barbarian? Never heard of Florence! There is no city greater, unless it is Rome!"

"Ah! Rome!" said Carlos. "I have heard of Rome. The pope lives there. You must be an Italian. I know! Florence! Is that the home of our great Spanish navigator Columbus?"

"Spanish?" shouted Antonio. "Columbus is Italian! And he comes from Genoa!"

"Really?" asked the innkeeper. He seemed genuinely fascinated. "Genoa! Then what is Florence?"

"Florence is in Italy too," said Antonio disgustedly. "To the north of Rome." He heard light laughter coming from the corner. "Leave me alone, will you? Go away!"

"Yes, sir," said Carlos. "Sorry, sir. I am not an educated man like you, sir . . . Florence!" He retreated apologetically.

"Wait," said Antonio.

"Sir?"

"You may be able to help me. I am looking for someone."

"Ah! Then I am your man. I may not know much about the world, but I do know this city. Carlos Diaz knows everyone. Just give me the name!"

"The man I want," said Antonio, "is Diego de Villanueva."

The innkeeper's gap-toothed mouth fell open. "Diego? The Grand . . . You can't want him! People don't look for him; he looks for them!"

Antonio had had enough of this inn. He got to his feet and turned to go but found his way blocked by the massive bulk of Pedro Rodriguez, who pushed him back down to the bench and said, "What do you want with Diego de Villanueva?"

Antonio was on his feet again in an instant, his sword

half-drawn. "What is it to you?" he shouted. "Stand aside, fellow, or you die!"

"What is it to me?" said Pedro, stepping back. "Well, I am his familiar. And you, I take it, are an assassin!"

Carlos Diaz ran unashamedly for the far corner, where Pedro's daughters stood terrified. Pedro and Antonio drew their swords together and the naked blades shone in the dim light.

Something is wrong, Antonio thought. His own sword, a fine weapon, was the blade of a gentleman, suitable for duels and other affairs of honor. But this familiar was no gentleman—with both hands he brandished a war sword more than three feet long, with a heavy, triangular blade. It looked big enough to break Antonio's sword in two.

Still, there was no way out for Antonio. If he could strike the first blow, he might have a chance.

Pedro's huge sword swept back to gain momentum for a killing blow, and Antonio dropped to one knee. If he could get one quick thrust in under Pedro's guard, he might save his life.

Antonio jabbed upward, but the old soldier was too quick for him. His massive wedge of steel swept down with incredible force, shattering Antonio's blade in his hand. His arm vibrated with the impact, but at least the broken sword had deflected Pedro's first swing.

The war sword reared up again.

Antonio tossed his useless hilt away, fell flat on the dirty floor, and rolled under the table. He cracked a shin on the legs of the bench, but the thick oak above his head stopped Pedro's blade.

For just a moment the sword was caught in the wood. Pedro pulled and Antonio slapped both hands against the underside of the table. He braced his feet and thrust up with desperate strength.

The table flew end-upward and crashed into Pedro, sending him sprawling back against the wall. But Pedro's sword was free, and Antonio's oaken shield was gone.

Antonio scampered back across the floor and stumbled over the metal cup that had held his wine. On his knees, he clutched at it, cursing.

Pedro advanced with his sword and a smile.

Teresa screamed.

"Thank you, lady," said Antonio. And he threw the cup.

Its heavy base caught Pedro above the right eye and he dropped without a groan.

Antonio leaned over his fallen adversary. The man was unconscious but still breathing. A trickle of blood ran into his eye.

"Thank God he's alive," whispered Antonio. He had never killed a man, much less in front of his daughters. He picked up Pedro's sword and, just for luck, the cup. His knees were shaking and the sword was almost too heavy for him to lift.

Breathing hard, he walked to the corner where Carlos Diaz stood with Pedro's daughters.

"He'll live," he told Teresa, and then he turned to Carlos.

"You," said Antonio. "Diego de Villanueva. Tell me. Where is he?"

Carlos looked at the sword and the blood-stained cup and tried to get behind Dolores.

"Ask for him at the Holy House. Two streets down. You'll find it with no trouble. The only great building that's not on the plaza. The Holy House."

"What sort of a place is that? Who is he?"

"You don't know him? He is the Grand Inquisitor!"

"Christ!" said Antonio. "The Inquisition? What sort of kinsman do I have here?"

"Kinsman?" echoed Carlos, but Antonio ignored him and turned toward the door. Teresa and Dolores rushed to their father's side.

Kneeling beside Pedro, Dolores shook him and called on him to wake up. Teresa only stood and stared at the young stranger dressed in a suit the color of the sky, who walked out of the inn with her father's sword in his hand.

Carlos Diaz could not have cared less about the sword, but this foreigner was leaving the Inn of the Golden Cup with some of the furnishings.

It took a moment for Carlos to swallow his fear, but

then he rushed for the door. "Wait!" he cried. "If you please! The cup! You're taking my cup!"

Diego de Villanueva made his way toward the inn in a state of cold fury. Tomorrow was the day of the *auto-dafé* and Pedro Rodriguez, who was indispensable, was missing. Diego had sent his vicar, Miguel, to look for Pedro, but the young idiot would never think to look in the obvious place, and it was not the role of the Grand Inquisitor to disillusion his underlings by informing them that a familiar of his august institution might spend his mornings drinking in a low tavern.

And so, to preserve decorum, the Grand Inquisitor must play errand boy. It was a curse to have such colleagues. His temper was not improved by the knowledge that the witch in the dungeons had yet to confess. His only hope lay with his brother Sebastian, a godless monster. Still, Sebastian might make Margarita talk tonight, and at least he would finish the book soon. But it was enough to make a man nervous.

As the Grand Inquisitor turned the corner he heard someone shouting, "The cup! The cup!"

It made no sense, but something in the word chilled him. He was reminded of something that Sebastian had told him but he could not quite remember it.

There was the inn, and in the doorway Carlos Diaz; the voice was his.

What caught Diego's attention, though, was the sight of a young man with dark curly hair and a neatly trimmed beard running along the edge of his jaw like a shadow. He sat astride a gray stallion and in his right hand held a sword. In his left hand was a cup dripping blood.

The Grand Inquisitor turned in his tracks. He had seen this man before. His picture was on one of the cards he had seen in the castle. Sebastian had warned him. The card was the Knight of Cups.

This was no time to stop at the inn. Diego knew it was nonsense, but something in the sight of this man had rattled him. He would return to the Holy House. Pedro would show up eventually.

The Grand Inquisitor hurried back along the dusty street to the Holy House, one hand lifting the hem of his white robe as a woman might lift her skirts. He was suddenly afraid to be alone in the streets, and his head was filled with stories of Inquisitors who had been assassinated. Behind him came the slow steps of a walking horse.

He turned and saw the stranger riding behind him. Torn between dignity and panic, Diego resisted the temptation to break into a run, but he was walking so quickly that he looked as if he were in some sort of grotesque race. He had no idea who the man in blue might be, but he could not forget the cards or Sebastian's mockery. Somehow the image of the rider with the cup was connected with the grinning skeleton and the angel of judgment: it was an omen.

There could be no doubt that the rider was following him. The worst of it was that the fellow moved at such a leisurely pace, for all the world as if he were a casual visitor admiring the sights of the city. Diego lost his nerve and bolted into a side street. He turned again, into an alley, and leaned gasping against the side wall of a small house, his feet resting in slop someone had thrown from a window. A pig, set loose to forage for garbage in the streets, stared up at him quizzically.

The maneuver was successful; at least, the man with the cup did not catch up with him. The Grand Inquisitor hid in the alley until pride overcame his anxiety. Then he peered timidly around the corner of the house. There was nobody to be seen. He stepped out, assumed the pompous air suitable to a man in his position, and made his way to the Holy House.

Once inside, he was immediately accosted by Miguel, who was visibly agitated. The Grand Inquisitor attempted to brush him aside, but the young monk would not be denied.

"There is someone here to see you," said Miguel. "A stranger, a foreigner. His name is Antonio Manetti. I told him how busy we are, but he says he has come halfway across Europe to see you, and he has waited long enough.

He seems to be a young man of breeding and says he is your kinsman. It hardly seems possible, but he says he is here to claim the estate of your brother Don Sebastian!"

Diego was too stunned to betray his emotions. He blinked once, but his face retained its customary bland expression. Inwardly he was reeling. An heir to Sebastian's castle! It was impossible! In a month or two it would not have mattered, for by then the book would be finished and Sebastian destroyed forever. But now! Nobody could be allowed near the castle until Sebastian's usefulness was at an end. Something would have to be done to keep this heir from his inheritance. It would be a pleasure to kill him, but it might not be prudent.

The Grand Inquisitor steeled himself. He would have to invent a story and devise delays to keep this interfering foreigner busy. Meanwhile, he would have to interview the fellow. Tomorrow's *auto-da-fé* would provide enough of an excuse to buy a little time.

It was not really a surprise, but it was no less of a shock for Diego de Villanueva when he entered his chambers. There, seated beneath a crucifix, was a dark young man dressed in blue, his hand still absent-mindedly clutching a battered metal cup.

8. The Goat

"WE SHOULD arrest him at once!" said Pedro, pacing the floor of the Grand Inquisitor's chamber as if imprisoned himself.

"No," said the Grand Inquisitor.

"But how can we let him run free? He has attacked an officer of the Inquisition, your own familiar! What will the people think?" Pedro's weathered face was flushed with shame and anger. The purple bruise on his forehead was still clotted with dried blood. His huge hands gripped the edge of the table as he leaned heavily over the seated monk.

"There is nothing we can do, Pedro. His claim seems to be good. He may be only a distant cousin, but he is my kinsman. We cannot touch him."

"Well enough for you, Diego de Villanueva! He is part of your family, and you will not have your honor besmirched. But what of my honor?"

"You are right that family matters enter into this business, Pedro, but you must understand. He is related not only to me but to Sebastian—in fact, he is Sebastian's heir. If this young fellow becomes our prisoner, what will happen to his property?"

"His property?"

"Exactly, Pedro. We have seen often enough how wealthy men are condemned to enrich the royal coffers. If Antonio Manetti is taken prisoner, his inheritance will go to the Crown. And his inheritance is Sebastian's castle."

"The castle?"

"If we arrest Antonio, then the king's officers will be at

the castle in a matter of days, and that must not happen, not yet. We will have to wait."

"I don't like it," said Pedro sullenly.

"Do you think I like it? Now, of all times! I don't know how we'll delay the transfer of property, but nothing must happen until the book has been completed and accepted by the authorities. Then there will be time enough to take care of this upstart and of Sebastian as well. But we must wait!"

"We could murder the rogue," Pedro suggested diplomatically.

"We dare not risk it," answered the Grand Inquisitor. "No one wants him dead more than I do, Pedro. He will be a terrible thorn in my side. But we must be patient and we must protect Sebastian. You will have to swallow your pride for a few weeks."

Pedro acquiesced. "He is stopping at the Inn of the Golden Cup," he said.

"I know," said the Grand Inquisitor. "I suggested that he should. At least there we will have Carlos Diaz to watch him and we may get some evidence that will be useful when we are ready to prosecute. Besides, there was no other place he could afford to stay. This lord of the castle has hardly a ducat to his name. But enough of Antonio Manetti. Tonight we must deal with the present lord of the castle."

"Don Sebastian?"

"He is coming. In fact, he should be here shortly. Sebastian will question the prisoner Margarita de Mendoza. She will be abandoned to the flames tomorrow, and Sebastian is our last chance to get a confession from her. You may leave now, Pedro, but first prepare the way for him."

Pedro turned silently and left the room, but he returned in a moment with an armful of the wooden crosses that decorated the halls of the Holy House. These he placed in an ornate chest, along with the crucifix Diego had removed from his own wall.

"Very well, Pedro," said the Grand Inquisitor. "Sleep well. We will have a busy day tomorrow."

Pedro stopped at the door. "You should be sleeping too," he said.

"Not tonight. There is too much to do. I will sleep tomorrow."

Pedro walked slowly through the dark, bare hallways and let himself out of the Holy House, leaving the door open behind him. The night was clear, but as he looked up he saw a shadow pass across the stars. He crossed himself. Something was soaring through the sky. He shuddered, shrugged, then trudged stolidly toward home.

A moment later Diego de Villanueva came to the darkened doorway and stood there waiting for his brother. If he was an eager host it was only because he was cautious. Visitors in the hours after midnight were best admitted quietly; a knock on the door of the Holy House might rouse a drowsy monk, and a corpse discovered standing on the threshold would be something of an embarrassment.

So the Grand Inquisitor kept his post like a common gatekeeper, peering eagerly into the darkness. His anxiety was half fear of Sebastian and half eagerness to see him. Diego's pulse raced but the minutes dragged; he was not fond of waiting. He gnawed nervously at his thumb, and his teeth caught a jagged bit of the nail. He pulled at it and ripped the piece away in a narrow strip that tore into the cuticle. He sucked in his breath at the sudden pain and stared at the bright drop of blood welling up in the self-inflicted wound.

As if in answer to a signal, Sebastian appeared in the doorway.

Diego started, and wiped his thumb surreptitiously on the rough folds of his white robe. "You come quietly enough," he said. "Don't just stand there. You might be seen. Why don't you come in?"

"You know," said Sebastian.

"Ah, yes. Well, then, enter, Don Sebastian de Villanueva, and welcome to you."

Sebastian, wrapped in his red cloak, crossed the threshold.

"Follow me," said Diego, turning toward the gloomy

shadows of the hall. "I can never understand that," he continued. "Is it really true that you cannot enter a building without an invitation?"

"You have seen," Sebastian replied, "but it need not be such a burden. Many mortals seem strangely eager for a visit from a vampire. We have ways of making ourselves welcome."

Diego turned at the door to his chambers. "But you really need to hear the words before you can take that single step? It seems impossible. Are you such a courteous creature?"

"There are only a few hours until dawn," said Sebastian, following his brother into the room where black candles burned. "Shall we spend them discussing my powers, or shall I question your witch?"

"You are right, of course," said Diego, "but I wonder at your sudden eagerness to see her as soon as I mention your weaknesses. You were in no such hurry when it came to getting here."

"I was writing, brother. I became so engrossed in a passage of your book that I forgot your invitation to dine. Whatever I do, though, it seems that I am working for you. I am more like a serf than the master of a castle."

"The castle. I have something to tell you about that," said Diego. "No, it will wait. We must hurry. Put this on, Sebastian." He handed his brother a Dominican white robe and black cowl.

"This disguise is more terrifying than anything I might hide beneath it," said Sebastian. "But I suppose it may serve to calm any wakeful monks abroad tonight in the Holy House."

"They should be asleep, Sebastian, and the guards have been dismissed. Yet the night before an *auto-da-fé* is a restless one, and there is nothing to be gained by taking a chance. No one must see you. Are you ready? Shall I go with you?"

"Stay here," said the voice from the black hood. "I will not have you spying on me. And I will know if you follow."

"So be it," said the Grand Inquisitor sullenly. He

turned his back to the door and when he looked around a moment later saw he was alone. He dropped into his chair with a sigh and opened a book, but it rested unread in his lap. He sat quite still, his chin supported by his left hand, eyes fixed on the spot on the wall where the crucifix should have hung. And he waited.

Margarita waited too. She sat in the cold slime that covered the floor of her cell and stared into darkness as black as the robes of her jailers. Her wrists and ankles were bound together by short lengths of chain, with the shackles clamped to lacerations left by the rack. The torn muscles and tendons in her arms and legs ached intolerably. Her shoulders, wrenched by the hoist, were so painful that she could not lean back against the stone wall, and the soles of her feet were covered with burns and blisters.

The Grand Inquisitor waited for dawn, but Margarita waited for death. She had been told repeatedly that an *auto-da-fé* was approaching and that her continued silence would leave her tormentors no choice but to burn her alive. Just a few hours ago, as nearly as she could reckon, the Grand Inquisitor's vicar, Miguel Carillo, had slipped into her cell to warn her that she had only one night left to live.

She had almost been touched by his pleading, which seemed more compassionate than his master's august ultimatum. The young monk acted as if he might really be concerned with the state of her soul, not just with her secrets. He had actually gone down on his knees in the filth at her feet and begged her to confess and be reconciled. She had begun to believe he was sincere, but then she remembered how calmly he had sat beside her, transcribing every scream and curse evoked by the turning of the rack, and the thought had made her scream again, this time in fury.

At that he had hurried from the dungeons, leaving her alone with the knowledge that the next voice she heard would summon her to die. She almost longed for it. She certainly would not betray the others in the coven to spare herself, but she dreaded the coming day. Her cell was always dark, so there was no way to tell if it was night or morning. Her heart staggered at any sound, for it might be summoning her to the flames, but the only noises were the scurrying of rats. There would be another sound soon, though, and her ears strained for it.

"Margarita!"

It was no more than a whisper, but she jumped when she heard it, and the links of her chains rattled. Her eyes searched through the darkness for the source of the voice, but it was impossible to see anything. There was nothing more to hear. Her suddenly tensed limbs began to relax again as she decided that the voice must have come from her own mind, but then it spoke again.

"Margarita!"

She was tempted to answer, but she reasoned that this must be another device of the Inquisition, so she kept her peace and only peered anxiously into the impenetrable gloom.

There was something in her cell—a faint glow, a spot of dull red that floated above her head. It grew brighter as she watched, then burst into flame. The sudden light blinded her and she threw an arm up to shield her eyes. When she lowered it a moment later she could see a burning torch and then the man holding it. His face was hidden by the folds of a black cowl, the top of which touched the dripping ceiling.

It was only reasonable to assume that he had come to guide her to her death, but his manner of entering made her wonder. She had never seen anything like it before, at least not in the Holy House. It was almost like magic.

"Do you know me?" he asked, thrusting the torch into a bracket on the wall.

His voice was deep, and cold enough to belong to an Inquisitor, but it did not sound like anyone who had questioned her before. Yet there was something vaguely familiar about it; even as she shook her head in reply to his question, she realized she had heard him speak before. But where? She tried to see his face, but it was hidden in shadows and folds of black cloth.

"If you do not know me, do you know at least that you are to die tomorrow?"

Margarita nodded. It was easier not to speak; her throat was still sore from the strips of linen she had been forced to swallow during the water torture. She was surprised to find herself answering the stranger at all.

"Would you bring more suffering upon yourself? Can you imagine the agony of the flames? Will you not accept the mercy of the Inquisition?" His questions rang hollowly in the confines of the narrow cell. "Your confession could buy you much, Margarita: more days of questions, more nights in the dungeons, and finally a rope to strangle you at the stake before your clothes catch fire. Will you refuse such blessings? And why? To prove your hatred for the men who hold you captive? To protect the naked wretches who danced beside you in the moonlight? To keep your promise to the Prince of Lies?"

Margarita's bewildered green eyes stared upward at the face she could not see. Something was wrong with these questions. They reflected her own thoughts too well, and that worried her more than the threats and arguments of the Grand Inquisitor.

"Who are you?" The words choked in her swollen throat. "What do you want of me?"

"I wanted to see you again, Margarita. You are foolish to be so brave, but it is bravery nonetheless."

"What else could I do?" she replied. "You have said it all yourself. I know your voice."

"And you know my face," said Sebastian. "This face, at least."

He pulled back the black cowl.

Whatever Margarita had expected to see, it was not what Sebastian showed her: flaring nostrils in a long gray muzzle, sorrowful brown eyes, and two long, sharp horns—the head of a goat.

She gasped, and her quick painful intake of breath turned to hysterical laughter. She crawled on twisted limbs toward the thing in monk's robes and embraced its legs. "The master," she whispered, and began to weep.

Fingers cold and hard as iron clutched at her shoulders

and pulled Margarita to her feet. She fell against Sebastian and felt his arms engulf her. The rough goat's hair brushed against her face as her head rested on his shoulder, and she inhaled the rich animal smell of him gratefully.

"You have come to save me," she said. It was not a question.

Then he held her at arm's length, and her mind reeled to see that his face had changed. He now had the head of a man and a gaunt pale face with sunken eyes. Black hair draped it, and a long mustache hung below the bony chin. It was the face of a corpse.

"Who are you?" Margarita asked again, panic in her voice. "Are you the master?"

"I am Don Sebastian de Villanueva."

"Don Sebastian? The brother of the Grand Inquisitor?"

"Even so, Margarita. And I am not here to rescue you. Rather you are here to rescue me. A witch should recognize the signs, my brave and beautiful Margarita. I am one of the undead and I have come for your blood."

Margarita stumbled backward out of his arms. "Satan!" she cried. "Am I betrayed again?" Her voice rose to a scream and her body was convulsed by sobs. "Then take my blood and welcome to it, for after this night I have no need of it!"

She threw back her head, exposing her long white throat like a sacrificial victim eager to be slaughtered. Sebastian's sluggish heartbeat quickened at the sight. He cast aside the monk's robe that disguised him and moved forward. As he glided toward her, his lips drew back in a bestial snarl, exposing his long ivory teeth, the canines sharp as swords.

Margarita's outspread arms reached to clasp him as he touched her, and she drew him closer as his cold lips sought her jugular. His teeth cut the warm flesh, and he felt the hot, salty blood rush into his mouth. She gave a little cry, half pain and half ecstasy. He felt her throat move under his lips. She grew limp beneath him and began to slide down the rough stone wall to the floor. Sebastian followed her, his arms supporting her weight, his eager mouth still fixed to the flowing wound, until they were on their knees together, almost like children at play. His white fingers tangled her long black hair; hers clutched and twisted his crimson cloak.

The torch above them sputtered; its flame sank into a ruddy glow, and then went out. There were small soft sounds in the darkness; they might have been kisses.

The Grand Inquisitor dozed in his chair. He had slipped into a nervous sleep in spite of himself. He had worked hard and he was tired. His dreams were vague but not pleasant; something in them startled him so that he suddenly sat bolt upright. His brother stood before him.

"Sebastian," he said. It took a moment for him to remember where he was. The first thing he realized was how much his brother had changed. Sebastian looked years younger, more like the soldier who had fought the Moors than the wizard who brooded alone in the tallest tower of an empty castle. He seemed taller and stronger. His face was flushed and the hollows around his dark eyes had disappeared, but the pale scar of the wound that had killed him was as vivid as ever. Diego had seen this transformation before, but something about it never failed to sicken him. He fought off his nausea and drowsiness.

"Well, Sebastian?" he said. "Well? I see you have supped—what else have you done?"

"Nothing, brother. I have failed you. She would not speak. I fear she will never speak."

"What? You haven't killed her?"

"No. She sleeps below. I leave her killing to you."

Diego sighed and rubbed his hand across his eyes. "I knew you would disappoint me. She is a stubborn wench. There is no way of understanding how she could resist everything."

"If you believe in witchcraft, brother, you must believe that witches have powers. Perhaps she has some trick that renders her insensible to pain. A simple trance would suffice. Surely she employed some power to defy you, Diego, for you have used her cruelly."

The Grand Inquisitor rose from his chair. "Do you dare reproach me, Sebastian? You, who still have her blood on your lips?"

Sebastian scowled. "I do what I must to survive, brother. But your work is past all understanding." His mouth twisted. "Keep away from the castle."

"But Sebastian! The book!"

"The work will continue. But for now, I have no wish to look upon your face."

"As you will, Sebastian." The Grand Inquisitor edged toward the door. "The sun will rise soon. You must leave at once."

Sebastian did not move. "There is one thing more," he said. "Margarita gave me a message for you."

"A message!" gasped the Grand Inquisitor. "What is it? Have you been fooling me? Is it a confession?"

"No, brother. Not a confession, only this."

Sebastian's hand lashed out with stunning speed and the back of it struck his brother full in the face.

Diego staggered from the blow, but he stayed on his feet. His hand flew up to his cheek. He stood in shocked silence as Sebastian vanished into the shadows of the hallway. Blood trickled from the corner of the Grand Inquisitor's mouth.

On the floor beside Diego's chair was a black-and-white Dominican habit. Someone had ripped it into shreds, and the pieces were spattered with fresh blood.

9. The Yellow Robe

THE BELLS woke Miguel at dawn. He sat up slowly and perched on the edge of his hard wooden cot, his bare feet dangling in the dried rushes that covered the cold stone floor. Hunched over with his head in his hands, he regarded the blank wall of his narrow room with bleary eyes and no affection.

"Too many bells," he muttered. They rang four times a day to summon the monks to services: at dawn, noon, dusk, and even at midnight, when everyone was asleep, so that he was awakened twice every twenty-four hours by their insistent pealing. Their sound, which had once seemed a hymn of praise, was now oppressive.

He steeled himself for another day of cruel monotony, then remembered with a queasy thrill that this morning would bring something different—the *auto-da-fé*. This day would be filled with pomp, processions, and preaching. It would be a spectacle and a celebration and would end with flaming death.

One of those to die would be Margarita de Mendoza. Perhaps then his dreams would stop. A few good nights of sleep might make his life more tolerable.

Miguel stood up to pull his rough robe over his head. As he tied the length of hemp around his waist he felt his stomach growl ominously, and he cursed under his breath at the thought that there was no breakfast in store for him, since the monks never ate until after High Mass at noon. What was worse, Miguel suddenly realized that today's special ceremonies would make even that meal impossible, so that he would have to go hungry until nightfall.

Still, there was nothing to be done about it. He stepped through the small, doorless archway and into the corridor beyond. At once he saw the Grand Inquisitor striding down the hall toward him, with Pedro close behind. Pedro was already dressed in the ceremonial garments the *auto-da-fé* demanded: a black suit with a white cross emblazoned on the chest to signify that he was a familiar of the Holy Inquisition. Pedro's face was clean and his beard combed, but his eyes were bloodshot and there was a purple bruise with a brown scab on the right side of his forehead.

Miguel bowed his head and tried to hurry by, but the Grand Inquisitor stopped him with a gesture. "Wait," he said. "We will dispense with your presence at the morning Mass, Miguel. There is too much to be done. Go with Pedro. He needs your help with the preparations. Here are your records." Miguel had time only for a glance at his superior, but he noticed that he seemed to have cut his lip. Then the Grand Inquisitor turned away, leaving Miguel alone with the grim giant in black.

"Come on," said Pedro, and led Miguel to a chamber where half a dozen monks and familiars stood silently waiting for instructions. In this storeroom were the trappings that made the *auto-da-fé* such a spectacle.

Above everything loomed the green cross, the emblem of the Inquisition. It was propped in a corner of the ceiling, held in place by a pole some ten feet long so it would rise above the heads of men and horses when carried in the procession that was to come. The cross itself looked rough and unfinished. It had not been smoothed and planed but seemed rather to have been fashioned from two rudely hewn logs of fresh wood symbolizing the living faith. In truth, though, it was dead wood painted green. One of the monks pulled it down and began to drape it in black velvet.

Another opened a chest and drew forth the banner of the Inquisition. It displayed an oblong field upon a black background, with the green cross in the center growing between an olive branch and a sword aimed toward Heaven. Inscribed around the oval was the legend

"Exurge Domine et Judica Causam Tuam, Psalm 73." The monk attached the banner to a pole while one familiar took from another chest what looked like a pile of yellow cloth. Miguel knew it was dozens of sanbenitos, the garments of shame that heretics wore to meet their punishment.

What drew his eye, though, was something more grotesque than any of these ceremonial objects—a group of ugly half-human figures huddled together in a dark corner. They were brittle and brown, their eyes black blots in empty faces. These were straw men, the effigies of those who had escaped the Inquisition, to be draped in yellow robes, carried through the jeering throngs, and finally burned at the stake along with the living bodies of those who had not fled in time.

But there was something worse, something Miguel had hoped he would not see. Stacked beside the sinners built of straw were three wooden boxes, each long and wide enough to hold a human body. Each box, covered with dirt and mold, had a name scrawled on its side in charcoal. These were coffins ripped from graves so that the corpses could be borne aloft to the flames. Not even death brought an end to the judgments of the Inquisition, and those whose heresies were discovered too late still merited posthumous punishment. Miguel knew this but had hoped to be spared the sight of those grinning, yellow-clad skeletons during the first *auto-da-fé* at which he was to officiate. He prayed that at least these newly uncovered heretics were long dead, so they would be no more than skeletons.

Miguel stared blankly into the dark corner and from far away heard the faint sound of hammering. "What is that noise?" he asked suddenly.

"The carpenters," answered Pedro, "putting up the scaffolds and benches for the *auto*."

"What? Are they still at work? They should have been done long ago. And nothing is ready here, either. We shall be late!"

"Calm yourself," said Pedro. "This is not Madrid, where there are so many heretics that the ceremonies take up the whole day. We have plenty of time."

"But we must be finished by dark," Miguel protested. "The people are always so excited by the end of the ceremonies, and we must not have an act of faith turned into an occasion for a night of revelry."

"They are excited by the flames, you mean," said Pedro. "Never fear, though; we should be done by dusk, with time enough to send them home before darkness falls. Anyway, the Grand Inquisitor has ordered a late start today."

"Why should he do that?" asked Miguel. The idea of a break with tradition worried him. In Madrid, the *auto-da-fé* always began at dawn.

"Politics," said Pedro. "Or something like it. You know that the parish priest always delivers the sermon at the *auto?* Well, today he will not. The Grand Inquisitor has reserved that honor for himself. Something to do with the witch, I think. He wants to speak to the people about witches. So the good priest has had his feathers ruffled, and he complained. Of course, he could hardly defy the Inquisition—he is only a priest—but the Grand Inquisitor decided on a compromise. Since it is a Sunday anyway, he declared that a High Mass be held as usual, where the priest may speak to his heart's content. When he dismisses his congregation, the *auto* will begin."

"I see," said Miguel, but he was not pleased by these irregularities.

"No matter whether you see or not," said Pedro sharply. "All this talk wastes the same time you're so worried about. Where are your records? How many have we today?"

Miguel fumbled with papers. "Thirty-seven in all," he said.

"Three of them dead already," said Pedro. "You there!" he shouted to a pair of the familiars. "Break open those boxes, and dress the dead ones in their golden gowns." He smiled at his pleasantry.

Miguel turned his head away as the black-clad familiars attacked the coffins with crowbars, but he could not block out the sound of tearing wood, or the sudden musty odor that filled the room. He heard the clatter of bones as they spilled onto the stone floor.

"Careful with those!" Pedro shouted.

"Three dead," said Miguel. He was almost shouting himself, as if trying to drown out noises he had no wish to hear. "Three dead. Seven fled, that is, seven contumaciously absent, to be burned in effigy. Twenty-seven living, of which four are impenitent and one relapsed. These five will be abandoned to the secular authorities."

"Five to be burned alive!" shouted Pedro to the familiar who held the yellow robes. He began to sort through them for those bearing the markings that indicated that the prisoner was condemned to death.

"No! Wait!" said Miguel. "The relapsed heretic has repented."

"Oh, yes," muttered Pedro, "the old woman." He turned again to the man with the sanbenitos. "Four to be burned alive and one to be strangled before burning!"

Miguel winced. He hated to hear the judgments of the Inquisition bawled out as if they were orders for goods in the marketplace. He watched the man in black lay out the yellow robes, covered with crude drawings in red paint of dancing devils and bursts of fire. On four of the robes the flames pointed upward, but on the fifth they pointed down, a sign for the executioner that he should use his strangling cord before applying the torch.

"Of the twenty-two remaining..." began Miguel, as he heard the nails ripping from the half-rotten wood of the third coffin. In spite of himself he turned to look. The two familiars, white crosses emblazoned on their black doublets, dragged two withered arms from the shattered wood. A stench of decay seeped into the room.

"Christ!" said one of the familiars. "This one is too fresh!"

"Not fresh enough!" said his companion, his face set in a grimace of disgust. He pulled again and a face emerged from the splintered box. Withered and brown and eyeless, it looked like one of the effigies, but it had been a man.

"Of the twenty-two remaining!" shouted Miguel. His stomach lurched.

"What a stink!"

"Get that thing on him before he falls apart!"

Miguel turned away from the sight of three men attempting to dress the rotting corpse. "Of the twenty-two remaining," he repeated, "six are lightly suspected, seven are gravely suspected, and nine . . ."

"Hold on a minute! Which is the one for the gravely suspected?"

"Fools!" bellowed Pedro. "The plain yellow for the lightly, the ones with half a cross on them for the gravely, and the whole cross for the violently suspected!"

"Six are lightly suspected!" screamed Miguel. "Seven are gravely suspected! And nine are violently suspected!"

He was grateful now that there had been no breakfast.

"The roll of those to be abandoned!" he continued, keeping his eyes on the paper. "One Margarita de Mendoza, shepherdess, of this parish, impenitent, guilty of witchcraft and sorcery . . ."

By the time the monks came to take her away, Margarita was past caring. Her mind was cloudy and she could hardly think. She saw clearly enough what was happening to her, but she did not seem to be a part of it. The voices around her were dim and distant, the men who dragged her to her feet only moving shadows. They were almost carrying her, since her twisted legs and blistered feet could hardly bear her weight.

"I will never walk again," she thought, and a voice in the back of her brain laughed at the idea. Of course she would never walk again—she would be dead by sunset. What did it matter if she had been crippled?

Nothing mattered but the throbbing where Sebastian had kissed her throat. Had he betrayed her? Why had he come? He had whispered to her in the darkness, but the memory of the words drifted away. Something about the sunset, but she would be dead by then. She could not remember, but she had been drugged by his kiss and would not suffer. For that at least she was grateful. His voice still rang in her ears, but all he seemed to be saying was her name: "Margarita. Margarita. Margarita."

It was only a whisper, perhaps only the memory of a whisper, and yet was more. He was somehow still with her and she with him, in a place that was small and cold and dark, yet somehow vast and radiant with silver.

"Margarita," he said. Then a voice spoke again. "You did not betray me."

But was it his voice or hers?

All at once the dimness of the dungeons vanished and the world turned bright as day. The yellow light was almost blinding, but she saw devils dancing in it.

Miguel sighed and lowered the yellow robe. The woman must have gone completely mad. Even when he held the sanbenito before her eyes, she did not respond. Everyone in Spain knew the emblem of infamy, and surely the demons and the flames emblazoned upon the robe were plain enough, but Margarita only looked at them and smiled.

"Cover her," said Miguel to one of the familiars. Her shift was so torn and frayed that she might as well have been naked, but the sanbenito would remedy that. Miguel turned to the next prisoner.

When the devils dropped away from her eyes, Margarita had a brief glimpse of a sunny courtyard full of people. Then something dropped over her head and she was plunged back into darkness.

"Margarita," said the voice.

Hands pulled at her and she squirmed, then her head popped through an opening and she could see again. She realized that someone was dressing her, which had not happened to her since she was a child in her father's house.

There was a man beside her who looked like her father. She tried to focus her eyes.

"Is it you?" she asked him. "Are you here too?"

The man turned to face her but did not answer. There was no need to; it was another old man. But he had the same white hair and flowing beard, same strong nose and sad brown eyes. He tried to smile at her, but his thin lips only twitched.

The devils were all over him, all over the long yellow robe pulled over his head like a poncho. Margarita looked down and saw the same red demons dancing on her breast. She realized all at once that she was wearing the sanbenito, as was the man beside her. She glanced around and saw dozens of the yellow robes, some like hers, some marked with crosses, some with no insignia at all. Scurrying among the robes were others, dressed in black suits with white crosses on the front. There were Dominicans, too, with their white cassocks and black hoods and black cloaks trailing behind them. She recognized one of them, the frail young monk who was always writing. There were others she had seen in the dungeons, but the Grand Inquisitor was not among them.

The men in black and white bustled about like characters in a play, but the people in the yellow robes were strangely still. None of it seemed real. Seeking out others like herself, Margarita found four whose sanbenitos bore the same markings: the old man who looked like her father, two younger men who might have been brothers, and an old woman who stood in a corner crying and looked very odd. She was certainly plump, almost fat, but her face was drawn and thin as if she had been starved. She has no trouble standing, thought Margarita; she must have given in almost at once.

So we are the five who will burn, said Margarita to herself. She closed her eyes against the morning sun and listened for the darkness. Someone whispered her name.

Someone grabbed her by the throat. She opened her eyes and recognized the giant who had arrested her. She had not seen him since that night, but she remembered him. As he tied a rope around her neck its rough surface scraped against the small wounds in her throat. The other end of the rope bound her hands together in front of her. As he tied the last knot tightly, the man with the gray beard and black suit grinned at her. "More fuel for the fires. What a waste." Then he was gone.

A monk came by and thrust a huge green candle into her hands. She tried to drop it, but he laced her hands together with a piece of cord.

Monks stood on either side of her, urging her to repent while there was still a chance, but she hardly heard them. She was listening for another voice.

A man in black led a string of mules into the courtyard and someone lit the green candle.

10. The Green Cross

ANTONIO STEPPED out of the dim shadows of the cathedral and down the marble steps to the sunny plaza below. The crowd flowed around him, moving with what he took to be unseemly haste, though he had to admit that the service had been all but endless. Indeed, he might have been tempted to forego the Mass if he had known just how interminable it would prove to be; but he was a pious man, up to a point, and would have been a madman to act anything less than devout while a stranger in Spain.

But how the priest had raved! He had shouted and whispered, threatened and cajoled, smiled and wept, and his sermon alone had lasted well over an hour. Antonio had distracted himself by admiring the rich interior of the cathedral, the first halfway-impressive building he had seen since entering Spain, though it was nothing compared with the glories of Rome or even Florence. In all fairness he acknowledged that this was not one of Spain's great cities, but it was the city where he was forced to stay, a fact that had begun to disturb him.

He hoped that the castle of Don Sebastian de Villanueva was worth his journey and certainly wished that somebody would help him find out. So far he had discovered almost nothing except that this was a city where a man could end up fighting for his life in the very hour of his arrival, an intelligence that had been anything but reassuring. Antonio's kinsman, Diego de Villanueva, had taken great pains to assure him that the quarrel with Pedro Rodriguez had been based on a misunderstanding and would not be repeated, but beyond that the tall, grim-faced monk had been irritatingly incommunicative. He had lapsed into Latin, which Antonio understood little better than Spanish, and had conveyed nothing more than the advice to be patient, along with some half-intelligible remarks about some imminent event that rendered further discussion impossible. No doubt it was a monkish sort of failing to speak dead languages, but Antonio had found it a most unsatisfactory interview.

At least he was happy to be free of Pedro Rodriguez. Antonio had seen Pedro's daughters at the Mass sitting almost directly below the pulpit, but they had not acknowledged his presence, and indeed he had no reason to think they were aware of it. He doubted that it mattered much, after the incident at the inn yesterday, and cursed his bad luck. Teresa was the prettiest girl he had seen yet in the city and he had taken a strange fancy to her, even though they had not exchanged a word. And now they probably never would. Why did women have to have fathers?

Antonio had descended the steps of the cathedral lost in thought, but when he raised his eyes to look at the plaza he was astounded. During the few hours he had spent at Mass, the public square had been transformed into some sort of amphitheater, although no one but Antonio seemed surprised to see it. A gigantic wooden platform had been erected forming three sides of a square, and tiers of benches rose from it. Pulpits, altars, and lecterns stood in the center of the square, along with a small structure that looked unpleasantly like an empty cage. Dominican monks were hurriedly draping everything in black cloth.

Something in the appearance of these friars disturbed Antonio. Monks were common enough; in fact, the man who had told Antonio about his inheritance had been a Dominican in Florence, who had seemed perfectly friendly, even genuinely pleased to be the bearer of good tidings. But these men were different. Perhaps there was nothing more to his feeling about them than the discomfort he had experienced in the presence of his kinsman the Grand Inquisitor, but after all, the Dominicans here were the officers of the Inquisition, and their reputation had cast a chill over all of Europe.

He realized now what sort of pageant was being prepared here. He had heard talk of it last night and this morning, but everyone spoke Spanish, and so rapidly that he had hardly known what they were saying. Now he understood without being told. He was about to witness an *auto-da-fé*.

Reluctantly he admitted to himself that his curiosity was stronger than his indignation; he would stay and watch. At least it would be something to tell his friends about when he was home again, he thought, then realized with a chill that this city was to be his new home. If all went well, he might be here for years, or never see Florence again. He looked at the busy friars so eagerly covering their world with black crepe. What was he doing here in this bleak country?

He wandered off the plaza for a moment; there was nothing happening yet to keep him there. He was thinking of food and believed he was going in the direction of his inn, but realized his mistake almost at once. He had turned into the wrong street and was about to retrace his steps when he smelled something that stopped him. There was a little stall built on to one of the houses here. A scrawny old woman stood behind a counter on which were several small, steaming pies. Antonio watched a ragged man purchase two and walk away munching one with every evidence of enthusiasm. He decided to follow suit. The transaction was quickly accomplished, but he was startled and a bit disturbed when the old woman slammed the shutters in his face and closed up shop a second after serving him. She must be off to see the show, thought Antonio, as he wandered back toward the square.

The pie was too hot to eat, too hot even to hold, and he was forced to toss it back and forth between his hands to avoid burning his fingers, even though he felt a bit of a buffoon.

"Are you going to eat that thing?"

Antonio looked up from his cooling dinner and saw Dolores Rodriguez, Teresa's little sister. "What?" he said.

"The empanadilla!" she said. "Are you going to eat it?"

"What did you call it?" asked Antonio. "Of course I am. What else would I do with it?" Matching the word to the deed, he bit into the tough crust, which was yellow in the center and burned on the edges. A spicy sauce that dribbled down his chin was so hot that tears sprang into his eyes. At least there seemed to be some sort of meat in it, but the seasonings masked the flavor completely. "It's very good," he said.

"It's terrible," said Dolores. "Nobody but a fool would eat one. They say the public executioner provides the meat for those things."

Antonio's mouth dropped open and the pie fell out of his hand into the dust. "What?" he said again.

"It's only a joke," said Dolores. "At least I think it is. But they're made from bad meat, covered with spices so you can't taste it. Everyone knows it. You're lucky you dropped it."

Antonio kicked at the dusty pie.

"You're funny," said Dolores. "Why are you here?"

"Why, to see the *auto-da-fé,* like everyone else."

"That's not what I mean, stupid. Why are you here at all?"

"Oh, well, I am an heir. I have come to take possession of my castle."

"You? A castle?"

"Me," said Antonio, but he couldn't help smiling. The idea struck him as unlikely, too. "It was the castle of Don Sebastian de Villanueva, but now it will be mine."

Dolores looked up at him quizzically. "It hardly seems possible," she said. "You, a relative of the Grand Inquisitor!"

"Only a distant cousin of some kind," said Antonio, not sure whether to be proud or ashamed.

"You should have seen his brother, Don Sebastian," said Dolores. "He was a hero. I think I saw him once when I was a little girl."

"And what are you now?"

"I'm thirteen, stupid! I'm not a little girl anymore."

Antonio, who was twenty-two, allowed himself a condescending smile.

They were just on the edge of the plaza, but it was filling with people: not just the congregation of the cathedral on the square, but the parishioners from two other churches in different parts of the city. Dolores turned to look at the crowd. "Here comes my sister," she said. "I've been hiding from her. She's stupid, too. I think she likes you."

"What?" said Antonio, wishing fervently for something else to say. "Even after what happened yesterday?"

"You mean because you hit our father? That doesn't matter. He hits us all the time. He deserves it. But nobody ever hit him before."

Teresa broke through the mob and put both her arms around Dolores. "Where have you been, Dolores?" she said. "Father would kill both of us if you were running loose, today of all days."

"Good day, señorita," said Antonio, doffing his hat and bowing low. "Your sister has been safe here with me."

Dolores squirmed indignantly in her older sister's grasp. "Come on, you," said Teresa. She took her little sister firmly by the hand and led her into the throng. Just before she was gone, though, she turned to Antonio and smiled. "Thank you, sir, for looking after the little one."

She vanished into the crowd while Antonio stood and grinned, looking at the summer sky. "I think she likes you," he quoted. In his exhilaration he kicked the pie so hard that it stuck to the nearest wall.

From somewhere in the distance he heard a drum beating. He craned his neck, but it was impossible to see anything from where he stood, so he began to press his way into the mob that stood between him and the center of the plaza.

He found that his knees and elbows were more effective than apologies, but he did not make any real progress until the people around him began, one by one, to drop to their knees. Trumpets sounded a melancholy fanfare.

With everyone kneeling, Antonio had a clear view of the plaza. It was still empty; in fact, even the monks who had worked there were gone. The platforms and benches stood starkly in the brilliant sun of a summer noon, waiting like the setting of a play that was about to begin. Several of those nearest at hand were glaring indignantly at Antonio, who suddenly realized how conspicuous he was as the only standing man among hundreds—or was it thousands? Everywhere around the platforms were multitudes of men, women, and children on their knees. Antonio hurriedly joined their number. By now he was close enough for a good look at the grotesque procession that marched ponderously into the public square.

First came the drummer, beating a slow dirge on the taut skin of the low-sounding instrument that hung from his stooped shoulders. Behind him were three trumpeters blowing minor chords. These, merely heralds, dispersed into the crowd as the procession proper came into view.

A Dominican strode into the square, bearing on a long pole above his head the green cross of the Inquisition. Sable drapings fluttered from its branches, moved not by the breeze but by the exertions of the laboring monk who sweated in the still summer air.

Following the friar was a platoon of familiars, grim men who marched with military pride, each with a white cross on his suit of shining black. At their head walked Pedro Rodriguez, eyes gleaming, his battered face thrust out and upward toward the yellow sun.

Behind the familiars came a monk ringing a bell. The people murmured at the sight of him and many crossed themselves. His bell signaled the arrival of the parish priest, who entered the plaza on a mule. Four acolytes surrounded him; above his head they bore a canopy of red and gold. The priest might not deliver the sermon at this particular *auto-da-fé*, but he had no intention of relinquishing his ceremonial position in the parade. Another company of familiars, lesser men than the first, perhaps, but no less conscious of their own dignity, followed him.

Then came the prisoners, who moved in ranks according to their depth of infamy. The twenty-two who were spared at least the ultimate punishment stumbled along, tripping over their long yellow robes, all marked to indicate the degree of their disgrace. Some wore the plain sanbenito; others were marked with half a cross, and still others wore the cross complete. But all hung their heads in shame, and on each head was the final mark of shame, the pointed yellow cap called a coroza. In each pair of hands, tied together, was a flaming green candle. The ropes that held the candles in place ran back to encircle the necks of the heretics.

At the sight of the prisoners a shout went up from the mob. People leaped to their feet to shout insults and curses. A barrage of fruit, vegetables, and even stones rained down upon the helpless heretics.

Antonio looked on in horror lessened only by the relief he felt as his knees came up off the hard flagstones. It was good at least to be standing again, and in any case there was nothing he could do about what was happening, so he determined to be philosophical.

A second group of prisoners entered the plaza. Their robes, covered with demons and flames, showed that they were bound for a fiery death. Antonio did not recognize the meaning of the insignia, but even he could tell that these were special cases. They each rode on mules between two monks, if only because they could not walk after their stay in the Holy House. These monks, starkly black and white beside the red and yellow of their charges, spoke continually to the prisoners, with fervent gestures that might have been for the benefit of their audience. Everyone but Antonio knew that they were urging the heretics to repent even now and exchange the agony of the flames for the mercy of the strangler's noose.

Surrounding the monks and their prisoners were a number of armed guards who bore on their shoulders long, lethal halberds, weapons that combined the deadliest features of spear and battle-ax. They were well designed to discourage any vain attempt to escape the justice of the Inquisition. Some that had been polished gleamed in the sun.

There were only five condemned to death in this small

city on this one Sunday, out of the thousands who died for the glory of the Inquisition and in the name of Christ. The crowd was more subdued in the presence of these heretics, not perhaps because of pity but because it was impossible to throw anything without the risk of hitting a monk or a soldier. The citizens might have even been worried about the danger of striking an innocent mule.

Antonio's gaze was drawn to one in particular among these five prisoners. This was a young woman distinguished not only by her haggard beauty but by the way her lips twisted in a vague, vacant smile. He could hardly bear to look upon her but could not bring himself to look away. Her face was pale, her downcast eyes green, and her tangled hair black as a raven's wing. There were white streaks in it, though, flowing down from her forehead like lightning in a stormy sky. She was almost as pretty as Teresa, Antonio thought, but in a very different way. And she was doomed to die.

She was the last of the heretics, or so it seemed, for after her came a collection of friars bearing more long poles. From these seven poles dangled hideous effigies of straw, their painted eyes staring blankly at the multitude, their withered bodies encased in yellow robes. Upon these the mob vented its greatest fury and the air was black with missiles. A large rock broke the neck of one of the straw men. Its head sagged and its pointed cap dropped to the ground.

The three monks who followed bore a more ghastly burden. Suspended above their heads was a trio of yellow-clad corpses. Antonio could hardly believe his eyes. He strained to see in hopes he had imagined the sight, then wished he had not looked. Two of the three were skeletons, but the last was unspeakable.

Behind it rode his kinsman, Diego de Villanueva, the Grand Inquisitor. Before him was a banner bearing the arms of the Inquisition, with the arms of Ferdinand and Isabella on its other side. The Grand Inquisitor, mounted on a handsome mare, stared sternly ahead at the banner, looking to neither right nor left. His aristocratic features were composed and he seemed lost in some profound meditation, utterly oblivious to the grim relics that swayed above his shaven head. At his entrance the crowd grew still. His appearance climaxed the procession, but a few monks, the most prominent officers of the local Inquisition, rode behind him.

Among them Antonio recognized the young friar, Miguel Carillo, who had admitted him into the Holy House. Antonio was aghast at the thought that Miguel, certainly no older than he was, appeared to have such an important position in the councils of the terrible Inquisition. What sort of young man could he be?

The parade concluded with a group of civilians, the secular authorities to whom the Grand Inquisitor would abandon the condemned with pleas that the law be merciful. Lest there be any doubt about the sincerity of these beseechings, the last man in the procession was the public executioner.

There was a moment of confusion as all these people and animals were massed into the open-ended square formed by the three platforms, but order came quickly out of chaos. The prisoners were hurried into the benches in the platform on the right, and city officials and some prominent citizens took their places in the benches on the left. The Grand Inquisitor, along with his entourage of monks and familiars, took his seat on the central platform. The green cross and the banner of the Inquisition were planted in small stands before him, with the effigies and dead heretics placed beside the benches where the prisoners huddled between monks still urging them to repent. Those who were to die sat on the topmost bench where everyone could have a good view of them.

Finally all were seated and the little parish priest hurried out from a corner and began to celebrate the Mass. Bells rang, incense rose, and sorrowful chanting filled the square. The people stood or knelt together as the occasion demanded, and when they crossed themselves in unison a great rustling echoed through the plaza. Antonio followed suit, bristling a little at the idea of two Masses in as many hours but hardly being rash enough to ignore the ceremony. His sidelong glances showed him that the crowd was taking only a perfunctory interest in this phase of the *auto-da-fé* and that they, too, were waiting for its conclusion. At last it was over and the priest left the altar, where six black candles burned.

The mob stirred. Antonio looked around for Teresa and Dolores, who were nowhere to be seen, though he felt sure they must be among the spectators. Their father was visible enough; seated high on the central benches near the Grand Inquisitor, he seemed to stare straight at Antonio, who felt uncomfortably conspicuous in his sky blue suit. As the people in the crowd began to mill around nervously, Antonio took the opportunity to step back a few paces.

He felt a bit safer now that he was no longer in the front ranks of the spectators but began to regret his position almost at once, when the murmurs of the crowd and his own partially obscured view informed him that the Grand Inquisitor was approaching the pulpit.

Antonio hardly knew what to think. He was a little proud, perhaps, that his relative should be such a great and powerful man, but at the same time he was sickened and ashamed to see his kinsman presiding over such a spectacle. At least there would be a chance to hear him at his best.

The Grand Inquisitor waited with stoical patience until the plaza was completely silent. The afternoon sun blazed down on his shining head as he glanced down at the papers placed before him. He looked to right and left, then raised both arms above his head and began to speak.

Diego de Villanueva looked on the sea of faces rolling around him and was pleased. There was a substantial crowd, which was good, but then again the crowd was always good. Few indeed were bold enough to stay away from an *auto,* whatever the excuse. The whole city was there, and the Grand Inquisitor knew that somewhere in their number were a dozen witches. He had to find them.

He began his sermon mechanically, reciting the formulas that began every *auto-da-fé* while his eyes scanned the upturned faces. It infuriated him that he could not detect the witches, that their unholy features were not marked with some visible sign, like horns or black and bloody halos. But all he could see were blank, stupid countenances waiting for his words. They were like cattle, he thought, but it would be wiser to think of them as sheep and of himself as their shepherd.

The image of the silent Margarita rose before him; he thought of her and of her sheep and grew furious. The anger was useful, however, and he fed on it. His voice grew louder and more strident, but he modulated it almost at once. He felt the power rising within him but he had to save his strength, because this would be a long speech, and it was his chance to smoke out the rest of Margarita's coven. If he could frighten just one of them into confessing, or at least scare some information out of one of the innocent fools who knew them, then he would take them all and his fortune would be assured.

The sun was merciless, but the Grand Inquisitor did not care. Let the people sweat, let them burn, and he would burn with them. The heat drove him slowly into a frenzy.

He began calmly enough, preaching the glories of the faith and promising eternal bliss to all who adhered to it. Then he grew stern, warning against temptation and threatening endless torture to all who yielded to it. He described Hell much more vividly than Heaven.

He began to speak about heresy, railing against it. He defined it carefully for his audience as the sin of sins. All men were sinners, he said, and all women, too; especially women, for they were weak. But sin was inevitable and was forgivable. Why, even the Grand Inquisitor himself— but enough of that. What distinguished heresy from sin was that heresy was the sin of believing there was no sin in sinning, and for that and that alone there could be no forgiveness. It was pride, arrogance, and placing oneself above the laws of God and his ministers on earth. It would be punished, in this life and the next.

The people were with him now. He saw fear in some faces and a sort of glee in others. Pressing his advantage at once, he began to speak of the Jews.

The crowd loved it. The Grand Inquisitor condemned

the Marranos, the Judaizers, the backsliders—all who had been given the truth but would have none of it. They had crucified the Son of God, he said, and each of them would be punished for it. Here in Spain they had been offered the inestimable blessing of Christianity; indeed, they had been ordered to embrace it, but many had fled from this honor, and many of those who remained were Christians in name only. All these New Christians were suspect, said the Grand Inquisitor, and should be watched. There might be a woman who never ate pork or a man who changed his linen too often. And there were other signs by which they could be known. All the backsliders and heretics must be taken and punished. A first mistake might be treated with a light penance, such as confiscation of property and a year of the Shame, but a further relapse could be punished only by death.

Antonio, standing in the ranks of the enthusiastic onlookers, was appalled. Could these people really believe this? Could Diego de Villanueva, a man of God and Antonio's own kinsman? Where did such ideas come from? Didn't they know anything? Didn't they know what the pope himself had said and what he had done?

Antonio had been in Rome four years ago, in 1492, and had seen the thousands of Jewish refugees pouring into the city from Spain in the wake of the edict by Ferdinand and Isabella and Torquemada. He had heard what everyone in Rome had, the pronouncements of Pope Alexander VI, who had welcomed the Jews into the Eternal City, offering them refuge and tolerance, at least, if not complete acceptance.

Antonio wanted to speak out, to tell them all that they were mad. But he saw the yellow robes, the soldiers with their halberds, and the exceutioner. He held his tongue. He was hot and tired, and the sermon was already longer than the one he had heard this morning. Worse yet, there was nothing to indicate that it was coming to an end.

The Grand Inquisitor spoke next of the Moors, which was ill-advised, since the Moors still had dispensation to practice their religion, but no one here would object. It was also unnecessary, because all the Moors were in southern Spain, but the Grand Inquisitor knew they were hated, if anything, more than the Jews. For centuries, he said, these heathens had occupied Spanish soil and their last stronghold had fallen only four years ago. He spoke in veiled terms of the future, when their hateful religion would surely be outlawed. All the people knew what he meant and were glad to hear it. Until then, said the Grand Inquisitor, there were the Moriscos, who had embraced Christianity and were thus liable to prosecution as heretics. They should be watched as well.

There was not a Morisco within a hundred leagues of the city, but the mob in the plaza would have been happy to see one burn.

At last the Grand Inquisitor tore into his principal topic. The most damnable heresy of all, he said, had now invaded the city. "Witchcraft!" he shouted, and the people cried and moaned and screamed.

He mentioned astrologers, card readers, and other fortune tellers and diviners. All these, he said, and others like them, were damned, but they were nothing to what lay behind them: the worship of the Devil himself.

He likened witchcraft to a plague spreading across Europe. The spawn of Satan had been discovered everywhere, he said, especially in Germany, and in France, a mere mountain range away. It had seemed for a time that Spain might be immune, perhaps because it was such a pious nation, but now he, Diego de Villanueva, had found a witch in this very city!

The people gasped in horror and crossed themselves in unison.

They craned their necks to look for the witch, but none seemed to know who it was.

The Grand Inquisitor spoke of the paths of light and darkness and of those who embraced evil not from ignorance but from a passion for wickedness. He spoke of the powers of witchcraft, and the people shuddered.

Panic ran through the crowd as he swore in ringing tones that there were a dozen more witches in their midst. The people stirred, turned to look around, and each saw friends and neighbors as if for the first time.

The effect was splendid.

The Grand Inquisitor warned the people and the witches. There was still time for the evil ones to repent and confess, to receive the penance that would save their souls. Those who were innocent should be wary, for the tools of witchcraft were curses, poison, and death.

"But where are the witches?" bellowed the Grand Inquisitor. "I will show you one!" His bony forefinger stabbed through the air. Sweat poured from his contorted features and stained his white robe. "There!" he shouted, pointing at a dark young woman staring vacantly into the sun.

"There!" Hundreds of heads twisted toward the monster on the highest bench.

"There!"

11. The Field of Fire

PEDRO RODRIGUEZ shifted uncomfortably on the wooden bench and squinted at the sky. It was late. He could tell by the position of the sun that the sermon had gone on far too long. Nevertheless, Diego de Villanueva had done a good job; the crowd was half-mad, and very likely there would soon be more witches in the dungeons of the Holy House. So perhaps the delay had been worthwhile, but there was no possibility now of finishing the *auto-da-fé* before sunset.

There was still the oath of allegiance to come and the individual sentencing of each of the thirty-seven prisoners, then the formality of abandoning them to the secular authorities and the procession out of the city to the *quemadero,* the field of fire. It would surely be dark before the last of the five impenitents was aflame.

Pedro had no serious objection to this state of affairs; it would be exciting to see the lurid scarlet of burning heretics against the night sky And if the people ran wild in the darkness he would be among them and might even find a willing wench somewhere in the shadows. First, of course, he would see to it that his own daughters were safely at home. Other fathers would have to look out for theirs as best they could.

Still, something in Pedro's administrative soul was piqued by the thought that the ceremony was not proceeding with the utmost efficiency, and he determined to make an effort to speed things up, even if only as a matter of form. Turning slightly toward Miguel, he whispered out of the corner of his mouth, "We're running behind. Read your sentences quickly, or we'll never be done by dark."

"I know," answered Miguel. "I will do what I can, but there may not be time anyway. Quiet! The oath!"

The Grand Inquisitor, who had waited with his head bowed for a moment at the end of his sermon, slowly raised his arms above his head and administered to the multitude the oath of allegiance. This was to be the last act of his performance, which he rightly considered the greatest of his career.

"Swear!" he shouted, as all assembled in the plaza fell to their knees. "I will defend the Holy Inquisition against all enemies," he said, pausing while the great voice of the crowd repeated his words. "I will be faithful in life and in death," he continued, and the response roared back upon him like a gigantic echo. "I will yield whatever is asked of me. . . . I will pluck out my eye. . . . I will cut off my hand. . . . I will sacrifice my family . . . my fortune . . . my life . . . in the service of the Holy Inquisition . . . and this I swear . . . before God . . . at the peril of my immortal soul."

He turned with a flourish, his black cloak fluttering behind him as he moved with stately steps toward the platform where Pedro and Miguel sat waiting.

Miguel stood at once, the roll of prisoners clutched in his nervous fingers, but even as he opened his mouth to speak, a shout rang out from somewhere in the crowd: "The Grand Inquisitor!" And then another: "Diego de Villanueva!" Pandemonium broke loose as the mob took up the cry, and the name of the monk who ruled the city roared through the plaza until it rang from the buildings around the public square: the courts, the houses of the rich, the cathedral itself. The stained-glass windows seemed to rattle in their frames.

Miguel stood bewildered. Such a demonstration was most unseemly, but there was no chance to stop it, even had he dared try. The tumult continued unabated for a minute, then the Grand Inquisitor turned to lift one hand and with the smallest of gestures silenced the throng. His features were cold and composed, but his eyes glowed.

There was a brief flurry of activity in the stands as the

Grand Inquisitor resumed his seat. At his curt order, Miguel, who still stood indecisively waiting, made his way down to his proper place at the lectern. Pedro took the opportunity to escort the nervous young vicar, stopped for a moment to confer with one of the armed guards, then pushed his way unceremoniously through the surrounding crowd. Miguel had begun to read the first sentence, his high, thin, unsteady voice fading into silence behind Pedro as he reached the solitude of a side street.

Pedro sighed with satisfaction and scratched himself vigorously. It was a blessing to be away from the ceremony, from the obligation to sit still and look solemn. Of course, he had left on the Inquisition's business, but there was no great hurry about it. He estimated that the sentencing would run close to two hours, which left him plenty of time to inspect the preparations at the field of fire. Alone in the street, he relieved himself luxuriously against a whitewashed wall, thinking himself luckier than any man who sat in squirming ceremony upon the benches of the Inquisition.

He had a horse waiting at the Holy House. A few minutes of riding past dwellings of diminishing dignity brought him to an open field on the outskirts of the city.

The ground was barren and scarred with black patches where fires had burned before. Here and there scraggly weeds were forcing their way up through the charred earth, but it was a desolate landscape. Fifteen wooden structures stood upon it in a neatly spaced row. Pedro surveyed them from horseback and found the symmetry pleasing. And the number was correct: there were seven effigies, three corpses, and five living human beings to be burned today.

Workmen were arranging logs at one end of the field. Their job was nearly done, and there was no need for Pedro to urge them on. Instead he stopped to admire their handiwork. The funeral pyres were neatly made, each constructed around a wooden box about half the height of a man. Three steps rose to the top of the box, which served as the base for a stout wooden shaft six feet in height. The firewood was no careless pile of logs and kindling. It was laid in front of the box with geometrical precision, each row of bound logs piled atop the last, with wide planks in between. The fires would burn well and slowly so that the prisoners would have ample opportunity to repent before they were hopelessly aflame. Heretics were less likely to be burned quickly than carefully cooked into oblivion.

A huge white cross was planted in the field opposite the row of stakes so that the Inquisition's victims would have ample opportunity to contemplate it through the smoke. Pedro stopped his horse under one arm of the giant cross; he surveyed the field of fire and recognized someone among the workmen who had no business there. He kicked his mount into a walk and approached the group preparing the last of the fires.

"You! Carlos Diaz! What are you doing there? Come here at once!"

A bald, bedraggled figure shuffled reluctantly toward Pedro. The innkeeper was decked out in a kind of wretched finery that looked shoddier than more humble garments would have. His black suit seemed to be a relic of his forgotten slender youth, a great expanse of dirty shirt showed between the fastenings of the coat, and the hose were torn, apparently by the sheer bulk of the short, heavy legs that bulged unattractively through each rip.

He was also stinking drunk, which would have been apparent even if he had not approached Pedro proffering a wineskin.

"What am I doing here?" muttered Carlos. "Doing my duty. Citizen. Want a drink? All these fellows here—working all day. No food. Brought them bread and wine. No one else cares. Duty. Wanted to come anyway, wanted to see. Want some wine?"

"You are a fool," said Pedro, but he took some wine. "How do you think it looks," he continued, wiping his wet mouth with the back of his hand, "for you to be hanging around here like some sort of ghoul? You're making yourself conspicuous and someone may suspect you. You should be at the *auto* like everyone else. What will people think? Do you expect the Grand Inquisitor to tell everyone that you have special privileges because you're a valuable informer? And how long would you live if he did?"

"You're right," said Carlos, hanging his head in an alcoholic parody of repentance.

"Then get back where you belong. Now! You'll be back here in plenty of time, along with the rest of the people. You won't miss a thing."

Carlos trudged off toward the city but turned back after a few steps and cried plaintively, "What about my wine?"

"I'll keep it," Pedro said sternly. "You don't need any more, and you can't bring it to the *auto* anyway. It's a sacred ceremony, not a drunken revel."

Carlos shrugged acquiescently and shuffled away while Pedro watched the work in progress with the fascination that comes only to those who have nothing to do themselves. He tipped back his head and poured a thin stream of sour wine into his gaping mouth.

Miguel found reading the sentences a terrible strain. It was his duty, since he was the Grand Inquisitor's notary as well as his vicar, and no doubt it was an honor as well. Yet Miguel felt almost embarrassed to be condemning these people, not because he doubted their guilt but because he knew he lacked the authority to pass judgment impressively. He felt small and alone in the arena bounded by the tiers of benches, and he sensed that his voice was weak. The people grew restless; he could hear them stirring. They were as anxious as he to adjourn to the field of fire.

At least the worst was over. The twenty-two minor heretics had been no problem, except that it had taken so long to sentence them all. Each had been escorted down to stand in the cage and hear a catalog of crimes, but it had not bothered Miguel to see them sweating in their grotesque sanbenitos, especially since most of them seemed so grateful for their punishments. Some would suffer the Shame and some imprisonment; all would have property confiscated, but at least none would die.

The effigies were different. They too were propped up

in the cage at the center of the plaza, and they too had to be sentenced. Sometimes the flat straw faces fell against the bars, and Miguel stared at them uneasily as he read the charges. Of course it was only a matter of form, but he disliked addressing these ugly objects as if they were living men.

Still, the effigies were better than the corpses, which were pulled down from the poles on which they had been carried to the plaza and carried one by one into the cage for the condemned. There they lolled, their heads adorned with pointed caps, withered limbs draped in yellow robes, empty eye sockets gazing up reproachfully at Miguel as he condemned their bones to the field of fire and their souls to the flames of Hell. As he looked over his records, Miguel discovered to his disgust that one of the skeletons had been a woman. Her fleshless skull seemed to grin at him as he called out her name.

After that it was comparatively easy for him to deal with the last five, those sentenced to death. The old woman had cried a little, but the two brothers had betrayed no emotion and neither had the old man. All four were Judaizers.

The fifth and last heretic of the day was Margarita de Mendoza. Miguel was almost startled to see her name. He had been reading for so long that he had begun to feel doomed to read forever. Yet the last came none too soon. The sun was sinking, it was almost dusk in the plaza, and the long shadow of the gray cathedral fell across the cage where Margarita stood.

Miguel thought to look upon her face for one last time, but it was obscured by the growing darkness. Already torches had appeared, to light the square. They would be needed soon for the field of fire. As he called out the sentence, Miguel heard a murmur run through the crowd. This was the witch. Miguel cringed inwardly, anticipating some sort of demonstration, but nothing happened. It was too dark, perhaps, or too late. The people were strangely solemn and subdued; perhaps they were afraid.

Miguel condemned Margarita to death in his most ringing tones, hoping the Inquisitor would be pleased with his enthusiasm. As she was led away, Miguel concluded his services by reciting the formula abandoning the prisoners to the secular authorities. The Inquisiton was not responsible for their punishment; indeed, it beseeched the civil law to deal leniently with these enemies of Spain and of God.

Even as Miguel mouthed the ritual phrases, the prisoners were hoisted onto the mules that would carry them to the field of fire.

In a daze, Margarita rode in the twilight through the narrow streets, where she was pressed on both sides by somber friars earnestly beseeching her to repent. She hardly heard them; she was listening to another voice.

For hours she had sat in the sun, half in a trance, drugged by the kiss of a vampire. The blessings, prayers, speeches, sentences had all flowed past her like a dream. But with the coming night, she had drifted back into consciousness. She was stronger now and her perceptions keener, but that only served to bring the terror of her position home. She was being carried away to be burned alive. She would have screamed, but she was too busy listening. The voice within her had grown stronger, too.

All day it had whispered and shown her strange, cloudy pictures in black and silver. Now the voice was louder and the pictures clearer. A bright night, a shining darkness, flashed and fluttered against that other vision of yellow robes and scarlet skies. The voice echoed unintelligibly down vast caverns with silver sides; it sounded a note of triumph. The note sang of death and of something beyond it, yet only one word rang clear the sound of her own name.

She closed her eyes to hear it better and saw hardly anything of what happened at the field of fire.

But Miguel saw it all.

More than half the mob streamed behind the procession, eager for the climax to the solemn ceremony. Attendance at the *auto* itself was virtually compulsory, but those who ventured out into the field of fire did so for their own amusement. Among the many who turned away toward their homes were Teresa and Dolores Rodriguez.

Miguel watched them go, wishing he might go with them. He had no stomach for executions. He did see someone accompany them, however, a sight that startled him, for their escort was none other than Antonio Manetti, the young man who had announced himself the day before as heir to the castle of Don Sebastian de Villanueva.

Miguel had no time to consider the meaning of this singular occurrence, however, for he was swept along in the procession. The people behind him were more raucous now, their shouts and cries clashing with the doleful chanting of the Dominicans marching before them. Miguel rode with the Grand Inquisitor at the head of the grim parade, followed by the five prisoners, mounted on mules and surrounded by monks and soldiers.

The mob in the rear dispersed into gesticulating groups as the procession reached the black and blighted field. Here, beyond the shadows of the city, a lurid sunset flamed against the mountains. Miguel shuddered at the sight of the crimson clouds; they would have reddened soon enough from the fires of the *auto-da-fé*. He reined in his mount and waited with the Grand Inquisitor beneath the great white cross at the edge of the field, watching soldiers, friars, and familiars as they rushed their charges to execution.

In a matter of minutes the effigies and corpses were aflame. There was no need for ceremony with these, no chance that they might confess or repent before the fire caught them in its cruel embrace. Smoke poured into the sky as the straw men, bathed in glowing orange, turned black, glowed for an instant as vivid embers, than sank into nothingness. A breeze from the west sent the smoke drifting across the field toward the white cross and Miguel's eyes began to water. When the corpses were set aflame, a darker cloud rushed toward him and started him coughing.

"A bad wind," he said.

"But a good day," said the Grand Inquisitor.

The old woman was first. The monks around her had no special interest in her, for she had already confessed.

Two of them led her up the steps of the platform to the stake, then one monk helped the executioner bind her while the other offered her a cross to kiss. As they descended, one gave a laconic signal to the executioner. His black hood nodded and he stepped up behind the old woman with a cord in his hands. He wrapped it once around her withered neck and yanked at the ends. A roar went up from the crowd as she kicked and twitched, but the spectacle was short-lived.

Miguel wanted to look away, but some fascination kept him watching. When the torch was applied he saw to his relief that the dead woman burned no differently from the effigies. Perhaps he would be able to stand this after all.

The deaths of the two black-bearded brothers were more dramatic and afforded the spectators some real amusement. The first one refused the cord and the cross and stared stoically at the monks, who retreated, shaking their heads at his stubbornness. The fire was lit and for some moments he regarded it with apparent indifference, though he began to choke on the smoke. But the flames grew higher and all at once he was seen to be screaming. He could not be heard, for at his first cry he had been drowned out by the cheers and laughter of the mob.

By this time the second man had been bound to the stake. The sight of his brother's agony undid him. It appeared that these two had resolved together to defy the Inquisition, but the second brother shouted out his repentance. A monk rushed forward to absolve him and the executioner reached for his cord. The spectators were delighted at this development, but their glee knew no bounds when the first brother, already blackened and blistered, saw the pact betrayed and cried out his own confession. The executioner hesitated between the two men, and by the time he decided to deal with the first the roaring flames were too high. There was no way he could approach without being burned himself, so the first brother expired in writhing anguish while the crowd cheered.

Miguel could think only of Hell as he gazed aghast at the roasting bodies and frenzied onlookers. The air was thick with smoke and the shifting light made the scene bend and quiver before his smarting eyes. An odor assailed his nostrils and his empty stomach lurched as he realized that his mouth had begun to water. He had not eaten all day and he smelled meat cooking. But the meat was human flesh.

He almost fell from his horse in his hurry to reach the ground, and he rushed off toward the city, choking and retching dryly.

Thus employed, Friar Miguel Carillo missed the final act of the drama played out that night upon the field of fire. In his extremity he had forgotten about Margarita de Mendoza, but the executioner had not.

The fourth prisoner, the old man, was already aflame by the time Margarita was seized and forced up the three steps to the stake. As she was tied to it, she opened her eyes and saw death staring at her. The whole field was alive with fire. In its garish light shone a multitude of eager, upturned faces bathed in sweat and soot. The yellow robe had been torn from her body so that it could be perpetually displayed in the cathedral to keep her infamy alive, and the people jeered and pointed at the nearly naked flesh beneath her pitiful rags. She looked past them and beheld a white cross planted at the top of a slope. A dark horseman lurked beneath it. She recognized him as the Grand Inquisitor.

At the sight of him a fury rose within her. She screamed and snarled curses, promising him a fate worse than her own. Diego de Villanueva could not hear a word of this, but the monks who still pleaded for her repentance were staggered and stepped back from the force of her invective. The executioner himself turned pale beneath his black hood. He had never burned a witch before, and he feared her powers as much as any man. The torch dangled uselessly in his limp hand.

A big man in black pushed the monks aside. "Fools!" he shouted. "She will die as easily as the others! What are you waiting for?" As he snatched the torch from the executioner, Margarita recognized him as the one who had arrested her.

She spoke to him calmly as he approached. "You will die," she promised him, "and your master there will die, and then your torments will begin."

"You cannot frighten me," said Pedro, and thrust the torch into the pitch-soaked logs.

Flames sprang up with amazing speed. Margarita closed her eyes against them. The people waited open-mouthed for her cries to begin, but they were disappointed. She stood quite still, her lips moving slowly as if in prayer. A blast of heat rushed over her, but a triumphant voice rang in her ears: "Margarita! Now, Margarita! The night! The night!"

From his distant vantage point the Grand Inquisitor saw it first. The people looked only at the witch, but he saw the sky and the vast black shape that hovered there.

"Sebastian!" he shouted, but no one heard him, for the crowd was in a panic. Something huge swept down out of darkness toward Margarita. Its leathery wings wrapped around the silent woman, and it sharp claws slashed at her bonds. Some of the people screamed and ran; others sank to their knees in prayer and were trampled in the rush from the field of fire. Only a few had the courage for more than a glimpse of the gigantic bat, whose red eyes gleamed brighter than the fire as it snatched up the Grand Inquisitor's greatest prize. Like a demon from the pit the thing writhed through the rising flames. When it soared above them again, Margarita de Mendoza was clutched in its massive talons.

Diego de Villanueva sat frozen beneath the white cross as the mob raced screaming past him. He gazed upward in amazement as the great wings flapped through the purple sky, until the black beast and its pale burden were lost in darkness and distance.

His rearing horse recalled him to his senses, and he turned to address the fleeing populace.

"Behold!" he shouted, in a voice so strong that many stopped to hear him. "Behold and tremble, for such is the fate of witches! Satan himself has claimed her for his own, and she burns in Hell tonight! Behold and repent, you sinners, for only I can save you from such a doom! Behold and despair, you witches, for you have seen your destiny!"

His voice turned to a maniacal wail until the onlookers fled from him as if he were another monster. His arms were raised to Heaven and his fingers clutched at the empty air.

12. The Crimson Cloak

MARGARITA AWOKE the next afternoon in a room she had never seen before. It was furnished in the Moorish style, and for a moment she thought she had been transported into another land, but the exotic embellishments could not completely disguise the fact that the cold stone walls were those of a fortress.

She lay on her back groggily, looking up at the high gray ceiling and trying to understand how she had come to be here. She remembered the field of fire, the jeering crowd, and the shadowy figure of the Grand Inquisitor. And there was something more: a monstrous creature that was at once a source of horror and delight. There was a memory of the earth dropping away beneath her, as in a belladonna dream, then nothing.

She propped herself up on one elbow and felt a silken sheet slide down her shoulder. She was lying naked on a pile of velvet cushions and was covered with silks and furs. Rich carpets in intricate patterns overlapped upon every inch of the floor. The walls were hung with tapestries showing almond-eyed men and women dressed in strange clothing and posed with amorous delicacy. The furnishings were few. There were cushions in profusion, especially around a low table inlaid with arabesques, and a large chest of the same design stood in the corner. Otherwise the chamber was empty.

Margarita sat up slowly, gathering the silk around her like a robe. She looked toward the wooden door and tried to rise. Her head swam as she stood erect, and sharp pains ran through her feet and legs. She threw one hand toward the wall to support herself and leaned against it, gasping—not so much from the pain as from the knowledge it brought. Tears filled her green eyes as she realized again what the Inquisition had done to her.

She might be free, but the torture chamber had left marks upon her body that not even time could heal.

Shaking her head fiercely to counteract her anguish, Margarita made her way slowly along the wall until she reached the door. It was locked. She leaned against it in an anxiety of bewilderment. Then her gaze fell upon a low table across the room.

On it she saw a silver bowl piled high with fruit, two silver jugs, and a silver goblet. At the sight of these she realized that she was weak with hunger. She stumbled gracelessly over the carpets and dropped on a cushion before the table, snatching at a pear as she sprawled upon the floor. Its sweet juices dribbled into her mouth and down her chin. She had tasted nothing so good for weeks. One jug held wine, the other water. She filled the cup with wine and poured it down her grateful throat in great sensual gulps.

A set of silver combs lay beside the basin, with a single sheet of parchment beneath them. On it were only two words: "Wait," it said, and was signed "Sebastian."

She picked up the note and stared at it intensely, as though expecting a further message to appear, but nothing happened. The room was silent.

Finally she dropped the parchment and dipped both hands into the silver basin. She splashed water on her face and shook it off in ecstasy; she cast her silken wrapper aside and rubbed her naked flesh with wet hands. Streaks of grime and soot ran in rivulets down her shoulders and breasts, until she impatiently picked up the second jug and poured the water all over her body, unmindful of the cushions and carpets growing damp beneath her. She spilled the basin over her head and gasped with delight, then gathered up the silk sheet and rubbed herself till it was damp and clinging.

This improvised bath refreshed her more than the food or drink. She felt that she had washed the stains of the dungeon away and almost believed it when she kept her gaze from her burned and twisted legs.

Kneeling by the table, she ran a comb through her tangled, dripping hair until it was clean and straight again. She looked for a mirror, but there was none to be found, and the reflection she saw in the silver pitchers was dim and distorted. The room was growing darker.

She thought of the chest and slid across the floor to reach it, another cupful of wine in her hand. Beside the chest she hesitated for a moment; she had no idea what might lurk within and was almost afraid to open it. But curiosity overcame her doubts, and she raised the carved inlaid lid. At first she could see nothing but darkness within; then she realized that it was filled with a woman's clothing. She pulled forth gowns, robes, and dresses in eager handfuls—brocade, velvet, taffeta, silk—each garment more splendid than any she had ever owned, even in the sadly distant days when she had been a young lady of some quality. She held them up before her in the fading light, longing again for a looking glass.

The dim chamber might have been a prison of sorts, but it seemed to Margarita her private preserve, designed and appointed for her pleasure. She had no doubts about the wisdom of putting on these clothes, only wondering which garment she would choose. At length, inspired perhaps by some premonition about the night ahead, she selected a white gown of smooth cool silk, its waist embroidered with silver threads. She slipped it over her head, pleased with the fit, then crept across the floor to the pile of cushions and furs that had served as her bed. There in the growing gloom she waited.

She heard footsteps and watched a dim finger of light slide under the door. Her heart raced and she held her breath. The door swung slowly open. There in its pointed arch stood Don Sebastian de Villanueva, wrapped in a crimson cloak, a golden candelabrum in his hand.

Margarita wanted to speak but could think of nothing to say. Sebastian was silent too. He placed the candelabrum on the table and stood beside it, staring at her. Margarita watched the dancing lights and the trickling red wax that ran down the side of the candles.

"This was my wife's room," said Sebastian, "before she died. And that is her dress you are wearing."

Margarita started, her hand clutching nervously at the white bodice.

"It becomes you," Sebastian reassured her. "That was a stupid way to start a conversation. I rarely speak to anyone now, and I have lost the habit of conversing politely."

"You speak well enough," Margarita said softly. "And you saved my life." She paused for a moment. "This is your castle, then?"

Sebastian nodded. "If a dead man can be said to own anything."

"And your wife?"

"No, she is not here with me. The Inquisition took her, as they did you, and I was not here to help her." His pale face twisted. "I was fighting for the Crown."

"What was her name?"

"Her name was Gracia. But it is senseless to talk of her. She is gone forever, and we are still here, Margarita."

"Why did you rescue me?"

"You think it was in memory of her. Well, perhaps it was in part, but there was more." He came closer and kneeled beside her in the shadowy glow of the candles. "I have known you for months, though you have not known me. I have seen you dance naked in the forest, the most beautiful of all my witches and the one whose rage and hatred matched my own."

"It may be that you hate the Inquisition as much as I," Margarita retorted bitterly, "but you seem to have made your truce with them, and with your brother, the Grand Inquisitor." The last words were spoken with a sneer.

"And for you I have broken that truce," Sebastian said grimly. "I can only guess how Diego will respond. It would be easy enough for him to destroy me, but I think he will not. Not for this. He has need of me."

"To frighten the wretches in his dungeons?"

"There is a better reason. He plans to become an

authority on the black arts, and I am his tutor."

"How can you?"

"He is my brother, though that means little enough now. But I have need of him, too. He has kept me safe in this castle for many years. Without him I would be a dead man, if I am not already."

"And is death the worst thing you can imagine?"

"I know that it is not for you, Margarita, and that is why you have been spared it, but I thought you might be more grateful."

"I am grateful," said Margarita in a gentler tone. Silk rustled as she moved to take his hand in hers. She bent to kiss his jeweled fingers. "You taught me what I know of witchery, or the goat did. If I seem surprised, it is only that I thought you a demon, a spirit, and now I find that you are still a man."

"I am more human than I knew," said Sebastian, "and I feel for you something I never thought to feel again." Their right hands were still clasped. With his left he reached out to stroke her damp black hair. Margarita closed her eyes and rubbed her cheek against caressing fingers.

"When you came to my cell," she whispered, "I thought ... no, I don't know what I thought. When I saw the goat, I was sure you were there to spirit me away, and then when I saw that you were undead ... I remembered what I was told when I was a little girl, how Lucifer is a seducer who torments even those who serve him. But your kiss was sweet." She touched her throat and slowly drew back from Sebastian. "What are these powers that govern us? I have seen them work, but what are they?"

Sebastian considered her question. "You might know more," he said at length, "if you were a creature such as I. And I have more to learn as well. What I see now is like a dream. There is no way to tell if what I see is the truth or only my own vision. I wonder if there is a truth at all. Yet the fact that I am here, after suffering a mortal wound on the plains before Malaga, is proof enough that magic can be wrought, even if its source remains a mystery. We are like mariners, Margarita, who cannot see the wind but know full well that it drives their ship toward some distant shore."

"Have you never spoken to Satan?"

"I doubt that he exists; certainly not as my brother would have the people believe. The power that works curses is the same one that works miracles, and the light that mortals seek casts the very shadows that they fear. There is only one source, its manifestations molded by the wills of men and women. Good and evil are not causes but effects, and the same force fills everything."

Margarita said nothing, just stared at the bright points of flame above the candles.

"But this is too high a doctrine," continued Sebastian. "The force can be used; perhaps it can even be known. But still, it does matter how we use it. To have it is not enough, for it may still produce a monster like me or my brother Diego. We both sought wisdom and power, and we have not been utterly denied, but what has it brought us? The universe is a mirror that reflects back upon us all our thoughts and deeds. Perhaps that is why I have become a vampire, to be free of my reflection at last."

Margarita looked at Sebastian intently. "Is it peace, then?" she asked. "Is it peace to be dead?"

"It may be," answered Sebastian, "but if it is, I am not dead enough to know. There is no peace for me now, only an unquenchable thirst."

"A thirst for blood?"

"For blood, for knowledge and power and for life, which I will never know again. Sometimes it is a thirst for death and for an end to all this thirsting."

Margarita took his hand again and held it against her heart. "Sebastian," she said. "Is there nothing for you?"

"Only when I sleep, in the crypt below the castle. To crawl into a coffin every morning should be a horror, but when the sun rises my dream begins."

"What happens?"

"Almost nothing, except that I am transported. The sensations can hardly be described. I lie as still as the corpse that I am, but somehow I move. It feels something like falling, but without the fear. Is it possible to fall upward? A sensation of flying, or floating down a stream. And a high, clear sound like bells or children singing, almost a melody but never quite. All around me grows a radiance and I flow toward it—into it—until I become one with the light. Then I see the power and am the power, but it matters not at all, for every desire is dissolved in the light."

"And is the light silver?" asked Margarita.

He looked at her in surprise. "How can you know?" he asked.

"I have seen it," she said, smiling at him faintly. "You showed it to me. Show me again."

He touched her forhead gently with his left hand. "Wonderful," he said, "that you should share my dream." He leaned toward her for an instant, then gently took his hands from her head and her heart.

"We must stop this," said Sebastian, "stop and consider, for tonight your fate will be determined. You are not a prisoner, you know. You are free to leave this castle."

"Free?" echoed Margarita. "Free for what?" Surprise showed in her pale green eyes and disappointment tightened her full red lips. "What could I do? Did you take me from the fire only to cast me out into the darkness?"

"I agree that you can hardly stay in Spain," said Sebastian, "and certainly you can never return to your home."

Margarita nodded. "I have no home," she said.

"You might be safe, though, if you fled across the mountains into France. Of course, they do not love witches there, either."

Margarita jammed a fist into a pillow. "How can I go anywhere? Look at my legs, my feet! Your brother has left me a cripple!"

"Yet still you have a choice," said Sebastian, "though I am reluctant to recommend it. I have saved you from one death; now I can only offer you another."

"Death?"

"And what lies beyond it. Stay with me, Margarita, and

be one with me. Live as I do and die as I do. Be my bride, and mistress of this empty castle, and one of the living dead."

His head was close to hers. She gazed into his eyes, thinking to find them burning with the fires of Hell, but they were dark and dull and dead.

Sebastian stood abruptly and turned away from her. "Do not look at me," he said. "My power is such that I could bend you to my will, but I have no wish to do so. Choose for yourself, Margarita, but choose carefully."

Margarita looked at his back and at the crimson cloak that covered it. "What could I be to you," she asked, "but a wretched wench with twisted legs?"

"Those are the afflictions of a mortal woman, Margarita, and they can be remedied. Let me bleed you as the surgeons do and you will find me a notable physician."

"Then you can make me whole again?"

"That and more, Margarita. I offer you eternal life."

Sebastian heard the rustle of silk and felt a hand on his arm. Margarita stood beside him, swaying on her tortured legs.

"I accept," she said.

Sebastian drew her to him, holding her up with his strong arms. "There is no safety here," he warned; "no peace."

"There is no safety anywhere," Margarita said. "I choose to stay with you." She pressed her lips against his and pulled him gently down to her bed. She slipped off the dress of white silk and knelt before him naked, her body bathed in light and shadow from the warm glow of the candle.

"You are more beautiful than I remembered," Sebastian said. His cool fingers ran along her bare back and pressed into the aching muscles of her shoulders. Margarita sighed and let her head roll back ecstatically. Tender kisses covered her long white throat, but the sharp sting she awaited did not come. Instead, Sebastian drew away to stare into her glowing green eyes. She saw that by some magic he was naked too, his crimson cloak lost among the silks and furs. His flesh was lean and muscular, but as pale and cold as a distant star.

He lifted Margarita and laid her down again upon the bed of cushions, his velvet cloak spread beneath her. He hovered over her, his black hair streaming down, and his long white fingers tracing patterns on her torso. He bent to kiss her trembling breasts and to caress her slender waist. Margarita's arms reached out to embrace Sebastian, and her pink fingernails sank into his back as she felt his fingers slide into the warm, wet curls between her thighs. She opened the way for him and dragged him down upon her. As she took him into her their eyes met, and she sank dizzily into the depths of his darkness.

Margarita felt a momentary panic as he entered her, awed by the strength of the uncanny chill that filled her warm human body. She froze for an instant, ready to recant, then an icy wave of ecstasy swept through her and she was lost.

Sebastian's head sank onto her shoulder and their bodies throbbed together in cold communion. Margarita felt a passion overwhelm her that was more than human. She gasped acceptance. As she did, the bright teeth of her lover sank into her throat. A spasm shook her to the very soul and she was cast into the void.

Something shimmered before her in the infinite blackness, a vast net of pulsating silver strands. Falling away behind her were a man and a woman in each other's arms; rushing toward her was a vibrant gleam that swelled into a blinding flash.

It absorbed her, and she became the light.

13. Two Sisters

"SPLENDID, PEDRO! Three in one day! Even better than I expected!" The enthusiasm of the Grand Inquisitor was so great that he could hardly stay in his chair. His hands waved expansively and his thin lips were pulled back from his yellowing teeth in an expression that on the face of any other man would have been a smile.

"All three of them came to the Holy House willingly and confessed without even a question from me. One of them even volunteered the names of several other witches, Pedro. There will be work for you tonight."

Pedro stood sullenly and looked at the floor of the Grand Inquisitor's chambers. He was not overly impressed by this good news. At yesterday's *auto-da-fé* he had done the work of two men, so he was not anxious to spend the coming night arresting crazed women. He had planned to be drunk in his own bed.

"I had no idea it would work so well!" continued Diego.

"You had no idea it would happen at all," countered Pedro bitterly. "I saw your face when that thing came down out of the sky and you were as amazed as anyone. I admit, though, that you recovered quickly."

"All right, Pedro," sighed the Grand Inquisitor. "Not even your impudence can anger me today. I suppose I could hardly expect to deceive you who have known me so long and known my brother even longer. I wonder why Sebastian did it. Could he have realized how well he was serving me? Not that it matters now, but I wonder. I almost think he meant to spite me by stealing her away in front of everyone, yet all he did was to frighten more witches into timely repentance. What a story for the book! Hundreds of witnesses saw her carried off by a fiend from the pit. What stronger proof could I wish for?"

"What do you suppose has become of Margarita de Mendoza?" asked Pedro.

"I have no doubt that she lies dead in the castle, her heart's blood drained away to sustain my enterprising brother. We shall not see her again, Pedro. Sebastian did seem to have a taste for her. I can hardly begrudge him for indulging his whim, since I would gladly exchange one silent witch for a whole coven of confessions. We have three already, and there will be more. My fortune is made."

Pedro scratched his nose with his thumb. "You have the names of the ones you want me to visit tonight?"

"Miguel has them. You can pick them up on your way out. The boy is not well today; something disturbed him at the field of fire. Sometimes I doubt whether he will ever have the stomach for this work."

"He's not the boy I'm worried about," Pedro replied. "I want to know what you plan to do with this one who claims to be the heir of Don Sebastian. He was seen yesterday after the *auto* talking to my daughters. I will not tolerate that!" His big fist smashed down on the table like a hammer.

The Grand Inquisitor picked up an overturned candlestick and replaced it with infuriating equanimity. "Surely you can take care of your own daughters," he said.

"I could take care of that boy easily enough, too, but you tell me I must wait."

"And I mean it, Pedro. If you cross me in this before Sebastian's work is done, I promise you not only the fate of an assassin but the hospitality of the Holy House. Be patient, Pedro. Our real problem will be to keep this Antonio patient as well. We can hardly have him inhabiting the castle before the book is completed. Perhaps your older daughter could be of some use to us."

Pedro's face turned purple, but the Grand Inquisitor ignored it. "What is her name? Teresa? There's no need to fume at me like that, Pedro, unless you doubt the girl's virtue. If Antonio likes her, she may be able to help us by giving him something else to think about."

"If he comes near her I'll kill him, in spite of all your threats."

"Stop and consider, Pedro. This young fellow has wonderful prospects. The castle may be an obsolete fortress, but its furnishings alone are worth a modest fortune, and the lands that go with it include most of the farms in this district. A family could live in grand style on the rents alone. Teresa could easily find a worse husband."

"You forget what he did to me at the Golden Cup," insisted Pedro, all the more adamant despite the doubts beginning to show in his eyes. "My honor is at stake!"

"Honor is as others perceive it. Who knows what happened there? Only Antonio and your daughters. Oh, and Carlos Diaz, too, but I am sure you have seen to it that he will keep quiet about the incident. None of them will care, and surely it will add to your honor to have your daughter made a noblewoman. You must think of the future, Pedro. I promise you that there are great things before us. I asked to be named Inquisitor of this little district because I was sure it contained what I wanted, but I shall not be here forever. A few more weeks and I shall be the talk of Spain, the great witch hunter of the kingdom. All the great cities will welcome me as I come to drive out their devils. There will be great honor in it, Pedro, and fame, and no doubt riches too. You will be at my right hand. How much better it will be for you to go with me and leave your daughters in luxury than to throw all this away for the sake of a tavern brawl!"

"You talk well enough," mumbled Pedro, more than a little dazzled in spite of himself. "But I like something I can see. This is only talk, and I'll believe it when it happens. For now, I have only a list of names and the promise that I will spend the night chasing hags."

Antonio waited in the shadows of an alley, watching a house across the narrow street. He had been there since nightfall, dressed in drab traveling clothes he hoped would make him less conspicuous. The summer night was warm enough but he was chilled, both by the danger of being abroad after dark and by the growing conviction that he was making a fool of himself.

The house, only a few streets away from the cathedral, was more substantial than those surrounding the Inn of the Golden Cup. It had two stories and its earthen bricks had been whitewashed not too long ago. The massive ironbound door was closed and the windows shuttered, but a faint glow between the shutters held Antonio's attention.

Then the door opened, and Antonio slipped hastily back into the depths of his alley. A gigantic black silhouette of a man stood out against the light for a moment; then he stepped out and shut the door behind him. He waited there for a heartbeat, apparently listening to something behind him—perhaps the sounds of locks and bolts falling into place—then he plodded down the street in the direction of the Holy House.

Antonio continued to wait, but his spirits were higher. Pedro had left home, so there was reason to believe that the waiting had not been in vain. In no time at all the door opened again. A small hand appeared holding a strip of white cloth, then shut the door upon it. Antonio saw the signal and immediately stepped out into the street. He paused for a moment, embarrassed by his own eagerness, then shrugged to himself, hurried up to the house, and knocked.

Dolores answered his knock. "You didn't take long," she said archly as she let him in. Antonio looked around him at the chamber that served the family as kitchen, dining room, and living room. He saw a huge fireplace with no fire in it, a heavy table, and several chairs and stools. A mirror hung on one wall above a brassbound chest; another wall was covered with shelves holding plates, cups, and pitchers. Cooking utensils hung beside the fireplace. A painted screen stood in one corner and in the opposite corner a miniature shrine constructed around an image of the Virgin. Antonio saw everything in the simply furnished room except what he had hoped to see.

"Where is Teresa?" he asked.

"Upstairs," answered Dolores. "Does it matter? I thought you came to visit me."

Antonio smiled. "I am very pleased to see you, but I hope to see your sister, too."

"Sit down," said Dolores, and Antonio obeyed. "She'll be down eventually, though I don't see why you should care. I'm as pretty as she is."

"Indeed you are," agreed Antonio, "but your sister is taller. I have a weakness for tall women."

"Do you like her?" asked Dolores, perching on a high stool across the room from Antonio's chair.

"Of course I do," said Antonio, glancing nervously toward the narrow stairs as if he imagined that Teresa might be listening upstairs. "Why else would I come here? Does she like me?"

"She hardly knows you, you know. She's hardly spoken to you. But she must like you a little, since she arranged for you to come here. We're all being very wicked, and father would be furious. I love it. Want some wine?"

"Well," said Antonio. "Perhaps a little. Did you hear what happened yesterday after you went home? Everyone has been talking about it."

"They burned some people, I suppose. I never get to see it. Father forbids it and Teresa doesn't even want to watch."

"She's right. It's nothing for a young girl to see, nor anyone else, for that matter. But last night they say there was something else. A woman was to be burned for witchcraft, but a devil flew down and carried her off."

"A devil!" said Dolores, filling a cup with sour red wine. "I never get to see anything! I suppose you missed it too. Do you believe it?"

Antonio took the cup from her and sat quietly for a moment, trying to create the impression that he was giving her question profound consideration. "I don't know," he said at last. "I can hardly deny the existence of devils that would be blasphemy but I wonder how often they appear to men. Still, there must have been something."

"You're right," said Dolores. "You don't know. I suppose it is hard to know the truth, though. Could you believe a stranger who claimed to be the heir to a fortune?"

Antonio inhaled a mouthful of wine and stared red faced at Dolores while he coughed. "Do you think I'm lying?" he finally gasped.

"I can hardly deny the existence of devils," said Dolores sweetly, "and I have to watch out for my sister. Sometimes she has no sense at all."

"Dolores! Do you think you're a matchmaker?" Teresa stood at the bottom of the stairs, doing her best to look angry with her little sister but at the same time trying to suppress her laughter. "I'm sorry, sir," said Teresa, "that you should be exposed to such an inquisition. My sister is an apprentice shrew, and she belongs in bed."

"No!" cried Dolores. "I'm your chaperone. Would you disgrace yourself? A lady must never entertain a gentleman without a duenna to keep an eye on her."

"Sometimes a duenna can be bribed to look the other way," replied Teresa, moving across the room to stand beside her sister in an attitude of mocking menace.

"And how would you bribe me?" asked Dolores.

"I might be persuaded to let you live," Teresa answered. She took her sister by the arm and pulled her not too gently from the stool.

"You can't make me go! I'm not a child! I'll just listen from upstairs anyway."

Antonio looked into his cup and pretended he was not in the room.

"Please, Dolores," said Teresa, speaking more softly. She bent down to embrace her sister and draw her away from Antonio.

"He wouldn't even be here if it weren't for me," said Dolores sulkily.

"I know," whispered Teresa, kissing Dolores on the cheek. "Please."

Dolores walked slowly toward the stairs, stopping only

long enough to wish Antonio a good night, and then was gone.

Antonio smiled nervously. He was suddenly conscious of the bedraggled garments that had seemed such a clever disguise when he had put them on a few hours before. Teresa was equally embarrassed by her own costume, a plain dark dress she had not dared to change for fear of exciting her father's suspicions.

"You shouldn't have come," she said.

"But..."

"I know. I asked you, and I arranged the signal—or was it Dolores? It's too dangerous, though. My father might come back for something. He'd kill you."

Antonio would hardly have left under such a threat even if he had been inclined to do so. However, he was beginning to feel decidedly uncomfortable. This was an odd courtship and quite likely inadvisable as well. "Your sister is a clever girl," he said inconsequentially.

"She's an imp," said Teresa, seating herself on the stool Dolores had vacated.

"She's certainly not shy," said Antonio, who had no desire at all to talk about Dolores.

"Isn't my behavior scandalous enough for you?" Teresa asked testily. "Are the women in Florence so bold?"

"I didn't mean anything," Antonio said, inwardly cursing the Spanish language and his inadequate command of it. "You are very good to see me. It is not pleasant to be a stranger in this city."

"I understand that you are soon to be one of its greatest men."

"Will I be any less lonely? You seem more real to me than this castle I am to inherit."

"You will find it as real as the mountains around it."

"I wonder. When I told people in Florence that I was heir to a castle in Spain, they laughed at me. You know, the very words 'a castle in Spain' are a sort of joke there. People say it when they talk about a dream or a wish that will never be granted. I thought to prove them wrong, but now I'm not so sure. I have not felt welcome here, and even Diego de Villanueva doesn't seem to want to see me."

Teresa felt some compassion for him, mingled with a certain surprise at his apparently impractical nature. "You should have no trouble proving to yourself that the castle is no dream," she said. "It stands to the north of the city. Go and look at it."

"I will. Tomorrow. But somehow I thought there would be somebody to show me."

"You will wait a long time for the Grand Inquisitor to give you his attention, I think. There is no one more important here than he is."

Antonio sighed and took another sip of wine. "What was Don Sebastian like?"

"A soldier," Teresa said. "A dark, brooding man. I saw him several times in the city. My father was his lieutenant. He died when I was a little girl."

"I don't really want to talk about him," said Antonio abruptly. "I want to talk about you. Why did you ask me here?"

"Dolores is right. Sometimes I am very stupid. And why did you come?"

"I don't know. Yes, I do. I thought it would be gallant and daring. And you are beautiful. I wanted to see you again. I wanted to know you better."

Teresa smiled. "I am not beautiful," she said.

Antonio smiled too. "Please do not dispute with me about beauty. I am considered a connoisseur. I had planned to be a painter, before I determined to become a nobleman."

Teresa shifted on her stool. "I wanted to see you, too. But now I wish you would go. I'm afraid to have you here."

"I'm not afraid," said Antonio, "and I don't want to go, but I will if you wish it. Soon. Just a few minutes more. How can I meet you again?"

"It seems impossible," Teresa said. "I thought he might be going out tonight, but I can't have you standing outside the house all the time waiting to see a white cloth stuck in the door."

Antonio stood up. "There must be some way, Teresa. Don't you want to? If I didn't have to speak in Spanish, I would make a wonderful speech to you, but now I don't know what to say that won't make me sound like a clown. I want you for a friend, and more."

She looked at him gravely and reached out a hand to him. Antonio took it, then kissed it with more passion than politeness. He looked up into her eyes. Something he saw there encouraged him to kiss her again, this time upon the lips. His first attempt was brief and gentle, as if he expected her to protest. When she did not, he tried again. Her lips were tender, and when she opened them her breath was sweet. For a moment their bodies were pressed together, then Teresa turned away.

"Please go," she said.

Antonio stood behind her with his hands around her waist. "First you must tell me that we will meet again."

"I don't know what to do," she said, while he kissed her hair, her ears, her cheeks. "We're hardly ever allowed to leave the house. Wait. The inn. Perhaps I could leave a message there."

"I don't trust that innkeeper," said Antonio, burying his face in her honey-colored hair.

"I don't mean him. There's a boy, a friend of Dolores. In fact, I think he's in love with her. He will give you a letter when I know where we can meet."

"Bless the boy," whispered Antonio, "and bless Dolores. Love conquers all. Send for me soon, Teresa." He kissed her neck and shoulders and drew her back toward him firmly. Teresa raised one hand to caress his dark, curly head as he bent over her shoulder to kiss her throat. His hands slid up from her waist to clasp her small, high breasts. Her hands covered his, pressing them to her for an instant, then she pulled away from his embrace.

"Please go," she said. "I'll send for you when I can. I promise." She ran to the door, unbolted it, and looked out into the street.

"Come on," she said. She kissed him quickly and pushed him out into the night. The sky was full of stars.

14. The Mountains

MARGARITA'S EYES opened but she saw only darkness. She was lying on her back and sensed rather than felt that she was stretched out upon some cold, unyielding surface. She knew she was awake, but still it seemed she was in a dream and curiously detached from her own body. She tried to move one of her hands, which lay crossed upon her breast. It responded, but it might almost have been someone else's hand, even when it struck something above her and she realized that she was enclosed in some sort of box. Caught up in a cold, remote tranquillity, Margarita was serenely indifferent in the knowledge that she lay in a coffin. She had been transformed.

Sounds of grating and scraping drifted down to her as if from a great height, and a faint light flooded over her. The coffin was open. A pale face floated in the distance, then all at once was close to her own, kissing her cool skin and whispering her name.

Sebastian grasped her shoulders and raised her until she was seated in the long box. Margarita looked around her. She knew instinctively that it was too dark for anyone to see, yet her surroundings were nonetheless visible to her, pulsing with a blue and silver glow that seemed to originate within her own mind. Even Sebastian was luminescent, as was the smile of mild mockery that bared his long white teeth.

"Are you surprised?" he asked. "You are a creature of the night now, and you will see as such creatures do, not like the mortals lost in the darkness. Now the light is your enemy, and the sun a foe who would strike you blind. But you are safe here, Margarita, in the final home of my illustrious family."

The ceiling of the crypt was low and vaulted, its several arches supported by narrow columns of moldering masonry. The floor was thick with dust, the pillars interlaced with the webs of spiders. Stone slabs stretched out in rows each bore a casket, some adorned with the images of those who lay within, portraits in stone dressed in the fashions of generations gone and forgotten.

"I sleep beside you," said Sebastian, "and my brother Diego has a place prepared for him on my other side, when he is ready for it."

"How does it happen that there is a place for me beside you?" Margarita asked.

"It would have been my wife's," Sebastian said, "but the Inquisition burned her body. There has been no one to lie near me for many years."

Margarita thought she should be jealous of this other woman, but in fact she felt nothing. She was too conscious of the changes in herself to worry about anyone else. "I feel very odd," she said. "Will that pass?"

"What you are feeling will not pass," Sebastian answered; "only the sense that it is strange. You have much to learn, Margarita. But tell me how you feel."

"I hardly have the words to express it."

"Never mind. We will have time to talk. The night is ours. Come from the casket." He gathered her up in his arms and let her feet drop down toward the floor.

"No," she cried. "Don't let go of me. My legs will never hold."

"Trust me, Margarita. I promised to cure you. Have you no faith?" He stepped away from her and she found to her amazement that she could stand. She took a few tentative steps forward, then threw herself laughing into his arms.

"You are a wonderful magician."

"The magic is in you, Margarita. You are one of the living dead now, and beyond all human ailments. Even the streak of white in your hair is gone."

Margarita put a hand to her head. "Was my hair white?"

"I forgot that you could not have known, and now there is no way for me to show you. Believe me when I tell you that you are beautiful and your tresses as black as this tomb. From tonight you must put vanity aside. You will never see your face in a looking glass again."

"I have not looked into one for years," she said. "You will be my mirror, Sebastian."

"And you mine," he said. "Come, Margarita."

He led her through the crypt to narrow, crumbling steps that reached upward into the shadows. They climbed the steps and came out into the ruins of a room that might once have been a chapel. There were benches, an altar, and a pulpit, but every sacred image had been removed. Margarita shuddered a little at the sight of it and hurriedly followed Sebastian through another door that led out into the courtyard of the castle.

At once she was enveloped in the radiance of the moonlight, which shone for her as never before. The walls of the castle rose around her in shimmering patterns of silver and icy blue, each stone and crevice alive with its own unnatural luminescence, each of the four round towers a shaft of cold, pale light. Above them all loomed the great square tower, its ancient battlements aglow against a dazzling sea of stars.

Awestruck, Margarita threw back her head to gaze into the shining skies and whatever lay beyond them. She hardly heard Sebastian when he spoke. "What?" she asked in some bewilderment.

"I asked you to tell me your dreams, Margarita. Tell me what you saw when you were asleep in the crypt."

"What did I dream? What could I dream? I was a dead woman."

"There are those who would say you are dead even now," Sebastian suggested.

"Then they would be fools, for I have never felt more alive." She spread her arms wide and spun around in a giddy circle.

"Then what is death?" Sebastian asked her.

Margarita was suddenly still. "I have seen death, and it is an emptiness. It is a slaughtered sheep that becomes a piece of meat. The mind is extinguished and the senses stilled. Nothing remains. Death is oblivion. This is not death."

"Have you always believed this?" asked Sebastian sadly.

"What else would I believe? The words of those pious murderers who preach of an afterlife? I believe what I can see, and I have seen that death is an end to everything. When Margarita dies, she will never see the stars again."

"And you saw nothing when you slept in the tomb?"

"Nothing," said Margarita.

Sebastian turned away and stared at the ground.

"What is it?" she asked. "Have I said something wrong?"

"No, Margarita, nothing wrong. You have only told me the truth, but it was not the truth I expected to hear. You have given me something, though: the answer to a question my brother the Grand Inquisitor has often asked. He will want it in the book."

"The book?"

"Something I am writing for him. It is almost finished; now it will be finished that much sooner. I will show it to you. But first I will show you some magic."

"The sabbat?"

"Not that, Margarita. I fear the coven will never meet again, and I suspect that most of the others are in the dungeons of the Holy House. What happened at the *auto-da-fé* must have frightened them, and I have no doubt that my brother has taken advantage of their fear. What they saw was some sort of demon flying away with you, and a sight like that must have sent the weaker ones screaming to confess and be saved."

Margarita looked at Sebastian in amazement. "Did you know this would happen?"

"I thought of it," he said, "but I was determined to save you no matter what the cost. Have you ever played chess?"

Margarita wrinkled her forehead in perplexity. "No, but my father did. What has a game to do with this?"

"I played with my brother until he grew weary of it. He would tell you, if he knew who the master of the coven was, that I sacrificed my pawns to protect the queen."

"I don't understand this game," said Margarita, at once flattered and dismayed. "Was there no other way for you to help me?"

"There might have been, if I had decided on it sooner. As it was, I almost let you die. But I dreamed of you after the night in the dungeons, and when the sunset came..."

"Then you do have visions, even when the sun shines and you lie in the tomb! Why should it be different for me, Sebastian?"

"That may change," he said sadly, "with the passing of time. There are so many things I must teach you. You must beware of the second death, from which there can be no awakening. You must be warned against the sun and against fire. They can destroy a vampire, as can a shaft of wood through the heart. Except for these, we are all but invulnerable. There are certain other limitations. You must return to your coffin before the morning comes and sleep in your native soil. You must beware of running water and of several herbs. It is said, too, that there are religious artifacts that are dangerous to such as us."

"Do you believe it?"

"I have never made a sufficient test, but it seems likely that there is some truth to it."

"Nothing from their religion could frighten me," Margarita insisted. "But is our whole existence to be restrictions?"

"There is one more," Sebastian said. "To survive, we must feast on the blood of the living."

"That much, at least, will be a pleasure. I can think of many I would be glad to kill."

"They are the very ones you must spare," Sebastian said. "The greatest weapon of the vampire is secrecy. If we leave a trail of bloodless corpses behind us, we shall surely be discovered and destroyed. Only the pact I made with my brother has kept me safe for so many years."

Margarita's full lips twisted in a grimace. "I feel a strength greater than any I ever imagined," she said, "yet you tell me that we are thwarted at every turn. Why did you choose to become what you are, Sebastian?"

His expression was grave. "Because I did not wish to die," he said. "There are few who do. If every man and woman had the knowledge I possess, the world would be full of vampires. But we do have strengths as well as weaknesses, Margarita. Let me show you."

He stepped toward her, his crimson cloak almost black against the unearthly phosphorescence that Margarita's transfigured vision cast upon the gray walls of the tower. "The power is within you," he said, "but I must call it forth."

He gripped her shoulders in cold hands, and her gaze was drawn to his dark, dead eyes. No fire burned in them, but there was a fathomless depth, an essence not within Sebastian but beyond him. Mesmerized, she sank into its endless vistas. She was losing herself.

Abruptly she broke from his grasp in a spasmodic effort that threw her to her knees upon the ground. She longed to be free of his power, even as she longed to make it her own. Her back heaved from her breathless gasps, and her bare shoulders thrust toward the moon. The power of the spasms shocked her. They seemed to be jolting her to her feet. As she stood erect, a tremendous wrench threw her head back and her arms aloft. The walls of the castle reeled past her startled eyes and she felt her naked feet pulled into the air. She had never felt such strength as surged through her shoulder blades. From the corners of her eyes she could see the tips of the great wings that had sprouted behind her, webbed and leathery, yet smoothed with a soft gray fur like that of a bat.

She soared into the sky.

"Flying!" cried Margarita. "I am flying!" Peals of hysterical laughter echoed against the glowing walls and out across the silent countryside.

She saw Sebastian's figure dwindling below her as she flew in dizzying spirals among the towers. Then he rose to join her, his wings flowering out behind his billowing cloak. The two figures circled in the sky beneath the silver moon and the castle dropped away below them. Margarita watched the effortless surging of Sebastian's wings as he swept toward her. For a moment they hovered together, exchanging cold kisses in the icy air. Then he led her in a downward swoop and they came to rest upon the battlements of the topmost tower.

"Sebastian!" she gasped. "This is wonderful! Why did you stop me?"

"Rest, Margarita. Soon a weakness will come upon you." He sat on the edge of the parapet, wings furled behind him and feet dangling far above the ground. "Beneath us is the chamber where my work goes on," he said. "There is much to see there."

"Why should I grow weak?" asked Margarita, but even as she spoke she swayed against the purple sky. "It is nothing," she said as he caught her in his arms.

"You are drained of life," he told her, "and you will need more. I must find a way to feed you."

"There is a whole city nearby," she said.

"We must avoid it," Sebastian insisted. "Nor can we count upon my brother to provide you with victims. It will be safer if he believes you are gone forever."

"Then what are we to do? You were right, Sebastian. I felt a terrible thirst when you mentioned it, and I feel it now. A thirst for blood."

Her pink tongue darted out over her red lips. Sebastian smiled to see it. "Perhaps we can find something there," he said, "over the mountains. In France, where they have witches of their own, nobody will think to suspect this castle. Are you too weak to fly?"

"I want to fly again!"

"I might be able to bring something back to you," he suggested.

"No. I want to fly, and with you beside me I will have nothing to fear. If need be, you can carry me. Come on!"

Her wings caught a current of air that carried her over the battlements and into space. Sebastian circled anxiously around her until he saw that she was safe. The exhilaration of flight was so intense that Margarita left any feeling of faintness behind her. She remembered only the powerful thrust of her surging shoulders and the burning hunger that drove her onward.

Like two gigantic bats they soared upward, their great gray wings flapping against the wind or catching breezes that carried them effortlessly aloft. The castle disappeared behind them, and the forest, and the dry sandy plains. Jagged purple peaks rose up to meet them: bare, forbidding mountains capped with snow and dotted with scrubby cypress trees. To an army the Pyrenees were all but impassable, yet Sebastian and Margarita passed over them as easily as the clouds, leaving no more trace than the shadows they cast on the icy summits.

Swiftly and silently they flew, and purposefully, but sometimes one of them swept playfully close to the other for a kiss or a caress. Once Margarita shouted.

"When I have tasted blood, Sebastian, then I will share your dreams!"

His wing brushed hers, but he did not reply.

Hours passed in the flight beneath the shining stars, until at last the mountains sank away into rolling hills and valleys. Sebastian flew lower then and kept his eyes upon the ground.

He circled lower still and suddenly shot out one long arm, his finger pointing toward something below. Margarita saw only a spot on the ground, but as she swept down for a closer look, she realized that something about it was unique. Everything around her had glowed with blue and silver, but the speck moving beneath her pulsed with a faint ruddiness. It was the first living thing she had seen that night.

Margarita dropped out of the sky like a stone. She had time to glimpse the startled, upturned face of a young man with fair curly hair. He looked toward the sky in surprise as a black shadow passed over his head, then Margarita was upon him.

She attacked her victim like a wild beast, and looked like one to the man who fell before her savage onslaught. He saw green eyes like a cat's, a black mane of streaming, wind-blown hair, and a gaping red mouth filled with gleaming fangs. His head struck a rock as he tumbled backward, and he offered no resistance as Margarita crouched over him and tore ravenously at his throat. Blood streamed and spattered from his mangled jugular. Margarita feasted on it eagerly, teeth slashing, lips sucking, and tongue licking at the crimson fountain. Her head reeled and her body quivered with delight until at last her thirst was slaked.

She rolled over and lay on her back beside the dead man. Both of them, covered with blood, stared upward at the distant stars. Margarita's face was a lurid mask of red rivulets trickling down her neck and over her naked shoulders. Her bosom heaved and her fingers ripped at the long blades of grass around her. Her eyes were glazed and almost sightless, so that she hardly noticed Sebastian when he dropped down at her feet.

If she had been looking at Sebastian, she might have noticed the strange expression on his face. He could hardly turn paler than he was, but his dark eyes were wide and his mouth hung half open as he surveyed the gruesome scene.

Finally he knelt beside her, his gray wings sheltering her body. He whispered her name and ran his white fingers through her hair. She stirred then and turned her dazed eyes toward him, a sleepy smile on her gory lips. "What bliss," she murmured. "Better than flying. Better than anything I have ever known." She smiled more broadly. "Except, perhaps, for your embrace."

"You will have more of both," he said, wiping her mouth with a corner of his cloak. "And you will learn to be less savage. These pleasures should be savored."

"And you will learn to be less of a hypocrite," she said, still smiling. "Others taught me savagery, and I will not forget the lesson. When I killed that man, I wished he had been another. I can think of several who owe me a debt that can only be washed away in blood."

"Be careful, Margarita, and remember my warnings." Sebastian's face was grim. "We must stay hidden from the world." He helped her to her feet and kept his arms around her, shielding her from the butchered corpse outstretched on the blood-flecked ground.

"You need not spare me from that sight," she said. "I am no stranger to slaughter. I have killed sheep and seen men burned alive. I was never a weak woman, Sebastian, and now I am stronger. You have given me that gift of power, and I promise you that I will be careful with it. I will not risk my life, now that I can live forever."

"Forever," echoed Sebastian, pressing her close against him. They were briefly lost in each other's arms, then Sebastian stepped back. "We must return to the castle at once," he said. "You will fly faster now, and so you must, for it will be morning soon. These summer nights are short."

15. The Book

NEARLY TWO weeks passed before the letter appeared at the Holy House.

These were difficult days for Diego de Villanueva, who was forced to maintain his outward composure despite a steadily growing anxiety about the book nearing completion at the castle. More than ever he longed to have the manuscript in his hand and taste the power he believed it would bring him. The wait would have been frustrating enough in itself, but it became almost unbearable when aggravated by the presence of the young man who was Don Sebastian's heir. Antonio visited the Holy House almost every day, each visit bringing new demands for action in the settlement of the estate. The Grand Inquisitor temporized as best he could, but his stratagems were not infinite and he knew that much further delay might bring about the collapse of his ambitions. His only consolation during this trying period was provided by the coven of witches imprisoned in the dungeons of the Holy House, who felt the full force of his impatience.

So when Miguel entered with the letter in his hand and the Grand Inquisitor recognized the writing, he had some difficulty containing his excitement.

"This was found under the door this morning," said Miguel. "It is addressed to you."

Diego restrained an impulse to snatch at the letter. "You may leave it with me," he said.

Miguel put it down on the table, a simple piece of paper, folded and sealed with red wax. Then he stood beside it. "Perhaps it is something important," Miguel suggested. "It might be from a witness who is afraid to show himself but still has important information. Or it might be . . ."

"Speculation is futile," interrupted the Grand Inquisitor, "when the answer is so near at hand." He reached out for the letter, his heart racing. "You may leave now, Miguel."

And yet, even after his vicar was gone, Diego de Villanueva could hardly bring himself to open the paper. Too much depended on it. He was almost certain that it contained the news he was anticipating, but he could not be absolutely sure. It was difficult to fathom Sebastian's motives at the best of times, but more so now that the Grand Inquisitor had been forbidden to visit his brother. Could Sebastian be such a fool as to finish the book? Did he imagine that he would be allowed to survive once his work was accomplished? Still, the hand that had written the Grand Inquisitor's name and title was certainly that of Don Sebastian de Villanueva. And there was more proof. The red wax sealing the paper bore a cloudy impression. No one else would have recognized the mark, but the brother of the man who had made it read it easily enough. Evidently Sebastian had sealed the letter with his signet ring, then recognized the imprudence of a dead man's continuing the habit of a lifetime and effaced the wax impression.

This was interesting enough, but inconsequential. The Grand Inquisitor drew a deep breath and broke the seal.

For an instant the words swam before his eyes, but he managed to read them, then read them again. There was no signature. The message was simple and direct, only five words: "It is finished. Come tonight."

The Grand Inquisitor sank back in his chair, the paper fluttering in his trembling hand, great waves of relief washing over him. He had hardly slept for days and had not relaxed for a month, but now he sprawled like a drunkard, smiling idiotically at the crucifix on the wall. He had done it. He had won.

• • •

"*Vires Malorum*," Sebastian said.

His brother did not reply and gave no indication that he had even heard. Utterly absorbed, he ran his fingers over the thick sheaf of paper on the ivory-and-onyx chessboard, almost as if he feared that the manuscript might be an illusion. Then he looked up distractedly.

"What? What did you call it? *Vires Malorum?*" He considered the title carefully. "I think not, Sebastian. It reminds me too much of Kramer and Sprenger, with their *Malleus Maleficarum*. We must have something different. Certainly this work is unique, not to be confused with any other. Let me think."

Sebastian sat quietly in his high-backed chair.

"*Vires* . . . *Vires Tenebrarum*," said the Grand Inquisitor. "Yes, that will do. What do you think of it?"

"*Vires Tenebrarum, The Powers of Darkness*. Not bad, brother. Use it if you will. It is your book. I still prefer *The Forces of Evil* myself, but let it pass. Your title is less dogmatic, and less insulting, too. I have no cause for complaint."

"So be it," said the Grand Inquisitor. "Well!" He was at a loss for words. This moment, which he had experienced so often in anticipation, now left him somehow dissatisfied and ill at ease. Perhaps it was because he knew that he would never visit his brother in the tower again. He cast his mind back over the years of secret meetings and almost found it within himself to grow sentimental. He would miss the nocturnal duels across the chessboard, the debates on the great mysteries; he would even miss Sebastian and the jealous hatred for him that had driven Diego de Villanueva from boyhood. It saddened the Grand Inquisitor slightly to think that his brother had to die. He wanted to snatch up the book and flee with it but realized it would be unwise.

"So!" he said. "It is really finished! I am quite overcome, Sebastian. There were times when I thought you would never do it. More than once I compared you with Penelope, the wife of the great captain Ulysses, who wove her tapestry by day and undid it by night so that after ten years it was still incomplete."

"This tapestry took only nine years," Sebastian said. "Have you no wish to look upon it, brother?"

"Of course I do. But I can hardly read it here."

"Is the light too dim?"

"No, Sebastian, but it will take me days to read all this. After all, it took you years to write it." The Grand Inquisitor lifted the bulky sheaf of papers in both hands as though to indicate the enormity of his brother's effort.

"No doubt you think me a fool to be done with it," Sebastian suggested. His brother's fingers slipped involuntarily and the uppermost sheet of paper floated gracefully to the floor.

"Let me take that," said Sebastian, rising from his chair. "It is the title page, and I must change it for you." He produced another piece of paper from a shelf above a row of books, and a quill wet with ink. *"Vires Tenebrarum,"* he muttered as he wrote. "I should be writing this in blood, no doubt, but I have none to spare."

"You must have had your fill of Margarita de Mendoza," said the Grand Inquisitor.

"Yes, brother, but that was many days ago."

"And where is she now?"

"She is dead, brother. Where do the dead go?" Sebastian smiled. "You have asked me yourself more than once, and now I have the answer for you. I could not resist the temptation to give this answer to you, and to the world, whatever the cost might be to me, and that is why the book is finished. Even I am surprised at what I have discovered."

"You know?" asked the Grand Inquisitor. "You really know? How did you find it out?"

"Come, brother, leave me a few secrets. Let us say that I found the truth through meditation. I should have seen it sooner." He placed the new title page atop the pile of papers on the black-and-white chessboard. "If I had known, all this could have been finished long ago. But sometimes simple truths are the most difficult to grasp. Even now you have not asked me for the answer but only for the method by which it was discovered. Perhaps you would prefer to know nothing about it." He sank again into his shadow-shrouded chair.

"Tell me, Sebastian. You have written it anyway, and I will know it soon enough whether you speak or not."

"Very well, brother. What I tell you is what I believe, and I am certain of it. But in the book I could do no more than offer it as a belief prevalent among sorcerers and witches. Otherwise, *Vires Tenebrarum* would be condemned as the vilest heresy."

"Yes, yes," urged the Grand Inquisitor. "Tell me what it is."

"Let us suppose that the religion you profess is the true one," Sebastian began. "It teaches that those who believe in its doctrines will be saved and will live on after death in a fashion that preachers love to describe. But those who break the rules and are not reconciled are promised an eternal life of another sort, which the preachers depict even more eloquently. Is it not so?"

"More or less," granted the Grand Inquisitor.

"But even your religion admits that these futures hold true only for those who embrace the faith. For those who remain outside it, another destiny awaits, a sort of vagueness outside your universe, which you call limbo."

"You are making it all too simple, Sebastian."

"I admit it, brother. What I tell you now is not as closely reasoned as the passage in the manuscript. Shall I stop now, and let you read it for yourself?"

"Continue, Sebastian. I will not object again."

"So much, if I may say so, for your orthodoxy. But consider the others, Diego. Every religion teaches something about the life to come. The Jews believe one thing, the Moors another, and who knows how many other beliefs there are in the world? Who knows what the natives of the New World believe? You, of course, dismiss them all as pagans, but consider, brother suppose that every one of them was right."

"Now you are speaking nonsense, Sebastian. How could every one be right?"

"Bear with me another moment. You know something of what I believe, Diego, and know that these beliefs, called witchcraft, sorcery, alchemy, or magic, are almost universally condemned. Every religion warns its followers to beware the men and women who follow the left-handed path. Might it not be because we know the truth about all of them, or because we could know it?"

"What are you driving at, Sebastian? Where is the answer you promised me?"

"Simply this, brother. Those who practice magic know, if they know anything, the importance of the will. We learn early that the power we seek is already within us and that our task is to express it, nothing more. Through concentration, through faith, we can accomplish anything. Even your religion teaches that faith is the key to everything and the one who believes will be saved. But you claim that the doctrine must be correct. I believe it need not be. In fact, I believe that there is no correct doctrine at all. There is only faith and the power of the will."

"What are you saying, Sebastian?"

"You understand me, brother, though you may pretend you do not. I am saying that the eternity a man imagines for himself is the one he will experience. Those who believe in your Heaven and believe they are worthy of it will find themselves there. Those who have faith in another future will find themselves in it, whatever it may be. The truth is that there is no truth. The world of spirits is infinite. Each man and each woman creates an individual destiny, which neither curses nor blessings can alter. Those who believe in nothing will taste oblivion, and those who wait for Hell will surely find it waiting for them."

Sebastian paused, but his brother did not answer. Instead, the Grand Inquisitor stared silently at the papers piled before him and at the black and white squares of the chessboard. He looked at the flickering red candle and the yellow skull supporting it. He saw the gray stone walls of the tower, and the Moorish tapestry that blocked the narrow window. And he saw the dark figure of his brother, sitting in shadowed silence like an emperor of evil.

"But how can you be sure, Sebastian? This is only a theory!"

"There is no way for me to prove it to you, brother. Believe it only if you will. But when you die, remember me."

"When I die . . ." said Diego de Villanueva.

"It may not be soon, Diego, if you are careful. And that reminds me. Do you intend to kill me, now that you have the book?"

"Why, Sebastian!" said the Grand Inquisitor nervously. "Do I seem so ungrateful?"

His brother answered him with a smile that looked like the grin of a skeleton. "I am reassured," he said. "I had imagined that you might decide you had no further use for me now that you have the book, and now that your dungeons are filled with witches."

"How could you know about the other witches? I have said nothing."

"When one witch is snatched away by a winged monster, confessions among her colleagues are certain to increase. I knew that what I did at the *auto* would be of some help to you. So you see how useful I can be, brother. Will you let me live a little longer? Perhaps I can help you again."

Something in Sebastian's mocking tone made his brother uneasy. Did he suspect that the Grand Inquisitor planned to destroy him while he slept? No. That was impossible. He would hardly be fool enough to hand over the manuscript if he understood that its last page was his death warrant. But why was he talking about it this way?

"There is still much for me to teach you," Sebastian continued, "and more for me to learn. A mere month ago I could not answer your question about death and its mysteries."

"I am less than certain that you have answered it now."

"But suppose that I have! Might you not need me, if only to teach you how to control your own mind? What do you believe now, brother? What would your fate be if you died tonight?"

The Grand Inquisitor stirred uneasily on his hard wooden bench. "My faith will sustain me," he said.

"Come Diego. I am your brother, not one of those superstitous souls in the city below us. Do not preach to me. How sure are you of Heàven, you, who have spent your life creating Hell on earth? I believe—and you believe it too—that you have only enough faith in your theology to become one of the damned."

The Grand Inquisitor had no reply to this.

"But do not despair," continued Sebastian. "If I have time enough, perhaps I will be able to enlighten you. There is always hope, and that is the beginning of faith."

Diego de Villanueva made an unsuccessfull attempt at a sneer. He was becoming angry as well as agitated.

"No?" asked Sebastian. "There is another reason for you to spare me, brother, at least for a little while. Take your *Vires Tenebrarum* and study it. You may find something in it that you will want to change. I will be waiting to assist you, and even when you have satisfied yourself you may find that you have further need of me. No doubt you will send the manuscript to your mentor, Torquemada, the Inquisitor General. You will need his approval and endorsement, but they may not be easy to obtain. What will you do when he questions you on some obscure argument in the text? What but run to your older and wiser brother for advice? It would be a shame for you to risk everything when you are so close to success."

There was something in this, much as Diego hated to admit it even to himself. The book might bear his name, but it was Sebastian's work, and very likely only he could understand it all. The Grand Inquisitor tried to calculate the amount of time necessary to deliver the book to Torquemada and receive his reply. Miguel would have to be sent with the manuscript and it would take him many days to return, even if he was able to obtain an immediate audience with the Inquisitor General. It might be possible, though, to keep Antonio away from the castle for a few more weeks, and Sebastian was right when he said that it would be wiser to wait.

Suddenly the Grand Inquisitor was very tired. This night, for which he had waited so long, did not mean the end of his worries after all. There would be more delays, more intrigues. He was not yet free.

Sebastian stood up and put a cold hand on his brother's

shoulder. The flickering candlelight made him look as if he were laughing, but he made no sound. "You are weary, brother," he said. "You must sleep. Your hours are not like mine and you are busy with your torture chambers. Think on what I have told you and read your book. I will be here when you need me."

He ushered the befuddled Grand Inquisitor through the arched door of the topmost room in the topmost tower and followed him down the dark stone steps. Neither spoke until they reached the courtyard, where a chestnut mare was tethered. Sebastian obsequiously offered to help his brother into the saddle, but the mare shied away from him and the Grand Inquisitor was obliged to mount her unassisted. He did it clumsily, with one hand clutching the bulky manuscript.

Diego de Villanueva rode slowly across the open drawbridge and soon vanished into the darkness. "Good night, brother," Sebastian called after him. "Sleep well."

Sebastian reached for the windlass to raise the bridge, but before he could touch it Margarita stepped from the shadows.

"You should never have given it to him," she said. "It was your protection."

"I hope you are wrong," Sebastian said. "I could hardly keep it from him forever or he would have become dangerous from sheer frustration. As it is, I think I have convinced him not to act too hastily. Even so, you are right; we must be on guard."

"But how can we protect ourselves when we must lie in the crypt?"

"Trust me, Margarita. If all goes well, we shall have nothing to fear. The book is poisoned."

Margarita smiled, and her lover was amazed anew at her ferocious beauty. "You have poisoned the pages?" she asked. "What did you use?"

"Not the pages, Margarita. This is something subtler still. I have poisoned the words. *The Powers of Darkness* will be Diego's undoing."

Margarita seemed to have lost interest in the Grand Inquisitor. She stepped back into the shadows. Her voice spoke to Sebastian quickly from a corner of the courtyard. "I heard what you told him. Was it true, what you said about faith and the future?"

Sebastian looked toward her but saw only a faintly glowing phantom. "I did not mean for you to hear that," he said, "but I believe that it is true. You taught me."

"When I told you that I did not believe in a life after death, and when I told you that the daylight did not bring me dreams like yours?" The voice from the darkness was almost a whisper.

"Yes," said Sebastian.

Margarita ran from the shadows and threw her arms around the tall, silent figure in the crimson cloak. "I don't want to lose you, Sebastian," she cried, "and I don't want to die. You must show me how to believe. You must show me how to have dreams like yours!"

16. The Second Voyage

MIGUEL STARTED out for Madrid, but he never reached it.

Only two days after he began his journey with the manuscript of *Vires Tenebrarum*, he began to hear stories about the king and queen that caused him to change his plans. Rumors said that the sovereigns were no longer in Madrid. For some reason they had decided to hold court at Burgos, or so Miguel was told. Perhaps the move meant nothing more than a desire to be in the north where the weather might be a little cooler. Who could understand the whims of royalty?

For Miguel the reason was unimportant. It was enough for him to know that his goal was so much closer than he had expected and that he would be spared weeks of traveling alone through the provinces. For if Ferdinand and Isabella were at Burgos, then Tomás de Torquemada would surely be there as well, since he was not only Inquisitor General of the whole kingdom but confessor to the queen as well. And it was Torquemada whom Miguel had set out to see, for Diego de Villanueva had given strict instructions that the book should be delivered directly to the one man in Spain whose influence was sufficient to guarantee its success.

Elated by the discovery that his journey would be so short, Miguel hurried toward Burgos. His timid nature made him uneasy on the road, and he continually imagined himself set upon by thieves, even though he realized there was not much reason for anyone to waylay a monk bound by vows of poverty. Still, it was a great relief to him when he passed through the gates of Burgos with the manuscript still safe in his saddlebag. Almost at once a new source of trepidation occurred to him. Now that he had arrived, he would be obliged to present himself at court, and he realized that he had no idea what to do. Of course, the Grand Inquisitor had given him instruction in deportment, but Miguel forgot everything in his first rush of panic. He was only a humble friar alone in a strange city that was not even the one he had been ordered to visit. He needed help, or at least some idea of where to go.

For a while he rode aimlessly through the streets. He passed any number of people and more than once determined to ask for directions, but he never did. The citizens, no doubt worthy enough, looked suspicious to him, and he could not bring himself to ask anyone the way to the king and queen, if only for fear that anyone he asked might reply with a burst of laughter. Miguel Carillo did not look like a courtier.

As the afternoon turned into evening, the young friar decided it would be wisest to postpone his mission until the following day. Relieved by this decision, he made for the nearest inn. His horse was soon stabled, but Miguel took the saddlebag with him when he entered the common room. A goat was roasting on the open fire and several fellows of various classes were enthusiastically imbibing. It was a rowdy, smoky place, and Miguel wondered if he might be able to find shelter at a monastery instead. Then he saw a Franciscan friar sitting alone at the end of the long table and decided that he would stay at least long enough to get some information.

The Franciscan was a tall man with a long red face. His aquiline nose was freckled, his eyes extraordinarily blue. He seemed no more than middle-aged, yet his hair and beard were white. But the eyes were certainly his most unusual feature. Their color alone was remarkable, at least in this district, and their expression was more remarkable still. Seamed and weathered and saddened, they nonetheless appeared possessed by a vision. They were not fiery and penetrating like Diego de Villanueva's; instead, they gazed outward dreamily, as if they saw something invisible to others. Miguel concluded that the man was a mystic—no doubt a commendable calling, but not very useful to anyone looking for practical advice.

Miguel had almost decided to look elsewhere for help when the blue-eyed Franciscan spoke to him. "Sit down, young man," he said. Miguel was a little surprised, since he was almost certain that the friar had not even looked in his direction, but he did as he was told.

"Are you lost?" asked the Franciscan. "You look as if you might be."

"I know where I am," answered Miguel, "but I am not quite sure where I am going. I came in here to get directions."

"It is a terrible thing to be lost," said the Franciscan, toying with the empty cup in front of him. "I feel that way myself. It is only when I don't know where I am that I feel really at home, and right now I am only too aware that I am in Burgos."

Miguel was certain now that he was talking to the wrong man. This one made no sense at all. Miguel's expression must have given him away, because the Franciscan reacted to his thoughts. "I am not mad, young man," he said, "or at least I do not think so. I only meant to say that I am wanderer, an adventurer if you will, so that I am happiest when seeking something new. I have just returned from the Indies."

"The Indies!" said Miguel. "Then you know the great admiral of the ocean sea? Columbus?"

"I know him as well as any man does."

"So the second expedition has returned," said Miguel. "We have heard nothing of it, though I suppose that is not surprising, since our city is a small one on the northern border. Few dispatches come our way."

"You may have your own news, though. There have been reports of battles with the French in the region of the Pyrenees."

"Battles!" gasped Miguel. "Are we invaded? I knew nothing of it. Are we at war?"

"Hardly a war, as I understand; not here. But we have been fighting the French over the succession in Naples, and they lost with bad grace. Some of their troops have been making forays across the mountains, but it will not amount to much."

"It may not be much to you," Miguel retorted, "but if you lived there you would feel different." He imagined hordes of soldiers rushing into the Holy House and was glad to be far away in Burgos.

"Of course," said the Franciscan apologetically, "I have been gone for so long that none of this seems real to me. I have been in another world. Three years! But even there we lived with warfare, and treachery too."

"Tell me about the New World," urged Miguel.

"They call it that now, don't they? But it is not a new world. It is the Orient, which will surely be proved in time, though even this second voyage did not penetrate far enough to reach the great cities of the khan. There should be a third expedition at once, but now there are delays and doubts and politicians. The people cheered when the *Niña* and the *Pinta* returned from the first voyage, but they laughed and jeered at the men who came ashore this June. I admit that the men were a sorry sight. They had come through war, disease, and starvation, but by San Fernando! they had come through! The only thing anyone wanted to know was how much gold had been discovered. May God take them! Is gold everything?"

"Then the second voyage was a failure?" asked Miguel tactlessly.

"It was not! By San Fernando it was not! But I fear it will be considered one," the Franciscan said, lowering his voice. "It was the crew. On the first voyage there were real seafaring men—tough, hard-working sailors. But once the stories of that expedition began to spread, a crew of fops and dandies appeared, eager to seek their fortunes on the second voyage. They should have stayed at home! As soon as they discovered that they could not pick up handfuls of gold on the first beach, they grew surly and rebellious."

"There was a rebellion against the admiral?"

"Worse than that. There was treachery. The trouble began before we sighted land. Men who had been left behind at the colony of La Navidad disobeyed the admiral's instructions. They treated the Indians brutally, raped and looted, and fought among themselves for the spoils. Finally a native tribe rose up against them and the settlement was destroyed to the last man. When we arrived with a fleet of seventeen ships there was no colony, and we had to begin again."

"Were the Indians punished?"

"They were punished and more. Perhaps too much more. The leader of the uprising, a king named Caonabo, was captured by Margarit, one of the most headstrong of the lieutenants *worse* than headstrong. He was left in charge of the new colony at Saint Thomas while the search went on for other lands, and he treated the natives abominably. These Indians are simple, peaceful people for the most part, and they should be converted, not exterminated. But too many greedy men had come from Spain, and they could not be controlled. The order was finally given that each native should produce a tribute in gold every month, even though the conditions were impossible. There is not much gold there, only farther inland, and the Indians grew desperate. Some tried to fight and were killed. Others fled into the hills and were hunted down with dogs. The worst of all were those who lost all hope and poisoned themselves. I believe close to half of them must have died since the second expedition arrived."

"And did the admiral approve all this?" asked Miguel, more interested than appalled.

"What else could be done? Could a man take the part of these savages in opposition to his own lieutenants? But it hardly mattered. No concession was great enough. These fair-weather sailors became indignant at every turn. They thought themselves too good to cultivate the land, even though it was obvious that the ships could not carry enough supplies to feed them for years. And always there was the cry for more gold. Finally, Margarit took one of the ships stole it. He headed back to Spain with a crew of malcontents to poison the minds of the sovereigns against the expedition. The result of this treachery was the appearance of another Spanish vessel at Saint Thomas bearing a fellow named Juan Aguado, who was named crown chamberlain, with authority to oversee the whole enterprise, an unacceptable situation. We returned to Spain at once, or would have, but there was a delay when a terrible storm arose. Three ships were sunk. I think it was a judgment of God. Finally, two ships limped back to Cadiz with a cargo of slaves to compensate for the gold that could not be found. King Caonabo, who was among them, died like a dog aboard the *Niña*, though he had been a mighty ruler in his own land. And here we are, awaiting the royal pleasure."

"What did the king and queen have to say?"

"Oh, they were polite and attentive and promised to outfit a third expedition. But what good are promises? Already months have passed. Now there are no men to volunteer for another voyage. Even men in prison prefer confinement to the dangers of the Indies, and they refuse pardons rather than brave the unknown. And ships? There seem to be none, though an armada of one hundred and thirty took the Princess Juana to her marriage in Flanders."

"Then you have been at court?" asked Miguel, suddenly remembering his own mission.

"I have, and it appears that I will be again," answered the Franciscan.

"Then you can help me," said Miguel. "How do I get there? And what should I do to gain admittance?"

"You must not expect much from Ferdinand and Isabella. They have a war to contend with and royal weddings. They have little time for such as you or me, my friend."

"They are not the ones I seek," said Miguel. "My business is with the Inquisitor General."

"The Inquisitor General? Torquemada?"

"Yes. Tomás de Torquemada," said Miguel reverently. "Why do you look so surprised?"

"You will be more surprised, my friend. I am glad you have not traveled far, because you will not find Torquemada at court."

"What? He must be. He is the queen's confessor."

"No longer," said the Franciscan. "He is old and ill and has his troubles with the Holy Office. You will find him at Avila. He has retired to the monastery there that was built on his instructions years ago."

"Retired?" Miguel could hardly have been more bewildered. "Is he still Inquisitor General?"

"I suppose he is. It is said that he is at work on new instructions for the operation of the Inquisition."

"Avila!" Miguel said in despair. "Where is Avila?"

"Almost half a kingdom away," answered the Franciscan. "At least three times as far as you have already traveled. It lies to the west of Madrid."

Miguel looked crestfallen. "Then I am for Avila," he said unhappily.

"Cheer up, my friend. You have an adventure ahead of you. A young fellow should be happy to have a chance to see something of the world."

"This is no adventure," Miguel answered glumly. "It is a duty and one I would gladly be spared. But someone had to deliver the book and I was chosen."

"A book. It must be a wonderful thing to have written a book."

"It is not mine. It is the work of the Grand Inquisitor Diego de Villanueva, who wishes to bring it to the attention of the Holy Office. I am only a messenger."

"Well, you are still young. No doubt you will write your own someday. Learning is a wonderful thing. I am a simple seafaring man myself, but I believe my son Ferdinand will be a scholar."

Dumbfounded, Miguel stared at his companion. What sort of a monk was this who claimed to have no learning and openly acknowledged that he had broken his vow of chastity? It was known, of course, that there were monks who had fathered children, but few of them were intemperate enough to boast about their indiscretions.

Again the bright blue eyes seemed to look into Miguel's mind. "You need not look so startled," said the man in the rough brown robe. "I am quite prepared to acknowledge my ignorance and my children, too. I had no wish to deceive you, my friend, but I am no Franciscan friar."

"But . . ." said Miguel, completing his sentence with a gesture toward the stranger's costume.

"This?" said the false Franciscan, holding up the hem of his habit. "I wear it for a penance. I fear that I have much to answer for. And it has other uses. I might be recognized if I wore other clothes, and I have troubles enough."

Miguel started to speak but was interrupted.

"You have troubles, too," said the man, "even if they have not turned your hair white. Mine was red not too long ago; but never mind. We must speed you on your journey, my friend. This tavern is no place for you, nor for me either. There is a Franciscan monastery on the road just south of here. If you leave at once, you can reach it before nightfall. They will be glad to shelter you and you will be a little farther along on your journey. I wish you well."

Miguel stood up with his head in a spin. This stranger, whoever he might be, was the oddest man he had ever encountered. Still, that was no reason for Miguel to be discourteous.

"I am Miguel Carillo," he said, "vicar to Diego de Villanueva, Grand Inquisitor. I thank you, both for your help and for your tales of the Indies. May God be with you."

"And I thank you, Miguel Carillo, for your company and for your blessing." The stranger took the young monk by the arm and leaned forward. "My name," he said in a whisper, "is Don Cristóbal de Colón."

Miguel was out of the smoky tavern and in the street before he realized what he had heard. He looked back toward the inn as if it were a vision.

Cristóbal de Colón   Columbus   the admiral of the ocean sea.

17. The Twelve Apostles

THE MONASTERY of Saint Thomas was renowned as the most beautiful in Spain. More than ten years, as well as a considerable portion of the revenue confiscated by the Inquisition, had been consumed in its construction. Building this magnificent edifice was a personal project of great importance to Tomás de Torquemada; it was said that the Inquisitor General had stood humbly beside the common laborers and worked on it with his own hands. He was certainly responsible for the legend engraved upon its walls: *Pestem Fugat Haereticam*. No heretic, no one who was even a descendant of a Jew or a Moor, was ever permitted to enter its sacred precincts. The only exception made was for those who were carried into its dungeons.

The monastery stood outside the town of Avila in the rich green lands along the Adaja River. The countryside was so different from the bleak one beneath the Pyrenees that Miguel began to wish he might never have to return. At the same time, though, he was anxious to be off. He knew all too well that Diego de Villanueva would grow more impatient with every second wasted in unnecessary delay and that only a foolish vicar would use a pleasant landscape as an excuse for a protracted stay. Not even his fear of an impending war along the border could keep Miguel within the tranquil cloisters of Saint Thomas. His mission was too important to be forgotten for reasons of personal safety. He sensed obscurely that his master's future rode with him, and loyalty was Miguel's cardinal virtue. If he waited, it was because he had no choice.

He was waiting for Torquemada.

Miguel had been naive enough to imagine that he would be granted an immediate audience with the Inquisitor General, but he was soon disillusioned. Evidently, the name of Diego de Villanueva, Grand Inquisitor, did not carry as much weight here as it did in his own district. In fact, nobody seemed to have heard the name at all. Miguel was even persuaded, against his better judgment and in contravention of his previous instructions, to surrender the precious manuscript that had never left his side during his entire journey. He had been told to deliver *Vires Tenebrarum* into no other hands than Torquemada's, but the order was impossible to follow. Torquemada was not to be approached so easily. Still, the monk who took the manuscript assured Miguel that it would be placed before the Inquisitor General and that an interview might be arranged soon. Meanwhile, Miguel was left to entertain himself as best he could.

For days he wandered aimlessly across the wide courtyards and down the pillared passages surrounding them. He ate, slept, and read, worshiped, prayed, and meditated. He worried and waited. On the fourth day he was summoned.

Miguel followed another Dominican down long, tiled cloisters supported by marble columns, past paintings of saints and angels. At length they reached a plain plank door. Miguel passed through it and was alone with the Inquisitor General.

The austerity of the room surprised Miguel. The whitewashed walls were bare except for a large silver crucifix, and the furnishings consisted of no more than a pair of chairs and a plain table. Still, Torquemada was renowned for his severity. It was only natural to suppose that his surroundings would be simple. This might have been Diego de Villanueva's chamber in the Holy House, except for two incongruous notes. There was an open window in the far wall, through which Miguel could see a flower garden and hear the distant song of birds. And, even though it was summer, logs burned in the fireplace behind the man seated at the table.

It was this figure that caught Miguel's attention and held it so that he absorbed the appearance of the room without really looking at it. He was not fully aware of anything but Tomás de Torquemada. At first glance, the Inquisitor General was something of a disappointment. Miguel had tried to picture him during the long days and nights on the road but had not been able to imagine anything more impressive than a bigger version of Diego de Villanueva. What he saw instead was a wizened old man, small, frail, and evidently in very poor health. He was dressed, like Miguel, in the black-and-white robes of the Dominican order. The fringe of hair around his shaven head was sparse and grizzled, his grim face a mass of quivering wrinkles. Only the brown eyes, liquid and unusually large, seemed alive.

The Inquisitor General gestured Miguel into a chair with a thin, unsteady hand. The manuscript was on the table between them. Sunlight poured in through the open window, its radiance turning the pale pages yellow. The room was filled with the scent of flowers.

"Miguel Carillo," said Torquemada. The voice was more powerful than the body that produced it. Miguel was disturbed by the discrepancy, and he fancied for a moment that there might be someone else in the room. Then he collected himself.

"Vicar to Diego de Villanueva, Grand Inquisitor," said Miguel.

Torquemada said nothing for a moment, but something like a smile touched his thin lips. "I remember him," he said finally. "He studied with me for some time. When he was ready to become an Inquisitor, he asked to be sent home. It was most unusual, and at the time I wondered why. Now I know. He was an ambitious boy."

Miguel could hardly believe that Diego de Villanueva had ever been a boy. Somehow the thought upset him.

"Have you read this?" asked Torquemada, tapping the manuscript with a thin forefinger. His voice was suddenly sharp and cold.

"What?" gasped Miguel guiltily. "No! I wanted to, of course, but I did not have permission. I am only a messenger."

"Good. Obedience is a virtue. In your case, virtue will be rewarded."

"Rewarded?" echoed Miguel nervously.

"I meant that you are fortunate not to have read this book," said Torquemada. "What do you know about it?"

"Only that it concerns witches."

"Witches and more. Sorcerers and soothsayers, Miguel Carillo, and devils and demons. Vampires, werewolves, ghouls—every fantastic horror spawned by the Devil is in this book, each abomination described in incredible detail, and with an intimate knowledge of the subject that might frighten any man. You are very lucky not to have read it, my son, and for more than one reason. What do you think of all this, Miguel Carillo? Do you believe this kind of story?"

"It must be true," said Miguel. "We have witches in the Holy House now. I have seen them."

"No doubt you have seen something," replied the Inquisitor General. "But what was it? No doubt you have women in your dungeons, but how do you know they are witches?"

"The Grand Inquisitor said there was a letter for you, sir, describing the case of Margarita de Mendoza, who..."

"I have read the letter, with its fabulous tale about a demon from the pit. But let us put that aside for a moment. I want to tell you a story. Perhaps you will learn something from it."

Miguel waited uneasily. Somehow this interview was not proceeding according to plan.

"This is a true story," said Torquemada, "and what I tell you happened not just once but many times. A band of men traveled through the countryside, stopping here and there at lonely inns. There were thirteen of these men, strangely dressed. They appeared at an inn and one of them ordered a meal. He was the only one who ever spoke. The others sat quietly, looking with adoration at one who seemed to be their leader: a tall man with long hair and noble features. The behavior of these men was very strange, almost frightening. When the meal was served, the one who had ordered it announced to the innkeeper that he was playing host to Jesus Christ and His twelve apostles."

Miguel crossed himself. Torquemada watched him with huge eyes, then went on with the story.

"Of course, the landlord was awestruck. Miracles do happen, even to the simplest of men. As certainly as a man may see a witch, so he may see a saint, or even the Lord Himself. The innkeeper washed the feet of the thirteen guests and knelt beside them as they ate. When the meal was over, he was called upon to confess his sins. There is probably not an innkeeper who does not cheat his customers when he can, and he would certainly admit as much to visitors like these, along with whatever else he had on his conscience. After the confession came the penance. The one who spoke instructed the innkeeper to bring forth all his money. The man was too frightened to hold any back, and before long every ducat was on the table where the Last Supper had been reenacted. Then came the judgment. All this money was tainted with sin. Some of it would be returned to the landlord, in payment for the meal. As for the rest of it, nobody would touch it, for it was declared to be the Devil's money. But no sooner were these words spoken than the door of the inn burst open and a horror rushed into the room, its face black and hairy, its head bearing horns. This thing gathered up the money and ran out into the night. Then the thirteen guests departed silently, leaving the innkeeper to give thanks that his life had been spared and his tavern blessed."

Torquemada stopped speaking and stared at Miguel as though passing judgment on him. The wrinkled face of the Inquisitor General was contorted with some indecipherable emotion.

"There are now fourteen men in the dungeons of the Inquisition," said Torquemada. "Fourteen thieves. Twelve played the disciples, one played Christ, one the Devil. They robbed many an inn with their masquerade, and it was only when the reports of miracles became widespread that we were able to capture them. But there was no miracle, Miguel Carillo. Only greed and stupidity."

Bewilderment showed on Miguel's thin face. His eyes goggled and his mouth gaped. He had believed every word of the story and would have been willing to tell anyone that Christ and His twelve apostles were making a tour of Spanish inns. How could he doubt it, considering the source?

Torquemada continued, blandly overlooking his young visitor's evident confusion. "So you see," he said, "how easy it is to deceive people. Most men are fools. And women, too; they may be worse. I wonder. The witches who have been taken in France and Germany are usually women. Whether one believes in witchcraft or not, it is certainly unwise to practice it. Have you ever wondered whether it might be unwise to prosecute them? Consider, Miguel Carillo. There has never been a trial for witchcraft in all the annals of the Inquisiton. Do you think this is an accident? A mistake? Have you read the *Reportorium Inquisitorium* of 1496?"

Miguel shook his head.

"Diego de Villanueva should have read it," said Torquemada. "It contains a thorough discussion of this matter of witchcraft and concludes that these witches, these *jorguinas,* are laboring under a delusion. It may be their own delusion, or may be wrought by demons, but for purposes of our discussion it is hardly worthwhile to distinguish between the two. The point is that these wretched creatures have no power to perform magic, whatever they may believe. Witchcraft is folly. Of course, it is still a heresy. The fact that nothing comes of the spells these wretches try to cast is immaterial. They are still guilty of rejecting the true faith and are still liable to prosecution by the Holy Office. But what would be the result of these prosecutions?"

Miguel was dumbfounded but was spared the problem of answering the Inquisitor General's rhetorical question. He looked out the window and saw a fountain among the flowers.

"We have studied the witchcraft trials throughout

Europe," continued Torquemada, "and have drawn our own conclusions. It appears that nothing encourages the spread of this cult as much as the attempt to suppress it. Every trial leaves in its wake a new band of witches. The people are weak and stupid, their minds ready to be inflamed by any passing fancy. Let them know that there is such a thing as witchcraft and any number of them will rush to embrace it, heedless of the danger to their bodies and souls. This is human nature, Miguel Carillo. It is not comforting but it is true, and there should be at least a little comfort in it, for when we know the truth we can use it for our own ends. We know that the lives of the poor are empty and futile and that they are ready to follow any illusion that offers them the hope of power and excitement. What does the Inquisition matter to a peasant woman who hears that she can lie with the Devil and then rise up with the power to blight her enemies?"

"Then the book?" asked Miguel, looking at the fire. He would look anywhere but at the Inquisitor General. He was cold and shaking like the old man across the table.

"The book," said Torquemada. "Diego de Villanueva's book. I can imagine what he thought while he was working on it. He asked to be assigned to the district where he was born, on the French border, and he was certain that he would find some evidence of witchcraft there eventually. No doubt he saw this cult flooding down from the mountains over the entire kingdom, with himself riding the crest of the wave. I wonder if he realized that the flood would be of his own making. No doubt he was too busy counting the honors that would be bestowed upon him as the Inquisition's authority on witchcraft. How many men do you suppose there are nursing the same ambition?"

Miguel's face was pale. He had nothing to say.

"There are ambitious men everywhere, Miguel Carillo, and everywhere there is the struggle for position, even in the Holy Office, even in a sacred order where every effort should be made to maintain the discipline that will sustain the faith. I assume you have heard of my own recent difficulties."

Miguel made a feeble effort to look wise, but had no

idea what the Inquisitor General was talking about.

"As you know," said Torquemada, "much of our work has been directed toward rooting out heresy among those in high places. It is much more important to drag down the heretics with wealth and influence than it is to burn some lunatic peasant, but it is also much more difficult. It has been my policy to spare nobody, not even men of the cloth. If I were a politician I might have fared better, but I am only a humble servant of the truth. Some of those who fell under suspicion were men in high places; one of them was the bishop of Segovia, whose grandfather was a Jew. He appealed to Rome and the result was a decree from this new pope, Alexander VI, that the Inquisition could proceed against him only with the consent of the Vatican. Others complained, too, whose positions counted for more than the purity of their faith. It has been two years now since Alexander appointed a pair of men to assist me. Assist me! He made them my equals in authority. The only reason he gave was concern for my health and my advancing years, but that was diplomacy. Now the bishop of Avila and the archbishop of Messina have the support of the pope and are here to implement his policies. They want to force me out; I know it. They might have waited; I have only a little time left before my work on earth is done."

Torquemada sighed theatrically and assumed the air of a martyr. Miguel felt some sympathy for the old man, but it was lost in his bewilderment over the conflicts within the Holy Office. If even the most powerful prelates could not agree, then what was a simple vicar to think?

"But I will tell you something," said Torquemada, his voice growing stronger. "They have not beaten me yet, Miguel Carillo, and as long as there is life in this body I will not see the Inquisition turned away from its duty to pursue phantoms like those concocted by Diego de Villanueva."

Miguel tried to react. He cast his eyes on the pile of papers sitting in the sunlight and remembered how important they had seemed to him only a few minutes ago.

"But surely there must be more to it," Miguel protested timidly. "What about the evidence?"

Torquemada looked at him grimly. "Even if I believed in the evidence, I would deny it rather than encourage people to accept the idea of witchcraft. We have enough to do with the Jews and the Moors."

"But something came down from the sky," Miguel persisted. "A terrible creature with wings!"

"Did you see this yourself?" asked Torquemada.

"No," admitted Miguel. "But there were dozens of witnesses."

"Men may be deceived. I would not be surprised if this were some trick of Diego de Villanueva's. I will have to question him about it."

Something in Torquemada's last phrase chilled Miguel. He felt his stomach drop, yet still he tried to argue.

"So many saw it," Miguel said weakly. "It will be told. A tale like that will go down in history."

Torquemada shook his head wearily. He was so surprised at this young man's stupidity that he almost forgot to be angry with him.

"History is made not by those who experience it," said Torquemada, "but by those who write it down. There will be no record of this event, I promise you. I will see to it. And in a few years it will be forgotten, Miguel Carillo. No one will believe that it ever happened."

Miguel tried to speak but was dumbfounded. He produced only a sort of inarticulate noise, but Torquemada had the wit to interpret it.

"You would be well advised to stop this futile defense of the book and to consider your own position. This is a very dangerous document."

Miguel looked again at the pile of sun-drenched papers but saw nothing frightening in them. He was afraid not of the book but of Tomás de Torquemada. He realized, however dimly, that his mission had failed and that both he and Diego de Villanueva might be in serious trouble with the Inquisition.

Torquemada's blue-veined hand caressed the pages of the book. "Suppose that everything written here is true," said Torquemada, "even the outrageous blasphemies purporting to describe a sorcerer's beliefs concerning the afterlife. Can you imagine what the effect would be if such a heresy were published?"

Miguel could not imagine. He could only stare stupidly at the Inquisitor General and imagine himself being put to the Question.

"Suppose even that it might be advisable for the Holy Office to engage in a campaign against witchcraft," Torquemada continued. "Not even that could excuse this book. It is so full of information about the spawn of Satan that no one could read it without beginning to wonder about the author. I have wondered myself. How did Diego de Villanueva learn so much about these horrors? It would be easy enough to believe that he had lived among them. Of course, that is not a comforting thought. I hope to ask him about it soon."

Miguel understood these words only too well. He might have tried to defend the Grand Inquisitor, but he was speechless.

"I am glad to see that you have nothing to say," Torquemada remarked in a more soothing tone. "I believe you when you tell me that you had nothing to do with this *Vires Tenebrarum,* and I will respect your innocence. I know that I have been called a bloodthirsty fiend, but you have nothing to fear from me, Miguel Carillo. Go back to your work. Go back to Diego de Villanueva and wait. You will hear from me."

Relief poured over Miguel like sunshine, momentarily washing away his panic at the realization that his master had been found unworthy.

Torquemada stirred in his chair as if impatient to conclude the interview. He turned to look at the fire behind him. "Perhaps you have wondered about this fire," he said pleasantly. "I find that it soothes me. I am an old man, Miguel Carillo—seventy-six—and I find that my old bones are cold and stiff even in the summer. The fire warms me. And it has other uses."

Miguel stiffened.

Torquemada turned back toward the table and picked

up the manuscript. "Six years ago," he said, "in 1490, I had another fire, a larger one. But this one will do. On that day, when I was younger and stronger, I burned six hundred volumes that smacked of heresy. They made a lovely blaze, Miguel Carillo. Yet none of them, I think, was as damnable a book as this."

Tomás de Torquemada shifted his chair so that he faced the fire. He crumpled the first page of *Vires Tenebrarum* and tossed it into the flames. It caught almost at once, burning with a blue-and-yellow flame. In an instant it was gone, leaving only a thin black tissue that writhed and glowed with red as it collapsed into ashes. A second page followed the first. Miguel's head was ringing with the echoes of the screams he had heard weeks ago at the *auto-da-fé*, and he saw blistering faces in the flames as another page caught fire.

Hunched over before the fireplace, Torquemada tired of his game at last. He might have spent an hour burning the manuscript one sheet at a time, but he had other matters to consider. He tossed the entire book into the fire. It landed with a thump and a shower of sparks. For a moment it looked to Miguel as if the weight of the paper might break up the slow-burning blaze, but the pages slithered away from each other and ignited one by one. The bulk of the manuscript began to smoke and smolder.

"You may leave me now," said the Inquisitor General.

Miguel backed away on shaking legs and felt behind him for the door. He took a last look at Torquemada but saw only an old man warming himself before an open fire, his face red and sweating, huge eyes gleaming with reflected light.

18. Judgment

DIEGO DE VILLANUEVA, Grand Inquisitor, stood before his brother's castle and screamed.

He cried out his brother's name and called on saints and demons. He raved and shouted until his horse took fright. When the beast bolted and ran off through the forest to its stable at the Holy House he did not even notice that it was gone. He saw nothing but the castle, its towers black against the cloudy, starless night, and he listened for nothing but an answer to his cries. He cared nothing for his frightened mare or for the city to which it fled. He was a pilgrim seeking sanctuary.

The drawbridge dropped down. The Grand Inquisitor heard its groan and was as grateful for the sound as he would have been for the song of an angel. The entrance gaped before him like a hungry mouth and he rushed headlong into it.

The dark in the courtyard was impenetrable. The Grand Inquisitor glanced nervously around but saw only shadows. The rattle of heavy chains came from a black corner: the sound of the drawbridge closing behind him. Diego de Villanueva was shut up in the castle and was grateful for it. Here he might be safe. The castle had protected Sebastian for years, and they were sons of the same father. Now these towers would have to be his refuge too.

"Sebastian?" whispered Diego. Now that he stood within the walls, there was no longer any need to shout. Yet he was still terribly agitated, as only a man can be who has seen his highest hopes shattered and who finds himself at last a victim of the very tyranny he has inflicted on others. Fear of the unknown is not always the most powerful: the Grand Inquisitor knew only too well what the Inquisition might do to him, and that knowledge made him something less than cautious concerning the reception he might expect to receive from his brother Sebastian.

An icy hand grasped Diego's wrist. He jumped at the touch of it. "Sebastian?" he said again. He could see only a dim form but knew it for his brother and followed willingly as he was pulled across the courtyard toward the keep.

"They burned it, Sebastian," muttered Diego incoherently. "We are lost. Lost in the flames. They burned it. You must save me."

Sebastian kept his silence as he led his brother slowly up the long stone stairway, but Diego could not stop talking.

"They want to kill me," he said. "The old man is jealous of me. That must be it. I know too much. I have surpassed him, and I deserve to be Inquisitor General. They are afraid of me, and they want to kill me. But they will never find me, Sebastian. I will be safe here."

Sebastian stopped at the top of the stairs and pushed open the door to his study. As Diego entered, he felt two hands drop on his shoulders. Sebastian pushed him back against the wall so that his head struck the unyielding rock.

"Speak sense if you must speak at all," said Sebastian harshly. "What do you mean by howling outside the walls like a lost dog? Would you destroy us both? Sit, and calm yourself. Has the world ended?"

Diego dropped down upon his usual bench and sat like a stone. "You are not far wrong, Sebastian," he said. "I think the world has ended, at least for me."

"You are still among the living," said Sebastian as he seated himself in the huge chair across the chessboard from his brother.

Diego's glance dropped to the chessboard and remained frozen there. The onyx and ivory board held only two pieces: a white bishop and a black castle. He looked up at Sebastian in amazement.

"A small problem in strategy," said Sebastian. "How would you play it out, brother? Or do you still prefer the cards?"

"Don't toy with me, Sebastian. You don't realize what has happened."

"Then tell me," said Sebastian. His long white fingers reached over the table and knocked the two chessmen to the floor. "You have my complete attention."

"It is the book. I sent my vicar off with it and he returned today. I saw at once that he was disturbed, and it did not take me long to find out what had happened, or at least the essence of it. The young fool was so frightened that his story made no sense at first."

"It would seem that you have trained him well," said Sebastian.

His brother ignored this gibe. "I suppose I am fortunate that he returned at all, considering what happened to him. I have no way of knowing if he came back to warn me, or only to keep an eye on me until the officers of the Inquisition could arrive. But he finally told me what I had to know. Torquemada read the book and condemned it. After all these years! He said the Holy Office had no interest in witchcraft and that in any case the book was heresy. Miguel thought he meant to prosecute me, and I have no reason to doubt it. Torquemada burned our book, Sebastian! And I am a fugitive from the Inquisition!"

Sebastian's dead eyes stared at the inlaid squares of black and white. "So much for *The Powers of Darkness*," he said.

"You did your work too well, Sebastian. There was more in that book than any man could have learned in a lifetime. You have ruined me!"

"And perhaps myself as well, brother. What do you intend to do?"

"Do?" shouted the Grand Inquisitor. "What is there for me to do? I came to you because there was nowhere else to go! You must protect me, Sebastian."

Sebastian ran a pale hand through his long black hair. "It might be better if you fled across the mountains," he said. "The Inquisition has no power in France."

"You would like that, wouldn't you? I would be dead before I crossed the border! Miguel had more news for me, Sebastian. We are at war with the French, and already they are making raids from the mountains. There is no safety for me there, Sebastian."

Sebastian sat slumped in his chair, his head bent, the heel of his hand supporting his brow. "You are a messenger of ill omen," he said. "This is something I had not anticipated. How safe do you think you will be here if there is a battle for this fortress?"

"It may not come to that. They say there will be only a little war and we may survive it. Miguel had his information from the mouth of Columbus himself."

"Columbus," said Sebastian. "I remember when you told me of him. We should be in his New World now, for this world has little room in it for you and me."

"The French may spare us, Sebastian, and then we will be safe enough."

Sebastian raised a sardonic face to his brother. "Your plight has made you forgetful," he said. "Let me remind you about Pedro Rodriguez."

"Pedro?"

"He has been my lieutenant, and he has been your familiar. But what master will he serve now that you are a fugitive? There will be a new order in the city with you gone, and he will be quick to curry favor. Pedro knows all our secrets, brother. What better way for him to prove his worth than to betray us? He will surely guess that you are here."

"Then you must kill him, Sebastian. Tonight!"

"I might be better advised to kill you," said Sebastian.

The Grand Inquisitor tried to smile. "You cannot mean that," he said.

"It would certainly be easier than killing Pedro," said Sebastian thoughtfully. "For one thing, you are here where I can reach you, whereas Pedro is doubtless locked up safe at home. You know that I cannot enter a house without an invitation, and I can hardly expect Pedro to offer me one. Even if all this had not befallen us, he would be too concerned for his daughters. No, Diego, the murder of Pedro is impossible for me.

"But it might be possible for you," Sebastian continued. "He would very likely let you in, and perhaps you would have a chance to take him by surprise. I am more than willing to risk it. In fact, brother, I will lend you my sword. Of course you will have to kill his daughters, too."

"You must be joking, Sebastian! I dare not go back to the city. It would be suicide!"

"I see," said Sebastian. He leaned back in his chair and pressed his palms together judicially, his steepled fingers brushing his long mustache. "Then we must consider my other suggestion."

Diego's eyes widened.

"Your death would have many advantages," Sebastian said. "If your body were found in the streets it would at least create a diversion, and no one would come looking for you here."

"Sebastian!"

"Please, Diego. I am thinking. I might be able to come to terms with Pedro; most men will do anything for money. And he would gain nothing by betraying me once you were out of the way."

Diego de Villanueva leaped from his seat and stood weak-kneed and trembling in the glow of the solitary candle. The skull beneath it seemed to be staring at him.

"You would not kill me, Sebastian? I came to you for help. I am your brother!"

"I know you are," said Sebastian quietly, "and I have frequently had cause to regret it. Tonight, for example. You could have stayed at the Holy House and accepted your fate, but instead you ran to this castle, even though you must have realized that your presence here would place me in jeopardy. You have less concern for me than you expect me to have for you."

"You could not do it, Sebastian!"

"Why not, brother? You would have done as much to me, if the book had been successful."

"Never!" Diego spread his hands on the chessboard and leaned across it to emphasize his words. "I promised you!"

"Spare me your promises, brother. I am not blind. I know what you planned."

"But you must have believed me! Why else did you give me the book?"

"I wonder. Part of it was pride, I suppose. I was pleased with what I had done, and I wanted someone else to see it—even you or Torquemada. And regardless, I was obliged to finish the manuscript sooner or later. You had been waiting for years and were growing more and more impatient."

"But Sebastian! All those reasons would have been worthless if you really believed I intended to destroy you." The Grand Inquisitor paced back and forth. He suspected that argument was futile, but it was still his only hope. He thought of running but realized he would not get far, and there was nowhere else to go.

"And there is something else, brother," Sebastian said. "You forget that I wrote *The Powers of Darkness* and that I knew what was in it better than any man alive or dead. It is no surprise to me that the book was condemned. I planned it."

"You planned it?" gasped Diego. His knees buckled and he sat down heavily. His face turned pale and drops of sweat appeared on his upper lip. "You planned to ruin me?"

"It seemed only fair, considering what you had in mind for me." Sebastian still sat quietly and spoke as if all these matters were of no more than passing interest. His apparent indifference infuriated Diego, whose anger began to overcome his fear.

"You think you will be safe if you kill me, Sebastian, but you are wrong. There is someone else, someone you do not know about. Whatever you do to me, you are doomed as well."

Sebastian gave no sign that he was impressed by this threat. "I have no doubt that you would say anything to save yourself, Diego, but why should I believe you?"

"Believe what you will," his brother answered bitterly. "I could save you with a warning, but why should I?"

"You will tell me," said Sebastian, "and perhaps I will spare you, though I hardly see how I can arrange it. Still, it is your only hope."

Diego realized all too well that he was playing his last card. Yet it seemed impossible to use it to good advantage. If Sebastian knew nothing about the heir to the castle, he would not take the warning seriously. But once he learned about Antonio, there would be no reason for him to keep his brother alive.

"You ought to know the man I mean," Diego temporized, "since you predicted his appearance."

"I did?" asked Sebastian, touching himself on the chest and raising his eyebrows with such exaggerated innocence that his brother began to fear that the world had no secrets from Sebastian.

Diego was dizzy and stupid from sheer panic, but he had to say something. "Think of a way to save my life, Sebastian, and I will tell you. A fair exchange."

"It sounds like a poor bargain to me, brother, since I have no idea what you are offering me."

"I am offering you your life," said Diego, "or such of it as there is." He suspected that Sebastian might be weakening and pressed his advantage eagerly. "That must be worth something to you."

"A doubtful proposition, brother. I am weary of all this. My work is done and it has been destroyed. Yet there is a life I would spare if I could."

The Grand Inquisitor looked at his brother eagerly. "I knew you would help me, Sebastian. You love to taunt me, but I knew you would not take your brother's life."

A sneer flickered across Sebastian's lips. "If you believe that, brother, then you will believe anything. So be it. Tell me your secret, and I will spare you."

A faint hope grew within the Grand Inquisitor. His sudden reversal of fortune had left him half-hysterical so that he had to struggle to think, but still he understood the need for caution. "How can I trust you now?" he asked. "If I am to die, Sebastian, there will be some satisfaction in knowing that you will follow me. If you want me to speak, you must think of a way to save me."

"I know of no way to save you, brother. I can promise only that I will not kill you myself. Perhaps we will think of something later. But speak now, or you die at once."

"You must swear that you will not kill me."

Sebastian smiled. "What would you have me swear by? Is there an oath I can take that will convince you? Shall I swear by my immortal soul? And what would it be worth if I did?"

Diego's pulse raced and his mind with it. "Not by your soul, Sebastian. Swear by the soul of your wife, by the soul of Gracia, dead these many years. That is an oath I can believe."

Sebastian's dead eyes turned to narrow slits and he rose halfway out of his chair. Diego cringed. His life, like Sebastian's body, hung suspended for a moment. Then Sebastian sank down again and the Grand Inquisitor knew he had won.

"I swear," said Sebastian, as if the words had cost him much.

Diego could have wished for a more elaborate version of the oath but thought it wisest not to press his luck. The issue he had raised was a sensitive one. He watched his brother and gradually began to relax.

"What I have to tell you," he said at last, "concerns a young man called Antonio Manetti, lately arrived from Florence. He is the heir to your estate, and he intends to claim it soon."

Diego waited for his words to take effect, but Sebastian showed no dismay. "The Knight of Cups," Sebastian said, and it was Diego whose face fell.

"He was here not many days ago," continued Sebastian, "inspecting his inheritance."

"You knew of him already?" asked Diego incredulously. "How?"

"I know many things, brother, if not everything I could wish to know. I thank you for your warning, but the young man will not trouble me. Let him spend a night here and he will cease to be a problem. This information is not worth much, Diego. I think you cheated me."

"You swore!"

"Fear not, brother. My oath is good and I will not kill you. But I think you owe me something. Tell me another secret."

Diego looked at his brother quizzically.

Sebastian's voice was as cold as the crypt. "You killed her, didn't you?"

Diego was so startled that his eyes shot up to meet his brother's. His gaze remained there, held by an uncanny compulsion. Sebastian's black eyes seemed to grow, and their darkness was overwhelming. The feeble flame of the candle dwindled away into insignificance and Diego was lost in the depths of his brother's unblinking omniscience. He could not turn away.

"You killed her," said Sebastian slowly. "Not with your own hands. But you betrayed her. Your ambition would not let you rest, nor your jealousy of my happiness. You gave my wife to the Inquisition and thus won favor. You paid for your position with her life."

"Yes," said the Grand Inquisitor. He did not even try to deny it. He could not help himself.

The dark room grew slowly brighter. Sebastian was still sitting quietly in his chair. It was almost as if nothing had happened. Diego wished that were true, but he knew better. He tried to collect his wits.

"You swore," he said, the words catching in his throat.

"So I did," said Sebastian calmly. "I will not harm you. But I had to be sure. And you should thank me. Confession is good for the soul. Do you feel better now?"

Strangely enough, Diego did. The deed he had just admitted had worried him for years, if not because he regretted it then because he feared his brother's wrath. If even this were to be forgiven, there would be nothing more to fear. It was almost too good to be true.

In spite of himself, Diego spoke. "Don't you care, Sebastian?"

"I suppose I should, brother, but it was long ago and I am not the man I was. I am not a man at all. I am a monster and think only of monstrous things. I can hardly remember her."

Diego breathed a sigh of relief. "What is it like, Sebastian? Is there nothing more than what you wrote in the book? I have asked you a hundred times, but still I think that you have never really answered me."

"More questions, Grand Inquisitor?" Sebastian's voice had a hard edge. "Are you never to be satisfied?"

He reared back suddenly in his chair and it fell crashing to the floor. As he stood towering over his brother there was a terrible majesty about him. He was incredibly tall. He seemed to grow until he filled the room.

Diego felt the floor shake. Was this magic? Sebastian seemed a giant and his brother was afraid he might burst through the ceiling. The whole tower trembled.

Sebastian's voice was an icy echo. "Would you know what I know? Would you see what I see?"

The tower heaved like a storm-tossed ship. Shelves rattled. Cards and chessmen flew through the air. The candle slid across the table on its death's-head base. Diego closed his eyes and gritted his teeth, his hands gripping the sides of his bench.

Then, abruptly, there was silence.

The Grand Inquisitor opened his eyes carefully. The floor was steady. Sebastian had disappeared.

The room was a shambles, but somehow the candle was till burning, its red wax dripping into the eyes of the skull that held it. Beside the skull was a solitary chess piece standing alone on the squares of ivory and onyx—the black queen.

Diego raised his eyes. A woman stood in the shadows. She wore a white dress embroidered with threads of silver. For a moment he imagined that it was Sebastian's wife returned to punish him, but it was not.

It was Margarita de Mendoza.

Diego tried to back away from her and his bench fell over. He crawled into a corner. "You are dead," he whined. "You must be dead."

Margarita advanced upon him slowly. Her legs seemed

bound together and he could not see them move. Yet she glided toward him, her green eyes glassy, her red lips fixed in a rigid smile. Her teeth were sharp and he heard them grinding as she bent over him.

"I took no oath," she said.

The Grand Inquisitor whimpered and tried to bury himself in the cold stone wall. Margarita bent down and caressed his cheek.

"Do not be so afraid of me, Diego de Villanueva. I will not kill you yet. There are hours till dawn, and I have no wish for you to die quickly."

19. Three Hunters

THE SUN was setting by the time Miguel decided he needed help.

He entered the disreputable Inn of the Golden Cup with reluctance, but not even concern about the dignity of his position could overcome his conviction that Pedro Rodriguez was the only man in the city who would know what to do about the disappearance of Diego de Villanueva.

Miguel spotted Pedro immediately, but the sight was not reassuring. The big familiar sat at the dim corner table, gesturing with an overflowing cup. Seated beside him was the innkeeper, Carlos Diaz. Miguel tried to guess how drunk they were, but he was not an expert in such matters. At least there was nobody else in the tavern.

The young monk made his way across the dirt floor and put a hand on Pedro's shoulder. The corner reeked of wine.

Pedro turned around abruptly at Miguel's touch, then relaxed with a contemptuous smile. "It's the little vicar!" he roared. "When did you get back from your pilgrimage?"

"Yesterday," said Miguel. "I must speak to you at once."

"Well? Speak!"

"I must speak to you privately. It concerns the business of the Holy Office."

To Miguel's relief, Pedro achieved immediate sobriety. He put down his cup, cast a cold eye at Carlos, and gestured with his thumb toward the door to the rear of the inn. Every trace of his former conviviality had vanished. Carlos, looking more saddened than surprised, shuffled away, apparently resigned to the fact that he was not even the master of his own establishment.

"Wouldn't it be better if we went somewhere else?" Miguel ventured timidly.

"You are the one who wanted to speak at once," said Pedro. "One place is as good as another. Sit down."

Miguel obeyed. Uncertain of how to tell his story, he decided to plunge into it at once. Pedro was not a patient man.

"The Grand Inquisitor is gone," said Miguel.

"What do you mean?" asked Pedro, squinting at him ferociously.

"He hasn't been seen since last night. He is nowhere to be found."

Pedro considered this for a moment. "Assassins," he muttered darkly.

"I think not," said Miguel. "I believe he is in hiding."

Pedro looked at Miguel incredulously, but his expression changed to one of rough cunning as he heard the tale of Torquemada and the burning book. Perhaps, Pedro thought, it was time to find a new master.

"What should I do?" Miguel asked helplessly.

"The very question I was considering myself," said Pedro. He drained his cup in a single gulp, but it had no visible effect on him. "Are you sure that Torquemada means to arrest the Grand Inquisitor?"

"I'm not sure of anything," replied Miguel. "I don't even know if I should have told him what Torquemada did. But how could I keep it from him? I'm only certain of the things I saw for myself. Torquemada destroyed the book, and the Grand Inquisitor is missing."

"And you don't know when he left?"

"Not exactly. Sometime before dawn."

Pedro propped his elbows on the table and rested his black-bearded chin on two fists the size of hams. "You should have come earlier, that's for sure." He was thinking furiously. "Now that it's dark, it won't be easy to get him out of there."

Miguel's mouth fell open. "You know where he is?"

"That much was easy. The question is, what are we to do about it?"

The burly old soldier and the frail young monk regarded each other across the table. Finally Pedro spoke.

"We'll have to go after him. Any way you look at it, we'll be better off with him back where he belongs. He should have stood his ground. We'll have to go tonight, whatever the danger. He'll be dead tomorrow if we leave him there. He may be dead already, if he got there before dawn today."

"Where?" Miguel asked in a frantic undertone. "What are you talking about?"

"Look, my young friend. There may be nothing to this business with Torquemada. Maybe it will all blow over. In that case, we need Diego de Villanueva back here so things can go on as they always have. On the other hand, maybe he really is in trouble. If he is, someone will be here soon to take his place. And how will it look for you and me if we let him escape? We'll be taken for accomplices. We must bring him back."

"Back from where?" Miguel asked angrily.

"There's only one place he could be. At the castle, with the ghost of his brother Don Sebastian."

Miguel gasped and heard a similar sound behind him. Whirling, he saw Carlos standing there with a candle in his hand.

"I was just bringing a light for you gentlemen," the fat innkeeper said nervously.

"You were eavesdropping," Pedro retorted. He sprang from his seat and grabbed Carlos by the arm. "Join us," he said. "We have a new recruit!"

Pedro smiled maliciously through his heavy beard while the inebriated innkeeper sputtered a protest.

"Recruit?" he said. "I don't understand you. Let me go!" But Pedro's heavy hand dragged him down to the bench beside Miguel, who only sat and stared.

"You wanted to know what we were talking about," said Pedro sternly, "so you might as well hear it all. You will be one of us. The three of us are going to make an assault on the castle."

"Not me!" said Carlos. He tried to rise, but Pedro held

him down. Miguel was equally unenthusiastic, but he kept his seat.

"The pair of you make a fine army," Pedro said bitterly. "A skinny stripling and a fat drunkard. Still, you may serve to distract him for a minute. One good shot is all I need."

"I don't want to go," said Carlos thickly.

"You have no choice," Pedro answered.

Miguel passed a shaky hand across his brow and looked at Pedro. "What was that you said about the ghost?"

"Not a ghost, exactly," Pedro said. "Don Sebastian is a vampire."

The innkeeper's thick features showed only bewilderment, but Miguel turned pale and crossed himself.

"So, vicar, you know what a vampire is?" asked Pedro.

"A dead man," said Miguel, "who feeds on the blood of the living. The Grand Inquisitor spoke to me about them."

Carlos moaned weakly. The others ignored him.

"He told me even more," said Pedro, "because he had to. I was the one who brought Don Sebastian back here after that cannon blew his face away."

Miguel winced. "But how did he become a vampire?"

"Some trick he learned from the Moors, I think. I never heard of such a creature, but apparently those heathen lands are full of them. I don't know what he did, exactly, but when he knew he was dying he found a way to transform himself. I suppose he sold his soul."

"And the Grand Inquisitor let him live?"

"Let him live?" Pedro snorted. "His brother kept him alive! For nine years! Half the heretics in the Holy House have gone to the field of fire with holes in their throats."

"I'm not going," said Carlos.

"You volunteered when you crept up to hear what we were saying," Pedro said. "You can come with us or we'll leave you off in one of the dungeons of the Holy House."

"I'll come," Carlos said tragically.

"Come on, Carlos, buck up! You may even live through it." Pedro laughed.

Miguel was indignant at such levity. The very foundations of his belief were crumbling. "I cannot believe you," he said. "The Grand Inquisitor could never have tolerated such a creature, not even his own brother. Why would he do it?"

"Why?" said Pedro. He laughed again and brought his hand down on the tabletop so hard that his empty cup jumped into the air. "Why? Who do you think wrote the famous book that caused all this trouble?"

Miguel was too astounded to argue, and Carlos looked back and forth between his two companions as if they were speaking a foreign language.

"Diego knows nothing about witchcraft," Pedro continued, "but Don Sebastian knows everything, and they reached some sort of understanding. But if the book has come to nothing, they'll be at each other's throats at once. There's no love lost between those brothers."

Miguel started to speak, but Pedro stopped him with a look. "No time to argue now," said the old soldier. "We must move at once. I wish I had some better men, but nobody else must hear of this or we'll all be in trouble. You, vicar. What do you know about killing vampires?"

"Nothing," said Miguel.

"Well, the Grand Inquisitor told me a little. Ordinary weapons won't do it. Fire will, or a stake of wood through the heart. But Don Sebastian will be up and about by now and we can't expect him to stand still for that. If only we could wait for morning! I'll have to use my bow. An arrow's made of wood, so it should work. We'll need some crosses. I'll go and get them . . . no. You'll have to get them, vicar. I'll stay here and keep an eye on Carlos. You couldn't hold him. Are you game?"

Miguel nodded gravely. He had no choice, yet he could hardly help wondering whether he was going to rescue the Grand Inquisitor or arrest him.

"Bring three crosses," Pedro said. "And horses, too. You can get the bow from my daughter Teresa. Make sure you ask for the right one. Not the crossbow. Those steel bolts would be no good for this hunt, and besides, it takes too long to load. Get the bow I captured from the Moors, and a quiver full of arrows. Teresa will know the one I mean. It's a heathen weapon, but I know how to use it."

Miguel rose to go.

"One more thing," said Pedro. "I'm worried about my girls. If this night's work does not go well, Don Sebastian may resent it. So make sure you tell them to keep the door barred and not to open it for anyone but me. Not for anyone, do you understand? I don't think he'll be able to get in unless they invite him. At least that's what the Grand Inquisitor told me. Don't let them know where we're going! There's no need for them to learn about things like this. Leave that for experts on evil like Diego de Villanueva!"

Diego lay dead in a stone sarcophagus, yet he dreamed that he was floating down a river. He was stretched out on his back at the bottom of a tiny boat, and though there was no one to guide it, he was not afraid. Above him rose shimmering silver arches. He drifted through them drowsily, his eyes half-shut, and thought of nothing but the gentle motion of the water.

The curved ceiling of light grew lower and he realized that he was in a cavern. The walls dripped with glistening blue phosphorescence—and drew nearer to him. This was less a cavern than a tunnel, and he saw to his dismay that it was closing in on him.

He tried to raise himself but found he could hardly move. The stream below turned turbulent and the boat rushed forward. He slowly raised his head to look around him, then began to panic.

The boat was a coffin, adrift on a river of blood.

He reached for the sides of the coffin. They were wet and sticky, but he managed to pull himself erect. The glowing walls cast cold reflections on the rushing river. He tried to scream, but no sound came. The crimson tide raced toward the end of the cavern and the black pit waiting there. His fingers stretched frantically toward the narrowing walls, but he could not reach them, nor could he stop himself. The void loomed beneath him. With a sickening lurch he dropped into darkness.

He fell, in a long, slow curve that seemed endless. He clutched his knees and huddled in a ball, waiting to be shattered into jelly when his fall was over. His heart stopped.

Suddenly the coffin came to rest. Diego opened his eyes and found himself in a black grotto, its depths hidden by a stagnant lake of gore. This vast red pool was radiant. A light like fire rose from it to touch the towering stones on every side. Diego knew he was dead; yet still he feared the sinking of the casket, as if he knew that something waited in the depths below that might be worse than death.

Thick bubbles rose to the surface of the lake. A hand reached out among them, dripping blood. It groped blindly for Diego. Another hand rose beside the first. Something splashed behind him and he whirled to see the body of his brother Sebastian. Rigid as a statue, it oozed upward from the pool, its face a scarlet mask. It smiled at him.

Diego turned away in horror, but what he turned to face was worse. The bloody hands had clutched the side of his casket and were dragging him down. A head slid up through the steaming surface of the lake, its dark hair thick with gore. The face beneath the streams of red was pale; the eyes were green.

The surface of the lake was alive with hands, hundreds of them, all reaching out for him. Fires sprang up and the lake of blood began to boil. Clouds of smoke obscured Diego's vision, but still he saw a throng arise around him. Dead, dripping faces encircled him, some of them burned and blackened. Dimly he recognized his victims. A mass of crawling corpses weighed his coffin down, embracing him ardently as he sank into the thick crimson. Everything was red.

Darkness streamed into his eyes and awakened him. His dream was done. Night had fallen and he was in the crypt beneath the castle.

He saw his brother bending over him. "Sebastian?" he said weakly.

Sebastian's pale face was expressionless. "You have been dreaming," he said. "Tell me your dream."

Diego made an effort to sit up, but all the strength seemed drained out of his body. He could see nothing but his brother's face and the low stone ceiling above it.

"I am thirsty," said the Grand Inquisitor.

"That will not last long," Sebastian said.

"Why am I so weak?" asked the Grand Inquisitor.

"Don't you remember what happened last night?" asked Sebastian. "Don't you realize where you are?"

Diego glanced anxiously from side to side and saw that he was lying in a low, narrow box. The memory of his nightmare rushed over him again.

"No, no, no," he said sadly. His terror gave him strength and he began to rise. He caught a brief glimpse of the tomb of the de Villanuevas; then his brother's pale strong hand was pressed against his chest, pushing him back into the sarcophagus.

"You remember now," Sebastian said. "You are one of us, brother."

Diego shook his head in denial, but he knew that it was true.

"You would not be here now," said Sebastian, "if Margarita had been satisfied with a quick kill. But she took her time with you. I had no chance to put you in the streets of the city where you belong."

"Margarita?" whispered Diego, his eyes darting back and forth.

"She is not here, brother. She is up on the tower, watching for three friends of yours. They are coming to rescue you, but they are too late and I am ready for them. Yet still you are a thorn in my side, brother. Who would have thought that you would inspire such loyalty?"

"Three friends?" repeated Diego, his mind almost destroyed by horror.

"The Inquisition," said Sebastian. "But you have no reason to fear them. Forget them. They will not take you, nor will I leave you in this sorry state. It is not fit that a Grand Inquisitor should become a creature of the night, prowling through the dark in search of food. I will spare you that, at least, though you have spared me little. I could forgive you everything, I think, if you had not killed my wife. If not for that, perhaps none of this would have happened. You might have stayed a humble friar, and I would not have sought relief in sorcery. You have much to answer for, brother."

The Grand Inquisitor thought of his dream and began to moan.

"I watched you sleeping," Sebastian said, "and you did not seem happy. What did you see while you slept?"

Diego shut his eyes. "What are you going to do to me?" he said.

"I will spare you the misery that I have known," Sebastian said. "But I cannot spare you that which you have brought upon yourself."

The Grand Inquisitor felt something sharp against his chest. His eyes shot open. Sebastian was bending over him, a thick wooden stake grasped in his hands.

"Please," said the Grand Inquisitor. His fingers fumbled at the stake.

"What did you dream, Diego?" Sebastian's voice was almost tender.

"A lake of blood and fire. Blackened hands reaching out for me. Hell."

"What else could you expect, brother?" Sebastian's eyes were dead, but his mouth twitched and grimaced. He raised the pointed stake above his head.

"Sebastian," said the Grand Inquisitor.

"Your dreams will be your destiny," his brother told him.

The stake came crashing down.

The last thing Diego de Villanueva felt on earth was the splintered wood tearing into his heart. The last thing he saw was his blood spattering over his brother's face. And the last thing he heard was the sound of his own scream.

20. The Lightning

MARGARITA GAZED over the battlements to the forest beyond. The moon shone with a pale blue light that turned the sky purple, yet already storm clouds had begun to appear.

The last of the water dribbled out between her fingers. She scooped up the embers of the burning herbs in her wet hands and scattered them over the tower in a descending shower of sparks. The incantation was complete.

Her lips moved silently as she watched the clouds boil and multiply until they covered half the sky. The pale moon vanished and the night turned black. One by one the stars were blotted out. She raised her hands to the heavens and was answered by a sullen rumbling. A wind rushed down from the mountains, ruffling her long black hair and blowing the banks of dark clouds toward the forest.

She waited for the approach of the enemy, hoping the coming storm would help. She knew she did not have Sebastian's powers, but any witch could raise a tempest and sometimes direct its thunderbolts. Yet it hardly seemed enough. She was obscurely troubled by the threat to the castle and more than a little doubtful about the impending battle.

The night turned white for an instant and thunder boomed among the mountains like the sound of cannon fire.

She thought of escape. Sebastian had given her the power of flight, and there was nothing to prevent her taking wing to flee from the castle and the men who moved against it. Yet they were her foes, perhaps even more than Sebastian's, and she felt bound to stay.

Still, the mountains tempted her. She had the gift of immortality and could pass it on to others. For all Margarita knew, she and Sebastian were the only ones in creation who had such power. Could she let it die with them? How could she be sure that either of them would survive this night? She envisioned a legion of the undead, spawned by her unquenchable thirst and wreaking vengeance on a world full of perfidy and persecution.

"Margarita?"

Sebastian stood beside her, his crimson cloak blown wildly by the rising wind. She could not face him.

"I thought of running," she said, "but I will stay."

Sebastian put his arm around her. "I wish that both of us could flee," he said, "but things are not that simple. There is nowhere for us to go. We must sleep each night in our native soil, so we dare not venture into France. There might be a cave in the mountains to shelter us. We could live there like animals, Margarita, preying on the villagers till we were hunted down. Perhaps you would prefer it. But this is my castle, and I will not yield it so easily. I will stay and fight. If I can kill them all, perhaps we will be safe."

"I will fight beside you," Margarita said.

Thunder cracked its whip across the sky as she embraced him.

"You will stay here," Sebastian said. "There is no need for you to risk your life."

"But you are weak," said Margarita. "You need blood."

"I am strong enough for them," Sebastian said. "They will be sorry they came here, long before they die."

"And your brother?"

"Dead," answered Sebastian.

The first drops of rain fell upon them and a misty wind billowed over the battlements.

"I can help you, Sebastian. I have magic too. Look at the sky and see what I have done!" Margarita spread her arms and a blue swath of lightning cut across the clouds. "I will strike them down before they reach the moat."

Sebastian traced the line of her cheek with cold fingers.

"Do what you will," he said, "but stay in the tower. None of them knows that you are here, Margarita, and they will not hunt for you. Even if they destroy me, you can still escape. They must not find you. I at least have hopes of something yet to come, but you . . ."

"I know," she said, silencing his lips with a caress. "But there are worse fates than oblivion. At least it would mean peace."

He kissed her fiercely and wild breezes mingled his dark hair with hers. His passion drew a drop of scarlet from her lip and he stepped back from her. She smiled at the wound. The blood was the Grand Inquisitor's. A gust of wet wind washed the drop away. The rain rushed down upon them and rattled on the stones.

"Come," he said, "and wait in the room below."

Margarita smiled. "Are you afraid I will catch cold?"

Her dripping hair streamed to her shoulders and her pale face gleamed in the rain. The white silk gown clung damply to her slender body, and her green eyes glowed.

"Leave me here, Sebastian," she said. "I want to watch the storm and to command the thunderbolts."

She reached out a hand to him and he held it for a moment, then he was gone.

Margarita stood alone on the topmost tower of the castle, water running down her cheeks. She turned toward the forest, raised one finger to the sky, then swept it downward until it pointed to an outlying tree.

A ragged streak of lightning ripped the purple sky apart as if it were a piece of paper, and the shattered tree burst into flames.

"Christ!" said Carlos. "That was close."

The proprietor of the Golden Cup stood beside his horse and shuddered. The storm had started only a minute ago, but already he was soaked to the skin. He watched the driving rain extinguish the burning stump of the thunderstruck tree and felt acutely uncomfortable.

Pedro Rodriguez was swearing too, but for another reason. He was wrapping something in his cloak. "Best bow in the world," he muttered. "Even better than the

English longbow. Shoots farther. But not if it's wet."

"What did you say?" asked Miguel. The young friar had been staring through the downpour at the forbidding black edifice that lay beyond the forest.

"This Moorish bow. Made of horn and sinew as well as wood. Takes them years to put one together. A fine weapon, unless the water hits it."

"I wonder about this storm," said Miguel. "It was clear enough when we started out, but I've read that a magician can raise a tempest. Could he know that we are coming?"

"It wouldn't surprise me," answered Pedro. "Don Sebastian seems to have a way of knowing things. Tie up the horses here. We won't take them beyond these woods."

"We should take them right back to the city again," said Carlos. The moisture on his fat face looked more like sweat than raindrops. "Are you so anxious to die? You say yourself that he's waiting for us. Who knows what a sorcerer can do? I say we should go back, and to hell with the Grand Inquisitor!"

"Nobody cares what you say," said Pedro curtly. "If you didn't always talk so much, we might have risked leaving you at the inn. But now you're here, so make the best of it. Put this bundle under your robe, will you, vicar? We have to keep it dry."

The innkeeper was becoming frantic. "What do you think we're going to do, Pedro? Just walk up to the castle and knock on the door? We'll never get into the place. You'd need an army!"

Pedro ignored him and peered through the trees at the long stretch of open ground between the forest and the rocks on which the castle stood. He gestured with a thick forefinger. "See those rocks over there, friar? The ones to the left of the castle? That's where the escape tunnel comes out, and that's where we're going in."

"Escape tunnel?"

"It runs underground from the keep. Been there for centuries. If the castle ever fell, it was a way out for the last defenders. Tonight it will be a way in for us. I only hope Don Sebastian has forgotten it."

Miguel finally admitted to himself that he was really going into the castle. His heart sank. Things were moving too fast for him. He no longer believed in the Grand Inquisitor or in witchcraft or the Inquisition. The only thing he could be sure of was that his life was in danger. His faith was failing, and he wanted to run. He tried to pray but heard himself saying, "I am ready."

"Good," said Pedro. "We'll make a dash for the rocks. There's a big stone that we'll have to move to get at the tunnel. It won't be easy, but that's one of the reasons why I brought this fat fool along. His weight ought to be good for something. We'll need you later, friar. For now, just hold on to that cross for dear life. And for God's sake, don't drop my bow!"

Carlos lurked behind them, looking as if he were ready to run back into the forest. "You first," snarled Pedro, grabbing the innkeeper by the scruff of the neck. He shoved Carlos between the trees and into the clearing. "Let's go!" he said.

Carlos stumbled forward a few steps and slipped in the mud. Pedro was right behind him, though, pulling him to his feet and pushing him forward.

They ran. The full force of the tempest hit them as they left the shelter of the trees. Rain lashed their faces and the screaming wind fought them for every inch of ground. Yet Pedro, bulky as he was, moved with surprising speed. He forced Carlos along before him. The innkeeper's shouts were lost in the fury of the storm. Miguel followed them, his black hood flapping in his eyes and both hands clutching the precious bow. He had more faith in that than in the cross dangling from his neck.

They reached the rocks. Carlos, gasping for breath, fell back against a sizable boulder and let the rain fall into his open mouth. Pedro stood with hands on hips and surveyed him disgustedly.

"At least you've picked the right rock," Pedro said. "That's the one we have to roll away."

Carlos and Miguel looked at him in amazement. The job seemed all but impossible, but Pedro was apparently immune to doubt. He stood tall and strong, indifferent to the buffeting of the storm that made the others duck their heads. Miguel was suddenly impressed with him. Pedro might be no Grand Inquisitor, but there were moments when a forthright and determined ruffian was worth any number of scholars. This was adventure, and Miguel began to feel he had been born for it. The wind exhilarated him.

Pedro turned his back to the castle and dropped his heavy hands onto the side of the rock. He pushed at it tentatively, then nodded.

"Come on, innkeeper," he said. "Get up here beside me and put your weight into it. You too, vicar. You might make the difference. Come on now, shove."

Despite his exhortations to the others, it was apparent that Pedro was doing most of the work. Thick legs braced, back bent, beard thrust toward the sky, he struggled forward. Miguel's fingers slipped on the wet rock and his sandaled feet slipped in the mud.

"Push!" shouted Pedro.

"I'm pushing!" Carlos answered. "Anything to get out of this accursed rain!" He grunted and threw himself against the stone. Slowly it began to move.

"Harder!" Pedro said. Veins bulged ominously in his forehead. The boulder tottered on one edge, overbalanced, and went crashing end over end into the clearing.

The three breathless men stood together watching its descent. Then Pedro dropped to one knee to examine the uncovered ground. He scraped some mud away and smiled. "Here it is," he said. "We'll have to pry it open."

"You two do it," Carlos said. "I've had enough." He took a few paces backward to demonstrate his independence. Pedro ignored him.

Miguel and Pedro squatted together beside the stone trap door. "How could they ever have moved that rock from below?" asked Miguel, raising his voice against the wind.

"This door worked like a sort of lever," Pedro answered. "But it was never meant to be opened from above. Maybe we can pry it up. See if you can get my knife under that edge. Just lift it a bit, and I'll do the rest."

He handed the monk a short, heavy dagger and Miguel slipped its point into a muddy crack. The blade slipped down to the hilt. Miguel looked up at Pedro's face with its dripping beard hardly a hand's breadth from his own face. "Go ahead," Pedro urged him. "Don't worry about breaking the blade. I still have my sword."

Miguel leaned against the hilt, feeling the grating of stone against stone. The trap door lifted and Pedro caught its edge with his fingers just as the dagger snapped in two.

"Got it!" said Pedro. "Good boy!" Miguel might have felt insulted, but he was proud. Pedro heaved the door back, revealing a set of rough stone steps that dwindled into impenetrable darkness.

"You! Carlos Diaz!" called Pedro.

Miguel glanced up. The fat little innkeeper was only a short distance away, a dripping and bedraggled figure standing on a rock and watching them work. He took one step toward them.

A blast of blinding white shot out of the sky and split his skull. His body was alive with light for an instant, twitching spasmodically against a landscape suddenly brighter than day. Thunder rolled down from the mountains and the night turned black again. Carlos fell without a cry and smashed his face against a rock. The rain splattered down upon his broken body. Steam and smoke rose from his sodden clothing.

Miguel crossed himself. His first impulse was to run, but his training overcame it. He moved toward the corpse, intoning a prayer for the dead.

Pedro grabbed his robe, yanked him toward the opening in the rocks, and threw him halfway down the steps. "Pray later!" bellowed the old soldier. "That was no accident!" He bolted through the hole behind Miguel just before the lightning struck again.

Miguel saw Pedro come tumbling down the steps in the sudden glare and heard the sound of splintering rock. Something fell into the opening above them with a tremendous crash. Miguel listened to a heavy thud and the noise of broken stones rattling down. One of them hit him in the leg, but he could not see it. The tunnel was plunged into darkness, and the roar of the storm turned to silence.

"Pedro?" whispered Miguel.

He heard someone moving. "Pedro?" he called again, his voice breaking.

"I'm here," said a rough but reassuring voice. "And I'm not likely to leave. The last blast sealed the entrance, vicar. I can feel it."

"Where are you, Pedro? I can't see anything."

"Behind you. Reach out your hand."

Miguel groped blindly. There was no light at all. "Are you hurt?" he asked.

"Not much. I got a good crack on the shoulder. How's my bow?"

"I have it. It seems to be all right."

"Good. Hand it over. We might as well get going."

Miguel felt Pedro bump into him and jumped. He had lost his taste for adventure, but now there was no way to back out. He was trapped beneath the ground, with enchanted thunderbolts behind him and horrors he could hardly imagine lurking ahead. He thought of the tons of rock looming over him and imagined them pressing down to crush the life from his thin body.

"You'd better go first," he told Pedro.

Miguel moved into the tunnel and immediately ran into a wall. He reached out and felt for the other, hardly an arm's length away. Both were wet with slime. "It's hardly wider than I am," Miguel said nervously "And I can't stand up in it, either. I wish I could see."

"You lead the way then, vicar. It's for your own good. If the tunnel is that small I might get stuck in it, and then we'd both be trapped. Just stay calm and move ahead slowly. I'm right behind you. And watch out for snakes."

Miguel felt panic rising within him. He had never been so frightened in his life. He wished himself back in the monastery of Saint Thomas, where there was nothing to face but the wrath of Torquemada. He could not bring himself to take a single step.

Pedro reached out to touch Miguel and felt him shaking. A monk with hysterics would be no help now. He thought of pushing Miguel through the black passage by main force but decided that persuasion might be more effective.

"Go ahead. It won't be so bad. I know it's dark, but the tunnel can't be very long. I'm counting on you, and so is the Grand Inquisitor. We'll be out of this in a minute or two once we get moving. You don't want to stay here forever, do you?"

Pedro's voice was calm and authoritative at the same time, and his last argument was convincing. Miguel wanted very much to be out of the tunnel. Head bent, hands pressed to the clammy walls, the monk moved forward.

There was a foul, damp stench in the tunnel that grew worse with every step. Miguel began to think of suffocation.

"Smells like something rotting," Pedro said, trying to keep up a steady flow of conversation to calm the quivering monk. "Go slowly. It won't be long now. Be careful, vicar. Don't stumble. Something might have fallen down. Just feel your way along. You're doing fine."

Pedro did not mention his own greatest fear, that the far end of the passage might have collapsed. If it had, they were buried alive. His broad shoulders scraped against the narrow walls and he shuddered. His plan had seemed better back at the inn when he was a little less sober. Would this tunnel never end? And what would they find at the end of it?

"Stop," said Miguel. "There's something here."

Pedro's heart sank. "What is it? Can you get past it?"

"I don't know," said Miguel. "I just ran into it. It's on the floor."

Miguel leaned down. The passage was still darker than the darkest night, and he was forced to use his fingers instead of his eyes. He had run into something hard, but now that his hands reached down, it felt softer—a protruding lump covered with rough cloth. He ran his fingers along it until they reached something bigger and softer that seemed to fill the whole tunnel. He touched a piece of wood and something sticky. His other hand touched cold, damp flesh.

Miguel let out a yell and stumbled backward. The two men fell in a heap.

"A dead man!" shouted Miguel. "It's a dead man!" His voice echoed hollowly up and down the black corridor. "Go back, Pedro! Get me out!"

Pedro made a grab for Miguel's flailing limbs and forced him to the muddy floor. He found the monk's mouth and put a hand over it.

"So it's a dead man," Pedro said. "He can't hurt you. You've seen dead men before. We have to keep going. Calm down. I'll lead the rest of the way. I'll have to move him. He's nothing to be afraid of. I'm going to take my hand off your mouth now. Don't shout. Just say yes if you're ready to follow me."

"Yes," Miguel said weakly.

Pedro reached back until he found the bow he had dropped, and he sighed with relief that it was still intact. Only a few of the arrows seemed broken. He crawled over Miguel and put his arms around the corpse.

"Follow me," he said. The floor inclined upward, which he took as a good sign. He was not even disturbed when the body in his arms flopped against a blank wall. "We've come to the end," he said.

Pedro leaned the corpse against the wall and pushed against the low ceiling. It yielded with a groan and Pedro stuck his head up through the opening. The darkness above was less intense; and he could hear rain driving against the walls.

"We're in the castle," he announced. "This should be the keep." He pulled himself up through the floor and hauled the body up behind him. He threw it down beside the trap door and stooped to give Miguel a hand. He was examining his weapons when he heard the young monk groan.

Miguel was pointing at the dead man.

"I thought so," Pedro said. "We have come for nothing."

Sprawled on the stones was the corpse of Diego de Villanueva, his face contorted with agony, a wooden stake protruding from his chest.

21. Two Swords

MIGUEL KNELT beside the body of the Grand Inquisitor, yet could not bring himself to look at it. He listened to the muffled thunder. He wanted to pray for the dead, but the only prayers he could think of were for himself. He begged every saint in the calendar to spirit him away from the castle, but when he finished, he was still inside.

Pedro was willing to ignore Miguel for a moment, even though he considered the young monk's display of piety ill-timed. At least it gave the big familiar time to think. He carefully unwrapped his bow and examined it as best he could in the dim light. Determining that the weapon was unbroken, he braced one end against his foot and leaned on the curved bow until it was bent enough to loop the loose end of the string into the notch that held it. Then he chose an arrow and fitted it to the bow. All the while, his eyes darted around the shadowed room, on guard for the slightest hint of motion.

The trap door had opened into an empty anteroom at the bottom of the great tower that dominated the castle. There were no windows, but there was a door—and it was open, which made Pedro uneasy. Against the opposite wall was the first level of the steps that led upward to Don Sebastian's chambers. Pedro, considering the steps, decided they were a trap and a temptation. He felt the same about the open door, through which lightning flashed. He looked down at Miguel.

"What are you doing with that cross?"

Miguel turned to Pedro with an expression that was half insane. His eyes were wide and he was smiling. "I'm going to leave it with the Grand Inquisitor," he said. "He doesn't have one of his own."

Pedro grasped Miguel by the arm and pulled him to his feet. "Are you mad? Hold on to that! He doesn't need it now, but it might keep you alive. I told you about that, didn't I, that the cross will keep Don Sebastian away from you?"

Miguel looked genuinely bewildered. "That doesn't matter now," he said. His voice was like a child's. "Aren't we going home?"

"Wake up, you fool! How do you think that body got into the tunnel? Don Sebastian knows we're here, and we'll have to fight our way out. Do you think you can just walk through that door over there and go free?"

Pedro regretted the words as soon as they were out of his mouth. Miguel took one look at the open door and his eyes went wild. He pulled away from Pedro, rushed across the room, and disappeared into the storm.

"Damn!" said Pedro. He hesitated for a heartbeat, then took a firm grip on his Moorish bow and hurried after Miguel.

A deluge greeted him, rain so heavy he could hardly see, and the water in the courtyard was ankle-deep. "Vicar!" he shouted. "Stay away from the drawbridge! He might be lurking there! Come back!"

Then Pedro remembered the bow. He had to keep it dry, no matter what the cost. A wet string would be the end of him. He ran for the nearest doorway and waited in its shelter, an arrow at the ready. The downpour was blinding.

Rapid footsteps slapped toward him across the courtyard. He almost fired, but the lightning stopped him just in time. It blasted the spot where he had stood a moment before, and in its glare he saw a disheveled figure dressed in black and white. It was Miguel, racing away from the drawbridge like a man possessed. He barreled into Pedro and knocked him through the doorway.

The room they fell into was not the one they had just left, but Pedro liked it even less than the first. It was awash with lights.

● ● ●

Margarita leaned over the battlements and stared at the empty courtyard anxiously. She could hardly believe what she had seen. Somehow, the two remaining invaders had made their way into the castle, and they had not come through the only entrance she knew of. In fact, she had seen them run out of the keep, directly below her. How did they get there, and where was Sebastian? Did he know they were inside? Could they have killed him? She forgot her promise to stay in the tower. It was impossible to wait there and do nothing. She knew where the men had gone and knew she must follow them. They were only human and should be easy enough to kill. The lightning was useless now that they were inside, but her teeth were still sharp.

"I heard him." cried Miguel. "Out by the bridge. I heard him laugh! And I saw him too. You should have seen him, Pedro! He is ready for you. You will never kill him. Never! Never!"

Pedro pushed the raving monk away from him to keep his hands free for fighting. There was no time for lunacy like this. Perhaps it was true that Sebastian had waited by the bridge, but that was no guarantee that he would still be there. Besides, Miguel was mad and not to be trusted. It might be better to make a stand here. Yet this room had clearly been prepared for them. Why else were all the candles burning?

They were in the great hall of the castle, a gigantic room where men had met to prepare themselves for battle. A long black table sat at one end, heavy chairs surrounding it. Candles, all alight, covered the table. There was a fireplace across from it, where flames crackled hospitably. This last touch disturbed Pedro most of all, for he sensed the mockery in it. Above the fireplace was a shield bearing the arms of the de Villanuevas. A red hand severed at the wrist stood against a field of black, the emblem of an ancestor who had lost a limb upon the field of honor. On the wall across from this was a tapestry, a peaceful picture of a knight kneeling in obeisance before his lady.

Pedro kept his bow ready and surveyed the scene.

There were three entrances to the hall: the one they had come through from the courtyard, and two others at opposite ends of the room, each leading off into black corridors. Both of these doorways were elevated and short flights of steps led from them to the flagstone floor. The entrances themselves were lost in darkness, and Pedro watched them anxiously.

Miguel sat on the floor and babbled. "He's coming for us, Pedro. He promised me. He shines! You will never kill him. He shines too brightly!"

This talk had no meaning to Pedro, yet it was far from reassuring. He considered killing the crazed monk, if only to stop his wild babble. The man was useless now; he had even left his cross beside the body of the Grand Inquisitor. Pedro's own cross was still with him, hanging from his neck by a golden chain. Its presence comforted him and gave him some pity for the mad Miguel, but if Pedro did not kill him, it was only because there seemed no harm in letting him live.

There was danger enough to consider. Pedro sensed that he was in the wrong place, but he did not know where else to go. Every entrance loomed before him darkly and he turned warily in a circle, desperate to keep the whole hall in view.

Miguel began to laugh. "There is a devil, Pedro. I have seen him! Even the Grand Inquisitor had his doubts, but I have none, He is there, outside the door!"

Pedro spun around to look, his fingers tight on the feathers of the arrow, but the doorway was empty. He listened to the rain spattering down upon the stones.

"He is coming, Pedro, he is coming for us, and she is coming too! She is beautiful!"

Pedro wheeled around to see the monk crawling across the flagstones toward the entrance near the fireplace. "Shut your mouth!" Pedro told him. "Would you wake the dead?"

And then he spied the figure on the threshold, a woman dressed in white. Even as Pedro turned, she leaped down the step toward Miguel. Wet black hair was plastered to her head and her eyes were green, like a cat's.

"The witch!" gasped Pedro, and drew his bow. It was impossible that she should be here, but there was no time to think of that.

Margarita had not seen the bow, but suddenly she realized what it was. She saw the long thin shaft of wood and the cold gleam of the sharp steel arrowhead that pointed at her heart, but she had no chance to stop her headlong rush.

The bowstring sang and Margarita reeled across the floor, the arrow buried deep in her left breast. Bright blood spilled over her white gown. Clutching at the shaft, she dropped to her knees, her head thrown back, lips parted in a silent scream. She slumped over on her side and let forth a moan that rose into a horrifying high-pitched wail. Convulsions shook her slender body and rolled her on her back. Then her bloodied fingers slipped from her wound. She was still at last.

As Margarita died, the storm she had summoned died with her. The thunder stopped, and the whining of the wind, and the roaring of the rain against the walls of the castle. Throughout the great hall fell an abrupt and awesome silence.

Miguel heard only the sound of his own breathing and the distant drip of water from the courtyard. He tore his gaze away from the dead woman and glanced around the vast chamber, searching the shadows cast by the flickering candles. The sight of Margarita's death agony had startled him into a semblance of sanity and he was grateful now for the presence of the giant behind him, a soldier who could kill without compunction and who seemed stolidly indifferent to the terrors of the night.

Pedro stood waiting with muscles tensed, another arrow ready, his mind weighing various plans of attack and defense for this battle against demons. They seemed to him as easy to kill as any other enemy, but it was best not to be foolhardy.

A faint sound came from the courtyard, a cold, metallic creak that chilled Miguel.

The noise was repeated and joined with sounds of scraping and clanging. Whatever it was was coming closer. Miguel's fear was of the unexplained, but Pedro, the old soldier, was frightened because he recognized the noises for what they were: the sound of a man approaching in full suit of armor.

Sebastian appeared in the doorway, clad in shining steel. A black shield emblazoned with a crimson hand hung on his left arm, and he brandished a gleaming broadsword.

"See how he shines, Pedro?" screamed Miguel. "You will never kill him!"

Pedro realized that the monk was right. The old soldier knew it better than any man alive, for he had been Sebastian's man-at-arms and had tested the heavy plate of this very armor years ago when it was new. Arrows would not pierce it, unless a lucky shot penetrated one of the joints, yet there was nothing else for him to do but try. He fired.

The arrow tore through the black shield, for the power of Pedro's bow was great, but it glanced uselessly off the curves of Sebastian's thick breastplate and rattled on the floor.

Sebastian's laughter echoed eerily from his visored helmet as he advanced toward Pedro like some huge machine. Then he saw the body of his mistress sprawled on the floor beside the fireplace.

"Margarita," he whispered. He gave a cry of fury and frustration, then rushed toward the man who had murdered her.

Pedro shot again, but his aim was wild and the shaft shattered on the crest of Sebastian's helmet.

Pedro dropped the bow and drew his sword, wondering whether this weapon would help him. His cross hung from his neck, but he had forgotten it; his fighting instincts were too strong.

"He is coming!" Miguel shouted from the flagstones.

Sebastian's massive sword whirled through the air and whistled downward, but Pedro's blade was there to meet it, and the clash of steel on steel rang through the great hall. Pedro stepped back as the force of Sebastian's blow drove both weapons toward the floor, and he slipped his own blade free. He made a short slash up and out and cut the great black shield in two. Sebastian shook the pieces from his arm and gripped his hilt in both gauntleted hands. Pedro hacked at his helmet. Pedro's broadsword rang and quivered from the impact but slithered off the armor plate, leaving hardly a dent.

Pedro jumped backward, and four feet of fine Toledo steel whirled past him so close that he felt the breeze on his face. He began to panic. He could not pierce Sebastian's armor, and he doubted if his sword could hurt the demon beneath it. He had only a second to realize he was doomed, then Sebastian struck again.

Pedro parried, giving ground with every blow. His breath was coming hard and sweat dripped into eyes. He held his battered blade upright before him and tried to save himself. Sebastian was driving him toward the fireplace with a hail of blows that increased in intensity as the swordsmen neared the spot where Margarita lay.

The furious onslaught wavered for an instant and Pedro spied an opening. He brought his heavy wedge of steel down with all the power of his huge shoulders and caught Sebastian in the armored joint just above the left knee. The plate was thin there, and it gave. The blade bit through Sebastian's thigh, all but cutting it in two.

Pedro paused for a moment as he pulled his broadsword free, but Sebastian did not cry out, did not bleed, did not fall. Pedro watched in horror as the butchered flesh above the vampire's knee grew whole again. Sebastian's sword was pointed toward the flagstones with an indifference all the more chilling because it was so evidently justified.

Pedro leaped forward with a roar and hacked frantically at Sebastian's chest. Metallic clanging echoed through the room, but that was all. Pedro would have fled, but he was not a coward, and he knew too well what a target his broad back would make.

He flailed wildly with his huge blade until his arms were weary. He was so close to the roaring fire that there was hardly room to run. Sebastian blocked his strongest strokes without apparent effort. Pedro decided he was a dead man, but then he heard Miguel.

"The cross, Pedro! The cross!"

Pedro's eyes dropped to the golden emblem dangling on his black doublet. He felt a surge of hope, but the distraction was his undoing.

Sebastian's sword flashed in a glittering arc and sliced off Pedro's head.

The sweep of the blade sent the head tumbling across the room, and the unsupported golden chain slipped over Pedro's severed neck. The cross clattered on the flagstones and the stump on Pedro's shoulders spewed forth blood like a fountain.

Sebastian's sword was so sharp that the headless man was not knocked down. Pedro stepped forward and his hands reached out. A rain of pumping red fell upon Sebastian and great gouts sputtered as they struck the fire. The bleeding thing advanced blindly and its killer stepped from its path. It stumbled toward Miguel, who scrambled backward up the short flight of stairs behind him. Blood splashed over the monk and he wailed at the touch of it. The dead man struck the first step, staggered, and pitched over at the foot of the stairs.

Sebastian kicked the gory bulk aside and loomed above Miguel. The monk's eyes were mad. He did not try to move.

"I lost my cross," he said sadly. "I left it with your brother."

"Pray," said Sebastian, and Miguel obediently clasped his hands.

The dripping sword rose and fell and the young monk's melancholy upturned face was split in half. Cold steel chilled his fevered brain as he slithered down the steps to land atop the corpse of Pedro Rodriguez.

Sebastian left his sword embedded in the friar's shaven head and turned wearily toward the fireplace.

Pale green mist poured from the slitted visor of the helmet and grew into the shape of a tall man. The empty suit of armor toppled with a resounding crash, and the gaunt figure of Don Sebastian de Villanueva staggered from his enemies and toward the body of his lover.

"You were right, Margarita," he said. "I am weak. I need more blood. There are others who must die tonight. Pedro has not been punished enough. His daughters are living still."

He looked down at Margarita's outspread black hair and staring emerald eyes. He saw the feathered shaft that pierced her heart and the blood that stained the bosom of her silken gown. He kneeled beside her and took her hand. One by one he pulled off all his shining rings and slipped them on her fingers.

"Are you dreaming, Margarita? Or is it only sleep? Whatever it may be, sleep well."

He tried to rise, but found he could not. His strength was almost gone. He twisted his head toward the carnage by the stairs. A puddle of crimson had formed beneath the bodies and oozed across the floor.

Sebastian crawled toward the spreading pool of blood, lowered his head, and began to drink.

22. The Cathedral

TERESA LIFTED her head when the storm stopped and listened to the sudden silence. "You should leave now," she said.

"Shortly," said Antonio. "You are the cruelest lady I have ever courted. I wonder that you didn't throw me out into the rain!"

Teresa smiled. "I let you stay till it was over, but now you must go, Antonio. It's getting late, and it really isn't safe, for you or for me either. He's bound to be home soon."

Antonio sighed and shifted in the chair he had drawn up beside Teresa's. "Rather than endanger you, Teresa, I will leave almost immediately. But is there still so much risk? You said yourself that you thought your father might be persuaded to give us his blessing."

"Not if he comes in and finds you doing that," she said, slapping his hand gently. "But I think I can win him over. He was quite impressed to learn that you were an heir and soon to be a man of some importance."

"You were impressed yourself," said Antonio. "Sometimes I think you love me only for my castle."

"You are no gentleman, sir," she answered, pushing his hand away.

"If I were a gentleman like some I have known, I would have bedded you already."

"What? Here? With Dolores just upstairs?" Teresa rose in mock indignation.

"Here or anywhere," said Antonio, stretching his legs out before the cold fireplace. "Dolores! She is the most mercenary Rodriguez of all. You should hear her question me about my inheritance!"

"She is only a child, Antonio." Teresa stepped behind him and rubbed his shoulders soothingly. "And certainly somebody should be concerned about the estate. You seem to have no interest in it, or in anything but pleasure."

"What would you have me do? I rode out to look at the castle, but it was hardly worth the effort. A pile of black stones. Not very attractive, and hardly the airy palace I had dreamed about. It made me uncomfortable somehow. I was almost glad I couldn't get inside. At least it's locked up tight enough. The drawbridge was up and a man would need a siege ladder to get over the walls. Still, I want to see what's in there."

"What does the Grand Inquisitor say?"

"The Grand Inquisitor! I've spent the best part of the summer listening to his excuses, and now it seems I can't even have those! I was at the Holy House today, and all I got out of it was some story about the Grand Inquisitor being away. They tried to tell me they didn't know where he had gone!"

"There's something wrong," Teresa said. Her hands were quiet on Antonio's shoulders. "Something may have happened to the Grand Inquisitor. A monk was here tonight, the vicar, in fact; he came to get my father's bow. They have gone to seek some enemy of the Inquisition. I'm afraid."

"Your father! The vicar! The Grand Inquisitor! To hell with all of them!" Antonio jumped out of his chair and stalked across the room to the locked and bolted door. "I'm going back to the Golden Cup. At least the lice are glad enough to share my bed with me!" He pulled irritably at a heavy bolt.

The door creaked open.

"Antonio," Teresa said. "Aren't you going to kiss me good night?"

He looked at her. Her lips were trembling and her eyes shone with tears.

"I'm sorry," she said. "I can't help it. I'm worried, and I don't know what to do. Do you hate me?"

Antonio had grace enough to take her in his arms.

"I didn't mean anything," he said. "It's just that I hate having to wait. But I love you, Teresa. I swear I do. Don't worry about that."

He kissed her tenderly. It was easy enough for him to show passion, as Teresa knew, but this kiss showed something sweeter.

"I don't even care about the castle," he whispered. "I try to be practical, but what is it worth? You are the greatest treasure I have found in this accursed kingdom."

He kissed her again, ran his fingers through her pale hair, and hurried off through the muddy streets.

Teresa held back her tears until the door was closed again. She locked and bolted it, then stood in the middle of the room and wept for joy and sorrow. She kneeled before the image of the Virgin in the corner and prayed as best she could, but the only words that emerged between her gasps were, "Please. Please. Please."

In a few minutes she composed herself. She stood up, straightened the chairs, and washed the two cups she and her suitor had used. When she finished there was no evidence that Antonio had been there, but still she sensed his presence in the room. Even if she had not been waiting for her father, she would not have been ready to climb the stairs to the bed she shared with her sister Dolores. Instead she sat in a chair to dream of Antonio, and her dreams were not as virginal as they might have been.

She was roused from them by a sudden pounding at the door. It startled her for a moment and her heart jumped, but then she realized who it must be.

"Father?"

"Let me in, Teresa."

It was certainly her father's voice. It sounded hollow and strangely sad, but what did that matter? He had come home.

"Teresa. Let me in."

The voice was weak and Teresa wondered if her father might be hurt, but the power of the blows on the door reassured her.

"I'm coming," she said, inwardly thanking Heaven that

Antonio was gone. Her hands were trembling with relief and she could hardly hold the key. The bolt was stiff. The impatient knocking never ceased.

"All right!" said Teresa, pulling at the heavy door. "It's open! Come in, and be quiet!"

A man stood in the doorway, wrapped in a crimson cloak. His face and hands were splashed with blood.

It was not her father.

His face, beneath the damp black hair, was as pale and gaunt as a skull, and there was something in his hand.

Teresa stepped back from the door, too bewildered for real fear. Where was her father? She had heard his voice.

All at once she recognized her visitor. She had seen him long ago, when she was a child.

He had been dead for nine years. She stared at him in disbelief, then saw what was in his hand.

It was her father's head.

Teresa did not scream, but she clutched her stomach with both hands and stumbled back against the wall. Her throat made soft, dry sounds.

Sebastian held the dripping head by its shaggy hair and raised it slowly. Its eyes were open and its lips began to move.

"Teresa," it said.

Teresa moaned sickly and looked at the man in the cloak. He was smiling and his teeth were much too long.

"Sleep, Pedro," he said. He tossed her father's head into the street and she heard it slap into the mud. Then she began to scream.

Sebastian's long white hands reached out for her, seeming to stretch across the room. The candles flickered out and the darkness in his eyes was everywhere. Teresa's screams died down to a whimper.

"Teresa?" The sleepy voice came from the stairs. "What's going on?"

Dolores came down into the dark room. Her voice broke Sebastian's spell and Teresa turned to see her little sister standing at the foot of the stairs, rubbing her eyes. Sebastian saw Dolores too. He lunged toward her.

"Dolores!" cried Teresa. "Run!"

Even as she spoke, Teresa realized that there was no one between her and the door. She glanced at the bloodstained monster and saw his hands busy at her sister's throat.

Teresa ran. She heard a short, sharp cry from Dolores and answered it with a heartfelt moan, but still she ran.

She tumbled through the door and fell into the muddy street. Her first thought was of Antonio and she jumped up, heading toward the inn.

What she met in the road blocked her as surely as a wall. Her father's head sat in the mire grinning up at her.

Teresa wailed and spun around. She saw the dead man in the doorway, with Dolores in his arms. Teresa knew she should stop and try to help her sister, but she could not bring herself to stay. The horror on the threshold was more powerful than love or loyalty. She sped down the narrow street toward the public square. Behind her were Antonio, Dolores, and Don Sebastian de Villanueva.

Teresa gasped and groaned as her strong legs rushed her through the dark, deserted thoroughfare. Her mind was with Dolores, but her body had its own will and was bent on survival at any cost.

She looked behind her as she ran and saw what followed her—the image of a nightmare. The thing with the white face bounded along behind her, its long hair streaming, its cloak billowing into the air like gigantic wings. Dolores dangled in its grip like a broken puppet. Its movements seemed supernaturally slow and graceful, yet it was surely overtaking her. Teresa looked away from it and rushed forward.

She dashed into the great plaza that was the heart of the city and there she stopped, the clatter of her shoes on the wet pavements echoing away into silence. The square was vast and vacant, bathed in the cold light of a waning moon. Teresa whirled hysterically, an awful emptiness around her. She saw the buildings spinning past, sanctuaries of the rich and strong that held no hope for her. She would have called for help but could not catch her breath. The dead man floated toward her with uncanny speed.

"Sweet Jesus!" cried Teresa. She turned again and the cathedral rose before her eyes. Its twin towers loomed above her and the spires touched the skies.

She stumbled up the marble steps. The man in black was in the plaza now, only a few steps away. He shouted something at her but she did not understand. Her heart throbbed wildly and her eyes were dim, but her feet moved doggedly up the slippery stairs until she fell against the door.

It was open.

Teresa dropped into the cathedral like a soul falling into Hell. She sprawled on the floor and raised her eyes to the vaulted ceilings. The spaces above her were huge and dark, utterly devoid of life. No one was here to worship and there was no priest. She crawled down the wine-colored carpet that covered the aisle and passed the stiff stone images of melancholy saints, their hands raised in benediction. She thought of their ghastly deaths and waited for her own.

In the light of candles glowing faintly before the distant altar she saw the great carving of Christ in agony upon the cross. She had seen it many times before but had never really understood that it was the image of a dying man.

The tortured face gleamed darkly and drops of painted blood glistened on the brow. Teresa struggled to her feet and tottered down the aisle toward the carving, muttering prayers for herself and her sister. She expected the doors to burst open behind her, but nothing happened. The ghost of Don Sebastian had abandoned her.

To the right of the dying Christ was the statue of a woman, her arms outspread, her robes painted blue. Teresa turned toward her and her compassionate eyes. A deep voice called to Teresa from the plaza, but she would not hear it. She embraced the image of the Virgin and sank dizzily down before it.

Sebastian cast a cold eye on the cathedral. Its twin towers, taller than the ones that sheltered him, were topped by crosses.

He put his boot on the first step, then stopped. The

child hung in his arms like a corpse, but she was still alive.

Between the towers and below them was a great round window of stained glass. Its outer rim was divided into twenty-four separate sections, in the center of which was a flower with twelve petals. The flower began to glow, light streaming outward from the central circle.

Sebastian tried to look away.

The whole cathedral shone. The rest of the world he saw was a dull silver, but this was gleaming gold. The radiance spread until the great round window was aflame with it, its multicolored panes alive like some omniscient eye.

Sebastian mounted another step.

This was the place where he had worshiped as a boy, and now he was obliged to enter it again, not as a man but as a monster. The girl who hid within it had to die, or else Sebastian's unnatural life was over. If she survived, the secret of the castle would be exposed. Sebastian pictured himself, helpless in the crypt, surrounded by a mob of pious monks bearing pointed sticks.

He took another step.

The towers of the cathedral reeled dizzily toward the heavens. They were not like the turrets of his castle, though they were nearly as old. The castle was stark and spartan, but these spires were ornate, airy squares of arches and arabesques topped by tapering fingers that pointed toward the stars. The golden glow rippled upward till the towers were dazzling.

Sebastian took another step.

The taste of blood was bitter in his mouth. The child he held was a pathetic thing, but she too would have to be destroyed.

He thought of himself as a child and remembered mounting these steps before. He had held his little brother by the hand and they had laughed and joked and teased each other, indifferent to the emblems of death and resurrection that lurked within the gray walls.

Sebastian grew sick at heart. He shouted for Teresa to come forth, but the words caught in his throat.

The cathedral was as radiant as the gates of Heaven.

He had dreamed of such a night before. The cross had seemed to him a sorry thing, and he never doubted that he could surmount it. The idea that two sticks of wood could repel him was ridiculous; he was not that weak. But this golden edifice was strong.

It was not that he could not enter it but that its presence saddened him. The images of martyred men and women rose before him and he pitied them. He pitied the young woman who had fled from him and the beautiful child in his arms. He thought of Margarita, her body pierced and bleeding, of himself, groveling toward a pool of blood, and he was ashamed.

Sebastian dropped back a step.

He was furious when he realized what he had done. He could not allow this pile of golden stone to defeat him.

"Teresa Rodriguez!" he shouted. "Come forth, or your sister dies!" The sound of his voice was ugly to him, as were the things it said. The unconscious child was heavy in his hands. Yet who was she that he should pity her, and who was her sister? They were the daughters of the man who had murdered Margarita.

He steeled himself and climbed three steps toward his prey. Yet the doors of the cathedral still seemed distant and were alive with light.

The flaming mass that blocked his path was an image of the coming dawn. There was time enough for what he had to do before the sun rose, but the burning spires were an ill omen. He teetered on the marble stairs and his foot slipped down again.

"Come forth, Teresa!"

There was no reply.

The golden gleam was blinding. Sebastian turned his back to it and looked into the soothing silver of the empty plaza. He staggered down the stairs and let his burden rest upon the bottom step. He gazed abstractedly at Dolores and his fingers brushed her blond hair. His head was bowed.

A horror came upon him. His thirst for blood and vengeance had waned, but there could be no turning back now. If he spared Pedro's daughters or failed in his siege of the cathedral, he would surely be destroyed. He sat on the cold marble beside Dolores and put a pale hand to his face. A great sorrow overwhelmed him.

He stepped resolutely into the plaza and whirled to face the golden sanctuary. Its dazzling brilliance stunned him. He raised his arms above his head and let out a titanic howl of fury and frustration. He lurched toward the cathedral, then stopped and threw his hands before his eyes.

A light came on in one of the houses across the square.

Sebastian stooped to gather up Dolores. "I am undone," he told her. "I should have stayed at home and mourned my dead."

Dolores could not hear him and could not see the black wings sprouting from his shoulders.

"There will be another death," Sebastian said, "before the next day dawns."

He rose into the gray sky, the child in his arms.

23. The Castle

TERESA LAY huddled at the foot of the statue in an agony of suspense and shame. A hundred times she rose to leave and a hundred times sank back sobbing and groaning. Whatever she did, the sad wooden eyes of the Virgin looked at her with the same tenderness.

Teresa sensed obscurely that she was safe from Don Sebastian in the cathedral, but the thought brought her no comfort, for she had abandoned her sister. She told herself that there was nothing she could have done to save Dolores, but still she felt that it might have been better to stay and die than to hide and feel such overwhelming guilt. She reproached herself for the very pain she felt, which was nothing beside the horrors Dolores might be facing.

Still Teresa could not abandon her sanctuary. And so the last long minutes of the night slipped away, and with them all Teresa's hope. The sky turned pink and pearly gray and the faint light of the coming sun brightened the cold colors of the stained-glass windows surrounding her.

As dawn drew near Teresa's spirits rose. There was no reason for it that she understood, but the promise of day warmed her heart as if the sun's rays had touched it. Light shone through the windows and cast spots of blue and red and yellow on the walls of the cathedral. Teresa stood again and swayed with weariness, but this time she did not sink down. The night seemed an ugly dream. With faltering steps she made her way down the long purple carpet.

She stopped on the threshold, hands on the doors, and

tried to imagine what she would see if she opened them. She pictured the dead white face that had haunted her throughout the night, then the face of her little laughing sister. Dizzy with exhaustion, Teresa pulled at the iron rings in her hands and the portals yawned before her.

There was the plaza, just as she had seen it a thousand times before. A faint radiance rose in the east and a few sleepy people trudged across the square. There was no sign of Dolores or of Don Sebastian. It was as if nothing had happened.

Teresa walked giddily down the marble steps. A man passed her and looked at her strangely, but he did not speak.

Teresa crossed the plaza without thinking to talk to anyone. She thought only to reach Antonio. There was no one else left for her. She approached the inn by an elaborate route, carefully avoiding the street where she lived. She had no wish to see what might still be lying there.

Her emotions had exhausted her, as had lack of sleep. Her progress was slow. More than once she stopped to rest against a whitewashed wall. Her odd behavior drew stares from the people in the streets, but Teresa was beyond embarrassment.

At last she reached the inn. The sky in the east was pink and gold, but still the sun was hidden. Teresa collapsed on the barred wooden door and beat on it with slow monotony.

A boy appeared in the entrance and looked aghast at Teresa's appearance. She recognized him as the friend of Dolores who had carried messages to Antonio for her.

"Bring him," said Teresa. "Bring him to me at once. Oh God, please hurry. It's Dolores."

The bewildered boy scampered obediently away and Teresa leaned against the doorway, awaiting his return.

Somewhere bells were ringing. Teresa's eyelids drooped and she nearly fell.

"Please hurry," she said to no one. "Hurry, hurry, hurry."

She staggered in the doorway, but Antonio caught her just before she dropped.

"Teresa!" he said sharply. "What is it?" He was shocked to see her tangled hair, haggard face, and disheveled clothing.

Teresa looked at Antonio through half-closed eyes. He was heavy with sleep and his appearance was not much better than her own, but he was sweeter to her than the statues of the saints who had guarded her through her dark vigil. She went limp in his arms.

"Teresa!"

She would have sold her soul to sink into oblivion, yet she blessed Antonio's insistence. With a tremendous effort she roused herself, to find that she was seated on a bench inside the inn. Antonio held her. She began to struggle against him.

"It's Dolores!" she cried. "He has taken her. We must go at once. He killed my father. Save her, Antonio!"

"What? Who has taken her?"

"Don Sebastian! Master of your accursed castle!"

Teresa was on her feet again, as if her own words had restored her strength. Antonio stared at her in disbelief.

"Don Sebastian?" he repeated. "But he's dead!"

"I know he's dead, but he still walks. I saw him, Antonio! Don't argue with me!" She pulled him up from the bench, her hands working frantically. "Must I show you my father's head in the street?"

Antonio did not understand, but he could hardly doubt her. He was suddenly wide awake.

"My sword," he told the boy. "Bring it to the stable. And be quick about it!"

He ran into the street, Teresa right behind him.

"Where could he have taken her?" he asked. "To the castle?"

"I don't know, he could be anywhere, but we must try the castle. Oh God, Antonio, I know he meant to kill her! I think we are too late!"

"When did it happen?" asked Antonio.

"Hours ago, it seems. What must you think of me? I hid

from him in the cathedral, and I was afraid to come out. I abandoned her."

"Thank God that you at least are safe. What could you have done against him? And what manner of man is he, to walk abroad years after he has died?"

"He is not a man at all, Antonio. He is a ghost, he is a demon, he is a monster! You should have seen him.... No. Stop. You should not follow him. He will kill you, too."

Antonio stopped outside the stable and looked to the east. "The sun is rising," he said, "and these spirits are strongest in the night. I will stop him if I can. Besides, I cannot have trespassers on my estate." He almost managed a smile. "Where is that boy with my sword?" He stepped through the shadows to the stall where his horse waited.

"What is a sword to a dead man?" Teresa asked. "I should never have told you! Don't go!"

Antonio calmly saddled his horse. "Wait here for me," he said, for all the world as if he were not afraid.

"Wait?" shouted Teresa. She almost slapped him. "I'm coming with you. It's all my fault, and I will not be left behind. Antonio!"

"I have only one horse," he said, taken aback by her passion.

"Then I will ride behind you," declared Teresa. "But hurry!"

Had Antonio reached the forest sooner, he would have seen two figures among the trees. One was a tall man dressed in black; the other was a small blond girl in her nightgown. Shafts of golden light broke through the leafy branches above them, but the dark man avoided these, skulking in the deep green shade. The child was crying.

From time to time he pointed out dead sticks of wood to her and she dutifully picked them up. Her arms were filled with fuel, and rotting bark darkened the front of her white gown. He bent over her and whispered in her ear. Her lips trembled with every word, and tears streamed down her cheeks.

He kneeled before her in the shadow of a great oak tree, his dead eyes level with her own. His hands touched her shoulders and his words came rapidly. She did not turn away from him.

Birds sang in the forest, heralding the dawn. The sun struggled up behind the purple mountains and cast its beams on the black towers beyond the forest.

The man stood up and put one arm around the child. She was all but lost in the folds of his crimson cloak. Together they walked through the trees until they reached the rocky clearing between the forest and the moat. They struggled up the stony path, the girl bent by the weight of her burden, the man lowering his head before the warm rays of the sun.

At length they reached the castle. He took some of the wood from her and helped her arrange the pieces into a circle.

Then he leaned down and kissed the weeping child.

The sun rolled majestically up into the sky, but the shadow of the castle fell upon Dolores and Don Sebastian. Trembling, they embraced.

Antonio lashed the reins mercilessly against the neck of his gray stallion. The beast responded nobly, but it could hardly gallop through the thick forest, such efforts as it made serving only to punish its riders. Low branches whipped Antonio's face into a mass of cuts and bruises. Behind him, Teresa wrapped her arms around his waist so that his body helped to shield her, but more than once a springy bough slapped out at her. Their progress was maddeningly slow.

Antonio cursed the trees, his mount, and the woman who clung so feebly yet still screamed exhortations upon him.

"Too late! Too late!" Teresa shouted. A branch struck her shoulder and nearly threw her from the horse.

Antonio pulled up his mount and turned to look at her. "I will leave you here," he said. "We are almost at the castle, and I will make better time without you."

"Damn you, Antonio! Ride on! We will be there in

another minute, and now you would leave me behind!" She hit out at him with both hands, her eyes wet, her face wild.

Appalled at her ferocity, Antonio made no answer but to spur his steed.

Near the edge of the forest, where the trees grew thinner, rocks rose up from the ground to bar their way. The foaming stallion leaped over some and stumbled over others, but the two riders kept their seats. Finally, they broke through the outlying trees.

They saw the bleak black castle, its towers silhouetted against the rising sun, its dark bulk looming majestically against the purple ranges of the Pyrenees. Antonio reined his horse against the very sight of its grim strength.

Teresa screamed in insupportable anguish.

Antonio turned his head to look at her and saw a face hideously distorted by misery and pain. Turning back, he saw what he had missed.

A fire burned before the castle, just outside the distant moat. In its scarlet flames a body writhed.

Antonio turned sick and dropped his reins. Teresa groaned, unclasped her hands from his waist, and slipped off the stallion to the rocks below.

Antonio dropped down beside her. He feared for his mount, but the beast apparently had no wish to approach the castle. It stood shivering among the stones as Antonio kneeled at Teresa's side.

She lay in a sobbing heap upon the ground, flailing her arms against sharp stones.

"She's dead, she's dead," Teresa cried. "Everyone is dead!"

Antonio reached out toward her carefully, almost afraid to interrupt her grief. He glanced toward the castle, thinking for a moment to drag the burning body from the flames, but he knew he would be too late. It was better to stay with Teresa and comfort her as best he could. He gathered her up and rocked her in his arms.

As they huddled together on the outskirts of the forest, Antonio saw all his dreams destroyed. The wailing woman in his arms was suddenly a stranger; the estate he hoped to claim, a mausoleum.

A shadow fell over him.

Antonio looked up and saw a figure standing dark against the sky. Its hair was wild, its arms outspread.

It was Dolores—tear-stained and bedraggled, but certainly alive.

Antonio choked and gasped and tried to speak, but for a moment no words came. Teresa, her face hidden on his shoulder, had not seen.

"Teresa," he said weakly, then again, "Teresa."

When she did not answer him, Antonio spun her around until she faced her sister. He shook her fiercely. "Look," he croaked. "Just look."

Teresa opened her eyes and fainted dead away.

Antonio held Teresa and stared at her sister. Her face had changed; she was not the child he had known.

"Help me with her," said Antonio. They propped Teresa up against a boulder and brought her back to consciousness with shouts and slaps. "We thought you were dead," Antonio told Dolores.

"He let me go," Dolores said.

Teresa stretched her hands out to Dolores and drew the child down to her. She held the little golden head against her breast, and the sisters wept together.

Antonio felt lost at the sight of their communion. He stood aside to let the sisters cling to each other and raised his eyes to the black towers.

"Don Sebastian!" he said. Spurred by some impulse he could not have named, Antonio ran toward the castle.

"What happened, Dolores?" asked Teresa.

"He killed himself," Dolores answered solemnly, "and he made me help him. He said he was already dead. He was very sad."

"Poor Dolores."

"He said it was a penance, that I should gather wood for him. He meant to kill me, but he changed his mind. He said it was enough that father died. Is father dead, Teresa?"

"Yes."

Dolores was silent for a time. She craned her head to see the castle and the fire that burned below it.

"I saw him once before," she said, "when he was alive.

Why was he still here?"

"I don't know, Dolores."

"He didn't like it, being here. He said to tell you he was sorry. He would have killed us both, Teresa, but you stopped him when you hid in the cathedral. He said you saved me when you did that."

"Oh God," said Teresa, and she crushed her sister in her arms. "Oh Christ. Oh Jesus."

"He said he would confess to me, since there was no one else. He told me things, but I couldn't understand them. Then he said it didn't matter."

"What did he say, Dolores?"

"I don't know. I don't remember. I don't want to know. He made me pray for him. I was scared, but I was sorry for him. Then he stood where we had piled up the sticks, and he lit them with his fingers. he stood there and caught on fire. I ran away then and found you. I want to go home."

"Oh, Dolores," said her sister, "what home have we now?"

Antonio scrambled up the rocky incline and stopped before the wide gray walls of stone. From there he watched as his dead kinsman died again.

Don Sebastian did not die like any ordinary man. He was not chained or tied, and there was nothing but the strength of his own will to keep him in the fire. His body was bathed in flame, but still it stood erect. The crimson cloak blazed behind him and the black velvet suit smoldered.

Sebastian saw a dim image of the young man who approached his funeral pyre. It was his heir. Then smoke filled Sebastian's eyes, and the golden flames before them turned to molten silver.

Awestruck, Antonio stared as Don Sebastian was consumed. The dead flesh boiled and blistered, and the long hair turned into a torch. The dark eyes bubbled in their sockets and ran down the blackened cheeks in bloody streams. The skin dropped away in dusky strips until the bones were bare. The blaze wavered and the stripped skeleton gleamed and glowed. Its bones shone like some precious metal.

The naked skull still glistened, but the ravaged corpse did not collapse. It gestured to Antonio with a desiccated arm.

Antonio stepped back in horror.

The grim jaws gaped and the long teeth glistened as the dead thing spoke.

"Here is your castle," said Don Sebastian.

The hot spine snapped and the silver skull dropped into the flames. Bones tumbled down behind it, and their weight put out the fire. As the flames sparked and sputtered out, they sent the bright skull spinning from the embers of red and black.

The dead grin rolled toward the dark walls of the castle and the head of Don Sebastian de Villanueva sank with a splash into the waters of the moat.

Black smoke floated up above the towers and was lost in the bright blue of the heavens

24. The Cannon

THREE DAYS LATER, French troops crossed the Pyrenees and occupied the castle. This maneuver was part of a series of minor border skirmishes arising from the conflict between France and Spain over the control of Naples. The French were driven back, but not before cannon fire had shattered the walls of the castle, toppling its great tower.

Antonio Manetti fled back to Florence. With him went the daughters of Pedro Rodriguez. There they lived out their days in peace, if not in plenty.

The castle fell in a few hours. Torquemada took two years to die, and Colombus was carried back in chains from his third voyage; but the Inquisition endured for another three hundred and thirty-eight years.

The Silver Skull

1. City of Gold

THE man with the skull in his sack looked down from the mountains toward the city in the lake.

Tenochtitlan was the most astonishing sight that Alfonso Martinez had ever seen. The lake, of salt water, was vast, stretching for miles in all directions; its borders were rich with fields and forests, and with gigantic gardens where flowers bloomed in dazzling profusion. A gleaming city rose from the waters, its pyramids mirrored in the shining surface of the lake. The brilliant sunlight and the thin air gave the panorama the quality of a vision, but however Martinez shook his head and blinked his eyes, Tenochtitlan would not disappear. The city was real, and Alfonso Martinez was about to enter it. It was a city of water, but to him it was a city of gold.

The men around Martinez stood awestruck, yet there was a disturbance among the soldiers far ahead of him, that handful of veterans who had first followed Cortez into Tenochtitlan months ago. What was wrong? The city seemed placid enough. No hordes of feathered Aztec warriors stood ready to attack the Spanish troops, and no war canoes skimmed the surface of the lake. And yet, as word drifted back to Martinez and the other new recruits, it became apparent that this very lack of activity was an ominous sign.

Last November, when Cortez and his men had approached Tenochtitlan for the first time, the inhabitants of the Mexican capital had greeted them with curiosity and even enthusiasm. The towers along the causeway had been thronged with onlookers, and the lake had been covered with boats. It had been almost a festival, but now there was no welcome at all. The quiet, shimmering city was suddenly frightening.

Like all the others, Martinez had heard talk of trouble in Tenochtitlan, and he knew that he and his companions in the second expedition were partly to blame for it. They had come to Mexico months after Cortez, their army led by other Spaniards who intended to take control of the newly discovered territory and its riches. Determined not to let these interlopers subvert his authority, Cortez had marched away from Tenochtitlan to stop them before they could reach the city, and such was his skill as a tactician that he had defeated their larger force in a few hours. Moreover, he had spoken to them so persuasively that he soon rallied his former rivals to his cause, thus doubling his forces. But the absence of Cortez had left Tenochtitlan in the hands of underlings who had not been equal to the task. Fighting broke out between the Aztecs and the tiny Spanish garrison; the messengers who reported it sent Cortez hurrying back from the coast to secure the city. Yet he still had only about a thousand Spaniards against a city so huge that Alfonso Martinez could hardly guess at the number of its inhabitants.

Nervously he fingered his pack, and felt the reassuring roundness of the skull hidden within it.

"What do you think, physician? Ever see anything like it?"

"Never," answered Martinez, turning to look at his companion. The man beside him was rangy and sunburned. His face, where it was not concealed by shaggy black beard, was scarred, and his armor was equally battered. Thick eyebrows met above his flat and broken nose.

Martinez squinted at the soldier suspiciously. "Should I know you?"

"I am Luis Garcia. Captain Cortez sent me to keep an eye on you."

Garcia grinned, exposing broken teeth, and Martinez wondered if he were already under suspicion.

"Cortez says you may be the most valuable man in this second expedition," continued Garcia. "The rest of these fellows are fortune hunters, not fighters—we proved that fast enough. You're a bit of a runt yourself, of course, but that's why I'm here to look after you. We can always use a doctor, and there will be work enough for you soon, if I'm any judge. Looks like there's trouble brewing here."

Martinez breathed a sigh of relief. It would be intolerable to come this far from Spain only to be exposed as an impostor. He was no physician, although he had signed on as one. It might prove troublesome to live up to his lie, but every alchemist had some knowledge of medicine, and it would be easier to mix a potion or even amputate a leg than to return to Spain and face the tribunal of the Inquisition. Those who traded in sorcery had no place in Spain; the skull he carried with him was proof of that. Martinez hoped that it would have important uses: its magic, and his own, small as it was, would have to protect him in this strange land. He reached back again to fondle the cowhide sack, and the bone beneath it that had once encased the brain of the greatest wizard in Spain.

"What's that you're playing with?" asked Luis Garcia, his long face showing friendly curiosity.

"Tools of my trade," said Martinez, smirking at the small joke of deceiving this lout by telling him the truth.

"Good enough," said Garcia. "I'll wager there are a score of men in that city who need them. These heathens' swords are made of stone, not steel, and they make messy wounds. There will be work for you."

As he fell into step beside Garcia, Martinez attempted to adopt the swaggering attitude of a soldier of fortune. His muscles ached from the long march, and the tropical heat had sucked the strength from his bones, but he was determined to prove himself as tough as the next man.

"If there are wounded," he said, "then some will live and some will die. I will do what I can for them, but I am not here seeking sainthood."

Garcia looked at him with a narrowing of the eyes the alchemist could not interpret. "There are only two reasons for a man to come to this land of devils," said Garcia. "Gold or glory."

"You noticed yourself that I am no soldier."

"Gold, then. Well, there is plenty here for you. It's not hard to find, but it may not be so easy to carry away with you."

"Is there really so much?"

"More than you have ever dreamed of, physician."

"You have never seen my dreams."

"No. But I have seen the treasure in the palace of the king, and a man could hardly dream of more. And yet, great as it was, this king Montezuma seemed to think it a pittance. He gave us permission to construct a chapel in the palace, and we found the treasure hidden behind a wall. It was the fortune of his father, they say, and no man had ever bothered to look at it for years. There was a great hall hidden behind the plaster, piled with gold and silver and pots filled with jewels the way you might fill them with water. There were wheels of gold, and bars, and nuggets just scattered on the floor. And there were statues and ornaments made of it, but we melted most of them down when we came to divide it. They use gold as a white man might use wood or marble!"

"You've already divided it?" asked Martinez.

"Yes," answered Garcia. "I gambled it away in a week. But there will be more. These savages don't know the value of anything. Montezuma hardly seemed to care if we found the gold or not. I wonder if he even remembered it was there. It couldn't have meant much to him, for he gave it all to Cortez of his own free will."

"What kind of fool is king of this country?"

"So great a fool that he has lost his throne as well. And so great a fool that he thinks Hernan Cortez is some sort of god."

Alfonso Martinez, stumbling down a mountain slope, had nothing to say. What he had heard made no sense to him. He broke his clumsy descent by falling against Garcia's solid back, instantly drawing himself up with a show of dusty bravado. "You are mocking me," he said. "They say Cortez is a good commander, but he is a long way from being a god!"

Garcia took a step back. "Cortez is lucky," he said, "and luck is worth more than skill or sanctity. Every soldier knows as much, and you will learn it too, if you live long enough. Look at that city! Do you think we took it by force of arms? There are not many of us now, and we were fewer still when we first arrived. But these Indians have a legend that one of their gods will return to them, and they have decided that Cortez is the very fellow they were waiting for. A white god, they say, and Cortez looks pale enough compared to these brown bastards. Of course it makes no sense. I have seen statues of the god they speak of, some sort of a dragon, but covered with feathers. How they could take Cortez for him I couldn't say, but it has kept us alive, and that's all I ask."

"Then they have more gods than one?"

"Hundreds, I suppose, and each more bloodthirsty than the next. Thousands die on their altars every year, and the congregations eat their flesh. Men, women, and children die; and men, women, and children devour them. They worship idols that look like devils. They know nothing of Christ. Whatever else a man comes here for, he learns soon enough it is his duty to wipe out these horrors."

"Is it black magic, then?" Martinez asked eagerly.

"Call it what you will, it is an abomination."

Martinez paused for a moment, then asked, as if he were changing the subject: "Where does the gold come from?"

"From mines, I suppose. Where else could it come from?"

"Well, these Aztecs sound like a race of wizards, and I thought they might have found the secret . . ." Martinez let his sentence trail off.

The two men had continued to trudge down the slope as they

spoke, but now Luis Garcia stopped and turned to look at Martinez with the enigmatic squint the alchemist had seen before.

"The secret of what?" asked Garcia. "The secret of making gold?"

Martinez said nothing, fearing that he had already said too much.

"I never thought of that," said Garcia. "Nobody has ever thought of it. There must be a reason why they have so much, and why they seem to care so little for it. And there must be a reason for all those sacrifices to their demons. You are a clever fellow, physician."

"It was just an idle fancy."

"Best to hope it's not true, then. If the gold comes from the ground, we will have it all. But if it comes from those gods, it will go with them, and we will be the poorer for it."

Martinez was dismayed. Could his comrades be such fanatical Christians that they would seal up an endless stream of riches for no other reason than to satisfy their scruples? What good was any god except for the gifts he gave his followers? If it was true, as he believed, that these demonic idols rewarded their followers with the gift of growing gold, then they would find an ardent devotee in Alfonso Martinez.

Like every other alchemist, he had labored for years to find the way to turn base metal into glittering riches, and had grown old before his time in the search. Years spent peering into smoking crucibles had left his back bent and his shoulders rounded; years spent with an ear cocked for the officers of the Inquisition had left him with shattered nerves and shifty eyes. At thirty-eight, his hair was gray, most of it gone. His beard was thin and scraggly, his high forehead creased by constant anxiety. He was a small man, and even he would have acknowledged that he was a wicked one. Yet he had a vision, and it made him brave and strong enough to cross an ocean that few men had dared.

The vision was simple enough: Alfonso Martinez, seated on a throne, surrounded by piles of gold and caressed by adoring women. The world was at his feet—a globe, as every sensible man had learned by now—and even the globe gleamed yellow. It was a pathetically simple picture, as Martinez himself admitted in his more cynical moments. But it pleased him, it drove him onward, and it made him something more than just a coward or a rogue. He knew there were those of his calling who claimed that the gold the alchemists sought was only the symbol of a purified spirit; but Martinez would have none of this. He was true to his dream.

Garcia's voice drew Martinez back out of his vision. "Listen, physician," said the soldier. "I'm going to leave you for a minute. Just keep your place in line and march along with the rest, and you'll be fine. You're surrounded by fighting men, and there's no enemy about. Even these savages you see here are our allies. They don't like this city any more than we do. There's nothing to worry about."

Martinez nodded, still half lost in his own thoughts, his eyes on the silent city.

Garcia was still anxious to excuse himself. "Did you see that canoe that came across the lake just now?"

Martinez had seen nothing, but pretended that he had.

"I think it was a messenger," said Garcia. "It can't hurt to find out what's going on, and I have a friend who's an aide to Cortez. Keep marching. I'll be back."

"Go," said Martinez irritably, reflecting that this Garcia must be a tenderhearted fellow to show so much concern for him. Either that, or he was afraid.

Martinez was anxious himself. He wondered what had happened to his countrymen in the city on the lake, and what would happen to him. His legs began to tremble. He had not forgotten Garcia's description of the room filled with forgotten treasure.

Yet there was little to protect him, or to lead him to a fortune, except the Aztecs' insane belief that Cortez was one of their gods. Garcia had forgotten the name, or was too sanctimonious to admit that he knew it, but the ugly word had been burned into Martinez's brain as soon as he heard it. Quetzalcoatl, the Feathered Serpent. How Cortez had acquired the identity might remain a mystery, but there was something to be learned from the simple fact of the impersonation. Martinez knew more than a smattering of the ancient theologies, and of the numerous deities that had struggled for power in the world of the Romans or the Egyptians. Might there not be another god here, one who rivaled the Feathered Serpent and who might prevent Cortez from enshrining Christ in the name of Quetzalcoatl? Christ gave no gifts of gold, and he was no god for an alchemist. The Feathered Serpent had his uses, evidently, but the mind of Martinez raced forward to a day when some other demon of Tenochtitlan might make him rich.

He wished, not for the first time, that there was more of the divine in his own appearance. This seemed to be a land where any man of commanding presence might proclaim himself the incarnation of a supreme power, but Alfonso Martinez knew all too well that he did not look like a god. The fates conspired against a man from the moment of his birth, and the shape they gave him was no small part of his destiny. If Martinez had been a dark giant like the man whose skull he carried, things might have been different. Such a man had commanded fear, even before he had transcended death.

Martinez had never seen Don Sebastian de Villanueva, but he had heard stories about him, wild tales that were hardly to be believed. But Martinez had believed, and he had stolen the skull. He took it one night from the workshop of another magician, and betrayed the man to the Inquisition before there was time to investigate the robbery. Unfortunately, his contact with the dread tribunal had put Martinez himself in jeopardy, and he had been forced to flee to the New World before he had found time to test the powers of the skull. Yet he never doubted its merits as a totem of true magic, and had guarded it jealously throughout his travels. There was something in the shape of the skull, and in the configuration of its long sharp teeth, which convinced Martinez that it was the key to his destiny. Even the blackest periods of poverty had not tempted him to have it melted down, although careful observation had convinced him, against all logic, that it was made of solid silver.

Martinez had long pondered the question of what sort of man might leave such a relic behind. Don Sebastian had been a warrior and a wizard who had destroyed himself in flames rather than become a prisoner of the Inquisition. That had happened twenty-four years ago, in 1496, but it was said that Don Sebastian had died years earlier, and had given himself a life beyond death by invoking dark forces and imbibing the bright blood of living men and women. In short, Don Sebastian had been a vampire, a brooding monster who lurked among the towers of his ancestral castle. His brother, the Grand Inquisitor, ruled the frightened city of their birth.

An unholy pact had been made between the brothers, motivated by their shared fascination with the mysteries of black magic; but something had gone wrong. No one living knew the entire story, but the Grand Inquisitor had disappeared and Sebastian's burning body was discovered outside the black walls of his castle. Some time later his skull had been dredged up from the waters of the moat, passing from hand to hand for years before it fell into the clutches of Alfonso Martinez. And now it was in Mexico, with its owner cursing himself because he lacked the knowledge once contained in the hollow, fleshless head he carried with him. Martinez swore that he would unlock the secret of the thing, that somehow its power would become his own.

"I think we'll be all right," said Luis Garcia. He startled Martinez by lumbering breathlessly up the hill, but his message was reassuring. "Only seven dead, and more wounded, of course. They'll be glad to see you, physician. It's not quite clear what happened, but it seems our men attacked some of these barbarians at one of their festivals and killed a bunch of them. And they fought back, for a while. I guess you and your comrades are responsible."

"Me?"

"These natives learned that you and your expedition had come to take command from Cortez. They expected you to win, and that made them bold, but when they heard you lost, they stopped fighting and settled for a blockade of our garrison. No real harm done, I suppose, except for a few poor devils who will have no tales to tell to their grandchildren."

A golden chord cut through the hot dry air.

"Trumpets," said Garcia. "Cortez ordered them, to signal the men in the city. You can see where they are, in Montezuma's palace—over there, to your left. He gave us quarters there, before we took him prisoner. The people and the priests may not like it much, but Montezuma knows who we are and what the future holds for his people. He knows that we were born to be his masters, and those who doubt it will learn soon enough."

Artillery fire echoed across the great salt lake, and along the nearer causeway, that led from the city of water toward the mountains.

"They've heard us," said Garcia. "They're answering as best they can, with gunfire. They're still alive, our brothers, and soon we'll be in command of the city again."

"With the help of the Feathered Serpent," mumbled Martinez. He shifted his pack on his weary shoulders, and followed the long line of conquistadors down the slope to the city.

2. The Palace

THE false physician had been sent to visit the casualties as soon as he reached the sprawling palace of red stone. Inside, he had been led through endless rooms and corridors until he reached the wounded. Stifling his awe at the alien surroundings, he had adopted an indifferent air and set himself to examining the stricken men. The charade had not taken long. Martinez had contemplated dozens of hideous injuries with apparent satisfaction, and had commended the makeshift work of the Spanish priest who had done what he could to bind up the stumps and gashes. Martinez himself treated only one man—and that because he could not stand the screaming. He hoped the fellow would die before the sleeping draught wore off.

As soon as he could safely claim his work was done, Martinez had demanded an escort back to the great hall where Luis Garcia waited. It was the only room of the palace that rose above one story, and it was big enough to house more than a hundred men. Beds of matting, each with its own canopy, lay in long rows on the floor, and braziers burned, filling the air with sweet, smoking incense. The Spaniards were anxious, and none more so than Martinez, who was driven into a suppressed frenzy by the strange splendor he saw all around him. Nothing he had seen in the New World had prepared him for the magnificence of Tenochtitlan, and he was more convinced than ever that magic had played a part in the growth of the city on the lake.

Without supernatural intervention, reasoned Martinez, it would have been impossible for this race of small, dark men to engineer the wonders he saw around him. The complex of palaces and temples that formed the heart of the city looked like the work of a giant; the low building in which he stood covered acres of ground. The architecture was inhuman to his eye: vast interlocking rectangles of some unrecognizable stone lying close to the ground, these interspersed with towering layered pyramids that seemed even stranger than the legendary monuments of Egypt. To a man who had never before left Spain, Tenochtitlan looked like the landscape of a fever dream. Far easier to imagine it the handiwork of some uncanny force than to believe that these pagans had constructed the three causeways, each miles long, that ran through the city and across the blue water to the shores beyond.

The lack of furnishing in the countless chambers of the palace confirmed his hypothesis that the Aztecs were merely the tenants of some dark god's domain. There were no beds; even the nobles slept on woven mats. The chairs were sorry things, so close to the ground that one sat upon them cross-legged. There were a few low tables and decorated screens, but in all it seemed a bare and empty edifice, one whose inhabitants might well be interlopers.

The bright murals on the walls, all the more vivid in contrast to their bleak surroundings, provided further evidence that this was a city built by spells. The walls were alive with monsters. Whatever artists worked here had seen horrors, and had delineated them in a style so unearthly that this thrilled Martinez more than the images themselves. The figures were outlined in bold strokes of black, the outlines filled with unshaded patches of violent color. The drawing was flat, without perspective, and Martinez was wise enough in the ways of magic to recognize that every image was a symbol of some unknown power. These were not portraits but portents, and Martinez struggled to grasp their significance.

There were men in the murals, but they were paltry beside the hideous demons they served. These devils announced themselves in lurid shades of red and yellow, blue and green. They were shaped like dwarfs, with outsized heads and shrunken bodies, striped faces and bared teeth; their eyes were cold. From head to foot they were enmeshed in strange designs whose meanings seemed as if they might be hidden in some forgotten corner of the mind. They tantalized Alfonso Martinez until he thought he would go mad.

"Garcia," he said. "Take me out of here. Show me the city."

"Too dangerous," said Garcia stolidly. "We're safer here."

"I would never have taken you for a coward, Garcia. Are you afraid to show your face to the sun?"

Martinez had his answer as Garcia's sunburned hand took him by the throat. He was lifted into the air, his feet barely scraping the floor.

"No man calls me coward," said Luis Garcia. Martinez felt the man's hot breath in his face. "I'll show you a few things, and then we'll see how brave you are, physician."

He lowered Martinez slowly, unaware of the fact that the alchemist no longer wished to go anywhere in the company of such a hot-blooded soldier.

"But you're not such a bad fellow at that," Garcia said, giving Martinez a slap on the back that nearly knocked him to the ground. "I'll bet there's not another man in this palace with the nerve to go outside. And you're not even on duty. Just want a look around, do you? You shall have it."

Martinez felt a heavy arm thrown about his shoulder and was half carried across the great hall to its entrance. The man on guard at the door was evidently a friend of Garcia's.

"Listen," Garcia said. "We have a scholar here. I want to show him the city. If things don't go well, this may be his last chance for a look at the place. He should see the temples, and Montezuma's menagerie. And the skulls. He's a little cocky, and that should calm him down. Let us pass, will you?"

Garcia winked broadly, and seemed on the verge of nudging

the man in his armored ribs. The short, stocky guard returned the wink and stood aside.

Martinez winced at the mention of the skulls, but nobody seemed to notice. He had no idea what they were talking about, but he was all too aware of the silver skull buried in the sack that had never left his side during the long voyage which had brought him to Mexico. In fact, he would have sworn that something had bumped against him when Garcia brought up the subject of skulls, but he was more than willing to attribute the thump to an imagination inflamed by heat, hunger, and the subtle horrors of Tenochtitlan.

"Lead on," he told Garcia. This was no time to lose face, especially now that he was aware of Garcia's mercurial temperament. Martinez might lose more than face if he tried to back out —the dangers in this strange land were not only those of the spirit. Yet everything he saw convinced Martinez that this was indeed a country of conjurers, where his own minor magic might work wonders and where the native necromancy had in fact revealed the secret of making gold.

Garcia worked his own more mundane magic on several other sentries until at last they reached the final portal of the palace. The afternoon sun beat down upon them.

"That's not really Montezuma's palace," said Garcia. "It's his father's, but it seems that each of their kings has to build his own. Anyway, it's been Montezuma's since we took him prisoner and brought him over to the place he appointed as our quarters. Now it looks like maybe nothing is his anymore. But at least you'll have a chance to see what he's lost."

Martinez blinked in the sudden brightness of the day and squinted down the long street that led into a causeway and toward the distant shore.

"It's a trap," said Garcia. "The whole place is a trap. But we've been hoping they won't have the sense to spring it. There are three ways out of this city, each one a line of bridges over the water. And each one of those bridges can be drawn up in a matter of minutes, leaving us stranded on an island in the middle of a lake. You may think you're tough because you're willing to come out here, and you may think I'm tougher. But only Hernan Cortez has the balls to march into a place like this, where we're outnumbered at least a hundred to one, and where a dozen idiots can cut off our retreat at a moment's notice. After you've seen what sort of barbarians they are, maybe you'll realize the kind of risks we're taking."

The two men stood in the great plaza near the center of Tenochtitlan. The square, paved with huge flagstones, was deserted save for a few Spanish sentries, yet Martinez felt the presence of the Aztecs everywhere. They were in the city, waiting.

"That red pile to the south is the palace where we kidnapped Montezuma," said Garcia. "I'll take you down that way so you can see his pleasure gardens. To the west, there, is the biggest of their pyramids. We'll circle around and come past it back to where we started. It's the temple of their war god, I think, and they make sacrifices there for his glory. You've heard of that, I suppose—how they cut the living hearts out and feed them to the flames? That's just one of the ways they have of killing people, and that's just one of the places where they do it. There are temples all over this city. In fact, there's another one right beside the one you're looking at, but you can't see it from here. Some black god with an unpronounceable name. I don't know what he stands for, but he's the ugliest one I've seen, and that's saying something."

They walked south as Luis Garcia continued his monologue. "This plaza," he said, "is the only part of the city where you can walk any distance without running into one of their damned canals. They use canals instead of streets, the way they do in Venice, I suppose. These Aztecs come and go in canoes, and they use barges for transporting goods. I guess boats seem like a sensible way to travel to men who've never seen a wheel or a horse. We won our share of battles on our way here because the fools scattered in panic at the sight of a stallion. But they have strange beasts of their own, and Montezuma has collected them. This is his menagerie."

They were in a garden, the most beautiful that Martinez had ever seen. It stretched out so far that he could not see the end of it, and it was filled with fruit trees, flowering shrubs, and beds of herbs and blossoms. Stone walks intersected the garden, running between the gleaming marble buildings arranged about the grounds. And from their white walls came ungodly screams.

"The animals must be hungry," said Garcia. "Their attendants seem to be busy elsewhere. You won't believe it, physician, but I swear to you that this Montezuma has hundreds of men who do nothing but look after his pets. I don't know what's happened to them all."

"There's one," Martinez said uneasily, as a figure stepped out from behind a distant stand of trees. The man saw the two Spaniards, stopped, and hurried off in the opposite direction. Martinez was glad to see him go, but cringed at the thought of furtive savages lurking in the shrubbery around him.

"Forget him," said Garcia. "Look at that." To the left of the walk was a sunken area, and in it was a large stone pool full of brightly colored fish. "He has dozens of pools like that, some for fish and some for fowl. And the pools are filled with fresh or salt water, whatever suits the creatures best. Whoever heard of such a thing? Montezuma's beasts are treated better than men, and what he feeds them every day would serve an army."

The soldier stopped at the entrance to one of the white buildings. "Let's go in here," he said. "I think these are some of the stranger animals."

A cacophony of howls and roars poured through the doorway. To Martinez, the place looked like a tomb, but he went in. He was so afraid the building might be filled with armed men that he could hardly spare a glance for the beasts. Nevertheless, he and Garcia were the only human beings there.

When he finally began to study the animals, Martinez was tantalized by their similarity to the creatures he had seen in Europe, yet his eye was keen enough to recognize the differences, even through the elaborate latticework that masked the roomy cages. Some of them seemed to be wolves, foxes, and lions—but they were not. Others looked like nothing he had ever imagined. In spite of his fear, he was fascinated.

"Look out for those," said Garcia, pointing.

"The ones that look like spotted lions? Why? Do they roam through the streets?"

"No. But if you see a man wearing one of those skins, keep away from him. They call those beasts 'jaguars,' and the men who bear those spots are their most dangerous warriors. They have two sorts of knights here: these jaguars, and the 'eagles,' who wear feathers. Each serves one of their gods. The eagle knights belong to that feathered serpent we spoke of before, and they are bad enough. But they are with Montezuma, and their god is the one whose mantle Cortez wears. The jaguar knights know no master but that black god whose temple stands beside the great pyramid. When you've seen their shrine, you'll know why I warned you."

One of the black-and-gold creatures clawed at the latticework cage. Its red mouth gaped, snarling. Martinez stepped back involuntarily; the fear he felt was something more than a dread of its bright fangs.

"Let's go," he said. "I've seen enough."

"I must show you the birds," said Garcia. "You've never seen anything like them. They're like rainbows. The Aztecs use their feathers for decorations."

"I can see birds enough to suit me from here," said Martinez as he stepped out into the sunlight. He began to wish that he had never left the palace.

"The serpents, then. There's a whole house full of them. There's one that's a marvel. His tail is covered with little bells, and he rings them before he strikes with his poison."

"No serpents," said Martinez.

"Getting jumpy, are you?" Garcia grinned. "Well, there's one more place here I have to show you before we visit the pyramid. This is sure to interest a man in your line of work. Come on, now. I insist."

He grasped Martinez by the arm and all but dragged him

forward. The alchemist knew that he was being mocked, but there was nothing he could do. He thought of running, then thought of himself lost in the city.

"They're a strange people," said Garcia, brutally, indifferent to his companion's protestations, "those knights I mentioned. When there is no war, they fight among themselves, the eagles against the jaguars. And I don't mean tourneys such as civilized men might have. They take the losers and sacrifice them to their gods. Their best men! They're crazy. And wait till you see what Montezuma keeps in here."

He stopped outside the white walls. Martinez heard strange cries from within, but he could hardly imagine what sort of animal might make such sounds.

"Look at those plants before we go in," said Garcia, obviously enjoying himself. "I've heard the herbs that Montezuma grows here make good medicine. Things we've never learned about. You should study them, physician. They might be of use to you."

Martinez stared stupidly at the ground and made a show of examining the leaves and flowers. For all he knew there was magic here, but now he could not bring himself to care. "Fascinating," he said at last.

"Come inside," said Garcia. "You'll love this."

"Are these buildings always left open? Shouldn't they be locked?"

"These people have no locks. It seems they have no thieves, either. I told you they weren't civilized. Look!"

For a moment Martinez could hardly see in the dim light of the menagerie. There were braziers and torches here but, unattended, they had gone out. The faint shapes he saw, and the jabbering and screaming he heard, convinced Martinez that this must be a house of monkeys. Then his eyes adjusted to the light.

It was a house of horrors.

"Montezuma keeps his monsters here," said Garcia, and he laughed.

A dwarf leaned his huge head against the latticework. He was unconscious, if not dead, but his head lolled back and forth as he was rocked in the arms of a wailing albino whose white eyes were wild. A naked hunchback groped out through the bars, speaking frantically in an unintelligible tongue.

Alfonso had seen misshapen men before, and their appearance had never disturbed him. He had known a dwarf who was a master magician. But he had never seen a collection of such people before, and he had never seen them caged like beasts. There were dozens of them.

"I think they're starving," said Garcia. "Nobody has time for them now."

A woman with no arms or legs squirmed like a snake in the corner.

"How do you like them?" asked Garcia. "I thought they would interest a man of science like you."

"Enough," said Martinez faintly. He pushed past his guide and staggered out into the fresh air. "They are human, Garcia. Can't something be done for them?"

"They were well kept, my friend, until this rebellion started. Now their keepers are in turmoil, like everyone else, and have other things to worry about. If they trouble you so much, you can feed them your next meal—if you can find one."

Martinez did not reply. He tried to blot the grotesque menagerie out of his mind, and to find consolation in the fact that he and Garcia were going back the way they had come. Their shadows were long in the afternoon light, and the palace loomed before them.

"Not so fast, physician. You're going the wrong way. The temples are over there, to your left."

"It's late, Garcia."

"They have no need of you in the palace. And you told me you wanted to see the city. I wouldn't want to disappoint you. Behold the great pyramid."

"I've seen it."

"Look again. This is the heart of the city, where the hearts of men are torn bloody from their ribs."

The white pyramid stood to the west of the palace, and its bulk blotted out the sinking sun. It rose in five stages, each taller than a house, but it did not reach a point. The top of the great pyramid was flat, and on the terrace at its summit stood twin shrines. A double staircase ran up the steep side of this imposing temple; the railings were twin serpents made of marble, whose fierce faces rested on the ground while their tails stretched toward the sky.

"How big is it?" Martinez asked at length.

"Who knows?" said Garcia. "It's the biggest thing in the city—that's for sure. There are a hundred and fourteen steps to the peak, and those two shrines at the top aren't small. Want to go up?"

"No," Martinez said nervously. "Have you been up there?"

"Montezuma took us once—me and Cortez, and some of the others—to show us the shrines and the view of the city. The second time was only with our men. Cortez took an iron bar and smashed the idols, and we rolled the blood-stained things down the steps and shattered them against the stones you're standing on."

"What did the Aztecs do?"

"Well, they didn't like it much, but Montezuma smoothed things over. For a while, anyway. I told you he thinks Cortez is a god, and the one who founded the city, at that! So he decided that if Cortez didn't like the sacrifices there must be something wrong with them, and he let us put the image of the Virgin up there. The priests wouldn't accept it, though, and they predicted that their god would punish us."

"And?"

"You and your accursed second expedition arrived. Since then, things have been going to hell. We had to leave the city to put your expedition in its place, and while we were gone this rebellion broke out. The Devil is no weakling."

"Which god dwells in this thing, Garcia? The jaguar or the eagle?"

"This is their war god. Everyone worships him without really caring one way or the other. It's the two below him who cause the trouble. One, the patron of the eagle knights, is that feathered serpent that Montezuma follows. He stands for peace or some such foolishness, but they think Cortez is his incarnation, so I suppose we should be grateful for him. It's the other who worries me. Come, I'll show you his temple. I don't know much about this, physician; you should ask our priest. He's studying their religion—he thinks it will help him to convert these savages."

Martinez felt his pulse quicken. He had pieced together his own version of Aztec theology from Garcia's ramblings, and he felt certain that this was the god he wanted. A god of darkness and mystery, who cared for neither war nor peace. A god of sorcery, and perhaps one who made gold.

"What is his name?"

"I don't remember. None of their names can be spoken by any Christian tongue. But it does have a meaning—something about a mirror. Not a looking glass, more like a crystal. They say he looks into it and sees the future. But see for yourself."

The temple stood south of the great pyramid and west of Montezuma's menagerie. Its central position alone gave a clue to its importance. Smaller than the sanctuary of the war god, it rose on three levels to a bare platform. There were none of the carvings that adorned the base and the summit of the larger pyramid. Stark and cold, the black stone structure stood in the twilight.

"I think it's bigger than it looks," said Garcia. "They say this is the only temple in the city that goes down into the ground farther than it rises toward the sun. You can see the door there; it's open. But not even Cortez wanted to go through it."

Carved on the side of the black pyramid was a gigantic face; its mouth was the entrance to the temple of the dark god, and it yawned open as though beckoning visitors to step between its jagged teeth. The face, Martinez suddenly saw, was really a gigantic skull. He stepped back from it and thought of the skull of the sorcerer Don Sebastian de Villanueva, buried in the sack that was still strapped to his back. A shiver ran up his spine.

"It's getting late," said Alfonso Martinez. "Let's go back, Garcia."

"I've one more thing to show you, physician. Tales don't mean much, and I doubt if you realize how evil these gods are. But this should convince you. Come into the shadows, here, between the pyramids."

Martinez felt himself forced onward, although he had no wish to go. He was relieved at first to see that the gathering darkness held nothing more than another pyramid, but before he could speak he realized that this one was composed entirely of human skulls.

"These are the relics of their gods," Garcia said. "This pyramid, and those two towers flanking it. One of the men sat here for a day, when times were better a few months ago, and he counted a hundred and thirty-six thousand skulls. How do you like the city now?"

Martinez stumbled out of the shadows and toward the square. "Look!" he gasped. "Someone's coming!"

"Our own men," said Garcia. "One of our patrols. Nothing to worry about, but we'd better get back to the palace just the same. You act like you've caught a fever."

A handful of armored men rushed past them. A few were on horseback, but most were on foot, and some of them moved as clumsily as Alfonso Martinez.

"Those men are hurt," said Garcia. "Something has happened. We'd better get back."

Wild shouts came from the twilight at the other end of the eastern causeway.

"They've risen again," Garcia said. "Come on, physician. We'd better run!"

3. The Jaguars

MARTINEZ kept to the palace. The whole city, led by Montezuma's brother, had risen against Cortez, and by the third day of fighting the alchemist would have sworn that he had treated every Spanish soldier for at least one wound. Even Cortez came to him with a gash in his left hand. Martinez thanked the fates that had protected him alone from injury. He realized that he had been spared because he stayed far from the battle, yet he could not suppress the conviction that he was also under the protection of the grisly talisman hidden in his pack. The skull had power, and he believed that it was saving him for some higher destiny than an encounter with an Aztec arrow.

For now, though, he wished it would teach him medicine. He feared that his disguise was slipping. The courage of the Spaniards and the stoicism of their Indian allies had helped to keep his secret safe, and the situation of the besieged palace was so desperate that none of the soldiers had any time to keep an eye on the activities of the company's physician. The men accepted his crude treatment and returned to battle. Only those who were too severely injured to fight on had a real chance to observe his incompetence, and those he drugged. They would either die or heal themselves. Many of them had died, but it had not always been the fault of Alfonso

Martinez. The Aztecs fought viciously for their city.

Martinez looked ruefully at his diminishing supply of sleeping powders and prayed to the silver skull for a change in his fortunes.

On the first day after the Aztecs attacked, Cortez had ordered four hundred men to move out of the palace and restore order; but the Spaniards soon found themselves attacked by a wave of warriors so numerous and ferocious that no progress was possible. Cortez had underestimated the city that had endured his orders so patiently for so many months. Neither armor nor guns were of any use against the onslaught of Tenochtitlan's rebellious population. Stones and spears poured down from every rooftop, and the Spaniards were forced to retreat to the palace with their attack scarcely launched.

The Aztec advance was heralded by thousands of voices crying wildly, by the sound of piercing whistles that signaled assault, and by the unearthly wailing of the conches that served as native trumpets. Spaniards fell under the cloud of missiles that flew over their defenses, while flaming arrows set fire to the palace and the timbers that shored up the wall around it. The flames and smoke created havoc, and the Spaniards were near panic. No one could hear orders, but everyone heard the ominous pounding of the great logs battering against the walls. Even Martinez heard it as he hid in the innermost recesses of the palace, finally having given up, in his terror, all pretense of offering aid to the wounded men.

Finally Cortez was forced to do what his enemies could not. The sole way to put out the flaming walls was to knock them down with cannon fire. The Aztecs poured through the breach, and only the coming of the night slowed their invasion. They drew back as the sun set, and left the starving Spaniards to spend the night repairing the broken wall and digging in the ground for water.

On the second day Cortez himself led an attack, but the Spanish onslaught was stopped completely when it reached the canals beyond the central plaza. All the bridges had been drawn up or broken down, so that it was impossible to move forward through the water. Canoes were everywhere, and Spanish riders who moved too close to the water's edge were gutted by upthrusting spears. The Spaniards took revenge for the previous day's disaster by burning several native houses, but the canals prevented the fires from spreading, and before the day ended Cortez was driven back to the palace. His own troops were decimated, but the ranks of the enemy seemed untouched. The entire population of the city was in arms, including the women, and reinforcements were pouring in from neighboring cities under the control of Tenochtitlan. The Aztecs numbered at least a hundred thousand, perhaps two or three times more. Cortez realized too late the consequences of releasing Montezuma's brother, Cuitlahuac; he had unleashed a demon, and there would be no calling him back.

That night, Cortez determined to begin the construction of towers that would protect his men when they ventured forth from the palace. But it would take time to construct these from the available timber, and he had no guarantee that they would serve their purpose. Still, it was an idea, and the exhausted men willingly fell to work.

By the morning of the third day Alfonso Martinez was close to madness. The hollow pain in his stomach was gone, but he felt a giddiness that was surely a symptom of starvation. He had not slept. He was exhausted, yet too nervous to rest, and in any case he had no time. During the day, the severely stricken were carried in to him, and at night their comrades staggered into his stronghold with what they thought were only minor injuries. Martinez had never seen so much blood in his life. From time to time he dozed against a wall, but these moments of unconsciousness brought him no peace, only enough strength to endure further tortures.

What worried Martinez most was the constant presence of the expedition's priest. He was the only man except the alchemist who spent all his time among the wounded, and his sturdy, resolute figure was too often beside Martinez when it was time to treat an especially urgent case. He asked difficult questions, and his eyes gleamed with a curiosity in which there was a growing measure of suspicion.

A party had gone out at dawn; shortly afterward they were back, bearing their fallen comrades. Some of these were easy enough to deal with. In fact, Martinez was surprised at and sometimes a little proud of the crude skill he had developed in two days of practice on helpless patients. But there was one man with a wound so terrible that it was impossible to believe he was still alive. His belly had been slashed open by a jagged stone sword, and over his legs poured yards of intestines, glistening except where they had dragged in the dust. Martinez turned away, sick to his stomach. He had never seen anything like this before, and he could not bear to look at the man, much less try to help him. His own face felt as white and cold as that of his patient.

The priest hurried up. He looked at Martinez and at the stricken man. "What's the matter?" he said. "Help him!"

He spun Martinez around to face the figure on the floor. Martinez spared the twitching, gasping man one glance, then averted his face again.

"Do something!" said the priest. "We can save him. I've seen them live through worse than this." He dropped to his knees, gathered up the soldier's spilled intestines in his hands, and began to stuff them back into the wound.

"He's yours, Father," said Martinez as he stumbled away. "Give him the last rites."

As he turned his back on the priest and his charge, he saw Luis Garcia among the men hurrying out to rejoin the battle. The tall soldier wore a dirty bandage under his helmet, and on his face was a wolfish grin. "Hello, physician," he roared. "My head's fine. And there's a good fight brewing. You should come and join us. They've got men on the great temple now, and we have to clear them off before they shoot down enough arrows to kill us all. Cortez is leading the next charge."

Martinez could imagine nothing that would appeal to him less, until he heard the voice of the priest in his ear: "That man is dead, and you could have saved him. At least you could have tried! What kind of a doctor are you? I've been watching you, Martinez. I don't think you know what you're doing!"

Martinez ran from the accusing voice. "Hold on a minute," he said, as he fell into step beside Garcia. "I'm going with you."

"Good enough," said Garcia. "I can't figure you out, physician, but I'll say one thing for you: you're game."

Martinez ignored the comment and hurried from the indignant priest. He snatched a helmet from a corpse and clapped it onto his own head, then stooped again to pick up a battered shield. At the door he turned for an instant and addressed the priest.

"You take care of them, Father," he said. "I've had all I can stand. There's a war to be won, and a man can only stand by for so long."

Bolstered by his own courageous claims, Martinez made it through the gates and into the plaza before he realized what he had done. His stone sanctuary was behind him. He was in the thick of the fighting, in the midst of a battle so fierce that he gasped at the sight of it. Rocks and arrows fell all around him. Not three feet away a man dropped, howling, to the ground.

Martinez ran back for the gate, but it shut in his face. He put his shield over his head and huddled beneath the wall of the palace, waiting to be killed.

He was surprised to realize, as the minutes passed, that he had been spared. In fact, it seemed that the missiles had ceased dropping around him. The sound of the conflict was distant now. Cautiously he lifted his shield and peered out from under it. What he saw amazed him. Hundreds of men, Spaniards and Aztecs alike, stood quietly in the plaza with their arms at their sides, their weapons trailing on the ground. Like Martinez, they had become observers. A truce had come into being without negotiations, as all those on the edges of the fray turned their attention toward the great pyramid, where the day's glory was to be won and lost. Martinez lowered his shield to the level of his nose and looked over its top toward the struggle for the towering temple.

Cortez himself led the attack, his injured left hand protected by a shield strapped to his arm. He and hundreds of his men charged the pyramid, the fire from cannon and musket cutting the way through the ranks of the defending Mexicans.

The pyramid was alive with Aztec warriors. They represented every rank, and seemed to be dispersed upon the five receding levels according to their status. At the base of the temple were hordes of common soldiers, wearing loincloths. Above them stood the proven warriors, their station indicated by the red bands around their heads, and by the quilted cotton armor that was sufficient to deflect almost any native weapon. On the third and fourth levels were the knights of the eagle and the jaguar. Their bodies were protected by plates of gleaming metal; on their heads they wore the insignia of their knighthood. The Knights of the Feathered Serpent were adorned with feathers, and their rivals, joined with them in the war against the invaders, were adorned with spotted skins, the heads of wild animals forming rude helmets that masked their warlike features. At the summit were the chiefs, bearing feathered cloaks of such ornate intricacy that they seemed utterly inappropriate for fighting—visible proof that these arrogant Aztecs never expected to meet their enemies in personal combat. Among the chiefs ran the priests of the native gods, their hair long and their beards wild, their black robes embroidered with skulls.

Cortez, followed by his own men and their Indian allies, stormed the steps. From the heights came a shower of missiles: arrows, spears, stones, and also timbers, some of them afire. Many men fell in the attack, but many more pressed onward. Continual blasts from the guns opened a path for them, and they struggled up the double stairway to the first level. Once they had reached it the battle was more than half won, for the Aztecs above them were obliged to stop the hail of weapons to avoid injuring their own troops. In hand-to-hand combat, the Aztecs were no match for the invaders. Spanish steel and Spanish armor had already forged a young empire in the New World, and the natives had nothing but courage to stand against the onslaught.

The higher the Spaniards went, the wilder the struggle grew.

The knights of the eagle and the jaguar fought with ferocity and skill that seemed inspired by the black-clad priests who raged above them at the peak of the pyramid. Since the Aztec knights wore armor too, here the contest seemed more equal. By now the battle was more than a hundred feet above the ground, and Martinez watched in sick horror as men on both sides dropped, wailing, from the temple to be shattered on the rocks below.

The distant rattle of muskets echoed through the plaza and another handful of Tenochtitlan's defenders tumbled down the steps. They could not fight the guns, and one by one they withdrew to the terrace atop the temple. There they waited for Cortez.

He was not long in coming. The broad pavement at the peak of the pyramid became a battleground from which there could be no retreat. A dozen Spaniards were thrown backward down the steps as they swarmed over the last step of the stairway. The guns on the ground grew silent; like their enemies, the Spaniards could no longer afford to send death rattling into a mass of men that was half friend and half foe. The fight for the pyramid would be decided by those who struggled on its summit.

Martinez watched the battle with an interest that was almost abstract. He knew as well as any man what was at stake, but there was something so bizarre in the spectacle of the small figures murdering each other atop the gigantic temple that he began to view it as a show designed for his own amusement. Not much time passed before he began to enjoy the beautiful symmetry of the arcs made by men falling from the terrace to meet death on the stones below. He noticed with some interest that more Aztecs than Spaniards were dropping, at least on the side that he could see; but then again, there were more Aztecs.

He spotted Cortez just once, recognizing the tiny man in the distance only by his armor and his shield. The commander teetered on the brink, an Indian clutching each of his arms. Martinez held his breath then, suddenly aware of his own vulnerability, and of how dim his chances of survival would be if this one man fell. Cortez dropped to one knee and twisted his body, and all at once the man on his right arm was hurled over the precipice, plummeting like a shot bird in a mass of feathers. His sword arm free, Cortez slashed at the man who held his other arm, and in an instant he was alone. He stood there for a heartbeat, then dashed back into the fray.

Martinez felt like applauding, and indeed he heard a cheer rise up from the throng gathered around the base of the pyramid. The alchemist felt a surge of power rush through him. He could not contain himself. He glanced around quickly, determined that he was unobserved, then rushed from the wall and slipped his sword through the naked back of a native near at hand. The man crumpled, and Martinez felt his weight on the blade; then the body slid off the sword and collapsed. No one had noticed. Feeling more of a soldier, Martinez stepped back behind his shield. It was his first kill.

Unexpectedly, he found himself shaking. Some part of this was excitement, but more of it was fear. He did not regret killing the man, but somehow it had reminded him of his own mortality. He sensed that he had been out of the palace for too long, and he wondered how many hours had passed since the gate had closed behind him. The sun was certainly lower, and while it seemed to Martinez that there was less activity now upon the high terrace, it was impossible to tell what that might mean. He could only see what was happening at the nearest edge, and that was next to nothing. He saw a great many corpses, but almost no one who was moving.

He looked toward the two shrines rising up from the top of the pyramid, then realized that his eye had been drawn to them because they were aflame. At the sight of the smoke, another roar ran through the ranks of the troops on the ground. A few Spanish soldiers moved warily down the highest steps, and more followed. The shouts around Martinez grew louder. Cortez had won. His men streamed down the double stairway, hundreds of them, almost as many as had fought their way to the top. They brought prisoners with them: bloodied knights, feathered chieftains, and two stiff, black-robed priests.

To retreat after this triumph seemed like insanity, but Alfonso Martinez knew that Cortez had no real choice. He had shamed the Aztecs, and the initial effect was strong enough to render them immobile, but it could not last. Better to return to the palace and hope that the battle for the pyramid would make the city of Tenochtitlan more malleable.

But would it? Martinez had a sinking feeling that nothing had really been accomplished, unless it were the loss of more precious Spanish blood. They had had a victory of sorts, but its ultimate result was that the forces of Cortez were weaker than ever before. The men who had survived were now marching away from the temple toward the palace, and no attempt was made to stop them. Martinez wondered how many of them had wounds for him to treat. Then he thought of the angry priest he had left not many hours ago, and wondered what his own life would be worth if he returned, to be denounced as a charlatan. Panic fell on him like a dead weight. The palace might be more dangerous than the plaza.

Someone touched him lightly on the shoulder. He whirled, expecting his uncouth companion, Luis Garcia, but saw instead the head of a jaguar. The man's eyes were shadowed by the black and gold, but his mouth was grim. Martinez moaned. "Not now," he said. "We've won."

He whirled and saw another jaguar knight behind him. Four hands reached out to hold him, and a third man dressed in jaguar skin caressed his throat with a black stone blade. One of them spoke, but Martinez could not understand.

"Open the gates!" screamed Martinez, but even as he spoke he knew that only the trumpets of Cortez could gain admittance to the palace, and that the heroes of the pyramid were still long minutes away.

"Open the gates!" he cried again, but nothing happened. He spoke to the masked men who held him. "You don't want me," he said. "They need me inside. Let me alone."

Gently but firmly the three jaguar knights pulled him away from the gate. They drew him toward the south, away from the palace. His feet dragged, but the blade beneath his chin was most persuasive. He tried to argue, but understood that his words meant nothing to the trio dressed in the skins of predatory beasts. He nearly wept when, just before they dragged him around a corner, he saw the gates of the palace swing open. Then he was in another street, and could not even see his sanctuary. These were the knights of the black temple. He knew where they were taking him.

4. The Skull

ALFONSO Martinez did not give up hope entirely until the three jaguar knights shoved him through the jaws of the skull that formed the entrance to the black pyramid; but when he stumbled into that dark hole, he knew that he was lost. There was no chance that the Spanish troops would find him here. He staggered down a shadowy inclined plane, his captors close behind him. The depths of the temple were honeycombed with passageways, and the men in the spotted skins hurried him through one after another. They were not so gentle with him now that there was no possibility of anyone noticing his abduction; more than once he lurched into walls or tumbled to the floor as he was driven through dim tunnels that seemed to lie at crazy angles to each other. His knees were scraped, his face was bloodied, and he was delirious with terror.

When they finally stopped, he was grateful for a moment, then filled with an even greater fear as he realized how close to death he must be.

He stood in a black stone room. The walls and ceiling tilted grotesquely, but the floor was level. It was made of glistening, translucent mica. Flaming braziers stood in the corners, and five stiff figures waited in a row against the farthest wall. Before them stood an altar with a small statue on it, and a stone slab big enough to hold a man. Martinez looked at it and groaned. He tried to back away, but the warriors held him.

The little idol was made of obsidian, the same gleaming black stone that gave the Aztecs blades for their swords and knives. A golden band encircled its head, and in one hand was a dark shield, so highly polished that Martinez saw himself reflected in it. The black mirror was surrounded by feathers of blue and green. In its other hand the idol held four arrows.

Martinez peered beyond it to the silent figures waiting by the wall. One by one they moved toward him, and he knew them for the priests of the dark god. Their robes were black, the borders embroidered with white skulls, and below the hems were feet and ankles hideous with bloody scars. The lobes of their ears had been slashed too, and their long hair was matted with gore. Their coppery faces were almost as black as the robes they wore, for their features were smeared with dark, resinous pitch. Only their eyes were bright.

When the last of the five stepped toward him, Martinez saw to his amazement that it was a woman.

He saw no scars on her body, no pitch on her face, no dried blood in the black hair that flowed gleaming to her ankles. She wore the same costume as the others, but her face seemed less menacing than the craggy features of the four men who surrounded her. Her huge eyes gleamed, her nostrils flared, yet her full lips were twisted into something like a smile. She looked nothing like the pale women of Spain, but there was a dark beauty in her that kept Martinez entranced. He forgot his fear in the wonder of her face.

"I am Toci," she said. "This is the house of Tezcatlipoca, the Smoking Mirror."

"Toci . . ." echoed Martinez. "Tezcatlipoca." The alien words seemed suddenly important to him. The name of the priestess was simple enough, but the name of the god reverberated through his rattled brain. "Tezcatlipoca," he said again. "The Smoking Mirror." This was what he had sought, and he began to feel less frightened than fascinated. Then he realized what she had said to him.

"You speak Spanish," he said. "Do you know what I am saying?"

"Cortez has a woman," answered Toci. "She learned to talk for him. The Lady Marina. She talks for Cortez, and she talks for Montezuma. She talks for the Feathered Serpent, the god of Cortez and Montezuma. I heard, I learn, and I speak for Smoking Mirror, the god of this house. The great god."

She was no more than a foot away from him. He wanted to take hold of her, to shake her, to make her explain herself, but a glance at the men around her dissuaded him.

"What will you do with me?" asked Martinez. "Will you kill me?"

"You do not know me, but I know you, and Smoking Mirror knows you. You are here for him. He spoke of you."

"Of me?"

"You are Martinez, the magic man. Cortez has a priest, but he is like the priest of the Feathered Serpent. You are the priest we want. You bring Tezcatlipoca with you. Your name for him is Smoking Mirror."

Martinez thought of the skull in his pack and his knees quivered. He was too amazed to speak anything but the truth. "I am Martinez," he said. His words came simply; the last thing he wanted was to confuse this woman, especially since she was the only one in this distorted room who seemed to understand him. "I am the magic man. I came across the sea when I heard of you. I want to see your god." He wanted to ask about the gold, but he was still too afraid. His head spun. He was torn between fear for his life and the hope that this woman with the golden skin was the key to his destiny.

"This is Smoking Mirror," said Toci, and she pointed toward the black statue. "But he is more. You bring more, Martinez. You bring him."

"What do you want from me?" asked Martinez.

"You know," said Toci. "Smoking Mirror." Then she said something he could not understand. Her face betrayed neither anger nor impatience, but at her word the men in jaguar skins forced Martinez facedown on the floor. He felt his nose crushed against the stones and hands ripping at the pack on his back. Then he heard a chorus of shouts and gasps. Some of the weight fell away from him, but one hand was still on his neck, pressing his head down, and he did not resist it.

Something rolled across the flagstones and came to rest before his upturned eyes. It was the silver skull of Don Sebastian de Villanueva. Its empty sockets seemed to stare at him. The three jaguar knights drew back from it, and the four priests dropped to their knees. Martinez remained where he was. Only Toci stood erect. She crossed her brown hands on her breasts and chanted again and again the name of her dark god.

Martinez stared at the skull, and at the skulls embroidered on the hem of Toci's robe. He could only guess what was happening, but his instincts told him that this was a time for boldness. He snatched at the skull, and, struggling to his feet, held it out to the priestess. "Tezcatlipoca," he said, staring at her with all the strength of character he could muster. The skull seemed to quiver in his hands. Its cold vibrations numbed his fingers.

As he reached out to the priestess the seven men sprang up to surround him, but she stopped them with a word. She stretched out her arms to Martinez, and her fingers touched his as she took his offering. Her hands were warm, but his were icy.

Martinez tried to speak carefully. "This is the skull of the greatest wizard who ever lived in my land," he said. "I carried it across the waters because I know its power. But its power is too great for me. I give it to you, if you will give me my life."

The priestess cradled the silver skull in her arms while the four priests gathered silently around her. Their faces were masks of malice. The three warriors stood between Martinez and the door, but at least they no longer held him. At last Toci answered.

"Your life?" she said. "You have your life. I have Smoking Mirror. He said he would come. The stars said he would come.

And you bring him. I do not want your life. I want you to exchange for our great priest."

Martinez felt his heart sink.

"Cortez took him today," continued Toci, and Martinez remembered the sight of the sullen idolators who had been led away from the battle on the pyramid. "Cortez has the priest," said Toci. "I have you. I want the great priest of Smoking Mirror, and Cortez wants you. You have your life."

Martinez let out an involuntary sigh of relief. Suddenly the tilted black room and the red glow of the braziers lost some of their menace, but the reassurances of the mysterious woman who held the fleshless head of Don Sebastian only served to set his mind racing off in another direction. If there was to be an exchange of prisoners, then he was safe, but that meant he had only a short time to fathom the secrets of the Smoking Mirror cult. What did they want with the skull? And was there a way for him to use his knowledge of its origin for his own benefit? A risky game, thought Martinez, but one in which the rewards might include secrets for which any risk was justified. If the secret of the Aztec gold was anywhere, it was in the bowels of this black temple. He watched the priestess as she clutched the silver skull to her heart, and he thought of her as one of the countless beauties who would adorn his throne when he was master of the world's riches.

"Tell me of it," said Toci abruptly. She turned her back to Martinez and placed the skull carefully on the long stone slab. Her four pitch-smeared priests gathered before the slab and hid the death's head from Martinez.

Martinez tried to answer her but could not find the right words. He wondered what she would understand. He longed to concoct an ingenious lie, but was forced to settle for the simple truth.

"I said that he was the greatest magician of my land. He died in battle, but he lived after he died. He lived on blood; others died to make him live. Fire killed him again. This is all that is left of him. But few know of him even in Spain. His power is a secret. What do you know of him?"

"He is Smoking Mirror. He talks to me. Cortez came to be Quetzalcoatl, the Feathered Serpent, the god who fights in the sky with Smoking Mirror. The Feathered Serpent is a bad god for us. He talks peace and he makes Montezuma a woman. Now I have Smoking Mirror. He loves war and we want him. He is good for us, bad for Cortez. He comes from far and you are his servant. Smoking Mirror comes to fight for us."

Martinez surmised from her enigmatic remarks that there was a cult in the city ready to combat the influence of Cortez. The alchemist was happy enough to have his theory vindicated, but the enthusiasm of the priestess disturbed him. He knew that the skull was strong, but what could the relic of even so mighty a magician do that would satisfy her expectations? And what would she think of Martinez when she realized that she had hoped for too much?

"What will you do with it?" he asked nervously, gesturing toward the four grim priests and what lay concealed behind them.

"Watch," said Toci.

The four priests stepped away from the black slab, revealing the body of a man stretched out upon it. He had not been there a moment before, and Martinez thought at once of magic, but dismissed the idea as quickly as it came to him. The man was mortal, and he was alive. Martinez guessed there must be another entrance to this chamber, and his guess was confirmed when he saw that now five of Tezcatlipoca's dark priests were gathered around the idol. The fifth held a jagged knife of gleaming black, its hilt the head of a monster.

There could be no doubt of what they planned to do. Martinez had heard of these ceremonies before, but had no wish to see one. He stared at the victim, amazed that he made no struggle, then concluded from the uneven rise and fall of his chest that the man must be drugged. He was nearly naked, with only a bit of white cloth wrapped around his waist. As the color of the pathetic garment registered in his mind, Martinez suddenly realized what he should have noticed long before: the man was white, too—he could only be a Spanish prisoner.

The priests remained silent, but the priestess sidled up to Martinez and whispered proudly. "See," she said. "Smoking Mirror wants blood. Blood of his people. Blood of his land."

She held up a large bowl decorated in black and white. "And more," she said. "His land. Your land. The trees bring it."

Martinez saw to his bewilderment that the bowl was filled with ordinary dirt. He tried to piece together Toci's puzzling remarks, and began to remember something. There had been trees, Spanish trees, saplings that the priest of the second expedition had nursed throughout the voyage so that he could try growing them in Mexican soil. And on the first night in Tenochtitlan the trees had been torn out by their roots, the pots emptied. So the dirt in this bowl might have been dug from Spanish ground. It was possible, but it made no sense. What good was dirt?

Only one sort of creature could care so much for its native soil, thought Martinez, and that was one that could not survive without it. But how could the servants of Smoking Mirror have known that the silver skull was the relic of a vampire? And what good was a bowl of earth to a wizard who could never rise again for long enough to seek peace in the ground?

"Look," said the priestess, clutching the alchemist's arm.

Four priests took the captive by each of his arms and legs. The fifth stood at his head, holding the black knife aloft in both hands. The prisoner stirred. Toci moved away from Martinez. She reached into the bosom of her robe and pulled out some sort of dried flower, which she held beneath the nose of the man on the slab. He coughed and kicked, and his eyes opened.

"Help me," said the prisoner, looking straight at Martinez. "Stop them."

For an instant Martinez thought of doing something, but before he had a chance to make even a futile gesture the three jaguar knights stepped forward to surround him. He could only turn his head away.

He heard a scream, and against his will he looked back across the room. The flames from the braziers cast gigantic shadows on the wall, and the biggest of them was the image of the priest who held the knife aloft in both his hands. The black blade dropped down and ripped into the body of the man, who writhed and squirmed in the grip of his captors. His gasp was cut off as the knife tore into the flesh below his ribcage, and he was nearly dead when the priest reached into his chest and pulled out his heart.

Martinez winced, but his fascination was greater than his fear. He watched as Toci stepped forward to scatter earth over the twitching corpse, and he even watched when the priest thrust the dripping heart between the jaws of the silver skull she held.

Something was wrong with the room. The walls began to shimmer, and at the sight Martinez realized how terrified he was.

One of the warriors stepped forward, and with a single blow of his obsidian sword lopped off the head of the body on the black slab. He dropped it into a flaming pot beside the idol of Tezcatlipoca. The brown hands of the priestess put the silver skull down where the head had been. Her hands were red, and the skull was red, and the walls were red. Blood was everywhere.

The five priests stepped back from the black stone. The young priestess remained beside the scene of sacrifice, and she held her hands over her eyes. The three warriors lowered their heads. Only Alfonso Martinez was fool enough to look.

The sloping ceiling slid downward; the flames that lit the room rose to meet it. There was a flash, and everything turned white and cold. The people in the pyramid were insubstantial shadows; the black idol turned to gold. Then it disappeared. There was nothing in the room, nothing in the universe, but a flat black stone awash in blood.

The skull grinned up at the sky while tendrils of red crept up its cheeks. It grew thick with gore while the body beneath it seemed to waste away. Blood traced crude features on the gleaming bone, it glistened in the hollow sockets where once eyes had shone. Black hair bristled on the silver brow, and the silver face turned white as death beneath the crawling crimson. The decapitated corpse grew long and thin, and its hands reached slowly up to claw at the face of a man dead for a generation. Pale fingers with black nails clutched at the head as if intent on claiming it, and when they slipped away they exposed dark, dead eyes. The horror on the slab raised itself and turned its gaze on Alfonso Martinez. A silver silence overwhelmed the temple of Tezcatlipoca, and finally Martinez turned away.

When he looked again, the room beneath the pyramid was as it had been before. The warriors were gone, though, and the five priests of Smoking Mirror lay facedown on the floor. Even the priestess Toci was kneeling, before the altar that held the small black idol. Beside her stood a tall, gaunt figure draped in robes of red and black and white. His dark hair hung to his shoulders, his long black mustache almost reached his chin. A pale scar ran down the left side of his face.

Martinez had never dared to imagine such a feat of necromancy, but he could scarcely doubt that this was Don Sebastian de Villanueva, the warrior, the wizard, the vampire, the man who had been destroyed in flames twenty-four years ago.

The dead man smiled at Martinez.

"See," said Toci. "Smoking Mirror."

Martinez tried to answer her, but darkness overwhelmed him. He was only a minor magician. He took one step forward and fell in a faint at the feet of the monster he had carried halfway around the world.

5. A Rain of Stones

MARTINEZ awoke to find himself being dragged through the twisting corridors of the black pyramid. Before he had time to realize where he had been, he was outside in the great plaza. The morning sun blinded him, and he realized that he had spent the entire night in the temple of Smoking Mirror.

As soon as he could see again, he began to squirm in the hands of his captors. Thousands of soldiers stood in the square, Aztecs and Spaniards alike, and their presence convinced Martinez that he was being thrown out to die. Then he realized that none of the men were fighting. In fact, he saw a narrow corridor between the silent ranks of the warriors, and it seemed to lead toward the palace of Montezuma. It looked like a road to freedom, and Martinez would have been glad enough to take it, especially when he remembered the horrors he had seen not many hours ago. Yet he had seen magic, and now no power on earth could persuade him that he had not left behind him the secret of making gold.

He twisted his head to look back. A pair of jaguar knights were holding him; they looked like two of the three who had taken him the night before. Behind them walked Toci, the priestess of Tezcatlipoca. Martinez almost expected to see the tall, pale ghost of Don Sebastian looming above her, but she was alone.

"Where are we going?" he asked her.

"Cortez," said Toci.

"They'll never let us through," protested Martinez. "They'll kill us."

The priestess did not bother to answer him. Martinez scrambled to his feet, but the men who held him were strong. There was no chance of running back into the pyramid. Martinez was a little shocked to realize that he was capable of considering such a move, but the dark secrets behind were less immediately frightening than the thousands of armed men who waited ahead. At least there were laws for magic; but who could predict the behavior of so many unruly mortals, any one of whom might strike him dead on a whim?

Deciding that resistance was impossible, Martinez pulled himself up as tall as possible and tried to walk as if he wanted to. His eyes darted right and left, searching the crowd for a man who might be ready to strike him down. He and his guards passed into the opening between the troops of Tenochtitlan, and Martinez felt a frantic pounding in his head which he knew came from the beating of his heart. The blistering white sunlight was intolerable. Martinez passed row upon row of dark faces, their expressions a strange mixture of passivity and hatred. He thought that Toci was still following him and hoped that her presence might guarantee his safety, but he was afraid to look back, since that would mean taking his eyes off the silent soldiers who surrounded him.

He reached the great pyramid of the war god. Beyond it was the palace of Montezuma. The feathers and skins of the Aztecs gradually gave way to Spanish armor, and Martinez began to believe that he might survive after all. But he still had a long way to go, and there was still an array of deadly weapons at his back. He put one foot in front of the other and tried not to think.

Sooner than he would have believed possible, he had a clear view of the palace walls, and then of the small group of men who stood before the gate. The metal plate armor they wore had lost its polish beneath a covering of dust and dents; some of them were bandaged; and all of them sagged with exhaustion. They were a sorry lot, but they were his countrymen, and that fact meant more to him than it ever had before. He would have hurried toward them, but now the jaguar knights beside him held him back.

An alien figure stood in the midst of the Spanish soldiers; by his black robe and matted hair Martinez recognized him as the captive high priest of the Smoking Mirror cult. He wore an elaborate headdress of bright feathers, bound in enough gold to keep a man alive for years. Hanging from his neck on a thick gold chain was a gleaming disc of black obsidian. Like Martinez he had a guard on either arm, but he did not seem to care. His predatory features were rigid with indifference, his head was thrown back proudly; he seemed to be gazing into the sun. Only when he came closer did Martinez realize what that fixed stare into the source of all light must mean. The high priest of the black pyramid was blind.

This revelation was lost upon Martinez when he recognized one of the men who stood beside the priest. Beneath a battered helmet loomed the long, flat face of Luis Garcia. Martinez was astounded by the strength of his emotion at the sight of this ungainly lout. The man might be a bully and a clown, but he was the closest thing to a friend that Martinez had found on this accursed continent.

"Garcia!" shouted Martinez.

The bearded soldier looked up and smiled a slow smile. "Hello, physician," he said. "I thought we'd lost you."

"If you'd seen what I've seen," Martinez began, then stopped himself. It would be stupid and even dangerous to describe the unholy resurrection of Don Sebastian de Villanueva, and nothing was worth discussing if it delayed his access to the safety of the palace. "Let's go inside, Garcia."

"Take it easy. You've nothing to fear. There's a truce on. Didn't they tell you? It's Montezuma's truce. He's going to talk to his people and see if he can get them to lay down their arms. You can thank him for calming things down enough so that we could trade this blind idolator for you."

"Well, make the exchange, will you?"

"You know," said Garcia, "I think you're glad to see me."

"I'd be glad enough to see you inside. What are you waiting for?"

"These things are tricky, physician. Everyone has to move very carefully. You can run for the gate if you want to; it's only a few feet away. But I'll bet you don't make it."

Martinez decided to stand still. He watched Toci lean forward to whisper something to the high priest. Martinez thought she could be planning treachery, or even discussing him, but somehow he was sure that what she spoke of was the skull that had spawned a walking corpse.

Garcia nodded, and the blind priest was released. He walked unerringly toward the knights who served his god. At the same moment, Martinez felt his arms go free.

"Come to me, physician," grinned Garcia, and Martinez stepped cautiously across the few feet of open ground between them. He saw to his surprise that Toci still followed.

"This one is worth more than you and that heathen put together," said Garcia, leering at her. "But for some reason the natives insisted that we take her along with you. She's part of the deal, and we're supposed to deliver her to Montezuma as soon as he's finished his speech. I guess their black god wants to be sure he's got somebody to talk to the king, even though he's not really king anymore."

"Not really king?" said Martinez. "What do you mean?"

"I'll tell you later. They're opening the gates."

Martinez was the first man through, and the first person he saw was the Spanish priest.

Martinez winced at the sight of him, remembering what he had forgotten during the dangers outside the fortress. This was the man who had seen him for the fraud he was, and whose shouts had driven him out into the arms of the jaguar knights. He was as great a threat as any man in the city, and he was rushing toward Martinez.

The stocky priest's honest face was flushed. He reached out both hands to Martinez, who could not bear to look at him.

"Thank God and all the saints you're safe," said the priest. "I could never have forgiven myself if you'd been killed. I know it was my tongue that drove you out into the battle, and I beg your pardon. These wars make men mad, physician, and I lost my head. I had no right to speak to you the way I did. I've prayed for your return, and for your pardon."

Martinez was at once delighted and embarrassed by this unexpected apology. He smiled sheepishly. "I was not myself either," he murmured diplomatically. "These are difficult times for all of us."

"Worse than difficult," said the priest. "Our situation is impossible."

"And this Martinez is just the man for an impossible situation," roared Luis Garcia. "He's performed a miracle. Physician, you're the first man to be taken prisoner by these pagans who lived to tell about it. How do you account for that? You lead a charmed life, that's for sure."

"I owe my life to Cortez," said Martinez, "or to whoever took that blind priest. They wanted him more than me. It wasn't pleasant, however. They had plenty of other prisoners. I saw a man sacrificed, and I might have been next. There was no magic about my escape. Only luck—and maybe the prayers of a good priest."

Garcia turned to the priest. "You'd better take this woman," he said. "She speaks for Montezuma's god, or at least one of them, and you seem like the man to bring her to him. Martinez and I may be needed here if things don't work out."

The priest walked away, and Toci calmly followed him.

"She seems to know what we're saying," said Garcia. "Maybe he can convert her."

"I doubt it," said Martinez. "That's a dangerous woman. I'd feel better if she was back in her pyramid. I don't know why she's here, but she's up to something, you can be sure of that."

"Well, she won't see Montezuma for a while. He's going to be up on the walls in a minute or two, and if he says the right things to his people we just might get out of here alive. She'll have to wait her turn if she's worried about the state of his soul."

Again Martinez was reminded that he was the only Spaniard in the city who knew what had happened last night, even though he could only guess what the ghastly resurrection might mean. And he did not dare to speak of it. Meanwhile, though, there were things for him to learn.

"What were you saying about Montezuma?" he asked Garcia. "What did you mean about him not being king?"

"More Aztec treachery," mumbled Garcia. "You remember the day you got here, when Cortez released Montezuma's brother, Cuitlahuac? He was supposed to be an emissary, but when he was freed the Aztecs took him for a new king. He's been leading this uprising, and by now there's no way to tell if anyone cares what Montezuma has to say. But he's been their king for years, and he should still be good for something. The important thing is that he's on our side. If he can calm them down, we might be all right. But if he can't, we'll have to fight our way out. And then God help us all!"

Martinez tried to decide what he hoped would happen. An end to the fighting would save his neck, and that was certainly desirable, but it would probably mean a retreat from the city, away from the black pyramid and its mysteries. He could hardly bear the thought of running away when he was so close to the secrets he had sought for years. The pale face of Don Sebastian de Villanueva haunted him. He was afraid to see it again, but almost more afraid that it might disappear forever, leaving Alfonso Martinez no wiser than before. But the worst of it was that it hardly mattered what he wanted: events would take their course with no concern for his wishes. The Aztec gold seemed very far away.

A blast of trumpets drew Martinez from these unhappy thoughts. Something was happening on the top of the wall, and there was a vast murmur from the crowd that stood outside it. Martinez gazed up and saw a small group of men moving to take a central position overlooking the plaza. Towering above the clustered Spanish helmets was a crown of eagle feathers.

"Montezuma," whispered Luis Garcia. "We might as well wait here and listen to him. Plenty of men inside need your help, physician, but if this doesn't go well it won't much matter what you do for them."

"Is there actually any chance that he can get them to let us stay?"

"Not much hope of that. In fact, that's not even what he's going to ask for. Our best hope is that they'll lay down their arms for a day and let us crawl out of here."

Martinez felt his heart sink. Could this be the end of the adventure, an ignominious retreat just when the technique of making gold was within his grasp? Had he carried the silver skull across the ocean only to abandon its magic to a race of dusky heathens?

"Here's your chance for a look at a king," said Garcia. "And maybe your last. They know how to dress them, that's for sure. You could buy a city with what he's wearing."

A hush had fallen over Tenochtitlan. The entourage of armed men stepped aside, and Montezuma stood on the parapet in solitary splendor. His heavy, pointed crown was wrought of solid gold, and Martinez was impressed to see how high he held his head beneath the weight of it. Feathers sprouted from the crown like rays of the sun, and a long, rich robe of intricate featherwork flowed down Montezuma's back. He looked something like a bird, something like an angel, and something like a god. The mantle he wore was blue and white, and in the clasp holding it together was a green stone as big as a fist. His robes were adorned with a multitude of gems that sparkled in the hot sun, and in his hand he held an ornate wand of gold and precious stones. Even his sandals were of gold.

Martinez tried to count the jewels, to estimate their worth, and to decide how many were emeralds or diamonds. The stones were too dazzling for any close calculation, however, and he was finally most impressed by the way in which Montezuma's costume duplicated the one he himself dreamed of wearing when he had mastered all the mysteries of alchemy.

Montezuma began to speak. Martinez guessed he was about

forty years old. He was tall and thin, paler than most of his race. His thick black hair was cut shorter than was customary among his people, and unlike many of them he had a beard, thin and wispy except at his determined chin. Martinez could not see the king's expression clearly, but there was dignity in his bearing, and an air of resignation. He did not gesture when he spoke. Something in his demeanor suggested a gaudily dressed puppet, moving stiffly at the insistence of some hidden master. Martinez wondered if Montezuma still believed that Cortez was a god, or if he spoke only to save his own life.

"What is he saying?" he asked Garcia.

"Who the hell knows? Do you think I speak their ugly tongue? Nobody does, except Marina, Cortez's native woman. I'm sure she's listening somewhere and telling Cortez what he says. But it better be the right thing. If we have to shut his mouth, we'll be worse off than before."

Someone in the crowd below Montezuma shouted. The deposed king continued his oration, but not before Martinez had seen him stiffen. The shout had not been a friendly one. The soldiers around Montezuma stirred nervously.

"It's not going to work," Garcia said.

As if inspired by his prediction, a series of angry cries rose up from beneath the walls around the palace. Montezuma was silent, but his head began to droop under the weight of his golden crown.

"Damn it," said Garcia.

Martinez stared upward at the splendid feathered figure on the battlements, and saw something arching through the sky from the multitude hidden behind the wall. It was a stone, and it struck Montezuma's arm. The king did not flinch as it hit him. His head was bowed. He did not move. Martinez saw a gleam that might have been another jewel below Montezuma's eye, then there was a sudden shower of stones.

Spanish soldiers rushed toward the king, their shields held high, but they were far too slow. Spears and arrows rattled off their armor, but they were better protected than the man they guarded. Rocks fell like hail on the abandoned king. He staggered as a black rock bounced off his temple, then dropped into the arms of a frantic Spaniard, and all at once there was a wall of shields around him.

"This is the end," Garcia said. "We're done for!"

A handful of steel-clad men stumbled down from the parapet like some ungainly beetle, carrying a drooping, weaving mass of feathers.

"Have they killed him?" asked Martinez.

"Don't ask me, physician. You'll be the one who gets a chance to look at whatever's left of him. But it doesn't much matter now. They didn't like his speech, and that's the end of it."

Martinez felt his stomach tighten and his mouth go dry. He realized that there were worse fates than the loss of a fortune. He remembered the dead smile of Don Sebastian, and now he perceived the mockery in it.

Men rushed back and forth chaotically within the confines of the fortress that had been Montezuma's palace. They shouted without any real purpose, but their anxious screams were nothing beside the wail of anguish that rose from the square outside. Too late the Aztecs sensed that they had killed their king. Their keening drifted away, and Martinez needed no sentry to tell him that the inhabitants of Tenochtitlan had fled from the enormity of their deed. For some reason, Martinez thought of the beautiful and enigmatic priestess Toci, and of the ghastly form of Don Sebastian de Villanueva, who had stood beside her in robes of red and black and white.

"We're all doomed," said Garcia. "Look at me, physician, and look well. I'll wager this is the last time you'll ever see a dead man walking."

6. The Dead King

MARTINEZ was soon summoned to treat Montezuma's wounds, and Garcia escorted him to the royal chambers. Once again Martinez found himself in an impossible situation; he felt the emptiness in his belly that was a fear too great for panic. He was groggy from too much tension and too little sleep. He could barely think of a way to keep his disguise intact, and was almost past caring. It was one thing to pass for a physician when the men he doctored were nonentities, but something else again to have a king under his care. Incompetence could hardly pass unnoticed here, and its punishment might well be death. Of course, he had little hope of surviving, no matter what he did—the hundreds of thousands of Aztecs surrounding the palace would see to that. Yet even an hour of life was precious, and there might be a small chance for escape from the Aztecs if he gave his own countrymen no reason to execute him. Martinez entered Montezuma's chambers hoping he would find the king dead.

The first thing he saw when he crossed the threshold was the black-clad figure of Toci. Her presence did not entirely surprise him, but it was disconcerting nonetheless. Memories of murdered men and the creatures that rose from their blood were the last things Martinez needed now, when all his concentration was necessary to preserve even the illusion that he knew what he was doing. And behind Toci stood the Spanish priest. The sight of these two together unnerved Martinez completely.

"I'm not well myself," he said, not daring to look at anyone in the room. "I've been a prisoner, you know. I haven't slept. There must be someone else who can do this. I won't be responsible in my condition. . . ." Martinez had intended that this speech would ring out with increasing forcefulness, but instead it tapered off into a whimper, and nobody took any notice of it except Garcia, who pounded Martinez on the back with rough affection.

"You can do it, physician," he said. "We all have to do the best we can." With that he turned and left Martinez alone with the king and his two comforters.

The room was not Montezuma's own, but one of those that had been assigned to him when he became the prisoner of Cortez. Still, the furnishings were rich. The low stools and tables were inlaid with gems and gold; the walls were bright with hangings of intricate featherwork.

Montezuma lay on a low straw mat, in itself no different from the bed of any man in the palace, although its canopy was beautifully woven. His robes had been stripped off, and his body was covered with bruises. These seemed to be minor injuries, but there was an ugly wound on his temple, black and oozing blood. Even from across the room Martinez did not like the look of it. The king was breathing raggedly, but was not nearly dead enough to suit his physician.

"Some of his women tried to bandage his head," the priest said to Martinez, "but he would have none of it. They did wash that spot on his temple, but you can see that it's still bleeding. And he won't take any food or water."

"Is he conscious?" asked Martinez, reluctantly approaching the royal bedside.

"He was, but I don't know what's happened to him since."

"I'll take a look," said Martinez.

The priest watched him with intense interest, while the woman

Toci remained indifferent, as still and stiff as one of the enigmatic figures on the wall.

Martinez reached gingerly across a low table covered with red earthenware dishes full of fresh fruit and stewed meats. The thick brew of chocolate and spices had grown cold in its golden cup. His hand hesitated over the wasted food; he could not remember when he had last eaten. Reluctantly he restrained himself, and his fingertips brushed the sleeping Montezuma's forehead in what was meant to be the delicate touch of a born healer.

For a moment there was no response. Then suddenly Martinez felt the grip of a strong hand on his wrist. Montezuma's eyes were open and fury was in them. Briefly Martinez felt the touch of a king, then he was unceremoniously hurled away. His foot caught the edge of the table as he fell and sent the bowls crashing to the floor. Martinez landed sitting down, his clothing covered with the food he had wanted so badly.

"He's awfully strong for an injured man," said Martinez petulantly. He stood up clumsily and tried to brush himself off. There was food on his fingers, and despite his best intentions he found himself licking them.

"He has refused all help," said the priest, "even my offer to pray for him. He seems to want to die. Not even Cortez could cheer him."

The king had sunk back on his bed again. He might have been asleep, or perhaps just waiting patiently.

"He is dead," Toci said abruptly. Martinez turned to look, but saw the king's chest still rising and falling unevenly. "He is dead soon," she continued. "Tonight."

"Is she right?" asked the priest.

"It's possible, Father. I hardly had a chance to look. He's badly hurt, and he should be treated, but it will do more harm than good if he fights like that every time someone goes near him. There is nothing I can do."

"You could drug his food, but that won't help if he won't eat any of it. There must be something you can do!"

"Listen, Father. These head wounds can be complicated. The most important thing is to keep him still. I can't make him eat, and I can't even go near him, without the risk of killing him at once. Anyway, if he lives, it will be a miracle."

"And if he dies," the priest said solemnly, "he will die without Christ. I must get his consent for baptism."

Toci stepped away from the wall to stand with folded arms between the priest and Montezuma. "The king has gods," she said firmly. "Not your gods. Not the Woman and the Boy. *They* have killed him."

The priest was stung at this insult to the Virgin and Child, but he answered as calmly as he could. "His own people tried to kill him," he said.

"He wants death, he waits for it. He waits for Smoking Mirror."

Martinez raised his eyes nervously at the sound of the name. The priest and the priestess looked at him, and he had the feeling that they expected him to settle their dispute.

"A man's soul is at stake," said the priest.

"Smoking Mirror wants blood," said the priestess softly.

Martinez did not really understand her argument, but there was something very persuasive about it nonetheless. She frightened him more than the priest, and he was more concerned with his own neck than Montezuma's soul.

"Perhaps what she says is true," he suggested. "He has his own gods, Father, and no reason to be grateful to ours, whose emissaries have brought him to this sorry state. She says he has refused you. Would you force him on his deathbed to become an apostate, and to suffer an eternity far more horrible than the one reserved for an innocent pagan?"

Martinez, startled by his own eloquence, discovered that his exhaustion had suddenly given way to a euphoric energy, as if he were a runner who had caught his second wind. The edges of everything he saw were unnaturally sharp and bright.

The face of the priest turned stolid and sullen. "Would you argue theology with me? You have not even wit enough to do your own job well."

Martinez felt giddy, at a loss for words, but Toci rescued him.

"Marina," she said.

"Of course," said Martinez. "If you don't believe the priestess, then ask the Lady Marina. You said Cortez was here; she must have been with him, interpreting for him as she always does. Ask the Lady Marina. Cortez trusts her. Ask her what Montezuma wants."

"So be it. But I will not leave you and this evil woman alone with the king. I will ask Cortez to order guards for him."

Martinez saw a frantic gleam in Toci's eyes and interpreted it as best he could. "You will ask for no one," he said, with all the authority he could muster. "You have seen how the king reacts. Will you be accountable for his behavior if a troop of armed men rush into this room? Do it, and the responsibility will be on your head."

The priest stopped in the doorway, scowled, then left without answering. But Martinez thought that he had made his point. He turned to Toci for approval, and saw her squatting down to pick up a piece of fruit that had fallen to the floor.

She rose and offered it to him. "Eat," she said. "You want it."

Martinez did as he was told. He had no idea what he was eating, but it was good. He sat on a stool in a corner, as far as possible from both Toci and Montezuma. A bowl had rolled to the foot of the stool. He scraped out what was left in it with his fingers and stuffed it into his mouth. He was thinking that the Aztecs were more generous than his own people; he had returned from the pyramid as if from the dead, but no Spaniard had thought to offer him food. He looked at the king, apparently unconscious on his straw mat, then at the priestess, who had resumed her place by the wall near the entrance to the royal chambers.

"How did you become a priestess?" he asked her suddenly.

"How?"

"Don't you remember? How did you choose this god to serve?"

"Smoking Mirror chooses," Toci said. "All my life I am his."

"You mean since you were a child? What about your mother and father? Did they give you away to the priests?"

"I do not know. All my life is for Smoking Mirror. No mother, no father."

"Are they dead? Don't you want to know who they are?"

"No."

Martinez stared at Toci. "This is no life for a girl," he said. "You should have yourself a husband. Someone to love."

"I am bride to Smoking Mirror."

"Not much love in that." Martinez leered sleepily at her. "You should have a man you can hold in your arms."

Toci's gaze seemed utterly devoid of guile. "But Smoking Mirror is here," she said. "You have brought him to the temple. The story said he would come. All my life I dreamed of him. Now he is here for me."

Martinez gave up this line of questioning, with a mixture of confusion and dismay, but he soon embarked upon another. "What are you doing here in the palace?" he asked her. "It isn't safe, you know. It might cost you your life."

"I am here for Montezuma. I am here for Smoking Mirror."

"Smoking Mirror? Do you mean your god, or do you mean Don Sebastian? What is Montezuma to him? And what have you done with him?"

"Smoking Mirror sleeps," Toci said. "Montezuma sleeps. But Montezuma dies, and Smoking Mirror lives this night. Smoking Mirror wants blood."

Martinez at once rejected the idea that came to him, then stopped for a moment to consider it. Don Sebastian de Villanueva had been revived by Aztec sorcery, and he was still a vampire. Was it really possible that the cult of Tezcatlipoca planned to feed him with the blood of their deposed monarch? How could they hope to smuggle a living dead man past the walls and through the passages that would bring him to this apartment, a floor above the ground in the only part of the palace taller than one story?

Sunlight streamed through the open window, but Martinez was shuddering.

"So you believe that Don Sebastian is Smoking Mirror," he

said. "I suppose that makes a certain sort of sense, especially when you consider that Montezuma thought Cortez was this other god, the Feathered Serpent."

"Quetzalcoatl."

"Yes," said Martinez. "And he is the rival god of Tezcatlipoca, isn't he? So now you propose to teach Montezuma a lesson by feeding him to Don Sebastian."

He was talking to himself really, trying to piece together the intrigue that had enveloped him, but Toci answered.

"Montezuma knows," she said. "Montezuma knows Smoking Mirror."

This much, Martinez thought, was impossible. He himself had seen the resurrection of Don Sebastian, and he would have sworn that there had been no time for him to visit Montezuma. But what of the other Smoking Mirror, the one who had existed long before Spanish feet had ever touched this soil? Could it be that Cortez really was the Feathered Serpent, and that Don Sebastian really was the Smoking Mirror? The alchemist's mind was unnaturally bright but still far too exhausted to consider the implications. There was magic here, yet in what strange channels did it move? Was there some dark parallel between what happened here and what happened a hemisphere away? Or was it only that the Aztecs had the gift of prophecy, and that their attempt to explain auguries had created relationships where none had really existed?

"Montezuma told you, I suppose," he said sleepily.

"Montezuma said it, this day. Montezuma knows, for many, many days. Before Cortez comes here, Smoking Mirror tells him."

"How does he tell him?"

"A bird. Many days, Cortez not here, a bird comes here. A bird in the palace, not black, not white."

"A gray bird," said Martinez. "Long before Cortez came, Montezuma saw a gray bird in his palace. Well, what of it?"

"A black mirror on his head. Smoking Mirror. Mirror of sky, mirror of stars. Stars go. Mirror of men. Men in gray gold.

Cortez. Montezuma sees him. Montezuma knows. Smoking Mirror tells him."

"So Montezuma knew that Cortez would come," Martinez said slowly. "He should have paid more attention to this bird with the black mirror on its head. It showed him Cortez; no doubt it showed him everything. A remarkable bird. He told you this himself, did he?"

"This day."

"Well," said Martinez. "Your king should have paid more attention to his vision. If a man is lucky enough to know the future, he should have sense enough to act on it. Then again, if he's really seen what lies ahead, I suppose there's nothing he can do to change it. That's why oracles are always enigmatic, so you can't tell what they mean until it's too late. Visions. A bird bringing visions, reflections of Hernan Cortez in a smoking mirror."

He gave a quiet snort that had been intended for a laugh. His head lolled against the wall. His eyes closed. "Smoking Mirror," he said. "Smoking Mirror sleeps."

He sat up with a start. "I'm falling asleep," he said. "I can't do that now." The colors of the tapestries were so brilliant that it hurt to look at them.

"Sleep," said Toci, still standing by the wall.

"It's the food," said Martinez. He tried to get up, but his head swam, and he sank back down again on his stool. "The food was . . . drugged. Of course. I would have done the same thing myself. Even . . . the priest thought of it. And Montezuma wouldn't touch it. He knew they'd try to knock him out. But not Alfonso Martinez —he's a fool. . . ."

He smiled drowsily. "A fool," he mumbled. His head fell back.

"Sleep," said Toci.

Night had fallen by the time Martinez stirred. His neck was stiff and his head was throbbing; in fact, it was discomfort that awakened him. He had not dreamed. The room was dark as he looked around it, and for a moment he imagined that he might be back in a Spanish garret. Then he remembered, and winced at the recollection. He turned his head to peer around, and the slight motion sent a long, dull ache through his brain. Nothing had changed.

Montezuma still lay face up on his mat; his chest rose and fell. And Toci stood like a statue against the wall. Martinez would have sworn that she had never moved, although hours must have passed since he had last seen her. The only difference in the room was the light. The pale, cold rays of a dim and distant moon slanted through the window.

Martinez wondered if Toci had heard him move. Her rigid figure seemed hardly human in the shadows by the wall. He wished his head would clear, so that he could determine his position in the dark affairs of Tenochtitlan. He had cooperated with the priestess in keeping guards out of the royal apartment, but now he wondered why. He sensed that something would happen in this room soon, and considered calling for help. Toci had all but promised him that Montezuma would have a visitor tonight, and such a visit could have only one purpose. But would it help or hinder the fortunes of Alfonso Martinez? Did it even matter now what became of Montezuma? Was there anyone who cared about the king except the people of the black pyramid? And was Martinez one of them?

"He wants death," said the priestess suddenly.

Martinez jumped at the sound of her voice. She knew he was awake. Nothing escaped her, not even in the dark.

"What are you going to do?" he whispered. "Will you kill him? Don't do it. We'll be caught. We'll be punished. They'll blame us, no matter who kills him. What are you going to do?"

"See," said Toci.

Martinez glanced wildly around the chamber of the king. There was nothing to see, nothing moving. And then there was a flicker in the white light of the moon. Something had passed before the window. Martinez felt his scalp tighten and heard his own breathing drown out Montezuma's.

Martinez looked toward the window. He saw the purple sky, the cold shimmering of stars, and the flat white disc that cast its glow upon the floor. Then he saw the long fingers that groped over the sill. It was the upper sill. Something was crawling down the side of the palace and into the room, something that moved as no mortal man could ever move. Now there were two hands, each clutching one side of the window, and now there was a dark head silhouetted against the sky. The head hung down, and long black hair streamed toward the floor. Martinez burrowed into his corner as Montezuma's visitor slithered through the window like some gigantic snake.

Martinez could not bear to look, but he could not shut out the sound of sandals slapping down heavily on the stone floor. Don Sebastian was in the palace, and now Martinez was afraid not to look.

The dark form of the dead sorcerer from Spain stood at the foot of Montezuma's bed. His face was black against the moonlight that illuminated his Aztec robes of red and black and white. He turned slowly toward the dying king, and as he did so the left side of his face was illuminated. The long scar running down over his eye was almost glowing, but the right side of his face was lost in shadow. A disc of black obsidian dangled from the golden chain around his neck, and his naked forearms were bright with gold and jewels.

He stepped to the center of the room. He moved toward the priestess of Smoking Mirror, but only for long enough to acknowledge her presence with a stately bow. Then he turned toward the false physician.

"Do you know me?" he said.

Martinez gibbered.

"I hear that I have much to thank you for," said Don Sebastian de Villanueva. "You cherished my bones, or what was left of them, and you carried me across the sea to this New World, where I am to be a god. Tell me your name."

Martinez complied.

"Alfonso Martinez," said Don Sebastian. "Your reward will be what you deserve. You have done me a strange service, Martinez. You have drawn me back from a world you could not imagine, and set me down in a world that even I could not imagine. Were I more of a philosopher, I might resent your interference. But there are mysteries here for me, and I confess that I am intrigued. I never thought to see this earthly plane again, and I never thought to be a god. I have been on a long journey, and I never thought to see my home again. How long has it been, Martinez? What year is this?"

"Fifteen twenty," said Martinez.

"Twenty-four years. A generation. I am old enough to be dead, Martinez, and now I find that I am born again. And I have you to thank. It is a mixed blessing but I am not ungrateful, for my last stay on earth ended before I had achieved my goals. To make more time for myself I became one of the living dead, but still there were not nights enough."

"Enough for what?" asked Martinez.

"To learn, Martinez. To find a way out of this life that would be more than merely death. For years I studied, and wrote what I discovered in a book. My brother meant to publish it under his name, and thus gain favor with the Inquisition, but he proved treacherous and I was obliged to let him die. The book was burned. Only I know what was in it, but I need to know more, for my spirit is not yet free. Perhaps I shall find what I seek in this new land. In Spain I fed on the blood of criminals and outcasts, provided by my brother, the Grand Inquisitor. It was safer. But here I find magic such as I have never seen before, and I am offered the blood of a king."

Montezuma stirred uneasily, and Toci stepped from the shadows.

"If you kill him," said Martinez, "then you kill me. They think I am a doctor, and he is in my care."

"Be calm," said Don Sebastian. "I learned caution long before you were born. I shall not leave him dead, but only dying. I would leave him altogether but for the urging of this woman. She has plans for me, it seems, and a touch of royal blood will endear me to her."

"Drink," said Toci urgently, and at her words Martinez's mind began to race.

He had seen Toci and Don Sebastian as allies, himself as an expendable interloper, but now he thought again. Did he have any less to offer this exiled vampire than that brown woman? She might be beautiful, but she could hardly speak his tongue, and her magic was utterly alien. Alfonso Martinez and Don Sebastian de Villanueva, on the other hand, were countrymen and colleagues. They were versed in the same school of mysticism, and they spoke a common language. Toci's stilted speech was enough in itself to mark her as a heathen witch. If the Spanish occupation of Tenochtitlan was doomed to end in failure, then there was no reason why a man should not ingratiate himself with the one whose triumph might well prove to be his own.

"Yes, Don Sebastian," said Martinez. "Drink." He stood shakily over Montezuma. "If they want royal blood in your veins, why should you deny them? They think you are their god, and there is no reason to gainsay them."

"This woman has told me of the Smoking Mirror," said Sebastian, "and what it means to them. She says he is their primal god, and that the other gods are only masks he wears. I can hardly argue with her—and not only because she offers me shelter. The god of blood and war and sacrifice is always the first god, Martinez. And I am more than willing to be his incarnation."

"And may you be their king," said Martinez. He felt a weird exhilaration in speaking with a corpse. He had dreamed of necromancy; raising the dead was every wizard's dream, and Martinez felt an awesome power rising within him, even though the wizardry he saw was not his own. Two forces waited in this room with him: the dark sorcery that he knew, raised to unimagined heights in the person of Don Sebastian, and the black magic of an alien race, incarnated in the body of the dark and beautiful young woman who stood silent by the door. He thought of a scale, with two differents sorts of sorcery balanced in it. The weights were

Toci and Don Sebastian, but Martinez was the scale itself. If he could keep them in equilibrium, then both might be made to serve him.

"I am your servant," said Martinez, spreading his arms wide to embrace both the dusky priestess and the pale vampire. At his gesture they moved toward him. Each took one of his hands. His right hand felt warm soft flesh; his left hand felt cold hard fingers. The white moonlight streamed down upon them, and in its glow a pact was sealed. Martinez was enraptured.

Don Sebastian was the first to step away. "There is another here," he said. "We have a priestess, a magician, and a rogue. But what does the king say?"

Montezuma, emperor of the Aztecs, stirred uneasily. He rose halfway up from his bed, and then he spoke.

"Tezcatlipoca," he said.

"The god who warned him," said Sebastian. "The god I am to be."

For a moment Montezuma's eyes were bright; then he sank down upon his woven mat. His face turned toward the wall, exposing his strong brown throat.

"He has spoken," said Martinez.

Don Sebastian did not reply, but he drifted toward the bedside of the king. He kneeled beside it, like a man paying homage, and then his head dipped lower.

Martinez stared. His hand gripped Toci's, and his nails dug into her palm. Yet she remained impassive. He looked into her eyes and saw that they were radiant, but he realized that the light in them was not for him.

Martinez was with his companions, and they had sworn fidelity to him; yet he was lonelier than he had ever been before as he listened to the sounds of a vampire feeding. Toci held Martinez's hand, but she was lost in an ecstasy he could not share. He looked to the walls and watched the woven images of gods he could not name.

7. The Bridge

AFTER Montezuma's body had been burned, the siege of the palace began again. Morning had found the king minutes from death, but still refusing the ministrations of both priest and physician. Cortez himself had stood at Montezuma's bedside, and when the king died he mourned sincerely, as did all the Spanish troops. Montezuma had been their only ally in Tenochtitlan; they had lost their one hope for a safe retreat. As soon as the corpse of the emperor had passed through the lines and into the hands of his people, his brother Cuitlahuac stormed the walls with unbridled ferocity.

The fury of the assault was inspired, at least in part, by the city's belief that the Spaniards had murdered Montezuma. The Spanish soldiers, who had seen the king fall under a rain of stones thrown by his own people, could only view this accusation as another symptom of Aztec madness. Just one man in Tenochtitlan knew the truth about the death of the king, and Alfonso Martinez thought it best to be discreet.

Toci was gone. As soon as he had pronounced Montezuma dead, Martinez had been hurried off to treat the wounded, leaving her behind in the royal chambers. His next glimpse of the priestess came hours later when he stood atop the palace walls with Garcia, watching the funeral procession move through the gates. Cortez had given up Montezuma's body as a mark of respect, and because he hoped the sight of it might sober the Aztecs. Cortez did not get what he wanted, but neither did Martinez.

"Look, there!" Garcia said. "Isn't that your sweetheart?"

Martinez, who had been regarding the spectacle with a combination of guilt and grogginess, followed the direction of Garcia's pointing finger. The sun was in his eyes, and he could hardly recognize the distant figures below him, but something in the bearing of the one Garcia indicated made him fear the worst. As he stared down in dismay the woman turned for an instant to look up at him, as if she had known all along that he was there. It was Toci.

Martinez wondered if there had been any expression on her normally impassive face in the glimpse that she had granted him. He would not have been surprised to see her laughing. As it was, Martinez was more than ready to laugh at himself. He had been betrayed. Of the three who had arranged the death of Montezuma, he was the only one left in the palace to face the wrath of Tenochtitlan. Don Sebastian had disappeared last night, sated with the blood of a king, and now the priestess of Smoking Mirror was marching out to safety as one of Montezuma's mourners. Martinez cursed himself for a fool, and his face flushed with anger and humiliation.

"Don't take it so hard, physician," Garcia said. "Nobody blames you. I'm sure you could have saved him if he'd let you near him, but as it was, what could you do? I'll admit things look black for us, but it's not your fault that Montezuma's dead."

"Idiot!" snapped Martinez, his frustration spilling over on the man next to him. "Do you think I care if he's dead or not?"

"It's the woman you're angry about, then. What were you up to in that pyramid?"

"We were raising . . ." Martinez began, but he stopped himself in time.

"I can guess what you were raising, physician," chuckled Garcia.

Martinez, flattered and furious at the same time, was still attempting to formulate a suitable reply when the first rock sailed past his head.

"Damn them!" roared Garcia. "They're at it again!" He threw up his shield and deflected an arrow with a casual gesture that amazed his companion. "Get down, physician." He knocked Martinez to his knees and covered him with his own huge body. "Start crawling," he said. "We've got to get off this wall."

Martinez could have sworn that he did not even breathe again until he stood beside Garcia in the comparative safety of the courtyard. "Don't go up there again," said Garcia. "I'd be in a hell of a lot of trouble if anything happened to you. I had a barrel of explaining to do when it looked like you'd been caught and sacrificed. We'll need you, physician, at least as long as there are any of us alive."

Garcia's talk was rough, but Martinez sensed a touch of sentiment beneath the bluster, and he was more moved than he would have cared to admit. "Isn't there any hope?" he asked.

"If I could predict the future, then I'd be a hell of a lot better gambler than I am."

Martinez looked across the courtyard. Work on new engines of war had begun days ago on the order of Cortez, who had apparently guessed that all would not go well with his plans to make peace. There were three of them, each almost as tall as the walls of the palace. The towers were wooden, two stories high. Each would hold two dozen men on its upper level, men with muskets. Loopholes studded the sides of the towers near their roofs, which were high enough to reach many of the terraces where the Aztecs stood to drop rocks on their enemies.

"Will they work?" asked Martinez.

"We'll know soon enough. We should be able to kill some of the bastards we couldn't reach before, but I don't know if it'll make any difference. There are just too many of them."

Martinez squinted at the towers, trying to create the impression that he was making an intelligent estimate of their chance for success. "I see the rollers at the bottom," he said at last, "and I see the ropes, but who's going to pull them?"

"Our noble native allies," replied Garcia sardonically.

"They'll be slaughtered."

"Maybe not. I admit it's not a job I'd like, but they're apparently impressed with the ingenuity of the thing. None of these heathens has ever seen a wheel before. Besides, they're not real men like us. They don't seem to care if they live or die."

"That might be their religion," ventured Martinez.

"Maybe so, but it doesn't seem like enough of a reason. Our own religion promises about as much as it can to a man who dies fighting for the faith, but you won't see any Christians pulling on those ropes. Still, they'll have some defense from our cavalry. If we don't protect them, those towers won't be going anywhere."

The shouts and whistles of the Aztecs made a roar outside the walls. "It's too damned hot," Garcia said. A stone the size of a fist fell out of the sky, and he sidestepped it nonchalantly.

Martinez began to watch the walls for signs of death dropping down. He was not in armor, like Garcia.

"Is there anything to eat in this accursed palace?" Martinez asked.

"Maybe," said Garcia. "Go ask the priest. You should be inside anyway. The wounded need you more than I do now. There's nothing for you to do out here but get killed. I'm going for a ride in one of those damned boxes."

Night was falling when Garcia shuffled back into the improvised hospital, followed by dozens of wounded men. He found Martinez stretched out on a pallet among the injured and the dying. The alchemist was asleep, and Garcia had trouble waking him.

"Come on, physician, there's work for you. It's lucky you had a rest, because you're going to need it."

Martinez felt himself hauled rudely from a beautiful dream. He whimpered at the touch of a strong hand on his shoulder and the sound of a rough voice in his ear.

"Go away, Garcia," he said, turning over onto his stomach and burrowing into his straw mat.

Garcia tried to smile, but it turned into a grimace when it reached the bruise on his cheek. "Get up," he said, sharply. "Soldiers have died to keep you safe for this little nap, and now it's your turn to do something for them. What's the matter with you, anyway? You act like you've taken one of your potions!"

He pulled Martinez to his feet and shook him. There was more truth than Garcia imagined in his guess that the physician had spent the day soothing himself with drugs, but Martinez still had a strong sense of self-preservation, and he managed to achieve a semblance of sobriety when he felt Garcia getting rough with him.

"I'm awake," he said. "Stop shaking me. What happened out there?

"Nothing good, physician."

"The towers?"

"Well, they worked, as far as they went, but they didn't go far enough."

"What do you mean?"

"It's the canals. You can't drag a tower through a canal, even with the best will in the world. Those bastards have torn down all the bridges on the causeways that run over the lake."

"And out of the city?"

"Yes. We couldn't go more than a few feet in any direction without running into a stretch of water. We're completely cut off."

Martinez stepped back against a wall and ran his hand over his mouth. "So we're really finished," he said. "I wasn't counting on that."

"Well, it's not so bad. We killed a lot of them. You should have seen us. They couldn't get near the towers at first; they didn't know what was going on. We rolled up to one rooftop after another, and it was heaven to watch the musket fire rip through the animals who've been dropping rocks on us for days. They must have thought they were pretty safe up there, I guess, or they wouldn't have had so many women and children doing the dirty work. You should have seen their faces when we opened fire! It's the first time I've felt right since we came back to this accursed city."

"So at least the roofs are cleared," Martinez said without enthusiasm.

"Only some of them. The towers weren't tall enough to reach the highest roofs, and one tower was just about smashed to pieces when it came too close to the great pyramid. The second one fell into one of the canals. Ours got through, though, or I should say it got back here to the palace. But what a fight it was, physician! There'll be ten of them in Hell tonight for every man of ours who died."

Martinez stepped away from the wall and thrust his face toward Garcia's. "What do I care how many you killed?" he screamed. "However many it was, it wasn't enough. They're still out there, aren't they? Who cares about those heathens? What I want to know is how many of us are going to die!"

"Quiet down," said Garcia. His voice was calm and cold. "I can't have you worrying the men." He moved deliberately toward Martinez, who backed away.

"Keep your distance," Martinez blustered. His voice was quieter. "It looks like I'll be dead soon enough without any help from you."

"Listen, physician. I like you. I don't want to hurt you. But I can't have you talking that way. There might be a chance, you know. There's always a chance."

"Tell me about that, then, and not about how many you killed." Martinez slumped down and sat on the floor, his head between his knees. Garcia squatted beside him.

"We're going to make a portable bridge," he whispered. "Out of the timbers from the tower we saved. One of the reasons we had to go out today was to see how big the gaps in the causeway are. If we can move the bridge across from one hole to the next, some of us will get away. We'll be setting out tomorrow night; they don't seem to like fighting at night. It's a chance."

"It sounds like a sorry night to come," said Martinez, but he adopted Garcia's conspiratorial tone. "So that's it, is it? We're going to run. No gold, no empire, no magic. Some of us may survive, and that's it."

"Do you like it here so much?"

"I could have liked it," muttered Martinez, more to himself than his companion. "It could have been a paradise, if all the promises were kept. But you're right, Garcia. I don't like it here. I don't like it anywhere."

He pulled himself to his feet and looked toward the wounded. "All right, you men," he barked. "Who's hurt the worst here?" The men stirred, and two of them stepped forward, holding a third between them. His right foot was gone, the stump wrapped in a dirty shirt.

Martinez worked throughout the night, improvising the best treatment he could give his patients, and noting with surprised satisfaction that even a week's experience had given him some sort of skill in treating wounds. He had proceeded by trial and error until his successful cases had taught him what to do; his failures were buried. He dispensed most of his drugs, but saved some for himself in case the next night found him alive outside the city. The doses he gave were bigger than usual, since it seemed unlikely that he would have more patients in the future, and the men were sleepily grateful. For Martinez, it was satisfaction enough to know that they would not bother him again, at least not until morning.

Remarkably few men, though, spent the night in the hospital. Most of them, despite their injuries, were in the courtyard working to transform the last tower into a portable bridge. They had caught the enthusiasm that Cortez felt for the idea; Martinez alone thought they had caught a disease called madness. He sat in the sickroom and envied Cortez, whose will was so strong that men would follow him in any enterprise, however fantastic. Martinez had seen the commander infrequently, and spoken with him scarcely at all, but still he sensed the power in the man, and hated him for it. The fools building the bridge were not working out of panic, but out of faith in their leader. The sound of axes and hammers rang through the night, penetrating even the dark recess of the palace where Martinez sat alone among his dead and dreaming patients.

Yet he thought of Cortez less than he thought of another. Cortez might have let his ambition betray an entire army, but that hardly bothered the alchemist compared to the resentment he felt toward Don Sebastian de Villanueva for leaving him behind. He tried to remember exactly what the vampire had said to him. Still, it hardly mattered. Whether the promise had been stated or implied, it had been there. He should not be here now in this charnelhouse; he should be in the black pyramid, sitting at his ease between a living corpse and a warm brown woman, running his hands over great slabs of gold and laughing at the plight of Cortez. Instead, he was no more than an animal caught in the cage of Tenochtitlan. He had countenanced the slaughter of Montezuma, and now he had nothing to show for it but his own plight.

Martinez wandered through the empty halls until he found a window. He sat in the corridor across from it, searching the sky for a sign from Don Sebastian. Even now, there was nothing to prevent his rescue, if that was what the sorcerer he had carried across the sea intended. He looked for black wings, but saw only glittering white stars. His eyes began to sting from the strain of peering into the night, and he thought it would be safe to close them for a few seconds. He opened them once or twice without seeing what he wanted; then he drifted off.

When Garcia found him, it was late morning. Martinez woke reluctantly, the brightness of the day proof that he had been abandoned by his nocturnal allies. He stood quickly, nevertheless, if only to prevent Garcia from shaking him.

"The bridge is ready," said Garcia. "It looks pretty good. We'll be setting out in a few hours. There's something to do first, though, and I think you'll enjoy it."

"And what might that be?"

"Gold, physician. Free gold. All you can carry."

"What?" said Martinez. He was suddenly very much awake.
"You heard me."
"Impossible," said Martinez.
"It's true. Orders from Cortez. There's a room full of gold in this palace. I told you before that we got shares of it. But there's still more left than all of us can carry out of here. The officers have had their share, and Cortez of course, and the royal portion has been set aside; but nobody has taken more than a part of what he could have. We're going to be running for our lives, and it's too heavy. There's just too much gold and too many jewels. But the order is that every man shall have what he wants."

"Let's go," said Martinez.

"Wait a minute, physician. You're supposed to take the men in your charge, at least the ones who can get up, and bring them with you to the treasure room."

"To hell with them, Garcia! From what you tell me, nearly every man here has had his pick of this treasure while I've been asleep, and now you expect me to share the dregs with a bunch of cripples who won't even have the strength to walk out of the city! Are you my friend or aren't you? Take me there now, and then we'll see about the wounded."

"You would hide in this hallway," said Garcia, "and now you blame me because you were nowhere to be found. I looked for you. But it doesn't matter, physician. There's plenty left, and we'll be leaving more behind than we take with us."

Martinez refused to believe there was that much gold. Garcia, he thought again, had no imagination. "If there's so much left," he said, "then there's no reason why you shouldn't take me first. Let me have my share, Garcia, and then I'll see to the wounded."

"It's damned irregular," said Garcia. Then he laughed. "But what the hell, I can see you won't believe me till I show you. Come on."

Garcia led the alchemist through long passageways and empty apartments until they reached the room, near the center of the palace, where Montezuma's father had hidden his treasure.

"There's where we broke through the plaster when Montezuma said we could build our chapel," Garcia said. "And there's what he gave us. Is there enough for you?"

"Oh," said Alfonso Martinez. He could say nothing more.

"Somebody figured it at a million pesos. Maybe more, maybe less. Who can tell? I can count to ten, or twice that if I take off my boots, but a million! A lot of it is gone now, but you can't say you've been cheated, can you?"

Martinez stared. At one end of the long, low hall was a rough-hewn statue of the Virgin. Beside it was a pulpit, and a crucifix hanging on the wall. But Martinez hardly noticed them. At the other end of the room the wall was shattered, the hole in its plaster revealing the secret chamber hidden beyond. And below the hole, a fortune.

Gold was piled on the floor like kindling. Much of the Aztec treasure had been melted into small bars, which were stacked as high as a man and many times as wide. There was a great wheel of the yellow metal in one corner, elaborately engraved. Martinez lusted after it, but realized that he would never be able to lift the thing. Here was half of what he had dreamed of, yet more than fate would let him have. He saw pots full of shining stones, and wished that he knew more about them. Were they really precious, or just the baubles of a primitive tribe? They glittered, but so did the gold. And there were pieces that combined both gold and jewels. One of them was an ugly figure that reminded him of Smoking Mirror.

It was shaped like a skull, and was about the same size. It seemed to be made of beaten gold, but there was a wide band of blue stones around the eyes, and another around the mouth.

"I like this," Martinez said. He picked it up. The eye sockets were filled with gleaming black stone, but as he held it he recognized the teeth as unmistakably human. "It doesn't weigh much," he said, ignoring the uncomfortable fact that the thing was undoubtedly the head of a man, however embellished it might be.

"Might not be worth much for the space it takes," Garcia suggested.

Martinez shrugged and thrust it into his pack, into the same place where the skull of Don Sebastian had rested. "So you're a jeweler, Garcia," he said. "Show me what you took."

Garcia removed his battered helmet and pulled out a package wrapped in cloth. He unwrapped it modestly and displayed a dozen pale green stones.

"That's all? What are they?"

"I've been told the natives prize them. Gold doesn't seem to be worth much here. They only like it because it's soft, and it's easy to make toys from it. I'm thinking that if I make it out of the city, these green rocks may help me get back to the coast."

"You're a fool, Garcia. What if you make it back to Spain? Will you be happy with a few pretty rocks?"

"I'll be happy if I make it back at all."

"That's not enough for Alfonso Martinez. How many times do you think a man gets a chance at a prize like this?" Martinez picked up two heavy gold bars, one at a time, and dropped them into his pack. He did this gently, so as not to break the skull.

"Those things are too heavy, physician. Only an idiot would try to carry them. Gold isn't worth much if it costs a man his life."

"And a man's life isn't worth much if he has no gold," said Martinez. He looked Garcia squarely in the eye and took two more of the small gold bars. Then he took a handful of the green stones out of an earthenware pot. "Listen," he said. "If things get too rough, I can always throw away the gold. But to leave it here, without even trying! I'm not philosopher enough for that."

"You may be right," Garcia said. "Our men have been laughing at yours, the ones from the second expedition, because they were greedy and took too much. Still . . ." he said, and he picked up one of the gleaming ingots, "I guess we can always throw it away."

"Of course," said Martinez.

"Though I think it's easier to pick up gold than it is to let go of it," said Garcia. "Still," he added, selecting another heavy bar.

"Absolutely," said Alfonso Martinez. "If these savages are going to send us home again, the least they can do is pay our passage." He chuckled uneasily, but felt a little better when

Garcia joined him. Their laughter echoed through the empty chamber, and the sound of it silenced both of them.

"I can't see what you want with that skull," Garcia said. "It's too big."

"It reminds me of something. And it doesn't weigh much. It's hollow, like your head, or mine. I think it's an emblem of that god of theirs, the one who played host to me in the black pyramid. I wouldn't want to forget him, would I?"

"Whatever you say," replied Garcia, suddenly grim. "But I'd rather forget those gods now, and pray to our God to get us out of here." He walked slowly toward the crucifix and knelt before it.

"Garcia," said the alchemist. He tried to follow his companion, but something stopped him. Garcia's head was bowed and his lips were moving silently.

Martinez took another step forward. His burden was heavier than he had imagined. It was difficult to move. "Maybe I've taken too much," he said to himself. He wanted to stand beside his friend, but found that he could not.

"Christ," said Martinez, calling on a name he had all but forgotten. He could not cross the room. "It's the skull," he muttered to himself. "Maybe it really is Smoking Mirror. Or Don Sebastian."

Whatever the skull represented, its dead weight appeared to be dragging Martinez down. Perhaps there was nothing more to this sudden immobility than his own realization that joining Garcia would be an affront to the dark god of the Aztecs—the one whose power had brought a dead man back to life—but Martinez decided that he had no further business in the treasure room. While the soldier prayed, the alchemist crept quietly away.

8. City of Water

A LIGHT rain began to fall shortly after sunset. To everyone else in the palace, the coming of the night meant that it was time for the escape from Tenochtitlan; but for Martinez the darkness meant that Don Sebastian had risen. If the vampire intended to rescue him, this was the time to do it. In a few hours it would be too late.

The alchemist was almost frantic as he watched the preparations for departure. Men moved swiftly and silently through the palace and the courtyard. The Aztecs had retired; the city was quiet. If everyone worked carefully enough, they would not betray their intention before the moment when the gates were thrown open. It was this that worried Martinez. No one outside the walls knew what was happening. Even if the Smoking Mirror cult did have plans for him, they had no way of knowing that this might be his last night in Tenochtitlan. More than once Martinez was tempted to cry out, to shout a warning that would rouse the city. It would be worthwhile if his scream for help reached the black pyramid, but by now he was not sure whether Smoking Mirror and his followers cared what became of Alfonso Martinez. Still, he might have tried it, even at the cost of every life in the palace, but he realized that he would be cut down as a traitor as soon as he opened his mouth.

As it was, he had no choice but to follow Hernan Cortez out of the city, risking his neck and leaving behind him all the wealth and power that could have come within his grasp.

"We don't have enough to worry about," Garcia said. "We have to get wet, too."

Martinez whirled. Lost in his own thoughts, he had not noticed the big soldier.

"Does it matter?" asked Martinez bitterly.

"It might be good, come to think of it. These savages usually don't like to fight at night, and the rain may be just the thing we need to send them all home to bed. Maybe Botello was right."

"Botello?"

"An astrologer, or so he says. Just a soldier, really, but he's made some good guesses before. Or maybe he actually knows something. Anyway, he predicted that this would be the best time for our retreat."

"There's no good time for a retreat," Martinez said, still full of regret, and angry with himself for not thinking to make his own reading of the stars.

"Spoken like a soldier," said Garcia, grinning. "But what else is there to do? We've got a whole city against us. We're not ancient heroes like the ones you read about in books."

"Horatio at the bridge," muttered Martinez, looking toward the wooden structure in the middle of the courtyard. "But we have to carry our own bridge with us."

"Well, it's solid enough. Nothing wrong with the way it's built. The hard part will be moving it."

"I'm not really looking forward to this, Garcia. What's the order of march to be?"

Garcia looked at him quizzically. "I never knew you were a strategist."

"I'm just trying to figure out the safest place to be when we march out of here. For the wounded, you understand."

"You've got me, physician. I can tell you how things are set up, but I'm damned if I can tell you the best place to be. It all depends on what happens. The advance is under Sandoval. They'll be the first out if things go well, but the first to fight if things don't. The rear is under Alvarado, and he's a good man, in spite of the way he messed things up when Cortez was gone. He might be in a good spot, if the advance has to fight its way through, but he might still be in the city when the Aztecs are aroused, and then he'll be in trouble. That's assuming they're not going to be waiting for us. It's hard to say."

"Where's Cortez?"

"In the middle. He has the king's share of the treasure, and Montezuma's son and daughters, and most of the artillery. That might be the best spot, but it might be the worst. I'm no astrologer. The middle won't have to break through, and they won't get stuck in the back, but they won't have the advantages of either. Your guess is as good as mine."

"I don't like the rear," Martinez said. "They might catch the brunt of the fighting if the city isn't ready now; and if the Aztecs are waiting for us beyond the city, they'll have no advantage except the chance to fall back to the palace and be killed a little later."

"True," said Garcia.

"And I don't like the front much. I'm not the man for charging into a rank of stone swords, and of course my patients won't be worth much in the vanguard. Then again, the front may be the only ones to get through. But I think I like the middle best of all. Moderation in all things, Garcia. Besides, that's where Cortez is, and he is where the gold is."

"You should have been a general, physician. I'll see if I can set it up. What are you going to do with the wounded who can't walk?"

"Somebody will have to carry them, I guess, but it won't be me."

"There are some horses, but I think they want them for the gold. I'll see what I can arrange for you."

"When are we leaving?"

"Midnight. You'd better get your men ready to travel, physician."

Garcia started off toward a group of officers standing in the courtyard, and Martinez ducked back into the doorway. The sound of the rain faded as he wandered with dragging feet toward his hospital and the dozens of men who waited there. He had no idea what to do with them; the only feeling he had for them was resentment.

When he entered the hall where the wounded lay, the first thing he did was to look to his own welfare. He gathered up all his possessions, sorry that it took no longer. His pack was on his back, and he was wearing all the armor he had been able to scavenge from the dead. He owned nothing else. The pack, which he had sewn himself, had been on his back for most of his adult life. He had walked the roads of Spain with it, but never before felt the weight of gold bars within it. He should have been happy, but he was too afraid of what lay before him and too sorry about what he left behind. He stood in the doorway and shouted to his broken army.

"Get up, you men! Get up, if you can, because we're getting out of here!"

The priest celebrated mass at midnight. Thousands of men stood in the courtyard to hear him, a comparative handful of Spaniards and a horde of their Indian allies who had no idea what the ceremony meant. The warm, thin rain fell on all of them.

Alfonso Martinez shuffled nervously back and forth. He was surrounded by the walking wounded, many of them standing only because they had another injured man to lean on. A few were on stretchers, accompanied by healthy soldiers who had volunteered to carry them, at least as long as seemed practical. Martinez doubted that any of them would get through, and he was not much more hopeful about himself.

"Everyone seems so cheerful," he whispered to Garcia. "Do they really think we'll just walk out without a fight?"

"They don't know what to think, and neither do I. Ask me again in an hour. Meanwhile, we might as well be cheerful. At least we're doing something, and not just waiting to be starved or slaughtered like pigs."

Martinez looked skeptically up and down the line. The center, where he stood, was the most congested section. The artillery, the ammunition wagons, and the carts filled with baggage were in front of him. Ahead of these was a company of selected officers, all mounted, with Cortez at their head. There were horses in this group that did not bear men, but gold for the king of Spain.

"I'd like to be on one of those horses," said Martinez.

"So would I, physician, and so would every man that's walking. But what would you have? They're carrying gold, and so are you and I. Admit the truth. That money is worth more to the crown than any one of us. Why do you think we came here in the first place?"

Martinez did not reply. Instead he peered off toward the distant head of the caravan, where the portable bridge stood, obscured by mist and drizzle. A squadron of bold cavaliers waited behind the bridge to lead the attack.

"There should be three bridges," said Martinez. "You told me yourself that there are three gaps in the causeway for us to cross."

"We've done all we can. Why don't you shut up?" Garcia turned away.

Martinez looked toward the rear. The priest was making his way along the line, blessing the men as they stood ready for action. The officers of the rear guard bowed their heads. Martinez felt his spine quiver. The raindrops falling on his helmet suddenly sounded like gunfire. The priest came closer, and his droning Latin cut through the rustle of the line of nervous soldiers. Martinez retreated rapidly into the shadows.

He waited against the wall until the priest had passed, then made his way back into the line. "Call of nature," he said to no one in particular.

"You all set now?" asked Garcia. "I swear you're the jumpiest man I ever saw. You must have a fever or something. I'd look after myself, if I were you."

"Tomorrow," said Martinez.

"Tomorrow, is it? Tomorrow. I've never known a man like you. Well, here's luck. They're opening the gates."

Horses stirred restlessly, their hooves echoing throughout the courtyard. The rain hissed down, and thousands of men drew their breath at once in a great gasp. From where Martinez stood, the gates made no sound, swinging inward like an image from a dream. Beyond them lay the silent city.

Martinez froze for an instant, waiting for a horde of savages to rush into the palace, but they did not materialize. The plaza was empty.

The bridge rolled out into the night, and the advance party followed it, moving like ghostly riders through the mist. They were lost from sight by the time there was room for Martinez to take his first step forward. His feet moved reluctantly, and he winced at every creak of wagon wheels, every cough from an injured man. Then he moved resolutely forward, his eyes fixed on the back of Hernan Cortez. He dared not stop to search the sky for dark messengers from Smoking Mirror.

As they passed through the gate, he glanced at Garcia, who grinned at him and winked. Martinez began to feel a conspiratorial glee. If they really did succeed in sneaking out of Tenochtitlan, it would be a triumph of guile and stealth, qualities that Martinez found much more to his liking than boldness or bravery. He crossed the plaza in an ecstasy of fear and pride.

The path of the Spanish army lay along the Tacuba causeway. It was not the way they had entered Tenochtitlan, but it was the shortest route to the shores of the lake that surrounded the city. The long line of soldiers turned west.

"We should have been in the front," whispered Martinez. "Where do you think they are by now?"

"On the causeway, probably," said Garcia.

Martinez followed him out of the great square and into a narrow street black with shadows. At the instant when he stepped into the darkness, the alchemist thought he saw something drift over his head. If he had been a little more certain, he would have screamed. As it was, he stopped dead in his tracks and looked anxiously upward until the man following ran into him.

"Get moving, will you? What are you waiting for?"

"I thought I saw something," Martinez said to the voice whispering behind him.

"I know, I've seen a million Aztecs since we left the palace. Forget it, you're imagining things. They won't sneak up on us."

Martinez moved ahead without answering, and finally passed through the street of shadows. The causeway stretched out before him, pale and faint in the misty downpour. Men were moving along it in dim rows; beneath them the waters of the lake gleamed like black obsidian.

Suddenly the line of soldiers stopped. As far ahead as Martinez could see, no one was moving. "What's going on?" he asked Garcia.

"They must have reached the first gap the Aztecs made," Garcia said. "They're putting the bridge into place."

Martinez waited while the minutes passed.

"Why don't they hurry?" he whispered frantically.

"I think they've done it, physician. Look. We're moving again."

Martinez went limp with relief. He looked around and saw smiles on the faces of even the most badly injured soldiers. There was a general rush forward. When Martinez stepped onto the causeway, he felt that he was halfway home. The feeling lasted only a moment.

"What's that?" he said to Garcia. "Are they crazy up there? Why are they shouting?" The unmistakable sound of men's voices drifted back across the lake.

"I don't think those are our men shouting, physician. I think we've been seen."

The wail of the conch shells the Aztecs used for horns cut through the falling mist. And from behind the Spaniards, deep in the heart of the city, came the echoing boom of a gigantic drum, the one that stood on the pyramid of the war god. Martinez cringed, anticipating an attack, but nothing happened.

"They've sounded the alarm," Garcia said, "but we might have a minute or two. We've got to get across that bridge." He cupped both hands around his mouth and shouted: "Move, you sons of snails! They're right behind us!"

All need for caution gone, the army of Cortez raced for their bridge. Thousands of rushing feet thudded on the stone of the causeway, yet hardly a man spoke, as if each hoped that silence might still save him. Martinez was in sight of the bridge when the crowd ahead forced him to stop. Instantly his patients bunched up behind him. Caught in a crush, he could scarcely move.

"Keep going!" he screamed to the men ahead of him, squirming up and down against the crowd to see the wooden planks that waited just out of his reach. "Run!"

"They can't," grunted Garcia, half embracing him. "Why do you think they've stopped? The advance has reached the second hole in the causeway, and the bridge is still back here."

Martinez, near panic, tried to force his way forward, and someone's flailing arm struck him in the face. He would have fallen, but there was no room. Slowly the mass of men struggled onward, less through their own power than the weight of the mob behind them. Martinez stumbled onto the bridge.

"They'll be here soon," Garcia said. "If we can get everyone across and pull up the bridge, they won't be able to follow us. Unless they take to their canoes . . ."

As the men struggled silently, Martinez heard a sound like the flapping of a hundred wings. He thought for an instant of a plague of vampire bats, then thought again, this time of paddles in the water of the lake. He looked from side to side, and saw a flotilla of Aztec canoes bearing down on the causeway. The sound of their progress was like the whisper of the warm rain, and so was the sound of the arrows that showered down upon the bridge.

"Garcia! Stay by me."

"Don't worry. I can't leave."

Martinez felt two arrows rattle off his helmet. Screams rang out all around him, but he ignored them and pushed on toward freedom as soon as he realized he had not been killed. The man he pushed against slumped backward unexpectedly, and Martinez found himself face to face with a corpse. He turned in terror, and saw the soldier with the missing foot forced off the bridge and into the water.

"Get me out of this!" Martinez wailed. The dead man in front of him dropped into an unexpected opening, and Martinez stumbled over the corpse without a second thought. He would have gladly slashed his way through the ranks of his comrades, but had no room to draw his sword. Someone thrust a shield above the crowd and Martinez grabbed it, holding it just above his head. The impact of arrows jolted his arm.

All around him men were slipping off the bridge. Some were slain, most forced off by the thrashing of the mob. Martinez kept to the middle. Thrown forward by a gigantic surge from the rear, he found himself beyond the bridge. The ranks of the Spanish forces were in chaos, and the order of the march was broken. Martinez felt himself smashed into a baggage cart that had started out a dozen yards ahead of him. Six arrows stuck out of it.

"Get over it!" roared Garcia. His huge hand grabbed the alchemist's arm and hauled him up. Martinez felt the arrows break as Garcia pushed past the obstacle. He fell on his knees and was almost trampled, but he fought his way to his feet with the help of the big soldier. A woman staggered past him, one of the prisoners. She might have been Montezuma's daughter. She had an arrow in her face.

"Nearly all across," shouted Garcia. Martinez risked a look back and saw the horsemen of the rear guard rushing across the bridge, trampling living and dead alike. And he heard the cry from one of the captains: "Bring up the bridge!"

The war canoes had reached the causeway. The fall of arrows was unceasing, but now it was augmented by the attack of long spears from the boats. Black stone blades shot up from below, slashing men and gutting horses. The silence of a few minutes before became a roar of agony.

Everyone was screaming for the bridge, and Martinez could see why. He was within sight of the second gap himself. Someone's blood splashed across his face. There was no room to move, no room to hide. And there was no bridge to span the hole ahead of him.

"It's stuck," screamed somebody from the rear. He looked back and through the rain saw dozens of men working to free the bridge. He could hardly believe they were still there. Nothing on earth or anywhere else could have persuaded Martinez to stay behind. They were soldiers. But they could not dislodge the bridge. The weight of frantic thousands had driven it too far down. Heartsick, Martinez turned away from it, and realized that he could not find Garcia.

He had never been so frightened. Better the purposeful approach of a monster than this random slaughter that respected no one. He longed for the horse-faced veteran as a man might long for a lover.

"Garcia!" he cried. "Garcia!" An arrow glanced off his hand. It was a wound too small to consider, but it convinced Martinez that he was vulnerable. He was cold all over. He looked toward the gap ahead of him, and saw the officers of the advance leap into the lake. Their horses were tall enough to keep their heads above water, but the canoes were bearing down on them. Still, the officers had no choice. Their own men were driving them toward death.

A man in gleaming armor rode down into the water, and Martinez recognized him as Cortez. When he struggled up to the other side of the gap, a cheer went up from the ranks of the soldiers, and Martinez joined in it. Crossing the gap was not impossible, and Cortez had proved his worth again. Martinez was grateful for the lesson, since every second drove him closer to the edge of the precipice where the Aztecs had broken the stone ramp leading to the shore. Then again, Cortez had a horse. And there was a third gap still to come.

A big man careened toward him and broke his fall with his fingers in the alchemist's face. Martinez stumbled toward the edge of the causeway, but stopped his cursing when he recognized his unwilling assailant.

"Garcia! Luis! You're alive!"

"Just. I've been looking for you."

Feathered warriors streamed up from the lake, their black blades slashing. They were dangerously close. The causeway was already insufferably crowded, but somehow they found room to stand.

"Look out!" Martinez yelled. He clutched Garcia and spun him half around, right into the path of a stone sword. The black blade hacked at Garcia's shoulder, and he dropped to the gray rocks of the causeway.

"Sweet Jesus," said Garcia. His right arm flopped away from him, and someone kicked it into the lake.

Martinez dropped to his knees beside his friend. Red spattered everywhere, and was as quickly washed away by rain. Screaming soldiers would have trampled them, but Martinez fended them off with his stolen shield.

"Garcia!"

"Fix it, physician. I'm really hurt this time."

"I know, I know."

"Stop the blood! Do something!"

Someone kicked Martinez. "Listen, Luis," he said. "I'm no doctor. I'm a fraud. I don't know what to do."

"Really?" asked Garcia, offering up a caricature of the smile Martinez had so often seen before. "Damn you, Alfonso Martinez, you're more of a rogue than I suspected."

"What can I do?" wailed Martinez. Blood pumped out onto the feet of the soldiers rushing past.

"Nothing, physician," said Garcia. "You certainly fooled me."

Tears tore into the alchemist's eyes. He looked for something to stop the flow of blood. "I'm sorry, Luis."

"Forget it. A better man than you are couldn't do much now."

"I liked you," said Martinez.

"Yes . . ." said Garcia. He twitched spasmodically and rolled toward the edge of the causeway. Rain splashed into his upturned face.

A dozen men rushed by, kicking Garcia closer to the water.

Martinez drew his sword and slashed out at them hysterically. "Bastards!" he screamed. The thrust of the retreat was driving him away from Garcia. An Aztec warrior leaped up, and Martinez split his skull without a second thought.

"Well played, physician," Garcia said. He slipped closer toward the edge.

A careening horseman came between them for an instant, and when he passed, Garcia was gone. Martinez rushed to the edge of the causeway, and beyond it he saw his friend's face, no more than a pale blur against the black water. A canoe swept over the spot, and Luis Garcia was lost in the lake of Tenochtitlan.

"Garcia!" shouted Martinez. He felt a moment of overwhelming grief, then noticed all at once that he was hanging half over the brink, with the canoe and its warriors bearing down upon him. He forgot Garcia in the scramble to regain his footing while he dodged a barrage of arrows.

When he finally reached the gap, Martinez found it filled with broken wagons, upturned cannons, and dead horses. Corpses floated everywhere, and a strongbox, no doubt full of gold, was wedged between two shattered carts. Yet there was no clear path to the other side, only islands of debris emerging from the surface of the water. Martinez tried to estimate its depth in the seconds he spent poised miserably at the end of the causeway—until a spear flew past his head, reminding him that this was no time for speculation. He stepped gingerly onto the bottom of an upturned ammunition wagon.

The boards lurched ominously when his foot touched them. Martinez waved his arms frantically and jumped for the first shape he saw. He landed on the barrel of a cannon, the breath knocked out of him. His hands slipped on the wet iron, and he slithered down toward the waiting lake. Martinez caught the spokes of one of the cannon's wheels, but it spun around, dropping him up to his neck in dark water. He looked desperately from side to side, and screamed for help when he saw another Aztec canoe, filled with half-naked men dressed in spotted skins. Their paddles cut through the water with grim regularity.

If he held on to the wheel, they would reach him in a matter of seconds. He took the biggest breath he could and dropped down into the lake.

He heard a splash and a gurgle, then was overwhelmed by silence. As he sank into the depths of the lake, a dim and peaceful sanctuary, he watched the bottom of the canoe pass over him. He held his breath for as long as possible, then kicked upward for the surface.

He barely moved. Something was holding him back. His ears and nose were clogged with water; half his air rolled up in bubbles before he realized he was trapped. Then he remembered the gold. He had forgotten it for hours, but now it was dragging him down to the bottom of the lake. His feet touched mud; his hands worked hysterically.

He remembered his advice to Garcia. It had sounded so reasonable to say that the gold could always be thrown away if necessary, but now he was drowning and his fingers could hardly reach the fastenings of the deadly container on his back. Struggling to untie wet knots, Martinez felt his lungs exploding. The last of his air streamed out in glistening globes that rushed upward past his face. With one arm twisted behind him, he reached into the pack. His head was throbbing.

He grasped one of the golden bars and wrenched it through the opening. He kicked feebly, but he was still too heavy. He reached back again, his hand groping desperately in the layers of cloth. He was half unconscious when he yanked out the second gold bar, but he felt a little lighter. Suddenly inspired, he tore off his helmet, and then the shield still strapped to his left arm. He felt himself drift upward, but far too slowly.

His fingers scraped at the pack, then slipped inside once more. He felt something round and hard: the jewel-encrusted skull. On the brink of death, his senses were unnaturally acute. His fingers traced each blue-green stone, slipping over the surface and into the sockets where the eyes had gleamed. Alfonso Martinez was dying. His hand twitched and slipped down to the death's head's teeth. The teeth of Smoking Mirror and of Don Sebastian.

The touch of the thing shocked him, and his body reacted to the pain with a paroxysm that propelled him, flailing, to the surface of the lake.

He had time to inhale only once, then a strong brown hand caught him by the throat and dragged him up. More dead than alive, Martinez dimly sensed that he had been pulled into a war canoe. Someone had saved him from drowning; he wanted to know nothing more. He slumped into the bow, his head in someone's lap, and sensed dimly that the fighting was over. Strong strokes carried him toward one shore or the other.

The night was quieter, though distant shouts still drifted feebly across the lake. The light rain fell on his face, and Martinez opened his eyes. He was cradled in the arms of someone whose face he dimly recognized. He was too weak for fear. He looked at the face, but it was upside down. Its eyes betrayed it, finally, for they were blind. The man who held Martinez was the high priest of Smoking Mirror.

All the men in the canoe wore the spotted black and gold of the jaguar. Martinez stirred, and tried to raise himself. The canoe bumped against something. It was not the distant shore, but rather the stone side of a canal. He was back in Tenochtitlan.

The spotted knights lifted him from the boat. A woman walked toward him. Her face was grave; her skin was golden. Martinez longed to embrace her, but hardly had the strength to take a single step. She gazed on him with a thoughtfulness that touched him more than the playful looks of many women he had known.

And then she stepped aside. Behind her was a tall, dark man. His face was white, and he was dressed in robes of black and white and red. His hair hung to his shoulders; a disc of obsidian hung from his neck by a golden chain.

"You need not have run," said Don Sebastian de Villanueva.

The false physician slumped in the arms of the men who held him. The fighting was finished, and Alfonso Martinez had found a new home.

9. The Black Knife

"SIT, Alfonso Martinez. And tell me what you know of Smoking Mirror."

Don Sebastian de Villanueva stood in the same room in which he had been revived less than a week before. His long, pale fingers stroked the miniature idol of the Aztec god as it sat upon its pedestal in the depths of the black pyramid. He smiled, but it only made him look more sinister.

"Sit, Martinez. You have nothing to fear from me."

Martinez had his doubts about the promise, but he obeyed. His stool was the only piece of furniture in the room, unless he counted the stone slab where he had watched one man die so that another could be reborn. The slanting walls and ceiling still disturbed him, but he was glad to see that at least his armed guards had been dismissed. Nonetheless, he found it disconcerting to be alone with a man who had died two dozen years ago.

"Longer than that," said Don Sebastian. "I left the earth then, but I met what men call death nine years before, at the siege of Malaga."

Martinez nearly knocked over the stool when he realized that Don Sebastian could read his thoughts, but he managed to catch himself before he tumbled to the floor. "Clairvoyance," he said in an undertone. He had learned as a boy that things were less threatening when he had a name for them, and understood that it would not do to appear untutored in the ways of wizardry. "Can you always do that?"

"Not always. But when I am alone with a man, and waiting for his answer, sometimes I do not have to wait. Such a gift is doubly welcome in a city like this one, where the inhabitants all speak an alien tongue."

"All but the priestess," answered Martinez. "Do you understand her?"

"I hear more than she tells me."

"I wish I did. She sounds like she's making sense, but I can't be sure."

"We have much to learn from her, Martinez. But I confess that it is a pleasure to converse with a man who knows my own language. You would have been worth saving for that alone, though I hope to find other uses for you."

"I am conscious of the honor," Martinez said uneasily. "I am happier here than at the bottom of the lake. And a man with my interests could hardly hope for a wiser teacher than you. It took me years to get your skull, and even then I thought it no more than a talisman. I never dreamed that I would speak with you. Well, perhaps I did dream it, but nothing more."

"And perhaps I dreamed that you would be the cause of my resurrection. I hardly remember. But tell me. How did you acquire this . . . What did you call it? A talisman?"

"I stole the skull from a dwarf. He was a master magician, the greatest I had found in Spain. And you were legendary as the source of his power."

"Did you kill him?"

"Not really. I hit him a few times, but I don't think he died. I robbed him and fled to the New World, masquerading as a physician."

"Then you know nothing of medicine?"

"I knew enough to fool Cortez."

"I wish you knew more. There is a sickness among these people; the Spaniards brought it with them. The pox. I fear it will kill many, and I hoped that you might work against it."

"I might do something," offered Martinez, suddenly fearful that he had been tested and found wanting.

"No matter. I am less concerned with the health of these people than with their knowledge. The magic that brought me here exceeds anything I have ever experienced, and I would know more of it. I understand you witnessed the ceremony."

"I did," said Martinez.

"You must tell me of it. This woman Toci has done what no witch in Europe could do. It is one thing to raise the dead, but quite another to raise the dead who have died a second death. There is magic here, Martinez, such magic as you and I have never encountered. And I mean to master it."

"To what end? Those who study the supernatural do so most often for some purpose. They want wealth, or fame, or power. Some even do it for love. What do you want?" Martinez was suddenly abashed. "I only ask, you understand, so that I may help you."

"It would be pleasant, certainly, to rule this city," said Don Sebastian. "That should be motive enough for you, Martinez. I see that you are still very much of the earth. There are pleasures here, to be sure, and I would not place myself above them. But the greatest pleasure of all is knowledge. There are secrets in this city that I have yet to fathom."

"I believe that they have found the philosopher's stone," said Martinez. A second later he wished he had kept silent, for fear that his motives might seem too mercenary.

"Do you think so?" asked Don Sebastian.

"Where else does all this gold come from? They have so much that they scarcely value it. Montezuma gave Cortez a king's ransom. Tons of it—more than an army could carry!"

"And you lost your share," said Don Sebastian. His tone was unsympathetic, but his gesture was generous. He stripped a thick gold bracelet from his arm and offered it to Martinez. "Take this. I will find you more."

Martinez reached out eagerly. He was conscious of a certain

shame, intensified by a reluctance to touch dead flesh, but the gold was irresistible.

"So you think they make the gold," said Don Sebastian.

"Is it true?"

"I had not thought to ask. It hardly matters, Martinez, for they do not value it as we did in Spain. Power is the coin of the realm in Tenochtitlan, and it can only be won in warfare or witchcraft. There is no way to steal it."

Don Sebastian stepped away from the idol and moved toward Martinez. His white hand crept into his robe to withdraw an Aztec dagger, and Martinez cringed involuntarily at the sight of it.

"Look at this," said the wizard. "Look at the blade. Obsidian is worth more than gold in this land. The people call it 'tezcat' —from Tezcatlipoca, Smoking Mirror, the god whose incarnation I am destined to achieve. The black stone makes the mirrors, too, like this one I wear. The knife and the mirror, Martinez. These are the keys to power. Forget the gold."

Martinez did not forget, but did his best to think as though he had. It would not be easy to deal with a man who could read his mind. Yet Martinez was enough of a magician to have learned that one of the first secrets of sorcery was the technique of creating a vivid mental image. He filled his mind with the picture of the sacrificial dagger, confident that only this would be transmitted to his interrogator. Don Sebastian looked at him intently, his pale face devoid of all expression. Then he handed Martinez the knife.

"Is this . . . the one?" asked Martinez.

"It is. The woman Toci gave it to me—a small gift compared to the life that it restored. Examine it."

Martinez held the knife gingerly in both hands. The blade was short, with ragged edges, as if it had been hacked out, stone against stone, centuries before human hands had learned to work in metal. The hilt might well have been made of the same black stone, but there was no way to tell, since it was covered with a mosaic of jewels and precious stones. The handle took the form of a kneeling figure, bent over double with its hands reaching toward the blade. The head was crude, and thick with brilliant colors, but it looked like a skull to Martinez. He ran his right hand nervously along the edges of the figure, and the knife slipped suddenly, scraping his fingers against jagged blade.

The cut was small, yet it bled profusely. Martinez rubbed the blood away with his sleeve, but more welled up at once. He looked up at Don Sebastian and saw the dead eyes staring down. "Blood," said Martinez, wishing at once that he was mute.

The vampire spoke. "Have no fear," he said. "I am well provided for, and have no need to feed on you. I am not a wild beast, Alfonso Martinez. Blood sustains me, but it is not the reason for my being. Think of me not as a monster, but as a fellow magician."

The argument was persuasive, at least as long as Martinez kept his gaze averted from the lean, pale face, the lank black hair, the dull and dark eyes, the long bright teeth. As if to prove himself, the vampire turned his back and walked away.

Martinez was more grateful for the gesture than he would readily admit. He would have gladly been alone. He wanted time to decide whether he had found a wonderful opportunity or a terrible dilemma. What good was Aztec gold to him in a city where it counted for nothing? And how far could he advance himself in a world where wisdom and courage were the only virtues? He knew he was not much of a sorcerer, and no hero at all.

"You have a place here," said Don Sebastian, speaking to the farthest wall of the dark, angled room. "I have need of you. I am a creature of the night, Martinez, and this is a world awash in sun. You will be my eyes. There is much to learn here, more than I can learn in the hours of darkness. I depend on you to witness that which I cannot see, and to report it to me faithfully. You will be my colleague, and between us we shall master the magic of Mexico. I ask you to trust me. I have never betrayed one who was true to me."

"What would you have me say?" Martinez asked boldly, hoping that his cynicism would work to good effect.

"You have no choice, of course," said Don Sebastian de Villanueva, "as the only Spaniard left alive in the city, I believe, and here only by the sufferance of a walking corpse and a band of bloodthirsty savages. Remember that your isolation makes you unique. The rewards your position might bring are incalculable, and you are invaluable to me, at least for now."

"I am yours. But I am not such a fool as to imagine that my welfare is your principal concern."

"Of course. I like a man who worries. To do less is to confess stupidity. Be cautious, Martinez, if it pleases you, but remember that too much caution is another sort of folly. Believe in me, and you will find me a generous master."

"And me a devoted servant," said Martinez, making a bow that turned into a nervous stumble when the vampire turned again to face him.

"It must be as you say," replied Sebastian, "for these people believe I am a god."

"And you?" Martinez asked despite his fear. "What do you believe? Are you a god?"

"What is a god?" asked Don Sebastian, seating himself on the stone slab where he had found another incarnation. "Only a being with more power than its followers. And one who gains strength from their devotion. In short, a creature much like a vampire."

"Of course, of course. The powers are inside us and outside us, and they grow stronger from the correspondence. But much of this is sophistry. I ask you outright: Are you the Smoking Mirror they have waited for?"

"I like it that you are rash enough to challenge me."

"Not a moment ago you promised me your patronage. Am I to begin by doubting you?"

"If I am to answer your question, you must answer mine. Let me ask again. What do you know of Smoking Mirror?"

"Precious little. These people are like the ancients; they have many gods. And Smoking Mirror is their dark god, the power of evil, the source of black magic."

"Nothing you say is wrong, Martinez, but you do not say enough. Smoking Mirror is more than just another name for Satan. The Aztecs are more sophisticated than Europeans; they see the virtue in the powers of darkness. The priestess, Toci, told me a story about this god; let me tell it to you."

Martinez doubted that the tale would answer his question, but he listened nonetheless.

"The gods of this country are said to walk among the people," explained Sebastian. "Of course; how else could they accept me? It is said that Smoking Mirror, if he is seen at all, will be seen at night, and with that I cannot argue. And he is most likely to be encountered along a lonely road, near a forest.

"Imagine yourself walking outside the city at midnight. If Smoking Mirror is near, you will hear the sound of a man chopping wood. That sound alone, known for what it is, would send cowards into flight; but if you are brave, and ambitious, you will step off the road into the woods. There is a threat, but there is a temptation too, and even a promise such as I have made to you. A man with the courage to face the god may hope to gain from the encounter."

"And what may he gain?"

"Much. But only after he has faced the Smoking Mirror. If you follow the sound of chopping wood into the forest, you will see a dim glowing in the darkness. And if you do not run from it, you will meet the god face to face. You will see him standing among the trees, a gleaming skeleton, with eyes afire and a long tongue lolling between his gaping jaws. And he will challenge you, not with words or actions, but by his very presence. The sound you hear is not an ax, but the noise of the god's ribs, swinging open and shut like a door caught in a vagrant breeze. Behind those banging ribs is the living heart of Smoking Mirror. If you have the strength to reach out and clutch that throbbing heart in your bare hands, then this god of bones and blood will reward you with riches and glory. But if you turn away from him, then you will be blighted forever."

"What do you suppose they mean by it?"

"Probably they mean nothing, Martinez, for they do not see it as a piece of fancy, but as the simple truth."

Nonplussed, Martinez looked down and noticed that he still held the black knife in his left hand. He offered it to Don Sebastian.

"Another way of reaching hearts," said the vampire, as he took the weapon. "No less effective, but suitable only for a priest. Yet Smoking Mirror is willing to appear to any common man and give him the chance to grasp pulsating power in his naked fingers. You may never be a priest, Martinez. But tell me: What would you do if you met the god in the forest?"

Martinez considered for a moment. "Easy enough," he said, "to swear that I would be bold and resolute. Such boasts cost a man nothing. Yet I will not proclaim myself a coward in advance of the evidence. How can I know what I will do until the challenge confronts me?"

"I can put you to the test. What say you, Alfonso Martinez? This room is not a forest, to be sure, yet it is certainly a setting in which the god might appear. Are you ready to face him?"

Martinez stood, suddenly afraid that he had pushed his luck too far, and dropped his eyes. "My hand," he said. "I have hurt my hand. You can hardly expect me to reach between the clashing ribs of a skeleton when I can barely hold a coin in my fingers."

He kept his gaze averted from the figure across the room, but he could not block out the short, sharp noise that came from the shadows. It might have been the blade of an ax chopping into the trunk of a tree, or it might have been the sound of a trap springing shut.

"This is not the test!" shouted Martinez. "I will not look! I have not seen the god!"

He stared resolutely at the mica floor and concentrated on the way in which its gleaming surface both absorbed and reflected the light from the burning braziers. He strove to hold the shifting images in his brain and think of nothing else.

"So be it," said the voice of Don Sebastian. "You have not entered the forest, Martinez. Remember, though, that such a chance comes seldom. Still, you are not compromised. Come, have faith in me. Raise your eyes. You need not spend the rest of your life in contemplation of a floor."

Reluctantly, Martinez did as he was told, and saw to his relief that his companion looked no more uncanny than before. Yet once more the pale face wore its mocking smile.

"You need not be embarrassed, Martinez. A man should have the right to choose his moment, although in truth the world is not always so generous. But let it pass. For the moment you have eluded the god in the forest. Perhaps you will never face him."

"When I am ready."

"Even so. But you have not answered my question, and so you have denied yourself an answer to your own. Unless you are willing to take the god's heart in your hands, I fear that you will never learn whether I am Smoking Mirror."

Martinez sat again. "You might have answered me directly," he said sullenly.

"Gods seldom do."

10. The Temples

IN the months that followed, Alfonso Martinez became a student of Aztec theology. It was an uncomfortable education. His schoolroom was the city of Tenochtitlan, and his teacher was Toci, the priestess of Smoking Mirror. He did not learn from books or lectures, even though Toci's Spanish improved with remarkable speed; instead, he learned from demonstrations. She showed him the rites of the gods of Mexico, an apparently endless series of lavish displays that would have delighted the eyes of any observer if they had not so frequently ended in death.

By day Martinez stood under the white sun and watched innumerable wretches sacrificed in ceremonies of blood and fire; by night he reported his observations to a living corpse. Don Sebastian had an insatiable appetite for detail; he was evidently engaged in a systematic analysis of the countless cults that controlled every aspect of life among the Aztecs. He brooded over manuscripts filled with the strange, flat drawings that Martinez found so disquieting, and he fingered the huge circular stones covered with apparently indecipherable hieroglyphics that represented the Mexican calendar.

"These people are fools," Martinez told him. "Look at that thing you're studying. Look at the shape of it. It's a wheel, isn't it? They have skill enough to make such a thing, but they don't have sense enough to know what to do with it. They still drag their burdens through the streets, and cover the only wheels they have with those meaningless scrawls."

"This may well be the most useful wheel ever invented," said Don Sebastian, but he would say no more.

Martinez grew increasingly impatient as the days passed. In his mind there was only one secret in the city worth uncovering, and that was the source of its gold. Yet whenever he mentioned the subject to Don Sebastian, he found himself turned away with an enigmatic remark, which was often accompanied by another gift of the precious metal. It was not long before the alchemist possessed a fortune. But he was still a virtual prisoner in an alien environment, one where his constantly increasing hoard was all but worthless.

The irony of the situation did not escape Martinez. He was not humorless, and more than once he laughed as he accepted another ring, bracelet, or necklace from his master, each ornament cold from contact with the flesh of a vampire. Yet the laughter was bitter. For years he had dreamed of accumulating such a fortune; its image had haunted him, and he had never doubted that somehow it would be his. But he had concentrated so intently on the mere accumulation of wealth that his mental projections had included nothing of the surrounding circumstances. He was certain that the intensity of his visions had produced the desired result, but equally certain that his failure to imagine sufficiently detailed conditions had caused his present predicament. The worst of it was that Don Sebastian seemed to know; the dead smile with which he bestowed the trinkets was proof enough. And indeed there might be a lesson in all this. The vanity of riches was an old sermon, but not one that Martinez wished to hear.

Still, he could not ignore the simple sensual pleasure that his new wealth provided. In his room in the palace, away from Toci and Don Sebastian, he found his principal diversion in playing with his golden toys. The mere touch of the objects was a promise of power; it only remained for Martinez to fulfill that tantalizing promise. Apart from this, his life was as empty as an alchemist's purse. The priestess and the undead wizard were his only companions, except for the servants who brought him the food he could not name and spoke to him in words he could not comprehend. Sleep on a straw mat under pictures of the hideous Aztec gods became a luxury, one that his keepers allowed him too infrequently. He began to think with nostalgia of the days when he had served in the Spanish army.

Cortez had fled the city in the early morning of July 1, and somehow his ragged army had fought its way through the outlying territory held by allies of the Aztecs. On July 2, while his former comrades struggled to save themselves, Martinez observed the first day of the festival of Xilonen, the goddess of young corn.

As the new corn ripened, the chiefs of each district gave freely of the food stored from the last harvest. The people feasted and danced in the streets. Martinez could not help reflecting that their recent victory gave them more to celebrate than the coming of a new crop.

Toci pointed out a young woman, one whom Martinez had already noticed for himself. She was dressed entirely in flowers. Her body was covered in white and yellow blossoms, and he found the effect so delightful that he was willing to overlook the red paint smeared on her face. More forbidding were the three ancient crones who accompanied her everywhere. Robed in black, their gray hair streaming in the dust, they seemed to have no other purpose than to feed her and to keep her dancing.

For days Martinez watched this lovely creature, enjoying both her presence and the images she inspired in his mind. He all but convinced himself that Toci had singled her out for his attention because she was to be a gift. But when he finally asked about her, he was disappointed. "She is the goddess," Toci said.

A charming custom, thought Martinez, still hopeful that the end of the celebration would leave this surrogate divinity free for earthly pleasures. Toci also drew his attention to a young man who was dressed with uncommon splendor, but the alchemist found him considerably less interesting. He preferred to direct his gaze toward the flowered image of the goddess, especially on the final day of the festival.

On that day, the goddess and her withered handmaidens mounted the steps of the temple, and there the object of the alchemist's desire began a frenzied dance.

In an ecstasy she tore the blossoms from her body until she was half naked, whirling on a carpet of yellow and white. Her torso gleamed with perspiration, her brown back arched, her pointed breasts thrust toward the sun. Martinez, who had often regretted the civilized garb of these savages, stared with undisguised delight. Not even the grave countenance of the priestess beside him could dampen his enthusiasm.

He was still staring when the three old women dragged his goddess down and hacked a hole in her chest with a blade of black obsidian. One of them held something up above her head, her hands dripping.

Martinez heard the voice of the crowd raised in a tremendous shout, but it seemed to come from a great distance. His lust gave way at once to horror, but there was an unforgettable instant where the two were mixed, and a lingering sensation that the tragedy he had witnessed was somehow ennobling. His feelings terrified him far more than what he had seen.

"The corn is ripe," said Toci.

He turned to her, half expecting to see in her eyes the mockery so characteristic of Don Sebastian. Instead, her face was sweetly serious, her eyes shining with unshed tears. "Xilonen is dead," she told him, "but she will rise again. The corn will rise again. It is good."

That night, a troubled Martinez spoke to Don Sebastian. He would have preferred to be reassured by Toci, but her acceptance of the ceremony was so complete that he could hardly expect her to discuss it rationally. And so Martinez, half ashamed of his own squeamishness, sought comfort from a being whose very existence was dependent on bloodshed.

Sebastian put aside his manuscripts and looked at Martinez

thoughtfully. "We are born to die," he said. "You have seen death before."

"But not like this," protested Martinez, sensing as he spoke that the creature before him had cast its cold eyes upon his inmost thoughts.

"You desired her, but death cares nothing for that, Martinez. The beautiful must die, as must the brave. Nor are the weak and ugly spared. All die."

"But the manner of her death!"

"All deaths are cruel; but I see that you mean something more."

"I almost think she chose it willingly. And the city cheered her slaughter. This is something I have never seen before—a nation that rejoices to see its daughters slain."

"Surely you know of such things, though you have never been a witness to them? Consider the creed of our native land, and the worship of its martyrs. It is a glory everywhere to die for a cause, to die for the gods and thus receive their favor. And there is a certain logic in it, since death is inevitable in any case. Would you not sacrifice yourself for a guarantee of endless bliss?"

"I might, if I believed in it."

"I strongly advise you to believe in something, Martinez. You are wise enough in the ways of the world to know the importance of faith. Years ago in Spain, my studies convinced me that the afterlife a man envisions is the one he will experience. I learned it from a woman. She was a vampire, like me, but her fate was not like mine. She expected only oblivion, and now she is no more. But somehow I have survived."

Martinez squirmed on his stool. "Then did you know that you would awaken in Mexico?"

"Perhaps. I knew, at least, that there was more before me. It seemed expedient to abandon this world temporarily, lest others should wreak their will upon my spirit. The secret of my undead existence had been discovered and I would no doubt be destroyed when the sun rose. My plans had gone awry; there seemed to be no escape. And so I set myself aflame before the walls of my black castle. But I never doubted that I would return someday."

"Return from what?" asked Martinez eagerly.

"I cannot easily tell you. And I wonder if I should. But I see that you have been chastened by this sacrifice, and I would show you what I can while you are still less worldly than you were. I dreamed in a sort of limbo—one of my own devising. I had peace there, and a beautiful darkness. But it was not enough. Not enough for eternity."

"Then you hope to find more here?"

"I must, Martinez. Why do you suppose I became the creature that you see before you? To revel in murder? To seek pleasure in a bed of earth? There may be some strange delights in it—such as the moment of madness you experienced when you saw the heart torn from the maiden you coveted, but there are more of shame and sorrow. If I endure these, then I must.

"Time, Martinez! I need more time. That black-and-silver world I constructed for my soul was not enough. I must have more. I will not spend the ages there alone."

Sebastian's face was contorted with emotions that Martinez never expected to see there, and he felt a pity for the lost soul that stood before him, mingled with a terror he had never known before. His own world was much simpler, but he felt to his dismay that it was shattering around him. He had always thought of himself as a young man, with time enough to worry about the state of his spirit.

"I have much to learn from you," he said.

"That is why we showed you the ceremony. It is easy enough to talk of mortality, but such a demonstration is worth more than words. It was Toci who guessed that it would change you. Dozens have died during this festival, but she knew that this one life meant more to you than most. Do not forget it, Martinez."

For a while Martinez did not forget. Yet the next festival, celebrating the birth of the flowers, was more pleasant. It followed immediately after the celebration in honor of the young corn, and Martinez began to understand that the life of the city was an endless cycle of religious rites, a pattern of continuous devotion that might dismay even the most devout Catholics of Spain.

"There are eighteen of these ceremonies," said Don Sebastian, "each lasting twenty days. They are something like our months."

"But they have forgotten five days," said Martinez. "That makes only three hundred and sixty. Or can't they calculate the length of a year?"

"Their calendar is exquisitely calculated, Martinez, and so complex that it will require months of study. Each day has its significance. I will show you when I know more. The five days you mentioned are not forgotten. They are called the five days of misfortune, and anyone born then is considered to be cursed. They fall in February, during those short, dark days when it seems that winter will never end."

"But does it all make sense?" protested Martinez. "Take this current celebration. Toci tells me that it honors Huitzilopochtli, their war god, the one whose temple dwarfs all the rest. But there are no blood sacrifices, and not even a mockery of warfare. There is only joy, and such abandon as I have never known here. The men and women even hold each other when they dance, something I have never seen before. And there is drunkenness. I had guessed that their strict morals were part of the discipline that produced warriors, yet they honor war by forgoing all decorum. They are mad."

"Perhaps they believe that Huitzilopochtli sees enough of killing, and can easily be spared more. That may be the nature of his holiday. Yet discipline is not altogether lost. Observe, and you will notice that only the old people are granted the gift of drunkenness. For all others, it remains a capital offense. Yet I grant you the paradox. Their beliefs are so complicated, so full of contradictions, that sometimes I despair of ever mastering them. And yet, if I can correlate them with the European systems, with our Zodiac, I believe that I will have the key to more power than any man has known before."

The thought intrigued Martinez. Time enough had passed, however, so that he was once again less concerned with his afterlife than with what he could acquire while still a man.

"Old habits die hard," Sebastian said, and by now Martinez was so accustomed to this mind reading that it disturbed him little more than the fact that he was conversing with a living corpse.

"The incongruities are intriguing," said Sebastian. "Tell me. What strikes you as the most appropriate time for the festival of Smoking Mirror?"

"I don't know. Scorpio, I suppose—the sign of death and transformation."

"And the time of All Hallow's Eve? The sign under which I was born. I would have guessed the same. Yet the feast of Smoking Mirror falls a full month earlier, when Libra rules the heavens—the sign of grace and balance, and the one ruled by Venus. But the Aztecs call Venus the star of the Feathered Serpent, the god whose mantle your Cortez assumed, the god who stands in opposition to Smoking Mirror. What do you make of that?"

"Nothing," replied Martinez. "This is superstition, not science. I suggest that you forget it all, and turn your efforts toward the conquest of these savages. To celebrate the spirit of the unknown so early in the year is against all precedent. Libra!"

"There is more. The constellation they ascribe to Smoking Mirror is not the Balance, but rather the Great Bear."

Martinez thought for a moment. "Ursa Major. . . . There is some sense in that, I suppose. But there's no system to it. You are embarked on the study of an illusion."

"I might agree with you, yet the mere fact that I am here argues against you. Their magic is potent, and there must be a methodology behind it. They say their gods come from the stars, from stars so far away that we can scarcely see them. Perhaps we are too much concerned with the lumps of stone and fire that spin around our own sun. There is an infinite universe beyond them, Martinez, with powers we have never dreamed of, much less summoned. You must forget your gold, and look to the glittering lights in the sky."

Martinez rarely saw the stars. He spent his days witnessing the rites of the Aztecs and his nights in the bowels of the black pyramid with Don Sebastian. And his discontent grew. Both Toci and Sebastian considered it sufficient to hint at their secrets; he was not really one with them, and he felt with some resentment that they considered him a novice in the quest for mystery.

The middle of August brought the celebration of the falling fruits. Martinez at once forgot the name of the god it honored, but he could not forget its rituals. The god was a god of fire, and the sacrifice was multiple. The greatest soldiers of the nation appeared, each bringing with him a prisoner of war. The pairs of men danced together, the captives no less dedicated to the ritual than their captors. In fact, Martinez found it necessary to ask Toci which were which. After a day of dancing, the prisoners were dragged up the steps of the god's temple, to its summit. A bed of coals burned there, and one by one the men were thrown into it. Toci assured Martinez that the victims were drugged to the point of insensibility, but still it came as a relief when the priests of the fire god dragged the half-roasted captives out of the flames with hooked poles and cut out their hearts.

The next ritual began on the last day of August. By now Martinez was sick of these gruesome celebrations, but he saw no way to escape them. And he had not yet lost all hope that there was a meaning to them. He asked Don Sebastian the name of the next god to be honored.

"Toci," said Sebastian.

"Toci!" cried Martinez. "You can't mean it? She is a priestess. They can't mean to kill her!"

"Toci is a goddess, who gave our Toci her name. There is no more significance in it than when a Spaniard is named in honor of some saint. She tells me that the name means 'Heart of the Earth.' Another fertility rite, now that the harvest is so near. Our Toci will not die. There is another woman who will assume the role of the goddess, and I understand that she will not be so lucky. Or perhaps she will be luckier, if she believes."

"I should have known," said Martinez. "You would not let your woman die, even if she had been chosen."

"You mistake me, Martinez. Toci is no woman of mine, whatever you may think or I may wish. She is a virgin, sworn to Smoking Mirror."

"Then you are not Smoking Mirror."

"That is as may be. Toci revived me and she sheltered me. She believes in me, and serves me in every way but one. Perhaps Smoking Mirror is beyond desire."

"But not Don Sebastian, eh?"

A twisted grin crossed the vampire's pale, scarred countenance. "Are you lonely, Martinez? There are maidens here for you to wed."

"I want no bride. I will not be tied to a savage. I am a Spaniard!"

"The city is not so ascetic as it seems. I understand that there are harlots here, though I know little of them. Ask Toci. Perhaps she will help you."

Now there was no doubt about the meaning of Sebastian's smile. He knew well enough that Martinez would never ask the august Toci to procure a savage slut for him. Martinez had some consolation in the thought that the great sorcerer was as lovelorn as the lowly alchemist, but no real satisfaction.

"Are they feeding you, at least?" asked Martinez.

"I am as you see me."

Martinez surveyed the gaunt figure standing between two flaming braziers at the foot of the black slab where he had been reborn. The face was white, and split by the old scar that ran down over the left eye; but the long hair was still black, and the dead flesh was firm. In his robes of red and white and black, adorned with ornaments of gold, Don Sebastian de Villanueva still possessed an unholy strength.

"You don't look starved," said Martinez.

The festival of the earth mother was the most elaborate Martinez had yet witnessed. It was called the Month of Brooms, and began with a ritual sweeping of the entire city, which made a bit more sense to Martinez when he learned that one of the titles of the goddess Toci was a term indicating she was a grandmother. In another manifestation of the goddess her name was Tlazolteotl, which meant "Eater of Filth"; she consumed sins, and pardoned them. The city's prostitutes were her wards, but the entire population exposed their failings to her in a ceremony Martinez could only regard as a parody of the Catholic confession. Somehow the goddess and the priestess who stood beside him were mixed up in his mind; he was tempted to confess to her and find redemption in her shining eyes, but he was too embarrassed, and hardly knew what she would regard as a sin.

Her beauty subdued him as much as her air of severity, and he was fascinated by the thought that she was still a virgin. He tried to guess her age, but could do no more than guess. The women of Tenochtitlan did not show their years, but he would have sworn that she was closer to twenty than thirty. Too young, certainly, to hear the sort of story Martinez had to tell. In any case, there seemed no profit to be gained from making sordid confessions to a creature who functioned more and more in his mind as a temptation. Martinez looked at her and longed for purity.

The ceremonies continued. The young man in the gaudy robes was there again, this time accompanied by four lovely young maidens who clustered around him as eagerly as brides; but Martinez was much more interested in the woman who played the role of the goddess.

She was a handsome woman, with strong features, but much older than the one whose death had shocked the alchemist. She had the air of a matron, which was further emphasized by the role she assumed. Dressed in white, like the image of the goddess in the temple, she sat amid a throng of dancers and worked on her weaving.

Four gigantic poles had been constructed in the courtyard before the pyramid, each of them so tall that they seemed to tower over the temple. Martinez could only guess their length, but they were certainly well over a hundred feet high, and close enough together that each set of two could be connected by numerous cross beams, so that they looked like two ladders reaching toward the sky.

On the last day of the festival, the mock goddess passed between these ladders, borne on the back of a black-clad priest. He carried her up the steps to the summit of the pyramid while the citizens of Tenochtitlan gathered at its base. As they reached the top—the woman in white with her face to the sun—another priest stepped forward, a black sword in his hand. The sword fell, and the woman's head fell with it. Blood spilled over the man who held the decapitated corpse.

Martinez had expected something like this, and tried to tell himself that he was past caring. But he was not prepared for what came next.

The priests bent over the body, their knives busy. They stripped off the woman's clothes, and then proceeded to remove her skin. Martinez felt his stomach lurch. The crowd was silent, and the sun shone down unmercifully. A naked man appeared, and stood motionless while the priests dressed him. His coat was the skin of a woman, peeled off her corpse from throat to thigh.

"She is born again," said Toci.

Martinez was nauseous, choking back his vomit as he turned away. When he had the strength to look again, he saw that the priests had covered the man's abominable garment with the white clothes that the woman had woven in the days before she died. Blotches of her blood were seeping through the cloth.

He made an effort to collect himself, remembering his duty to Don Sebastian. "Why is she a man?" he asked halfheartedly.

"She will fight," said Toci. "Now men will die."

Her remarks made Martinez expect something further from the hideous man-woman, but instead the creature disappeared into the depths of the temple, and two new priests took the stage as they crawled up the gigantic ladders in front of the pyramid. When they reached the top, they lashed themselves into place with ropes.

Captives were herded into the square formed by the four poles, and one by one were forced to climb upward toward the waiting priests. There was a brief flurry of arms and legs as each man reached the summit, then the captives dropped, shattering like ripe fruit on the flagstones below. A priest was waiting for them;

he cut off their heads and collected their blood in a golden bowl.

When it was finally over, the man in the woman's skin stepped forward from the crowd. He leaned over the bowl, dipped one finger into the blood, and licked it.

The gesture was a signal to every man, woman, and child in the great plaza. They bent down, touching their fingers to the ground, and then tasted the earth. Martinez stood erect while countless thousands stooped toward the ground. The goddess, he remembered, was an eater of filth, but he had hardly expected the populace of Tenochtitlan to follow her example. And certainly he was not prepared for what came next. Later, he tried to convince himself that it was an illusion, induced by horror and the heat of the sun. For what he felt was nothing less than an earthquake.

The ground he stood on shook; the long poles before the pyramid swayed dizzily. A vast rumbling rolled through the city, jolting Martinez so that finally he fell to his knees. He looked at Toci, and saw her slender figure thrown back and forth by the cataclysm. Her eyes were closed, her face ecstatic. The heart of the earth was throbbing, and Martinez clutched the ground to save himself.

Abruptly, everything was still. Martinez lay outstretched for a moment, then guiltily put a dirt-streaked finger to his mouth. He looked up, and saw the white-clad goddess surrogate advancing into the plaza, followed by a small army of soldiers dressed in golden skins spotted with black. They were the knights of Smoking Mirror.

More warriors rushed out from the mob to meet them: the Knights of the Feathered Serpent. This was the mock combat Martinez had heard about, though what it had to do with an earth goddess was more than he could guess. The enthusiasm of the fight appalled him—this was more than ritual. Men fell bleeding, and the air was filled with stones.

Martinez swore as a club flew past his head. He clutched at Toci. The city was in chaos. "Do they mean to kill each other?"

"Some die," said Toci. She took his hand and led him along

with the crowd toward the small shrine of the goddess with her name. Martinez saw that the battle was working its way toward the same objective. The twilight rang with shouts.

Night fell before the knights of Smoking Mirror and the Feathered Serpent reached their goal. On the edge of the city, with the shore in view, the fighting stopped. The man in the guise of the goddess, face streaming from a dozen wounds, struggled to the top of a black building where a straw dummy waited. He pulled off his woman's clothes, and then the woman's skin. He stood naked for a moment while the people streamed through the street to witness his abdication. He put the skin on the straw figure, then the white blouse and skirt. Devoid of his finery, he jumped down and disappeared into the ranks of battered warriors.

A ladder led to the rooftop. A young man in glittering robes stepped forward and pulled it to the ground. Four young women stood beside him; together they lifted the ladder and cast it into the nearby canal.

"It's him again," said Martinez, now totally bewildered. "Who is he?"

"He is Smoking Mirror," said Toci.

The alchemist felt something snap inside his head. "Smoking Mirror, is he? Then what of Don Sebastian?"

"The god has many faces," said a voice behind him.

Martinez whirled. The sky was dark, but he had never thought to see his teacher in the streets of the city. Martinez could not speak.

"There is another name for Smoking Mirror," said Don Sebastian. "He is the dark part of every soul, and sometimes they call him 'He Who Stands at the Shoulder.'"

"You deserve the title," said Martinez. "You haunt me like the horror that you are, and I have seen enough of horrors."

"Then perhaps you are ready, Martinez. For tomorrow begins the feast of Smoking Mirror."

11. A Box of Earth

THE festival that began near the end of September was called the Return of the Gods, and the first to return was Smoking Mirror.

Although Martinez was unnerved by the appearance of Don Sebastian at the conclusion of the festival for Toci, he could not suppress the fascination he felt at the news about the next celebration. He held his peace as he followed Sebastian to the black pyramid, speaking only when he was again seated in the subterranean chamber with the tilted walls.

"I suppose they'll be killing that boy."

"He will die in time, but not yet," replied Sebastian. "Tezcatlipoca is a god of such great importance that he is given two feasts. His representative is chosen a year in advance, but is not to be killed until the celebration marking the end of the drought, in May. Until then he is treated like a king. He does no work; all his wishes are granted. Those four young women with him are his brides—until the spring."

"I can wait."

"The death of Smoking Mirror is a ceremony worth waiting for. But this will be more than public spectacle—something that takes place late at night atop this very pyramid, with only the priests of this cult to witness it, something worth more to me than the slaughter of a thousand pampered boys. On that night the gods return from their journeying among the stars, and Smoking Mirror manifests himself."

"Exposing you as a fraud."

"Then you have decided against me, Martinez?"

"Should I acknowledge you as the god of a race you never dreamed of?"

"You have never seen my dreams," said Don Sebastian, and Martinez peered at him intently. "You would be well advised to trust me, Martinez. I will assume that the sacrifice today disturbed you. You know that without my protection you would not live long in Tenochtitlan. And you know that I offer you an opportunity few magicians of your rank will ever have. What more could you want of me?"

"The truth. I know you saved me, but for what? I live an endless round of horrors and frustrations. I have no friends, no position, no home, and no women. No one even speaks to me, except a woman made of ice and a man who should be dust. It's like living on some distant planet. And don't tell me how many magicians would be grateful for just such a chance. I've had the chance, and I know what it's worth. This city is no more to me than a dunghill covered with flies. What I want from you is not promises but the truth!"

"In your present state of mind, you would hardly be receptive to great truths. I almost think you mean to make me angry, though what you hope to gain from that I cannot guess. I am disappointed in you, Martinez. Ask your questions, and I will answer them if I can."

"Tell me about the gold," said the alchemist.

Sebastian moved across the room and stopped beside the idol of Tezcatlipoca. "Not the question I had hoped to hear," he said.

"You know what I mean. I came to this accursed continent in search of gold. And more than that, the secret of its source. They have so much, and prize it so little, that I guessed they might have found the philosopher's stone."

"I think not, alchemist," Sebastian said, and Martinez sat as if he had been turned to stone.

"It might not be beyond their powers," continued Sebastian, "but they would call a man mad for wasting his efforts on such an endeavor. It is pretty stuff, I grant you, and it gleams with a yellow like the sun. But what use is it? A soft metal, most valued here because it can be fashioned into ornaments. The art of the jeweler gives it what worth it has. It comes from mines, Martinez. It is a toy, a trifle. It answers no need. Any man in this city would tell you that a good blade of Spanish steel is worth its weight in gold, and more."

"I suppose you knew this all along," Martinez muttered. "You knew what I wanted, and you knew it wasn't here."

"I hoped that you would grow wiser. You already have gold enough to satisfy a man of your class. What would it matter if you could learn to manufacture it?"

"In this stinking city, not much. In the real world it would make me someone to be reckoned with. If I could return to Spain with the secret, I would be the wonder of the age!"

"I doubt if you will see Spain again, Martinez. Yet I won't deny you. Will you take this ring?"

"You think I will refuse it—you think you have taught me a lesson. But all the seers say that no man can predict his own future, however great his skill. Perhaps I will get out of here somehow; and if I do, I will be rich." Martinez took the ring.

"The last time you tried to carry a treasure out of this city, it all but killed you."

"Then I will have to be more careful."

"Let me show you something else, Martinez."

"Another sacrifice? Another magic trick?"

"I think it may impress you. I show it to you with the warning that it is guarded through the day by more jaguar knights than you would care to meet."

Sebastian led the alchemist across the crooked room to the wall that slanted over the sacrificial slab. His pale fingers ran along the dull black wall, and suddenly a portion of it dropped away. Martinez had seen panels hidden in other buildings, some of them counterbalanced so that they would spring open soundlessly at the slightest touch, yet this concealed chamber was like no other he had seen. Perhaps it was the oblique angle of the ceiling that made the long and narrow niche seem strange, but he could not shake off the notion that it was the entrance to another dimension —the work of a sorcerer, not an architect. Yet what it held was commonplace enough, no more than an open wooden box half filled with dirt.

"Your coffin," said Martinez.

"Mark it well. Whatever your ambitions, Alfonso Martinez, they will all end in a box like this."

Martinez turned away from the coffin and the dizzying crevice that contained it. "Your very presence shows me that death need not be the end," he said.

"It is not death that should concern you, but what comes after it. If you should die tonight, what would become of you? I have died twice, and twice returned to life, and still I am searching for a way to meet eternity. Your life should be a preparation for what will come."

"But who are you to tell me? You admit that you still know nothing, and you are in your third life. It would be wonderful if you could show me how to guarantee myself eternal bliss. What formula should I recite? Which incense should I burn? But for all I know, the path you want me to take leads to the void. I'll admit your way might be best, but only when there's proof that it goes somewhere. Meanwhile, I'll settle for the pleasures of the earth and let my soul fend for itself!"

"Come, Martinez. Every alchemist's apprentice knows that faith must come before the fact. I admit it is a difficult doctrine; indeed, it is devilish. If you believe in nothing, you cannot expect much else. Which leads us to your next question. Ask it."

Martinez sat on his stool and looked at the gold ring in his hand. "I can't believe that you will give me a good answer," he said. "I have asked before. And for this question I hardly know the answer that I want. I don't even know what the question means anymore."

"Can it hurt so much to ask?"

"You know I am a coward in many ways, and I confess that you can frighten me. That's what you've always done when I've asked questions. You are a magus, and you are undead. But are you Smoking Mirror?"

Sebastian touched the tilted wall, and watched the black stone swallow up his coffin. "Then you have not entirely renounced me, Martinez. I am grateful for what belief remains."

"What do you care what I think? Why don't you just kill me and be done with it?"

"I might have, years ago," Sebastian admitted. "But you have been of help to me. And for some reason I want to help you. Your skepticism is a rock to hone my thoughts. Your doubt strengthens my belief. And you are not such a fool as you make yourself sound. You are something like me, Martinez, and I will not kill you unless you drive me to it. And I will continue to protect you from the Aztecs. I will even try to answer your question."

Martinez stirred uncomfortably, then stood and paced across the mica floor. "Now you would shame me," he protested. "I don't know what to say."

"Then I will say it. Admit this: I am as much Tezcatlipoca as Cortez is Quetzalcoatl."

"Granted." Martinez stopped his pacing and stood against a distant wall. "But the comparison is instructive. Where is Cortez now?"

Sebastian glided from behind the black slab to stand again beside the obsidian idol. "I fear we have not seen the last of him. He fought his way out of the city, and now there are reports that he is active in the countryside. One by one, he is subverting cities that are chafing under Aztec rule. I believe he means to rise against Tenochtitlan again. He is still a god to many."

Martinez's mind was racing feverishly, but he tried to keep his thoughts from Don Sebastian.

"It has a bearing on our argument," Sebastian went on. "An

upheaval of the kind that I envision will interfere with my quest. I am fighting time, Martinez, and now I must fight you as well."

"Then you really do believe that you are this Aztec god?"

"What is the nature of these gods? The stories say that they are tangible beings, creatures who have appeared here before. The Aztecs have been waiting for us, Cortez and me, and their belief in us is unquestionably a source of strength. Cortez employs that strength strategically, as you would have me do. Perhaps I am mistaken in my hope that such strength can affect the spirit, but I shall stand by my judgment. Could it be true that these gods once walked the earth? And might their incarnations reappear?"

"I don't know," admitted Martinez. "But I ask you again: How can you cling to the hope that you are Smoking Mirror, and at the same time hope to see him in this ceremony that you spoke about? If he appears, then you will be discredited."

"Theology is subtle, Martinez. Think of Spain and its religion. What they worship is threefold, a trinity of power, each part separate and yet inseparable. Learned men debate such paradoxes, but I am willing to accept them. And when Smoking Mirror comes, I hope that he will not expose me but embrace me, and that his power will be mine."

Martinez rubbed his hand across his mouth. "There is a risk, even if your premises are sound. You hope to absorb the power of this god. It seems more logical to expect that he will absorb you. You might be lost forever, leaving me alone among these savages."

"We shall be obliged to take our chances," said Sebastian. "I choose to believe in their gods, and to assume that what they have of value here comes from the stars."

"Then you think these gods came from the stars?"

"The documents suggest it. And the idea makes more sense than the story we were told as boys, of one force in the clouds and another buried in the bowels of the earth. The universe is infinite, Martinez. Dimensions beyond dreaming lie around us. Who knows what powers careen through the vast gulfs that spin around this ball of earth we stand on? You could speed among the stars for eternity, Alfonso Martinez, and never reach your journey's end. Somewhere in those endless reaches there must dwell forces of such magnitude that they would shatter our poor human visions. Perhaps all the gods of men are such—titanic entities that pass us on their travels through unknown realms. Gods beyond good and evil, gods who long to find strong souls to join them in their cosmic dance. Gods like Smoking Mirror."

"Perhaps," said Martinez.

For days Martinez watched the preparations for the return of the gods of Tenochtitlan. There was merrymaking in the streets; the ban against drunkenness seemed to be forgotten. Young men and women carried leafy branches, using them to decorate the shrines and temples of every god and goddess in the city. There were no sacrifices.

Each night Martinez reported on the day's events to Don Sebastian, and on the eighteenth night Toci followed him into the crooked room where the vampire waited.

"Smoking Mirror comes tonight," said Toci.

Martinez, who had done his best to forget Sebastian's ravings about monsters from infinity, felt a sudden chill.

"There will be four of us," Sebastian told him, "we three, and the blind high priest. And if things happen as they have been written, there will be a fifth."

"You really expect something?" Martinez asked, apprehensively.

"I have studied the stars and find them propitious. I might have chosen a later night, but this is the one that is prescribed. If we find less than I anticipate, I have another plan, based on my own calculations. Yet the Aztecs have studied their god for generations, and I will not challenge their traditions."

"What will happen?"

"What they expect is a small thing, though not without significance. But I expect much more. I may be disappointed, but I think the presence of a creature such as I am may encourage further manifestations."

"Just tell me what the small thing is," Martinez said.

"A footprint."

"A footprint?"

"The legends say that he has only one foot. He lost the other when the gods battled for possession of the universe. Four of us will wait at the summit of the pyramid, seated around a bowl filled with flour. And in the darkest hour of the night, Tezcatlipoca will stream down from the stars and leave his footprint there."

"Then he is invisible?"

"On this night he is, unless he honors us with more than he has granted before."

"A footprint," said Martinez. "I know a dozen men in Spain who could do more. I could do it myself, with the right equipment. Have I come across the ocean for a footprint? You should turn yourself into a bat for them, and they would make you king of all their continent."

"I am here to learn, Martinez, not to put on pageants. This is not magic as we know it. The priest will not impose his will upon the world of matter, but wait receptively until the great god comes."

"Then he won't gain much by it," said Martinez.

"He may not, but we might."

Martinez had forgotten Toci, but she stepped from the shadows to offer him a golden cup.

"More bribes?" he asked Sebastian.

"She is not offering you the cup, but its contents."

"What is it?" asked Martinez, trying to ignore the solemn gaze of the priestess, whose face was only inches from his own.

"A sacred potion," said Sebastian. "You should be flattered to receive it."

"Drink," said Toci.

"What is it for?" asked Martinez. He looked at the dark liquid below the golden brim, but turned away from Toci's shining eyes.

"It brings visions. Toci has told me it liberates the spirit, and sets the mind vibrating with the music of the spheres. Most of the ingredients are native plants. The seeds of the flower we call the morning glory, the essences of several mushrooms, and the buds of a plant called peyote."

"Have you tasted it?"

"Experiments years ago convinced me that it is unwise for me to consume anything but human blood. You are more fortunate."

"If you won't take it, then I won't," said Martinez. "I prefer to be sober while I await the coming of a god." He shook his head at Toci, then turned his back.

"You need not hide from it," Sebastian said, and when Martinez looked over his shoulder he saw Toci draining the golden cup. He watched for some spasm to run through her, but he was disappointed. She stood quite still, holding the empty cup between her breasts.

"You have lost an opportunity," said Sebastian.

"How will we reach the top?" asked Martinez. "By the stairs outside?"

"Toci knows the way," Sebastian said. "Follow her."

The path to the top of the pyramid ran through dark passages, lying at crazy angles but leading inexorably upward. Some of the rough-hewn ceilings were so low that Martinez had to stoop to pass beneath them. He sensed rather than saw that Toci walked somewhere ahead of him, but he was all too aware that the cold form of Don Sebastian was at his heels. It was a relief finally to step out into the night.

The blind priest sat alone on the bare summit; before him was a golden bowl. Martinez stopped beside the black trapdoor and watched Sebastian crawl out into the night. The peak of the pyramid was nothing but a bare black platform. Martinez found that no matter where he stood, he felt uncomfortably close to the edge. The city spread out before him; he stood above both pyramids and palaces. Only the great temple of the war god blocked his view. Canals reflected the dull light of the waning moon. Beyond them lay the dark lake, its surface masked by wisps of fog.

Here and there a light shone, but most of Tenochtitlan was dark. A few stars glimmered, but the night was cloudy, and the scene above him was much like the one below. Martinez felt as though he was standing on a mirror—a tiny mirror drifting through a sea of stars. In this setting, even the footprint of a god was not a matter to be taken lightly.

As he looked at his three companions, he was suddenly aware of an isolation he had not known before. Their garments were an outward symbol of some more subtle truth. Martinez alone wore Spanish clothing. The priest and priestess were draped in the black robes of their cult, with white skulls embroidered on the hems, and Sebastian was resplendent in his raiment of red, white, and black.

Sebastian and Toci sank to their knees on either side of the high priest; like him, they faced the golden bowl. It was left for Martinez to complete the square, which put him opposite the blind and clouded eyes of Smoking Mirror's priest.

They sat in silence while the stars moved slowly overhead. Sebastian kneeled, and the priest and priestess sat cross-legged. The others stayed quite still while the night crawled past; each of them seemed lost in a trance. Martinez squirmed with boredom and discomfort. He began to wish that he had taken the drug, and he would have asked for the golden cup if he had not suspected that silence was expected of him.

He tried to watch the bowl, but there was nothing there to interest him. At length, for lack of anything else to hold his attention, he began to stare at Toci. He wondered, not for the first time, how she would look without the grim black robe that covered her from throat to ankle. He guessed that her body would be slim and girlish, with smooth skin like polished gold. He dreamed of slight, exquisite breasts and strong, supple thighs. She seemed completely unaware of his relentless gaze, and her indifference was hardly encouraging, but it gave him a chance to study the woman as he never had before. Her huge brown eyes were radiant, and the high, wide bones of her cheeks looked like the work of a sculptor. Martinez was filled with melancholy, squatting beside a goddess, knowing he would never possess her. Yet somehow he was soothed and almost ennobled by her very presence.

And then he noticed what any sensible man would have noticed hours earlier. If his rapt inventory of her charms did not distract the priestess, it was because she was lost in contemplation of Don Sebastian. The brown woman and the pale man were caught in a communion, an exchange of souls so evident that it almost shamed Martinez. He was embarrassed by his own desire, and embarrassed to be witness to a rapture he had never known. He would not have been surprised to see light streaming between the dead and living eyes.

And what was he to do? Stare deliriously into the clouded cataracts that blocked the vision of the old high priest? Caught for an instant between jealousy and reverence, between lust and distaste, Martinez unexpectedly felt the presence of the god called Smoking Mirror.

There was no change in what he saw, and yet everything had changed. No monster roared down from the skies, but every detail Martinez looked at was thrown into some strange relief, as if the universe had dropped ten feet away. Both light and shadow seemed more vivid, and the faces of his three companions were like flickering hallucinations. Their faces spun around him: the dark forbidding beauty of the priestess, the wrinkled wisdom of the old high priest, the unmoving ivory features of the dead magician. And then the three merged into one, a misty creature with six eyes, part blind, part living, and part dead. The stars were bright as suns.

Martinez felt his scalp crawl. He lowered his gaze to the golden bowl, a solid presence in the midst of so much instability. He glared at the object as if it were all that kept him anchored to the earth. He was so dizzy that he would not dare to shut his eyes. He watched as the grains of flour in the bowl began to move. One by one they dropped away, some pushed toward the sides, some pressed down. A pattern formed in the smooth surface of the flour. It might have been a footprint; perhaps it would have been, if Martinez had waited. But when he realized what was happening, he jumped up.

His legs were stiff and clumsy; his left foot caught the golden bowl and sent it rattling over the peak of the black pyramid. He heard it crashing down the layered sides of stone until it reached the ground.

"It's here!" Martinez screamed. "It's here! I saw the footprint!"

Whatever spell existed had drifted away. The world looked right again, but Martinez was past caring. He stumbled back and forth upon the summit of the pyramid until he felt cold fingers grip him by the throat.

"Fool!" said Don Sebastian.

The strong right hand of the vampire lifted Martinez off his feet. Martinez tried to speak, but found that he could only gasp and choke. Sebastian strode to the edge of the small platform and held the alchemist aloft. Martinez felt himself suspended more than a hundred feet above the ground. He struggled for a second, then realized that breaking free would mean his death. The grasp that strangled him was all that kept him from smashing onto the stones below. He looked down, then wished that he had not. His pleas for mercy were unintelligible, and he was half unconscious.

Dimly he sensed two black-clad figures rushing toward him. He heard the old man speak in the language he had never understood.

"Stop!" said Toci. "Do not kill him. He has seen the god."

"And driven him away," Sebastian said.

"Did you see Smoking Mirror? We saw only one another. The priest saw only darkness. But the little man knows Tezcatlipoca. Do not kill him."

More dead than alive, Martinez loved Toci as he had never loved another woman. He hung in the air for another moment, then felt himself released. He started to scream, then stopped abruptly when he realized that he had fallen only a few feet. He lay crumpled on the summit of the temple of Tezcatlipoca.

"True," Sebastian said. "Too true, and my disgrace. You and I saw only one another. Martinez alone saw the footprint."

Toci hung her head.

"What does the high priest say?" Sebastian asked Toci. There was a brief exchange in the language of Tenochtitlan.

"He says that we are four, and four are needed."

"So," Sebastian said, "you are spared, Martinez. I am not happy with you, but there is much I do not understand. Get below, and sleep while you can. Tomorrow we set out for Texcoco."

"Texcoco?" whined Martinez. "What is that?"

"It is the city sacred to Smoking Mirror. There, the legends say, he first appeared, and there his temple towers above all others. We must reach the city before this festival is done."

"But how will you travel?"

"You have seen my box of earth. The jaguar knights will carry it. Now go below."

"I'll lose my way."

"We shall follow you, and we shall find you."

Martinez crawled to the trapdoor and disappeared into the depths of the pyramid.

Toci looked again at Don Sebastian. "I saw you," she said again. "I did not see Smoking Mirror."

"You have seen him," said Sebastian, his voice not as sure as it had been. "What passed between us made a road for him. Together we are the god. Believe me, Toci."

He reached out his hand, and it was shame rather than reluctance that prevented her from taking it. "Ask the priest," Sebastian said.

A few words passed between the servants of the god, then Toci took a step forward. "You are the god," she said.

She had never touched Sebastian before, but now her hand held his. She peered into his eyes, then twisted her head away, but her body moved toward his. And all at once she held him fast. He felt her soft, strong body pressed against his own. His dead flesh tingled.

"We go to Texcoco," Toci said. "You are Smoking Mirror."

12. City of Ghosts

THE city of Texcoco lay to the east, beyond the borders of the gigantic lake of which Tenochtitlan occupied the southwest corner. As their expedition started out in the bright morning, Martinez learned from Toci that the lake itself was called Texcoco.

He was surprised to hear that this lake and the second city shared the same name, yet there was certainly some logic in it, especially since Texcoco was a community sacred to Smoking Mirror. And Martinez could no longer doubt the importance of the god, not after what he had seen the night before. The footprint in itself was next to nothing, but the atmosphere in which it had appeared was something he could not forget. For an instant he had felt that a hole had been torn in the cosmos so that a solitary footprint could drop through. Martinez had seen the living die, and the dead live again, but neither sight had prepared him for the overpowering otherworldliness of the night atop the temple. Don Sebastian might not be Smoking Mirror, but something was.

The alchemist was subdued enough to keep silent during the preparations for the pilgrimage. He watched a squad of jaguar knights assemble, heavily armed and dressed in spotted skins. There were eighteen of them. Six carried Sebastian's coffin, six marched before it, and six behind. The high priest, blind as he was, seemed to direct their operations. Finally Toci stepped out of the dark doorway that was hidden in the mouth of the black skull at the base of the pyramid. She led Martinez to a position at the rear of the coffin, and waited there beside him until the march began.

The alchemist's pack, heavy with treasure, was strapped to his back. He might have moved more easily without it, but he could not bear to leave his gold behind him.

"Where is Texcoco?" he asked Toci.

"There," said the priestess, extending a brown hand toward the east. The day was clear, and Martinez thought that he could almost see the distant shore.

"But we're going south," protested Martinez. "Must we walk all the way around the lake? Why not take boats and cross the water?"

"Smoking Mirror says no."

"He does, does he?" Martinez lapsed into silence. He shifted his pack and took another step. Already, only a few paces from the temple, he felt that he had been transformed into a foot soldier again. His months in Tenochtitlan had brought him only another forced march, and one that did not promise wealth, just further horrors. He knew who had given the order to take the long route, and was irritated to hear Toci speak of Sebastian as if he were undoubtedly Smoking Mirror. He wondered at Sebastian's decision, then recalled something he had heard about a vampire's fear of running water. A legend said the undead could not bear to cross a stream or river. The lake was not really running water, but apparently Sebastian wished to take no chances, even if his skull had already crossed an all but endless sea. And Martinez understood the dangers. A canoe might well capsize; and if the waters of Lake Texcoco did not destroy Sebastian, they would surely wash away the precious bit of Spanish soil in the box, the dirt that was said to keep the living dead alive during the hours of daylight.

Martinez cursed the ignorance of the Aztecs, whose civilization had no place for either wheels or horses. "How long will this little walk take?" he asked.

"Two days," said Toci.

"Wonderful," said Martinez bitterly. "Just enough time to reach Texcoco before the festival of Smoking Mirror ends. Smoking Mirror!" He spoke the name as if it were an oath. "Tell me, priestess, do you really believe that Don Sebastian is Smoking Mirror?"

Toci smiled. She gave no other answer, but it was enough for Martinez. He had never seen her smile before.

Trudging down the southern causeway beside her, Martinez decided that the priestess had become Sebastian's lover. The vampire might not have lied to him; it could have happened as recently as last night, but Martinez was certain the expression on Toci's face could have only one meaning. Fuming with jealousy, he peered at her throat for telltale signs while she walked placidly along. He could not find the two small wounds he searched for, but their absence did not alter his conviction.

He did not speak to the priestess for the rest of the day. His silence seemed to have no effect on her at all. It bothered Martinez, though, and as the march wore on his thoughts turned inward. The evident understanding between Sebastian and Toci made him feel more isolated than ever before. His stay in Tenochtitlan had been a disappointment; the trembling sense of expectation with which he had greeted the revival of the magus had come to naught. Without Alfonso Martinez, Don Sebastian would still be a silver skull grinning on the shelf of a sorcerer's den somewhere in the back alleys of Madrid. Yet last night the vampire had almost killed him, for nothing more than a small display of nervousness. Toci had saved him, of course, but that was not exactly flattering. The two of them might have been parents bickering over the education of their child, and Martinez was not happy with that role. He was sick of being patronized, especially since he had been the only one to see the footprint.

Sebastian might talk of the search for Smoking Mirror, he might have his coffin hauled around the shores of Lake Texcoco, but it was clear to Martinez that the vampire cared less for the god than for the slim girl whose hair hung to her ankles. It was easy for Martinez to envision the future. There would be more invocations, more failures, more threats. In time Sebastian would tire of his quest, take Toci as his bride, and make himself immortal emperor of all the Aztecs, sustained by freely offered sacrifices. Martinez would become a sullen court jester, denied the doubtful gift of living death, then grow old and die among barbarians.

It would not do.

For some reason Martinez found himself thinking of Luis Garcia. Perhaps it was the long trek through the unremitting sunshine that reminded him of the battered veteran. They had marched together down causeways like this one, and a rough companionship had sprung up between them. Some of this feeling was nostalgia, no doubt; Garcia was a bully and a clown, and frequently Martinez had feared or hated him. Still, Garcia was human. He had joked, bragged, and blustered, but Martinez could deal with that. Garcia had been easier to comprehend than this clandestine couple, this pair of austere and sinister stepparents whose very whims meant life or death. Garcia had almost been a friend, certainly more of one than Martinez had known since that sad night when the rain fell and the bridge failed.

The alchemist, who loved to think of unearned miracles, tried to guess what he would do if an angel or a devil suddenly appeared before him and offered him a choice. The decision was surprisingly easy. He would pick the army of Cortez, with all its risks and hardships, over an exile's life in Mexico. With Cortez, who lurked somewhere in the hinterlands, there might still be a chance to see Spain again.

Martinez thought of Spain. He might return with gold, if not the secret of its origin. And even if he returned empty-handed, he would have tales to tell. He pictured himself, a grizzled adventurer, sitting safely in a tavern among his awestruck colleagues, regaling them with tales of Mexico. He would tell the story of the wizard resurrected from the skull that he himself had carried from the Old World to the New, and of the beautiful native priestess who had loved Martinez with most of her heart and all of her body. He would speak of her streaming eyes when he abandoned her; perhaps he would make her a princess. He would talk about the women he had seen skinned and disemboweled; and the whores would giggle and shiver and draw closer to him. And he would save at least one relic, a bit of stone or jewelry to prove that everything he said was true. It was a brighter picture than the one he had imagined for himself a moment ago: Martinez as the lackey of a monster and his mate.

But it was only a dream. Or was it? Martinez thought again of what Don Sebastian had offered him, and tried to decide what it was worth. If everything the sorcerer said was true, Martinez might be abandoning eternal ecstasy. But what were the odds? It was easy to believe that a man might have a pleasant life, and horribly difficult to think that an omniscient god might sweep out of the skies to gather him up and grant him unhuman bliss.

Martinez cursed himself as a man of little faith. He knew what he wanted—he wanted everything. But what could he expect to get? He felt little prepared for the gifts of Smoking Mirror, however much he might desire them. And he wondered if they were real. Perhaps in a later incarnation, Martinez would know more. There were levels of spirit, and a soul could only go so far in one lifetime. He was out of his depth. Still, he would give the god one more chance. Tomorrow night, in Texcoco, the destiny of Alfonso Martinez, an aging alchemist, would be determined.

The route to Texcoco took the expedition for several miles down the southern causeway, then east until they reached solid ground. There it was necessary to turn south again, following a narrow strip of land that ran between Lake Texcoco and the adjoining Lake Chalco. The jaguar knights kept close to the shore of Texcoco, and gradually they turned northeast. Slowly the cultivated fields and forests gave way to wilderness, confirming the alchemist's guess that sensible travelers approached Texcoco by the shorter route across the salt lake. The path along the water's edge was narrow, sometimes overgrown. The woods, when they appeared, were vaguely menacing, but somehow Martinez liked them more than the long stretches of arid wasteland, the sandy stretches where nothing grew and the trees in the distance looked like hiding places for tribes of savages. It was hellishly hot in these little deserts. Martinez felt the sun searing his armor, and wished he had not worn it, nor the sword that slapped against his leg. The Spanish steel was heavy, but Martinez did not feel safe without it.

He waited for the jaguar knights to stop for rest and food, but waited in vain. A brief pause came about midday, which lasted only long enough for Sebastian's six pallbearers to be replaced by six fresh men. He wondered what the coffin weighed.

His stomach rumbled, and he cursed himself for neglecting to bring food. At least he had a skin of water. He drank from it incessantly and finally, against his better judgment, he offered some to Toci. She accepted it, and Martinez was furious when he realized how touched he was by her generosity in deigning to notice him. Nonetheless he drank after she did, feeling for a moment as if he had stolen a kiss.

At last the sun began to fall. Martinez watched his shadow lengthen, eagerly anticipating the moment when darkness would put an end to his suffering. Weak and weary, he was amazed by the stolidity of the warriors who carried the coffin on their sweating shoulders.

At sunset the expedition stopped abruptly. No one spoke, and yet the knights of Smoking Mirror seemed to know when they reached the place: a clearing by the shore, surrounded by tall trees. Martinez did not question the decision; he dropped to the ground. He tossed his helmet and his sword away, and then eased off his pack, but stayed close beside it. He shut his eyes and tried to forget the trees. All day, even though he had feared a hostile ambush, he had hoped that Spanish soldiers might break through some patch of woods, kill all his companions, and rescue him. Now it was enough to rest. Cortez was evidently elsewhere.

He almost slept. He heard people moving, and smelled a campfire burning, but he ignored it all as best he could. He was lost in a dreamless trance, more free from fear than he had been for a long while. He thought of nothing—until some unidentified disturbance jolted him back into awareness. He sat up all at once, his eyes wide. The night was black, relieved only by the orange flicker of the nearby fire. At his feet stood the figure of Don Sebastian.

"There is food for you," Sebastian said.

Martinez sat where he was. He rubbed his eyes, then looked up thoughtfully at Don Sebastian.

"What will you do if nothing happens in Texcoco?" asked Martinez.

"I shall try again."

"And so on," said Martinez. "Where is the food?"

Toci slipped from the group of men around the fire and silently handed Martinez an earthenware plate.

"You gave her water," said Sebastian.

Martinez grunted. He looked at the steaming stew on the plate, picked out a piece of meat with his fingers, and put it in his mouth. It was probably dog, but he was used to it. Sebastian and Toci watched him eat, but Martinez never raised his eyes.

"What are you staring at?" he finally asked. He set his empty plate aside, and at once the priestess snatched it up and carried it away.

"I have been thinking about you," Sebastian said.

"And I have been thinking about you."

"What have you determined, Martinez?"

The cries of animals drifted out of the distant trees, echoing across the lake. "I don't know," said Martinez. "I wonder if you will ever succeed in your efforts, and I'm not even sure what you're trying to do. That footprint last night is as much as anyone expects to see of Smoking Mirror, and I can't see that it was any use. Yet you noticed that it was enough to frighten me. I don't know if we can ever find this god, and I don't know if I want to."

Sebastian sank down to his knees beside the alchemist and spoke to him earnestly. "Remember what I told you, Martinez, about those who meet Smoking Mirror but are afraid to reach out to him. It may be only a parable, but there is truth in it. My own studies have convinced me that belief in these powers is demanded of those who would receive them. Perhaps they grow from human thoughts, or perhaps such thoughts attract and nourish them. But surely they will never summon one who doubts."

"Even if it's true," protested Martinez, "what can I do about it? How can I make myself believe? How can I concentrate my will on something I cannot imagine and am afraid to see? I'm not like you. I'm just an ordinary man with ordinary dreams. The most I ever hoped for, even with the aid of alchemy, was to have a life of pleasure. I might have thought of death later, but not now. I'm afraid of Smoking Mirror. And I'm afraid of you."

"I know," Sebastian said. "I am a horror. Why do you think I seek to solve these mysteries? Because I must. There is no other hope for me. I can never turn back, and never be human again. I must go forward, wherever it takes me. This god, this force, this power may be the one thing in the universe with strength enough to lift me out of this decaying shell and set me free."

Martinez shifted his position to look into the shadowed face of his companion. Sebastian's dead eyes were as dark as his streaming hair, as dark as the gleaming mirror that hung from the golden chain around his neck.

"Maybe tomorrow," said Martinez.

"Tomorrow," said Sebastian, rising. "You must sleep now, Martinez. Everyone must sleep but me. I stand guard. Good night."

Martinez rolled over on his side and clutched his pack as if it were a pillow. It was hard and heavy, stuffed with gold and the last few vials of the potions he had brought from Spain. He shut his eyes, hoping he would not dream.

On the last evening of the twenty-day feast of Smoking Mirror, nineteen men, a woman, and a corpse reached the outskirts of Texcoco. There they waited for the sun to set. The eighteen jaguar knights sat quietly, their burden on the ground, while a restless Martinez peered anxiously toward the city.

"It's getting dark," he said. "You'd think there would be lights to be seen. What are they up to? Are they keeping the city black to honor the approach of the god?"

"They do not know we come," answered Toci, but she would say no more. She leaned over a small fire. Above it was suspended a small stone bowl filled with salt water from Lake Texcoco. When it began to boil, she dropped things into the water. Martinez watched her carefully, trying to keep track of the ingredients she put into her brew. He noticed flowers and seeds, roots and mushrooms, and small brown buds.

"It's that same stuff again, is it?" he asked, but the priestess did not answer him. Instead, she chanted to herself in an unnerving undertone.

"Maybe I'll try some of it tonight," offered Martinez, but when Toci continued to ignore him he turned away. He walked toward Sebastian's coffin and looked down at it speculatively. "Think you can do it?" he asked the wooden box. He was suddenly surrounded by half a dozen Aztec warriors. Two of them took him gently by the shoulders and pulled him back from the coffin.

"It's all right!" protested Martinez. "Do you think I'm going to kill your god? I was only looking." Despite his explanations he was dragged away, and not released until a contingent of armed guards had stationed themselves around Sebastian.

Spurned by Toci and Sebastian, threatened by the jaguar knights, the alchemist stood alone in the growing darkness and cast resentful eyes on his companions. Steam rose from Toci's potion, drifting on a breeze until it reached Martinez with an odor that was at once sweet and sickening.

And then Martinez saw another sort of smoke. Green and glowing, it poured from Don Sebastian's coffin. The men surrounding it dispersed before they were enveloped in the luminescent mist, and as they stepped into the shadows they bowed before the billowing cloud. Martinez watched as the cloud coalesced into a pillar of pulsating fog. He guessed what was happening, and wondered if the others did. Even Toci was transfixed by the unearthly sight, and Martinez had to remind himself that this was merely a more dignified way for a vampire to leave his coffin than crawling out.

The smoke drew in upon itself until it formed a grotesque parody of the human form. Wisps of haze turned into locks of hair, and gaps in the mist transformed themselves into a pair of dark, hollow eyes. Fog became flesh, and Don Sebastian stood at the edge of Texcoco.

The thing that might be Smoking Mirror looked around. "A dark city," he said. "Let us proceed."

They were more than a mile from the lake by now. The sun was gone, and when the fire had been extinguished Martinez found that he could barely see. The city they approached was a gloomy mass of indistinguishable buildings. One landmark rose above the rest against the purple sky: the pyramid of Smoking Mirror.

The formation of the march was much as before, except that now Sebastian walked with Toci and Martinez behind the empty box which six warriors carried on their shoulders. Six others walked before it, and six more behind. Martinez was more grateful than ever for their presence. "Something's wrong here," he said. "Where are the people?"

"There may be none," Sebastian said.

"What do you mean?"

"There are only rumors. Yet Cortez had the king of this city executed months ago for inciting a rebellion against the Spanish occupation. And when Cortez was driven from Tenochtitlan, the army of Texcoco stood against him in his flight. But Cortez broke through, with horses and guns. Since then, there has been little word from Texcoco. Some say the people fled in fear of Cortez, convinced he was the Feathered Serpent, the ancient enemy of Smoking Mirror. Some say they fled to join him, wherever he may be. But it matters not at all to us, Martinez. We are here not for the city, but for its god."

The humble buildings they were passing were utterly devoid of life. Martinez felt his skin crawl. "There's nobody here," he said. "A whole city, and it's been abandoned. Did you know this?"

"I feared it," said Sebastian. "It matters little for this night's work, but it bodes ill for the future. There was an alliance between Tenochtitlan and Texcoco, and even an apportionment of interests. Tenochtitlan was the military capital and Texcoco the center of culture. The most revered of the poets and priests were here. It was a more civilized city, but also weaker. And now it seems that there is nothing left of it."

"But surely Smoking Mirror is the god of blood, and the Feathered Serpent the god of art and learning . . ."

"Another paradox, Martinez, and one that I cannot explain. Yet what has happened is beyond doubt. This is a city of ghosts, and one haunted by the image of Hernan Cortez."

At Sebastian's words, a dim shape raced across the street in front of them. Toci gave a sharp command that Martinez could not interpret, and three soldiers rushed off in pursuit of the phantom.

A moment later they were back, a prisoner within their grasp. By the faint light of the sliver of moon, Martinez saw that it was an old woman. The shadows made her wrinkles look like black war paint.

"Question her, Toci," said Sebastian.

A terse exchange followed, and if Martinez could not understand the words, he understood something from the tone of the old woman's voice. They were well into the city and she was the only human being they had found.

"She is alone," said Toci finally. "Texcoco is gone. All are gone. She says Texcoco is her home. She stays. Where can she go?"

"She is mad," Sebastian said, and Martinez thought he saw his mouth twist in the moonlight. "Let her go."

The old woman scurried off into the darkness.

"There may be others," said Sebastian, "more dangerous than this one. Watch carefully, Martinez. Watch the shadows."

Martinez looked anxiously around. There was only light

enough to frighten him. "Perhaps we should turn back," he said. "Who knows what powers rule here now? An empty city. There will be scavengers. Perhaps entire tribes of savages, armed with spears and arrows. Weapons made of wood."

"If that wood strikes my heart," Sebastian said, "I will be no worse off than before you brought my skull across the seas. We must press on. This may be our last chance. Cortez is still in Mexico, and stronger than before. His strategy is clear. One by one, he will subvert both tribes and cities, until he has an army even Tenochtitlan cannot withstand. Our time is running short. Tonight we have the opportunity to meet with Smoking Mirror. We may never have another."

13. The Pyramid

THE pyramid of Smoking Mirror blotted out the waning moon, and its gigantic shadow fell upon the twenty-one pilgrims who waited at its base. To Martinez its black bulk seemed much more imposing than the temple of the god back in Tenochtitlan; he would have sworn that it was higher than the great pyramid of the war god. An all but endless row of steps led up one side to the distant peak, bordered by carvings whose details were obscured by darkness. The shrine looked as dead as the empty city that huddled around it.

"We should build a fire," suggested Martinez.

"I think not," Sebastian replied. "As you said, there may be scavengers about. Not beasts—who fear the flames—but hungry men, who might be drawn to them. If our presence here remains a secret, we will be the better for it."

"Then tell me what is to be done. You have said nothing of your plans. Only that you hope to raise the god."

Sebastian stared at him steadily but did not reply.

"I thought I might take some of that brew tonight," continued Martinez uneasily, "the seeds and buds and mushrooms. Perhaps it will show me something I cannot deny."

"No, Martinez."

"No? What would you have of me? Two days ago you all but

ordered me to take it, and now you deny me! Don't you want your apprentice to meet this fabled god? Are you ashamed of me?"

"Too late, Martinez. You are too late."

"Too late for what? I am here and I am ready. I will do what you say."

"Precisely. And I say that you will wait here with these warriors while Toci and I ascend the pyramid."

The alchemist looked wide-eyed at Sebastian, and then at Toci. Neither of them spoke, but Martinez began to sputter incoherently. "You can't mean to leave me behind," he finally blurted out. "Why did you bring me all this way?"

"You would not be safe alone in Tenochtitlan. You know that. And in truth, I did not decide what would be done with you until last night, when we camped by the shores of Lake Texcoco."

"Last night? Why?"

"Remember your own words. You told me once again that you could not believe, and that you were afraid to try. You have no faith, Martinez, and your will is set against the god, when faith and will are all we have to draw him down to us. The presence of an unbeliever is too great a risk. We must succeed tonight, regardless of the cost. I am sorry, Martinez. I did not hope for this."

Martinez shook with indignation. "Was it for this I took your side? Was it for this I carried your accursed skull halfway around the world? I was good enough to be your brother then, but now that you stand on the verge of triumph, you find you have no need of me. Just you and the woman, is it? Up there alone in the dark, with her drugged past caring? I doubt she will come down alive, and I pray your thrice-accursed Smoking Mirror will carry off the pair of you!"

He turned away in fury, but before he had taken a step he felt Sebastian's strong hand fall on his shoulder.

"Take care, Martinez," Sebastian said. "I have no wish to make an enemy of you, and you would be wise to feel the same for me. This decision is your doing as much as mine, and it is only for tonight. If we find Smoking Mirror, you will share his blessings.

And for now, you are spared the dangers of courting him. Do not cross me, Martinez."

The face the alchemist presented to Sebastian was empty of all expression. "So be it," he said.

Sebastian gazed at the blank countenance for a moment, then he stepped back toward Toci. He stood protectively beside her as she raised a small flask to her lips, then put an arm around her shoulders and led her to the first step of the pyramid.

"Just a little fire?" begged Martinez. "Only for a minute. I want to brew some chocolate. It will help to keep these men awake."

The two devotees of Smoking Mirror ignored him and moved slowly up the narrow stairs. Martinez watched them carefully until they reached the summit and, stepping onto it, were lost from sight.

The shadow of the pyramid dropped behind Sebastian when he reached the peak; the square platform that he saw was lit by the weak rays of the low crescent moon. He helped the priestess up the last step, more out of gallantry than any need, then stepped away from her to pace the perimeter of the stone terrace. He surveyed the darkened city on all sides, but the dim and distant buildings were no more to him than the lonely landscape that might surround an isolated mountain. And at its top stood two small figures who were utterly alone. Somehow the dead city pleased Sebastian, yet he was troubled by the feeling that there might be an omen in its desolation. An image of Texcoco's sister city swam before his eyes and disappeared.

"The potion," he said. "Is it working?"

"No," said Toci. "Soon." She walked across the broad platform to stand beside him.

"You know what I must do," Sebastian said. "There is no other way. I can drink nothing but blood."

"I said yes," Toci replied. There was no recrimination in her tone.

"I have seen the priests do as much," Sebastian continued, "bleeding themselves as penance to placate the gods. Smoking

Mirror needs blood. And only when his drugs run through your veins may I taste of them."

"Soon," said Toci soothingly. She touched his arm and led him to the center of the terrace. There she sat cross-legged as she had two nights before in Tenochtitlan. Sebastian kneeled before her.

"I shall not kill you," said Sebastian.

"I know."

They waited together while the stars wheeled slowly overhead. Sebastian saw a change come over his companion. Her face turned pale, and a delicate film of perspiration gleamed on her brow. Her eyes grew huge, and they began to shine. Her breathing grew more rapid; Sebastian could see her breasts and shoulders rise and fall beneath the black robe. He found himself thinking too much about the priestess and too little of the god; but then, he had not yet tasted the god's potion.

Toci stretched out her arms behind her and leaned back. Her beautiful small head turned gracefully, and her long bright hair cascaded over the black stones. "I took more," she said, "for you."

Her golden throat throbbed, and Sebastian knew that it was time. He slid toward her, his anticipation tinged with an unexpected melancholy. Something in her willing youth and innocence called out to him for mercy, and he wished for a moment to be an uncorrupted Aztec boy who would offer this lovely woman nothing but affection.

He took her face in his hands and looked into her shining eyes. His fingers stroked her cheeks and slipped through her bright black hair. He kissed her lips gently, and when her mouth opened under his he felt her warm, sweet breath flow into him.

A mixture of regret and gratitude welled up in him when Toci pulled back from his kiss to offer him her throat, but he could not resist the offering. He kissed her there, and put his arms around her. The two of them sank down. Gently, carefully, his teeth slipped into the pulsating vein. Her blood was sweet.

She lay beneath him quietly at first, a sacrificial victim, but when his bite sank deeper, he felt her respond by digging her long, pale fingernails into his shoulders. Rapture overtook Sebastian.

He doubted that the drugs could act so quickly. Rather, it was Toci that intoxicated him—her bright blood, her unquestioning acceptance. Knowing he could never drink enough, he stopped himself and drew away from her.

She lay very still, and for an instant he feared that he had been too greedy. But she was still breathing, though now her gasps were deeper and more regular, as if she were asleep. She stirred, and he gathered her up in his arms. Two dark wounds glistened in her throat. He lapped the trickling blood away, and waited for her eyes to open. "Toci," he whispered.

Slowly she regained possession of herself, until finally she could sit opposite him again, trembling but erect. "The god will come," she said.

Sebastian wondered, but only for a moment. He felt a touch of giddiness, something draughts of blood had never brought to him before. The weight of his dead flesh began to drop away, as if his body were no more than a shell housing his spirit. This was something he had always believed, but he had never experienced it so vividly. He lifted his head toward the heavens. With no fires to obscure the sky, the stars seemed very close. They began to spin before his startled eyes, leaving glittering streaks of multicolored flame against the darkness. He felt as light and insubstantial as a ghost, and yet uncannily aware of every nerve and muscle he possessed.

His gaze dropped down to the small black mirror hanging from his neck. He recollected dimly that a vampire could never hope to see his own reflection, but nonetheless he raised the dark disk to his face. At first he saw nothing in its shining surface. Then, gradually, a glowing mist began to drift up from the black obsidian. He stared at it for centuries, or so it seemed, until the mist parted to reveal a bright unblinking eye.

"The Smoking Mirror," said Don Sebastian, hearing his voice echo from afar.

His very words took shape in gleaming arcs of molten metal;

he was seeing sounds and tasting colors. He closed his eyes in momentary weariness, but the pictures on his eyelids were more than he could bear. He looked into the smoking mirror once again, and there he saw the face of Toci carved in gold. He studied it intently, forgetting the living woman who sat a few feet away, only to see the gold slip down her face in rivulets, exposing the naked skull. He wanted to weep, so great was his sense of love inexorably lost, but then the skull transformed itself into a sad-eyed silver mask alive with fire. It was still her face, yet it was his own as well, and as he stared, it dissolved into a blast of pure white light so blinding that he let go of the illusive disc.

And there before him sat the priestess of his visions, her huge brown eyes absorbing him. A cool breeze slipped across the pyramid; it caught her long black hair and spread it out across the stars.

Almost aghast at her ethereal loveliness, Sebastian attempted to compose himself. "The food of the gods," he said. "And you have tasted it before. But it was never so ennobling, I venture, for it was never filtered through your precious blood." His voice cut glowing swaths across the air that kept Toci's face hidden from him, but when the silence came again she was still there, her lips parted, her face raised expectantly.

She moved her head, and he saw a thousand images of her embossed against the sky, each one a small part of that graceful motion, each one a frozen instant of perfection.

"Toci," he said. "You are more beautiful than the moon." He wanted nothing more than to reach out to her, yet he would not. Some small resolute part of him still held the hope of seeing Smoking Mirror, and he doubted that the god would come to them if they were lost in passion, however exalted it might be.

"I dare not touch you," said Sebastian, "but surely you can speak?"

"You are the god," said Toci. "I see it. Wait. Wait for the light in the sky."

"How long have we been here?"

"I know not. Wait for the god." Her words were low and clear, like distant bells. Each syllable surrounded Sebastian with luminescent rings. He felt an exultation rise within him, streaming up from his heart into a rush of raw energy exploding in his head. He reeled backward, a million galaxies away from Texcoco, and yet still close to Toci. His face fell toward the black stone terrace, and every speck of dust he saw became a universe.

Flat on his back, he watched the moon dance past him. Patterns danced in the streaming stars, cold white pictures of the god Tezcatlipoca. He saw the pale skeleton that rattled in the forest, and the dark idol that squatted in the temple, and the brightly colored image that adorned the walls of Montezuma's palace. He felt the huge bulk of the pyramid straining up beneath him, its massive stones extending upward to the cosmos through the small terrace where he and Toci worshipped. The few square feet of stone became an interface between the tiny earth and the infinities surrounding it.

"Toci," said Sebastian. "The god is here." He sat up suddenly, his head reeling, and as he did so his hand stretched out to take his dark companion's wrist.

The slightest touch of her was overwhelming. Deliriously, he felt her naked flesh and sensed the vibrant flow of rich red blood that coursed through her. His eyes caught hers, and they were locked together in a communion he could not undo. All thoughts of Smoking Mirror were lost in her. A still, small voice chastised him, but he chose to ignore it. If he was a god, then the privileges of a god were his.

He took the priestess by the shoulders and pulled her to her feet. She rose to meet him in a series of fragmented pictures, each more exquisite than any painting he had ever seen. "I have waited for the light," he said, "but you are the light. You are the god, and I am the god. Together we are Smoking Mirror."

"Yes," said Toci, and the word generated silver flames around them.

Tenderly, Sebastian kissed her glistening eyes. He had no thought of blood, no thought of domination. His only wish was to become one with her. He took her black robe in his hands and lifted it. Toci flowed toward him, her head bent low, and suddenly he held her only garment in his quivering hands.

The golden goddess stood before him, naked and unashamed. Her body shone like some forgotten antique statue in the moonlight, except that it was real. She was not marble, but rather an awesome amalgam of black and bronze. Her dark hair streamed behind her like a cloak; her frank and open gaze suspended him somewhere between the earth and sky. Her figure was exquisite. Plump thighs, slim hips, and gently swelling breasts chastened his lust while they inflamed it. For a moment he was afraid to touch her, but then he ran hands along her perfect cheekbones and stroked her full lips. His fingertips were afire. He ran his right hand down her throat, past the cruel wounds he had demanded of her, and traced a path between her small dark nipples. Her belly was firm and flat; as he sank down upon his knees before her, his pale fingers reached up to sink into the softness of her breasts. She was half a dream and half a woman, a vision sent by Smoking Mirror and yet a victim, too. He felt a love for her that he had never known before, as if she were part of himself that he had lost and then miraculously regained. His hand slipped down between her thighs and sought the crevice waiting for him there. He had no wish to hurt her, for she was not another, but himself. He caressed smooth round buttocks, and he kissed her tenderly. A white light roared around him, and he heard her moan.

Toci collapsed upon him in an ecstasy. Then the blinding light was everywhere. The night was gone, and the first rays of the morning sun streamed brilliantly across the surface of the pyramid.

"The light!" Sebastian screamed. The sun!"

He pushed the priestess from him frantically and pulled himself along the terrace toward its edge. The bright rays of the dawn seared his pale skin, and his howls of agony careened through the abandoned city. Toci rose to her feet in drugged bewilderment, watching her lover all but throw himself down the long stairway.

She stood at the brink and stared in horror as he crawled, head first, erratically down the narrow steps like some exotic insect.

His robes of red and white and black were steaming. Toci forgot her stunned surprise and raced naked down the pyramid behind him. Below her, she could see the bodies of the jaguar knights stretched out in sleep. Neither the sun nor Sebastian's anguished cries awakened them.

By the time the vampire had reached the ground, the shadow of the pyramid was long, but his coffin lay beyond it in the sunlight. He leaped out of the shade to grasp the wooden box, and his titanic wails seemed loud enough to shatter the sky. Toci screamed at him to wait, but he was past all reasoning. Limbs flailing, he dragged the coffin toward the shadow of the temple. In her rush to reach him, the priestess tripped over the bottom step and fell flat on her face upon the pavement. Gasping for breath, she raised her eyes and saw Sebastian creep tortuously toward the darkness, pulling the box of Spanish soil along with him.

The wind had been knocked from her, and her body felt like one long bruise, but she staggered to her feet in time to see Sebastian achieve his goal. He gave one final heave and fell into the shadow. And still the men around him did not move.

Toci called on them to wake, then ran to Sebastian's side. He was as immobile as all the others, but she knew that each dawn brought him death. When she reached him, however, she saw that he had not entirely escaped the sun. He lay sprawled on his back, but his sandaled right foot had fallen out of the shade into the blazing beams of dawn. The foot was gray and withered, and as she stared at it the flesh began to boil. Horrified, she grasped the vampire by his hair and heaved him out of the sun entirely. The foot was a blackened, blistered stump, but Sebastian was saved. Calling up all her strength, she dragged the dead weight of her lover to his coffin and rolled him into it.

For a moment she stood panting, a naked woman alone in a city of ghosts. Then she began to walk among the jaguar knights. All of them were dead.

They lay where they had fallen, their eyes staring, their faces white against the spotted skins they wore. The flower of Tezcatlipoca's warriors were here, and each one had been murdered. The lips of some of them were covered with a fine froth; it did not take a physician to see that they had all been poisoned.

"The little man," said Toci. Alfonso Martinez was nowhere to be found.

The naked priestess shivered in the sunlight. She was alone in Texcoco, far from home. Her knees were bleeding from her fall, her chin was bruised, and her head ached. Slowly she ascended the steps of the pyramid, and there retrieved her long black robe. She winced as she put it on, and yet the wearing of it gave her comfort. She was not just a frightened woman, she was the representative of a great god. She thought of the vampire's hideous foot, and felt a thrill run through her body that was something more than terror.

"He is lame," she said. "Smoking Mirror."

The god had come after all. The legends said that the gods had battled in the skies to gain possession of the earth when it was new, and that the struggle for supremacy had cost Smoking Mirror a foot. Now Sebastian bore his mark.

She walked slowly down the steps of Smoking Mirror's temple, her head bowed, her mind obsessed by visions. She dragged the coffin to the base of the pyramid and threw herself full length upon it. There, alone, she waited for the darkness.

14. The Bats

"THE god mocks us," Sebastian said. He sat on his own coffin below the pyramid, and Toci sat beside him. The night was only a few minutes old, but he had been awake for long enough to comprehend the plight in which Alfonso Martinez had left them.

"Martinez," said Sebastian bitterly, looking out at the dim, unburied forms of eighteen warriors of Tezcatlipoca. "I shall see Martinez again and I shall relish the encounter. I wish I were as sure of Smoking Mirror."

"But Smoking Mirror came!" protested Toci. "You said it, in the night."

"I thought for a moment that there was something, but what has come of it? Our escort has been destroyed and we are trapped in this abandoned city. The alchemist has turned against us, and the sun has crippled me."

He contemplated his withered right foot. "But I am to blame," he said. "More than the sun, more than Martinez, and more than Smoking Mirror. Perhaps the god might have appeared, had I not been intent on you to the exclusion of all else. I have betrayed myself."

Toci stared at the ground, her eyes averted from Sebastian.

"Smoking Mirror makes men want women," she murmured. "There is magic in it."

Sebastian stood up suddenly. He nearly fell, but slowly regained his balance and began to pace back and forth, at once expressing his frustration and testing his ruined limb. At least he was walking, however much more sinister his limp made him appear. Half sick with sorrow, Toci nonetheless felt a tenderness for Sebastian that she had never known before.

"Look," she said. "Look at you. You must believe the god has come. He left his mark on you."

Sebastian stopped. "The lame foot," he said. "I never thought of that, though you told me the story, and I told it to Martinez. So you think this new monstrosity I bear is a sign from the stars that I am chosen? I would have been content with less than this."

"Who knows the gods?" Toci replied. "I see you, and you are Smoking Mirror."

Sebastian sat down again. "A god of tricks and treachery," he said. "A god who tests his followers, who lures them on with dreams of love and power. It might be true. Perhaps this is his way of greeting me, for all that it is not a welcome one. I suspect that what I feel for Smoking Mirror now is what Martinez felt for us when he poisoned his guards and ran away. I will try to be more of a philosopher than he was, however grim our present plight may be. And it is grim enough."

Toci had nothing to say.

"I might have tried to carry the coffin myself," Sebastian continued, "but now I can hardly walk, and there would have been much risk in it, we two traveling alone through wilderness at night—especially when every man we met might be our enemy. There's no way of telling where Cortez may be, no guarantee that any Mexican is not his ally. Apparently Martinez was certain that the Spaniards are nearby; certainly he did not flee to find a new home in the jungle."

"Then will we go?" asked Toci.

"There must be a way. I thought of flying, by transforming

myself into a bat. It is a long way to Tenochtitlan, even if I fly across the lake, and I must have the coffin to take me every morning; without it I cannot survive. I would have to fly to Tenochtitlan, alert the high priest to our predicament, and then return again by sunrise. It would be unwise to risk it, and I cannot leave you here alone at night."

"You love me?"

"Suppose that I do," Sebastian said. "Or suppose that I care nothing for you. Suppose I want you only for your strength, for that firm purity of purpose that's born of your virginity."

Toci gazed at him earnestly. "What is this 'suppose'?" she asked.

"A word," Sebastian answered. "Only a word. Pretend you never heard it."

"And what is this 'pretend'?"

"Nothing," Sebastian said. "Forget I said it." He took her head in his hands and pulled it down upon his shoulder. "You were right the first time. I love you, and I would not leave you here, even if I could." Toci embraced him eagerly.

Despite himself, Sebastian summoned up the ghost of a smile, a mixture of derision and delight that Toci did not see. "Are you so eager to sacrifice your innocence?" he asked. "Remember, you are sworn to Smoking Mirror."

"I am sworn to you, then."

"There are more ways than one of showing love," Sebastian said. "Nothing would please me more than the chance to take you —to steal away your blood and your purity. And yet I need your life, and your maidenhead, because you are my only link to the god."

"I am here for you," Toci said simply. "Do what is best."

He kissed her fiercely and then drew back.

"You tempt me, Toci, more than I can say. But this is not the time. There may never be a time. You are Smoking Mirror too, a trickster and a tempter. Yet what you and I need now is not each other. We need a band of men, strong and faithful servants like the ones that we have lost. Men to carry my coffin."

A cool wind sighed through the deserted streets of Texcoco. It ruffled Toci's hair, and sent a shiver through her slim brown body. "There is no one here," she said. "We are alone."

"Perhaps. Yet there was something Martinez said that rang true. I have no way of knowing how long this city has been empty, but surely time enough has passed for someone to learn about it. There may be men in this city. Not its citizens, but those who come exploring. It seems most likely they would be enemies. But if we cannot find someone, we are in jeopardy here."

"The high priest," suggested Toci. "He will look for us."

"The blind man," said Sebastian. "I've thought of him. He will send a search party out for us eventually. But when? Until they come for us, there is no food for you, no blood for me."

"My blood is yours."

"Toci," Sebastian said. He touched her face. "You have given me enough. I need you as you are. I have no desire for more, and I will not see you transformed into a monster like myself."

"You are no monster," Toci said. "You are a god."

"A god with no subjects," said Sebastian. "Or only one. Come, Toci. We will be safer on the pyramid tonight: less visible, and more likely to see anyone approaching. My eyes are keen at night, but still it helps to have a vantage point."

He staggered to his feet and leaned heavily upon the priestess as she led him up the narrow steps. More than once he stumbled, but she never let him fall.

"Does it hurt?" she asked.

"No. It is dead."

At the summit, he let go of her and paced the edge of the terrace as he had the night before; but now his steps were slow and tortuous. He did not watch his feet, but kept his gaze on the silent city below him.

Toci stood in the center of the terrace and watched him grow straighter and stronger with each step he took. His eyes were never on her; he was struggling alone, still outwardly intent on his surveillance of the city.

He stopped abruptly, staring into the east. "Someone is coming," he whispered. "Get down, or they will see us against the sky."

Toci sank down on her bruised knees, then flat upon her belly. With her black robe and black hair, she seemed no more than a shadow slithering through the dim moonlight toward Sebastian. He had dropped down too, and lay prone upon the pavement, his face at the eastern edge of Smoking Mirror's pyramid. A night bird screamed somewhere in the distance.

"Do you see them?" asked Sebastian softly, as the priestess crept beside him.

"No. Where are they?"

"You will see them soon enough. They are coming this way. More than a score of men, and I would swear that they are heading directly toward us."

"There," said Toci in a breathless undertone.

The interlopers walked in darkness. They were small, swarthy men, naked but for loincloths, armed with spears and arrows.

"Weapons of wood," Sebastian said. "The only ones I fear."

The men walked single file through the narrow street until they passed into the courtyard at the base of Smoking Mirror's temple. They were almost directly beneath Sebastian and Toci.

"I know them," Toci whispered. "They are animals. A wild tribe with no king. I told you of them once before, and you laughed."

"Tell me again, quickly. They are going around to the other side of the pyramid, and I believe they mean to mount it."

"Animals. They kill for nothing. They have no god, only the bats."

"The bats?"

"I told you. Vampire bats. Animals that live on blood like you. You laughed when I told you."

"I am not laughing now. I hear them coming up the steps. We have only one chance. Can you understand their talk? Is their name for Smoking Mirror the same as yours?"

"Yes."

"Then lie there and wait for me. We shall see what kind of god I am." Sebastian rose slowly to his feet.

"Down!" gasped Toci. "They will kill you!"

"They will try," answered Sebastian, "but I shall change their minds."

Incoherent shouts came from below as Don Sebastian stood up against the waning moon. An arrow flew past him and rattled on the stones beside Toci. Sebastian raised his arms. A short spear seemed to strike one hand, but passed through it without apparent harm.

"Tezcatlipoca!" Sebastian shouted. He threw back his dark head and soared into the air. Two spears sped fruitlessly beneath him. His robe of red and white and black slipped limply to the ground; his pale flesh turned dark. Great webbed wings had sprouted from his shoulder blades. The hail of weapons ceased, and no one ventured to the summit of the pyramid. A vast silence embraced Texcoco. Half man, half bat, Sebastian floated hundreds of feet above the city claimed by Smoking Mirror.

He swept around the pyramid in a huge circle, then darted down, spreading more consternation among the terror-stricken men who sprawled along the steps. None of them screamed; none of them even moved. Sebastian skimmed the surface of the narrow stairway, and when he rose again one member of the tribe was caught in his strong hands.

The man kicked feebly, half dead from fright, and Sebastian climbed with him through the empty air. The huge wings flapped majestically, lifting man and monster until they were no more than specks against the stars. From above, the priestess heard a scream.

The cry was faint at first, like something heard in a forgotten dream, but it grew louder, and then louder still. Toci jumped up when she saw what was coming. The man Sebastian had chosen was plummeting through space, dropping like a stone from heights beyond imagination. His wail of horror rose till it was deafening; his flailing figure seemed to grow against the sky. Toci stepped back.

The man splattered on the stones atop the pyramid; his blood splashed over Toci. Nothing was left of him but split skin, shattered bones, and crimson jelly. Toci wiped his blood from her eyes and strode toward the stairway. Before she reached it, Sebastian swooped down beside her.

He became a man again. She touched his skin eagerly, ran her hands along his naked body, and kissed him fiercely. Willfully, she tore her lower lip against his fangs. She dropped down to her knees and kissed him once again, then rose to face the awestruck tribesmen, her face a mask of blood.

"This is your king!" she shouted. "This is your god! This is Smoking Mirror!"

Dozens of dark eyes looked anxiously up at her, but no one moved. Then, one by one, the men began to creep backward down the stairs.

"They are too much afraid," Sebastian said. "They will be no good to us or to themselves. I should not have killed that man."

"You did well, Tezcatlipoca."

Naked in the night, Sebastian felt his emaciated body stiffen at the sound of the name Toci had never called him before.

"You kept my life," the priestess said. "It is yours forever."

Sebastian wanted nothing more than to dismiss these men and take Toci at her word. But these might be the ones he had hoped for to replace his murdered escort, and he knew that he must win them to his side. "Tell them to stop," he told her, and Toci called out the command. Twenty-seven men froze like statuary.

"Where are these bats you say they worship?" he asked.

"At night, they are everywhere."

"Then I must find them. Keep these fellows here. They will obey you."

He ran his hands through her black hair, and he stared at her while his body changed again. Gray fur sprouted from his dead skin, wings wider than a man was tall sprang from his back. His face turned dark and blunt, and his still-human fingers traced a pattern upon Toci's breast.

"Keep them here," he said. Then he wheeled into the wind.

He was gone for long enough to worry his worshippers. Toci walked among them, up and down the steps, a blood-stained beauty they could scarcely comprehend. To some she spoke soothingly, to others she was sharp and threatening, but somehow she kept them together as the seemingly endless minutes dragged along.

At last Sebastian returned, and with him came a horde of little bats. They fluttered down in multitudes behind him, a swarm of miniature monsters, quick flapping bits of fur and leather. Their bright eyes gleamed where Don Sebastian's were dead, but their sharp teeth were very like his own.

Again Sebastian took human form, but still the black beasts clustered all around him. They covered his pale skin like a cloak of living leather. The men on the stairway looked at him with suddenly illuminated eyes.

"Tell them," said Sebastian, "these are my brothers."

The priestess spoke. Sebastian moved among the men, and Toci walked beside him. He bent to touch the men's heads, and more than one she kissed upon the cheek. And each man that either of the lovers touched rose up. Sebastian was alive with crawling creatures, each one nipping at his naked flesh. The tribesmen clustered round him eagerly, their faces flush with holy ecstasy. Red streams coursed down Sebastian's limbs, and Toci stood at his right hand.

"My brothers," Sebastian said again. Men and bats surrounded him. "These are my brothers."

15. The Feathered Serpent

HERNAN Cortez occupied the city of Texcoco on the last day of December 1520, in command of a great force, augmented by supplies and soldiers from the Spanish colonies of Cuba and Jamaica.

He issued orders that every native town owed him allegiance. All rebels were sold into slavery, except, of course, for those who died in the fight for their freedom; and the Spaniards never lost the allegiance of the Tlascalans, the tribe of Indians whose unswerving support had been theirs from the beginning. Perhaps they still adhered to the belief that Cortez was the Feathered Serpent, but as his power grew there was less and less need to bolster Spanish strength with claims upon the supernatural.

And yet the gods seemed to be with him. The hitherto unknown disease of smallpox had spread among the Mexicans, striking even the new emperor of Tenochtitlan, who was replaced by Cuauhtemoc, husband of one of Montezuma's daughters.

Cortez began to treat his men with some indifference. The gold that he had granted them on the night when they fled Tenochtitlan was gathered up, and most of it found its way into the coffers of the Spanish king and his commander. All Indian women captured were called in for branding, and none were returned to the common soldiers who had made wives or mistresses of them. His last order, before setting out for Texcoco on Christmas Day, was that his shipbuilder should begin construction of thirteen sloops that could patrol the waters of Lake Texcoco.

The Feathered Serpent from Spain appointed a puppet king, then set up his own headquarters in the palace. On the first day of 1521, he summoned Alfonso Martinez.

"The man is mad," the Spanish priest said. "He has been so for more than two months, since we first found him wandering around the lake. The tales he tells are past belief."

"No doubt," Cortez replied. "I have not seen him since he rejoined us. Yet I can hardly doubt his story that he saw Texcoco long before today it is certain, just because he is alive, that he is the last man of our race to have set foot in Tenochtitlan. The interview should prove interesting, at least. Perhaps it will be of some use as well. I mean to glean the truth from his strange dreams. However weak his mind, he is our best informant."

Hernan Cortez sat upon the throne of Texcoco. The royal room was nearly empty, stripped of almost every trace of Aztec embellishment, though there were plans afoot to refurbish it. Six tried and trusted men stood beside the throne, their armor dulled, their sharp swords battered but still intact.

"Bring in Alfonso Martinez," Cortez commanded. Two men stepped forth to do his bidding.

The figure they escorted back into the king's chamber was grotesque. He had been fed, of course, yet his face had the sunken, bony look of a man near starvation. His eyes darted nervously from side to side, his hands shook from the aftereffects of a fever that not even native medicine could cool. His shoulders were stooped; his beard was sparse and sickly. His skin was an unpleasant shade of yellow. He wore some mismatched bits of scavenged armor, and each piece seemed too big for his small frame. Yet the priest had said that he refused to take them off, even when he slept.

Martinez was unaware of his commander's scrutiny. He was too busy looking at the man who was apparently on the brink of toppling an empire.

Cortez was suited to the part. Even though he was sitting, he was a man of considerable height, with broad shoulders and a thick chest. His hair and beard were dark, his face surprisingly pale. At his ease, in a sober black suit with white ruffles at the neck and wrists, Cortez looked more of a grandee than his birth would indicate; but this was the New World, where a man was judged more by his deeds than by his antecedents. And at thirty-five, Hernan Cortez was fortune's favorite. Yet there was something about him that disappointed Martinez. The conqueror's eyes were narrow and close-set; his mouth was small. His face suggested careful calculation more than bold heroics, however much his history might argue against it. Behind him stood one of the banners he had ordered years ago in Cuba. Embroidered in gold on the black field were a cross and the royal arms of Spain; beneath them was this legend: "Comrades, follow the sign of the Holy Cross with true faith, and through it we shall conquer."

The soldier and the alchemist examined each other, one completely relaxed, the other teetering on the brink of hysteria.

"I understand that you have been in Texcoco before," began Cortez.

"I have," croaked Martinez. "On the last night of the feast of Smoking Mirror. It was then that I killed eighteen of his jaguar knights."

Cortez decided there and then that the priest was right about this fellow's state of mind. He hardly seemed capable of killing a mosquito, much less of defeating a band of such intrepid warriors.

"I had to do it," Martinez continued. "I had to get away from Don Sebastian."

"Stop for a moment, please. Identify this Don Sebastian."

"Don Sebastian de Villanueva. He is Smoking Mirror, or so he claims."

"Stop again, please. Who or what is Smoking Mirror?"

"One of their gods, or one of their devils. Some of the Aztecs think that Don Sebastian is the incarnation of this fiend, much as Montezuma thought you were the one called Feathered Serpent."

"Parts of your tale have reached my ears before, physician, but only from the lips of other men. Yet one thing is sure. We checked the rolls, for all that it was hardly necessary, and found no man in all our company who bears the name you mention."

"Of course not!" answered Martinez. "He has been dead for more than thirty years."

"Ah," replied Cortez, suddenly grateful for the presence of half a dozen men-at-arms. This Martinez was clearly a lunatic, and very likely dangerous. Still, his wild stories might provide an evening's entertainment. Cortez stood up, and made an unobtrusive signal to his guards to keep close watch. Martinez noticed nothing but the conqueror's bowleggedness.

"Tell me more about this dead man," said Cortez.

"The Aztecs brought him to life again. This time, at least. The last time he did it himself."

"Then is he not one of our men who died in battle? A friend of yours, perhaps?"

"Oh, no," said Martinez. "He never fought for you. I brought him here, from Spain. I brought him in my pack."

Cortez exchanged a flickering smile with his guards. "It hardly seems big enough to hold a man," he said.

Martinez touched his pack, which he was said to keep beside him always. "It was only his head," he explained.

"And you carried the head of a corpse from Spain? It must have smelled pretty bad, after a time." One of the soldiers snorted, but Cortez silenced him with a swift glance.

"It was only his skull," explained Martinez. "I kept it with me for . . . for my medical studies. Besides, it was made of silver!"

"Then it was well worth having," Cortez said thoughtfully. "What other treasures have you in your pack?"

"Me?" gasped Martinez, as if he hoped the question might be meant for someone else. His eyes moved rapidly; his hand reached back to clutch all he possessed.

"Show us," Cortez commanded.

"There is nothing, really. Only a change of clothing and a bit of medicine. Nothing more." Martinez took only two steps toward the door, then the soldiers were upon him. He felt them pull the pack away from him, and remembered a similar event when the jaguar knights had robbed him of Sebastian's skull beneath the temple of Tezcatlipoca.

"Not again!" Martinez wailed.

He watched in horror as a burly guard emptied the pack upon the floor. Myriad golden rings and bracelets spilled out, together with a few small figurines. A gold bar clattered down behind them, followed by a jewel-encrusted human skull.

"I guessed as much," Cortez declared. "From the condition of the clothes you wear, it was evident you have no others. My nose told me as much." He pushed a path through the precious trinkets with his boot. "And no drugs, either. Reports have told me that you have not been much use as a physician since you rejoined us. I can see why."

"I have been ill myself," said Martinez.

"This is bad, physician. The order went out weeks ago that every man was to turn in his gold, so that the royal share could be collected. And the penalty for failure to comply was clearly stated: that each one who held back would lose everything. You have not paid your taxes, Martinez."

"You would not take it all!"

"You have disobeyed me. I have an obligation to the other men, the ones who did their duty." Cortez pushed at the jeweled skull with his toe. "And what is this? Your comrade Don Sebastian?"

"No, no! I told you. Don Sebastian is alive again in Tenochtitlan. Unless I killed him too. I meant to. This skull is an image of Smoking Mirror."

"But you said that this Sebastian was Smoking Mirror. What is the difference?"

"Listen to me!" screamed Martinez. "I know what you think of me. I know what everybody thinks. But I am telling you the truth! I have important information. This is not the skull I spoke about. The skull of Don Sebastian was brought back to life by that damned woman!" He reached out to touch Cortez, but six strong men kept him away.

"It will be more pleasant to converse from a reasonable distance," said Cortez. "I am sure you understand."

Martinez nodded.

"Very well. Release him. Tell me about this woman."

"She is his mistress, though she claims to be a maiden. A highborn Indian girl, who speaks for him to the Aztec chiefs. She has learned Spanish. She worships him."

"Send for the Lady Marina," Cortez told one of his guards in an undertone. "This fellow's fantasies must spring from something, and I begin to see the pattern."

This time Martinez was listening intently. Like every man in the army he had heard of Marina, the woman who claimed to be an Indian princess, who had been rescued from slavery by Cortez long before he reached Tenochtitlan, and who served now as his interpreter and his mistress. He had never thought before how similar her station was to that of Toci, but the realization only served to show him how important his own knowledge was. Quite clearly, the struggle for Mexico was a duel between Hernan Cortez and Don Sebastian de Villanueva, between the Feathered Serpent and Smoking Mirror. That each man had a native lover was only one more proof. But Martinez still had sense enough to suspect that Cortez would not be easy to convince.

"Believe me," pleaded Martinez, "for what I say is true. Smoking Mirror has a lady much like yours. I have not dreamed her. He is set against you, and he is the greatest threat to your success. I would not be surprised to learn that he has rallied all of Tenochtitlan against you after so much time. The gods fight in the skies, Feathered Serpent against Smoking Mirror, as you and Don Sebastian fight in Mexico."

"Tenochtitlan will fall," announced Cortez.

"There are at least a hundred thousand there to be subdued," protested Martinez.

"No doubt," Cortez agreed. "But we will take them. You have been with us since we moved against the province of Tepeaca.

The reports say that we killed at least fifty thousand there. Of course, they were not all banded together in the same city. But they fell. Tenochtitlan will do the same, I promise you."

"But you must beware of Don Sebastian!"

"Let him do his worst," Cortez said tolerantly. "God is with us, and His favor is worth more than any number of demonic serpents or bedeviled mirrors. All the news we hear tells us that the Aztecs have fallen victim to the pox. It is a new ailment to them, and it kills them faster than we could hope to do. I think I could sit here for a year, and then walk into Tenochtitlan unopposed."

"The pox will not kill Smoking Mirror."

"I suppose not, since you say he is already dead. And yet it does its work. The Indians have an ugly sort of vengeance, though, in this new lover's ailment, syphilis. It is a curse. No wonder that the Aztecs are so chaste."

"There is a cure for that," Martinez ventured. "The Aztecs know it. Let me help you."

"I was speaking in theory," Cortez announced, but he was blushing furiously. The five remaining men-at-arms did all they could to keep their faces grim.

"The Lady Marina," announced the sixth man as he came in through the door. Cortez attempted to compose himself by sinking down upon the throne of Texcoco.

The woman who came into the room was beautiful, garbed in the beaded gown of a Spanish noblewoman. But Martinez did his best to look past that, and past the elaborate high dressing of her thick, black hair. Attempting to keep his mind free from prejudice, he did his best to imagine her naked, the way that he had always tried to think of Toci.

They might have been sisters. Both had the same full lips, bright eyes, and golden skin. Yet Martinez decided, with mingled regret and pleasure, that Toci was far lovelier. In every feature the mistress of Cortez was just a trifle coarser, so that, finally, she seemed a caricature of the exquisite virgin Martinez had known. Perhaps it was no more than the incongruity of her European dress, but Martinez sensed subtler discrepancies. The Lady Marina looked to him like an opportunist, and for some reason he still hoped Toci was something more.

"Is this the woman you spoke of?" Cortez inquired.

"Of course not!" snapped Martinez. "If you think I'm a lunatic, why do you question me at all?"

"You have paid well for whatever time you take. Would you like to speak to her?"

"I have nothing to say to her," Martinez said boorishly.

Marina laughed, and Martinez saw at once that she had adopted the airs as well as the garments of a Spanish lady. He suspected that Cortez had spent much time instructing her.

"They are not the same," said Martinez. "The woman that I meant is much more beautiful."

The laughter stopped, and the Lady Marina looked at Martinez with a savage anger. She swept out of the room.

"I am not pleased with you, physician," said Cortez. His voice was quiet, but a vein in his forehead was throbbing.

"I am a simple man," said Martinez, "and not much good at giving compliments. Perhaps I am the idiot you take me for. But I swear to you that every word I say is true. My only wish is to prove myself to you. Why else would I run away from Don Sebastian? I was an honored man among the Aztecs, because I had brought back their god, and yet I gave it all away to seek you out. That much, at least, you must believe. How do you think that I survived for so long in Tenochtitlan?"

"If you were ever there. Much simpler to believe that you were lost in the retreat, and foraged for yourself until you rejoined us. Yet I do remember that we lost you once before, and you were returned alive in exchange for one of their heathen priests."

"Of course!" said Martinez. "I had almost forgotten. That was the night Toci brought Don Sebastian back to life! You should have seen it. I am the only white man to have witnessed it, and I know many such strange secrets. Just listen to me."

"All right, physician, I have a mystery for you. You know the tallest pyramid in Texcoco?"

"Indeed I do. That is Smoking Mirror's temple."

"Is it?" asked Cortez, genuinely surprised. "I scaled it yesterday, with some of my men, and we found something puzzling there. It was the body of a man. He had been dead for months."

"Was there a woman, too?"

"No. Now listen, Martinez, for this is very strange. There was almost nothing left of this man, yet there was more at work than mere decay. It looked as if he had been smashed to pulp against the summit of the pyramid, as if he had fallen from some tremendous height. Yet there is no higher spot in Texcoco. You say you know dark secrets. How do you explain it?"

The face of the alchemist was crumpled and shaking. "Sebastian!"

"What do you mean, physician?"

Martinez put a hand to his face as if to keep his quivering features still. "Don Sebastian dropped him," he said tonelessly.

"Dropped him?"

"From the sky. Didn't I tell you that Don Sebastian can fly?"

Cortez turned from him in disgust. "I see. We thought the man might have been crushed with rocks in some sort of sacrifice. None of us knew your friend Sebastian could fly."

"Of course he can fly! He is a vampire."

Cortez froze for a heartbeat, and cast a glance at the gold cross embroidered on his banner. His nurse had told him of such creatures when he was a mere child, and something of his boyhood fear came back to him, but he shook off the chill. "We will watch out for him," he said.

"Be warned," said Martinez. "He means to summon Smoking Mirror from the stars, and with the monster's power to destroy you."

"I shall be careful, Martinez. You saw one of their sacrifices, did you?"

"I witnessed dozens."

"That might be enough to turn the head of any man."

"Indeed," said Martinez. "Sometimes I wonder that I am not mad."

"All right, physician. You may go."

Martinez looked longingly at the floor. "Must I abandon all my treasure? Isn't my information worth something?"

"I suppose so," Cortez said sympathetically, and his guards looked at him in surprise. "Take the skull of your friend Sebastian."

"I told you that this isn't Don Sebastian," said Martinez, stooping to retrieve his prize and return it to his pack. "But you have listened to me with more courtesy than any man in all your army, and I thank you for that, at least. There is more honor for you in it, since I know you think me mad. God bless you for a gentleman!"

The alchemist had touched the right note; Cortez looked on him with new favor. Martinez backed toward the door, a soldier at each hand.

"There is one thing more," said Martinez.

"Come on," said one of the men-at-arms. "You've taken enough time."

"Wait," said Cortez from his throne. "I will hear him out."

"There is another threat to you," said Martinez. "I almost forgot, since it seems so trivial compared to Smoking Mirror."

"Go on."

"There is a conspiracy against you."

"Wait there," Cortez commanded. He beckoned the captain of his guards and whispered in the man's ear. "This Martinez is evidently off his head, yet I cannot ignore this sort of accusation. I would not worry your men unnecessarily. Take them out with you and leave us here alone. I shall be safe with him. I have my sword."

The captain of the guards reluctantly complied, and Cortez was left with no one but the little man in his ill-fitting armor.

"You fascinate me, Martinez. Tell me more. But keep your distance."

"I don't know all that I should. I think their plans are not yet laid. But they consider me an idiot, and they are not as careful with their speech as clever plotters should be. I believe they mean to assassinate you."

"So." Cortez shifted uneasily in the king's seat. "This tale is less fantastic than the others you have told me, but it is equally disturbing. It could not be my veterans. It must be some of the new men. I don't know why I listen to you, Martinez; but give me a name."

"It is too early to say. Nothing may come of it. You would not have me condemn a man for a bit of idle talk?"

"Take back your gold bar. But don't come any nearer than you must."

Martinez scuttled across the floor to snatch up his reward. "There is a man here," he whispered from halfway across the room, "who is the protégé of Cuba's governor. He does not speak well of you."

"I think I know the man you mean. How sure are you of this?"

"I need more time."

"So, Martinez, keep yours ears open, and act as crazy as you can. If you learn anything, report to me at once. The order will be given to admit you to my presence at any time of day or night. We shall give out the story that you are my court fool."

"Very clever," said Martinez, as he retreated.

"Physician!" barked Hernan Cortez. "Come back here! You have forgotten half your gold!"

It was not until several weeks later, when the chief of the conspirators was hanging from a palace window, that Cortez was sure he had made the correct decision in the matter of Alfonso Martinez. Yet one thing troubled him. The physician's story of a plot among the officers had proven all too accurate. Could it be, then, that there really was a walking corpse in Tenochtitlan, one whose sole ambition was to summon up the hordes of Hell to snatch away the Crown of Mexico?

16. The Plague

THE smallpox epidemic raged through Tenochtitlan like an army on horseback. No one knew the number of the dead. A king had died of the disease already, and thousands upon thousands of his subjects followed him. The city was filled with corpses, many of which remained unburied and unburned. Whole families fell and went unnoticed until the stench from their houses reached the street. Even then they were frequently ignored out of superstitious fear or sheer despair. The dead lay rotting where they dropped.

Sebastian sat brooding beneath the pyramid of Smoking Mirror. The tribesmen who worshipped the vampire bats had brought his coffin back from Texcoco, and now they formed his personal escort. A band of naked savages, they were as awed by Tenochtitlan as the city was by them, but they were unswerving in their loyalty to Don Sebastian. Toci informed him that their name for him was "He Who Flies." The god had found his followers at last.

But the god had not found his own god, and time was running short. Each messenger from the surrounding cities brought news that promised imminent disaster. Cortez triumphed everywhere; the best guess was that his army of subjugated Indians was almost equal to the population of this final Aztec stronghold, or more than a hundred thousand strong. Soon he would begin his siege upon the city in the lake. Until he did so, the plague did his work for him.

Sebastian kept Toci by his side as much as possible. His greatest fear was that she would fall victim to the disease, and he hoped she might be safer in the temple, isolated from contagion. He warned her against the cold baths with which the Aztecs suicidally tried to counteract the pox, and racked his brain in search of Spanish remedies. He even found himself wishing for Martinez, although he knew the man was no physician. Yet he might have helped somehow, and Sebastian's hatred of the little man grew deeper as he imagined Toci pockmarked and blistering with fever.

Yet life in the city went on. In May, while Cortez supervised completion of the mile-long canal that would put his thirteen sloops into the waters of Lake Texcoco, the spring feast of Smoking Mirror came due.

"It might be better if you did not attend," Sebastian said. "I am the only one in Tenochtitlan who can be certain he will not fall sick."

"No," said Toci. "I must go."

"I suppose you must, even as you must remain a virgin. Yet neither decision delights me. Of course you are a priestess, but sometimes I think you care more for the Smoking Mirror in the skies than you do for me."

"What do you want?" asked Toci earnestly. "I am for you. You want to see Tezcatlipoca, and you fear the sun. I go to see the sacrifice and you sleep. I go to tell you. What else? I love you."

Sebastian stood in the distorted room with its dull black walls and looked tenderly into her shining eyes. "I would not worry if I did not care for you," he said.

"Why do you speak backwards?"

Sebastian smiled. "Stand beside me, Toci, and I shall be more direct."

She stepped forward with no hesitation, and laughed to feel Sebastian's teeth nipping harmlessly at her throat. And yet there was no malice in her laughter, only a childlike pleasure. She knew no blood would flow, but she also knew that her complaisance satisfied her lord. The wounds that he had left upon her throat in Texcoco had long since healed.

"Be careful, Toci. But how can you beware of a disease?"

"It will not take me. I wait for something else."

"And what is that?"

"I wait for you. I will not die till you are ready."

"Then you will live forever."

"Maybe. It will be what Smoking Mirror wants."

He stroked her face in a familiar gesture. By now she was accustomed to his cold fingers, and thought that she would find the hot flesh of an ordinary man repugnant. She stroked his hands as they ran along her throat and brought his fingers to her lips.

"You are a fatalist," Sebastian said. "Where did you get such thoughts?"

"I have faith," Toci replied. She pulled his hands down until they rested on her heart and stared into his dead eyes. "I do not think. I know."

"I wish I were as sure," Sebastian said, "at least about the pox. I would keep you from the ceremony if I could. I shall be asleep in my coffin, and you will do as you choose. I hope there is some profit in the risk. This is Smoking Mirror's festival, and we certainly have need of him now. If we cannot evoke his power soon, Cortez will overrun us. We can hardly sit with folded hands, waiting until next autumn when the god returns; but I wonder what killing this boy will mean to us. This is the public ceremony, the Feast of Dry Things—no more, really, than a plea for rain to grow the corn. Tell me, Toci. Do you think Tezcatlipoca will sweep down from the sunny sky at the first sight of blood in his temple, destroy the Spanish forces, and set Tenochtitlan free?"

"Tomorrow will tell."

"How is the boy?"

"They say he is afraid."

Toci herself had no role in the sacrifice, but she stood at the foot of the black pyramid among the celebrants and watched. The crowd was hardly a crowd at all. Thousands of the Aztecs were dead of smallpox, and thousands more were ailing. Even among those who were well enough to attend, there was such a fear of plague that many had chosen to hide themselves at home on this great day of the great feast. And most of those who did attend stood well apart from one another, as if they sensed that no more than a touch might end their lives.

The day before, the idol of Tezcatlipoca had been brought forth from the vault and paraded through the streets, the blind high priest following behind it. The black statue was dressed in robes and jewels as if it were a man, and all who saw it wept for their sins. The weeping was more than ceremonial, especially this year, when the streets were lined with corpses, their faces covered with scabs that would never heal.

The Spaniards had built up an immunity to the disease, yet even among them it was a horror, for the epidemics that swept through Europe had killed many of them. Yet they had a good chance of surviving it with nothing more to show for the experience than pockmarks. Among the unexposed Aztecs, smallpox was almost always fatal. Each citizen of Tenochtitlan waited for the signs. At first there was no more than fever, a weak and giddy feeling that might be a dozen other illnesses, but then the marks would come just a few days later. Initially they were tiny lumps, like insect bites; sometimes they bled. Eventually the eruptions turned to blisters, and then to running sores. They covered the face, the arms, the back, and the chest; and they meant death.

The Aztecs feared the smallpox more than they feared Cortez. It was small wonder that so few of them turned out even to honor Smoking Mirror.

A second procession preceded the sacrifice. The idol was brought out again, carried by the priests of Tezcatlipoca, who had abandoned their black robes for this one day to don brilliant red and green and gold. Their faces were darkened with soot, and blood streamed over them from self-inflicted wounds. They had been fasting for five days.

Young men and women who were the acolytes of the temple came forth next, their faces brightly painted, their arms and legs adorned with scarlet plumes. Around their necks they wore many necklaces of toasted corn, and they passed among the noblemen to offer them the necklaces. Toci sighed to see so many courageous warriors shrink even slightly back from contact with another human being, but at length this ceremony was performed.

The citizens of Tenochtitlan moved reluctantly forward to reach the lower steps of the pyramid. While the statue of the god sat silently between braziers of burning incense, they made their offerings. Jewels and gold and cloth and featherwork were laid upon the stairs; the poor brought merely food, but it was welcome, for only this charity could end the fast of Smoking Mirror's priests.

The gifts were gathered up and carried into the temple, where a band of maidens, each with a black circle painted around her mouth, walked among the dignitaries of the cult, serving the sacred meal. Toci ate with all the others whose lives were dedicated to Tezcatlipoca, sitting cross-legged in the crooked chamber in the depths of the black pyramid. Sebastian slept among them as they feasted.

The afternoon was well along before the food was gone, and the time for the sacrifice was near. When Toci stepped again into the day, she was surprised to see how little light there was. The sun would not set for some time, but it was now overcast with clouds. Anxiously, she scanned the ominous sky, remembering Sebastian's question, and half expecting some uncanny being to drop down on Tenochtitlan.

The high priest and five of his underlings waited at the summit of the temple while the crowd made way for the young man who was to die. Unlike other sacrificial victims, he had been chosen an entire year before, the handsomest of all the prisoners of war on hand. Toci studied his appearance, not for the first time, and decided that he was a most suitable offering for what she knew to be the greatest of the gods.

His headdress was made of gold, covered with white plumes

that hung over his face; his bracelets, rings, and earrings were of gold as well, as were the small bells on his ankles that jingled when he walked. Garlands of flowers covered him; jewels flashed on his throat and wrists. A disk of white stone hung at his chest, reversing the image of the smoking mirror that Sebastian wore. The boy had a fringed white loincloth, and a richly woven blanket of black and red.

Toci had concluded that Tezcatlipoca would be pleased with such a splendid sacrifice, but when the young prisoner moved past her, she saw that he was trembling. This was unthinkable. It would never do to send a coward to meet Smoking Mirror. If this youth could not contain himself, he should have been drugged; but now it was too late for that.

No doubt it was hard for him to bid Tenochtitlan farewell, since for a year he had been granted all the honors of a king. His four brides walked behind him weeping, and at the foot of the temple they abandoned him. In his right hand he held a small bundle of flutes, the very ones that he had played throughout the city, symbols of his leisure. And now, as he mounted the black stairway alone, he cast the flutes down one by one and broke them on the steps beneath his feet. He faltered only when he reached the top, teetering dizzily at the edge of the platform as if his body had rebelled against his forward progress. Toci held her breath for an instant, then watched him right himself and step forward to meet the priests.

Drums played, and music sounded from around the pyramid. This was the greatest of the Aztec sacrifices, its victim the most honored. His body would not be cast coldly down the steps like all the others, but carried in reverence back to the ground by solemn priests. There would be no feasting on fragments of his flesh; only his heart would be removed, and after it had been held aloft by the high priest, it would be burned.

The old blind priest, still dressed in black, stood at a distance while his five aides surrounded the young man bedecked with gold. They led him toward the sacrificial stone, while Toci prayed that this offering might win Smoking Mirror's favor. Yet the gift to the god was shaking once again when he kneeled before the high priest, and when the others lifted off the brightly colored blanket that covered his back and chest. They stretched him out upon the stone, and then they stopped.

One of them shouted; another pointed. Then, one by one, they moved away from the young man. Toci peered up at them in bewilderment. The crowd stirred anxiously. The priests were staring at their hands in horror.

The young man was no coward. His trembling had not been caused by fear, but by a fever, for he was a victim of the plague. His feathered headdress and his robe of black and red had hidden the telltale spots on his face and shoulders. A priest ran screaming down the pyramid; another followed him. The people rushed back from them as they would from wild beasts. Panic filled the public square.

Smallpox put an end to the ceremony honoring Smoking Mirror. With cries and wails the worshippers departed, some of them fleeing headlong through the streets. They mourned not only the presence of the plague, but also the fact that they had offered up a tainted sacrifice. The city had offended Smoking Mirror. The nobles left more slowly, with flourishes of feathered cloaks, but most of them had cast aside their necklaces of corn as if they were contaminated.

Toci stood alone in the great plaza while the world grew dark. Tezcatlipoca's victim sat up on the great stone slab, demanding to be killed. He could hardly be blamed for preferring the black knife to the pox, yet his behavior had disgraced Tenochtitlan and he had frightened off the very men who might have stopped his suffering. He got up, looked around the terrace atop the temple, and saw no one there but the old high priest, huddled in upon himself like an ancient embryo.

The young man picked up the blanket that had covered him and then cast it aside. He stumbled down the steps and walked away to die alone.

Toci shivered in the dim shadow of the pyramid. The city seemed so deserted that it reminded her of Texcoco. Her thoughts were black, and nothing drew her from them until she heard the shouts that echoed through the empty plaza. They came from the peak of the temple. Toci turned her head to look, and saw the blind high priest crawling across the high terrace. Without hesitation she hurried up to him, and saw his old hands grope along the black stones in search of something he had lost. He screamed out his frustration, but ceased abruptly when his fingers touched the sacrificial dagger. Then he stood, a black figure against gray clouds, tears streaming down his wrinkled face. He held out his left hand and slashed the palm.

Toci stared as the black blade flashed again, this time hacking at the priest's forearm. She gasped to see how deep the wounds were; this was no ordinary penance. When he began to slice open his face, Toci could stand no more. She threw herself at the priest, grasping his right arm. The stones were slippery with his blood.

He fought frantically against her, even when she screamed her name. His bleeding hand clawed at her face and he kicked at her shins, but she was stronger. She pulled the knife out of his hand and pushed him away. He crumpled on the flagstones as Toci turned desperately to the sky. The sun was sinking and the clouds were darker than before. She panted heavily, her neck craning upward.

A raindrop struck her on the cheek.

Toci reached up to touch it, her eyes wide. The god had not forgotten them. The rain had come. She looked toward the old man at her feet, and what she saw showed her why he was the high priest. Gritting her teeth, she dug the black stone blade into her right arm. She could do no less than he had done. The rain was falling faster now, washing away the blood that ran from the gash in her arm, rattling on the pavement as she cut into the back of her left hand. Thunder boomed like Spanish cannons, and the storm broke with a vengeance. The priestess was drenched; the force of the downpour was so intense that it seemed to press her toward the earth, as if a giant's hand had stretched out from the sky to push against her.

"Smoking Mirror," she said.

The blind high priest was laughing. She could not hear him over the fury of the cloudburst, but she could see his mouth spread open in a toothless grin of triumph. His long gray hair was plastered over his eyes, his fingers stretched out to catch the raindrops.

Toci kneeled across from him, and she too reached out her hands to gather up Tezcatlipoca's storm. The old man and the young woman prayed together at the summit of the black pyramid while night fell imperceptibly on Tenochtitlan, hidden by the darkness of the clouds. They might have been the last remaining devotees of Smoking Mirror, except for one other buried hundreds of feet below. Wind whipped at them, and rain lashed at their faces.

They remained until a third figure appeared suddenly at the peak of the pyramid. Toci glanced up, and a flash of lightning showed her the face of Don Sebastian. He glared down at them for a moment, then reached out to grab the priestess by her shoulder, catching the high priest in his other hand.

"Get below!" he roared, his angry voice much louder than the driving rain. "Would you kill yourselves?"

He hurried them down the narrow steps and through the yawning skull that was the entrance to the pyramid "To think I should be saddled with such a pair of allies!" Sebastian bellowed. "To sit out in the rain and court the pox! And this one an old man, already weak enough. Are you mad?"

"It rained," Toci protested, as he rushed her through claustrophobic corridors. "It rained!"

"That much is evident," Sebastian snapped. "Did it take you so long to notice it?"

"Listen to me," said Toci, her voice so full of feeling that it gave Sebastian pause.

"I will listen," he said more softly, "but only after you have dried yourself and changed your clothing. You will also see to the high priest. Then come to my chamber. I have news of my own, which also concerns the rain."

Toci did as she was told, leading the blind priest away. At each juncture of the twisted hallways she met anxious men who rushed by her without a word: priests, acolytes, jaguar knights, and even Sebastian's savage tribesmen. Oddly enough, each one of them carried a vessel: a jug, a bowl, or a vase.

Toci did her best to ignore this puzzling behavior until she had left the old man in the care of some temple maidens, and changed her dripping black robe. That done, she ran to meet Sebastian.

"Stand by that brazier," he told her, "and warm yourself."

Flattered by his concern, Toci moved closer to the flame. She pulled her long, damp hair over her shoulders and dried it by the fire. "The boy was sick," she said. "He had the marks. There was no sacrifice. The people ran away. The high priest gave his blood, and then the rain came."

"He was not the only one to give his blood," Sebastian said, reaching out to examine her hands and arms, "and I suspect that what you offered Smoking Mirror was most precious of all. No god could be indifferent to such a gift." He kissed her wounds, his tongue catching the last drops that lingered there.

Toci arched her back ecstatically, feeling again the now familiar mixture of pleasure and pain. "Smoking Mirror came," she said. "There was no sacrifice, but still he gave us rain."

Sebastian raised his head and spoke. "The god has an undoubted gift for irony. This is almost as amusing as the morning he announced his presence by leaving me a cripple. Damn Smoking Mirror, if he exists, and damn Hernan Cortez!"

"If he exists!" repeated Toci. "What else brought this rain?"

"Whatever always brings the rain," Sebastian said.

"What is wrong? We failed the god, but he gave us his blessing."

"He gave us no more than an ugly joke. This may be the last water Tenochtitlan will ever see."

"What is wrong?" Toci asked again.

"The water is stopped," Sebastian said. "You saw the men go out with jugs not long ago? I have given orders that every man and woman in the city should do the same. What we collect from

Smoking Mirror's rain may be the only water we shall have, unless the people try to drink the salty sludge of Lake Texcoco."

"But the aqueduct—"

"Exactly. The aqueduct—the city's only source of fresh, clean water. For weeks I had a tribesman stationed there, with no other order than to report to me. I had no doubt of what Cortez would do. Any general would do the same. I warned King Cuauhtemoc to guard it, but his army has been decimated by the plague. It would not have mattered much in any case, for the men who attacked the aqueduct today were insurmountable. Tens of thousands of them, mostly rebellious vassals of Tenochtitlan. They think the Spanish Crown will treat them better, fools that they are! While Smoking Mirror smiled and gave us rain, Cortez cut off the aqueduct."

Toci put her arms around Sebastian. "It begins," she said.

"It does indeed. While you and that blind fool sat up there bleeding into the rain, they took the western causeway and cut off the city's sole supply of water. And they did more. Another force has cut off the causeway to the south. Only the northern route out of the city is still open, and I can promise you that it will be shut soon. We are besieged, Toci. We are surrounded. And you tell me that Smoking Mirror came!"

The priestess raised her head, her eyes awash with tears.

"Forgive me, Toci. You did all you could do, and what you bought with your sweet blood may save the city yet. But what kind of god is this, to grant us little favors while he lets our enemies run wild? I'd like to meet him face to face, the way the legends say one can. If all it takes is bravery and will, he'd see his dripping heart in my cold hands and feel his bones disintegrate beneath my rotten foot. Where is this Smoking Mirror?"

"He is here," said Toci as she wept.

Sebastian tried to smile, then turned away toward the black stone wall.

17. City of Blood

ON June 1, 1521, thirteen newly constructed Spanish brigantines slid down the waters of the canal Cortez had built and floated off across the waters of Lake Texcoco. A roar of triumph went up from the assembled army, and on a nearby island the Aztec outpost set off a signal fire. The battle for Tenochtitlan had begun in earnest.

The ships swept toward the city in the lake, their long oars flashing, their white sails billowing. And from the city, close to a thousand Aztec war canoes set out to meet them, the warriors gazing in awe at the line of vessels which, however small by European standards, loomed over them like eagles over hummingbirds.

The canvases swelled, and the monstrous ships built by the Feathered Serpent bore down upon the Aztecs. There was no battle; there was only slaughter. The huge bows of the brigantines plowed through the light canoes, leaving little but splinters in their wake. Hundreds of men were thrown screaming into the salty water, crushed and drowning. Muskets and artillery sent smoky explosions from both sides of each ship, sinking more of the small boats and killing more of their crews. The surviving Aztecs turned tail at once, not even taking time to shoot a single arrow. Most of them ignored the cries of their sinking comrades, and those who did stop to take drowning men on board were sitting targets for the Spanish guns. Yet even flight did not bring safety. The big sailing ships were faster than canoes, and they cut continuous swaths through the ranks of their beleaguered enemies, while ceaseless volleys sank the stragglers. Under a sunny sky, the Spaniards took complete command of Lake Texcoco. Only a handful of canoes crept back to Tenochtitlan and slipped into the narrow canals where brigantines could not pursue them.

Sebastian took the news with little grace, but less fury than Toci had anticipated. "I warned them," he said bitterly, "but they would not listen. I suppose it was impossible for them to imagine just how badly things were bound to go, and I suspect they would have tried it anyway. Your people have courage, Toci, if nothing else, and they could not sit idly by and grant Cortez their lake. Their courage cost them much. Perhaps now King Cuauhtemoc will be ready to take my advice."

"What will you tell him?"

"About the ships, nothing. Even if we could get the timber, the skill to build our own fleet does not exist here, nor would there be trained men to sail. I am no sailor myself, nor am I a shipbuilder. I wish at least I were human again, so that I could go out by day and lead troops into battle. This Hernan Cortez would learn a few things about fighting then, I promise you."

"You will fight in the dark, as Smoking Mirror does."

"And as the Aztecs never do, unless I change their minds. At least I have my own platoon, a band of savages who love the night. We will give the Spaniards something to remember before the city falls."

"Then must it fall?"

"It appears inevitable. They have as many men as we do, and also ships, guns, food, and water. The only thing we have that they do not is plague."

"We have the gods," said Toci firmly.

"We shall need them. What maddens me is that each night I spend in warfare will mean another night lost to the search for Smoking Mirror. And yet we may at least gain time by fighting. I hope it will be time enough."

"Smoking Mirror is with us. It rains again tonight."

"Thanks for that. The rainy season will hamper Cortez, I think, and for a while the city may not die of thirst. Yet we must have food as well, and I see only one way to get it. The causeways are cut off, and apparently the lake is lost to us as well. But thirteen ships cannot guard so large a lake, especially at night. Canoes could slip through and reach the shore. There must be towns there where Tenochtitlan has friends. Surely the king will see the logic in at least that sort of night maneuver, and from it others may spring."

Toci nodded, then walked across the subterranean chamber to stand before the idol. "He will help us," she said.

"He seems to favor you as much as I do. We have that much in common. It was your blood that brought the rains, and I like it myself. But if we were really brothers, Smoking Mirror would send me some guns, or some ships. I am not fond of either, really. A cannon first took my life, and left this pretty scar across my eye. Yet they are useful things. And those damned ships! I would as soon fight soldiers armed with wooden stakes."

Toci reached out to stroke his arm, but Sebastian did not notice. He was lost in thought. "Stakes..." he said, and then fell silent for a moment. "It might work. Send for my men, Toci, and send for carpenters. There will not be time enough tonight, but we can be ready by tomorrow. It cannot solve all our problems, but if the first attempt succeeds, it will help a bit."

"What is it? Tell me."

"You will see soon enough."

On the next night she did see something, but still could not understand it. Sebastian set out for the lake, accompanied by his personal guard and a number of jaguar knights, all of them struggling under the weight of numerous gigantic wooden stakes, as thick as tree trunks and almost as long, one end of each cut to a sharp point. And still Sebastian would not explain their use.

"If the plan succeeds, you will hear of it," he said. "If not, I shall gain nothing by boasting of my ingenuity. Wait for us. There is no way for you to help, and there may be some danger. Look for us by dawn."

Cortez sailed around Tenochtitlan and made his camp near the southern causeway, the one that offered the shortest route into the city. Two of his most trusted lieutenants were stationed with thousands of men at the northern and the western causeways. Tenochtitlan was bottled up, and for the moment Cortez was content to wait, planning his strategy and watching the effect of his blockade.

The first attempt to break through it came almost at once, and close to Cortez. The southern waters of Lake Texcoco were thick with tall reeds, numerous enough to provide cover for canoes. Early one afternoon, a handful of the Aztec boats slipped from the reeds and headed for the distant shore. At once a trumpet signaled from the camp, where a lookout had been stationed in a captured Aztec tower near the foot of the causeway. Cortez himself climbed up to watch, accompanied by Alfonso Martinez.

"Good," said the commander as he peered across the lake. "Our two brigantines are coming already. We are too fast for them. These savages should have learned something from our last battle."

"They seem to have learned a little," said Martinez; "at least enough to cut and run. They're turning their canoes and heading back for the reeds."

"Much good may it do them. The reeds are no protection, and our ships will surely overtake them before they can reach real safety in the canals."

The brigantines tore through the stand of reeds in hot pursuit of the hidden enemy, then suddenly stopped dead, faster than any ship should, as if they had run into an invisible barrier. A tremendous noise of tearing wood echoed across the lake, joined with the bewildered shouts of Spanish sailors.

"Witchcraft!" said Martinez.

Cortez stared silently at the stranded brigantines. The shrill cacophony of the horns and whistles of Aztec warriors rose from the reeds, and hundreds of Indian arrows were launched into the air. Within moments, the decks of the stricken vessels were covered with fallen men.

"A trap," Cortez shouted. "Those ships are caught in something, and there's no way we can help. I can't see what's going on, but there must be a whole fleet of canoes hidden there. The ones that came out were only decoys. This is intolerable!"

He watched ashen-faced, while half-naked warriors swarmed over the sides of the ships. They did their work with astonishing speed; the long row of war canoes sped away for Tenochtitlan before there was any chance to summon other brigantines. The two ships trapped in the reeds were well aflame, certain to be destroyed before anything could be done. The two captains and most of their crews were dead, and Hernan Cortez was seething with frustration.

Hours passed before he determined the cause of the disaster.

Some time ago, probably before his men had first approached the southern causeway, the Aztecs had floated a collection of huge logs out to the reeds and driven them down into the bed of Lake Texcoco, so that their tops were a foot or two below the surface. They provided no impediment to small canoes, but when the low-riding brigantines ran onto the stakes, they were as helpless as if they had run aground.

"Ingenious," said Cortez. "Who would have thought these savages could be so clever?"

"It was not the savages," said Martinez darkly.

"What? No matter, they will pay for their audacity. Tomorrow we march on Tenochtitlan."

"March carefully, then, and march by day. I see the hand of Don Sebastian in this."

The hand of Don Sebastian was clenched in triumph when he heard the news. Toci had assembled all the tribesmen to awaken him at sunset, and he rose to walk among them, embracing each one in turn as if he were a happy soldier and not an animated corpse.

"It means next to nothing, of course," he said at length, "yet it delights me nonetheless. A few Spaniards will have cause to remember us, and now perhaps the Aztecs will see the virtues of fighting at night. We should prepare tonight, and make a raid after the sun falls tomorrow."

Sebastian's plan did not come to fruition, however, for Cortez struck shortly after dawn, and his attack left the city reeling. The assault on Tenochtitlan came from all three causeways at once. The troops in the north and west had longer distances to go, and succeeded in no more than distracting large numbers of the defenders. Cortez, however, penetrated into the heart of the city.

The emperor Cuauhtemoc had ordered his men to break down each of the many bridges that interrupted the causeways, so that the Spaniards and their thousands of Indian allies marched only a short distance before they reached a gap. Across the water from the gap Cortez saw a strong stone barricade. Hundreds of Aztec warriors stood behind it, loosing clouds of arrows against their enemies. The fire of the besiegers could not destroy the rampart, but Cortez did not despair. He called up two of his brigantines, which sailed unimpeded around the wall of stone to use their guns on the defenders. The Aztecs retreated with great losses, and the attackers made their way across the gap. Cortez left orders that the breach should be filled with the stones that had defended it, then led his men toward the next broken bridge. Cavalry and cannon followed him over the rough reconstruction.

Each of the defense posts fell in the same manner until the Spaniards stood at the outskirts of Tenochtitlan. The people of the city were appalled to see how quickly all their barricades were broken; the besiegers seemed unstoppable. Yet within the city itself the Spaniards had no chance to use the ships. Now the fighting would be man to man, or so it seemed. But supplies from Spain had left Cortez well armed, and withering gunfire drove the Mexicans steadily backward while hundreds fell before the onslaught of the small harquebus and the huge cannon.

In their enthusiasm, the Spaniards overlooked the danger in their new position. Inside the city, they were surrounded. The Aztecs were not only in front of them, but on every side. The Spanish ranks were broken as hordes of screaming soldiers rushed down on them, and Cortez was forced to retreat. But that night, as the rain began to fall, he had cause for satisfaction. In one day he had destroyed the most important Aztec defenses, and proved that he could enter Tenochtitlan when he pleased.

The next morning, he set out again. Alfonso Martinez marched close beside him, encouraged by the stories of the preceding day's success and determined to take his share of loot. He expected to walk straight to Montezuma's treasure house, but he was disappointed. As in a dream, Cortez discovered that he must relive the deeds of yesterday.

"The bridges are down again," he muttered to himself. "Don't these people sleep?"

"Sebastian," whispered Martinez, only to be rewarded with a glance so withering that he sought refuge in the rear.

Methodically, Cortez proceeded as he had before, and by noon he reached the public square, in the heart of the city. There he sent his men to the sprawling palace where they had been housed by Montezuma almost a year before. The building was made of stone, but its beams and roofs and towers were made of wood. The Spanish torches caught.

Flames streamed through the interior and the fire burst into view, a blinding sheet of red and gold, so hot that men retreated from it smelling their singed beards. The long beams turned to cinders, and the home of Montezuma's father collapsed upon itself with a roar like thunder.

Torches blazing, the Spaniards rushed on to the menagerie. Here, where Montezuma had collected all the creatures of his world, the buildings were unfortified. The house of birds, an airy structure delicately fashioned from thin shafts of wood, went up like kindling. The uncanny screams of the trapped creatures rose like voices from the pit of Hell. Birds struggled toward the sky, half-burned and trailing smoke. A few flapped weakly on wings that were afire, then plummeted to earth. Only a handful escaped, among them a pair of eagles that soared through the flames, exchanged harsh cries, and glided toward the distant mountains.

Sebastian crawled from his coffin with the smell of smoke in his nostrils, and listened grimly to Toci's report. Cortez had dropped back again at nightfall, so there was no one to challenge the dead wizard and the young priestess as they mounted Smoking Mirror's pyramid. They stood under the cloudy sky and watched the smoldering wreckage of Tenochtitlan's treasures. Embers glowed crimson in the shadows, while groups of men and women ran back and forth between the ruins and the canals, shouting to each other as they carried water to put out the flames.

"Too late for that," Sebastian said. "Will it be this easy for Cortez?"

"No," said Toci. "We build again."

"Of course, Toci. And really he has damaged nothing of significance. No doubt he thinks the loss will bring despair to the city, but from what you tell me, he has done nothing but steel the resolve of his enemies. Yet I don't like those fires. It is not pleasant to imagine that this pyramid might be consumed while I lie beneath it."

"Stone," said Toci, stamping her foot on the terrace. "No wood. Nothing that will burn."

"It is well. Then I have nothing to fear except cannon balls bringing the pile of black stone down upon me. Better not to think of it; better still to prevent it if I can. We must begin the counterattacks tonight."

Sebastian's first assault caught the Spaniards entirely off guard. He chose the southern causeway, more out of hatred for Cortez than from any strategic reason. Down it crept a small army of archers, led by the phantom many of them called Smoking Mirror. In support came dozens of canoes, sliding silently through the waters until they were within shooting distance of the Spanish camp.

Alfonso Martinez, never a good sleeper, was one of the few awake when the feathered shafts began to fall. He jumped up screaming from the muddy ground, thanking every power in Heaven and Hell that he was never without his armor. For more than a minute the effect of the attack was devastating. The arrows came so thickly that they might have been hail, and countless men were killed before they could awaken. Martinez, after his first shout, put both hands over his head and rolled himself into a ball, never looking up until he sensed that the attack was over. Sebastian's warriors had come and gone as quickly as a summer shower, but what they left behind was death.

Martinez ran to the tent where Cortez slept, and found the commander outside, buckling on his sword. "You see?" said Martinez. "I warned you they would fight at night. You cannot expect them to be like other Indians, not when Don Sebastian leads them. And now you see why I wear my armor all the time. You never can tell, can you?"

Cortez rubbed the sleep from his eyes and squinted at the corpses all around him. "You weary me, Martinez," he said. "You seem to be an idiot, yet time and again you turn out to be right. I will give orders for the men to sleep in their armor. Our native allies will have to do the best they can; sometimes I think we've too many of them anyway. Now, get away from me. Go ply your trade among the wounded!"

For days the war continued as before, with maneuvers by the Spaniards in the sunlight, and sorties from the defenders, inflicting vengeance when the sun was gone. For all his assaults, Cortez felt himself stalemated. He gave orders that his native troops should construct rude buildings to house his men, and for a time he ceased to make attacks. Each night, the Aztecs broke down the bridges once again. He thought of posting guards, but gave his reasons against it in a dispatch to the Spanish emperor. His Indian allies would not do battle after dark, and his few hundred Spaniards were too valuable to be deprived of sleep. He decided on a war of attrition, waiting to see what smallpox and starvation might do to the spirit of Tenochtitlan.

He stood by his decision until the last night of June, when the enemy launched a devastating attack on all three causeways. Many were slain; this was the anniversary of the *"noche triste,"* that sad night a year before, when the Spaniards had been driven from the city in disgrace.

Cortez saw the little physician the next morning. "Mention that name," he growled, "and I shall have you thrown into the lake. We have enough to worry about, without you trying to frighten the men with your old wives' tales."

Finally, Cortez decided to move. His goal was the marketplace in the northwestern corner of the city. Once established there, the Spanish forces at the northern and the western causeways could combine, forming an impregnable outpost within the city itself. The last orders Cortez gave before the march concerned the necessity for filling in the gaps where the bridges had been, which he said was much more crucial than a quick advance. With luck, all would go well, but it was always vital to leave a path in the event of a retreat.

Martinez wisely decided that he would keep well to the rear and supervise the work of filling the canals. Dead men have no use for gold, and he suspected that the day might be a hard one, especially because he sensed that the commander had made a decision against his own better judgment.

The advance went well at first—so well that it worried Cortez, who watched the Aztecs fall back with such alacrity that he began to fear a trap. The commander took a small group of men and abandoned his own post to reconnoiter. As he rushed to meet the rest of his scattered forces, he heard the blast of a horn from atop the great pyramid, the horn that could only be blown by the emperor of Mexico.

When he reached the path that most of his men had taken, Cortez found his worst fears confirmed. Before him stretched a broken bridge, the surface of the water interrupted by only a few boulders, not even enough to serve as a footpath. As he stood cursing, he heard the sound of running feet, followed by the distant sound of Aztec war cries. Before he had a chance to move, Cortez was overwhelmed.

His own forces rushed wildly down upon him. It was not a retreat, but a rout. Hundreds of men threw themselves into the canal, only to be trampled and drowned by comrades running frantically for safety. In a moment the Spanish forces were mixed with those of the Aztecs, and suddenly a dozen brown-skinned men had Cortez in their hands. A black stone sword chopped into his leg, and he fell writhing into the mud.

Two of his aides rushed to his defense, and paid for his life with their own. Someone's arm flopped down on the half-conscious Cortez, the blood from its stump spattering his face. The roar of battle made him dizzy, and the air was thick with spears and arrows.

More dead than alive, Cortez was escorted back to camp, surviving only because he had been on the right side of the gap his men had neglected to fill. He slipped into the ranks of his Indian troops and disappeared from the scene of battle.

The forces of Cortez had fled in disarray, and it was only the gunboats that prevented their foes from overtaking them. The expedition was a calamity. There was no record of the Indian allies slain, but the number must have been in the thousands. Seven precious horses and two of the cannon had been captured, and the Spanish soldiers had been decimated. The deaths would have been bad enough, but subsequent events showed that more than sixty had been taken alive.

Beyond the lake, Cortez sprawled on a blanket while Martinez cleaned his wound. "Sebastian," muttered the commander. "Don't say it! He had nothing to do with it. The sun was shining, physician. It was nothing more than savage strength, and our own incompetence. There is no Sebastian."

"You could see him now, if you could stand," replied Martinez, as he wrapped a bandage around the commander's wounded leg. An Aztec drum throbbed in the distance, and Cortez felt his leg respond in kind.

"What? Show him to me, physician. I challenge you!"

"You won't like what you see, no more than your soldiers do."

"Stand me up, Martinez! Call for men! Where is he?"

"Far off, but not far enough," said Martinez, offering Cortez his arm. Two pages joined him, and together they dragged Hernan Cortez into the night.

Cortez had insisted that he be carried to the camp on the western causeway; he was less than a mile from the great plaza. The night was clear, and torches illuminated the distant pyramid of the war god. With all the clarity of fever, Cortez saw black-robed priests dragging naked white men up the steps.

"See that one?" said Martinez. "The one at the top there, whose robes are red and white and black. The one with the knife. The one who's cutting out their hearts. That is Don Sebastian."

Cortez was almost convinced that he could hear the screams of his slaughtered comrades, and he knew without a doubt that some of those dying men had been his attendants.

"That little man?" he sneered. "I can hardly make him out. That doll? That puppet? He is some priest, and not a ghost."

"Whatever you say," replied Martinez. "But that is Don Sebastian."

The drumbeat rolled across the lake as Cortez sank down upon his blanket. That night he had a dream.

A glowing green mist filled his tent, and then a man stepped out from it. His face was dead white, his eyes sunken and dull. His black hair hung to his shoulders; his black mustache drooped below his chin. A hideous pale scar ran down the left side of his grim countenance. His robes were as Martinez had described them.

Cortez attempted to cry out. He heard a feeble croak, and knew it for his own voice. His skin crawled as if a family of snakes were creeping over it. He tried to raise a hand, and found that he could not.

"I could kill you now," Sebastian said, "but gentlemen do not fight wars that way. I need not explain, I trust. I shall pretend that you are a man of honor, whatever I hear to the contrary. I long to meet you in single combat, Hernan Cortez, but it will never be. We are both cripples, I fear. You may recover, but I shall not. Look."

The ghost raised up its robes and lifted up one leg. Cortez turned sick at the sight of it. The foot was gray and withered, as if it had been dead for a lifetime. Bones gleamed faintly through the rotten flesh.

"We share the same wound," Sebastian said, "but mine is permanent. It came not from a man, but from the sun. From a god, perhaps. From Smoking Mirror. I am your opposite, you know—I might almost say your mirror image, except that I cast no reflection. But the Aztecs take us both for gods, and the two they name us for are ones that struggle in the sky. Tell me, Hernan Cortez, do you feel like a god?"

Cortez managed to shake his head.

"Nor do I. But we do not choose the roles we play. And yet I think you crave divinity, or at least the power you think it brings. In that, at least, we are much alike. But you are too much of this world; your ambitions do not extend beyond this life. I have been a soldier, like you, and I learned that conquest comes to nothing. What matters is what the mind conceives for the future. Not the next battle, but the next life. And so I cling to belief in Smoking Mirror, however alien it may be, in the hope that I may achieve his incarnation and be free at last of this accursed planet."

Cortez could only stare in disbelief.

"I have known men like you before," Sebastian said. "My brother was one. He believed too much of what he was told, and death caught him unprepared. He was burning in the hell that he devised while you were still a boy. Wordly power is all vanity, you know. Of course you do. Even your priests say as much, but few men believe them until it is too late. Consider this, Hernan Cortez. I came here as a naked skull. I have been dead for decades, and still my trials are not done. I promise you this much, that you will return to this city as I first approached it. A man will bring your fleshless head to Tenochtitlan, and you will know it. I imagine you will win this war, but it will bring you nothing. You will never know peace, unless the gods are kinder than I think."

Cortez plucked weakly at his blanket, wondering when the dream would end, or whether it was a dream at all.

"I would not weary you," Sebastian said, his pale features dissolving into fog. "Sleep, conquistador. Tell Martinez that I was here, and that I shall see him again."

The green mist slipped away and Cortez collapsed. When the physician called the next day, his commander thought it wiser to say nothing. And after a while he forgot the dream.

18. A Wheel of Gold

THE Spanish troops were virtually idle while Cortez recovered from his wound. After their disastrous defeat, no one dared suggest that it was wrong to sit and wait, or even that it was wrong to endure the Aztec night attacks without reprisals. It was time for retrenchment, and a stricken commander was not the only problem. The supplies of powder and shot were running dangerously low, and the Indian allies were discouraged. Many of them had slipped away, their hatred for the Aztec overlords insufficient for the prospect of a long and fruitless siege. They began to believe the priests who shouted from the temples telling them that Tenochtitlan would never fall.

The expedition might have failed, if not for Spain. A ship arrived at Veracruz, and from that distant port came the ammunition that would turn the tide. Cortez was up to greet the first arrivals of these invaluable supplies, limping a bit, but clearly in command. He ordered a council of war.

"There is only one way to take the city," declared Cortez, "and that is to destroy it. We have been in and out of it more times than I can count, but nothing we can do has much effect. The causeways and canals impede us at every turn, and must be eliminated. The water must be converted into dry land."

His lieutenants stirred nervously and looked at him in some bewilderment.

"Some of you think, perhaps, that I am just as mad as my friend Martinez here. You wonder why I keep him by my side. It happens that his thoughts on this subject are much like my own."

Martinez smiled shyly and lowered his eyes.

"Our failures and successes in this campaign have depended almost entirely upon our use of the canals. When we have taken time to fill them, we have won. Surely none of you will dispute that." Here Cortez glanced pleasantly at several of his more careless officers. "So. We shall fill in everything, and then we shall have room to move. Work slowly; take one building at a time. And when you have it, tear it down! Cast the rubble into the water, and soon there will be land for the swift progress of the cannon and the cavalry. It seems a shame to lose this royal prize, but only when we level Tenochtitlan will it be ours."

"It won't be easy," someone said.

"But not as hard as you think," countered Cortez. "I have already spoken to our native allies, and the scheme delights their savage souls. They showed me a tool they have, something like a hoe, well suited to the work. They will be glad to pull apart the city that has ruled over them for centuries. Our guns will protect them, and there will be no stopping us. I only hope the Aztec king, Cuauhtemoc, will be humbled enough to surrender while there is still something left standing."

"Is this the festival of Xilonen?" Sebastian asked.

"Yes," Toci replied. "The goddess of the young corn."

"And a virgin is sacrificed?"

Toci nodded.

"I remember that Martinez did not enjoy it. It hardly seems possible that a year has passed since then. Will the sacrifice be made?"

Toci looked doubtful, but could not bring herself to answer.

"Cortez is near her temple, is he? Well, perhaps there will be time enough. It hardly matters. The way the war is going, there will be no one left to gather the harvest. And no one left to celebrate the gathering by greeting the return of Smoking Mirror in the fall. We cannot wait for that, or we shall certainly fail. Who follows the corn goddess?"

"The god of war," said Toci.

"The chief god of Tenochtitlan, the one whose pyramid rises above all the rest. No doubt the city needs his help, but it is slow in coming. What concerns me is that he is only another manifestation of Smoking Mirror."

"There is the red Tezcatlipoca, and the black. Huitzilopochtli, the war god, is their little brother. His name is Hummingbird Wizard."

"A wizard like his brother. And his holiday falls so as to coincide with Leo, perhaps the strongest sign in the Zodiac. And Smoking Mirror is the Great Bear."

"I do not understand."

"I am looking for the night, Toci, the best night when we may hope to conjure up your god to set us free. I doubt that even Smoking Mirror's magic can save the entire city now, but surely his power represents a chance for us to escape Cortez and the disaster he will bring, even if it means trading this world for the stars. So I study the stars, by the systems of your people and my own, searching for the most propitious time to summon Smoking Mirror. Consider it, and consult with your high priest. There must be another chance for us."

Toci nodded again, and Sebastian was so intent upon his own concerns that he failed to notice the expression on her face.

"Enough of this," he said, casting his charts upon the mica floor of the subterranean chamber. "I must look at the city."

"Again?" asked the priestess. "Cortez is there."

"The Spaniards sleep at night, Toci, and there is not much danger. I need to know how well the siege progresses. No, do not follow me. You see enough of this by day, and there is always the possibility that someone will be about. I will not have you raped and murdered by my countrymen."

Sebastian limped through the twisted corridors beneath the

temple, by now as familiar to him as the passages of his ancestral castle in the north of Spain. At length he reached the street. Nothing in his unnaturally prolonged life could compare with what he saw there.

The beautiful city of Tenochtitlan was in ruins. The outskirts had been razed, and from those ruins Cortez had proceeded inward, his troops attacking from the south, the north, and the west. Day by day the monuments had fallen, the buildings destroyed one at a time, and slowly the Aztecs were driven toward the marketplace in the center of the city. The great plaza where kings and gods dwelled together had been almost entirely destroyed; the palaces were gone, and only the gigantic pyramids of Huitzilopochtli and Tezcatlipoca still remained. Cortez had decided that they were too strong to be knocked down with ease, and almost impossible to burn. The two temples stood alone, huge piles of stone in a wasteland of devastation. The war had passed them by, if only for the moment.

Just a few priests remained with Sebastian and Toci in the black pyramid, together with what remained of the tribe they had found in Texcoco and a handful of the once-proud jaguar knights. Toci had pleaded with them, and the blind high priest had threatened, but only Sebastian's displays of wizardry had kept them out of the fray. They were the last defenders of a forgotten outpost.

More than once Cortez had offered terms, but the emperor Cuauhtemoc steadfastly refused them. He had learned too well the lesson of Montezuma, and his stubbornness was encouraged by the priests of every cult in Mexico. Better to die, said these seers, than to be slaves of the treacherous Spanish.

Almost two weeks ago, the plan to bring food into the city by canoe had failed. At first the men had come back empty-handed; then they had not come back. No friends of Tenochtitlan remained along the shores of Lake Texcoco, and now that the besiegers had moved in, there was no chance to use the lake in any case. There was now no food. The Aztecs fed on the roots and grass that grew within the city. The people captured vermin when they could, and sucked juice from the hard bodies of the insects that they caught. Women ate their babies. Yet still there was no thought of surrender.

Smallpox and starvation had done their work well. Corpses rotted in the streets and houses, and all efforts to dispose of them had been abandoned. The living lay beside the dead in humble dwellings, too weak to move when enemies approached to bring their roofs crashing down upon their heads. A pestilence sprang up from the corruption of the unburied dead, killing as many as the pox. The stench of mortality hung over Tenochtitlan.

Through these scenes of horror Sebastian stalked, his magic useless against the massed might of a continent. Cortez might provide the leadership, but the Mexicans were destroying themselves, the rivalry among their factions opening the way for a few thousand to take command of millions.

Sebastian saw an old man crawling down what once had been a street, and pitied him until he saw the bony hands reach out to catch a small green lizard. The old man smiled as he bit off the squirming head.

Sebastian stood beside him. "We must eat," he said in Spanish, but his companion did not understand. Nonetheless the old man nodded, the cold blood dripping down his chin.

The vampire was half starved himself, and he regarded the squatting figure with a speculative eye. But the creature that he saw was already in the embrace of death, hardly worth the taking. Sebastian needed not only sustenance for himself, but food for the dozens who waited in the pyramid. Smoking Mirror passed the old man by. Yet fires had turned the sky before Sebastian to the color of blood and somewhere ahead of him a dim figure scurried through the shadows. No doubt it was another starving Aztec; what the vampire wanted was a well-fed Spaniard, his fat face flushed with triumph.

More than once it had occurred to Sebastian that he could infiltrate a Spanish camp, transforming himself into a wisp of fog. The idea of killing Cortez tempted him, but he rejected it. It was too late. Not even the death of their commander would stop the invaders now. They had won. Tenochtitlan was a dead city, though too staggered to give up the ghost.

There was one man Don Sebastian hoped to see, but he was not Cortez. He was a smaller man, with a thin beard and stooped shoulders, wearing a pack that was most likely filled with gold. Hernan Cortez might lay waste to a civilization, but Alfonso Martinez had done something still more unforgivable. He had betrayed Don Sebastian de Villanueva, and that, at least, must be avenged.

Sebastian picked his way through the rubble in the streets. Some of the bodies were fresh, Sebastian observed, but what of it? He would never stoop to drink the blood of a corpse.

He wondered if there might be looters abroad at night. The wealth of Tenochtitlan might tempt any man, but Cortez kept good discipline among his own troops, and to his allies gold and jewels were merely trinkets. And only a fool of either race would wander through these ruins by himself. Sebastian's chance of meeting anyone was small.

He walked beside a broad canal, its depths so choked with stones and timber and corpses that he could easily have walked across it. The brackish water lapped quietly against the banks, and a light rain began to fall.

He was sick of the sight of death. It had been his companion on countless battlefields throughout his life, and it had slept beside him in his coffin through the long days since his transformation. He had killed before, and even now he was searching for an opportunity to kill again, but he had never seen anything like Tenochtitlan. The city was a charnelhouse. A cloud of corruption seeped up from the slain, who soaked in the rain all night and baked in the sun all day. Swarms of flies were their only mourners and rats their only heirs. Suppressing the first shudder he had felt in decades, he moved toward the scene of that day's battle.

Something splashed in the canal. The sound was weak, but Sebastian whirled to investigate its source. A heap of bodies clogged the intersection of two waterways, and from them came a bubbling groan. The vampire stiffened, then moved toward the carrion pile.

He spied a pale hand crawling over muddy rocks, and then an armored back that moved. Sebastian hurried forward, ignoring what his feet were forced to touch. He lifted up the Spanish soldier, as tenderly as a father with a stricken son. A bloody gash trailed across the man's forehead and his helmet had been battered in. One of his eyes bulged unnaturally. Still, he was alive.

"Don't die now," Sebastian whispered. "We need you."

He took his captive by the arm, relieved to find that it did not drop away, and dragged him through the human rubble to the street. There he leaned over to examine his find more closely.

"You'll live long enough," he said. "And your death, when it comes, will not be meaningless."

The soldier groaned again, then coughed. His mouth was full of blood and water.

"Just a few minutes more," Sebastian assured him. "We have not far to go."

Dragging his prize behind him, he shuffled through the ruins toward the black pyramid.

As July drew to a close, Cortez joined forces with his lieutenant Pedro de Alvarado, the man whose slaughter of the dancers more than a year before had begun the war between the Aztecs and the Spaniards. Cortez crossed the last canal between them, his progress impeded only briefly by a bedraggled crew of emaciated Aztec warriors. The Spaniards did not move too near the water until it had been filled in by the labor of their Indian allies, and if a number of those workers died completing their task, there were many thousands more.

As Cortez rode over the broken stones and broken bodies, he saw flames in the west. They seemed to be rising from a nearby temple, and for a moment he imagined that some cult was conducting an unholy rite there, perhaps a ceremony to curse the invaders. But when he drew closer to the fire, he realized to his delight that the conflagration was Alvarado's work. The armies of the south and west had joined, leaving behind them acres of utter devastation. More than three-quarters of the city had been completely leveled, and now the two paths of terror had merged into one. As soon as the remaining troops moved in from the north, the vise would close, leaving the surviving Aztecs with nowhere to hide.

The two contingents of the Spanish force rushed to embrace each other over the brown bodies of their friends and foes. They met in the marketplace of Tlatelolco, where in happier days the people of the city had exchanged their wares. Cortez and Alvarado took their horses into the huge enclosure whose countless porticoes and pavilions marked the sites where merchants traded their weavings and carvings for vegetables and grain. The square was empty, but despairing Aztecs lined the roofs.

Martinez watched from a safe distance. There seemed to be no fight left in the people of Tenochtitlan, but their spirit was not what worried Martinez. Reports of a most disturbing nature touched on a topic close to the alchemist's heart. Alvarado's men claimed that they had heard shouts from the vanquished priests, repeated so often that a translation had been possible. The Aztecs were taunting their conquerors with the information that they had buried all the city's treasure where no man would ever find it.

The thought drove Martinez close to madness, and his only consolation was that he did not entirely believe the story. Certainly the Aztecs were capable of such barbarism, but it seemed hardly possible that they had found the time to hide the wealth of an entire empire. They might do so in the days remaining to them, but surely some booty still remained. Where could they have put it all? He thought of the lake and its far shores and almost despaired, but then reminded himself that Cortez had controlled the waters of Texcoco for some time.

Martinez did not move, but his brain was working furiously. His mind was wracked by the horrors he had seen in Mexico, but still he knew what he wanted. The gold might be anywhere; the chance to seek it out might never come, but Martinez was determined to try for his share.

He kept well to the rear for the next few days, anticipating at least one more big battle. And at each sunset he cursed himself because he had not yet hit upon a plan for finding Montezuma's gold.

The battle he expected finally came. The marketplace was constantly filled with old men, women, and children—who offered no resistance, but seemed to form a shield for the soldiers who must be lurking somewhere. Three times Cortez called on them to surrender, promising to treat them well. It was imperative to clear the way, he said, and if they did not move he had no choice but to unloose his Indian allies.

The people stood quietly in the marketplace, as if they did not have the strength to move. They were like sheep awaiting slaughter, and at last their butchers came.

Martinez felt himself drawn irresistibly toward the scene, despite his fear, despite his disapproval. He had seen men kill each other before, but he had never seen anything like this.

A few rocks fell from the rooftops; otherwise the Aztec defense was negligible. Gunfire kept the Aztecs so well confined within the square that Martinez was able to observe the action with next to no danger to himself. He saw an infant smashed against a wall and its mother cut in two. An old man lay in the dust while half a dozen warriors flattened his head with their war clubs. A woman slumped in front of him, her back feathered with arrows. A small boy caught a cannonball as if it were a toy; it carried him into a canal.

These were the stragglers. Where the fighting was hottest, there was nothing to be seen except a flailing throng of flesh. The screams were deafening, the smoke blinding. Spears and arrows hissed like snakes; swords and clubs rose and fell like clockwork. Martinez turned away and noticed, to his surprise, that the water behind him had turned red. He had heard of such a thing, but always assumed that it was simply poetic exaggeration. This was real. The canals were bright with human blood.

The attack was so successful that the victors could hardly climb over the bodies of their victims to reach more. Even Cortez was shocked. He wrote in his reports that more than twelve thousand had been killed in this one afternoon, and then he called a truce.

King Cuauhtemoc offered to meet with Cortez, but day after day he failed to appear. It was clear to Martinez, as it would be soon to everyone, that the Aztecs were playing for time; they were evidently determined to fight to the bitter end, and then beyond.

The truce tempted Alfonso Martinez. Ostensibly there was no fighting anywhere; perhaps a man might be safe alone in the city. And certainly this was the perfect chance for the priests to make good their promise by burying the treasure of Tenochtitlan. For two nights Martinez held himself in check; on the third he slipped out of his quarters. A little piece of gold sufficed to bribe the guard. He would have let the lunatic physician out for nothing. The campfires burned behind Martinez. He was alone.

The city was black, its broken buildings like the ancient ruins of some forgotten civilization. A few minutes beyond the Spanish headquarters, Martinez ran into his first heap of corpses. The darkness obscured them, but he could not block out their reek. He tried to hold his breath until he passed them, but it was no use. The dead and their unholy stench were everywhere.

A light rain trickled down from the gray sky, drops pattering against his armor. The sound dismayed him; he began to fear that he was making too much noise. He knew he should go back, but something drove him forward. He had traveled thousands of miles for this. He had braved vampires and demons, endured war and famine, countenanced cannibalism and human sacrifice. The time had surely come for his reward.

He imagined how the guard would laugh at him if he crept back so soon, and he kept on. He scarcely realized where he was going. The gold might be anywhere, but he was moving slowly south.

The thought occurred to him that some of the bodies piled around him might be worth investigating. He spotted one covered with limp white feathers; perhaps it was a chief. Martinez sloshed through a puddle that he hoped was only water and reached out a trembling hand. He groped for an instant, then pulled away with an involuntary gasp. His fingers were coated with something thick and sticky. He ran for the canal and dipped his hand into the water, choking back his nausea as best he could. When he stood up, Sebastian was beside him.

Martinez drew his sword, stared at it for a moment, then handed it to Don Sebastian. The vampire tossed it carelessly away.

"You were coming to the pyramid," Sebastian said.

"Was I?" Martinez blinked against the water that dripped from the visor of his helmet.

"Nothing else but blight lies in this direction, and it would be a good place to look for gold."

"No doubt. Funny that I didn't think of you."

"Part of you remembered, Martinez. Part of you wanted me."

"There was not much else for me to do, was there?"

Sebastian did not reply. He beckoned, and Martinez fell into step beside him. Smoking Mirror's temple lay that way.

"I shall show you my treasure," Sebastian said. They walked together through the rain.

"The priestess," said Martinez. "Is she still alive?"

"She is."

"Shall I see her again?"

"I think not, Martinez. You disappointed her, you know."

"I am not like you. I told you more than once. I was not ready to reach out and grasp at stars. There was no place for me in your schemes, and Cortez was no better. I shall have neither gold nor glory."

"You shall have gold enough, I promise you."

They stopped before the black pyramid. The area around it had been cleaned of corpses.

"Has Smoking Mirror come to set you free?"

"Not yet, Martinez."

"He'd better hurry. I wish I could go with you. Perhaps in my next life."

"Perhaps."

"I should go," said Martinez; but he stood quite still.

"Come, Martinez. There is nowhere for you to go. You would not get far, and you would miss the splendid death that I have planned for you."

"Your treasure?"

"Wait for me here."

Martinez watched Sebastian mount the steps, a tall pale figure whose Aztec robes of red and white and black no longer seemed incongruous. He might have been a native priest.

Sebastian sat on the top step and then reached back toward the terrace. He pulled an object toward the ledge.

"Look at this, Martinez," he called down. "The Aztec calendar. One I never showed you. It was too precious. But I have learned all I can from it, and now it shall be yours."

The vampire stood on the brink of the terrace, the gigantic calendar clutched in his pale fingers. He lifted it above his head, a wheel of solid gold. No mortal could have carried it. Thicker than a man's arm, it was half as tall as Sebastian. Martinez expected him to throw it down from the pyramid at once, but Sebastian was not yet ready.

"See how it gleams, Martinez," Sebastian shouted. "It is the moon! It is the sun!"

"Let me look for a moment," Martinez said, his head raised toward the sky. "It is beautiful. You were right. That is the gold I wanted all along."

Time stopped for an instant, and in that span Martinez saw each marking on the disc in bold relief. And more than that, he read their meaning. Each hieroglyphic was a message from a god, and in their twisted symmetry he understood the secrets of his fate. He knew now what Sebastian had tried to tell him, and he would remember it. His quest was ended.

"Thank you," said Martinez, and even as he spoke Sebastian cast the glimmering disc from the heights of Smoking Mirror's temple.

The false physician bowed his head, and the heavy wheel of gold came spinning down on him like some gigantic coin.

19. Heart of the Earth

"THE eleventh night of August," Sebastian said.

"What is that?" asked Toci.

"It is the best night left to us for what we have to do, the night after the war god's festival is over. It seems to be a day of no importance, only the beginning of the feast you call the Fall of Fruit. Yet my calculations have convinced me that something will happen then. There is a discrepancy between your calendar and my charts of the Zodiac, and I have done what I could to correlate them. I believe I am right, Toci, but come and look."

She kneeled beside him on the mica floor, much of which was covered by two huge parchment sheets. On each of them was inscribed a circle, divided into segments marked with hieroglyphics. Sebastian leaned over the two charts, using the stick of charcoal with which he had drawn them as a pointer.

"This is the Aztec calendar," he said, gesturing to his left. "Beside it is a map of the stars as they will be on that night, constructed according to the rules of Spanish astrologers. You have eighteen months but we have twelve, each of them named for the constellation that is strongest in the heavens at the time. This is the month we call Leo; his name means a wild beast, something like your jaguar. The eleventh day of August is the twentieth degree of Leo, much more auspicious for our purposes than the nineteenth, even if it means bypassing the climax of Huitzilopochtli's holiday. The influence of the war god should still be lingering then, and in any case it is not war we seek."

Toci looked down at the charts, then up at Sebastian. She seemed puzzled.

"Perhaps this will help you to see it," Sebastian said. He gathered up the twin sheets of parchment and placed one over the other. Then he stood and held the two charts close to a brazier's flame. The light shone through, and suddenly both diagrams became visible, one against the other. Sebastian adjusted them meticulously.

"Now look," he said. "Your map of the year and my map of the stars. Can you see how the two of them are aligned? This line represents the change between the two feasts, and just after it is the night represented by this horoscope. Look at this mark, here. We call it Venus, but you told me that the same star represents the Feathered Serpent. When I learned that, I thought there might be a way to read the Aztec diagram against the European one. Actually, of course, it is Arabic. You remember when I told you of them? Well, never mind that now. The important thing is that it does all come together."

"Show me," Toci said.

"We call this Mars," Sebastian went on, "this glyph made of a circle and a dart. He is our god of war, and should correspond to yours. See how he stands in relation to the Feathered Serpent. I think it means Cortez will win the war, although we hardly need a horoscope to tell us that. But look at these other stars. This one, I believe, is Toci."

"Toci?"

"Your goddess, the one you call 'Grandmother,' or 'Heart of the Earth.' She is old and wise, and moves with great deliberation. She is the planet with the ring of light around her body, the one that we call Saturn."

"And where is Smoking Mirror?"

"I wish I knew. No planet that we can see corresponds to him, but certainly one exists. Our sorcerers insist that there are planets we cannot see, whose presence affects us nonetheless. I wish

I had my cards, or that I had taken the time to make some. Then I could show you his face. We cannot see his home, but we have a picture of him, and it is much like one of yours. He is a skeleton. I cannot chart his course, but the god we have who stands for Smoking Mirror is called Pluto."

"A dead god? And in hiding?"

"Precisely. But there are signs of his presence. I know from you that Smoking Mirror is the Great Bear; at least that is our name for the group of stars you showed me. That is a constellation that plays only a minor part in our astrology. It is marked here. By reckoning the attributes, Smoking Mirror should be Scorpio, and yet his festivals fall in Libra and in Taurus. But look again at the Great Bear. Then note this planet, Jupiter, the one we call the god of fortune. See how they have combined? And look at the moon. I have never seen a chart like this. I promise you this is the night when Smoking Mirror's power will be at its height."

"You see more than I see," Toci said, "but you do not see Sebastian. Your face tells me more than these pictures. I know you speak the truth. You have found the hour?"

"Only three more days," Sebastian replied. "I wonder if Cortez will grant them to us."

"Our king will fight."

"I want these final days, but I wonder what their price will be. There has been too much killing. How many more must die to grant me the opportunity for this last experiment?"

"No," said Toci firmly. "They have forgotten us. Tenochtitlan does not fight for Smoking Mirror. It fights to be free."

"Death before slavery," muttered Sebastian. "I wonder. It was not my choice, or I would never have become one of the undead. There is something to be learned here on this plane, and often a single lifetime is not enough. Nothing is enough. I stand here with my calculations and I believe in them. But what will happen when that night falls? How shall we summon Smoking Mirror?"

Toci took him by the arm with a surprising strength and turned him round to face her. "Smoking Mirror will be there. As you say, 'I promise you.'"

Sebastian stared into her shining eyes. "So be it," he said. "We shall trust each other, Toci, though neither of us understands just what the other means."

The priestess kissed his cold lips, as if to seal the bargain. Then she stepped away.

"Three days," Sebastian said. "King Cuauhtemoc has kept Cortez at bay with his talk of peace, but he will certainly be forced to fight soon, unless he chooses to surrender. And meanwhile the Spanish are constructing that damned catapult. It is a strange device, Toci; it might be strong enough to knock down Tezcatlipoca's temple."

Day by day the emissaries went back and forth between the Spaniards and the Aztecs. The uneasy truce was close to collapse. Cuauhtemoc promised to meet with Cortez, but did not. Some of his chiefs appeared, however, to explain that their emperor was ill. At the next appointment the same chiefs arrived, saying that Cuauhtemoc feared an ambush. Cortez agreed to give him one more chance, and warned him of the consequences if he did not comply.

There was a soldier in the camp, one Sotelo, who talked loudly about his experiences in the Italian wars. He had observed the working of the great siege engines there, and was confident that he could build one. It would be powerful enough to break through any building in Tenochtitlan, or so the self-styled engineer insisted. Cortez endured the fellow's boasting for as long as he could, then ordered him to build a catapult.

Lime and stone were hauled into the empty square, along with ropes and timbers. The carpenters set to work, and the sound of their hammers rang through the empty streets. A hideous structure of beams and pulleys rose above the roofs. Two gigantic slings were sewn together from carefully selected hides; they were big enough to hold a boulder. As an afterthought, Cortez ordered that the weapon be equipped with wheels. If it worked, there would be no point in confining it to this one locality. A hundred Indian allies struggled to lift the ponderous engine so that axles could be slipped beneath it. When the sun set, Sotelo was still making delicate adjustments of the ropes and cords, and promising that it would be ready by morning.

That night it rained again. Guards were stationed all around the catapult, grumbling at the drizzle, and the mist, and the sickening miasma that rose from the unburied bodies of their foes. The men felt extraneous; the Aztecs were completely cowed, and it was reasonable to assume that they had no idea what this machine could do.

None of the guards noticed the wisp of fog floating above their heads, its color more green than gray. None of them observed it hovering over the catapult, and none of them saw the long pale hands that materialized out of the cloud. Thin fingers reached forth from the mist to touch a pulley and draw back a cord. In a few seconds the hands were gone, and the green cloud drifted south.

The next morning, Cortez marched into the marketplace. He waited impatiently for the arrival of Cuauhtemoc, convinced that he would never come. When the Aztec messengers arrived with new excuses, Cortez was ready for them.

The command was given, and a platoon of Indian workers rolled a huge rock up the ramp. Sotelo supervised while it was set in place. The engine of destruction was aimed toward one of the temples that bordered the marketplace. The leather sling was filled. Windlasses turned, and ropes grew taut.

Sotelo released the stone, while his audience gave one collective gasp. The boulder flew into the sky.

Then it dropped straight down again, crushing the catapult to splinters.

There was a moment of stunned silence, and then the starving citizens of Tenochtitlan burst into laughter. The flight of the stone had been so ludicrous that not even the Spaniards could contain themselves. They laughed too; thousands of delighted voices rose in a sound that would never be heard in the city again.

Sotelo stood beside his ruined catapult, his protestations of innocence drowned out by the general hilarity. He blushed furiously and turned away.

Cortez was red-faced too, but more from fury than from shame. He ordered an immediate retreat, then made his plans for the final assault on the city. Cortez, who had been driving the Aztecs steadily to the north, now gave the order for the troops in the north to advance, supported by the entire fleet of ships. Cuauhtemoc's retreat would be cut off, and further defense of the city would be impossible. A few days' work would make the Spaniards masters of Tenochtitlan.

The massacres began again.

Sebastian brooded beneath the black pyramid. He stared at his charts for hours, alternately consoled by their exactitude and depressed by their apparent uselessness. His frustration took form in endless pacing back and forth, and his restlessness communicated itself to his men, who wanted nothing more than to go out and fight. Sebastian himself remained inside the temple; he had seen enough. Toci did her best to soothe him, yet Sebastian noticed a change in her. It was more than despair at the plight of her people. She was withdrawn and meditative.

Finally the night they had been waiting for arrived. At sunset Toci touched the panel in the dull black wall, and the stone turned back, exposing Sebastian's earth-filled coffin. The priestess lifted up the lid, and the master of the pyramid crawled out into the shadows.

"How goes the siege?" he asked at once, and listened to Toci's catalogue of horrors with no show of emotion.

"At least this pyramid still stands," Sebastian said. "The wreck of the catapult has left us enough time. Now there is nothing for us to do but to await Smoking Mirror."

"We must call him," Toci said.

"Indeed," replied Sebastian. "And have you found a way to summon him?"

Toci nodded, and Sebastian looked at her in amazement. Her eyes were unnaturally bright, her dark features a mask of fierce determination.

"How?" Sebastian asked her.

"You know," said Toci.

Sebastian did not reply. Instead he stared at her as if he hoped to read whatever mysteries were hidden behind her enigmatic expression.

"We shall speak of it later," he said at length. "For now, you may tell the men that they are free to go and fight if they still wish it. They can do nothing more for us after this night, and I would not deprive them of their pleasure."

Toci slipped out of the room without a word, and Sebastian gathered up his charts. He glanced at them for a few seconds, then rolled them up and carried them to the corner where a brazier burned. The parchments burst into flame almost at once; their fitful light sent Sebastian's shadow leaping over the sloping ceiling of the subterranean room.

"They left as soon as I told them they could go," Toci said as she returned to him. "The high priest is here, and four jaguar knights. That is all."

"The high priest," Sebastian said. "Does he know what you intend to do?"

"I told him today."

"And he approves?"

"He said it would be best, whether the god comes or not."

"And what will he do?"

"He will not come here. He said this is sacred, for us alone. He will go up on the pyramid and call on Smoking Mirror."

Sebastian took both her hands in his. "There is no need for you to do this thing," he said. "The Spaniards will not kill you; you are too beautiful. You could wait here until Cuauhtemoc surrenders, and perhaps your future life would be a pleasant one. Some chief might take you for a bride and make you a great lady."

Toci spat on the mica floor. "I am not the woman who sleeps beside Cortez," she said indignantly. "I have only one husband, and tonight he comes to me."

The vampire kissed her, and then stepped away. "I wonder what the chances are . . ." he said. "Surely Smoking Mirror has never had such a noble sacrifice, but it must not be offered for nothing."

"Not for nothing," Toci said. "For love."

"Listen, Toci. I have given this much thought. How do these gods approach the earth? And what are they? Are they beings like ourselves? Or are they bodiless intelligence? Perhaps they are pure energy, a force like fire or light. But whatever they are, they reach us through the power of our own wills. They do not travel through the stars in ships, as a sailor might, but through the minds of those who wait for them. Our strength feeds them, as the blood of living men and women feeds me."

"This is why you are Smoking Mirror."

"But even gods die, Toci. Consider the gods of Rome. No, you know nothing of them. The stars bear their names, the ones I told you of, like Venus and Jupiter and Saturn. And the city that worshipped them had conquered all the world. But men forgot those gods, who once walked among them, and now they come no more. I fear the same is true of Smoking Mirror. How many are there left to call on him? Only the two of us, and five men up above. Can that be enough to draw him down to us?"

"You say the gods are dead," Toci replied, "but they have become stars. And the stars still shine."

"Then this is truly what you want?"

"This is what I want, and it is what you want. You always wanted it. You know the story of Tezcatlipoca; you told it to Martinez. Smoking Mirror waits in darkness for someone to come, then offers up his heart. If you have the courage to take it, you will be blessed. He gives what you wish, if you are strong enough to wish it."

"His heart," Sebastian said. "The heart of the earth."

"Take what you want," said Toci, "and we shall see the Smoking Mirror."

She slipped out of her black robe and walked naked to the sacrificial slab. The virgin priestess sat cross-legged on the stone, waiting for the appointed hour.

20. The Smoking Mirror

A BAND of eager warriors rushed from Smoking Mirror's temple. Some of them were jaguar knights who had been assigned to guard the pyramid; the others were Don Sebastian's own troops, members of the savage tribe that worshipped vampire bats. They were fresh soldiers, who had been kept out of the battle of Tenochtitlan for many days, and not long ago Sebastian had fed them well.

Atop the pyramid, the blind high priest listened to them hurrying across the plaza. He guessed that they would not return alive, but nonetheless he sensed the same longing in the four men who had been ordered to stay behind and help him in his invocations. He felt the heat from their torches, and a cool breeze that promised rain before the night was gone. Aromatic incense helped to mask the odor from the streets beow, and the flavor of the sacred potion he had shared with Toci was still bitter in his mouth. Pictures formed behind his sightless eyes.

He envisioned the devastation of the city, and for a moment he was grateful that he could no longer see. He summoned up the image of the young men who were running off to die, then thought with more satisfaction of the two lovers hidden hundreds of feet beneath him. He turned his dead eyes toward the sky, away from them, and dreamed of Smoking Mirror.

His trembling fingers reached out into the air around him, as though it had a substance he could feel, and the four acolytes stepped back to give him room. One of them handed him the bejeweled skull that had been retrieved from the pack strapped to the crushed corpse of Alfonso Martinez. The high priest kissed the skull and fell into a trance.

Something called him from his contemplations, though, and he shook himself awake, uncertain of how much time had passed. There was a disturbance in the public square at the foot of the pyramid. He heard the sound of running feet, and angry voices shouting. At once his thoughts returned to earth. He did not need to ask his acolytes to understand what had happened. The attack of Smoking Mirror's men had turned into a rout. Jaguar knights would surely stand and die, but the tribesmen had no such training, and they had fled the onslaught of the enemy, leading their pursuers back to the only home they knew and to the god who would protect them. They had hurried back to Don Sebastian, and thus betrayed him in the final hour.

The old high priest cast the sacred skull down toward the noise of fighting men and listened to it splinter on the distant flagstones. For an instant the clash of arms was stilled, and he imagined all the soldiers staring up at the peak of the pyramid to discover the source of the strange missile. He called for his staff of office, a stout stick taller than any man, capped at one end with a heavy ornament of gold. Clutching this formidable weapon in both hands, he gave swift orders to the soldiers who stood beside him. If the Spaniards could be lured up to the platform, it would take them that much longer to find the secret chamber in the heart of the temple.

The torches were doused against black rocks, their pungent smoke filling the blind priest's nostrils. He heard men moving up the narrow stairway: first his allies, then his enemies. Swords clashed and soldiers screamed. He retreated from the steps as his four guards advanced, listening with satisfaction as a brazier scraped along the stones, and smiling at the howl of agony when its smoldering incense caught someone in the face.

The mixture of peyote, mushrooms, and morning glory seeds had made his senses unnaturally acute. The clash of armor, the gasps for breath, the bite of steel or stone in flesh, even the whistling of weapons through the air, all served to form a picture in his mind. No sighted observer could have been more aware of every detail of the struggle on the stairs. He judged that the Spaniards were more than halfway up the steps, but still he would not allow his quartet of jaguar knights to venture down. Each second that could be gained might make a difference.

He tried to count the number of those below him, studying the voices and their placement. He estimated half a dozen tribesmen, and at least twice as many Spaniards. But by the time the first man reached the summit, the numbers had grown smaller. Finally, he commanded his four knights to move forward. He had no doubt of who would win the fight; over his vision of battling warriors floated the hollow face of Smoking Mirror.

The wail of someone tumbling down the stairs was so distorted that there was no telling who had fallen, but his loyal soldiers shouted out the progress of the conflict to him when they could. It was not until the last of their voices died away that he stepped forth from the darkness beyond the stairs, the final defender of Tezcatlipoca's temple.

Their heavy breathing told him of several men, closing in upon him in a semicircle. He came to meet them, an old man leaning on his stick. And as he hoped, they tried to capture him alive.

When they were close enough, he lifted his long staff and sent it wheeling through the air. He heard the satisfying thuds and felt the impact in his arms as the golden figure at the far end of his stick caught two separate men. He spun in a circle, his weapon longer than any sword, and felt another enemy go down.

And then the steel shaft from a Spanish crossbow caught him in the throat.

Toci lay curled up on the stone slab, her body cushioned by her own black garments, and by Sebastian's robes of black and white and red. She looked up into his face as he leaned over her, his bright fangs bared.

"Not all at once," the priestess said. "Take my love before you take my life."

Sebastian kneeled beside the sacrificial altar so that his face was close to hers. She turned toward him, leaning on one elbow, her long black hair covering her like a cloak. Sebastian stroked it with pale fingers, then gently pushed it back, uncovering her golden flesh.

"Now is the time," said Toci.

She took one deep breath, then sank down upon her back, drawing the vampire to her with both hands. They kissed as gently as if they were strangers, their lips barely touching. She felt Sebastian slip up to lie beside her on the stone.

Sebastian kissed her once again, this time with more intensity. He clutched her shoulders, rolling on his side to pull the full length of her body close to his, her warmth against his chill. The still embrace continued for a moment, interrupted only by Sebastian's continual caresses. He felt Toci's warm breath against his cheek, and heard her shuddering sighs. He nipped her soft throat tenderly, then drew away, letting her sink down again, her bright black tresses like a blanket under her.

Sebastian kneeled between her open legs and gazed down at her familiar features, seeing them as if for the first time. Her brown eyes gleamed with anxious expectation, her nostrils flared, her full lips quivered. She arched her back, lifting her small, exquisite breasts to meet his eager hands. Her soft flesh seemed to writhe beneath his touch, and when her nipples hardened he bent low to give them delicate bites.

Toci reached out to touch his face, and as he raised his head, his black hair fell around it like a dark halo. The faint light from the braziers turned his pale cheeks red and gold as he ran his fingers along the inside of her thighs. His strong hands grasped her slim hips, and Toci felt him slipping into her. She gasped at the short, sharp pain, but then it passed away and they were one.

The priestess who had been a virgin saw the slanted ceiling

spinning overhead. Her intoxicated eyes went wide, and every fiber of her being pulsated with independent life. She rocked beneath her lover, her legs wrapped around his waist. Bursts of passion coursed through the drugged visions that she saw; Sebastian's eyes were stars. Smoking Mirror had taken her for his bride when she was still a child, and finally their wedding night had come. This was the sacrifice that would call the god down from the skies, the god whose only law was to take what he desired, the god who had already found a partial incarnation in the dead flesh of Don Sebastian de Villanueva. And now that Sebastian was pure appetite, there could be no barriers between his spirit and the dazzling force that was the Smoking Mirror. But Toci could no longer consider her decision; she could only watch the whirling images of the god, who was at once a dark statue, a pale man, and a silver skull. Her moans rose into an ecstatic scream, and she fell back upon the sacrificial stone.

Six Spanish soldiers stood outside the doorway to the pyramid, examining the black stone skull whose open mouth invited them to enter.

"Nothing in there," one of them said.

"No? Where do you think those five up top came from? This part of the city's supposed to be cleaned out, but those barbarians were guarding something. This might be where they hid the gold."

"And it might be where they hide their soldiers. Do you want to go in and see?"

"There can't be anybody left. They'd all have come out to fight us."

"Anyway, we should get back. We'll catch hell if any officer finds out we chased those men back here. It's against orders."

"They'll forget that if we bring Cortez a fortune, won't they? And a promotion wouldn't hurt, now the war's almost over and the fun's about to start."

"I don't like this place. I heard something about it. All their gods are devils, but this one frightens even the Aztecs."

"What was that? Somebody screamed!"

"I'm going back. We need a cannon for this accursed pile."

"And I'm going in. Women and gold sound good enough to me, especially when there's no officer around to tell us how to behave. Who's with me? Come on!"

"Your love is like your bite," murmured Toci. "It hurts at first, but not for long." She lay in Don Sebastian's arms, her skin covered with a shiny dew of perspiration.

"Is this not enough for you, Toci? Do you insist on death?"

"This is the night you chose. You took part of me; now take all. And Tezcatlipoca will welcome us."

"If he does not come, you will be dead."

"I die tonight, or I die tomorrow, when Cortez comes. Believe, Sebastian. This is the way, I promise you."

Sebastian's faith might waver, but his desire was unswerving. The lovely creature he embraced was begging him to take her blood, and even as he pitied her, he felt the hunger rise within him. He took her roughly by the throat, as if he hoped that she might stop him with a cry for mercy. But Toci only threw back her head and wrapped her arms around him.

Sebastian ran his fingers along her body, cherishing every touch. His lips were at her jugular. He thought of her dead, then imagined her rising the next night as a vampire like himself. But would there be another night? And what chance would two of the living dead have to survive in a city conquered by Cortez? They were not proof against the wooden spears and arrows carried by tens of thousands of the Indian allies. The only hope lay with Smoking Mirror, whose faithful followers had been reduced to a pathetic handful.

Sebastian cast his doubts aside and sank his sharp teeth into Toci's throat.

Even then, a protest from her might have stopped him. Her life was precious, and there was nothing he could offer her in exchange for it except the dream that something might sweep down from the stars to rescue them. But Toci held him closer than before, her body stiffening, her breath coming in spasms.

Her hot blood pulsed over his tongue with each throb of her wildly beating heart, its salty sweetness laced with the mysterious drugs of Mexico. A fever overcame Sebastian, and as he sucked the life out of his lover he saw the world turn red. Her fingers raked his face spasmodically; to him they felt as if they were already bones.

Then Toci's slim brown hands dropped down, and her blood came more slowly. Her heart was failing.

"The god is here," she whispered. "You are Tezcatlipoca, my Sebastian. . . . You are the only Smoking Mirror."

Her words reverberated through the black chamber, sending a shock of horror through Sebastian. He lifted up his head so suddenly that he tore a piece out of her throat. Her blood splashed over the altar.

"Toci!" he shouted. "What do you mean?"

A small smile twisted her lips; her eyes were glistening. There was no reproach in her steady gaze, only tenderness.

"Toci!"

The light went out of her eyes, and she slumped back against the stone.

Sebastian stepped away from her. Toci's golden skin had turned hideously pale; her slim body was unexpectedly gaunt. Clotting blood dripped slowly from the ugly rip his teeth had left when he pulled away from her. His intoxicated gaze distorted every detail so that he could hardly bear to look at her.

Sick at heart, he stood beside the stone slab while the moments passed, waiting for something he no longer expected. The black room was still. No god appeared.

The subterranean room was suddenly very small. The dull and twisted walls seemed to press in upon Sebastian. For the first time, he noticed every dusty cobweb and every puddle of dried blood. The chamber was a tomb, weighed down by countless tons of dark and heavy stone. The drugs from Toci's veins showed Sebastian no visions, only a pitilessly detailed picture of his own surroundings. A naked corpse limped back and forth inside this black and bloody trap, alone except for the woman it had murdered.

Sebastian's head throbbed and voices rang in his ears. They spoke in Spanish, and they were coming closer.

He realized abruptly that the sounds he heard were not delusions. Spanish soldiers had invaded the temple, and they were working their way through the twisting passageways toward the little room where their dead countryman stood alone.

Sebastian prepared himself to meet them. Shutting his eyes against the sight of the slaughtered priestess, he gathered up his robes and put them on. As he did so, he noticed to his dim confusion that the sacred disc hanging from his neck had changed from black to gold.

Sebastian shook off his surprise, determined to control his reeling brain. His first decision was to rid the room of light. It made no sense to guide his enemies directly to his lair. He knocked the two burning braziers to the floor and stamped on the burning coals with his naked feet, noting with grim satisfaction the way his gray, withered right foot began to smoke and smolder.

The voices were louder now, yet somehow they were more distant, echoing along endless corridors that seemed to stretch a century away. And the room had not gone dark. The fires were all out, but the chamber was illuminated by some faint phosphorescence. Sebastian turned toward the entrance; it was thick with shadows. He looked down at the glassy mica floor, and through its half-transparent surface he saw the full moon beaming up at him.

"Sebastian," whispered someone behind him.

He whirled at the sound, convinced that it was Toci speaking, and when he faced her corpse he saw that its bloodless flesh had been transformed into a figure of rich, black obsidian.

The shining statue spoke again; he saw its dark lips move. "Tezcatlipoca," it said, "Smoking Mirror." The sound of cymbals rippled through the pyramid, and spicy incense filled the stagnant air.

He staggered toward the altar, to gaze in wonder at the perfect replica of his beloved. She was as beautiful as she had ever been, each swelling slope and curve of her face and figure embodied in the gleaming stone. The muttering of Spaniards became as faint as the buzzing of insects, and he waited for the voice of the priestess to come again. Instead, the glistening statue rose.

He reached out to touch her cheek, but at his touch the living statue disappeared, leaving him with nothing to embrace but throbbing darkness.

Somewhere a bell rang. Sebastian raised his hands above his head and saw the ceiling of his dismal prison turn to glass. A universe of stars shone down upon him.

Sebastian spun around, and, as he did so, he saw each of the slanting walls of his dark chamber turn transparent. He was in the center of a jewel, bright and multifaceted. From each slanted wall there rose a flight of stairs, stretching off into infinity. He watched a silver skull bounce down each set of steps, rolling up gigantically against the glassy surfaces until he was surrounded by images of his own mortality.

Sebastian screamed, covered with filth and blood and death.

A cleansing wave of blue and green rolled down each stairway, washing away the multitude of skulls, and he realized that the waves were made of fire.

It occurred to him that he had experienced all of this before. He remembered it, and he was calm, even when his gemlike cell broke away from Tenochtitlan to drop dizzyingly into the sky.

He soared through the starry universe in a twelve-sided crystal cage, the distant points of brightness rushing by so quickly that they turned to flickering streaks of white. He spun head over heels in a giddy flight that put his wings to shame.

Toci appeared before him, her face so huge that it blotted out the stars. "We have won," she said. "Tezcatlipoca."

The shining polyhedron flew toward her and sank into the darkness of her eyes. Passing through the darkness, Sebastian felt himself turned round about, and what he saw behind him was his own gigantic face, fading into distance as he dropped away.

The stars were specks of gold and silver against a background of black silk when Sebastian came to rest. Suspended in infinity, he reached out to touch the translucent sides of his bright prison. One of the walls swung open, and the blind high priest stepped through. The hollow sockets of his eyes were filled with diamonds.

"We are the last," said the old man. "Gods never die, but men do, and they announce the death of gods who have forgotten them. Smoking Mirror has forgotten Mexico, but he has not forgotten us. His priestess waits for you, the bride of the stars."

The high priest touched his own forehead and dwindled away to nothing.

Sebastian heard Toci calling to him, and felt himself dissolving into light. His glowing body rose into a shower of dazzling brightness as he reached out to embrace the universe, and in each of its endless worlds he sensed the presence of his beloved. He had become the Smoking Mirror, and she was his reflection.

The walls around him shattered, and finally he was free.

21. The Conqueror

CORTEZ and several of his officers stood inside the tilted chamber at the bottom of Tezcatlipoca's temple. The night was far advanced, and outside the rain was falling heavily.

"Reprimand the men who left their posts," said Cortez. "There is no gold here, nor any Aztec warrior. Nothing but that heathen idol."

"Look at that dried blood, though," said an eager young officer. "It's caked to the floor. And the incense! The place smells worse than the street we passed through. How many lost souls have spent their last moments here, I wonder?"

"There shall be no more," Cortez replied. "Call up the cannon. This abomination must be destroyed. And if they have anything hidden here, we shall find it among the broken stones."

The men filed out, but the young officer lingered for a moment. "Look at the walls," he said. "They're made of that black glass. You can see yourself in them."

On that night, August 11, 1521, the heavy thunderstorm produced a rare phenomenon. A ball of lightning streaked across the sky, sparks trailing behind it, and disappeared into the darkness of the lake. It might have been a visitation from one of the gods, but in their present plight the Aztecs could only regard this sign in the heavens as an ill omen.

Two days later, King Cuauhtemoc surrendered the city of Tenochtitlan. Hernan Cortez and his allies took possession of the ruins eighteen days before the festival of the goddess called "Heart of the Earth." Her feast was not celebrated, nor were any of the others that had always followed. The gods were gone.

Cortez died in 1547, after years of neglect by the fickle court of Spain. He had his time of triumph, but political enemies kept him from the honors he sought, and he squandered most of his fortune. He was buried in Spain, but twenty-two years later his body was exhumed and transported to Mexico City, the capital he had built with slave labor on the ruins of Tenochtitlan. In 1823, after the war for independence, public indignation against the man who had conquered Mexico for Spain grew so great that plans were made to burn what was left of Cortez. Officers of the church were forced to hide the body, and did it so successfully that it was lost for more than a century. Archaeologists finally uncovered it in 1946, hidden behind the walls of an old chapel. The little casket was covered with a cross of gold; the broken bones inside it were wrapped in white silk trimmed with black lace. There was little left of the conquistador except a yellowed skull.

Citizen Vampire

1

The Last Cards

THE COUNTESS looked at the seven cards and raised a disdainful eyebrow.

"So much money for these scraps of paper? You have been cheated. Or perhaps you are trying to cheat me?"

Rollin shifted uneasily as he stood beside her chair and pushed back the twisted spectacles which were sliding down his long nose. Convincing a client to pay for his services was the most difficult part of his difficult business, but he had learned long ago that it never helped to apologize.

"It will cost you this much, Madame Countess, and a great deal more. These cards are relics, the last remaining tokens of a wizard who died three hundred years ago, and my colleagues bid wildly for the privilege of owning them. There was even an attempted robbery. But only Rollin was clever enough to see what they were worth. And only Rollin, I might add, has a patron wise and generous enough to pay the price, both for the cards and for the experiments we shall perform with them."

The Countess de Corville smiled. "I am immune to flattery, I hope; I have had a lifetime of it, and from men whose manners are far more polished than yours. Yet it amuses me to hear your rude attempts, Rollin, and I confess that other men speak less of my wisdom than they do of my beauty. You may continue."

"I am an old man, Madame Countess, and your beauty is

not for me, however much it may delight me to find so fair a flower here in this miserable garret. But you show your wit by seeing through my stratagems. Let me be honest with you." He shuffled around the sagging table to face the Countess and gazed intently into her luminous brown eyes. "I ask nothing for myself," he said, "except the opportunity to perform this great work for you. Magic is an expensive business, and the world is full of those who can see nothing beyond the gleam of gold. Trust me, I implore you, and I shall show you something that no woman in Paris has ever seen."

The flickering light of a single candle stump illuminated the face of the Countess de Corville as she sat considering Rollin's proposal. Most of what he told her was true, but not that he was indifferent to her appearance. He was a man of sixty-seven winters (he remembered the winters more than the summers), but only a woman half his age, as he guessed his visitor to be, could believe that a man of his years was immune to feminine charm. And the Countess breathed charm, as tangible and yet elusive as the spicy perfume that filled Rollin's cramped attic apartment.

Her hair was the color of honey, so lightly powdered that little of its natural beauty was lost, and it fell in a profusion of waves and curls over her bare shoulders. Her hat was broad-brimmed and black, adorned with ostrich plumes; it shadowed her large, dark, and liquid eyes. Her face was a painting in red and white, after the fashion of the time, and a tiny black patch highlighted her left cheek, but no amount of artifice could conceal the perfection of her delicate nose, her soft lips, and her slightly rounded chin. Wrapped tightly around her long neck was a choker of black velvet; hanging from it was a single pearl, its pale iridescence matched by the glowing flesh of an exquisite bosom only half hidden by her black velvet bodice. The rest of her costume was hidden in the folds of a crimson cloak, from which her long white hands emerged, covered with jewels. Rollin admitted to himself that he was old enough to care more for these gems than for the glamour of the woman who wore them. Any one of her rings would pay for a dozen experiments such as the one he proposed to her.

The Countess seemed to be aware that he was devouring her with his eyes, yet she was more entertained than annoyed. She shrugged her shoulders in a manner that seemed calculated to release her high breasts from their dark confinement.

"It is too expensive," she said. "What shall I tell my husband? It is bad enough when I have something to show him, a gown or a wig or a necklace. But I can tell him nothing of this. And he does nothing but complain about money. I think he will die if the king decides to tax the aristocracy. He tells me that the Estates-General will meet in a few days, and for no other purpose than to protest the shabby treatment that we nobles are receiving. Where shall I find the money?"

"The Countess will find a way," said Rollin as he sat again beside her. "She is already an astute practitioner of magic, and this final effort will give her the keys to wealth and youth and power. It is a wiser investment than a few more acres of land to be neglected by ungrateful peasants."

"I agree, Rollin, and I would gladly give you this pearl to pay your price." Her hand caressed her throat and strayed coquettishly into the soft shadow between her breasts. "But my husband is the sort of man who counts his wife's jewels when he has bad news from our estates in the country. Still, I suppose I shall find a way."

"I have faith in you, Madame Countess. You can control the Count more easily than we can control the magic in these cards."

"I suppose so. He is a fool. If he has the time to wonder where I am, he will only imagine that I am with a lover."

"Now you flatter me, Madame Countess."

"Indeed. But what have you been saying? Is there danger in these bits of paper?"

"Only for Raoul Rollin, who will see to it that you are safe."

"They are only Tarot cards, not much different from the ones you have had for years. What can seven cards do except to predict a future so misty that only a charlatan like you would have the audacity to interpret it?"

Rollin's watery gray eyes blinked behind the thick hexagonal lenses of his spectacles, and he ran his fingers through the long hair that hung sparsely from his balding skull. Then he wiped his hand absent-mindedly on a waistcoat that was already more than a little greasy.

"These cards, Madame Countess, are not for predicting the future, but for controlling it. As you say, there are only seven, and anyone who dealt them out would read the same fortune. The cards are only a blind. There is something hidden in them!"

"But what fortune do they tell?"

"Please, dear lady, listen to me. These cards were made by the hands of one of the greatest sorcerers who ever lived, a man who was powerful enough to conquer death. They were rescued from his castle in Spain after it was destroyed in 1496, almost three hundred years ago."

"Two hundred and ninety-three years, to be exact. This is 1789. Your exaggerations will not impress me."

"Three hundred, two hundred and ninety-three, what is the difference? The point is that this man, this Don Sebastian de Villanueva, knew more than any man alive knows, and that some of his secrets are hidden in these cards."

Rollin's enthusiasm pulled him up out of his chair and he began to pace around the narrow room. Each time he crossed the candle, it sent grotesque shadows flashing across the slanted ceilings of his garret. His body was lean to the point of emaciation except at the waist, where an incongrously round little belly swelled. His waistcoat and breeches were black decaying into green. His shirt, stockings, and cravat might once have been white, but there was no way of proving it. His costume was completed by oversized red slippers that flapped as he walked; his hat and coat hung on a peg in a corner. He was not dressed to receive a lady, and the Countess de Corville found it best to press a perfumed handkerchief to her delicate nostrils on those occasions when he came too close to her.

"So this Don Sebastian conquered death," she said. "Then where is he now?"

"Who knows? There is a story that he died in Spain, and another story that he died again nine years later. Some say that he survived even that, and somehow appeared in Mexico during the Spanish Conquest. Wherever he was, now he is lost. But Rollin has found him again! Look, Madame Countess. He is hidden in the cards."

Rollin spread the seven pieces of pasteboard across the scarred face of the table in front of his client. The Countess glanced at them without much interest; she had seen them before.

"You must examine them more closely," Rollin said. "You will need a glass. I have one somewhere. What did I do with it?"

He began to rummage through a pile of books stacked against the low wall, but found nothing except a scrawny cat which emerged from its nest with unruffled dignity. He ran his hands along a row of dusty bottles on a shelf, pressed his fingers to his face in exasperation, and then plucked off his spectacles. "These will do," he said. "Take a look at Death."

The Countess peered at him sharply for a moment, then realized what he meant and turned her attention to the card bearing the picture of a skeleton.

"Beautifully done, isn't it?" asked her host ingratiatingly. "Of course the ink has faded a bit after all these years."

She hardly dared to touch the antique card for fear that it would crumble to dust beneath her fingers. The skeleton walked across a field whose abundant crop consisted of human hands and heads. Some of the heads bore crowns, but the scythe the skeleton brandished swung toward them without hesitation. The sun was sinking behind the bony figure, and the sky was red, but its color had aged until it looked like dried blood.

"It is an old picture," said Rollin as he leaned over the table. "But observe." He placed his glasses over the ribs of the skeleton and adjusted the lenses as carefully as his weak eyes would permit. "These will magnify it for you. There is secret writing hidden in the lines of the drawing."

The Countess leaned forward over his shaking hand and stared through the dirty glass at lines of faded ink that swam before her eyes. For a moment she thought she law letters burried between the bones, but she could not read their message.

"What does it say, Rollin? The light is so weak."

"It is written in Latin, which I assume you do not read. There are so few ladies of your station who can. But Rollin will translate it for you. It says: 'Seek me among the stars.' "

"And what does that mean?"

"At first I was not sure. Even now I am not completely sure. We have only hints. Most of the cards are gone, but I believe I have enough of them to give me a key, the key that Don Sebastian left for me three hundred years ago. The first writing I saw was in another card, and I could not read them all until your generosity enabled me to buy them. The first thing I noticed was in this one. The Devil."

"These are not the most favorable cards, Rollin."

"But they are among the strongest. What would you have from a wizard? We are lucky to have what we do. And the Devil was what set me on the track. The message is in the chains that bind the naked woman to Satan. It says: 'Blood and bone imprison me.' And that sent me back to the Death card. As you know, it does not signify death in the ordinary sense, but a transformation or an upheaval. It also stands for Scorpio, which I believe to be the sign under which Don Sebastian was born. And I think there is more in that card than we have seen so far. Part of the clue was here."

His bony finger touched another card, one representing a tower struck by lightning, with two figures falling from it toward the rocks below.

"The Tower," said the Countess. "Another ill omen."

"It is only Mars, the planet that rules Scorpio. It is a blessing to have three cards of such power. The other four are comparatively unimportant, all from the minor arcana. Five of Cups, Ten of Wands, Ten of Swords, and Knight of Swords. Cards of small significance. I would trade them all to have the card called the Star. 'Seek me among the stars,' he wrote. But we must make do with these."

"And what do you propose to do with them, Rollin? These snatches of poetry seem to have no import. Why should I have paid so dearly for them?"

"That I hope to show you now. I waited for you to come before performing the next step. It has something to do with the message about blood."

His eyes twinkled happily as he picked up his spectacles and put them on; then he stepped away from the table for a moment. When he returned he was holding a knife with a long, narrow blade. The color of the blade was dull, but its edge was sharp. "This should do nicely," he said with a smile.

Instantly the Countess was up out of her chair and backing toward the door. "I have four servants waiting in the street below. The footmen were chosen for their strength, and they are armed. One cry from me will bring them at a run. Be careful with that knife, old man."

Rollin gave a wheezing chuckle as she shifted her chair to block his path. "My dear Countess," he said, "do not mistake me. This blade is not to draw blood, but to remove it. Still, stand where you are, if sharp steel frightens you. Stand and watch."

He picked up one of the cards—she could not see which one—and held it over a small copper bowl, then began to scrape at the paper with his knife. He worked slowly, and despite her caution the Countess found herself drawn toward him. Small dry chips of something were dropping into the copper bowl with each stroke of the steel.

"Ah. I knew it," said Rollin. "It was blood that painted this red sky behind the skeleton, and no doubt the blood was Don Sebastian's. And look, Countess. See what was hidden underneath that crust of blood. More writing!"

The old magician's feet were almost dancing with excitement, but his trembling hands went about their business methodically. "I knew this was the card," he muttered. "So simple, really. 'Blood and bone imprison me.' I can almost read a bit of it now. Looks like Greek. But there's something strange about the letters. Could it be Hebrew? No. What's wrong? Is it a code? No. I have it, dear lady. I have it!"

He brandished the knife gleefully in the face of the Countess, but she did not even notice.

"What is it, Rollin? What have you found?"

"It's the Tower. Did I tell you what was written on that card? It disappointed me at first. 'As it is above, so it is below.' Old saying among the alchemists, you know. Reflections. Just a commonplace, I thought, but now I understand.

It's Greek, all right, but it's been written backward. I need a mirror. Do you have one? I never use the things myself; don't like the way I look that much. No? Never mind. The window will do. Improvise. Ah. It's none too clean, but what are sleeves for, eh? There, that should do it. And there's your coach in the street. Five stories down. I never look out of this window. Too busy. And I shouldn't be looking out now, should I? Should be looking into it instead!"

He grasped the guttering candle and held it up against the pane of glass that looked out onto the streets of Paris. The night was dark, and the reflection of his face was clear in the small portion of the window he had polished. He stared at himself for a second and then turned away. "I was young once," he said.

Rollin held the card and the candle before his improvised looking glass while the Countess leaned over his sloping shoulder. "I can't see it," he said. "I can't hold it steady. Will you do it? Good. Only a few words showing. Have to work all night to get them all out into the open. Here's something funny. That word means reflections. And this is thirteen. Thirteen reflections. Does he want mirrors? Have to get them. Thirteen! So much glass! Magnifying lens, spectacles, mirrors, and the window, too. Here's another word. Blood. And there's something about earth. Dirt, really. Dirt of the native land. So much to read. And so much to do! That's enough for you tonight, dear lady. You'd better leave. Come back tomorrow. No, make it the night after. And come at midnight. Come a little before. Call me sentimental if you wish, but I think midnight will be best. And it might take me two days to gather everything we'll need. You'll have to leave me more money, of course. Quite a bit of it, in fact. It won't be cheap to get all this, especially the blood. I wonder what sort of blood it will turn out to be?"

"Rollin!" said the Countess. She was almost shouting, and he started at the sound of her voice as if surprised to realize that he was not alone. "What are you talking about, you old fool? What is this?"

"Don't you understand?" he asked in innocent amazement. "Didn't I say? This is the formula that will enable us to summon the spirit of Don Sebastian! He left it for me. For me, Raoul Rollin! And what a meeting it will be!"

His cackle of triumph turned into a cough and he staggered against the window frame. The Countess took the candle from his hand an instant before he would have dropped it, and led him to a chair. It was the first time she had ever touched him. She dropped the Death card on the table beside the others.

"Are you sure?" she asked. Gasping for breath, Rollin answered her with an enthusiastic nod.

"You need something to drink," she said. "Have you any wine? You must calm yourself."

"No wine. Not tonight. Must work. Must get ready for Don Sebastian!"

"Even if you can bring him back, what makes you think he will be happy to return? Will it be safe?"

"Of course he wants to come back. Wouldn't you? He left the instructions."

"But that was three hundred years ago. Could he really have expected to be returned to Paris in 1789?"

Rollin slumped in his chair. "I thought you would be delighted," he said, "but now I see you are afraid."

"Now you are acting again," replied the Countess. "You think to shame me into buying this Don Sebastian back from the devil. And I am afraid, at least a bit. I have wasted a fortune on you and others like you, men and women who promised me excitement and unholy knowledge but delivered nothing. And perhaps that is all I really wanted. I'm still half afraid that you will only cheat me, but I think I'm more afraid that you will do what you say. I've never seen you as excited as you were when you held that card up to the window, and I'm not sure I like it. Can you really do what you say? And if you can, what shall we do with a dead Spanish wizard?"

"We can only try, Madame Countess. I offer you not only my own skills, but also those of the man who made those cards, and I believe we shall succeed. As for what will happen afterward, I can only guess. I hope that Don Sebastian will be grateful to us for following his instructions, and that we shall learn much from him. And I choose to ignore your claims to womanly weakness. You have come too far with me, dear lady, and I know you well. You are not like all the others, those empty heads with full purses who swoon at the sight of manufactured ghosts and ask for nothing more. You want more than life has offered you, and you care nothing for the cost. Or the risk. Is Rollin right?"

"I suppose so, even though I suspect that you are only flattering me again."

"One must flatter the Countess de Corville if one is to speak the truth."

"Enough. I will send my maid Madeleine tomorrow, and you will tell her how much money you need for your materials. And on the next night, I shall be here before midnight."

"One more thing before you go. Did you read the book I recommended to you?"

"Father Calmet's *Treatise on Vampires*? That old thing? I read it when I was a girl. Half of Paris has read it. What of it?"

"I thought you would have guessed, Madame Countess, if only from all our talk of blood and magic and mirrors. How do you suppose that Don Sebastian survived his own death? And how do you suppose he acquired his unearthly knowledge? Our visitor, if he comes, will be a vampire."

2

The Countess

THE GILDED COACH rattled through the narrow cobblestone streets, each revolution of its wooden wheels jolting the two footmen who clung precariously to the rear of the conveyance. The coachman, dressed like the others in green livery trimmed with gold, flicked his whip lightly over the backs of the matched white stallions that were among the most prized possessions of the Countess de Corville. This rush through the spring night was hardly necessary, but the coachman knew that the Countess loved speed, and it was worth his position to give her anything less.

Inside the coach was the fourth servant who had attended the Countess on the visit to Raoul Rollin, her maid, Madeleine Benet.

"What will Madame tell the Count about this evening's business?" she asked.

"Nothing, Madeleine. My husband's head is so full of other worries that he will never ask where I have been. I have no need for excuses. In fact, he would have been furious if I had been present to intrude on his conference with the gentlemen who called on him tonight. The Estates-General will convene in a few days, and my husband's friends are working frantically to come up with a plan that will enable them to maintain their privileges. The Count worries less about me than he does about his money."

Madeleine reflected that the affections of the Countess lay in the same direction, but of course she could not say it. Instead she nodded, and as she did a wisp of bright red hair slipped from the hood of her black traveling cloak and brushed across her forehead. Madeleine pushed the hair aside, a flicker of irritability in her pale blue eyes. Her mistress caught the look, but it only amused her, for she had long since grown accustomed to Madeleine's sullenness. The girl was an excellent servant, far too efficient to be dismissed on a whim, and she seemed completely trustworthy, but she lacked that spirit, respectful yet convivial, which was the mark of the ideal lady's maid. Instead, Madeleine gave the impression that she was suffering under some unnamed injustice, although the Countess could not imagine what it was and had long ago decided that it would be preposterous for her to ask. The girl was simply sulky, and the only pleasure her company provided was the opportunity to provoke her until her eyes turned cold.

"Tomorrow, Madeleine, you will have the chance to visit Rollin's rooms yourself."

"I, Madame? For what purpose?"

"To pay him. I could have done it myself, tonight. . . ." The Countess paused and watched her maid's face. "But I have no money. I shall have to ask my husband for it."

Madeleine relaxed slightly against the cushions of the swaying coach, her brief spasm of annoyance subsiding when she realized that her mistress had not simply postponed the payment to Rollin for the pleasure of sending her servant on an unnecessary journey. Such things had happened before.

"This will be the last money that charlatan will receive from me," continued the Countess, "unless he delivers something more than promises. I have already given him enough to pay your wages for several hundred years."

With this remark the Countess de Corville turned away to glance out of the small window to her right. Her surroundings told her that she had nearly reached her destination, but her thoughts were not on home or husband. Instead she was thinking of Don Sebastian de Villanueva, the undead Spanish wizard whom Rollin had sworn he could revive. She wondered what such a man would be like, assuming that he actually existed, and assuming that Rollin could actually produce him, something which the Countess was inclined to doubt. Certainly he would not be like Rollin, a small, seedy man who smelled of something sadder than the grave. Don Sebastian would be the embodiment of magnificence and mystery, something more than any man she had ever known. He would be naked power, and he would show her secrets far beyond the world in which she had been trapped, a world in which everything was counted and nothing was measured. Her husband's wealth had not brought her the freedom she desired, but perhaps Sebastian would.

The wheels of the coach scraped to a standstill, and the Countess was startled to see a dark figure standing in the shadows around her home. It was a tall man, dressed in a slouch hat and a long coat with overlapping capes descending from the shoulders. He dropped back into the darkness, and for a moment the Countess thought of Don Sebastian, but then she realized who it must be.

"There is that young man who has been courting you, Madeleine. What is his name again?"

"Andre Latour."

"And does he work?"

"He is a lawyer, Madame."

"Ah. Yes. It seems that every young fellow these days is a man of law, unless perhaps he is a man of letters. Each one of them believes that the mantle of genius is about to descend upon him, and each one thinks that he will reform the world. I doubt if there have ever been so many fools intent on expressing themselves. But sometimes I wonder if they have anything to express. Does he make any money?"

"He will," said Madeleine, burying herself in a corner where she knew her features were all but invisible.

"No doubt," said the Countess. "I suppose you want to speak to him, even though you know I will need you."

Madeleine did not reply.

"Very well," said the Countess. "It is most inconvenient, but you may have an hour with him. No more. I expect you back to help prepare me for bed."

"You are very kind, Madame," said Madeleine as she

slipped hurriedly out of the coach, almost neglecting to shut the monogrammed door behind her. A moment later she was caught up in the strong arms of her lover.

Behind them, set far back from the road, stood the Paris home of the Count de Corville. The house itself was hidden behind a high wall whose top was adorned by small pillars and decorative sculpture. Enclosed within was a spacious courtyard whose shrubbery formed a maze long enough to lose a legion of lovers. And it was rumored that the Countess had had such a legion, or at least it would have been rumored if there were anyone among her acquaintances prepared to be scandalized by her behavior.

Madeleine waited to speak until the ornate gates had closed behind the coach carrying her mistress toward the mansion beyond the maze. And when she did speak, the sound of her voice was buried in the folds of her lover's coat.

"You'll have to do better than that," said Andre Latour. "I can't hear a word you're saying."

"I said she is a witch! I said she is a monster! I said I would be glad to strangle her!"

"As it is, you are all but strangling me, Madeleine. Your embrace is like a death grip."

Madeleine smiled fiercely up at him. "I am strong, aren't I? Not like that horrible skinny creature or her fat toad of a husband. I could break them both in one hand."

"But you won't," Andre replied. "Wait a few weeks, and the people will take their power away. Soon we will have them. Not just these two, but all of those damned aristocrats." He grinned back at her. "Meanwhile, suppose you show me just how strong you are."

His handsome face grinning even more broadly, he bent his head and busied his huge hands at her throat, undoing a clasp and pulling away the hooded black cloak that covered her from head to foot. Madeleine took a step back from him, plucked off her white mob-cap, and shook her head to free the shining strands of her red hair. She was dressed simply as befitted her station, but her small, sturdy figure required no embellishments. Her wide hips and full bosom made her look like a miniature Venus; and if her features were a shade too strong for perfect beauty, there was both a promise and a challenge in her wide lips, short nose, and bright blue eyes.

Andre, a tall, broad-shouldered young man with curly chestnut hair, stood in the dark and stared at her happily.

"You've looked long enough," she said at length. "Am I a prize cow? Come here and kiss me. We have only an hour."

The Count de Corville sat behind an ornately carved desk, his pale, puffy face lined with worry. One stubby hand wandered idly through a sheaf of documents; the other clutched a glass of brandy. There were empty chairs and empty glasses all around him. He raised his eyes distractedly when the door opened and a liveried footman ushered his wife into the stuffy room.

"Ah, there you are, Juliette," he said, draining his drink as the Countess made her way across the Turkish carpet and through the disordered furniture until she stood beside him. She kissed him dispassionately on the forehead and he waved her away from him.

"Must you dress the servants in green?" he asked petulantly. "It's a very fashionable color this year, you know, and it embarrasses my guests to find that they're dressed like our lackeys. You could be more considerate, my dear."

The Countess laughed. "They deserve to be embarrassed, if they have no minds of their own. What is fashion that they should follow it so slavishly? Should I dress as the Queen does? Would you have me look like an English milkmaid?" She removed her broad black hat with its ostrich plumes and tossed it into a chair. "I dress to please myself. And also, of course, my husband. Would you prefer it if I draped a kerchief over my shoulders, Henri, or do you like me as I am?"

"You are a lovely creature, Juliette, and your appearance pleases me as much as it does my friends. Wear what you wish. It may not be stylish, but you have the figure for it, and a woman's body will never be entirely out of fashion."

The Countess smiled and made a curtsy. "I knew what you liked when you bought me."

"Bought you? I didn't buy you, my dear. I married you."

"And what, pray tell, is the difference?"

The Count turned back to his papers. "It would have been cheaper to buy you," he muttered. "And to sell you again when the sight of you wearied me."

"You might not have tired of me if you were man enough to do more than look."

The Count de Corville sank wearily back into his chair. "Must we have this song again? I am an old man. I was old when you married me. Old, and tired, and ill. My life was as good as gone before I inherited the title, but it seemed to me that I was at least entitled to a beautiful wife. And in exchange, I have made you one of the richest women in the kingdom."

The Countess grimaced and dropped into a chair some distance from her husband. "You disgust me," she said. "Your frailty is all in your imagination. You love to whine and worry, Henri. You spend your life constructing phantoms to oppress you. We both know men far older than you who are still alive, who are still men. Have you no wish for an heir?"

"Perhaps one of your lovers will provide me with one. What would you have from me? Have I made you a prisoner? Do you want for anything? Am I a jealous husband? Do I have you followed? Do I ask you where you go? Do I care where you have been tonight?"

"No!" shouted the Countess. "You do not care. You care for nothing but yourself."

Her husband stared at her for a moment, then stood with a sigh and began to shuffle around the high-ceilinged room. "Look at all these candles. Dozens of them. Costs a fortune to keep them all burning. Like burning money. No need for all this light." One by one he blew out the small yellow flames until his desk was the last remaining island of cheer in a sea of shadows.

His wife sat in the dark. "You act like a peasant," she said.

"One of us should, my dear Juliette. We are not poor yet, but we may be soon. You say I think only of myself, but are you any different? All France is in turmoil; the very foundations of our fortune are threatened. Yet still you insist on behaving as if we had access to the national treasury. Not that it would help much if we did, of course. France is on the verge of bankruptcy, and we nobles have been named to make up the deficit. We face ruin."

The Countess sighed and shifted impatiently in her chair. Her husband could hardly see her in the dim light, but he heard the rustle of her gown. "Surely you exaggerate," she said. "The danger can hardly be so great. The King would not permit it."

"The King! He would betray us in a moment. I half believe that he already has. He needs money just like any other man, and he is beginning to think like a farmer or a tradesman. Harvests have been bad, and the people have no money to pay taxes. It would hardly do to tax the Church, so King Louis has only one choice, unless he is to suffer along with the rest of us, and that he finds unthinkable. And so, it seems, he means to tax the nobles. Of course he will not admit it, but why else has he called the Estates-General to meet for the first time in centuries? He means to have our blood!"

"A bit of our money, perhaps," suggested the Countess dryly.

"A bit! The whole structure of society will collapse before he's through. It's bad enough to see these wretched pig-breeders and shopkeepers voting to elect their representatives; it reminds me of the horrors of America. But the King has agreed to double the number of their delegates, so that they will be equal to the combined strength of the clergy and the aristocracy. The Third Estate has become too powerful. Grant them a few radical priests, and a soft-headed Marquis or two—Lafayette, for example—and they will win on every vote. And what do you suppose the result will be?"

"For you, Henri, I suspect the result will be a fit of apoplexy. You must be calm. Save your speeches for the Estates-General, and have a little more brandy. Shall I ring for the servants?"

"The bottle is there beside you, my dear. Would you be good enough to bring it to me?"

"Well, since you promise me that I shall be a poor woman

soon, perhaps the practice in serving a gentleman will be good training."

The Count de Corville managed a wan smile when his wife drifted into the pool of candlelight around his desk and leaned over him to fill his glass. "When you choose to be kind," he said, "you are the only pleasure that life has left me. Do you hate me so much?"

"Poor Henri," said the Countess, bending low to cradle her husband's round head against her perfumed bosom. "How could I hate such a sweet-tempered and generous man?"

He pulled his head away and looked up at her sharply. "It means only one thing when you tell me that I am generous," he snapped. "You want more money. I tell you, Juliette, you shall not have it. Don't you hear what I tell you? You are becoming more extravagant than ever. Have you been reduced to paying your lovers now? You are too young for that. I know any number of men who would be glad to pay you."

Ignoring his insults, the Countess kneeled beside her husband and stroked his jowls with long, pale fingers. "It's not for that sort of man, Henri. It's for something else. A secret. A surprise. Something that may change our fortune."

The Count gulped his brandy. "What is it, then? Some of your magic? No one would think to look at you that you are such a fool. What pleasure can there be for you in that except the pleasure of throwing away my fortune? You'd be better off with one of your young lieutenants. Magic, indeed! I agree that we need a miracle, but you will never get one from these charlatans you patronize. And you will never get money from me for any such nonsense."

"Never, Henri? I can make your life quite unpleasant, you know."

"My dear Juliette, I have learned to expect nothing less from you."

The Countess stood up and stepped away from him, then turned back to face him again. "You might as well give it to me, Henri. You're certain to, sooner or later, but this will not wait. And what you give now to please your wife will mean that much less that the Estates-General will be able to steal from you when they meet."

"Ah, that reminds me, Juliette. The night after next I will need you here to entertain some guests. You will be good enough to arrange your time accordingly. One evening away from wizards will do you good, especially since it will be spent with men who see which way the world is heading."

"Impossible," she said, barely suppressing a triumphant smile. "I have an engagement."

"You will break it. This will be the last meeting of our little group before the Estates-General convene, and I am depending on you to do with your charm what I cannot do with logic. There are several men to be persuaded."

"You should not depend on me for anything, Henri. And especially not for charm. I am a poor woman, and my tongue is sharp."

"You will be a poor woman, I promise you, if our cause fails. I am not asking favors for myself, but for France. Surely you understand what is at stake."

"I understand nothing except that I have a cruel husband who denies me innocent entertainment but still expects me to flatter his friends, as dull a crew as has ever been assembled under one roof."

"And I see what you have in mind, beloved. How much will it cost me for your services as a hostess?"

She ran her fingers over his head, pushing his powdered wig askew to reveal his naked scalp. "It will cost you a great deal," she said. "But no. It is impossible. I must be away that night."

"Must I beg for the privilege of being robbed?" roared the Count. "Do you honestly believe that your friends will refuse to wait for you when your gifts are all that stand between them and the gutter? Will you be here when I need you or will you not?"

"I am a dutiful wife," said the Countess.

"Then take the money and be damned," whispered her husband.

She hurried out of the room before he could retract his promise, the first flush of her success a trifle chilled by his final words. He had cursed her often enough before, to be sure, but the thought of damnation seemed suddenly more vivid when she recalled Rollin's garret and tried to imagine what she might meet there when the seven cards of Don Sebastian yielded their last secret.

3

Thirteen Mirrors

WAITING FOR the sound of midnight to drift from a distant clock tower, Raoul Rollin spread the seven cards again across the scarred surface of the table in the center of his attic room. Everything was ready for his experiment; now there was nothing left for him to do but wait for the hour or his client, whichever one of them came first. He had spent too long agitating himself about the tardiness of the Countess de Corville, but finally philosophy had come to his aid. There was really no cause for concern. He had her money, delivered the day before by a surly redheaded wench; he had his materials; he had his instructions. And he had the cards. The Countess could come or not as she pleased. Rollin was ready.

Yet something she had asked lingered uncomfortably in his mind. It was only the foolish whim of a woman untutored in the secrets of the occult, of course; Rollin knew what the cards were for, and she did not. Yet still her question remained: What fortune did the cards foretell? It was absurd, but in the last minutes before midnight Rollin suddenly decided to treat the ancient bits of pasteboard as if they were no more than the vulgar tools of a gypsy fortuneteller. It was a trifle odd, come to think of it, that he had ended up with precisely seven, the number used in the most common form of divination. And it was strange, too, as the Countess had observed, that none of the cards could be considered favorable. It hardly mattered what order he arranged them in; the prediction they made was unsettling at best. If Rollin had been willing to consider them seriously as a key to the future of his experiment, he would have been more uneasy than he was.

The Five of Cups was on the face of things the least threatening of the lot, but it was the one that worried him most. It promised nothing more intimidating than disappointment through self-indulgence, but that could be interpreted all too simply as an indication that all of Rollin's efforts were doomed to end in failure. He would almost have preferred to find his future in the Ten of Wands, which spoke of tyranny and oppression, or in the Ten of Swords, which signified loss or ruin. The Knight of Swords was better; it signified a clever man, and Rollin was willing to see himself in the vigorous armed figure of Don Sebastian's drawing; but the card also meant conflict, and even war.

The trumps were not much better. The Devil was a card depicting the bondage of fate, a man and woman chained at the feet of a leering demon. The Tower, with its falling figures and its flames, prefigured a violent upheaval. On the whole, Rollin was fondest of Death. He knew that it signified a change rather than an ending, and after all, it was the card that had taught him most. The blood-red sky around the skeleton had been entirely scraped away to reveal line after line of minuscule writing, and here Rollin had found the formula left three centuries ago by the hand of Don Sebastian de Villanueva. If there was not as much information as Rollin could have hoped for, he believed that there would be enough.

Rollin's old cat crawled up one of his legs, uninhibited in the use of its claws, and settled briefly in its master's lap. He stroked its sparse fur absently as the cat raised its head to peer intently over the edge of the table. Then it jumped lightly up to land upon the cards and pace among them on its padded feet. Its eyes caught the light of the candle for an instant and turned to glowing balls of phosphorescence.

"Careful, cat," said Rollin. "Those cards are worth more than you are." He picked the animal up by the back of the neck and dropped it to the floor, then brushed its gray hairs from his black suit. "And stay away from that bowl! There's nothing there for you. Haven't I fed you tonight? Even though I've been fasting to purify myself?" Rollin grabbed the cat, a bit more roughly this time, and tossed it across the room, away from the silver bowl in the center of the circle he had painted on the floor.

"Might as well get things in place while I'm up," said Rollin, speaking half to the cat and half to himself. "It can't be long now." He began laboriously to pull the sagging table across the room toward the window. "Got to make room. Make room for Don Sebastian. The Countess should be here to meet him. Not enough of a receiving line, really, just me and a cat. I wonder where she is. And I wonder if she could have been right about the cards?"

Gasping for breath, Rollin shuffled over to a chest in a corner where the ceiling was so low it almost touched the floor. "Woman's intuition," he said. "Of course it's only chance that I found those cards instead of others, but then it's only chance that picks the cards a fortuneteller deals. But whose fortune would it be? Hers? Or mine? Or Don Sebastian's?"

He pulled a filthy sack out of the chest. "Dirt," he said. "Bag of dirt all the way from Spain. Hope it's real. Paid plenty for it. Paid more for those damned mirrors. And what does he want them for? If he's a vampire, he won't be able to see himself anyway. And if he isn't, he won't come back at all. No, he'll come back; he said he would. It's in the cards, eh, cat?"

With the sack slung over his slumped shoulder and his spectacles slipping down his nose, Rollin rummaged in the chest with his free hand and pulled out a bundle of candles tied together with twine. These he carried across the creaking floorboards until he reached the painted circle. He put the candles down, dropped the sack, and returned to the chest. He drew forth a small earthenware flask and cradled it in both his trembling hands. "He'll like this, won't he, cat? Of course he will. This cost the most of all. Could have got it myself, I suppose, but Rollin's never been much when it comes to murder. Still, it's fresh. It was still warm when I paid for it. I'm sure he'll like it, especially after three hundred years! I'd pour it now, but you'd drink it, wouldn't you, my furry gray friend? Besides, I'm supposed to pour it last. Mustn't get excited at the last moment. What can be keeping the Countess? Stupid woman! No doubt she's dancing at a ball. Forgotten all about Rollin and Don Sebastian. Well, she's done her part. She's paid for this, and that's enough. All those aristocrats are good for, if it comes to that."

Rollin cut the twine that bound the candles together and put one of them down at each point of the star inscribed within the circle. He took the colorless wax stump from the table and let it drip on the floor at one point of the pentacle, then pressed the end of one of the new candles into the molten pool so that it would stand erect. Repeating the process, he shuffled on his hands and knees around the circle until five black candles were in place. He reached out for the bag of Spanish soil, and left a thin trail of it behind him as he crawled again around the circle. The gray cat followed him curiously.

"Don't mess up that line. It's not just ordinary dirt. There's still a lot left in the sack, but this should be enough. He may want the rest of it later, for his bed. How would you like to sleep in dirt, eh? Well, I suppose you already do. Both of us do. Look at us. A fine pair, aren't we? Let's look at ourselves in some mirrors. I wish you could help me move them. Heavy. It cost a fortune just to have them carried up four flights of stairs."

By now Rollin was so intent upon his work that he did not rise, but simply shuffled sideways across the dusty floor until he reached his doorway. Leaning against the wall was a stack of rectangular mirrors, each one taller than a man. Below them were an unruly pile of crude wooden braces, each of them as wide as one of the mirrors. Rollin encircled the braces with his arms and pushed them toward the pentacle. There he separated them and dragged them into place until they were evenly spaced around the painted circle.

"This will be the hardest part," he said as he rose creakingly to his feet, supporting himself against the wall. "I need an apprentice. Well, perhaps after this I'll be able to afford one. Someone to move the mirrors. They're too heavy for an old man."

Bending low in anticipation of his effort, he shuffled

toward his collection of looking glasses and pulled the first of them away from the rest. Keeping its base braced against the floor, he began to drag it across the uneven floorboards. He was looking into his own eyes, but his reflection was so close that he could hardly focus on it. He yanked the oversized mirror over an unruly knothole, and then gave vent to several colorful curses.

"Almost dropped it. Mustn't do that, must we? No spares, are there? I cut myself, though. Both hands. Well, it's all to the good. Can't have too much blood, can we? Even though I'm not an unbaptized babe, at least it's blood. And it hurts, too. Would have bought mirrors in frames, but then there would have been nothing left to buy food for the cat, and that would never do."

Rollin walked the looking glass across the room, his palms streaming red against its glittering surface, and hauled it up until it was securely fitted in its wooden brace. All the while his old gray cat slipped back and forth between his feet, always on the verge of tripping him, but always a bit too graceful to actually do it.

"We must be more careful. Still twelve more to go. I need something to protect my hands." Wiping his blood on his vest, Rollin stumbled wheezing toward the corner where his ragged coat was hanging. He wrapped his hands in the greasy black cloth and went back for another mirror. One by one he dragged them toward their appointed places until the painted circle on the floor had been completely surrounded by a curved wall of thirteen mirrors.

"It must be almost time," said Rollin, and as if in answer he heard the chimes ringing out from the clock that was almost too far away to hear. He counted every clear, faint tone.

"Twelve," he said. "And we're ready. To hell with the Countess. We're ready for you, Don Sebastian de Villanueva. Come wizard, come vampire, come giver of gifts. One question, though. Where is Rollin supposed to stand?"

The closed circle of gleaming glass shut him out completely, but Rollin had more work to do. He yanked one of the mirrors away until he had made a doorway for himself into the shining circle. "Not done yet," he said, "and it's midnight already. Must light the candles."

He snatched the guttering stump from the table, stepped into the universe of reflections he had created, and there lit each of the five black candles that stood at the points of the star within the circle.

"One more thing," muttered Rollin. "The blood." He stumbled out of the circle and returned again with the flask he had left on the table. He uncorked it and poured the thick red liquid into the silver bowl at the center of the pentacle. "Hurry, hurry, hurry."

He looked at the circle and he looked at the window. "Not enough," he gasped. "This won't bring him. Just a lot of props. I should have known. Better say something. Say it now. But what? No instructions in the cards. The cards! Maybe he wants them. Now. It's time."

Rollin snatched up the seven cards and stepped again into the circle of mirrors. The old cat ran erratically across the pentagram, butting its head into images of itself. "Get out, you," said Rollin. "Better get out myself, I suppose. Should I be inside or outside? Better leave room for him. But first the cards."

Rollin paced around the circle, and set one of the pasteboard scraps aflame in each of the five candle flames. The Devil, the Tower, the Five of Cups, the Ten of Wands, and the Ten of Swords, each caught fire and dropped back into ashes; but Rollin retained the Knight of Swords, the clever man, and also the card called Death.

"Enough," he said. He stepped out of the circle and pushed the thirteenth mirror back into place. "There's nothing more for me to do."

And yet, on an impulse, he blew out the candle stump on the table, so that the only light he saw came from the five flames reflected by the gleaming circle that he dared not enter.

"What else can I do?" shouted Rollin to the ceiling. "Should I pray to him?"

On the verge of panic, he paced in a circle around the wall of mirrors, half afraid of what might come, but more afraid that nothing would. The light from the five candles, multiplied by mirrors, crossed his face in narrow beams as he passed each gap between the thirteen sheets of glass. The effect was disorienting, and Rollin began to feel dizzy. He staggered to a chair and sat gasping while he stared at his handiwork.

Nothing happened. Rollin waited alone in the dark and gazed intently at the weird edifice of flame and glass he had constructed, but as the minutes passed his shoulders slumped. As a last resort he tried reciting the Lord's Prayer backward, a trick he had learned as a young man, but even that had no visible effect. He grew dejected, then bitterly disappointed, and finally bored. He was exhausted, and his tired eyes were filled with unshed tears, but at the same time a fury of frustration and disappointment was rising within him. He could hardly sit in his chair all night and wait for visitors who never came, whether they were countesses or corpses.

His knees cracked as he stood up and walked across the room to peer through an opening between two of the tall mirrors. The only change he could detect in his magic circle was in the five black candles, which had burned down leaving spidery pools of dark wax on the floor. Pushing his inquisitive cat away with a slippered foot, Rollin made an opening for himself and slipped into the circle. He stood dejectedly beside the silver bowl, mocked by an infinite number of Raoul Rollins who posed around him in the thirteen mirrors.

"He should have come," muttered Rollin. "He should have appeared right here." He stamped his foot ineffectually and made a theatrical gesture which was instantly repeated in the reflections all around him. "Don Sebastian," whispered Rollin dramatically, throwing his hands into a menacing pose and watching the countless images take up the gesture. "The vampire!" He snarled once or twice, but the mirrors did not echo that. The last two cards, still clutched in his hand, inhibited his performance. He dropped them contemptuously into the silver bowl of blood and continued to prance around the circle, baring his yellow teeth and rushing toward the surfaces of gleaming glass. Hysterical, halfway between laughter and tears, Rollin played the monster he had failed to summon.

He stopped quite suddenly when he saw a face in the mirrors that was not his own.

The face was pale and misty, hardly visible at all. Rollin

rubbed his streaming eyes and looked again. This time he saw a long white hand hovering above his head, its groping fingers heavy with golden rings.

Somewhere in the room the cat screamed, and Rollin whirled at the noise. Now there were two hands, or two hundred, or two thousand, each reaching out to touch his face. He spun in a circle while the candles flared. He was instantly terrified by the thought that they might go out, but not much better pleased when each tiny flame shot up into a long needle of light that touched the ceiling. Reflected all around him, the uncanny beams of radiance were like the luminous bars of some celestial prison. And through them stretched the hideous white hands.

Rollin screamed once and dropped to his knees. A multitude of Rollins dropped around him, and a sea of dead white faces smiled. He heard the sound of splintering in time to hide his head under his arms, and felt rather than saw the force that broke all thirteen mirrors in an instant and sent the jagged fragments pouring down on him like hail.

In a shower of shattering glass, Don Sebastian was reborn into the world.

It was some time before Rollin dared to move. He lay huddled in the center of the circle, and not even the pain of his wounds could make him rise. Countless cuts from the broken glass marked his head, hands, neck, back, and legs; he could feel blood streaming all over his body. And he heard someone walking in the room.

When Rollin finally raised his head he was half blinded by the blood that dripped into his eyes. One of the black candles was still lit, and now its flame was no longer than it should have been. Its dim illumination left most of the attic room in darkness, but still Rollin was able to see the thing that frightened and yet fascinated him so much that he crawled toward it. A shadowy figure was seated in his chair; it wore his ragged and rusty black coat with the bloodstained sleeves.

"You did come," said Rollin. "I did it. But what kept you?"

The creature in his coat answered Rollin with a moan, so deep and dark and full of misery that Rollin was ready to reproach himself. At what price had he summoned the spirit of Don Sebastian de Villanueva?

"I called you back," Rollin said. "The cards showed me how. The cards you made three hundred years ago."

The thing in the chair sat huddled, its long black hair streaming down into its face, but at the sound of a human voice it raised its head, and then Rollin began to wish that it had not. The skin was the color of old ivory; the long black mustache drooped over teeth that were thin and sharp. The sunken eyes, which Rollin expected to glow like fire, were dull, and dark, and dead. The face of Don Sebastian looked like a skull covered in parchment, draped with black funeral crepe.

"You were not wise to summon me," said Don Sebastian. His voice was low and dismal, so piercingly melancholy that it was a moment before Rollin realized that the thing in his garret was speaking to him in perfect French. There was an accent, to be sure, but the words were preternaturally clear.

"But you left instructions. They were in the cards." By now Rollin was ready to get up off the floor, but still his knees were not. He tried twice to stand, and then sank down again.

"Is this France?" asked Don Sebastian. "I fought here once." He turned his narrow head to gaze at Rollin's attic, then lifted his pale hands and held them up before his face. "I am earthbound again," he said. "I, who might have spent eternity among the stars."

"Where have you been?" asked Rollin breathlessly.

"Where am I now? What year is this?"

"This is Paris. The year is 1789."

"So. And who are you, this creature that squirms across the floor?"

Rollin had managed to reach the table, and dragged himself up to lean against it. "I am Raoul Rollin," he said. "A wizard. I found your cards, or some of them at least, and I followed your instructions."

"My instructions." Sebastian looked at him intently. "I suppose they were my instructions, but I should never have left them. Much can be learned in three hundred years. I wish that you and those accursed cards were burning in hell, Raoul Rollin."

"But you must have wanted to come back. I did it for you, and for my patron, of course."

"Your patron?"

"The Countess de Corville. She should be here to greet you, but she seems to have been detained. And so were you. Why did you not come when you were called?"

"I tried to resist. And it would have been better for you if I had succeeded. I am not happy to be trapped in flesh again. Dead flesh. Yet you used my own formula, and that I could not resist. Nothing we do goes unpunished, Raoul Rollin. Remember that, and forgive me for what follows."

"What follows?" echoed Rollin, suddenly discovering that he could hardly stand, even if he kept his old hands on the table.

"Tell me," Sebastian said. "What have you in that silver bowl?"

"Why," said Rollin, gesturing feebly, "it is the blood of an unbaptized child."

"And so it should have been. But it is not. Where did you get it?"

Rollin looked at the dead face and felt his stomach shrink. He also felt his blood dribbling from the countless cuts he had received when the mirrors broke. The half of him that faced Don Sebastian was whole, but his back was a maze of trickling gore. "That bowl is full of good blood, I promise you. I bought it from a colleague, just tonight. It's fresh. I would have taken it myself, but I've never cut the throat of a baby."

"You might have been wiser if you had, Raoul Rollin. Bring me the bowl."

Rollin did as he was told, though he had hardly the strength to move. He stumbled toward the silver bowl, and was on his knees when he brought it back. For some reason he found that he was searching for his cat, but the animal was nowhere to be found.

Sebastian took the silver bowl into his long pale fingers, and he dipped his head toward it.

"You have been cheated," he said. "This is the blood of a pig."

"No," said Rollin. "Damn him. I'll deal with that fellow tomorrow."

"You shall not," said Don Sebastian. "You shall not see tomorrow. You have brought me back to a future I never wished to see, and you have not even seen fit to feed me properly. But you know what I am, Raoul Rollin, and so you know what I must do. Take back your bowl."

Don Sebastian stood, and it seemed as if his head would scrape the ceiling of the tiny garret that had welcomed him. He was a giant, and he had a giant's thirst.

"But I brought you here," whimpered Rollin.

"For that alone you should be punished," Don Sebastian replied. He threw the silver bowl of blood into his host's face.

The heavy metal shattered Rollin's spectacles and sent splinters of glass flying into his eyes. The old magician howled and fell back upon the floor. He twitched and writhed so violently that Don Sebastian found it difficult to get a grip on the old man's throat.

"My mistake," the vampire said. "And yours. We both shall pay. But you should have left those cards alone."

4

A Patron of the Arts

THE COUNTESS de Corville stood in the midst of a glittering company and tried not to scream. Midnight had come and gone, but she was still in her husband's house, miles away from Raoul Rollin and whatever he might be conjuring. She had earned the money for Rollin's magic by agreeing to play hostess to this gathering, but now it appeared that she would be denied the fruits of her labor.

She maneuvered through the crowd with smiles and curtsies until she reached her husband's side. "Henri," she said, "let me take you away from this gentleman for a moment."

"Later," snapped the Count. "Later," he repeated more politely. "This is most important, my dear. See what you can do to entertain that group in the corner over there."

"But it is the entertainment of your guests that concerns me, Henri. You must spare me a moment, or I am afraid that our hospitality will be called to account. Excuse us, sir." She flashed her dazzling white teeth at the plump young man who had been talking with the Count, and at the same time she dug her long fingernails into the back of her husband's hand. He winced politely and drifted away with her, accompanied by profuse apologies.

She pulled him away to an isolated spot near the entrance

to the brilliantly lighted room; there was no one near them except a frozen-faced lackey dressed in green livery.

"Surely this is enough," hissed the Countess. "The hour is late, and I have served you well. Now I insist that you allow me to leave."

"Impossible," replied the Count.

"It is impossible for me to stay," the Countess said. "I have a fortune at stake, and I must see what I have paid for. Rollin is an enthusiast, and he will not wait for me now that he has the money."

"Rollin, is it? So that's his name. I shall have him arrested in the morning."

"In a moment, Henri, I shall begin to raise my voice. And it will grow louder and louder. I can promise you quite a pretty scene."

Already he could see her face flushing beneath its white powder, and the cords tightening in her slender throat. He turned toward the servant who was staring complacently across the room. "Get out of here, you," snarled the Count de Corville. "Go do something." The man moved off like a clockwork toy.

"The servants will be the least of your worries in a few more seconds, Henri."

The Count pulled a lace handkerchief from his sleeve and patted his wrinkled forehead. "But you can't go, my dear." His tone was almost apologetic. "I knew you would try to leave before your time, so I sent the coachman away and told him not to return until just before midnight. Now there's nothing to be done, so try to be patient."

"You miserable old fool, it was midnight half an hour ago. I told you it was late, and I told you I was leaving."

"All right," he said resignedly. "Ruin me, if you will. I can hardly expect anything else of you. But you could have spared me this one night."

"And you could have told me your plans. No doubt you had this evening arranged weeks ago, but you never bothered to tell me. You will not let me be a wife to you, Henri, so why should I try?"

"At least make some plausible excuse, Juliette."

"What would you have me do? Faint?"

"No, I suppose not. No one would believe it of you."

"They will never even notice I am gone, believe me. They are all politicians. Horrible men. Not a gallant in the lot. Good night, Henri."

The Count shrugged and assumed a woebegone expression. Impulsively she bent down and kissed his fat, sad face. For an instant he felt her tongue flicker in his mouth, and while he was still trying to recover from the shock she disappeared. The Count waddled back toward his guests in a daze, the future of the kingdom forgotten, and tried to concoct an excuse about some household crisis that had called his wife away.

The Countess raced down the long hallway through air that was cool and fresh after the stuffy, crowded, perfumed atmosphere of the room behind her. She raised the hem of her yellow satin gown in both hands as she ran, trying not to stumble in her impossibly delicate high-heeled slippers of jeweled brocade. She was furious and frantic, far too concerned about keeping her appointment with Rollin to consider what she might find when she arrived. Her head felt intolerably heavy, weighted down by an extravagant powdered wig festooned with feathers, pearls, and flowers. A shadowy figure dressed in green stood at the end of the corridor and opened the door for her mechanically as she neared him. She passed by without a word and rushed out into the night.

More servants stood on wide marble steps patterned with light from the small panes of many windows, but not the servant she hoped to find. She hurried down the stairs, the cool breeze of a late spring evening like a slap on her flushed face. A footman followed her at a discreet distance as she made her way along the gravel path skirting the border of the maze of greenery that was her private pleasure garden. When she reached the gate the man behind her dropped away; there were others here to attend to her. The gate was open, and her gilded coach stood before it. The coachman was ready, and so were her white stallions.

And there, in the shelter of a sculptured tree, was her maidservant, Madeleine. There was someone with her, a tall man in a slouch hat. Both of them looked up as the Countess approached; they conferred for an instant, and then the man slipped through the gate into the street.

The Countess slowed to a walk as she approached Madeleine. "Is that your lawyer?" she asked. "The fellow skulks about like an assassin. And he may end like one if he is not careful. Let us see less of him."

"Yes, Madame Countess." Madeleine's blue eyes were like slate in the moonlight. "I will certainly see less of him in the days to come. He is to be a deputy representing his district in the Estates-General."

"What? Serving in the same body with my husband? Incredible. You are lying, of course. Such a thing could never be allowed. What was his name again?"

"Andre Latour, Madame."

"Evidently the fellow is deluded, if he told you a story like that. I advise you to have nothing to do with him. Get into the coach. We have wasted enough time already."

Madeleine obeyed, taking care to let the Countess precede her. The wooden wheels spun as the coachman's whip snapped, sending gravel spattering against the high wall, and the coach careened into the empty street while the Countess de Corville shouted for speed.

Madeleine watched her mistress sit stiffly in the corner of the coach, her bare shoulders shivering. "The night is chilly," she said, "and Madame is not properly dressed. May I offer her my cloak?"

"Don't be ridiculous. And do be silent." In truth, the Countess wished to be warmer than she was, but she could hardly borrow clothing from a servant, and she knew that Madeleine was well aware of it. In any case, the Countess suspected that the cold she felt had nothing to do with the weather. Until this moment, she had hardly had a chance to consider her destination, so intent had she been on simply achieving it. But now that she had a chance to reflect she realized, perhaps for the first time, that she was on her way to meet a living corpse. She had a rendezvous with Don Sebastian de Villanueva, a man who had died three hundred years ago. She almost hoped that Rollin would fail her; yet surely anything was better than another disappointment. Whatever this monster might be, he would be exciting, she thought, exciting and alive. More alive than any man I know, she said to herself, and laughed aloud at the idea while Madeleine stared at her and the coach rattled through streets that grew darker and dirtier.

It dragged to a halt before a tall, dilapidated building, so old and crooked that it leaned forward as if it might drop at any moment into the narrow, muddy thoroughfare below. When the Countess stepped out of the coach, her foot sank into filth up to the ankle, but with her next step she reached broken wooden stairs. Rollin had left the door open for her, as he always did. "Wait," she whispered, to Madeleine, and she slipped into the house.

She paused in the passageway until her eyes grew accustomed to the dark, moving only when she could discern the cracks in the gray plaster that clung in scraps to the damp wooden walls. The low-ceilinged hall was heavy with the smell of the evening's cooking and less pleasant odors. The Countess de Corville, fresh from the society of some of the noblest families in France, stared up into the blackness beyond the foot of the staircase that stretched toward the attic apartment of Raoul Rollin, and steeled herself to begin the ascent. Something would be waiting for her at the top of the stairs. Perhaps it would be only Rollin, who might have postponed the experiment until she could arrive; or perhaps he would be alone amidst the shambles of a failure. Yet there might be someone with him, someone called back from a world she could scarcely imagine, and it was this thought that slowed her progress up the four flights to the garret. Each board on which she placed a foot creaked with its own individual note, creating a mournful melody that added to her trepidation. Fearing that she might lose her balance in the darkness, she stretched out both hands to brace herself against the crumbling walls.

After what seemed an hour of climbing the steep stairs she reached the door she wanted. There could be no mistaking it; the steps ended, and there was nowhere else to turn. She knocked, then waited for a moment, listening to the silence. She knocked again and then called out, shocked by the feeble croaking that issued from her dry throat; but still there was no reply. Could it be that Rollin was not at home? It would be intolerable if her husband was right about Rollin, if the old man had taken her money and run away with it. Suddenly infuriated by the thought that her pet magician had played such a trick on her, she groped for the handle and pushed her way into the room.

The light inside was hardly brighter than it had been in the hall. A black candle flickered on the floor, surrounded by the debris of what looked to her like broken glass, but it illuminated only one small corner of the garret. No one came forward to greet her. "Rollin?" she whispered, her anger giving way to uneasiness. Something stirred in the shadows. "Rollin?"

A figure was dimly discernible at the far end of the room, sitting stiffly in one of the chairs. It began to rise, and as it did Rollin's cat jumped lightly from its lap.

"Ah, there you are," said the Countess with a sigh of relief. "What have you been doing? Have you been asleep, you fool?"

"I have not been asleep," answered a hollow voice, "but I have been dreaming. And I am not the man you seek."

The Countess felt her skin grow cold and tight. She wanted to turn and run, but something held her.

"Do not try to leave," said the voice, "or I shall be obliged to kill you at once." The figure was standing now, and even in silhouette it was unnaturally tall and thin.

The Countess leaned back against the door to keep herself erect. "I believe you are the man I seek," she said weakly, "if not the one I expected to find. Are you Don Sebastian?"

"I am," he said, starting to move forward. "And you are the Countess de Corville?"

"Please do me the kindness to stay where you are," she said, stretching out a trembling hand as if to hold him back. "I am not ready to see you yet. And how did you know my name?"

"Your friend Rollin told me," said Don Sebastian, stopping where the darkness still hid his face.

"Rollin," she said. "Then is he here?"

"He is. Do you wish to see him?" He made a gesture toward the floor behind him, and the light touched his long pale fingers, gleaming on his golden rings.

The Countess pressed back against the wall as if she hoped to force her way through it. Both hands were pressed to her bosom to stop the hammering of her heart. It was a moment before she could speak again.

"Then you are not thirsty?" she asked as lightly as she could.

"Not any longer."

"I was lucky to be delayed, I think."

"Indeed," said Don Sebastian. "I could hardly have resisted such a beautiful creature if you had been here when Rollin summoned me. Even now you tempt me. There was not much blood in the old man."

"Enough, I hope," the Countess said, trying to appear calm despite her terror. "I did not pay a fortune to summon you so that you could feed on me. And I shall be more useful to you with my blood where it belongs."

"We made no bargain," replied Don Sebastian sternly. "And why did you pay to bring me here?"

"I seek knowledge, and the power it brings."

"Knowledge is just as likely to bring misery. Do you think you have the courage to learn what I can teach you, when you are not even brave enough to look upon my face?"

"Step forward then," she snapped impulsively, regretting her words almost at once. "But not too close."

"You are accustomed to command," he said, "but I am not accustomed to obeying. Still, I shall do as you wish, at least in this one matter. May you have as much pleasure in the sight of me as you have brought to my eyes."

There was blood on his lips, and on his chin, and clots of it in his long black mustache. His eyes were dark hollows where no light shone, and down the left side of his face ran the ragged seam of an ancient scar. Shining black hair hung down to the shoulders of the ill-fitting coat that the Countess dimly recognized as Rollin's. He was too big for it; pale arms and legs stretched out from the dark garment, which seemed to be the only thing he wore. He should have been hideous, and in fact he was, but something in his appearance pleased her. He could never have been handsome, even when he was alive, but his face was intelligent and strong. She had not dared to turn away from him, and had almost decided that she could look at him without flinching when he stepped back into the shadows.

"Are you pleased with your purchase, Countess? I am not pretty, as you see."

"Then I shall be the pretty one," she said, almost laughing. "There is not much merit in that, although there is more effort than you might imagine. I shall be satisfied if you are wise. And you are not as ugly as I feared. I imagine I shall grow accustomed to the sight of you."

"Do not imagine too much. And do not play the coquette with me. What makes you believe that you will see me again, or even that you will survive this first meeting?"

With tremendous effort she forced herself to take one small step toward him. "I put my faith in the legend that you are a man of unusual intelligence. It would do you little good to kill me, Don Sebastian. I am here to serve you, and you will need my help. What do you know of the world around you now? Do you know where you are, or even what year this is?"

"Your friend Rollin had time to tell me that much."

"I was not his friend. I was his patron."

"And now you expect to be mine?"

"In part, perhaps. I also expect to be your pupil. Perhaps we shall become friends, if such a thing is possible. You are a man of noble birth, not a common creature like Rollin."

"You will find me a most uncommon creature," Sebastian said. "I am not like the men you know, and you will not find it easy to use me." With startling swiftness he strode across the room to take her throat in his cold hands.

She stiffened at his touch, half prepared to die, but although he held her tightly, he did no more. She stared wildly into his dark, dead eyes, searching them for some clue to his intentions, but she saw only emptiness.

"I am a monster," he shouted into her face, "not one of your playthings." He ran his icy fingers over her face, and caressed her naked shoulders menacingly, yet she sensed something in his touch that was less a threat than a promise. She put her hands over his and held them to her.

"Monsters can be tamed," she whispered, "or so the stories say. Sometimes they are even transformed into wonderful lovers. A man should be part monster, or he is hardly worth having. Stay with me, Sebastian." Her pulse was racing, and she felt her flesh grow hot under his hands. "You are what I wanted, and you need me to survive."

"I survived in Spain under the Inquisition, and I survived in Mexico where the Aztec priests ate human hearts and the steel of the conquistadors toppled an empire. And for centuries, as mortals reckon time, I have dwelled among the stars, transformed into pure spirit by the grace of an Aztec priestess and her god. What can there be in France to threaten me?"

"Perhaps you do not need me after all," she said, "but surely you can take what I offer you. I can make you comfortable and keep you safe. I can show you this world you have never seen, and make a place for you in it."

"I have seen enough of this world, and there is no place for me here. I should slaughter you for bringing me back to suffer here again."

"It need not be all suffering," she said, drawing his hands down so that they rested between her breasts, "but if you choose to kill me now I cannot escape." The expression on her face seemed to suggest that she would find either alternative equally gratifying.

"Your husband must be a sorry fellow," said Sebastian as he stepped away.

"What? How did you know I was married?"

"I know many things. But surely this is obvious enough. Both your station and your behavior betray you, Madame Countess. It was hardly necessary to see your ring."

"You may call me Juliette," she said. "We must hurry. There are not many hours till dawn, and we have a journey to make. My coach is waiting in the street below."

"And who is with it?"

"Only the coachman and my maid Madeleine."

"Two more than I wish to meet. Do you trust them?"

"Madeleine knows everything I do. I don't like her, but she has never betrayed me, and she has had many chances. She will be certain to learn about you sooner or later."

"Only if I agree to follow you."

"You will not be fool enough to refuse me. You have

nothing to fear from me, and you have nowhere else to go."

"Perhaps you are right, but I will not trust my life to your maidservant. Dismiss the coachman."

"In the street? In the dead of night?"

"There must be an inn nearby. Send him there and bring me his coat. For tonight at least, I shall be your coachman. Tomorrow I shall decide if I will become your guest."

The Countess moved toward the door.

"Wait," Sebastian said. "First there is something I must show you. I am still not convinced that you realize what you are bargaining for. Before you decide to harbor me, come and look at Rollin."

She bit her lip as Sebastian picked up the last black candle and drew her across the room toward what lay crumpled under the table. Sebastian turned over the old magician's body with his foot. Rollin's dead white face was drained of blood and devoid of all expression, but there were holes in his throat and shards of glass in his staring eyes.

"It is worse to be a vampire than a murderer," Sebastian said, "for my victims rise up again to haunt me. This one will be walking again tomorrow when the sun sets, and I want nothing to betray my presence in Paris. I shall have to dispose of him. I dare not leave any trace behind. It is bad enough that I must trust you, but I shall not trust another vampire. Go now, Juliette, and do as I instructed you."

She hurried blindly down the dark stairs and out into the street, where she found Madeleine asleep in the coach. The drowsy coachman grumbled at her orders, but a few francs settled him, and the Countess was ready when the gaunt figure of Sebastian appeared in the doorway.

"Get in," Sebastian whispered as he slipped into the livery of the Count de Corville. She looked up as she stepped toward the coach, and saw flames in the window of the topmost floor of Rollin's house.

"Sebastian!" she gasped. "There are families inside! You will burn down the entire building."

"I hope so," he answered. "It will be for the best. Most of them will probably escape, but at least there will be no evidence of what happened in the attic."

The Countess de Corville felt a thrill that was only partly

horror. "Don't you care whom you kill?"

"Not if it means protecting myself. In any case, the sound of the horses will probably awaken them. Most animals don't like me, though Rollin's cat was an exception. A familiar, I suppose."

As if in acknowledgment, a fearful feline wail streamed from the fiery window above their heads. Already the streets were faintly tinged with orange light from the flames.

Sebastian pushed the Countess unceremoniously into the coach and crawled up into his seat. The white stallions began to buck and scream even before he cracked the whip, and muffled shouts came from the house. Madeleine's cold eyes opened sleepily as the coach leaped forward, and she looked with curiosity at the ecstatic expression on the face of her mistress. The coach raced through the streets, moving faster than it ever had before.

5

A Patriot

ON A MORNING late in June a young man with rising prospects sat waiting to keep a rendezvous in the Café Mécanique. It was not the most fashionable gathering place for members of his set, but he was there to meet a woman, not to plot political strategy. And something in the equipment of the café impressed Andre Latour as eminently suitable to a man in his position, even symbolic of the new order which he represented. The design of the place was so modern and so clever, thought Andre, that it was almost revolutionary. Machinery, not men, brought coffee to the customers.

There were still waiters, of course, but they delivered only cups. The tables themselves poured the coffee. Andre caught the attention of a sleepy-eyed waiter whose apron was still clean, held up a coin, and put it down ostentatiously beside his empty cup. The waiter merely nodded and remained lounging in his corner. He knew his customer, and that he enjoyed serving himself. Andre put his hand on the spigot that rose from the center of the table, pulled on a handle, and watched the thin stream of dark, steaming liquid pouring into his cup.

He hardly understood how the trick was accomplished, though he supposed it was a matter of steam and hydraulics, but Andre was satisfied to realize that it worked. He thought that the machinery of the Café Mécanique was much like the machinery at work beneath the surface of the Estates-General. He comprehended neither, but he was delighted with the results of both.

It had been easy enough for him to be elected as a representative of the people, but considerably more difficult for him to represent them. He knew that he was tall and handsome, with a booming voice, a gift for gestures, and sufficient wit to concoct phrases that shone with sincerity and rang with glory. Yet once in office he was lost. His ambition was to change the world, and to make himself a place in it, but he had no idea how these things might be accomplished. Instead he was obliged to watch the work of men who were older and wiser, who lacked his impressive appearance but had mastered the occult art of making things happen. They had less respect for Andre Latour than his constituents did, but they tolerated him because he had sense enough to cast his vote in accord with their policies. And Andre, despite a certain irritating intimation of helplessness, was content, at least for the moment. No doubt a crisis lay ahead, but thus far the common people of France, through their representatives of the Third Estate, had succeeded time and again in forcing their will on the nobles, and the clergy, and even the King. Yet it had only been a battle of gestures and declarations, and Andre wondered how long it would be before words were not enough.

He looked up from his cooling coffee and saw Madeleine Benet slip into the room. He signaled to the waiter for another cup and rose to greet her. Except for the two of them the café was almost empty at this time of day, and Madeleine made no effort to lower her voice as she sat across from Andre.

"I thought I'd never get away from the witch," she said. "I've hardly been asleep all night, and it's been like this for weeks. Ever since she took that new lover of hers she's been more impossible than ever. Any other lady would have the decency to dismiss the servants, but she's afraid she might need something, so she keeps me on call until dawn. You'd think she'd at least be able to put herself to bed in the morning without any help from me. But no. And she talks nothing but nonsense. Sometimes I think she's going mad, and of course the Count is not much better. You and your friends have him almost hysterical, Andre." She smiled and stifled a yawn as the waiter filled her cup.

"You should see him sweat," Andre replied, "at least when he and his fellow aristocrats have the courage to put in an appearance at all. Once he tried to make a speech, but he could only sputter. One of the greatest pleasures of being a deputy is watching the face of the Count de Corville. I wish you could see him, Madeleine."

"I see him too often as it is, but he is not suffering enough to suit me. And I won't be satisfied until the Countess wakes up and realizes what the future has in store for her. She is so besotted with her own intrigues that she hardly realizes that the world is collapsing around her. Even I hardly understand what has been going on, and my man is one of the leaders of the new age."

Andre bowed as well as he could while seated at the table. "Don't you read the papers?" he asked. "It's been a long time since you've seen me, but surely every citizen should be informed."

"The papers!" snorted Madeleine. "What good are they? Each one tells a different story. On the same day one will report a brilliant victory for the Third Estate, while another reports a dismal failure, and a third praises the virtues of a compromise proposed by the King's new ministers. What is happening, Andre?"

"Much," he said, adopting the air of an orator, "but not enough. I think we were already winning, although not many realized it, when King Louis granted our demand that the Third Estate should have as many representatives as the nobles and the clergy combined. Of course he only did it so that we could levy taxes against those damned aristocrats; he doesn't care where his money comes from, as long as it doesn't stop. But that gave us the leverage we needed. A few progressive priests and aristocrats gave us the majority, and when the rest tried to boycott our assembly they only made fools of themselves. We declared ourselves the National Assembly, and there was no one to gainsay us. Since then, they have been creeping back, a handful at a time, still dreaming that they can have a voice in our deliberations. Even the King was afraid of us, and tried to lock us out of the Hôtel des Menus-Plaisirs, but we met in the tennis court instead, and swore to stand firm. What does it matter where we meet? We are the people!"

"Then the aristocrats are finished?" asked Madeleine with an interest that seemed more personal than political.

"I'm not as certain of that as I'd like to be. The King is an obstacle. He seems to side with us, but only because he wants to tax the men with the money. He has no interest in our demands that the nobles should be deprived of all their other privileges, such as the right to control the law in their own districts, or to raise their own taxes, which will no doubt go up if they have to give money to the crown. And he has nothing to say about opening up government positions or the higher ranks in the military so that common men may hope to advance. He even said that the Third Estate could not expect to have equal representation in future voting."

"Then what have you gained, you and your National Assembly?" interrupted Madeleine indignantly. "You have done nothing but give the King what he wanted!" Her voice was shrill, and it occurred to Andre for the first time that the sounds she made were not always pleasant.

"Can't you see what we have achieved, Madeleine? We have given the people a voice, and we will never allow it to be silenced. The King and his nobles are in conflict, but we are united. And the people of Paris are with us. Thousands are in the streets already, and they are angry. Money is almost worthless, and the price of bread has never been higher. The mob may not understand everything we do, but they do understand fear and hunger, and they are ready to act. Either the King will learn to respect our power, or perhaps we shall learn to live without him. The choice is his."

"A world without a king," said Madeleine. "A world without aristocrats. It would be a wonderful thing, Andre, for us to live in a world where there was nobody to hold us back, where we could rise to the heights we deserve." She was talking to him, apparently, but he noticed that she was staring over his shoulder to a spot on the blank wall behind him.

There was a moment of silence; then Madeleine shifted her gaze toward Andre again.

"You must not expect too much at once," Andre said.

"You are becoming a politician," said Madeleine. "I expect a great deal, and so do the people of France. You and your colleagues will do well to keep us in mind."

"We think only of the people," snapped Andre, "and you should know it. But we must be careful, Madeleine. No one wants fighting in the streets."

"Some would relish it, and you should be among them."

Andre saw the weary anger in her eyes and decided it would be better to placate her than to defend himself. "I know you have suffered much," he said, "and I promise you that it will not last much longer. It must be hell to have the Countess for your mistress, but you will soon be free. I promise it. Has she really become so much worse?"

"Much," said Madeleine, and Andre was relieved to see that he had succeeded in shifting her anger toward another target.

"Tell me more about this new lover of hers," he said.

"Could it be important? Could you use it to drag her down?"

"It is nothing new for the Countess de Corville, of course. He would have to be a very special sort of man to interest the National Assembly."

"There's something wrong with him," said Madeleine eagerly. "I haven't seen much of him, but somehow he's horrible. For one thing, he's a foreigner. . . ."

The dusk that day was warm and full of flies, even in the courtyard of as important a personage as the Count de Corville. The Countess swatted irritably at the insects with her fan as she paced throughout the maze of shrubbery and waited for darkness to fall. She glanced nervously back to make sure that no solicitous servant was following her as she worked her way slowly toward the center of the maze and the bizarre little building that was hidden there.

The marble pavilion had been constructed to her specifications shortly after her marriage to the Count, who had never been permitted to enter it. And in fact he had demonstrated very little desire to do so. It was his wife's sanctuary, and he realized that any intrusion on his part would doubtless prove embarrassing to both of them, and very likely to a third party as well. For the Countess entertained her lovers there. But it was only recently that she had permitted one of them to actually take up residence.

As the Countess approached the small structure of pale marble, she congratulated herself on having chosen the ideal tenant. For the place might have been designed as a miniature palace of pleasure, but it looked more like a tomb. Purple shadows formed among its arches and pillars as the sun buried itself at the edge of the city. A swarm of glistening green flies buzzed outside the entrance as if in search of carrion.

She felt her lips twitch involuntarily at the sight of the eager insects, but ignored the momentary feeling of revulsion until it was replaced by a sense of sick excitement at the thought of what waited beyond the door. The key was already in her hand. Heavy steel bolts grated as the key turned and the door opened into darkness.

The air in the anteroom was stale and musty, and there was no sound except for the tapping of her heels on the inlaid floor. The windows of the chamber within had been covered with drapes of purple velvet, through which a single pale beam of lingering sunlight slipped, catching in its path a drift of tiny specks of dust. This last touch of light died as the Countess watched.

"Sebastian?" she whispered.

She moved cautiously across the room, her eyes still unaccustomed to the darkness, until she could lay her hands on the long, low marble chest that had been built into the farthest wall. It had been intended merely for storage, but now its installation seemed providential. It had been designed to hold gowns and linen, but it was big enough to hold the body of a man.

Glancing nervously behind her to make certain that no trace of sunlight remained to penetrate the room, the Countess de Corville pulled a key from her bodice and unlocked the chest, then sank to her knees as she endeavored to raise the heavy lid. She took a deep breath as she struggled against the ponderous weight, then was startled to feel it lifted from her hands by a strength much greater than her own. The marble slab crashed back against the wall, and the Countess felt her slim wrist grasped by the cold, dry fingers of Don Sebastian de Villanueva.

A pale face, draped with long black hair, reared up from the depths of the chest. Bits of Spanish soil dropped back as the figure rose, but others clung to the clothing, and even to the upraised hands. The dark, vacant eyes held the Countess for a moment, and then she looked away. The sight of Sebastian was so awesome that she felt driven, almost against her will, to domesticate his presence.

"You look more human, now that the tailors have done their work," the Countess said.

"Do not be deceived, Juliette," Sebastian replied. "I am not human, nor shall I ever be again."

"At least you are decently clothed, Sebastian."

"And I thank you, although such garb is alien to me. This is a strange world you have brought me to, and I know little of it, except what you have shown me."

"If you knew more of it, you would find it stranger still. You are fortunate to have me as your guide. In fact, without me you would be locked in this chest, a helpless prisoner."

"Do you really think I am so easy to entomb? Your key is to keep others out, not to keep me in."

"Then could you break through solid marble?" asked the Countess eagerly, reaching out to touch his arm as if she could absorb his strength through her fingertips.

"I could," said Sebastian calmly, "but it would be a shame to destroy such a handsome piece of handiwork, and it would be much simpler for me to become a mist and flow out into the air without disturbing anything except myself. Of course I would be obliged to leave behind this splendid suit of clothes." He touched the lace at his throat and glanced down at his red velvet frock coat, embroidered waistcoat, and black knee breeches.

The Countess stepped back and stared at him with shining

eyes. "Do it now, Sebastian," she said. "Show me. Change."

"I am not a juggler," Sebastian said, "and neither am I here to entertain you."

"But you are, Sebastian. We are here to serve each other. I offer you shelter, and I expect you to instruct me in the mysteries of the undead. I expect you to show me all your secrets."

"And I expect much more of you than you have provided. I need more than a place to hide. I need to know more of this world into which you have summoned me. And I need blood."

"But Rollin . . ." protested the Countess.

"That was long ago. I must be fed regularly, like any of your other household pets. Do you not see how pale and thin I have become?"

The Countess allowed herself a little smile. "But it suits you, Sebastian. How else should a vampire look?"

"This is not a comedy," replied Sebastian with a frown. "And I warn you, as I have before, that it will very likely end in tragedy. A creature such as I walks hand in hand with Death."

"Well, then, find your victims. Feed! We are in one of Europe's largest cities. Surely there is blood enough for you!"

"But there is a price to pay for it. When they die, my victims become vampires themselves and their presence might reveal my own. But if I let them live, they are all too likely to report what must certainly be a unique experience. Either way, I risk exposure and destruction. Centuries ago, I learned to be more circumspect. It is not enough to have a hidden tomb. I must make my very existence a dark secret, or I shall not suffer your hospitality for long. And I am an ungrateful guest when I am crossed."

The Countess took one step toward him, her head lowered. "But I am a generous hostess," she said. "And now that I understand, your fast may end. If you need not kill the one you feed upon, then feed on me, Sebastian."

"No. You do not understand what you are saying. And I must have others. Many of them. You could not safely nourish me for long, even if I were willing to accept your offer."

The Countess turned her back on him and walked across the room. "You are an ungrateful beast," she said, "and you are a fool. A child!" She spun around to face him once again, and her expression was a mixture of frustration, contempt, and fury. "This is not Spain three hundred years ago! This is Paris! This is 1789! Have you never heard of passion? Or debauchery? Don't you know what money can buy?"

Don Sebastian lifted one dark eyebrow. "I have seen men and women sell many things for gold," he said, "but never their own lives."

"Not their lives," replied the Countess, "only their blood. Very likely, too, there are others like me, who would give a bit for their own pleasure."

Sebastian sat down on the marble chest and cupped his chin in his right hand. "Explain yourself," he said.

The Countess sat beside him and stroked his long black hair. "You will have to tie that in a ribbon," she said, "or perhaps I should get you a wig. There is a man I want you to meet, and it is hard enough to make you presentable, with your white, scarred face. Fortunately, his residence is one where not much stock is taken in appearances."

"Speak more directly. What are you talking about?"

"The Bastille."

"The Bastille? Is that the man you mentioned? And will he sell his blood?"

"He lives there. And you are right that I have neglected your education, but I will make amends. He sells nothing, but he would be glad to drink blood if he could, at least if he speaks the truth. Certainly he will know where to find the sort of women you seek. Poor Sebastian. Do you know nothing of debauchery?"

"My brother was a monk, and I have heard him speak of it."

"These are not the Dark Ages of three hundred years ago. Monks are in disrepute, and pleasure is the only god, at least for those who can afford it. Have you never heard of those who find joy in pain?"

"I have. My brother was an officer of the Inquisition."

"I mean no such hypocrisy. There are those who inflict suffering frankly, for the sheer joy of it. And there are others who are glad to accommodate them, who take delight in their own pain. Do you know nothing of this?"

"I have never heard it offered as a replacement for religion. I know that there are men who satisfy their lusts with torture, but I would have guessed there were few enough who were eager to accommodate them."

"There are more than you might think. And still more who will do what they must to buy their bread. They will certainly not bother about it, provided you have sense enough to present yourself as a depraved nobleman and not as one of the living dead. My friend the Marquis will know where to find them."

Sebastian stared at her intently. "And are you one of these, Juliette?"

Under his scrutiny, the Countess came close to blushing, or closer than she had come in years. "Not precisely, yet I am willing to be. The Marquis will tell you that the greatest pleasure is to be found in attempting all things, in experiments to achieve ecstasy."

"Is he your teacher, then? And where may he be found?"

"He is in prison."

"In prison!"

"The influence of his wife's mother, who has friends at court. She hopes to prevent him from sullying the name of her family. He is a martyr."

"A martyr! Then this is indeed a religion! And Cupid must be its god, dispensing his darts for the faithful to give and receive as they see fit."

The Countess turned away. "Must you mock me? I have offered you much. Are you incapable of understanding?"

Sebastian put his cold hands on her bare shoulders. "I understand more than you imagine. I have sustained myself on the blood and suffering of others for longer than you have been alive. But it was a sacrament, and now you tell me that it should be no more than an entertainment. And so I ask you again: Is this a comedy or a tragedy?"

"That is for us to decide. Not by our desires, but by our deeds. Will you have me?"

"I will. Since I am here, I can do no less than follow fashion."

"I knew you would," the Countess said. "I came prepared." She threw back her cloak, revealing a filmy nightgown, but Sebastian had hardly time to look at it before she had pulled it over her head. She stood naked before him, her bright eyes on his. "Do I please you?" she asked.

"Perhaps I should have said Pan rather than Cupid. You are as slender and graceful as a woodland nymph."

"And twice as willing. Are you all ghost, or are you still a man?"

"I see that you want more from me than my teeth in your throat. But do you want a dead man for your lover?"

"A pleasure that few women have known," answered the Countess. Her hands were on his face, her quick tongue upon his throat. "There are men who love to lie with the dead, but I have never heard of a lady who accomplished it. Few have had my opportunity."

"Too few," replied Sebastian. He led her toward the carved and canopied bed in the corner.

"Wait," said the Countess. "Wait." She stepped to the curtain beside the bed and pulled it back, revealing a long and glistening mirror.

"Do you love to see yourself so much?" the vampire asked. "For you shall see none of me in this."

"I shall see myself," she replied, "and I shall see what you do to me. I have had paramours before, but none who was invisible." She looked into the mirror, examining with a calculating eye her high breasts, her slim waist, her long white thighs. She collapsed upon the bed, and as Sebastian sank down upon her, she began to tear the clothes from his body.

She felt his weight on her, and turned her head to see the effect in her looking glass. There she was alone, yet she could see the presence of her lover. She arched her back, looking not toward Sebastian, but toward the mirror where she could watch invisible fingers tousling her honey-colored hair and pressing down upon the soft warmth of her breasts. She shifted her position to behold the horror of an unseen lover taking her.

And through a chink in the curtain, her maid Madeleine watched as well. And the shudders that racked her body were only partly caused by fear.

6

Philosophy in the Bastille

"He is in the Tour de la Liberté," the Countess said.

"The Tower of Liberty?" Sebastian asked. "In the Bastille? A prison? Has your world constructed a dungeon where the inmate is free?"

"Not free, exactly, but more so than you might suppose. The Marquis has been here for more than five years, and he spent longer than that in another prison. But these are not the dungeons of your Spanish Inquisition. The King has agreed to keep the Marquis at the request of his family, since they find his behavior embarrassing. But he is not abused; in fact he is as comfortable as a man can be who has lost his freedom. And the Tower of Liberty is the one of eight in the Bastille where the prisoners enjoy certain privileges. They are exercised daily, for one thing; but more to the point, they are sometimes allowed visitors. I understand that his wife sees him almost every week, but he is less than delighted with such loyalty, since it was her mother who used her influence at court to have him put away."

"And what has he done to deserve such treatment?"

"Let him tell you. We have arrived, Sebastian. Behold the Bastille."

The coach of the Countess de Corville drew up on the rue Saint-Antoine. Beyond the walls, beyond the moats, beyond the drawbridges, the Bastille loomed darkly against the purple sky of evening. Its eight round towers rose above walls more than a hundred feet high.

"Come," the Countess said as she alighted from the coach. "Here, across the drawbridge. My servants have prepared the way, but no doubt more gold will change hands before we see my friend."

Sebastian paused beside the restless white horses and their sleepy driver. "I have no love for prisons," he said.

"Nonsense," replied the Countess as she drew him along behind her. "You have told me how you can flow through locks and fly over walls. You have less to fear here than any man in France."

"It is not fear that troubles me, Juliette. But I hate confinement, and the madness that it brings."

"Then you will like my friend. There has never been a man so bent on absolute freedom. Perhaps that is why he has so little of it. He will be disappointed that I have not come alone, and I expect you to console him with your wit. He claims to be a philosopher."

"I wonder what sort of philosophy these walls will breed."

"There is the emblem of the Bastille, Sebastian. Time and confinement." The Countess pointed upward as she whispered her name to a shadowy sentry while she slipped him a few coins. Across the empty courtyard was a huge clock, suspended between two towers, supported by an ornate group of statues representing hundreds of men and women, all in chains. "That tower to the left is the one we seek."

They crossed the moonlit stretch of ground alone, hemmed in on all sides by the gigantic barricades of stone, while the clock and its tortured supporters stared down at them.

Another man stopped them at the Tower of Liberty, and again the Countess quieted him with coins, while Don Sebastian stared up at the tower and thought of the Spanish castle where he had been the master, and yet a prisoner as well.

The turnkey opened the door into the Tower of Liberty and escorted them inside. There he consulted a thin-faced man who sat drowsing beside the stump of a candle. He looked half dead, but was revived immediately by the cold touch of the Countess de Corville's gold.

"Second floor," he muttered. "He has more visitors than any other prisoner we have. More trouble than he's worth. Wish he was back at Vincennes. Still, he pays for his fun, or at least someone does. This way . . ."

Stoop-shouldered, the flickering candle in his hand, he led them up a circular stone staircase until they reached a landing where they were greeted by an iron door. A faint light shone through a narrow, barred opening. The man peered in. "Could be asleep," he said. "No, he's writing. Might have known. You can go in." He produced a big key from the ring at his waist and opened the well-oiled door.

"Visitors," he said.

The man who sat at the desk in the circular cell looked up at them through bloodshot eyes. "Who is it?" he snapped irritably. "I am half blind from writing by candlelight. Send them away. I am working."

"But surely," the Countess said, "you would not dismiss your Juliette."

"What?" said the prisoner. "Is it you?" He stood so suddenly that he nearly overturned his candle, a short, fat, pale man who squinted desperately against the dimness. "Who is with you?"

"One is my friend," she replied. "The other is your jailer."

"Ah. I am still dreaming. I forget sometimes where I am, and I imagined that you might have come alone, Madame Countess. You are a Countess now? Well, at least dismiss the lackey."

A certain sly concern showed on the thin face of the turnkey. "Be careful, milady. He has shown violence to his wife, and even to the Governor of the Bastille."

"I could hardly do less myself," the Countess said. "How much will it cost to send you away for a while, fellow?"

"Send him for a bottle of wine," said the prisoner. "Send him for two, but expect to see only one of them."

"And don't hurry," shouted the Marquis as his jailer retreated with a fistful of money and closed the door silently. Sebastian listened for the sound of the key turning in the lock.

"I could gladly strangle him, Juliette. And not for the pleasure of the act, but simply to be rid of him. Who is this gentleman? An inspector of prisons?"

"An inspector of prisoners, perhaps. He has come far to meet you."

"Indeed! Have I admirers in distant lands? I certainly have none in France!"

"I fear that he has never heard of you. Nonetheless, you are the man he seeks. He is a Spanish nobleman, Don Sebastian de Villanueva. Sebastian, may I present the Marquis de Sade?"

The two men bowed stiffly, eyeing each other warily across the circular cell. Abruptly the Marquis sat down again behind his desk. "And what does he want of me?" he asked.

"He has an odd taste," replied the Countess. "He drinks blood, and he seeks those who can satisfy him."

The Marquis peered at the shadowy figure who stood beyond the glow of the candle. "So, sir. You are one of the brotherhood of libertines? Come closer, so that I may look at you."

"Libertines?" echoed Sebastian. "I have never heard the word."

"It signifies men such as you and I, who feel free to indulge their impulses without regard for law or custom. Society's criminals, and nature's heroes. You are pale, more so than I." He placed his pudgy hand against Sebastian's for contrast. "And you are cold. No wonder you want blood."

"It is more than a desire, Monsieur le Marquis. It is an absolute necessity."

"I have done little enough of that myself; in fact I have done little of anything for the past ten years. But I have heard of such men, and I have written of them. I have written of everything I could remember or imagine. It is the only vice I am allowed. I think all men of letters should spend time in prison, if only because it sharpens the concentration. And there have been many such hidden behind these very stones. Voltaire, for one. Have you read him? No? A very clever fellow. A challenger of kings and gods."

The Countess smiled. "If you were not here for making a scandal, you would be here for blasphemy or treason."

"One scandal! There were many, I assure you."

"Would you give Don Sebastian a catalogue of your crimes?"

"Small enough, I fear, for a man of his interests. I hired a woman to take a whipping, and she complained to the authorities, even though she was well paid. No doubt she hoped for further compensation, for when she received it the charge was dropped. Then there was the matter of the candies. They were only meant to excite the ladies, but some of them grew slightly ill. There was more trouble when I was charged with committing sodomy with my manservant. I was beheaded and burned in effigy for that; I wish I had seen it. But ultimately none of these charges was sustained. What undid me, I think, was conceiving a passion for my wife's sister, which so infuriated their mother that she used her influence with the King to have me locked up here on no charge at all. A government where such things are permitted is an abomination."

"In Spain," Sebastian said, "the accusations alone would be enough to guarantee you torture and very likely death."

"And am I not tortured? A man of my passions confined in this cylinder of stone? Could you bear it, sir?"

"No prison can hold me, except one of my own creation."

"So I thought. I have escaped. I led them a merry chase for years. But there is no escape from the Bastille, not until the people rise up and tear the accursed pile apart, stone by stone."

"And that is hardly likely," the Countess said.

"You think not, Juliette? Then you know less of the world than what I hear through these thick walls. The throne is threatened. Freedom is in the air. The people are unhappy as well as the nobles. There are riots."

"Well, there are always riots. Sensible people stay away from them."

"And what does the gentleman from Spain think?"

"I know little of conditions here, and so have little to say. I suppose that countries have risen against their kings; perhaps a few thrones have been toppled. But they have always been replaced by other thrones. I fear that we shall never see a time when men like us are free. Freedom is easier for those who expect little from life. If freedom were unlimited, then you would have to grant your King the chance to lock you in this tower. We are obliged to live outside the law."

"Then you see that we are brothers?"

"I know only that I am thirsty."

"Then is it your only passion? There are hundreds, you know. And I have taken it upon myself to create new ones. Let me show you what I have written." Unshaven, disheveled, the Marquis de Sade rose heavily from his chair and shuffled toward the wall, where he squatted and put his hands on a stone. The Countess sank into an armchair near the door, but Sebastian watched carefully while the Marquis worked the stone loose and withdrew a thick roll of paper. "My masterpiece," he said. "A single sheet, almost forty feet long, covered on both sides with the smallest writing my hand could make. Even I can hardly read it."

"And what is it called?" asked the Countess without much interest.

"*The 120 Days of Sodom.* There is a tale in it, I suppose, but in essence, it is a listing of all the passions I can conceive of, the simple, the complex, the criminal, and the murderous, making six hundred in all. Surely yours is here among them. I know I have something about blood. But only that? You are too particular, sir. I saw your face when I mentioned my experiments in sodomy. Surely one should try everything!"

"I understand that such practices were common among the Moors," Sebastian said, "but they were my enemies, and in any case I never felt the desire to emulate their fashion."

"Too proud to lie with a man, eh? But not too proud to kill a woman for her blood?"

"I prefer not to kill those who feed me."

"But you have, haven't you? It shows in your face. Here is something close to what you speak of, but it is only a fellow who likes to watch the blood flow. He does not even taste it." The Marquis had unrolled his scroll, which stretched across the cold floor like a pale ribbon. "Can it be that I have left you out? That will never do. And to think that I finished this almost four years ago. I was rushed toward the end, though, and described the murderous passions in less detail than I might have wished. I had to hide the thing, of course, or my keepers would have surely destroyed it."

"I killed only those who wished for it," Sebastian said. The Countess looked up in some surprise, sensing for the first time that there was some uneasiness in his manner.

"You serviced suicides? And none other?" asked the Marquis.

"I have killed enemies. But my passion, as you call it, has been reserved for those I love. And I have offered them not death, but life eternal."

"Ah. Sent them straight to Heaven, did you? And I thought I was dealing with a rational man! Who have you brought me, Juliette? Next you will tell me he is a bishop!"

The Countess stirred in her chair. "You misunderstand him," she said. "He is a vampire."

"Of course, of course. What else would a man who drinks blood be?"

"But I mean it," she insisted. "He really is a vampire, my dear Marquis. A living corpse."

"Nonsense, Juliette. If I believed in such things, I would be obliged to believe in God. And then where would I be?"

"Where you are now," Sebastian said quietly.

"If there were a God, then I would surely be in Hell."

"Are you so far from it?" asked Sebastian. "Am I?"

The Marquis began to retrieve his scroll. "The torture I endure," he said, "is of man's devising. And do not tell me that it is what I have chosen. I did not wish to be what I am, but since it is my self, I certainly will not deny it."

"Bravo," Sebastian said.

"I do not masquerade as some fantastic creature. And I have not killed. These are only fancies," said the Marquis de Sade, brandishing his catalogue of crimes. "In the world of ideas, there must be no laws. If we could see ourselves, if we could face our darkest dreams, then we would know that we are all villains. And we would all be in prison together, even as we three are. Or perhaps we might all go free."

"As two of us shortly will," the Countess said. "I have brought you some money, and I have paid as much to visit you. Will you be kind enough to help my friend?"

"Not for your money, though I have little enough. But for an embrace."

"You sound like a starving man," the Countess said. "What of your wife?"

"I would not touch her for my life," the Marquis replied. "Forget her. You are the first woman I have seen in years. Surely you will not deny me the chance to offer you some small abuse?"

The Countess turned to Sebastian.

"Do what you will," the vampire said. He took the manuscript from de Sade and sat with it in the chair beside the door, studying it intently, apparently oblivious to the sound of rustling silk behind him. He was examining a passage near the end of the scroll, in which a nobleman arranges to have fifteen young girls murdered simultaneously for his amusement, when he heard a sharp gasp from the Countess. Sebastian raised his head, but did not turn around.

"Enough," the Countess said. "Your jailer will be returning soon. This is not the time or the place."

"There is no other time for me," the Marquis said, "nor is there any other place. And you are as cruel as every other woman I have known."

Sebastian stood up and gathered de Sade's manuscript together. The Countess and the Marquis stood three feet apart. Both of their faces were flushed.

"Someone is coming," the Countess said. "Give us the names."

"I have been imprisoned for ten years, my dear Juliette."

"You know who can help us. Write their names here."

De Sade scrawled a few lines on a sheet of paper. "Give me that manuscript," he said. "I must hide it." He busied himself with the loose stone in the wall. "They must not burn it."

"A remarkable work," Sebastian said. "Guard it well. My book on witchcraft was burned three hundred years ago, something almost as complete in its own way."

"You would be wise to spare yourself these delusions," said de Sade. "We must face the truth before we can be free."

"I see now why this is called the Tower of Liberty. I have never met a man whose mind was so unfettered. Nor do I hope to do so again. I wish you well, nonetheless. Perhaps you will find the freedom you seek."

"Only if I can tear down these walls, Don Sebastian."

"Then you must do it."

A key rattled in the lock and the jailer entered, one bottle of wine in his hand and another one inside him.

"There is nothing I can do," said the Marquis, "except to write."

"Then do that," Sebastian said. "There is always something. There must be. We were not born to be prisoners."

The Countess glanced at de Sade, then hurried from his cell.

"Do you believe what you say?" asked the Marquis.

"I do. I must," Sebastian said. "My cell is larger than yours, but the walls are just as strong." He stepped onto the stairway behind the Countess.

They hurried down the steps while the jailer lagged behind to lock the door.

"You might have been more concerned," the Countess said. "I risked much for you."

"You risked nothing," replied Sebastian. "The man is harmless. A man who writes as he does has no need for human victims. Furthermore, I had no wish to interfere because I knew how much you were enjoying yourself."

The Countess looked up at him, tried to achieve an indignant expression, and failed.

"I remember only one night," Sebastian said, "when I have seen you so pleased with yourself."

Alone in his cell, de Sade sat before his flickering candle, staring into its yellow flame.

"There must be something," he said to himself. "Some way. Anything is possible, even freedom, in a world which sends a prisoner both a beautiful woman and a walking corpse. And one of them was real! But this Don Sebastian. A man who thinks he is a vampire! Perhaps I imagined him. Either way, the poor fellow must be completely deranged."

7

The Fortress

"POOR DE SADE," the Countess said. "I am afraid our visit upset him. I have a message here which says that he has gone quite mad. It's from Launay, the governor of the Bastille."

"What does it say?" Sebastian asked. His voice showed no emotion, and he continued to pace before the Countess through the dark maze of shrubbery that surrounded her marble pavilion.

"Apparently he attempted to start a riot among the people passing in the street outside the prison. I suppose he was lucky that no one was killed. It is easy enough to start that sort of trouble these days."

"Easy even for a man in prison?"

"What he did is too ridiculous to discuss, really. Yet it was dangerous enough so that he was removed a few days ago from the Bastille to the asylum at Charenton. Apparently he managed to fashion something like a megaphone out of a piece of drainpipe, and he used it to gather a crowd by shouting through the window of his cell. He told them that the prisoners were being slaughtered and urged them to storm the walls at once. And they might have done it, if he had not been silenced in time."

"When was this done?"

"The day after we saw him. And no doubt we are partly to

blame. You should not have urged him to fight for his freedom."

"Could I do less? In any case, I am in some respects much like your friend the Marquis. Too often I am tempted to make experiments, if only to see whether or not the results will please me."

"And are you pleased, Sebastian?"

"Five years is too long a time for a man to be kept anywhere. At least the Marquis succeeded in getting himself moved to new quarters."

"Locked up with lunatics! Though I almost think he belongs there, after what he has done. How could he encourage the rabble to rise up? He has betrayed his own class."

"Come, Juliette. You can hardly expect him to be grateful to a king who throws him into prison."

"Perhaps. But if the vermin of Paris run riot, de Sade may begin to wish that he was safe in the Bastille again. You don't realize how dangerous conditions have become." The Countess sank down on a wrought-iron bench near the outskirts of the maze. "Today mobs attacked the posts where taxes are collected on goods coming into the city, and burned most of them to the ground. They think such anarchy will lower the price of grain, but of course they were not content to wait, so they also broke into a monastery and stole all the food. And they freed all the criminals in another prison today. I tried to convince my husband that we should leave for the country; the city simply isn't safe. But the fool continues to believe that his intrigues at court will help to settle things, even though he and most of his party have withdrawn from the National Assembly now that the rabble of the Third Estate has taken control of it."

"Are there no soldiers to maintain order?"

"Soldiers! Henri tells me that the King is constantly ordering more into the city, and that itself is causing more unrest. But the worst of it is that as often as not the men throw down their arms, or join the mobs they were sent to control. It frightens me when I think of it. And so I try not to think." She touched the bench beside her, inviting Sebastian to sit, but he remained standing.

"I have seen war," he said, "but never anything like this. Is it really possible for the common people to rise up and rule themselves? How will they keep order?"

"Who knows? Perhaps they will find the biggest fool among them and make him their king. The point is that they will not keep order. They will destroy France!"

"More likely the rebellion will be quelled. But perhaps it would be safer to leave the city temporarily. Do you think you can persuade the Count to go?"

"If he does not agree soon, then we shall leave without him. I have no wish to be murdered in my bed." She looked at Sebastian and smiled. "At least not by a stranger."

"And not tonight, I hope," Sebastian said. "For I must leave you, Juliette."

"Again? So soon? I should never have taken you to see de Sade. Now you will not even sit with me. You think of nothing but those sluts and their blood!"

"At least the names he gave us proved to be useful, even if there was some difficulty in tracking the women down. And without them, we would have more to worry us than the state of the government in France."

The Countess stood and thrust her face toward Sebastian's. "Take me instead," she whispered.

"I need more than you can give me, Juliette. I need more than any single woman can give me, and that is why I must visit these others so often. If I took all that I needed from you alone, you would be dead."

"What does it matter? We may all be dead tomorrow anyway."

"You are becoming hysterical. Conditions can hardly be as desperate as you imagine."

"You know nothing at all of what is happening in France!"

"Then my travels tonight will give me a chance to learn."

"You shall not have my coach, Sebastian. The mobs will tear it to pieces before you have gone a mile."

"Then I shall go without it. But I must go."

The Countess turned away from him with a toss of her blond head. "Return soon," she said, "or you may find me gone."

"I would not willingly abandon you," Sebastian replied, "but I must be true to my nature, whatever the cost."

She felt his light touch on her shoulder, but waited for a moment before she responded. When she finally turned back toward him, the path was empty. She looked around anxiously, but saw nothing except the tall, shadowy hedges that surrounded her. She heard a rustling from the shrubbery. Something black soared into the summer sky on leathery wings and sailed across the ivory moon. The Countess shuddered and crossed her arms on her naked shoulders. She had often longed to see Sebastian transform himself, yet the sight of what he had done left her awestruck and more than a bit afraid. For long minutes she stared up at the moon; then she began to work her way through the intricate twists and turns that led out of the maze.

As she stepped out of the shadows and into the bright moonlight of the open courtyard, her fingers moved unconsciously toward her throat, where a black velvet choker hid the two small marks that were so slow in healing.

"A strand of pearls would do as well."

The Countess gasped at the sound of the unexpected voice, then noticed her maidservant Madeleine standing beneath a carefully pruned cedar tree. Something in the twist of Madeleine's lips disturbed the Countess, who nervously dropped her hand to her side. "What do you mean about the pearls?" she demanded.

"Nothing, Madame Countess. Only that you wear that black band so often now, when you have so many other ornaments that would serve as well to set off your beautiful throat."

The Countess looked at Madeleine as if seeing her for the first time. "I will consider your suggestion tomorrow," she said. "As for tonight, it hardly matters, since I intend to retire at once." She stepped rapidly across the courtyard, but stopped short when she realized that Madeleine was following her. "You are dismissed," she said curtly. "I shall undress myself. Go meet your lover. Do what you will. But leave me alone. And be advised that we shall leave for the country as soon as my husband has put his affairs in order."

Madeleine made an obsequious curtsy, but there was

mockery in her blue eyes. "Very well, Madame Countess," she said. "I hope the people in the streets will not disturb your rest."

The Countess de Corville did not reply, but hurried away toward the house in a state of obvious agitation. Madeleine's strange manner had intensified her concern about the risings in Paris, and also about the strange guest hidden in the center of the maze, whose presence might not be as much a secret as it should be. For the first time in her life the Countess felt threatened by dangers that she had not created for her own amusement. She rushed past a servant and through the door, calling for wine as she passed. And though she went to bed, she did not sleep.

Outside the house, Madeleine Benet waited by the gate. In the distance she could hear occasional shouting, and once a sound that might have been a shot. Such noises left her as nervous as her mistress, but Madeleine felt less fear and more excitement. She stared down the empty street before the residence of the de Corvilles, waiting for one man but hoping for a mob.

Finally Andre Latour arrived, alone and on foot. His curly hair was tousled, his face was smudged with soot, and one of his sleeves was torn. He embraced Madeleine eagerly, clinging to her as if she were his only anchor in the midst of a whirlwind.

"Is it safe for you to travel unprotected?" Madeleine asked him. "Surely you should have come here with a band of men."

Andre smiled. "And burned the place to the ground, I suppose?"

"Would that be such a bad thing?"

"We are hardly ready for that. We are still arming ourselves."

"But is tonight the night, Andre?"

"There will be many nights before this business is done. We cannot conquer France as quickly as all that, Madeleine. I have never known such a bloodthirsty woman! Of course I have heard that red hair means a passionate nature, but I hoped for love rather than hatred."

Madeleine shrugged. "You are much the same as I, Andre, for all your fine talk. You could have stayed in Versailles to carry on the debate with the National Assembly, but you prefer to be here in Paris, where men fight instead of only arguing."

"True enough. It is hard to dissemble with you. But I still say that I fight because I love freedom, and not because I hate anyone."

"You will find soon enough that there can be no difference, but I don't want to argue with you over principles. Tell me something I can taste, Andre. Tell me what has been done."

"The electors of Paris have created a citizens' militia. Our obvious motive is to control the rioting, but of course we mean to control it for our own ends. We have been collecting arms from various sources, but so far we have not found the ammunition for them."

"And the King?"

"He continues to send troops, but they only make our numbers stronger. He has some foreign soldiers who care nothing for the people of Paris, but there are not enough of them to stop us. When Louis replaced the ministers who were sympathetic to our cause, he did us a great service. Now almost all of France is against him."

"But you have no gunpowder."

"A little. And tomorrow we shall have more. We know where it is. In the Bastille. One of the prisoners broke loose from his captors not long ago and shouted to the people below that they must storm the place. He was stopped almost at once, but not before he had thrown down letters telling us that there were cannons ready to fire on the people, and that there was enough powder and shot in the Bastille to supply an army. I have forgotten the fellow's name, and in any case he has been transferred from the Tower of Liberty. A disaffected nobleman, I think, imprisoned on order of the King. Regardless, the man is a true patriot."

"But the Bastille, Andre! Can it be taken?"

"The soldiers there are Frenchmen, and we must depend on that. The governor of the prison is a fool, of course, but that may be to our advantage. A few of us may die, but we shall not be stopped. The Bastille shall be ours. And after that, all Paris."

"Take me with you, Andre. Now. I want to watch their power crumble."

"There will be little enough to see, and more danger than I would expose you to. Wait, Madeleine. Soon enough you will have everything you want."

"I don't want to wait! The Countess is planning to leave Paris, perhaps tomorrow. I will not be locked away with that bitch and her cuckold while France finds her liberty!"

Andre held her at arm's length and looked at her with all the sincerity he could muster. "If they reach the countryside," he said, "then you must be with them. You must not underestimate the Count de Corville. He is one of our most devoted foes. Our informants tell us that he is powerful at the Court, a member of the Queen's party who would rather see France invaded by the King's allies than see the monarchy fall. He must be watched. And our struggle must be spread beyond Paris. Half our support comes from those who are hungry. Unless we win over the peasants who produce the bread we eat, we are lost."

"So you would send me away." Madeleine stepped back from Andre and turned toward the gate, but she moved slowly enough so that he had no trouble catching her.

"Madeleine. I have no wish to lose you, not even for a moment. But a few more weeks may make all the difference. My cause is the same as yours. We must make sacrifices. If I spoke only for myself, there is nowhere I would rather have you tonight than in my bed. But the next few months may make all the difference in the lives we lead. Surely you can understand?"

"I understand that you ask much and offer little. I understand that I am only a woman, good enough for sneaking and spying and sex, but worth nothing when great deeds are to be done."

"Give me peace, Madeleine. You wrong me either way. I offer you a task and you refuse it. But when I offer you only my love, you tell me that I have given you nothing. What would you have me do?"

"If you give me nothing else, at least give me the hours until dawn, Andre. No doubt you think you have much to do, but who knows when we shall see each other again?"

"Nothing would please me more than to spend the rest of the night with you, Madeleine, but there are men waiting for me."

"Let them wait. No man is indispensable, except to the one who loves him."

Andre Latour stood silent for a moment. "You are right, of course," he said, "though sometimes I wish it was not true. I want nothing more than to rise to power. At least that is what I tell myself, but there is something I want more, and that is you."

"Then take me while you can, Andre, for you have exiled me. Surely France can spare you for a few hours."

"I fear she can."

"Then take me," said Madeleine. "If not to the battle, then to the boudoir." She pressed her full lips against his and felt the thrill of conquest, even if the King still reigned.

Sebastian drifted across the warm sky, dizzy with the taste of the blood that had served to stimulate him, but had not been enough to satisfy. Not for the first time, he cursed Raoul Rollin and the Countess de Corville for dragging him back from the edge of eternity. Rollin had paid for his audacity, but the Countess had not, perhaps because of the affection which Sebastian could not entirely withhold from her. Her rage for ecstasy fascinated him, and so did her beauty, but he realized when he was not hungry for her blood that there was no reason for him to trust her. And the world into which she had summoned him was one where nothing was secure. Yet everything was for sale. He thought of the girl, who could not have been more than sixteen, but who had been more than willing to slash her arm and spill blood into a cup for him. It meant nothing to her. Neither fear nor passion had shown in her face; she had been content with the money he had offered her. He realized that it was wiser to pose as a libertine rather than admit that he was a vampire, but what sort of world was this?

His wings, the wings to which this world could not give

credence, carried him over the grim towers of the Bastille. He thought of de Sade, that strange little man, fat and unhappy, whose writings nonetheless showed that he possessed an imagination more daring and more depraved than any Sebastian had ever known. It was impossible, of course, that the Marquis had created the scene below alone, but as Don Sebastian passed over the fortress, he could hardly ignore the crowd, ever increasing, which stood outside its stony walls. And like Sebastian, they were patient.

They were waiting for the dawn.

8

A Country Estate

THE COUNT de Corville stood on the terrace of his ancestral home and squinted against the sun as he surveyed his fields and vineyards. His property stretched away as far as the eye could see, but the view was barren. The land was brown, sun-baked, and unattended. There were no peasants working the fields; in fact there was no sign of life at all. Yet the Count scanned the landscape anxiously as if searching for a figure moving somewhere in the distance.

"How does the prospect please you, my dear Juliette?" he asked. "Are you happier here than in Paris? And do you think you are any safer? Things are quieter in the city now; in fact they were better before we left, even if it was necessary for the King to pretend he would cooperate with the rabble. At least the criminals of the Third Estate have too much sense to destroy Paris, but these beasts of the field you have brought us among have no such scruples."

The Countess glanced around nervously, torn between fear for herself and fury toward her husband. "You know what they did to the Bastille," she snapped. "How could we know that they would not do as much to us? You did not take much persuading when we fled here a few weeks ago!"

"I was wrong, Juliette, as I have been wrong each time I have listened to you. In the past, I had only to be concerned lest your extravagance ruin us, but now I think that you have brought us to our deaths. I have not received a letter for a week, but you know what the last one said."

"I know. That the people are rising in the countryside as well, and that we are in more danger here than we ever were in Paris. That houses are being burned, and the owners murdered. And I know that if you were any kind of man at all you would do something about it. Instead you only stand there, old and fat and frightened, just waiting for marauders to spring from the trees and slaughter us. You did nothing when the men abandoned the fields, and you did nothing when the servants ran away. No doubt you will do as little when you see me raped by brigands!"

"And what do you expect of me? Even if I were one of your sturdy young lovers, I could hardly subdue the entire countryside single-handedly. We are at the mercy of history, and she is not merciful."

"God! To think that I should have tied my fate to such a man! If Madeleine had not remained faithful to me, we would both have starved to death by now. I don't know how she finds food for us, but at least she has done it, while all your chosen men have abandoned us. And no doubt the stewards you left behind in Paris have looted the house there by now. We are ruined, with nothing to defend us but that crumbling tower that your ancestors raised three centuries ago. You are nothing but a sack of money!"

The Count de Corville looked at the ruined fortifications, and at the bright, airy building beneath them that had been constructed to please his wife. "If money had not been enough for you," he said, "you would not have married me."

"I was a child then, but now I am wiser. What I need is not money, but a magician."

The Count's round face turned red. "Will you be sensible? This is no dream, Juliette, nor are there any wizards here to rescue you. We must rely on ourselves. Perhaps judicious bribes will be enough to buy our way back to Paris. Or it might be best to run for the border."

"Do you think you can offer them a bit of money when there is nothing to prevent them from taking it all? A magician would be much more useful, I promise you. But it depends on the time when the attack comes. By day, we are helpless, but by night, we might have a chance."

The Count de Corville trudged away toward his barren vineyards. "Must I be burdened with a madwoman too?" he shouted back at her. "Do what you can, but don't tell me that my vigil on the grounds makes less sense than your nights on the tower."

"The tower?" called the Countess.

The stubby shape of her husband turned toward her again, dark against the setting sun. "I know where you are, at least, if not what you do there. If it pleases you to wave your arms at the moon, by all means continue. If you conjure up a demon with the power to transport us from this place, by all means let me know. I will be glad enough to sell him my soul, or anything else he wants."

The Countess watched him wander off, and there was something in the slope of his shoulders that moved her to pity, if not to the love that she had never really known for him. She would save him if she could, and she was even more determined to save herself. She thought of Sebastian asleep in the tower, and wondered if he had the strength to defeat an entire nation. It hardly seemed possible, especially now, when he was so weak from lack of blood. Still, she would give him his chance tonight. And even if he failed her, she would not give in to despair. There was always a way.

She stepped inside through the glass doors with their leaded panes, more conscious than ever of the fragility of her surroundings. She walked slowly to the kitchen, where she knew Madeleine would be waiting.

Madeleine stood there smiling, a butcher knife in her right hand. "I found a chicken," she said, "and some greens. You will not go hungry, Madame Countess, as long as I am with you. But the prices are outrageous."

"We have money enough," the Countess said, "but without you to deal with the people here, we would be lost. Madeleine . . ."

"I know, Madame Countess. Do not demean yourself. I was born to serve you." Madeleine smiled brightly, and cut one leg off the dead chicken. "I will have to prepare this as the peasants do," she said, "but at least you and the Count will dine."

"Will you share it with us, Madeleine? You have become our savior, and we cannot have you going hungry."

"That would not be seemly, Madame Countess. I hope I know my place." She sliced off another leg, cutting through the tendons with quick efficiency. Her long red hair shadowed her face.

"You have been more loyal than I had any right to expect, Madeleine. But I wish I could believe that we were friends as well."

"That would hardly be suitable," said Madeleine. Her hands were covered with blood.

"And your young man," the Countess said. "How is he faring?"

"Well, I hope. I have not seen him for some time. Strange that you should take an interest in him now, when you only mentioned him before to sneer at him."

"His name is Andre, isn't it?"

"It is. Now you remember. Pardon me, but I shall never finish here if you require my undivided attention. You see why we must not become too friendly."

"Even so," the Countess said, and she backed out of the kitchen while Madeleine continued to slice and to smile.

"And how is your friend in the box?" Madeleine called after her.

The Countess slammed the door behind her, both hands clutched to her bosom as if she thought she could stop the pounding of her heart with the pressure of her fingers. She had hoped to find an ally in Madeleine; instead she found only mockery. And for the first time Madeleine had done more than drop disquieting hints. Quite clearly she had found out about Sebastian, and her knowledge terrified the Countess more than the thought of an imminent assault on the house.

More than an hour of daylight remained before Sebastian would awaken, but already her thoughts turned to the crumbling tower where several crates had been stored by the servants who had long since vanished. There slept her last hope for salvation. Slowly she stepped out into the afternoon sun and made her way toward the long shadow of the ancient tower.

She opened the box as she arrived, but she knew it would still be a long time before Sebastian stirred. His long, pale face was gaunt, with shadows under the eyes and cheekbones that made it look like a fleshless skull. The room in the tower was musty, filled with the relics of forgotten generations. Outdated furniture, unfashionable clothing, portraits from the wrong side of the family, all were stacked like firewood into the narrow confines of the bare stone walls. Sebastian's mouth was open, and under the long black mustache his sharp white teeth protruded unpleasantly. The scar that ran down over his left eye looked as if it must have killed him, and the Countess knew that it had, but only for the first time, three centuries ago. Still, he looked exactly like a corpse, and nothing like the vigorous, sardonic creature she had taken for her lover. It seemed impossible that he would ever rise again. She had never seen him this way before, and even while she stared at his impossibly white skin, she wished that she had waited for him to rise. He was too dead, too helpless, too obviously incapable of helping her. He might be immune to ordinary weapons, but she was not, and it seemed impossible that he could protect her against the armed mob that she pictured descending upon her before the sun rose again. She put her hands on his chest, feeling desperately for some sign of a heartbeat, but there was none. She wondered if he would ever live again, despite the evidence of her own eyes over the last weeks.

She could not believe either that he would rise or that he could save her. She dropped the lid on him and turned away.

Sebastian woke in darkness, surrounded by the sweet smell of his native earth. For a moment he lay still, reluctant to shake off the silver dreams of peace and freedom that filled his sunless days, yet his senses were as alert as those of a hunted animal. He knew at once that he was still in the crate that had carried him from Paris, and that the Countess had not come to greet him as he rose. There was something in his hands. Abruptly he pushed back the top of his wooden box and leaped out of the coffin. He smelled danger, but evidently it was not in the tower. He stood poised for flight or battle, casting wary glances all around him, his undead vision casting a pale blue glow over the pitch blackness which surrounded him. Only when he was sure he was alone did he look down at the single sheet of paper which had been placed in his fingers while he slept. The message was in a woman's handwriting.

My Dear Sebastian,
You have taught me little, and I have helped you less. You were right when you said that I should not have brought you back from whatever world you were inhabiting, and I am sorry now to have done it, but I can see no way for me to repair the damage. France is devouring herself, and both of us seem to be caught in her jaws. I cannot keep you fed, and the sight of you lying dead in the earth has made me fearful. I am not ready to die and will not offer myself as your next meal. Below you will find my husband and my servant Madeleine, neither of whom has proved satisfactory to me. If one of them will serve to nourish you, at least let me offer you that one last act of hospitality, for when you read this I hope to be many miles away. I have taken a horse, and nothing else except the most disreputable clothing I could find in the trunks you see around you. I hope to reach Paris alive, and with luck I shall find friends to shelter me. I believe I shall not look much like a noblewoman, and anyone who stops me will find nothing to rob me of except my virtue, which I do not hold in high regard. For a woman who has made love to a corpse and the Count de Corville, men hold no terrors. But I intend to survive, my dear Sebastian. I regret that I can do nothing more to protect you, and that I cannot trust you to protect me. I wish you well. In better days, we might have known more pleasant nights than this.

Juliette

As he absorbed the contents of the note, Sebastian's grim mouth twisted into something like a smile. Mixed with his fury and frustration was an ironic admiration for the woman whose scruples were so easily sacrificed to self-interest.

"You would have made a splendid vampire, Juliette," Sebastian said as he crushed the note into a tiny ball and tossed it aside. He turned toward the stairway and hurried out into the night.

The air outside was warm and damp, faintly illuminated by the thin wedge of a waning moon. Sebastian studied the house and made his plans, thankful that he had been cautious enough to leave several sacks of Spanish soil in Paris. The city was the only place where he could hope to survive, and he had taken care to question the Countess regarding the distance he would have to travel. One night's flight on his bat's wings would leave him ample time, provided he was strong enough, but first he would need blood.

Only one light was visible in the house, dulled by drawn curtains. Sebastian walked slowly toward it and placed his cold hands on the small panes of glass. For an instant he stood poised against the window, then drew himself up to his full height and reared back.

The Count de Corville groaned with terror as shards of glass flew into the room and a pale gigantic man leaped in behind them. The Count fired his pistol, but its single shot went into the ceiling, sent there more by panic than any real hope of destroying an enemy. His grip on the bottle of brandy in his other hand was considerably firmer. He dropped the empty pistol onto the carpet, leaned back in his chair, and took another drink.

"You've come, have you?" he said. "Have some brandy. Have anything you want. But be good enough to leave me alone."

"I have not come to rob you," said Sebastian. "Where is the girl?"

"Girl? There is no girl. There was one, and there was a Countess, too, but both of them have run away. At least the Countess had the courtesy to leave a letter," said the Count, holding up a sheet of paper of the same kind that Sebastian had found.

Sebastian reached out for it, but the Count thrust it toward a candle and watched it catch fire. "Please," he said. "I have little enough honor left, but at least enough to stop another man from reading that. Where are the others? Surely you did not come alone!"

"You mistake me. I am not the first of a band of interlopers. Indeed, you might almost call me a friend of the Countess."

"Then I can hardly call you a friend of mine. Still, for your own sake, I advise you to leave at once. I expect an insurrection momentarily," said the Count, speaking with the care of a man half gone with drink, "and now that I have murdered the ceiling, we have no weapons."

"Good advice, no doubt," Sebastian said, "but I am thirsty."

"Something to speed the parting guest? Of course. But hurry. I can hear them coming now."

Sebastian had been advancing upon the Count, who might be old and plump, but certainly had blood in him. But he stopped suddenly and whirled toward the broken window behind him. Distant voices drifted into the dim room. He stood poised for an instant too long.

A dozen men forced their way through the opening Sebastian had made. Three of them held torches, and all the rest were armed with scythes and clubs and pitchforks made of wood. Sebastian stepped back when he saw the sharp wooden spikes. The men were unshaven and shaggy-headed, dressed in ragged clothes. They waited just inside the room, as if suddenly awed by the thought of what they had come to do. The Count sat in his chair and smiled foolishly.

"Kill the woman!" shouted a voice Sebastian recognized. "But capture the old man! He may know something of the King's plans."

A woman with red hair revealed herself to Sebastian's night vision, standing behind the men and urging them on. For a moment their eyes met. It was Madeleine Benet. "Watch out for the tall one!" she shouted.

Sebastian did not pause for a reply. He reached for the heavy table behind him, raised it above his head, and sent it crashing across the room. Two men fell beneath its weight, one of them with his skull crushed, and two more fell back through the splintering glass. One of them dropped his torch, and bright flame ran up the gossamer curtains. The Count stumbled out of his seat and toward the angry men who rushed through the flickering fire.

A squat, muscular man ran toward Sebastian, brandishing a scythe. The vampire caught the rusty blade in his right hand, and its owner had one moment of amazement in which to realize that the sharp steel could not cut Sebastian's fingers. Then he found himself in the tall, pale man's embrace, with long teeth slashing at his throat.

A small, flat-faced man rose from the floor, his coat smoldering. Inspired, the Count flung the contents of the brandy bottle over him, then stood back to watch in horror as the man burst into flame. Wailing, he staggered across the room toward Sebastian, who shoved his own victim, throat still gushing, into the writhing puppet of burning flesh. Blood sizzled as two dead men crashed into a corner, and Sebastian, his mouth red and dripping, turned to face the rest.

"Take them!" commanded Madeleine. "There are only two! And find the woman!"

Another man rushed through the mounting flames, and the Count calmly hit him in the face with his bottle. It was too heavy to break, but the man's face was not. The Count struck again and again, then dropped the bottle and stood stupidly beside the window. Arms reached out for him.

Goaded by an instinct he could not explain, Sebastian rushed to his side. The first man to reach the Count had his face ripped off by icy fingers, and Sebastian fell to the floor on top of him, slavering at the shower of crimson. He rolled away just in time to avoid the thrust of a wooden pitchfork and sank his teeth into his attacker's leg. And when the man fell Sebastian was upon him, smashing his head repeatedly into the carpet until it was pulp. He looked up in time to see the Count's round face, white with shock, disappearing into the smoke that obscured the window.

There was still one peasant in the room. Sebastian thought at first that he had frightened the others away, then realized that fire had done the job better than he could hope to. The room was like an oven, and orange flames were crawling up the walls. The black clouds of smoke were blinding. Sebastian's last opponent coughed and stumbled, dropping his club to rub his streaming eyes. He was easy to kill, and he was dead before Sebastian realized that he was little more than a boy.

The country estate of the Count de Corville burned like a house in Hell. Only memory told Sebastian where the window had been. He tore off his smoking clothes, feeling bright agony as his sprouting leathery wings were touched by fire, and burst out into the darkness.

He soared toward the moon, a gigantic bat carried aloft on currents of smoke and summer air. Below him were half a dozen men, holding an impassive prisoner in their arms. And Madeleine Benet, with her flame-red hair, screamed obscenities into the sky and rained blows down upon the helpless Count de Corville.

9

Dr. Guillotin

"I LIVED better when I was a servant! At least I was paid something for my work, and I was never buried in a hovel like this. When is your wonderful revolution going to start killing the damned aristocrats and giving their houses to the people?"

"Be calm, Madeleine. If we had a mansion, there would be still more work for you, unless you expect to have servants of your own."

"Of course I want servants! I want the Countess de Corville down on her knees scrubbing the steps of my palace!"

"First you will have to find her, Madeleine. And if you do, I fear she will end up in prison with her husband and the other conspirators against the National Assembly."

"No, Andre. If I find her, she will end up with her throat cut!"

"You should be going to see Dr. Guillotin, not I. Apparently you have theories on capital punishment that he might want to consider." Andre Latour reached for a peg on the wall and took down a three-cornered hat with a red, white, and blue cockade affixed to the brim.

"You know what my theories on the subject are, Andre. The King and the Queen and all their followers should be executed at once. There will be no freedom for us until we are rid of them all, but you and your friend Dr. Guillotin can find nothing to do but hire carpenters to build you toys."

"I hardly know him, Madeleine, but this is a very important committee, and I'm lucky to be on it. Surely a republican like you must approve of Guillotin's proposal that the same punishment should be inflicted on aristocrats and commoners alike?"

Madeleine turned from her washing and pushed a strand of red hair back from her face. "Why punish commoners at all? Haven't we suffered enough?"

"We must have some sort of order. What about thieves? And murderers? What about the one who's been killing all these women?"

"What?" Madeline looked up sharply. "Who?"

"I shouldn't have mentioned that. We've been keeping it a secret; the people are agitated enough. But several women have been found dead in the streets, horribly murdered. Their throats were slashed, and what's worse, their hearts had been torn out. We can't have any rumors started, but I'm glad you know now. I want you to be careful."

Madeleine stood quite still, her eyes wide. "Their throats? And their hearts?"

"I didn't mean to frighten you . . ."

"I'm not frightened."

"No? You should see your face."

"Don't be ridiculous. Go to your meeting, Andre. You'll be late." She put his hat on his head, running her fingers through his curly hair and kissing him absent-mindedly. Then she opened the door.

She listened while Andre's footsteps trailed off down the narrow stairway. Her hands were trembling. "He is in Paris," she said to herself. "All this time he has been here. And the Countess must be with him."

"Ah, Citizen Latour," said Dr. Guillotin. "Come in. Allow me to present my colleague Dr. Louis, secretary of the Academy of Surgery."

Dr. Louis sat in a corner of Guillotin's consulting room, enjoying a glass of wine which he raised in salute to Andre. Sunlight from a nearby window made the crimson liquid sparkle, and something of the same color showed in his ruddy face. He was a big, hearty man, and Andre had to look at him closely before he could believe the report that Dr. Louis was approaching seventy.

Dr. Guillotin, twenty years younger, somehow appeared older, a thin, nervous, fussy little man who was dressed entirely in black, while his colleague wore the richly embroidered clothing that had gone out of fashion after the fall of the Bastille.

"Well, take a chair, young man," said Dr. Guillotin. "We have much to discuss."

"And take some of this excellent burgundy as well," said Dr. Louis. "We must fortify ourselves, eh? This is a solemn business." Dr. Guillotin nodded as he sat behind his desk, but Andre noticed to his great surprise that Dr. Louis was winking at him.

"A solemn business indeed," said Dr. Louis, reaching out to touch the polished human skull on a shelf beside him. He took it down and held it in one hand. "Death, young man," he said. "That is our concern. Death and heads!" He tossed the skull across the room toward Andre, who caught it instinctively, nearly knocking over his chair in the process. He held the ugly thing gingerly in his hands, trying not to look at it too closely, and was relieved when Guillotin snatched it away from him with an angry look at Dr. Louis.

"Your levity is not appreciated," said Dr. Guillotin.

"But my talents are," said Dr. Louis. "It is easy enough for you to make speeches about a new method of execution that will be just and speedy, but when it comes time to do the job, then you send for me, eh? You are a philosopher, of course, and cannot be expected to soil your hands with the actual business. Really, Citizen Latour, you must drink some of this. No need to be as serious as our friend here. It is only a matter of life and death, isn't it?" Dr. Louis laughed explosively.

"Precisely," said Dr. Guillotin.

Louis took another sip of wine. "Wasn't there a philosopher who worried himself over the difference between the mind and the body?"

"Descartes," said Andre.

"And evidently Dr. Guillotin is his disciple, intent on finding the best way to separate them entirely. It is to be decapitation, is it not?"

"The Assembly is agreed on that," said Andre. "If decapitation is good enough for the nobles, then it is good enough for everyone. We shall have no more hangings, nor any more disgraceful spectacles in which men are torn apart by horses. We shall treat each prisoner with the same dispassionate, impartial justice. We want something quick, and neat, and democratic."

"But there are problems with beheading, too," said Dr. Guillotin, rummaging among the papers on his desk. "I have a letter here from Sanson, the public executioner. He displays a somewhat dubious sentiment by arguing that only criminals of high station have the dignity to bear themselves well during the last moments, and warns us that prisoners who do not cooperate will be able to create a most unpleasant spectacle. Apparently any struggle on the part of the condemned makes it impossible to do the business with one stroke of the sword. He also has the honesty to admit that even a willing prisoner is not always enough. He congratulates himself on his own skill, but warns that provincial executioners are likely to bungle the job. There have been cases where even three or four blows were not sufficient to remove the head, and it would hardly do for our new order to sanction something so clumsy. We must be efficient."

"And so you needed someone with a knowledge of anatomy," said Dr. Louis.

"I lectured in anatomy myself," said Dr. Guillotin.

"I hope I shall never be treated by one of your pupils, then. Your suggestion of having a flat blade drop down upon the neck is completely preposterous. Even the sword would be better."

Dr. Guillotin scowled, but decided to ignore the last remark. "The executioner has something to say about swords. Apparently they grow dull rapidly, and sometimes the blade is chipped in doing its work. He says it is impossible to use the same sword on more than one prisoner. This was no problem when so few were beheaded, but if we are to move forward, we must find something better than a sword."

"I don't understand, exactly," Andre said. "What is wrong with a machine to drop a blade from some great height?"

"Nothing is more welcome than honest ignorance," smiled Dr. Louis. "The basic idea is sound enough, but the blade must not be horizontal, despite my learned colleague's suggestion. Any honest headsman could tell you as much. Why do you suppose their swords and their axes are always curved?"

"I never thought about it," Andre admitted.

"You should study the edge of a blade through a microscope, my boy, so that you could see exactly what it is. No matter how carefully honed, it is still in reality a saw, and it is the sideways motion which does the job. The spine is easy enough to snap, but very difficult to sever. A curved blade, as it penetrates, has the same effect as a saw."

Andre swallowed his wine in one gulp, and Dr. Louis rose genially to pour him another glass from Dr. Guillotin's decanter.

"Of course the blade need not be convex like a sword," continued Dr. Louis, "although that is the design I suggest. It could just as well be concave, or slanted, or even pointed. The important thing, Dr. Guillotin, is that it must not be flat. Such a blade, even if it were heavily weighted and dropped from a great height, could do no more than smash the neck into a bloody pulp. And that, I assume, is not what you have in mind."

Dr. Guillotin took a pinch of snuff. "That is why you have been employed," he said. "I have not studied the physics of decapitation; I merely wish to see justice done. I have advocated this reform for years, but it took a revolution to give my voice the strength it needed."

"Your voice was always strong," said Andre, realizing at the same moment that Dr. Louis was filling his glass for the third time. "I read your pamphlet of 1788, advocating the rights of the Third Estate."

"I missed it," said Dr. Louis. "Wasn't it suppressed immediately?"

"Suppressed by a government that has been supplanted," replied Dr. Guillotin.

"In any case, I see that our young friend is a diplomat. I wondered why he was here. Perhaps he will enable us to work together. Let me show you my plan for the machine."

Dr. Louis reached into his coat and withdrew several sheets of folded paper from an inside pocket. "I understand you are anxious to move ahead, since there is now no provision at all for executions, and the prisons are becoming overcrowded. And if these arrests of political prisoners continue, we shall have to start building new prisons unless we construct this machine quickly. So I hope we shall have no argument about the plans. These specifications have already been submitted to Guidon, who has been employed for years to build the scaffolds for hangings, and he is preparing his estimate now."

Dr. Louis opened the pages and spread them out on Guillotin's desk; Andre rose to peer over his shoulder at the little drawing and the list of instructions. "I think ten feet should be tall enough for the uprights," said Dr. Louis, "and any carpenter should be able to construct the necessary grooves. The principal problem is still with the blade."

"I thought you had decided that it would be convex," snapped Guillotin.

"Of course, of course. But there is another problem. The blade must be narrow enough to cut neatly, yet heavy enough to penetrate by its own weight."

"Perhaps a spring might power it?" suggested Andre. He felt a trifle giddy from the stuffiness of the room and from the wine.

"Far too ingenious," said Dr. Louis. "We must keep things simple, to avoid the possibility of a malfunction. My suggestion is that we allow for a mechanism that will permit us to attach weights to the blade should it prove necessary. That is the significance of these marks here," he added, pointing at the drawing with a thick forefinger. "It should be easy enough for us to guarantee that the thing will drop like a stone."

Dr. Guillotin peered at the plans with rapidly moving eyes. "This scooped-out portion here at the base," he said. "Is that where the prisoner is expected to put his neck?"

"Precisely," said Dr. Louis.

"It will hardly serve," said Dr. Guillotin. "Remember what I told you about the danger that the prisoner might struggle? The executioner was very specific on this point."

"Yes," said Dr. Louis, "flinching is always a problem. It makes surgery difficult, and of course it would be completely unacceptable in an execution, which unfortunately must be done in public. Perhaps we will require men to hold the subject, as we do during a particularly delicate operation."

"Unseemly," said Dr. Guillotin. "It will not look efficient. It might even appear to be cruel."

"We mustn't have that, must we?" said Dr. Louis, chuckling. He wiped a thin trickle of wine from his chin. "Perhaps we will need to devise some sort of clamp, although making room for it will be difficult. It will be easier to tell after we have made a few tests."

"Tests?" sputtered Dr. Guillotin. "There must be no tests! Our first performance must be perfect, or we shall be disgraced."

"I never meant to suggest that we would experiment with prisoners, of course. I think a series of corpses, of different sizes and types, will serve us admirably."

"Corpses?" Andre echoed queasily. "Where shall we find so many?"

"The hospitals are full of them," said Guillotin.

"And fresh ones every day," said Dr. Louis. "Even in the hospitals where your pupils work, eh, Guillotin?"

Dr. Guillotin stood abruptly. "I think we are finished for tonight," he said. "There is nothing more for us to do until we receive the estimate from the carpenter."

"The machine looks as if it will be practical," said Andre, making for the door. He was beginning to feel ill, presumably from the effect of the wine.

"Of course it will," replied Dr. Louis. "And it will be humane. The prisoner will have only time to feel a cold little tickle at the back of the neck."

10

An Empty Street

ALONE, SEBASTIAN wandered through the streets of the city. The nights were cold, and the streets were almost empty. Yet from time to time a solitary figure wandered by, and such occasional victims were sufficient to supply his needs.

It was a brutal business, however, and not to his liking. If he chose young women when he had the luxury to choose, it was because their blood was sweeter, and because their throats were lovelier; but there was little of the pleasure he had known in his past incarnations, when his prey had been lovers and not strangers. He had known banquets, in which the cruelty his condition imposed upon him had been softened by bright eyes and willing hearts, but now he was no more than an assassin.

There was no love in what he did, and no poetry. His sharp, white teeth were inappropriate weapons in a world where his greatest concern was to conceal his presence. Instead, he carried a long, sharp knife, and its ministrations were all he could offer to those who crossed his path.

The thoroughfares were narrow in the dark quarter of the city where he looked for his unwilling lovers; the ancient buildings leaned forward, blotting out the sky, and the streets were little better than sewers. Those who intended to pass Don Sebastian did not go far. They were pulled into alleys, where cold hands smothered their cries, where cold steel slashed their throats, and the former master of a Spanish castle fell upon them in the mud of Paris. And there he gasped at their gushing life, tasting the shock as they struggled beneath him, until finally they were limp and he was satisfied.

And then there was more to do. The contagion that kept him alive was in their blood, and he could not risk the chance that they might rise again to betray the presence of one of the living dead. He had thought to pierce the hearts of his benefactors with wood, in keeping with the legendary prescriptions, but he realized that the evidence he left behind would betray him as surely as the marks of twin teeth which he had taken such pains to avoid.

And so it was necessary to rip away the clothing of those who had preserved him, and to use the dappled blade on their pale flesh. His knife dug deep beneath the curved ribs, leaving a red ruin where once there had been tender beauty, and when he staggered away there was a warm heart in his hands. The wounds he left behind were bloodless, as were the innocents who bore them, but they were no less hideous for that. Sebastian knew of the ancients who practiced such sacrifices, and in truth to him their lives were as close as yesterday. But those hearts had been offered up to glory, while the ones he held in his icy fingers were cast away in gutters, perhaps to be devoured by dogs. There were no gods left to accept such offerings, certainly not Sebastian, who cursed the day when he had been drawn back into the world where he was forced to pose as a lunatic in order to maintain an existence that had no purpose and little pleasure in it.

Don Sebastian had been transformed into a cutthroat and a vagabond, as low a creature as any in a city that teemed with misery and frustration. He was one of the dispossessed. The idea of theft had tempted him, but he had no use for money except to buy himself a home, which was hardly advisable in a time when strangers bearing large sums fell under immediate suspicion as fugitive aristocrats. Moreover, the thought of robbery was distasteful to him, even though killing had become part of his nature.

He slept in a tomb, among the dust of forgotten generations, in a neglected old cemetery on the outskirts of the city.

The Spanish soil he had hidden around the estate of the de Corvilles served him well; in his more reflective moments he was grateful to the old magician, Raoul Rollin, who had provided it on a night that seemed eternities away. As for Juliette, the Countess de Corville, Sebastian's sentiments were ambiguous. He cursed her as the author of all his misfortunes, yet he treasured her as the last companion he had known, a woman of some wit and daring, however untrustworthy she had proven. But it hardly mattered if he hated her or loved her, for it seemed unlikely that he would ever see her again.

In any case, there were more important matters to occupy his attention. Someone was approaching, and the light sound of the quick, small steps promised that the passerby would be a woman. Sebastian slouched against a crumbling building, half hidden by its shadows. The moon was dark, the distant stars blotted out by drifting clouds. Most of those who ventured out at night traveled in groups, and by torchlight, but this was a lone woman, making her way through the darkness. Sebastian fingered his long blade, waited for her approach, and bridled inwardly against the fate that had driven him to such a pass.

His long right arm reached out and caught the woman by the shoulder. She stumbled toward him as he pulled her back into the deeper darkness, his hand reaching for her mouth. She was strong, and as she struggled with him, he was surprised to realize that she had not begun to scream. His undead vision showed her to him in a pale blue glow: a handsome young woman with bright eyes and a strong jaw.

"Sebastian!" she whispered.

The sound of his name startled him, and for an instant he released his grip. The woman staggered back against a wall, and withdrew from her cloak a wooden cross. Sebastian stopped where he stood and considered her. He thought of throwing the knife, then recognized her pale blue eyes and long red hair. This was the woman he knew only as Madeleine, the maidservant of the Countess de Corville.

"I thought I would never find you," she gasped. "Even after I found out where you prowled, I had to walk the streets for weeks."

"You would have done better to stay at home," Sebastian said.

"I think this cross will protect me."

"It means nothing to you," Sebastian said, "and so it means less to me. Such protection is only for the faithful."

Madeleine held the cross aloft, but her full lips twisted when it began to crumble in her hands. The dry wood turned to dust and scattered into the air. Sebastian smiled at her and moved forward.

"Wait!" she said. "Don't kill me. At least listen for a moment."

Sebastian caught her thick hair in his left hand. "I have a moment," he said, "but I have a terrible thirst as well. Be sure that your remarks are entertaining." He held her close to him, the sharp blade of his knife close to her throat.

"I can hardly speak like this," she whispered. "If I wanted to die, I could have found an easier way."

"Your plight is no concern of mine," Sebastian said.

"But yours concerns me. I have come to help you."

The steel point dropped back a few inches, but still it hovered close to her throat, and to her face.

"You made a bargain with the Countess," Madeleine continued, "and she betrayed you. But I shall do better."

"And what have you to offer me?" The knife was lowered, but Madeleine found cold comfort in the knowledge that it was now pointed at her heart.

"Let go of me," she said, "and let me speak. Or kill me and be done with it. I cannot reason with a man who holds a knife."

"You forget that I am not a man at all," Sebastian said, "and that you have nothing to offer me half as precious as your blood. But speak. Sit down against that wall, and do not rise unless you wish to die at once."

Madeleine slumped down, her skirts trailing in the mud. "I shall not move," she said. "Your teeth fascinated me when I saw you, but the knife is less to my liking. Any man might wield one. Still, here we are, as those like you and I have always been. A nobleman holds a commoner in thrall. Don't you see that you are one of us?"

"There is none like me in all Paris. I have seen to that."

"There are thousands like you. Those who have nothing. Those whose whole existence is nothing but a struggle to survive. Can you take your stand with the aristocrats when they have brought you to this?"

"I stand alone," Sebastian said.

"Then stand with me," Madeleine said earnestly. She began to rise.

"Sit. You have promised me nothing worth having, only the chance to pretend I favor one faction over another. And in truth, neither interests me. There is no place in any order for one who feeds on blood."

"But we mean to have blood, and rivers of it. The blood of our oppressors. And if you agree to help me, I promise that you will not starve. I offer you shelter, and more blood than you can drink. You know that our cause is destined to triumph."

"I know nothing about it. I am a beast of prey, and that is what I shall remain. It matters little to me who rules."

"But it should matter to you. Those who rule have the power of life and death, and that should surely be of interest to you. Soon the enemies of progress will begin to die. I know. I am not the common wench that you think me. I have friends who mean to shape the future, and I offer you my help."

"You forget that I have seen your loyalty in action. Your face was among those I saw in the raid on the country estate of the Count de Corville."

"I never promised them my loyalty. I worked for them, and I was paid little enough. When a chance arose for me to be free, I took it. Would you do less? Now I have my liberty, and I want to share it with you. I can make a place for you in the new world we are building."

"The new world. I have heard those words before, centuries ago when men sailed west; but the new world proved to be much like the old, nothing but a scramble for power and gold. There are no new worlds, Madeleine, only those who proclaim them to disguise a viciousness that puts the old worlds to shame."

Madeleine sat in the shadows, hugging her knees and staring up at Sebastian with pale blue eyes. "You are no stranger to cruelty," she said. "How many have you killed since you came among us?"

"Many," said Sebastian. "But I had no wish to be here. And I do only what I must to survive."

"Surely you can see that the same is true for all of us. Did I ask to be born? And can you blame me if I seek to ease my pain?"

"You know nothing of life and death," Sebastian said.

"I grant you that I have never tasted death, but I know more of life than you do. At least I can see what is happening around me. Awake, Sebastian! The world you knew is dead. You are no feudal lord of ancient Spain. You are a victim, as surely as the rest of us, unless you choose to cast your lot with those who will surely be the victors. Look at me. Am I as beautiful as your Countess?"

Madeleine rose slowly, her back to the wall, her blue eyes on the keen tip of Sebastian's blade, but she never faltered as she stood erect and opened her cloak. Her white gown flowed, marked only by a tricolor sash around her waist. She pulled the flimsy cloth away with both her hands. For an instant her full breasts were bare, then her long red hair tumbled down to cover them. "Am I not worthy?" she demanded. "Am I too common to be your mistress?"

Sebastian's dark, dead eyes held hers. Then he looked at the knife. "What you offer me is already mine," he said.

"Only if you prefer a corpse to a lover. You are so alone, Sebastian. Surely you must be lonely, too. At least take me for a friend."

Sebastian said nothing, and his pale face was expressionless.

"I offer you my heart," said Madeleine, caressing his cold fingers and the blade they held. "Or would you rather have it in your hands?" She drew him to her, and stiffened as she felt the sharp point touch her skin.

The knife clattered as it dropped to the cobblestones.

Madeleine took a deep breath and covered herself with her cloak. "Then you are not dead," she gasped as she slumped backward. She could hardly stand. Sebastian turned away from her.

"What do you want in exchange for this devotion?" he asked.

"Much," said Madeleine. "What you denied the Countess. I want every secret you possess. I want your power. Everyone knows how the King opposes us, and how his minions plot against us. I want the power to expose them all. These compromises bring us nothing. I want the truth, and I want death for every man and woman who would stand against us. You will teach me how to find out what I need to know, and I shall use your magic to seek out the oppressors and destroy them all."

"And in return?"

"I will shelter you."

"I prefer to trust myself."

"I will tell you what you need to know. Do you realize that the citizens' militia patrols the streets in search of you?"

"Are they searching for a vampire?"

"Only for a murderer, but that may not make your lot more pleasant if they find you."

"They will not even carry crosses, then, and you have seen what they are worth in the hands of an unbeliever. Your warning is worthless in a city where the religion is atheism."

"Still, you should beware. If you invoke your powers to escape, the witnesses you leave behind will know you for what you are. There are still priests, you know, even though they are in disgrace because of the riches their Church has acquired."

"Your warning is worth little compared with the blood it has cost me."

"Is my devotion nothing?"

"Time will tell. I know that you already have a lover."

"Andre? He is a disappointment. He preaches the overthrow of the government, but he has little taste for blood, even though it is his task to punish the enemies of France."

"Is he an executioner?"

"He is their master, but I suspect that he would rather write laws than enforce them."

"You offer me cold comfort, Madeleine Benet."

"Tell me where you sleep, and I shall find a better place for you."

"No. Tell me where you sleep, and I shall visit you."

"As you say, Sebastian. The last house on that corner there, on the top floor. And do not think I mean to leave you starving."

Madeleine dropped to her knees, groping in the darkness for the knife. Sebastian made no move to help her, but watched with satisfaction when she drove the blade into her left arm, a few inches above the wrist. She lifted up her bloody hand, her face an enigmatic mask.

"Drink," she said. "And believe in me."

Sebastian's mouth fastened on her arm, and his hands stroked her red hair. They stood frozen for a moment, and then they heard the sound of men approaching.

"The militia," said Madeleine. "You must let me go. You must not be discovered." Sebastian raised a crimson mouth and looked at her with empty eyes.

"Is my blood sweet enough for you?" asked Madeleine. Sebastian did not answer. Instead, he turned pale, then gray. His long black hair turned to smoke, and he faded away before her startled eyes.

Trembling in every limb, Madeleine pressed her dark cloak against her flowing wound, then rose to meet the men of Paris.

11

The Hospital

"I UNDERSTAND that people are already calling it 'the guillotine,' " said Dr. Louis.

"I have heard others calling it 'the louisette,' " said Dr. Guillotin. "After all, you invented the thing."

"But you have demanded it for years, and it will be named for you, my illustrious colleague, no matter how many men you bribe to argue that it should be named for me. I am merely the mechanic, but you are the creator, and the credit will be yours."

Dr. Guillotin's face turned sour. "I have never asked for credit, and I want none. This project is for the good of France and not for the glory of any man."

"There is never any glory in this sort of business, and you were a fool not to have realized it long ago. Even the carpenters have more sense, which is why I had so much trouble getting the thing built."

"I know, I know. But to employ a German harpsichord-maker! It hardly seems appropriate. We must be careful not to excite laughter."

"We have very little chance of exciting anything else, except perhaps in the hearts of our victims. And we would have looked considerably more foolish if we had accepted the bid of your man Guidon. Over five thousand livres, when Schmidt offered to do the job for nine hundred! And that includes the cost of the leather bag to take away the head."

"Such details are disgusting. They should be left to the executioner. My only concern is justice, and I have no wish to worry about leather bags. Nor am I interested in seeing a parade of corpses butchered so you can find out if your revolting contraption will do its work."

"No, friend Guillotin. It is yours, not mine. You are the instigator; I am merely conducting a little experiment in physics and anatomy. Perhaps next time you will think longer before you rise to speak in the Assembly. I have heard it said that there is no greater curse for a man than to have his ambitions achieved."

Dr. Guillotin turned away. "Here comes the coach," he said. "I might have trusted that fool Andre Latour to be late. Being saddled with such a fellow is one of the worst aspects of this entire business."

"At least we have a pleasant spot to wait in," replied Dr. Louis. "The grounds of this hospital are wasted on the sick."

The hospital of Bicêtre, a few miles outside Paris, was a converted chateau, and its proprietor had maintained its parks and gardens beautifully, if more for his own pleasure than for that of his patients. Louis and Guillotin had wandered for more than an hour in the cool, sunny morning while their host prepared for the arrival of Andre Latour and his companions. Dr. Louis gave every evidence of enjoying his promenade, but Dr. Guillotin could not conceal his agitation as he hurried toward the coach.

"No wonder you are so thin," said Dr. Louis. "There's no need for all this rush, you know. The horses can move faster than we can."

"I want to get this over with as quickly as possible," snapped Dr. Guillotin.

"Come now. Let us enjoy our day in the country. Our host, Dr. Cullerier, has promised us an excellent lunch, and I will not have his hospitality abused."

Dr. Louis shuffled along with the dignity his bulk demanded, still pausing from time to time, to admire the view around him, but Guillotin paced resolutely forward to meet the new arrivals. Andre Latour stepped from the coach; his manner, as Dr. Louis observed, betrayed a nervousness even greater than Guillotin's. Another man followed Andre out. He was a little shorter than Latour, and considerably calmer. His shoulders were thick, and his hair almost colorless, but what struck Dr. Louis about him was his bland, expressionless face. The doctor could hardly imagine a countenance less distinguished, or less distinguishable. Dr. Guillotin hurried up to greet him.

"You are Schmidt, I suppose?"

"No, sir. I am Sanson, the public executioner."

Dr. Guillotin pulled back his hand, attempting to look as if he had never intended to offer it, while Dr. Louis smiled and clapped Sanson on the back.

"You did bring Schmidt, didn't you?" demanded Guillotin.

"I'm here," said a thin voice from the coach, speaking with a heavy German accent. A small, sharp, hairless head peeped out from the window. "The motion of a coach always makes me a trifle sick, you know. I think I might have had an accident if Monsieur Sanson had not been good enough to keep me distracted with stories about his exploits." Tobias Schmidt, a birdlike man in shabby clothing, stepped gingerly to the ground. "Monsieur the executioner is skeptical about this new device, but I promised him that we had hit upon something to make him happy in his work. Is everything in readiness?"

"You said you set up the machine yesterday afternoon," said Andre.

"I mean the subjects," said Schmidt.

"Our host has promised us a number of specimens," Dr. Louis assured him. "He is waiting for us in the courtyard on the south side of the hospital. Come, gentlemen."

"I am no gentleman," protested Andre. "I am a republican, a citizen of France."

"Very laudable, I'm sure," replied Dr. Louis. "Well, come along in any case." He cheerfully escorted Sanson and Schmidt down a flagstone path toward the hospital, while Andre and Dr. Guillotin hung back, clearly reluctant to be part of the group, yet equally dissatisfied with each other's company.

Andre was the last to enter the gate that Dr. Louis held open. And there he saw the machine that Tobias Schmidt had built. It seemed simple enough—a few beams of wood, some rope, and a curved steel blade that shone dully in the cold sunlight. Yet there was something in the sight of it that made Andre shiver. He looked away from it and saw a shapeless pile on the ground, covered by a number of soiled bedsheets. Dr. Louis shut the gate behind him.

"Of course it should be mounted on a platform," Schmidt explained apologetically. "And it will be when it goes into use. We must have it high enough so the people can see what we are doing, of course. But for today, I thought it would be easier like this, since of course our subjects will not be able to climb the steps, and it will be difficult enough to get them into place. A dead weight is a cumbersome thing."

"Guidon has been awarded the subcontract for the platforms," Dr. Guillotin said drily. "He has been constructing scaffolds for some years."

"Fair enough, no doubt," said Schmidt. "But the price he wanted to charge for building the mechanism! The man is no better than a thief himself, and I wouldn't be surprised if he ended up testing the machine with his own neck."

"Come, Schmidt," said Dr. Louis genially. "There will be a time and place for that. Let us attend to business. Ah, here is my friend Dr. Cullerier. Gentlemen, our host."

A middle-aged man with a pockmarked face entered the courtyard through a small door in one of the hospital's stone walls. Andre looked around apprehensively while the introductions were made. The walls were high, and the space dominated by the mechanical executioner seemed very small. Andre felt hemmed in, and would have excused himself if he could have contrived a suitable reason. But he could think of nothing but the truth, and he was not willing to admit that he was afraid.

Dr. Louis squinted up at the sun, which shone in the sky above but not in the shadowed courtyard. "I think there is no reason why we should not begin," he said.

"Please give me a moment to examine the machine," said Sanson quietly.

"Of course, my dear fellow. But you will see that it is simplicity itself. That is its great virtue, eh? Come, Schmidt."

Andre stepped back so that they could pass, and found himself uncomfortably close to the gray sheets and the bodies he knew must be beneath them. He moved away and leaned back against the wall behind him, raising his head while he took deep breaths, as if he hoped to draw in the fresher air above the courtyard. Only his desire to prove himself worthy of his position kept him from fleeing.

"There is really nothing for you to do but pull this rope," said Dr. Louis, his voice coming to Andre as though from a great distance. "That will release the catch and permit the blade to fall."

"Even the catch is a special feature," chimed in Schmidt. "But it will relieve you of the burden of holding up the blade by hauling on the rope."

"It does seem simple enough," muttered Sanson, "provided that it works. The blade seems to be sharp, and it has a good weight, but I wonder if the drop is long enough. With a good sword and a strong arm, I know what I am about."

"Nobody doubts your skill," said Dr. Louis. "But not every city is as fortunate as Paris, and with machines like this we will have efficient executions throughout all France."

Andre saw that Dr. Cullerier had joined Louis, Sanson, and Schmidt beside the apparatus, but Dr. Guillotin remained standing in a corner, his body rigid but one cheek twitching.

"I think I'm ready," said the executioner.

"We have a variety of subjects," said Dr. Cullerier, "as you requested."

Andre looked to Schmidt, hoping to see some uneasiness in his face. After all, three of the others were doctors, and the fourth was a public executioner, but Schmidt at least might have been expected to exhibit some signs of the distaste which Andre felt so strongly. However, the little harpsichord-maker seemed all eagerness to have his handiwork put to the test.

Dr. Louis lifted one of the sheets. "We should start with a small one, I think, just to demonstrate the soundness of the design. We may have to make some adjustments, of course."

"I have a small boy here somewhere," said Dr. Cullerier. He pulled a sheet unceremoniously aside, and Andre looked away.

"Surely not a child!" said Dr. Guillotin.

"No?" asked Sanson. "I have them often enough. Some of them take to crime quite young."

"Our new government will see that such tragedies are unnecessary," said Dr. Guillotin. "I will not have this device tested on the body of a child!"

"A woman, then," suggested Dr. Louis. "A thin woman, if you have one."

"I have several," said Dr. Cullerier. "One was especially scrawny. A pauper who died in childbirth. Here she is."

"The rigor has passed, has it?" asked Dr. Louis.

"Yes," replied Cullerier, "but she is quite fresh, and will offer as much resistance as if she were alive."

"Come, Citizen Latour," said Dr. Louis. "Help us carry her."

"I will not," said Andre.

"I am surprised you did not offer us her baby!" spat out Dr. Guillotin.

"You dishonor me," said Dr. Cullerier icily. "The child is still living, and I have every hope she will survive."

"Please, gentlemen," said Dr. Louis. "We shall do this poor creature no harm, and this is not the occasion for gallantry. Women sin as often as men, and much as we like to forgive them, we must have justice. It was justice that you wanted, eh, Guillotin?"

He moved toward the uncovered corpse, but Cullerier pushed him gently aside. "These are my patients," he said, as he helped Sanson carry the woman toward the waiting blade.

Despite himself, Andre could not turn away. The woman's dark hair was limp, and so was her haggard face. Schmidt stepped back beside him for a better view, and Andre sidled away until he was standing beside Dr. Guillotin. Neither of them spoke.

The corpse slumped beneath the blade, its neck resting in the hollow at the base of the machine, its hair streaming on the ground. Andre glanced at Dr. Guillotin and saw that his eyes were shut; then he turned back toward the executioner.

"Ready?" asked Dr. Louis.

Sanson nodded.

"Then proceed."

Sanson waited for a moment, then pulled as the rope with two strong hands. The blade flashed down.

Andre jumped at the sound of steel crashing against wood. The blade bounced, and something fell into the dirt, covered with hair. There was no blood at all.

"Bravo," said Tobias Schmidt.

Andre was trembling, but relieved to find himself relatively composed. The speed of the thing was startling, so sudden that it hardly seemed possible to end a life in such short order. It might have been much worse.

Sanson seemed to share Andre's feelings. He looked at the rope in his hands and the head at his feet as if he could not believe how easy it had been. His bland face showed mild surprise. "It seems quite efficient," he said after a while. "It might be best if there were something to catch the head, though."

"Indeed," said Dr. Louis. "We must not have them bouncing into the crowd, must we? Attend to that, Schmidt."

"It will cost a few more francs."

"Of course, of course. Shall we try another woman?"

"Get on with it," said Dr. Guillotin. "I acknowledge that it will take the head off any woman in France."

"How much more for the basket?" asked Andre, trying to represent his constituents.

"A few more francs," said Schmidt.

"I have several men," said Dr. Cullerier. "One of them died after a drinking contest . . ."

"Splendid," said Dr. Louis. "Let us have him." He picked up the woman's head by its hair and carried it back to replace it under the sheets, while Sanson dragged the rest of the body away and helped Cullerier put the new subject in place.

The man was fat and pale, with close-cropped hair. Andre watched with less trepidation and more curiosity as he was dragged into place.

"What worries me," said Sanson, "is that they are already dead. A living subject might be less willing to lie so still."

"We are working on a clamp that will hold the head in place without impeding the progress of the blade," said Dr. Louis.

Sanson interrupted him with a casual pull at the rope. This time Andre made a conscious effort to catch the falling steel, but the machine was too quick for him. It really was remarkably neat, he thought, although he was disgusted to see the severed stump flash by as the head rolled past him.

"Give us your best, Cullerier!" Dr. Louis called cheerily.

"I do have quite a brute here, killed in a duel. He has a neck like a bull. If he yields, your fortunes will be made."

"I think our report will be favorable," whispered Andre. Dr. Guillotin nodded, his lips in a thin grimace, as the bodies were exchanged

The curved blade rattled down again as Sanson tugged casually at his rope, but the satisfying crash Andre had come to expect did not follow. The sound was thicker, and duller. The big head, with its shaggy red hair that reminded him unpleasantly of Madeleine, did not drop to the ground, although it sagged unpleasantly.

"Oh, dear," said Dr. Louis.

"Not too bad," said Dr. Cullerier reassuringly.

Tobias Schmidt rushed forward to examine the results. "It certainly would have killed him," he said.

"I've seen worse," volunteered Sanson. "There was a case where it took more than a dozen strokes to get the head clean off."

Even Dr. Guillotin stepped up to examine the corpse. "Spinal cord completely severed," he said. "Only a few tendons left."

"But not good enough," said Dr. Louis. "Something like this could make a bad impression."

"Let me try again," suggested Sanson. "It was working so well that I hardly pulled the rope."

Andre listened as the blade creaked upward. For some reason he could not have explained, he found this failure much more horrifying than the previous successes. But the sounds he heard reassured him: the crash of steel against wood, and the thud of flesh striking the earth.

"That's done it," said Sanson.

"Still, there's room for improvement," said Dr. Louis. "We can add weight to the blade."

"Or make the uprights higher," Schmidt suggested.

"Still," said Dr. Cullerier, "a good morning's work. A most interesting experiment. Perhaps we should adjourn for lunch? I have two freshly killed capons, and a wine that I think will please you."

12

Two Prisoners

"ANOTHER QUIET night," said Madeleine as she looked down into the street. "Paris sleeps too soundly."

"It is hardly practical to have an uprising every night," replied Andre, "even if they do keep you entertained."

"They do more than that, although I would be the last to deny that they are exciting. But every one has meant more progress!"

"That is only because they are well timed, Madeleine. We must be patient. Sometimes you sound like a Jacobin."

"And so should you!"

"Those lunatics? If they ever came to power, they would destroy the country in a few weeks. Fortunately, there are far too few of them to do any harm."

"There should be one more, Andre. The Jacobins see which way things are heading, even if you don't. The compromises will never work. What we need is blood and more blood!"

"We are at war with Austria, and Prussia too. Aren't the battles bloody enough for you?"

"The wrong ones are dying," answered Madeleine. "Your Assembly was fooled into starting that war by the King, and the Church, and the aristocrats. They're more than willing to have France conquered if it will give them even a prayer of regaining their power. Yet you and your friends make speeches calling for more battles, when the ones who need killing most are here in Paris."

Andre sighed and pushed aside the papers he had been studying by the light of a single candle. He rubbed his eyes and turned to face Madeleine, his old chair creaking ominously. "Of course you know more than anyone else in France," he said, "but unfortunately the people elected me instead of you. And your constant complaints are not making the job easier."

"I am trying to help you, Andre. I only want what is best for France, and best for us. I want you to be a success. How else can a woman achieve her ambitions except through her man?"

"I almost thought you were going to say 'through her husband.'"

"We have discussed all that before, haven't we? Marriage is superstitious nonsense. Do you need a priest's permission to love me?"

"No, but sometimes I think I need God's help. You are never satisfied, Madeleine, not even now when our machine is well employed in taking the heads off the worst of the aristocrats."

"The guillotine? It is wasted. It should be working night and day, until there is not a powdered head left in Paris. You should be seeing to that, Andre, but instead you waste your time with figures."

Andre snatched the papers off the kitchen table and shook them at her. "These figures will determine my future," he said. "Apparently that swine Tobias Schmidt has been cheating us."

"Have you become a bookkeeper now? Must you concern yourself with such petty details?"

"This is no small matter, Madeleine. This is a report from the Minister of Finance himself. Schmidt's estimate was so much less than the first one we received that we accepted it at once, but it appears that we should have been more cautious. Our latest information is that the machines are faulty. The last beheading in Paris was not complete, and there have been complaints from the provinces about the quality of what Schmidt has been sending them. Now an architect has reported that the things could be built for a third of what we have been paying. He even offered an improved model, with brass grooves to keep the blade from sticking, for less than half Schmidt's price, and he promises to deliver it already painted red!"

"You are a fool, Andre. Men do not rise to prominence by counting the cost of brass and paint."

"This is my job, Madeleine, and if I cannot succeed in so small a thing as this, there will be no hope for advancement."

"Jobs are for little men. To be a leader, you must have a dream!"

"My dream is that I must see Dr. Louis tonight and discuss these charges so that we can explain our actions satisfactorily."

"And what about your precious Dr. Guillotin?"

"He has withdrawn. He says he is ill, and I think he means to retire."

"You should prepare to do the same, if you have no more vision than this."

"I will take it under advisement," said Andre quietly, but he slammed the door behind him as he left.

Madeleine stood in the center of the small kitchen and cursed quietly. She looked at the shabby furniture, and at the cracks in the walls that were only half covered with cartoons from the political journals. Then she picked up Andre's chair and smashed it against the floor. The weak leg splintered.

"Good!" screamed Madeleine. "Good!"

She kicked the pieces of wood away and leaned against the table, breathing heavily, her eyes fixed on the flickering flame of the candle. For several moments she did not move, then she rose and carried the light to the window. She drew back the curtains and placed the candle on the sill, searching the street again for signs of life. All she saw was the tall, sturdy figure of Andre Latour as he strode away from her.

"Run," she whispered. "Hurry. You mustn't be late, must you? And you mustn't be here when Sebastian comes."

She found it fascinating to notice how short Andre looked when viewed from several stories up. He seemed more like a clerk than a hero. She tried to imagine Sebastian passing him, and felt certain that there was no distance great enough to make the vampire look small. She longed to see him again, and hoped that the light in the window would bring him up the stairs at once, but at the same time she realized that she could not count on his coming at all: he might well be more interested in fresh blood than in her promises. Considering how little she had to offer him, his visits were puzzling, and Madeleine could imagine only one motive for them. Despite his awesome power, Don Sebastian was lonely.

Deep in thought, Madeleine sank into a chair to wait, wondering how much farther Sebastian's isolation could carry her, and how much farther it would be safe for her to go.

Three loud knocks rattled the door, and Madeleine jumped up to answer it, her schemes and speculations vanishing at the sound.

Sebastian stood on the threshold. A long black coat hung down to his ankles, and a broad-brimmed hat shadowed his features. He stood stiffly in the doorway while Madeleine reached out to embrace him, but as she drew him into the room she felt his fingers stroke her shoulder, and she realized with a shock of pleasure that his cold caresses were worth more to her than Andre's had ever been.

"You should be wearing that cockade I gave you," said Madeleine.

"It has been centuries since I wore another man's colors."

"But those colors are for every man. That is what they signify."

"Then they are not for me."

"But they will protect you, Sebastian. A stranger without them is more likely to be challenged by the night patrols."

"I prefer to protect myself."

"What is it, Sebastian? Why do you come if you mean to be so discourteous to me?"

"Curiosity, I suppose."

"About me?"

"In part. And your revolution fascinates me. It is as strange to me as magic is to you, and my thirst for knowledge is almost as strong as my thirst for blood. I have only two passions, but that is more than most dead men have."

"Three," said Madeleine. "You forgot that I saw you

with the Countess. Have you ever thought of making love to me, Sebastian?"

"As often as I have thought about making you one of my kind," he said. "But neither act would please you."

"Perhaps you are right. You do frighten me, but something in me loves the fear. How can you be so sure what I want when I don't know myself?"

"Your passions are of a different kind. You do not love pleasure much, nor do you long to solve dark mysteries. What you want is power."

"Of course I do. And who does not?"

"It is the emptiest of passions, Madeleine. There is neither truth nor beauty in it. Yet I think you will have to hold it in your hands before you realize that it is hollow. You sought me out because you think I can help you, and perhaps I can, but the result may not please you. Surely you can see where my efforts have brought me."

"Sit there," she said, "and have done with philosophy. Your practical instructions are of more use to me."

"It is as I said," replied Sebastian, but he took the chair.

"Why do you help me, then, if you think so little of me?"

"I think as much of you as anyone in Paris."

"You would rather be with the Countess, I think, even though she betrayed you."

"And should I be more grateful to you, Madeleine? The same night when the Countess fled, you were part of the rabble that attempted to destroy me."

"Then you do love her!"

"I love no one in this world, least of all myself."

"And you hate me."

"There is enough hatred here, without my adding to it. Neither of you could appreciate my position, I am sure, but I see you and the Countess as two sides of the same coin. Two masks, Madeleine, with but a single face behind them. And my only interest is to see which way the coin will fall. I am the lover who waits for midnight to see what lies behind the mask."

"You know that the Count has been imprisoned?"

"I guessed as much. I saw him captured."

"He has been found guilty of conspiring against the revolution. He was encouraging the invasion of France to protect his own interests."

"Very likely."

"He will be guillotined tomorrow."

"I met him only briefly. A surprising man. His wife had so much contempt for him that I did not expect him to put up any kind of fight at all."

"No doubt you will mourn for him?"

"I think not. But I respect him more than his wife did. The two of you are alike in that as well. You seem to care nothing for the men you swore to love."

"Love must be earned," said Madeleine.

"If that were true, which of us would be worthy of it? The world would be full of Sebastians, fit for nothing but seeking victims in the night."

"And so it is, Sebastian."

"How goes your search, then?"

"I have you, I think, and certainly I have Andre, although he does not really please me anymore. But perhaps that is not what you meant. My other search has gone well, too," she said, her blue eyes cold.

"The spells proved useful?" asked Sebastian. His hat rested on his knee, but his dead eyes were still shadowed by his heavy brows.

"More than you might imagine."

"You must not take me for a fool, Madeleine. Think what you will of Andre, but never imagine that I am your devoted servant."

"I have been a servant, and I know how devoted they are. I only meant to say that I put your spells to uses other than the ones you might have expected. My mother was a wise woman, and she taught me many things. With what I already knew, I was able to do more with your tricks than you intended."

Sebastian smiled, showing long white teeth. "Red hair is said to be the sign of a witch," he said.

"I do what I can," said Madeleine, and she was smiling too. "I am not a countess, and cannot pay wizards to do my work for me. It follows that I must do it myself."

"Then perhaps you have no further need of me."

"I need you more than ever. I have done a few small things to satisfy myself, but I am still far from the centers of power, and I see now that Andre will not be able to help me to get much closer. I must reach the Jacobins."

"The Jacobins? And who are they?"

"One of the parties in the Assembly. Sometimes they are called the Party of the Mountain, because they occupy the highest seats. And I think their position enables them to see more, for they are the only ones with the vision to realize what France must do."

"And what is that?" asked Sebastian.

"The King must die. And the Queen. And all their followers. They plot against us, and we shall not be safe until they are gone. Even when the royal family tried to get out of the country, the moderates who still control France would not realize the truth. They want to keep that treacherous coward Louis XVI as a figurehead, even though it's plain enough that he means to destroy them all."

"What has this to do with me?" Sebastian asked.

"You are a Spaniard."

"I have never denied it."

"And the King of Spain is our King's cousin."

"Indeed? The last time I saw Spain we were at war with France, but that was long ago."

"We are already at war, and there is reason to believe that a move against the throne would bring an attack from Spain. Nothing would please the Jacobins more than to think that Spain was on the brink of revolution."

"But is there any reason to think that this is true?"

"You are my reason, Sebastian. I mean to introduce you to the Jacobins as an agent of the Spanish revolution."

"A lie of epic proportions," said Sebastian, and for the first time Madeleine heard his laughter. The sound was enough to silence her for a moment. "Such a story could not be maintained for long," Sebastian continued.

"But long enough. Once we had their support, we could prove useful in other ways. I promise you, Sebastian, these men mean to rule France. There will be a new order, and when we have achieved it, you will never want. You told me how well the Spanish Inquisition served you three hundred years ago, and I can promise you that France will provide you with as many victims. You cannot mean to cast your lot with the aristocrats?"

Sebastian stood up and looked out of the window. "Their cause seems doomed," he said. "Once their claims to privilege are doubted, there is nothing to sustain them but the power their forefathers had, and that is long since dissipated. I might not believe you, Madeleine, but I have seen the mobs marching in the street."

"They will march again, Sebastian. Are you with us?"

"Your idea promises some entertainment," he said. "Do you mean to offer them sorcery?"

"Not to offer it, but to provide it nonetheless. Those who deny God have no faith in the Devil. But we shall know their enemies, and we shall find them, and we shall destroy them. With what we can do for them, they will soon forget all about Spain."

"Are you so sure of yourself, Madeleine?"

"I have reason to be. But can I be sure of you?"

"I have agreed to try your plan, have I not?"

"Then I am sure. I have proof enough already, if it comes to that. I was almost afraid to tell you, Sebastian, but your spells proved most useful. Now I am sure that we can serve the Jacobins, for I have found the Countess de Corville."

Sebastian raised one eyebrow, but made no other response.

"She was right here, in Paris. After all this time."

"She would have been wiser to emigrate," Sebastian said.

"She could not believe the truth. She still hoped to have her power restored. I almost wish I could have left her longer where she was, Sebastian. You should have seen her!"

"Where was she, then?"

"She had hired herself out as the serving wench in a common tavern, carrying wine to laborers, and each one had his hands on her. I never hope to see a prettier picture, not until I see her head drop into a basket."

"And will she die tomorrow with the Count?"

"The day after. Andre has some influence with the executioner, and I arranged for the postponement. I want her to see her husband die. I want her to know what to expect. She believes that she will be killed tomorrow, but I have given her an extra day. After she has seen that fat toad die, I expect her to spend a pleasant night."

"You are a remarkable woman, Madeleine. I regret that I must leave you so soon."

"Have I displeased you, Sebastian?" Madeleine's voice was anxious.

"Not at all. But I have other business."

"Stay with me a little longer, then."

"It is impossible. Your man will be returning soon, but that is the least of my worries. Look at my face."

Madeleine stared as he held the candle up. His skin was dead white, his cheeks were sunken, his dead eyes were little more than hollow sockets. "And look at this," he said, brandishing his knife. "If I spend the night with you, you will taste steel before the Countess does. I am dying, Madeleine. I must be fed tonight."

She stepped toward him, ignoring the jagged blade. "You are too weak to hunt," she said. She embraced him, and felt the blade catch her a few inches below her throat. She gasped as she turned to open the shallow wound. "I cannot give you all you need," she whispered, "but take this."

She opened her arms, and felt his head sink down upon her breast.

13

The Executioner

THE GUILLOTINE stood under the sun in the Place de Grève. The beams of wood that formed the uprights were taller now, and they had been painted red. The curved blade designed by Dr. Louis had been changed to one that slanted downward, but only after much debate. King Louis XVI, under house arrest but still the monarch, had demonstrated his interest in justice by suggesting that the blade should be slanted in two directions to form a point, but he had been ignored. The leather bags, supplied at no extra charge by Tobias Schmidt, waited to be filled, lying on the platform constructed by the disappointed contractor Girard. A clamp to hold the prisoner's head in place, demanded by Sanson the executioner, had been dutifully provided, but its design still needed further modification. Andre Latour was in daily conference with the architect Giraud, planning to make the machine cheaper and more efficient.

Only Dr. Joseph-Ignace Guillotin, among all these men, was doing nothing to advance improvements in the mechanical executioner. He was not even present. Yet his name was the one most frequently spoken by the thousands of men, women, and children who had gathered to gaze up at the invention he had inspired. He was perhaps the most famous man in Paris.

Sanson, his bland face imperturbable, stood on the platform and looked at the crowd like an actor counting the house. "More of them come each time," he said to his son.

"Give them a Count and they will come," replied the boy. "They don't seem to care for thieves and murderers anymore."

"Be sure to get a good grip on the hair. We don't want another accident."

"But they say the Count de Corville is bald! I can hardly hold him by his wig."

"Hold him by his ears, if you must, but don't let him pull back at the last instant. We are paid to remove heads, not to slice them in two."

Below the guillotine, Andre Latour conferred with Dr. Louis, both of them grateful for the armed guards that stood between them and the spectators. The sound of the impatient mob was like the vast whisper of the sea.

"I don't believe it," Andre said. "It can't be true."

"You should have talked to Sanson. He says he has seen their eyes move. I wonder what our friend Guillotin would think."

"I think we should forget all about it. The device is a great success, but we might have trouble if the wrong people heard about this. What good will it do us to know if the heads live on or not?"

"You are too practical," said Dr. Louis, his red face beaming. "Of course it will do us no good to know. But don't you wonder? It's only another experiment, my boy."

"And one I do not wish to see conducted. You will risk everything for the sake of your curiosity."

"Be calm. I am not a politician, and I have no wish to publish my findings. But I am a scientist, and I must know. It will be our secret, eh?"

Some members of the audience were spared the press of the crowd; the best seats were near the windows of the buildings that surrounded the guillotine. Visitors to the city, intrigued by the novelty, paid high prices for the chance to enjoy the view from above. But even on such heights there was democracy, for the windows of the nearby prison looked down on the same sight.

And in one of these narrow windows, the Countess de

Corville clutched at the bars, weeping in fury and frustration as the long blond hair was chopped away from the back of her neck.

"I would have left it till tomorrow, dear," said the old woman with the shears, "but orders are orders. Such pretty hair, too, but you won't miss it for long, will you? I wouldn't look through that window if I were you, though. There's nothing there you want to see. Just sit quietly and pray. There, that's done it. Would you like to see a priest?"

The Countess, held in place by two sturdy matrons, twisted her head around and saw her barber gathering the fallen locks of hair into her apron. "What are you going to do with that?" she screamed. "Cast a spell on me?"

"Oh, no, dear. I hope I'm a good woman, and I'm certainly no witch. But it's such fine hair, I thought I might sell it to a wigmaker."

The Countess lunged at her, but had hardly time to move before she felt four strong hands push her back against the bars.

"No sense in being mad at me," the old woman said as she retreated. "It's all for your own good. The hair catches the blade, dear, and that makes things much more painful. You're better off without it, and I'm a poor woman, aren't I? I don't mean any harm. In fact, I've brought you a visitor."

The Countess stopped her stream of tears at once. She tried to raise her hands to wipe her eyes and cover her shaggy head, but her guards made that impossible. She looked down at the shabby dress she had worn as a tavern girl, torn in her arrest and soiled by her imprisonment; she would almost have preferred to be naked. "Who is it?" she asked the walls. She stood a little straighter, and she shook her head to cast away her tears as best she could. "I knew they would not kill me," she said. "I have never done anything to anyone."

The old woman backed out through the heavy wooden door, grinning toothlessly, and disappeared into the darkness of the corridor. The only light in the cell drifted through the barred window behind the Countess, who looked anxiously toward the gloom outside the door for her salvation.

A dark figure waited there. The Countess de Corville

strained forward, and Madeleine Benet stepped down onto the stone floor, a small smile on her full lips.

The Countess did not speak, but she slumped down with such abruptness that she might have fallen without the aid of her warders.

"I wanted to see you once more," said Madeleine, "before I see that long neck shortened. That gown does not become you, Madame Countess; or did I tell you that the last time we met?"

The Countess raised her head. "How can you hate me so much?" she asked.

"It is not difficult. I have hated you for years."

"Was I so cruel to you, Madeleine?"

"It was enough. It was enough just to know that I was the servant, a person of no importance, who lived only to satisfy your whims. You remember Andre, and how you laughed at his ambition? He has become a man of some influence; in fact, he arranged for me to see you here. Soon I think you will be impressed with him; you could hardly be otherwise, since his work led to the creation of that machine out there, the one that will remove your husband's head today, and will do as much for you tomorrow."

"But you cannot want me dead! I have never plotted against anyone. I am nobody."

"True enough, but you should have realized it long ago. In twenty-four hours, it will be even more clear to you."

"You are mad. It is not so bad to work for another—you have seen me do as much."

"And no sight has ever pleased me more, except for the look on your face when the militia arrested you. To tell the truth, though, I am enjoying the present more than most. I wish I could watch you while the Count loses his head, but I want to be close enough to feel his blood splash into my face. My only consolation is that I know you will be watching too."

"I would not give you the satisfaction, you icy-eyed slut!"

"Of course you will," said Madeleine. "You will not be able to resist. In a moment you will be alone. You will hear the drums roll, and you will know whose death they announce. You will not be able to keep your skinny face away from the window, will you? That is why I saw to it that you should die the day after the Count. I know you cared little for him, even less than I care for Andre, but I know you will be compelled to see him die."

The Countess drew herself up to her full height. "I promise you that you will be sorry for this day's work," she said. "Not even my death will prevent my vengeance."

"The guillotine will quiet you, I think. You have no magic left, Madame Countess. I did not mention it before, but you should know that your friend Don Sebastian has now become my ally. You could expect no less, considering how you betrayed him. Rest assured, the executioner will be your last lover."

The Countess struggled fiercely against her captors, who dragged her down to the stone floor, pressing her face into the filth.

"Leave her," said Madeleine as she backed away. The Countess lay sobbing on the floor while the others withdrew. She thought she was alone until she heard the voice of Madeleine Benet ring out again: "You should have kept me on to dress your hair, Madame Countess. Your present style does not become you."

The door slammed shut.

The Countess had no way of telling how long she spent stretched out on the stones, but when she heard the shouts of the crowd below, the window beckoned to her like a mesmerist.

Far beneath the bars she clutched, the tumbrels rolled. Crude wooden carts crawled toward the guillotine, crowded with those who were condemned to die. And in the first, his head jerking from side to side like a puppet's, was the stubby figure of the Count de Corville.

"Henri," whispered the Countess. "I never wished this for you." She looked away, and then looked back at him again.

He leaned against the flimsy wall of the tumbrel, numbed by the gargantuan voice of the mob. He stared down in bewilderment at the red shirt he had been obliged to wear. A stone flew past his face, and he looked after it in fascination, wondering where it would land. The cart stopped suddenly, and someone took him by the arm.

"Not this one," said Andre.

"He is the best subject," said Dr. Louis. "At least we can be sure that he has some intelligence. He is not a common cutthroat like some of these others."

"I feel that I know him too well," said Andre. He would have continued if he had not been interrupted by Tobias Schmidt, who pushed his way through the guards and looked up beseechingly at Dr. Louis.

"Watch," said the little German, "and see how well it works. No improvements are required. I know I have enemies, and that they talk against me, but there could not be a better machine, and it could not be built as well for less."

"No doubt, no doubt," said Dr. Louis, his ruddy face beaming down on Schmidt. "Still, it might have been better if you had not applied for a patent. There has been some resentment. In any case, you are talking to the wrong man. I am only a scientist. Speak to Citizen Latour, here."

Dr. Louis moved toward the steps that led to the guillotine, only a step behind the Count de Corville and his guards. The murmur of the mob rose to a shout as the Count stumbled up the thirteen steps to stand upon the platform. He glanced up at the guillotine, then shut his eyes. When he opened them again, he was staring into the face of Henri Sanson, the executioner.

"Shouldn't you be wearing a mask?" asked the Count. "I always imagined that you would."

"There is no need for that," replied Sanson calmly.

"No," said the Count. "Now you are a hero."

"And I hope you are a brave man. If you try not to struggle, it will make my work much easier."

"Surely Dr. Guillotin has already done that," sneered the Count, but the last syllable caught in his throat, and he knew that he would not have the strength to speak again. It was all he could do to remain standing. His vision grew unnaturally keen, and he saw the bright blade above his head gleam against the sky like a picture etched in glass. The basket below the guillotine was new, and the design of the woven straw touched him with its simple beauty, while the splashes of dried blood beneath it seemed to be painted in patterns of obscure significance.

Someone tied his hands behind his back and pushed him gently forward into Sanson's waiting arms. The taunts of the crowd were no more than a high ringing in his ears, and the thought of death seemed less vivid to him than the fear that he might disgrace himself at the last minute by vomiting all over the executioner.

Below him, Dr. Louis was attempting to pull Andre up the stairs for a closer view of the proceedings.

"You can conduct your experiment without me," snapped Andre. "I must wait here for Madeleine."

"Nobody could get through that crowd now, my boy, so you might as well come and help me. Don't you want to know? It will be a splendid joke on all of us if it turns out that the thing is not painless after all."

"What?" wailed Tobias Schmidt in Andre's ear. "Of course it is painless! Has everyone turned against me?"

"If they have not, Schmidt, then they soon will." Schmidt whirled at the sound and saw the architect Girard standing behind him.

"You!" screamed Schmidt. "You dare to come here? Assassin! Hypocrite! Slanderer!" The voices of the crowd rose behind him like a chorus.

"You are a thief and an incompetent!" shouted Girard. "I wonder that you dare to show your face here!"

"Dr. Louis!" cried Schmidt, "I appeal to you for justice!"

"Citizen Latour," Guidon began; but Andre had already ducked away and hurried up the steps behind Dr. Louis.

Three men were pulling the Count de Corville toward the guillotine. The world spun around him as they dragged him down, and the high wall of the prison caught his eye for an instant. There seemed to be a pale face at each barred window, and one of them belonged to his wife.

The Countess pressed forward until her head was almost wedged between the steel bars. Horror compelled her; she could not turn away. The citizens of Paris seemed to be dancing around the scaffold to the solemn beat of a drum roll.

She stared with wide eyes as her husband was stretched out prone beneath the blade and carefully maneuvered into position, and she could almost feel her own throat pressing into the wooden hollow of the guillotine. She saw the executioner reach for the rope.

"Wait, father! The wig!" Sanson's son reached down and snatched off the Count de Corville's powdered wig. Shouts and laughter came from a thousand throats as it was held aloft, and the Count was surprised to feel the heat of a blush on his face. Above the noise he heard a hideous rhythmic squeak. At first he took it for the sound of the guillotine, but then he realized that what he heard was the sound of his own voice. He began to tremble violently.

The executioner's son waved the wig cheerily above his head, exuberantly careless of its resale value. He spotted a voluptuous redheaded woman pushing through the crowd, her arms raised eagerly, and he tossed the thing to her.

"Madeleine," said Andre, half sickened by the ecstatic expression on her face.

The Count felt someone grab him by the ears and yank his head forward. He yelped at the sharp pain, and his eyes filled with tears. As he tried to blink them away, something rough struck him in the face.

For a moment he could could not see at all. He felt the pressure on his ears again. Two hands seemed to be pulling him upward. Was it possible that he had been reprieved? Someone was staring into his eyes, a red-faced old man he had never seen before. The noise of the crowd was almost deafening; it made the Count feel dizzy.

"Look. The basket cut his cheek."

The Count wanted to squirm away from the hands holding his ears, but he found to his horror that he could not move. He tried to speak.

"Look, Andre. The lips are moving!"

The Count wondered for an instant how it was possible to hold a man of his weight aloft so easily. Then, all at once, he knew. He opened his mouth to scream.

"My God," said Andre. "He's still alive! He knows."

And at his words, the eyes turned in the dripping head that

Dr. Louis held in both his hands. Andre stood rigidly while the dead Count's bulging eyes studied him. The heavy lids began to droop.

"Come, Citizen de Corville!" Dr. Louis was shouting in the thing's right ear. "Another effort!"

The eyes blinked again, and a pink froth covered the thick lips. Then the face went slack.

"Less than a minute," said Dr. Louis. "Do you suppose he's done?" He waited for a moment, clearly discouraged, then let go of one ear and tweaked the Count de Corville's nose. At once the entire face contorted itself into a hideous grimace, its features writhing as it hung sideways in the air.

Dr. Louis was startled enough to drop the head. It bounded across the platform, the executioner's son pursuing it with an open leather bag.

Andre turned away and saw Madeleine beaming up at him. She was still clutching the wig. A yellow dog brushed past her and joined the pack of starving mongrels below the scaffold. Their pink tongues worked eagerly as they lapped the blood up from the cobblestones.

14

A Visitor from Spain

THE COUNTESS de Corville huddled in a corner on her bed of straw, her wide eyes staring through the window of her cell and into the empty darkness beyond. Nothing could be seen there but the night, yet the image of her husband's severed head seemed to float just outside the bars, its features wavering and changing to become her own. She had tried shutting her eyes, but even that would not blot out the flickering faces and their butchered necks. Nor could she dull the echo of a thousand voices cheering, not even with her hands over her ears.

She shivered against the stone walls, but not from the chill of the night. It was the darkness that terrified her, almost as much as the thought of the morning light that would soon announce the day of her own appointment with the guillotine. The back of her neck was cold where her hair had been clipped away, and she could almost feel the touch of steel upon it. All that sustained her was her fury at her fate, and her hatred for the woman whose machinations had condemned her. The Countess would gladly have given her life to rob Madeleine of this triumph, but it seemed impossible. A bloody bruise on her forehead was all she had to show for her frantic attempt to beat out her brains against the stones of the prison; she had not been able to bear the pain.

A ribbon of light slipped under the cell door and passed

away with fading footsteps; the jailer was making his rounds. The Countess heard muffled voices respond to the cruel rattling of his keys, then only silence. She wondered how many hours were left before morning. The night was long, but it could never be long enough. She turned toward her window and moaned when she saw a pale glow against the blackness of the bars.

Yet the light did not seem to be the sun's, nor was it like any she had ever seen before. A luminous, blue-green fog drifted into her cell, its tendrils stretching out from the night as if it were alive. It might not have been the dawn, but it was no less frightening. Its dim, pulsating light cast shadows on the gray stones as the Countess shrank back into her corner, her fingers stifling a scream.

The mist swirled into a shape, seeming to draw in upon itself as its light began to dim, and in the fading glow the Countess saw two dark hollows that might have been eyes. The last flickering wisps of fog became writhing fingers as the darkness fell.

"Juliette," said a deep voice.

"Sebastian!"

The Countess jumped up and staggered toward him, then suddenly stopped.

"And have you come to mock me too?" she asked. "I heard your name today from Madeleine."

"And I heard yours," Sebastian replied. "That was what decided me."

The Countess swayed dizzily, one hand to her heart. "Why have you come, Sebastian? I know I abandoned you, but can it please you so much to see me suffer?"

"I have not come to mock you, Juliette. I hope I am no crueler than I need to be. I came to offer you what little help I can."

She stumbled forward and wrapped her arms around him, her eager face upturned. "Then you have come to set me free?"

"That I cannot do. But I can offer you another prison in exchange for this one."

"What do you mean? Of course you can release me. We can be gone as easily as you came. Your magic will save my life, Sebastian. Take me where you will, as long as it is away from here."

"I cannot take you out, nor can I save your life. I can bring you only death, and a bondage more oppressive than the one you know now."

The Countess stepped away from him and studied his pale face. "What do you mean, Sebastian? Will you save me or not? Don't torture me!"

"I must. You have seen me drift through those bars, but you are still a mortal, and your flesh will not melt as mine does. I can be gone in a minute, but you could never follow me."

"The door, then! You have told me that you are stronger than any living man. Break it down, Sebastian. You will not leave me here?" She clutched at his cold hands.

"The door might be opened, Juliette, but there are many armed men between you and freedom."

"And do you fear them?"

"Not for myself; their weapons will not harm me. But they will surely kill you long before you reach the open air."

"We must try, Sebastian. Surely there is at least a little chance, and even if there is not, I would rather face a sword thrust or a pistol shot than lie under that hideous machine while the assembled vermin of Paris mock my death. Just to know I had cheated them would make my murder in these corridors seem sweet."

"I intend to cheat them," Sebastian said. "There is another way. It may be worse than death, and yet I think that you will choose it."

"What could be worse than death?"

"To be one of the living dead. To die in my arms tonight, and wake as a vampire when the sun sets next."

The Countess dropped his hands. She shuddered once, and hugged herself as if the touch of her own arms could keep her warm.

"How many hours are there till dawn?" she asked.

"It is not yet midnight," Sebastian replied.

"Must I decide at once?"

"Soon, Juliette. I have other work to do before sunrise."

"With Madeleine?"

Sebastian did not reply.

"How can you stay with her, Sebastian? Do you love her? And if you do, why have you come to me? She will not be pleased if I escape the guillotine."

"I owe you this much, I think. She used my magic to find you. And I do not expect her to find out what happens here tonight. If she does, she will discover you again, and there will be no way for me to bring you back from death a second time."

"Then you mean to return to her? You do love her?"

"I love no one. You and Madeleine have taught me how little love is worth in a world like this. And despite what you both think, there is little enough to choose between you."

"No, Sebastian. If you believed that, you would have left me for the guillotine."

"That would have meant choosing, Juliette, and I wish to see the game played out, whatever the risk may be."

"And do you know how the game will end, Sebastian?"

"It will end badly. I promised you that when we first met. The time to which you called me has been cursed, and those who summon dark powers to defy their destinies often lose more than they gain."

"And you say that, Sebastian, despite what you are?"

"I say it because of what I am. Be warned, Juliette. I shall return in a few hours for your decision."

"No! Don't leave me alone. I cannot trust you to return if you see her again. Take me now. I am ready."

The Countess de Corville reached for the rags below her throat and tore them away. Sebastian stepped toward her.

"Wait," she whispered. "Please. One minute more. I am still afraid to die, Sebastian. Do you promise me that I shall rise again?"

Sebastian nodded. "Even as I have done," he said.

"And shall I see you then?"

"I promise it. I have denied myself a companion for too long, out of nothing more than caution, but I put my faith in you."

"Then I am the chosen one?"

"See that you do not betray me, Juliette."

"I am yours, am I not? But I am terrified. See how my hands shake? What is death like, Sebastian?"

"Words cannot describe it. And they are not necessary. Soon you will know more than I can tell you. They will bury you, and tomorrow night I shall find your grave. By then death will hold no mysteries for you."

"I am not brave enough for this," the Countess said. "Will you be my lover while you take my life? At least let me die in ecstasy."

Sebastian's cold hands ripped away her last remaining garments. His pale face was grim. "Only death will conquer your fear," he said.

The Countess reached out with her slim arms, her high breasts trembling. She stood poised for an instant, then backed away toward her bed of straw. "Help me," she said. "I know what we must do, but I don't dare. You must force me."

Sebastian stretched out his white fingers toward her, but when he touched her naked shoulder the Countess ducked away. He lunged across the room, caught her by the throat, and pushed her down onto the straw. The Countess fell on her back, her long legs twitching, her face wild with terror. Her broken fingernails scratched at his scarred face until he caught both of her flailing arms and scraped them outstretched against the rough stones; she shuddered violently under him as his weight pressed her toward the floor. His head dropped down upon her, and spasms shook her body as his icy lips flickered over her soft breasts. Her head thrashed from side to side in protest, but her pale thighs opened to receive him, and he heard her sigh as her rigid muscles yielded to the luxury of passion for the last time.

For a long moment there was no sound in the cell except her heavy breathing and the rustling of straw. Then she whimpered and began to lick his cheeks and neck with her warm tongue.

"Do it quickly," she wailed, her voice rising. "Do it now."

Sebastian's bright fangs ripped into her jugular and he felt her hot blood fill his mouth. His hand closed over her lips before she had a chance to scream, but her teeth bit into his dead flesh. Her frightened eyes were huge, and her body bucked under his like a wild horse, but at the same time her clutching hands pulled him toward her. He stroked her slender body until her quivering limbs were almost still, but he kept his left hand pressed over her writhing lips, and as he took her down into his dark domain he felt her small teeth meet, tearing away a piece of his palm.

It caught in her throat as she died.

"Citizen Robespierre," said Madeleine.

Sebastian bowed, but he did not extend his hand.

"A late meeting," said Maximilien Robespierre. "I hope you will forgive me. The Jacobin Club had one of its sessions here tonight, and our difficulties are so great that I hardly thought it suitable to meet you under such circumstances."

"Late hours are congenial to me," Sebastian said.

"Indeed," said Robespierre. He ushered them through a spartan hallway and into a plainly furnished room. "I share the sentiment. When all the world sleeps it is easier to think, almost as if the fact that so many are at rest cleared the air of random thoughts and made room for new ideas."

"There are fewer thoughts in the air," Sebastian said, "but more dreams."

"Just so," said Robespierre. "Please be seated, both of you. It is as you say. When I sit up in the hours before dawn, I feel that I can sense the dreams of France. And in the daylight, I do what I can to fulfill those dreams."

"A commendable ambition," said Sebastian. He sank into a plain wooden chair, paying no apparent attention to Madeleine, who seated herself alone on a small couch near him. Robespierre remained on his feet, pacing back and forth before a small fireplace where a single log had turned to embers of red and black.

"Citizeness Benet tells me that you have come from Spain."

"I do," Sebastian replied. His dark eyes took in the small room, with its high ceiling and uncarpeted floor. The door they had come through was closed, and the only other exit, in the opposite corner, was covered by a curtain.

"No windows, as you observe," said Robespierre. "I have enemies. No doubt you can understand my position. There is no future in carelessness, is there? Perhaps that is why you have not removed your cloak, or even your hat. Do you realize that I can hardly see your face?"

"His position is precarious," said Madeleine. "Foreigners are not welcome here in France."

"Precisely," said Robespierre. "We are surrounded by enemies. We are already at war, and when we do what we must with the King, we shall have still more to contend with. It was easier for them in America, with an ocean between them and Europe; but when Frenchmen wish to be free, they threaten every crowned head on the continent. Do you think you can help us?"

"I wish to help my own people, nothing more."

"Well said. I can understand a man who looks after his own interests. If you had claimed a disinterested love for France, I would have been compelled to doubt you. And is there really hope for a revolt in Spain?"

"Are we any less oppressed than you have been? Or are we less courageous? And is our King not a Bourbon, of the same blood as yours?"

"Blood," said Robespierre. "There will be more of it. My party faces opposition from those who think that compromises will bring freedom, and we have yet to achieve the power we deserve. But our time is coming, and when it does, we shall have blood. How many thousands are there, in this city alone, whose hatred can only be satisfied with the death of their oppressors?"

"Too many to be subdued," Sebastian said.

"Even so. We must channel their thirst for vengeance, though, without allowing them to destroy the very basis of society. It is difficult. But it must be done, and it will be easier if we can depend on Spain to rise against her King instead of against us. What guarantees can you offer me?"

"None," Sebastian said.

"Excellent," said Robespierre. "You promise me nothing. Such a man might be trustworthy." His small, sturdy figure moved back and forth before the dim red light of the fire. "Of course you know that I have reports of your activities."

"Of course," Sebastian said. "Without Madeleine Benet, you would never have heard of me at all."

"But who is she?" asked Robespierre, his big, bright eyes moving back and forth between Sebastian and Madeleine. "Only the mistress of a very minor deputy. And what is her opinion worth? Especially when I consider that Andre Latour is too cautious to join our cause?"

"I have told you what I think of him," said Madeleine. "The guillotine has destroyed him, as certainly as if it had taken his own head. He has no stomach for what we must do to make France free."

"Then you are more use to the cause than he is?"

"I certainly hope so."

"And does he know what you think?"

"I have told him often enough."

"And you would prefer to put your faith in this Spaniard?"

"You see me here with him."

"And if he can arrange an uprising against the King of Spain, he will be more precious than gold. But how can we be sure? Do we even know that he is from Spain at all? And if he is, how can we be sure that he is not the agent of our enemies?"

Robespierre stood against the fire, casting a long shadow over both of them.

"You have my word," said Madeleine.

"And what has the visitor from Spain to say?"

"I shall answer my accusers," Sebastian said, his eyes fixed on the curtain that covered the door in front of him.

"You are certainly a clever man," said Robespierre. "I wish that did not lead me to suspect that you are a spy."

Madeleine stood, her face pale, her blue eyes cold. "What reason have you to suspect me?" she demanded. "I have offered you the help you need most."

"I have every reason," said Robespierre, "though I reserve my judgment. But I told you I had reports of this man, and only one of them came from you. The other came from a government official."

Sebastian slumped in his chair, his wide-brimmed hat pulled low over his face. "Open the curtain," he said wearily. "Or is he afraid to come out?"

Robespierre walked slowly across the room, but the curtain flapped out into the room before he could reach it, and a man stepped through.

"Andre!" said Madeleine.

Sebastian tipped his hat, then settled it over his eyes again. Robespierre looked at him in some surprise. Andre seemed to fill the room with his rigid shoulders and his big, curly head, but Sebastian only looked as if he were asleep. It was not the performance of a man haunted by guilt.

"You are a seducer," boomed Andre, "and a seditionist."

Sebastian appeared to be entirely unconscious.

"And you are an idiot," shouted Madeleine. "Who asked you here?"

"I invited myself," Andre replied. "How many times did you expect to meet this animal before I learned of it?"

Sebastian lifted the brim of his black hat as he sprawled bonelessly in his chair, and the sight of his dark eyes seemed to quiet Andre.

"You know nothing of him," screamed Madeleine.

"Quietly, please," said Robespierre. "There are guards all around this house."

"Quietly, then," said Andre. "Citizen Robespierre, I tell you that this beast in black seeks to subvert our revolution."

"It may be so," said Robespierre. "Or perhaps he has only stolen the heart of a young woman with red hair. This is not yet a crime."

"And the new regime cares little for old rights of property, Andre. I did not think that you would spy on me," said Madeleine. "But have you proof to offer except your own jealousy?"

"I loved you," Andre replied. "But now I see that serving the Countess has corrupted you beyond recall. The agony of France was not devised to serve your lust, Madeleine."

"And have you nothing to say?" Robespierre asked Sebastian.

"This boy has said enough for both of us. How much

credence can you put in the whining of an overgrown puppy?"

"Stand up when you speak that way of me!" shouted Andre. He jumped toward Sebastian, his strong hands clutching at his rival's throat.

And although Robespierre watched eagerly, he did not see Sebastian move. He saw only an indistinguishable flurry; but Andre flew away from it, to crash into the wall.

Sebastian sat quietly in his chair while Andre struggled up from the floor. "You are a dog," whispered Andre. "And that thing with the red hair is your bitch!"

"I cannot stand for this," Sebastian said. "Say what you will of me, but I cannot allow that." He stood slowly.

"These Spaniards are famous for their gallantry," said Robespierre. "You must answer him."

"Answer him?" hissed Andre. "I challenge him!"

Sebastian laughed, and Madeleine stared at him in horror.

"No, Andre!" she said. "You mustn't. You'll be killed!"

"You have done enough," Andre replied. "Would you make a coward of me too?"

"A duel," said Robespierre, looking quizzically at the imperturbable figure of Sebastian. "An aristocratic custom, I think, but perhaps this is a situation with no other solution."

"No!" shrieked Madeleine.

Two burly men in red caps burst through the door. Each of them had a pistol in his hand.

Robespierre stopped them with a gesture. "I am quite safe," he said, "but the woman is upset. There is no place for her in this affair, even if she bears some responsibility for it. Please remove her."

Robespierre's guards stood on each side of Madeleine and took her arms. "You can't do it, Andre," she said, her voice rising hysterically. "You don't know who he is!"

"Put her in my coach," said Robespierre, "and send her home. But return here at once."

"You can't," wailed Madeleine as she was dragged through the door. It slammed shut behind her, leaving three men in the quiet room. Sebastian continued to slouch in his chair, while Andre stood in the corner, his face red with rage.

Robespierre paced before the fire. "You have been challenged, I believe," he told Sebastian. "It is your privilege to choose the conditions."

"I have only one," Sebastian replied. "I must leave the city before sunrise, and in any case there is nothing to be gained by waiting. Let us have the duel tonight."

"In the dark?" sputtered Andre.

"It will be equally dark for both of you," said Robespierre. "And there is a moon. The weapons?"

"Since he is an aristocrat, no doubt he is a swordsman, too," said Andre. "And I know nothing of foils. But I will kill him anyway."

"Would you prefer pistols?" asked Sebastian. "I promise that I have never fired one, but the two we saw in the hands of the men at the door appeared to be serviceable."

15

A Duel Before Dawn

A CRESCENT moon spread its cold blue light over the park where five figures stood. Four of them were human, and the fifth was Don Sebastian de Villanueva.

Robespierre stood in the center of the group. "Then you both agree," he said, "that my guards will be your seconds?"

"I would prefer to have a friend," replied Andre, "but I can hardly call on one this late at night."

"What friend?" asked Sebastian. "Dr. Guillotin? Feel free to summon him if you will. As for me, I have no friends in France. I am content with these honest men, and with you, Citizen Robespierre, as our umpire."

"A democratic sentiment," said Robespierre. "Gaston, attend our visitor from Spain." The broad-shouldered young man with the long nose took his place behind Sebastian.

"See how easily he agrees?" demanded Andre. "I tell you that he is a hypocrite and a spy."

"We shall know soon enough," said Robespierre.

"Can you believe that, Citizen Robespierre?" asked Andre. "I hope to kill this cur, and it will please me mightily, but surely you cannot accept the idea that the result will be a judgment from on high. That is rank superstition."

"Men have believed it for centuries," Sebastian said. "It is the origin of the custom."

"You see?" said Andre. "Next he will tell us that he is a Christian!"

"Not I," Sebastian said. "But is it permitted to believe in a power greater than that of mortal men?"

"Even that is likely to be troublesome," said Robespierre judicially. "It leads to priests. Our prisons are full of them, and even here I think they have too much power."

"The same power he worships," said Andre with a sneer. "He expects God to save him."

"The challenge was yours," Sebastian said.

"Only because I expect to kill you, and because you deserve to die."

"No doubt I do. But if you have no faith, how can you be sure that justice will be done?"

"Enough," said Robespierre. "A few shots will settle this."

"Then you agree that justice will be done?" Sebastian asked. "It is not possible that the wrong man will win?"

"At least one or the other of you will be silenced," said Robespierre. "I hear enough debates each day, without keeping myself awake for another. Please examine the pistols." He offered one in each hand. Andre picked them both up, judging their weight as he examined them in the moonlight.

"They seem much the same to me," Sebastian said.

"I believe they are identical," said Robespierre. He glanced at Andre, who seemed earnestly intent on choosing the best weapon. "In fact, they are a pair of dueling pistols. I needed something to arm my guards, and the nobleman who owned these had no further use for them."

"Nothing to choose between the two of them," said Andre. His face was flushed, and his hand a trifle unsteady as he returned the pistols. One of them slipped through his fingers and fell to the ground.

Sebastian stooped to retrieve it. "This must be mine," he said.

"As you will," said Andre stiffly.

"A moment longer," said Robespierre. "I want the two of you to watch while they are loaded again. There must be no irregularities here. My honor is at stake, as well as yours. The winner of this contest will certainly bear watching, but at least he will win fairly. Gaston!"

Andre watched intently as the man took up the ornately engraved pistols. "There is only one way to empty them," said Gaston.

"Proceed," said Robespierre. "At least this will show that the flints are in good order."

The roar of the gunpowder igniting was almost deafening at such close range, and Andre jumped involuntarily. He steeled himself for the second shot, but still could not help noticing how the lead ball ripped through the branches of a nearby tree. And in the flash of the priming powder, he saw Sebastian's dark eyes for the first time.

The silence after the shots was overwhelming. A few insects chirped in the distance, and the moon made shadows among the trees. Andre stared at Sebastian while he listened to the broken branch that slowly fell.

"I would like to see my opponent's face," said Andre.

"Do you think that will help you?" asked Sebastian.

"It seems a fair request," said Robespierre. "And in truth, it would satisfy me to know that I could recognize you again."

"So be it," said Sebastian. He turned down the collar of his cloak and tossed his broad-brimmed hat into the grass at his feet. His gleaming face was whiter than the moon; his mouth was red. Black hair drooped over his hollow cheeks, and a crumpled white scar streaked down over the left side of his face. His empty eyes were sunk in shadows, and the smile under his drooping mustache showed long, sharp teeth.

Andre stepped back involuntarily. Gaston crossed himself, then looked up anxiously to see if Robespierre had noticed. But the leader of the Jacobins had not taken his eyes off Sebastian's face.

"Is that a dueling scar?" he asked at length.

"I won it in a war," Sebastian said. "Shall we proceed with the loading of the pistols?"

"At once," said Robespierre. "You are very pale. If I believed in such things, I might suspect that you were a ghost."

"It is best for both of us that you are too wise for that," Sebastian said.

Andre felt his knees turn to suet. The sound of gunfire had startled him, and the face of his opponent had unnerved him altogether. Whoever this Sebastian was, his countenance was grimmer than the executioner's, and there was something in his manner that indicated a man so accustomed to killing that he was almost tired of it. And Robespierre's suggestion that Sebastian was already dead did nothing to sooth Andre's nerves. He tried to remember Madeleine's warning, but could only recall how anxious they had all been to have her gone. He watched Gaston busy himself with wadding, ramrod, powderhorn, and two lead balls, but realized that his eyes could hardly focus.

"Why does my opponent's second do the loading?" Andre asked.

"Would you prefer Alphonse?" asked Robespierre.

"Let my opponent have the choice of weapons," offered Sebastian, "as long as I am done with this by dawn."

"By the first crow of the cock?" asked Robespierre, and Andre wished for less of his graveyard humor.

"Precisely," answered Sebastian, still smiling at Andre. His grin was like a skull's.

Gaston held the weapons out to Andre, their polished barrels gleaming in the light of the waning moon. "Choose," he said.

Andre looked to the right, and then to the left. Twice his hand reached out, and twice he withdrew it. He had witnessed the loading, and he realized that his choice should have no meaning, but he had grown suddenly superstitious. He did not wish to make a selection. Too much seemed to depend upon it. His hand wavered, and his curly hair sagged damply over his broad forehead.

"Come," said Robespierre. "Surely it is late enough already."

Andre shot out his hand and picked the gun at his right.

"So be it," said Sebastian as he reached out for the remaining weapon. For an instant his long fingers touched Robespierre's.

"You are cold," said Robespierre.

"It will soon be winter," Sebastian replied.

"Indeed," said Robespierre. "Do you both understand the rules? You will each take twenty paces away from each other. Then at my command, you will turn and fire. The ground is quite clear here."

Andre looked at the long expanse of grass, each blade touched with a gleaming drop of dew.

"There is only one ball in each pistol?" asked Sebastian.

"One will be enough for me," Andre said.

"And if we both miss?"

"That will provide an opportunity for a reconciliation," said Robespierre. "I understand that it is customary for gentlemen to find satisfaction in taking first blood."

"Only death will satisfy me," said Andre.

"Then I hope to see you satisfied," Sebastian said.

"Evidently words will not settle this dispute," snapped Robespierre. "Let us begin."

Andre and Sebastian turned back to back, but Andre was careful not to let their bodies touch. Somehow the thought of even the briefest contact with Sebastian frightened him, and in any case he did not want his opponent to detect the involuntary spasms that seemed to be shaking his spine. He saw his own shadow stretched out at his feet, and the longer shadow of Sebastian spreading over it.

"One," said Robespierre.

"Wait," said Andre. "I have the inferior position. When I turn, the moon will be shining in my eyes." He turned around as if to demonstrate.

"Come," said Robespierre. "What difference can it make? It is not the sun, after all."

Andre found himself staring into Sebastian's dead eyes, only two paces away, and almost wished he had not called a halt to the proceedings. Sebastian smiled again. "Let us change places by all means," he whispered. "I would not have it said that I won this duel unfairly." He stepped past Andre and took up his new position.

"Does this satisfy you?" Robespierre asked curtly.

"It does," replied Andre.

"The light of the moon is hardly blinding," he heard

Sebastian say, "but the silhouette of the man it shines behind makes an excellent target."

Andre could not move while he heard Robespierre count off the first step, and almost stumbled trying to make it up. He was beginning to realize that he might be dead in a minute. His hands were slippery with sweat despite the coolness of the night, and he wondered if he could hold onto his gun. Robespierre's thin voice seemed very far away; Andre began to take bigger strides, as if he hoped to leave the other men far behind him.

At the count of five he peered over his soulder and saw the dark figure of Sebastian striding away from him; but it was still dismayingly close. Robespierre glanced reproachfully at Andre, who quickly turned his head.

A grove of cedars stood not too far ahead of Andre; he wondered if he might reach their shelter before any shots were fired. He lengthened his steps again, even as he realized that the trees were too far away to do him any good.

"Nine," said Robespierre.

Andre's stomach turned to lead. He felt sick, so sick that he would surely be justified in postponing the duel. How could he be expected to fight when he was so ill? He decided not to move again.

"Twelve," said Robespierre, and Andre took another faltering step. He found himself staring at the moon, and in its distant glow he seemed to see the scarred half of Sebastian's face.

"Thirteen."

Andre clutched the pistol in both hands to make sure that he would not drop it. He thought of the guillotine. Not of the living men and women who were dragged under its blade, but of the pathetic corpses who had been used to test its efficiency. For the first time he could imagine himself as one of them, a helpless slab of meat. He thought of Dr. Louis subjecting his body to some hideous experiment and knew that he would feel each indignity, however dead he was. The writhing face of the Count de Corville seemed to float before his eyes.

"Seventeen," said Robespierre.

Andre barely caught himself in time. He shook his head to

clear away the pictures in his mind. There was no time left for dreaming, even if he seemed to hear a high voice calling his name. He took a firm grip on his gun and held his breath.

"Nineteen," said Robespierre.

"Andre!"

He whirled at the sound of Madeleine's voice and saw her running down a grassy slope behind Robespierre, the two seconds hurrying toward her. And in the same instant Andre saw Sebastian, his back still turned, his dark cloak trailing in the wet grass.

Andre raised his pistol.

And as Robespierre shouted "Twenty," Andre pulled the trigger.

The blast of the gun thrilled him, as if its power were his own. The dark, distant shape of his enemy was almost facing him, and he saw the black figure stagger backward as if it had received a blow from a leaden fist. It looked to Andre as if some scattered fragments had flown away from Sebastian's stumbling body.

"Foul!" shouted Gaston, releasing his hold on Madeleine and rushing across the slippery grass toward Sebastian. A cloud of bitter smoke made Andre's eyes water.

But Sebastian did not fall. He took two wavering steps and then righted himself. He waved his second away with his empty hand. "I am not hurt," he said. "Keep the woman out of range."

Gaston nodded grimly, then hurried back to help subdue the struggling, cursing Madeleine Benet. Sebastian raised his pistol.

Andre felt his legs buckle, and without time for thought he dropped to his knees on the cold ground. He looked amazed at his own shadow, but could not raise his eyes. "Don't shoot me," he murmured.

"Stand up, Andre," cried Madeleine, and Robespierre silenced her with a slap. Andre was too preoccupied to notice it.

In what he took to be a burst of inspired courage, Andre looked up in time to see Sebastian take one step forward. The man in black was taking careful aim.

"The next shot is yours," said Robespierre.

Andre was surprised to find himself crawling on all fours through the wet grass. The gleaming barrel in Sebastian's hand seemed to draw him like a magnet. He could hear nothing but the sound of his own breathing, and he did not wish to hear it stop.

Sebastian stood quite still, the pain he had felt subsiding as the hole in his dead side began to heal itself. Soon he would have the strength to fire his pistol. And while he waited, Andre slithered toward him.

"Stay back, for God's sake!" said Robespierre.

But Andre knew that his only hope lay in reasoning with the man whose face was white as the moon. He had almost reached him now. He wished he could make his voice louder, but his throat was dry. He held out his empty gun as an offering, then dropped it at Sebastian's feet. He wrapped his arms around Sebastian's knees.

"Please," said Andre. "Please, please, please."

He raised his head, and saw the hideous aperture of the barrel that was aimed toward him. The face behind it did not wear the smile he had feared. Instead, the twitching mouth was almost tragic, but that frightened him even more. As Andre raised an imploring hand, the gun went off.

He screamed and fell back on the ground. He screamed again, and again, until at last he realized that he was alive. The shot still rang in his ears, but he had not been touched.

Slowly, carefully, Andre took his hands away from his eyes. He saw Sebastian striding off toward a clump of trees, the pistol dropping from his hand. Andre smiled and turned on his side. Robespierre and his two guards were hurrying up the slope toward their waiting coach. Only Madeleine remained, the moon on her red hair. For a moment she stood without moving; then she followed Robespierre.

Andre lay on the cool ground for a long time, laughing quietly to himself and stroking the wet grass. Dawn was breaking before he had the strength to rise.

16

The Pit

THE RAIN that fell the next night provided some relief for those citizens of Paris whose homes were too close to the place where the guillotine had been installed. Already there had been complaints from the residents about the stench of the blood which covered the scaffold and the streets. The hole in the ground beneath the blade, designed to collect the blood, had done its work too well, becoming a repository for the noxious odors which had roused the indignation of even the most patriotic Parisians. It was a problem that no one had considered.

Alone in his rooms, the window buffeted by wind and water, old Dr. Louis raised his glass of port to the elements, thankful for at least a temporary solution to the dilemma. "Heaven's tears," he said to himself.

In a poorer quarter of the city, Andre Latour and Madeleine Benet sat quietly. They did not speak, and their eyes never met. All that passed between them were the damp draughts that found chinks in their walls.

And Dr. Guillotin sat wrapped in a shawl, wishing that he had another name.

The worst section of Paris had been chosen for the site of the pit where the decapitated corpses of the guillotine's victims were laid to rest. Christian burials might have been considered contrary to the spirit of revolution, and in any case there were few relatives willing to identify themselves to the authorities for the cold comfort of claiming a body in two pieces. So France's dishonored dead were tossed into a pit and covered with a thin layer of earth. The few who lived nearby feared that the constant increase in the number of half-buried bodies might breed pestilence, but their protests were few and feeble, and of course the corpses had to be put to rest somewhere.

This was a grave that had no visitors, except for the men who drove the carts that stopped beside the pit each evening, men who were there not to mourn the dead but to increase their number.

Yet on this night one figure stood beside the pit while the cold winds howled and the night turned black. His wet cloak was shiny and the brim of his slouch hat dripped; but Sebastian never moved, even when blasts of icy rain tore at his face.

"Come, Juliette," he whispered. Distant thunder muffled his voice, but he was not speaking to human ears. He was calling to a dead soul.

He stood at the edge of the pit and raised his hands toward the rolling clouds. Torrents spattered down upon the earth and transformed the grave into a pond of gleaming mud.

The surface of the wet ground broke. A section of the muddy grave fell in upon itself, then rose up again as if an animal were burrowing beneath it. Huge cracks appeared in the earth, and something pushed its way up into the storm.

Sebastian kneeled down at the edge of the pit, but what reared up to meet him was the body of a woman, its headless neck hideous as the rain washed it clean. The body slumped, and a writhing hand reached up behind it, the fingers stretching toward the angry sky.

"Rise, Juliette," Sebastian said.

Another hand appeared beside the first, then two thin white arms that squirmed like snakes. Sebastian grasped them and began to drag the Countess de Corville from her grave. Her small head emerged, caked with dirt, the face turned toward the clouds. Darkness ran down her cheeks in muddy streams, and blond hair hung damply over her eyes. Her mouth was an open square in which small, sharp teeth shone.

She wrapped her arms around Sebastian as he pulled her into the night, her teeth snapping weakly at his throat. He held her back and brushed her hair aside, revealing dead, white eyes that did not blink even when the raindrops struck them. He lowered her gently to the ground and let her lie there while the storm washed the dirt from her body.

The corpse he had left in the prison had been naked, but someone had dressed her for burial in a flimsy white shift. It was soon drenched by the downpour, clinging to her slender body like a second skin while she shuddered at the edge of the pit. Her eyes closed for an instant, and when they opened again her dark irises were visible. Sebastian stood over her while lightning lit the sky, then pulled her to her feet while thunder barked across the city.

The Countess de Corville swayed unsteadily and took a faltering step toward him. "Sebastian?" she said. Her hands groped toward him. "Am I dead or alive?"

"Neither," he said. "Or both."

"Hold me," she said as she stumbled against him. "I feel so strange, Sebastian. It frightens me."

"That will pass," he promised her. "Sooner than you think. You have found what you sought for so many years, Juliette. Now the magic is within you, and you are one with it."

She looked back toward the muddy pit. "It would be better not to think of that," Sebastian said.

"Not think of it? I shall never forget it. I woke under the ground with a head for my pillow and a corpse for my blanket. There are dozens of butchered bodies there, Sebastian, and I had to crawl through them to reach you. I do not intend to forget it."

"But you are free now, Juliette."

"Yes. Free to kill. Free to seek revenge."

Sebastian raised his head to the lashing rain. "And is that what you intend to do?" he asked.

"Others must die to keep me alive. It would be foolish not to choose my enemies when I seek blood."

"But it would be foolish, Juliette. It is the one certain path to destruction."

"You are wrong, Sebastian. I am too strong for them now.

I am no longer a weak woman. They have made me a demon, and they will taste my wrath."

"The strength you feel will die with each dawn, Juliette. You must be cautious. Forget France, and forget your enemies, or they will kill you again."

"What would you have me do, Sebastian?"

"Know yourself for what you are. I understand it is hard for you to believe so soon, but you are no longer part of that world, and its quarrels should not concern you. Now you are the night, Juliette, and you are mine. I have watched centuries of warfare, and I swear to you that we should have no place in it. Such struggles are for the living, and even they find little profit in it. You must cast off your memories with your life, and let me show you the secrets that hide in the darkness."

The Countess gazed into his eyes, dark even when the sudden glare of lightning touched them. She raised her hand to her head and pushed away a dripping lock of hair. "I remember now," she said. "Madeleine. She told me that she had befriended you. And now you want to protect her from me!"

"Then you intend to kill her?"

"I see that I was right, Sebastian. You mean to offer me nothing. You only want to protect that redheaded bitch!"

"You mistake me, Juliette."

"I do not think so, Sebastian. You mean that I have understood you all too well. You need not worry, though; she will not die soon. First she must be made to suffer."

"But why must you think of her at all?" Sebastian shouted against the thunder.

"Because she killed my husband, and because she killed me. Last night I was a living woman. Do you think I chose this fate gladly?"

"You must accept your fate, as I have mine. Did I choose to be summoned here from the peace I had found among the stars?"

"Will you reproach me for that again?"

"I meant only to remind you, Juliette. We are the playthings of destiny, and we must yield to what we cannot conquer."

"I shall never yield to her. I will destroy her, and you have given me the power to do it. That is the fate I shall accept!"

"You will destroy yourself."

"How can you love her so much, Sebastian?"

"I selected you from every woman in this bleak world, and not because I loved another more."

"You wanted my blood, and you have had it. You have made me what you are, and that is your revenge."

"If I had wanted only that, you would not have risen again. Others have not been so fortunate."

"You wanted a mistress, did you? Then go back to Madeleine! Or has she proved too cold for you? I hope not, for you have a few more weeks left with her. And you will not have me."

Sebastian put both hands on her throat as if he meant to strangle her, but he only shook her and then pushed her away. "I thought the last few days have taught you more," he said, "but you are a victim of your time."

He turned and walked slowly away, his cloak billowing in the wet wind, but stopped when he felt her touch on his shoulder. "Wait," she said. "You cannot leave me here alone, Sebastian. I am lost. You must help me." Sebastian stopped under a tree that offered some shelter from the storm.

"You are in your native city, and apparently quite capable of determining your own destiny. There is nothing I can do to help you now. I meant to rescue you, but I have only prepared you for further pain."

"You transformed me into what I am, and now you must instruct me. What am I to do?"

"Seek a shelter where you will not be discovered. Stay out of the sun. Feed on blood when you must, and be as inconspicuous as you can. There is very little else."

"And is this all? You make a miracle sound like a very small thing."

"So it is, for those who see it only as a weapon. There are dark dreams in it, and glimpses into the mysteries that lie beyond death. There is even the chance for freedom, the chance to learn the secrets that will bring another transformation, the chance to send the spirit soaring into another realm for which there are no words. There is a hope for peace, but that will mean nothing to those who want war. I have nothing to teach you, Madame Countess."

"But you have, Sebastian. I have seen you do things. You have transformed yourself into a bat, and last night you came to me as a mist. Show me how to do that!"

"You are as eager as a child," he said. "Such tricks will be simple for you now that your blood is like mine. Simply concentrate your mind upon the transformation you desire, and the strength of your will should do the rest. It is simpler than learning to walk."

"Is there no secret to it?"

"Do you want a verse to recite?" he said irritably. "I wish it were as easy for me to make you believe the other things I have tried to tell you, but they take longer to learn. This you can prove to yourself."

The Countess looked up at him doubtfully as a faint flicker of distant lightning illuminated his grim features. She raised her right hand and held it in front of her face where it blotted out Sebastian's features. The wind was weaker now, and the rain had become no more than an icy drizzle, but wisps of fog rose from the ground.

The Countess forced all her attention toward her fingertips, and as she stared at them they seemed to glow. Fog flowed up to touch them and they disappeared. Sebastian watched her expression of mingled delight and shock as her entire hand dissolved into a luminescent mist. She gasped and staggered backward, sighing with relief as the hand restored itself.

"It is true," she said.

"Everything I have told you is true. It would be better for us both if you believed all of it."

"I am not such a fool as you seem to think me, Sebastian. Perhaps your visions are worth more than my vengeance, but there is no need to choose when we have all eternity ahead of us. Let me taste my power before I renounce it. Our magic could save France!"

"I have heard the same thing said before, and only misery came of it. We will never control the world, but at least we can hope to be free of it."

"Who knows what I can do until I try? It might be more

than killing. I know from my own experience how easy it is for a living person to fall under the sway of a vampire. It is true, isn't it? Could I make a man my slave with my first taste of his blood?"

"A woman like you would hardly need the blood."

"I mean it, Sebastian. I can seek out my enemies and bend them to my will. I can change their minds as easily as I can change my hand."

"It might not be quite as dangerous as trying to kill them all," Sebastian said, "though in some ways the risk of discovery would be even greater. But it is futile, Juliette. This revolt is not the plot of a few conspirators. To defeat it, you would be obliged to enslave all of Paris."

"There are always a few who lead the others, and I shall find them. Will you help me?"

"I have tried to help you by telling you the truth. There is nothing more for me to do."

"Then I must act alone," said the Countess de Corville. She backed away from him, her mouth set in a straight line. "It seems that I must abandon you once more, Sebastian. Do you think we shall meet again?"

"If you succeed, you will have no further use for me. And if you fail, you may well destroy both of us."

For an instant their dead eyes met. The Countess ran across the grass and threw her arms around him. Her slim body, wet and almost naked, writhed against his while her cool lips kissed him ardently. Sebastian felt as if her flesh would melt into his own.

But as he gazed into her beautiful, pale face it faded away into the fog. She whispered something that he could not hear as she became a glowing mist that drifted out of his embrace and was lost in the cold rain.

17

Citizen Sade

A SHORT, heavy-set man with a cockade in his hat stood uneasily on a dark street corner and listened to the shouts of the approaching mob. He reached for the musket leaning against the wall beside him, held it gingerly in one hand, then shook his head and put the gun down again. The heavy footsteps in the next street sounded like an advancing army, but he could tell from their voices that these were only the citizens of Paris on their nightly rounds. Still, he could hardly repress a shudder when they rounded a corner and bore down upon him.

Hundreds of men and women were hurrying through the night, covering the cobblestones so completely that they looked like a moving wall. Most of them were grimly silent, but from time to time a cry broke the silence. "The priests!" called one man. "The prison!" answered another. And when a woman demanded the blood of an aristocrat, it was all the man with the musket could do to keep himself from running.

He stood his ground because he knew that flight would bring pursuit, and because common sense told him that he had nothing to fear from these people. In fact, he was their representative. He saluted smartly as they rushed past him, his gaze on the swords, pikes, and clubs in their hands. And when they were gone he leaned back against the wall and closed his eyes.

"Monsieur le Marquis?"

"What? Who are you? Don't call me that! I am Citizen Sade of the militia, and I am armed!"

Sade fumbled for his musket while his weak eyes searched the darkness for the man whose words had startled him.

"You have nothing to fear from me, Citizen."

"Then come forward, where I can see you," demanded Sade as he raised his gun.

A tall man in a black cloak stepped up to the nuzzle with complete confidence and politely removed his hat. "I wonder if you will remember me," he said.

"The Spaniard," whispered Sade. "Don Sebastian."

"Then you have not forgotten."

"I saw few enough faces in the Bastille. But what are you doing here? The city is not safe for you."

"You know what I am," Sebastian replied. "Such a creature is as safe in one place as in another. And there is certainly enough blood flowing here, though most of it is wasted. Dogs drink it in the streets, but I cannot."

Citizen Sade lowered his musket but kept a firm grip on it. "My dear man," he said, "it is all very well for you to call yourself a vampire, and I would be the last to discourage the pursuit of pleasure. But you are a Spanish nobleman, and Paris has little love for either foreigners or aristocrats. You are in terrible danger. Don't you know that we are at war? The Prussians are marching on us, and the people are in a panic, running wild through the city in search of imaginary enemies. It would be enough that you are not French, but you are not a commoner either. You'll be lucky if you live long enough to reach the guillotine. Haven't you heard what happened to your friend the Countess?"

"I heard that she was dead," Sebastian said.

"Guillotined."

"I believe she died before she could be executed."

"What difference does it make? If you are caught you will die, whether you have to wait for the executioner or not. Have you heard what is happening in the prisons?"

"I have heard rumors that angry crowds are breaking into the jails again, but surely this is nothing new. I remember that the Bastille fell only a few days after I met you there."

"But that was done to free the prisoners," protested Sade. "Now it is done to murder them."

"Indeed? It hardly seems necessary. I understand the guillotine is very quick."

"Not quick enough for the people of Paris, evidently. They prefer to bypass the courts, corrupt as they are, because trials take time. It is easier now to slaughter one's enemies in the street."

"You speak as if you did not love the revolution," Sebastian said.

"I hate this new regime almost as much as I hated the old one. The only difference is that this one got me out of prison. They seem willing to regard me as some sort of hero, just because I was incarcerated for so long on the orders of the King. They are even willing to overlook the fact that I am an aristocrat, though it chills my blood to think that they might change their minds. Meanwhile, though, they have made me secretary of my district, and I would hardly complain, except to a man like you."

"And is this one of the duties of your new office, to stand on a corner with a gun in your hand?"

"It's all part of their damned democracy. Every man must do his duty, and I may be an official, but I also serve in the fourth battalion, fifth legion of the national guard. And I have been assigned to twenty-four hours of guard duty here, despite the fact that I am old, and ill, and almost blind. This is no life for a man of letters."

"Then you still write, even now when you are free?"

Sade's face fell. "I thought you might have heard of me," he said. "I had a play produced not long ago, *Le Comte Oxtiern*, and it caused something of a sensation. In fact there was a small riot."

"I can imagine," Sebastian said.

"It was not what you think, my friend. The play was nothing like the work you examined in the Bastille. Quite respectable, I assure you. The problem was that I am an aristocrat, or at least I have been one, and some members of the audience took it upon themselves to protest the simple fact that my tragedy was presented. We had only two performances."

"You might gain even more notoriety with the sort of work you wrote in prison. I have read the classics, but I have never seen anything to compare with what you showed me that night."

"Perhaps you are right, but there are obvious difficulties. Have you heard of a book called *Justine*?"

"I think not. In Spain I had time to read a great deal, but here in France I count myself lucky if I survive."

"Indeed. This is not the best time to publish a book. But it is the sort of thing you might enjoy. It was published anonymously, of course, and already I have been obliged to disown it. What fame is there in that?"

"What of the book I saw? The one written on the scroll?"

"*The 120 Days of Sodom*? I fear it is gone forever. When I was taken from the Bastille and transferred to another prison, I had no chance to rescue it. At least that was buried in the walls, and sometimes I try to tell myself that it may still be safe. But the rest of my writing, the result of a decade's effort, has all been destroyed. My wife's fault. She had time to collect my belongings, but she procrastinated, fool that she is, until the place was ransacked. And now she has asked for a separation and taken herself to a nunnery. I wish she had been born there! My only consolation is that my actions may have helped to bring about the fall of the Bastille, however much it cost me."

"I heard about that from the Countess," Sebastian said. "May her soul find peace. What is *Justine*?"

"You should read it. The subtitle is 'The Misfortunes of Virtue.' It concerns an innocent young girl who is beset by libertines, and it ends only when she is struck dead by a bolt of lightning. A nice touch, I think. What else can purity expect from the heavens but death? There is no justice in this world, my friend."

"There may be a better world, Citizen Sade. I saw a man die in the way you have described, but he certainly deserved it."

"We all die, whether we deserve it or not."

"There are a few like me," Sebastian said, "who never die."

"You must not delude yourself, my friend. Paris will kill you unless you escape at once."

"I intend to stay," Sebastian said.

"You know what will happen to you?"

"I am almost looking forward to it."

"So be it, then. You realize what became of our friend Juliette?"

"I know more about it than any man in Paris."

"Really? I hope I am not talking to the wrong man. I wonder why I trust you. Perhaps it is because you are mad. But I do not think you are a Jacobin. Have I told you about the book I plan to write? No? I mean to name it after Juliette. It will be the story of Justine's sister. She will be a woman of no virtue at all, and consequently she will triumph."

"Things are simpler in books," Sebastian said.

"Of course. Why else should we bother to write them? I could try to tell the truth, but that story is hardly worth telling."

"One might almost think that the facts regarding life in Paris would inspire you, but apparently they do not."

"Of course not," de Sade insisted. "What do you take me for? Am I a monster? I may have committed murders on paper, but all my victims have been on paper too. I don't think I have ever killed anyone."

"It seems likely that you would remember if you had," Sebastian observed.

"I was a soldier when I was a boy. I fired a few shots, and it's perfectly possible that one of them hit somebody. But I have never murdered for the sheer voluptuous pleasure of it. It's a good idea, though, don't you think? In fact, it's the only acceptable motive I can imagine. There's no point in doing something unless it satisfies a passion. To murder as most men do, for some material advantage, strikes me as contemptible. And contempt is all I feel for this mechanical massacre of the finest men and women in the kingdom. Of course, it will not be a kingdom for long. . . . Did you see the mob that passed here before you arrived?"

"I saw them, but I waited until they had left. I did not come here to interview a mob."

"You mean you came here deliberately? I thought this was a happy accident. How did you find me?"

"Through the magic you deny. I sought you out, Citizen de Sade, to see if you could explain your world to me. I think you are a philosopher. And despite your odd tastes, I think you may be the only sane man I have met in Paris. Or at least sane enough to recognize your own madness for what it is."

De Sade bowed, and for a moment again he was a nobleman. "There is nothing for me to explain," he said. "You have seen it all. The world is mad. You should find a place here without any trouble. A man who thinks he is a vampire should have no problem believing that a few thousand murders will make France free."

"On the contrary," Sebastian said. "Part of the problem here is that France has lost its faith in magic. And even those few who believe are only looking for a weapon with which to smite their enemies."

"I am amazed that you have found even those few. We are rational now, although I admit that the results leave something to be desired. I have no use for priests, but I never expected to see the people killing them. That's what began these nights of slaughter, you know. A cartful of priests was transferred from one prison to another, but they never arrived. Since then, crowds have been attacking the prisons and dragging out priests, or aristocrats, or anyone they choose. The people are uncontrollable. Last night they invaded a women's prison and put dozens of innocent prostitutes to the sword. But why? Are they enemies of the republic?"

"Apparently. The priests surprise me more. In Spain, as I remember it, the Church slaughtered the people. My brother was an officer of the Inquisition."

"So. In Spain the priests kill the people, and in France the people kill the priests. But is there any difference?"

"Not much. Certainly none of them do it for love of their victims."

"No," de Sade replied. "They do it for love of something that none of them can touch or taste or even smell. They do it for liberty, whatever that is."

"But are we so different? Are our dreams less cruel than their actions?"

"The difference," said de Sade, "is that my dreams are only dreams."

"Perhaps," Sebastian replied. "But there are those who say that dreams fulfill themselves in life."

"I refuse all responsibility for this. The victims I envision are cherished before they die. The guillotine is no friend of mine."

"The people seem to find pleasure in its work."

"Then they are fools. It is too mechanical and too impersonal. If you had an enemy in your hands, would you hand him over to be butchered by another man playing with a foolish machine? A very unsatisfactory toy."

"I have never heard it called a toy before," Sebastian said.

"No? You should be more observant, my friend. You can see the children playing with them. The toymakers sell miniature models which the boys and girls use to remove the heads of mice and birds. There are pretty little children turning into executioners on every sunny corner. Their mothers are a bit more refined, of course. But there's many a lady in Paris with a little guillotine on her dressing table. It decapitates a doll, and the red liquid that gushes out is perfume. A pretty picture, don't you think?"

"Remarkable," Sebastian said.

"It is all a great game, except for the victims, of course. The whole country is in love with what they call the National Razor. In fact, it is becoming fashionable to attend parties designed to celebrate the work of this glorious machine. Such affairs are called *les Bals des Victimes*. I believe there is one scheduled a few nights from now."

"A dance of victims," Sebastian said. "Where will it be?"

"I don't know if you will be amused or depressed when I tell you. In any case, you would hardly be fool enough to attend. You would be safer walking into a den of murderers. But the truth is that the ball will be held at the former residence of the Count de Corville."

"You startle me," Sebastian said, but his features remained impassive.

"Nothing surprising about it, really. There are few men of means in the new order, so when they wish to celebrate, I suppose it seems reasonable enough to them to use the houses of those who have no further use for them. There is a certain humor in it; I wonder what Juliette would think if she could see her house crawling with the very rabble that condemned her."

"The same question just crossed my mind. Precisely what would she see if she were there?"

"The people of Paris mocking the corpses of their victims. They bedeck themselves in the discarded finery of dead aristocrats, almost as if they were ghosts. Some paint their faces white and dabble themselves with blood. The prettier women, though, are content with something milder. Not wishing to mar their beauty, they tie red ribbons around their necks to represent the kiss of the guillotine. And to complete the illusion that they are what they are not, all of the dancers wear masks. It must be an edifying spectacle, don't you think?"

"One that I can hardly deny myself," Sebastian said.

"One that might cost you your life, my friend."

"I abandoned that many years ago. But there is someone I would like to see again."

"Listen," de Sade whispered. "Gunfire. They are shooting them now."

"Is there a prison nearby?"

De Sade nodded. "Already they are becoming mechanical about their massacres," he sighed. "I didn't hear of any shootings yesterday, only stabbings and clubbings. I suppose this is more efficient. It takes time to tear a woman to pieces, as they did last night to the Princess de Lamballe. Men paraded through the city wearing parts of her body as a joke, and the same people who condone these crude obscenities condemn my little books, even though I do no more than report the facts about the loathsome human race. Let me send you a copy of *Justine*."

"I have no fixed address to give you, Citizen, and I do not expect to be here much longer."

"Very wise, even if it means that you will never read my book. Leave France if you can, and stay away from that masked ball."

"I shall remember your advice, whether I take it or not."

"I do not think I shall see you again. Will you stay a little longer? A night like this seems endless without company."

"I have stayed too long already," Sebastian said. "I have much to do before the sun rises again."

"I suppose you are safer in the dark."

"I am," Sebastian said. "Farewell."

"If you must dance with the dead," Sade advised, "at least be sure you are dressed as an aristocrat. Otherwise they'll be sure at once that you are one." He would have continued, but his visitor had dropped back into the shadows. Sade rubbed his tired eyes, shrugged, and sank back wearily against his wall. He began to think of another story.

18

A Masked Ball

A BLACK bat drifted over the wall surrounding the house that had once been the home of the Count and Countess de Corville, recently deceased. Armed guards stood at the gates, but they were less intent on their task than on the lights and music from which they were barred as effectively as any trespasser would be. None of them thought to look for an intruder from above, but in any case they would not have recognized the bat for what it was. And they were too far away to see the figure of a man which materialized atop the slanting roof. Instead they watched the clouds their breath made in the winter air while they cursed the luck that kept them as far outside the house as they had been before the revolution.

Sebastian crawled across black slate toward the edge of the roof, his strong white fingers gripping the shallow crevices as he eased his way down the slope until his head hung over the eave.

An open window would have made his task much easier, but that was too much to expect now that winter had overtaken Paris. A bat might fly through a window, but it took a man to open one. A stone cherub flanking the pediment smiled sadly at him as his long arms snaked down to touch an icy surface of polished glass. He saw nothing but darkness inside. He groped for a latch, pulled at the lead frame between the panes, but nothing yielded to his searching fingers. He looked across the shadowy maze in the courtyard toward the tiny figures of the guards, listened to the music and the laughter in the house below, then smashed his fist into the window.

The noise was less than he expected. A few fragments of broken glass shattered on the pavement outside the house, but he was certain nobody had heard them, and the cuts in his hand began to heal even before he had a chance to examine them. He pushed aside the twisted metal frame and slithered into an upstairs room.

Sebastian stood for a moment staring out of the window at the clear night sky with its scattering of stars. Then he turned and surveyed the chamber into which he had dropped. The room was dark and empty, stripped of all furnishings and decoration, not very different from the tomb in which he slept. And the sounds of revelry below him might have been a celebration in the depths of Hell.

He paused at the door hanging from a broken hinge and adjusted his clothing carefully. The suit which the Countess had given him so long ago was dangerously out of fashion, but he had kept it with him even though he had since replaced it with simple garments of sober black. Now he wore the red velvet coat again, the ruffled shirt, the black knee breeches with white stockings, and the waistcoat embroidered with silver. His long black hair was covered with a powdered wig. All of the clothing was musty and mildewed from months of storage in a closed coffin, but Sebastian hoped that would be appropriate at a ball where the guests were masquerading as corpses. He pulled a narrow black mask out of his sleeve, tied it over his eyes, and stepped out into the corridor.

Dust was thick on the bare floor boards as Sebastian moved quietly toward the dim light welling up from the staircase. A man lay sprawled on the steps, his gray face spattered with red. A woman in a fantastic white wig leaned over him; for a moment Sebastian thought she might be mourning her lover's death. Then he realized that she was laughing. The man on the stairs moved his hand and she shrieked with delight at his touch. They were too busy to notice when Sebastian slipped past them and stepped down into chaos.

The house was a hideous mockery of what it had been in the past. Only a few people stood in the hallway, lounging against the walls defaced by revolutionary slogans. The carpets were gone, the paintings had been removed, and the chandelier had been torn from the ceiling. A twisted candelabrum stood on the floor; there was nothing else left to hold it. Through the open double doors Sebastian could see the once luxurious reception room where his hosts had gathered. A small band of weary musicians scraped out a distorted tune as Sebastian entered.

The mingled scents of cheap wine and stale perfume were almost overwhelming, but that startled Sebastian less than what he saw. The hundreds of men and women crowded together in the room looked like an orgy of the dead. Every face he saw was paler than his own; those that were not white were gray or green or blue. Every costume was splashed with red, and Sebastian wondered if his was the only waistcoat bearing traces of authentic blood. The boisterous young man who staggered past him had a stain on his shoulders of such spectacular proportions that he certainly looked as if he had purchased his clothes from the executioner, but Sebastian could not get close enough to make sure. Dancers swept around him but seemed oblivious to his presence; at least no one challenged him. A woman with a bottle of wine examined another critically, then poured the scarlet vintage over her companion's dress, and the victim's shout of surprise turned to delight as she pirouetted through the crowd, red drops flying everywhere. Not even Sade's description had prepared Sebastian for this.

He tried to ignore the shouts on every side as his dark eyes scanned the masked faces around him, searching for familiar features among the ugly disguises that grinned up at him. He went where the crowd carried him, careful not to resist lest he draw attention to himself, yet he could not help wondering how many men and women had died to supply the bedraggled finery in which the dancers romped.

Someone pushed Sebastian into a corner, and at the same moment he noticed a woman across the room. There was a dripping crimson mask across her face, but no wig covered her gleaming red hair. Sebastian turned away, suddenly unsure of his disguise. He had not seen Madeleine since the night of his duel with Andre, and had no way of knowing what to expect from her. She was certainly not the woman he had hoped to meet at this dance of the dead.

Buffeted by the dancers, many of them less intent on the music than on wine or lechery, Sebastian studied the wall, noticing the cobwebs that hung from the ceiling. Candlelight cast distorted shadows against the shattered plaster. He wondered if Madeleine had noticed him, and the suspense was so great that he was almost relieved when he felt a hand on his shoulder.

The music stopped for a few seconds as he whirled to face Madeleine. Her gown of stained blue satin matched the eyes that flickered behind her bloody mask. "It's only paint," she said. Her face and shoulders were a dull green.

"Is blood so hard to find?" Sebastian asked, his face expressionless.

"I hoped to see you here," said Madeleine, "but I never expected it. Have you abandoned me?"

"It was not entirely my choice; but I thought it wiser to leave you alone after what happened when we last met."

"I thought you knew me better," Madeleine replied. "If you had killed Andre, I suppose I might have hated you, especially since you were in no danger yourself. But all you did was show me what a coward he is. I suppose you knew long ago, but sometimes women are blind."

"Then you have left him?"

"No. I should have, and undoubtedly I will. It would be easy enough to find another man. But I have been waiting for you."

"Do you still expect to conquer Paris with my help?"

"That was a mistake, and I admit it. But you still have more power than any man in this city, and there must be a way to use it, Sebastian. Your presence here is proof enough that nothing can stop you. And I know that you came to see me. How did you get in?"

"I flew over the wall."

"How simple you make it sound. But you know that it

is not. Imagine an army of men like you!"

A woman with a blue face stumbled into them. Her tongue was out, and both hands were clutched around her bloody throat. She giggled as Madeleine pushed her away.

"Then you wish to join the ranks of the undead?" Sebastian asked.

"I will be dead soon enough if I live a hundred years. And I think I am more useful as I am."

"But Andre is useless, is he?"

"Look at him, and answer for yourself."

Sebastian followed Madeleine's gesture, his gaze fixing on a tall young man across the room. Andre Latour wore a silly smile and a white wig that had fallen away from his dark curls. His mask was green and his skin matched it. One hand held a bottle, and the other groped toward a woman who danced away with a sneer.

"You can be certain that he will not recognize you," said Madeleine. "I doubt if he would recognize me."

"But he has retained his position?"

"Robespierre has nothing to gain by denouncing him now; he is still gathering his forces. But the time will come soon. Have you heard about the trial of the King?"

"Very little."

"He was finally condemned yesterday. And tomorrow he will lose his head. This is a celebration."

"Things happen very quickly here in Paris," Sebastian said.

"He asked for a stay of execution, but there is too much risk in that. He tried to escape once before, you know."

"It seems that you are gaining all your objectives without any help from me. And weren't you pleased when your lover voted for the King's death? He can do more for your cause than I can."

"Andre? He is hardly my lover; I haven't let him touch me since the night he crawled across the grass to beg you for his life. And he didn't even vote. He was drunk."

"Apparently he was not needed."

"He never is. His days are spent emptying wine bottles, and his nights are spent fighting his way out of dreams. He dreams of you, Sebastian."

"Then I must pity him," Sebastian said.

"That is more than I can do. He disgusts me. He sweats and screams, and he is haunted by visions of smoking pistols and severed heads."

"It must be quite uncomfortable for you."

"He sleeps on the floor," said Madeleine. "He doesn't even mind it. I doubt if he knows where he is most of the time."

"I wonder that you brought him with you," Sebastian said.

"It would have been impossible to keep him away. I think he feels safer where there are lights and noise and crowds; and he knows that the de Corvilles kept a well-stocked cellar."

"I hope your friend Robespierre did not come with you," Sebastian said as he looked around the room. "He has a keen eye."

"Robespierre has no time for affairs like this; he is too busy charting the destiny of France."

"You may be right about Robespierre," Sebastian said, "but you are wrong about Andre. He knows at least one of us, and he is coming this way."

Madeleine looked over her pale green shoulder, her face twisting with distaste as she watched Andre pushing his way across the room. "It must be me," she said. "I hope so. But you must get away from here, Sebastian. If he sees you, we are lost."

"I can hardly leave," Sebastian said as he stepped forward into the crush of people surrounding them.

"Will I see you again?" asked Madeleine; but if Sebastian replied, she had no chance to hear him before Andre was upon her. He spun her around and kissed her sloppily.

Madeleine tried to push him away, but the crowd had closed behind him and there was nowhere for him to go. The big curly head with its green mask pushed forward again, and Madeleine struck out at it. Andre staggered back a step, his painted face a mask of shock. Only the press of the people around him kept him on his feet; there was no room for him to fall. He swayed for an instant before he lunged toward her again.

"You shouldn't have slapped me," hissed Andre. "Is it a duel you want?"

Madeleine looked frantically around for Sebastian. He was only a few feet away, but his back was turned as he pushed through the people gathered around him. She opened her mouth to cry out for him, and then Andre's heavy fist smashed into her jaw.

Madeleine smashed into the wall, but Andre caught her before she dropped. He shook her angrily, far too drunk to realize that she was unconscious. Madeleine hung in his arms, her red hair streaming.

"Madeleine!" Andre shouted above the din. He was beginning to realize what he had done to her when he felt someone pulling her away. Andre looked up, trying to focus his eyes.

The face he saw was long and pale. Neither the white wig nor the black mask was sufficient to disguise it. The long scar on the left side was enough for Andre, who fell back screaming. He knocked down two dancers before he hit the floor.

Sebastian's black eyes were huge as he bent over Andre. "Be still," he whispered, "or the guillotine will come for you." Andre could only stare, his green lips twitching.

The mob of sham corpses opened a pathway to the hall as Sebastian lifted Madeleine. "Both of them are drunk," he said apologetically as he stepped over Andre.

"It's only Andre Latour," someone shouted, and laughter broke out behind Sebastian as he carried Madeleine out of the room.

The hallway was dim. Most of the candles on the floor had burned out, leaving an irregular pool of colorless wax on the bare floor boards. The couple on the stairway seemed to be asleep. A lone figure stood at the opposite end of the hallway. It was a woman. Her low-cut gown was yellow satin, and around her slender throat was a crimson choker. A pearl hung from the velvet band, almost as colorless as her gleaming flesh.

"I hoped to see you here," Sebastian said, "almost as much as I hoped you would be too wise to come."

"What is that thing you are holding?" asked the Countess de Corville.

"Your maidservant," Sebastian replied. "She is unconscious, for which we must thank the stars. How could you have worn that dress, Juliette? She would have recognized you at once."

"The wench knows every gown I ever wore," the Countess said. "It was her business, when she had one. Do you intend to kill her?"

"I only want to get her away before she wakes up and sees you. There should be someone to take her home. I have never wished for servants as I do now."

"She and her kind saw to that," the Countess said. "I would kill her myself, but it is too soon. She has more suffering ahead of her before she dies."

"You have learned very little, Juliette. Of course you are still young for one of our kind, but I hoped you might have grown wiser."

"I am learning, Sebastian. At least I know by now that I shall never change the destiny of France. There is not time enough. Tomorrow when they kill the King, the world I knew will be gone, and I can do nothing about it but lie in a box and dream of vengeance."

"Then you have abandoned your plan to gain control over the men who run the government?"

"It might have worked, if they had been men, but they are a cold, circumspect lot, and not much interested in dalliance. I found few who were willing to invite a strange woman into their homes. Most of them are well guarded, and you know that we cannot enter a house where we have not been invited at least once. So I have had to content myself with a pair of minor deputies whose lust for power had not entirely destroyed their other passions."

"And what became of them, Juliette? Did you change their attitudes?"

"I killed them outright. I didn't mean to, but I couldn't stop myself. I hated them too much. And I was thirsty."

Sebastian smiled. "You see why I advised you to forget politics," he said.

"I shall. But I cannot forget what was done to me, or to my husband."

"You thought little enough of him when he was alive," Sebastian said.

"A woman can have a great deal of contempt for a man

without wishing to see his head chopped off."

"Then you will not deny yourself revenge?"

"Why should I?"

"For your own sake. It has already brought you close to destruction." Sebastian felt Madeleine stirring in his arms. "In another minute she will recognize you."

"If she does," the Countess promised, "she will die at once. Take her out of here while you still can."

"Come with me, Juliette, and leave her to her fate. There is nothing left for us in this world."

The Countess glided forward and put a cool hand on Sebastian's cheek. "Just a few days more," she whispered. "Let me finish with my enemies, Sebastian, and then you can show me the stars."

Her voice was tender, but Sebastian saw her sharp-toothed snarl when she heard Madeleine moan and saw her eyelids flutter. Sebastian lifted Madeleine and strode hurriedly to the door.

"Are you protecting her or me?" the Countess demanded.

"To Hell with both of you!" Sebastian snarled. "You will find the man you want inside."

The door slammed behind him as the Countess rushed into the ballroom.

19

The Crimson Choker

ANDRE LATOUR, propped up in a chair by a few friends who wanted him off the floor, was staring into space, his foot twitching in time to the music, when the woman in the yellow gown entered the room.

She stood poised on the landing for an instant before she walked into the crowd, but in that brief time her image burned itself into Andre's eyes. She was a vision in gold and white, as radiant as the sun, and when she stepped down and was lost among the dancers, it looked to Andre's blurry vision as if night had fallen. He blinked, rubbed his eyes, and stumbled shakily to his feet. If he was barely sober enough to stand, he still had sense enough to wonder if she was a hallucination; but even if she was, Andre decided, she was the first of his dreams for weeks that was not also a nightmare, and thus well worth pursuing. He pushed a couple aside as he forced his way onto the dance floor, his big clumsy body gaining the strength that comes from inspiration. He could hardly have explained the power that drew him forward; it was more than the beauty of pale flesh or the splendor of gleaming satin. As his broad shoulders forced passage among the dancers, Andre felt like steel drawn to a magnet, and he could not shake off the impression that the eyes behind the woman's white mask had been staring at him.

All around him were the faces of the dead, their mottled

skins the sickening color of decay, their mouths gaping with hideous laughter, their throats dappled with dripping scarlet. And as he pushed them aside, Andre dimly recognized the same marks of mortality on his own painted hands. He fought his way through the grimacing phantoms that threatened to engulf him, his befuddled mind clinging to the picture of light and purity that seemed to promise him salvation.

From time to time he caught a tantalizing glimpse of gold behind the writhing figures of his companions, and once, as fiddles scraped out the last notes of a mournful tune, the crowd parted for an instant to show him the woman he sought as she made a graceful curtsy to her ungainly partner. By the time he reached the spot, however, the music had begun again and she was gone.

The noise was a torture to Andre's ears, and the atmosphere so close that he could hardly breathe. An old woman in a black dress whirled him around and sent him careening toward the doors leading into the hallway; he took the opportunity to stumble up the few steps to the landing where he could survey the entire ballroom. The woman in the yellow gown had disappeared. Andre shook his head and looked again, but she was nowhere to be seen. Feeling sick and dizzy, he staggered out into the peace and darkness of the hall.

The greasy stump of a single candle provided the only light, but even as Andre's bloodshot eyes focused on the yellow flame, an icy draft whispered across the floor. As the flame shivered and died, Andre looked up in time to see a sliver of the night sky vanish as the entrance at the far end of the corridor swung shut in a rustle of yellow satin.

Andre lurched toward the door.

Sebastian stood at the foot of the bed and watched.

"I want to go back," demanded Madeleine. "There's nothing wrong with me."

"I admit you weren't hurt badly," Sebastian admitted, "but I think you will be safer here at home."

"Safe from what? Is there more risk attending a ball with my friends than there is in spending the night alone with a vampire?"

"You know as well as I do what will happen if you return. This time he only struck you, but if you goad him further, he might be capable of anything. From what I saw and what you told me, I would judge that he is a little more than a lunatic."

"That's why I must go back," said Madeleine as she sat up. "Andre is in no condition to take care of himself. Anything might happen if no one is there to watch him."

"And does that matter to you now? A few minutes ago you told me how much he disgusted you. Would you care if you never saw him again?"

"You know something, don't you?" Madeleine crawled off her bed and took a firm grip on Sebastian's shoulder. "Tell me, Sebastian. What is it? What's going on back there? Why did you take me away?"

"I brought you here for your own safety, Madeleine, and you will wait here until the sun rises."

The winter night was cold, turning the perspiration on Andre's painted face to icy rivulets as soon as he stepped outside, and the shock of contact with the frigid air left him feeling very nearly sober. Light streamed through the windows behind him, creating pale patterns on the frosty lawn. Before him stood the maze, its thick hedges impenetrable even in January. There was no sign of the woman he had followed.

Andre gazed up at the clear night sky as if he might find her there, but he saw only the mocking stars. He moved forward hesitantly, not knowing which way to turn, cursing the fate that had shown him such a vision only to steal her away, when above his own harsh, angry voice he heard for one brief moment the musical tones of a woman's laughter.

He stood perfectly still, waiting for the sound to come again, his head turned toward the rough wall of the maze. For a long moment there was only silence, then the soft swish of cloth against the shrubbery. Half of Andre's mind told him that it might be anyone behind the hedge, that he might well be disturbing a couple whose passion had made them indifferent to the weather, yet he was absolutely if unreasonably convinced that the woman he wanted was hiding in the maze.

The laughter and music from the house grew muffled as

Andre pushed forward into the black opening between the bushes. Darkness engulfed him, and he realized for the first time that he was shivering. His outstretched hands scraped against branches on either side as he moved carefully into the maze, guided only by his sense of touch. He could hardly see, yet there was a delicate fragrance in the air, almost imperceptible, that kept him moving into the shadows.

Slowly his eyes grew accustomed to the darkness, but still the woman in the golden gown was nowhere in sight. A gap appeared in the wall of vegetation that surrounded him; Andre had no way of telling where to turn, but a sound too faint to be identified drew him through the hole in the shrubbery. The new passage in which he found himself had two more openings, and Andre realized that a few more turns would leave him lost. He felt as if he were freezing, and a wave of dizziness swept over him that nearly brought him to his knees. His mouth was foul with the taste of wine, yet he longed for another drink to fight off the cold. He hesitated, tempted to go back to the house for a bottle, but the lure of the elusive creature who had drawn him from the house was stronger than his love for drink or even his fear for his life. As he crashed through the hedge he thought he heard the sound of laughter once again.

Guided only by instinct and the faint, elusive noises that might have been his own imagination, Andre wandered on through the twisting passageways. Each one seemed blacker than the last; he recognized nothing but the narrow strip of sky above him, and when he looked at that, the stars seemed to be spinning. He stumbled through another opening, almost convinced that the maze was a trap that he could never hope to leave alive.

He found himself in a small clearing where a marble bench stood beside the path through the shrubbery. In the dim light that the open patch of sky cast on the scene, he saw the woman in the golden gown.

She seemed to him a creature of almost supernatural beauty. Her flawless skin was incredibly white, paler than the marble bench on which her delicate fingers rested, paler than the fragile mask of white silk that set off her fathomless dark eyes. A powdered wig adorned her head, but a few strands of honey-colored hair had slipped out to caress her cheek. Her gown left her shoulders bare, and scarcely covered the swelling breasts that seemed to gleam faintly in the starlight. She wore no jewelry except the crimson choker that encircled her graceful throat, a tribute to the mark of the guillotine.

And he could hardly doubt that she was an aristocrat. If not, she was a brilliant actress. Her bearing and her beauty made a stark contrast to the ugly mockery Andre had witnessed at the masked ball; even her gracefully inviting pose as she sat on the marble bench showed her nobility. She was nothing like the vulgar, screaming wench with red hair and a green face who had assaulted him so recently. The very sight of this lovely lady seemed to promise him the peace he had so long desired.

The thin red ribbon around her neck filled him with a strange sorrow, as if it were an emblem of the cruelty he had condoned, and of her willingness to forgive it all. There were no shrill reproaches here in the maze, only sweet silence. As he approached her, the woman raised her head and offered him a tender smile. He had only a glimpse of her small, sharp teeth.

Madeleine sat at the edge of the bed with blankets wrapped around her. Twice before she had tried to rise, and twice Sebastian had pushed her down again. Wine had made her too weak to struggle with him further, and she was half asleep, but she was determined to keep her red-rimmed eyes open. They glared at Sebastian wearily.

"Is it an assassination?"

"I tell you that there is nothing, Madeleine. My only concern is for you," Sebastian said.

"You are lying to me. You know something. And you certainly don't care whether I live or die."

"You are certainly wrong about that," Sebastian replied. "I believe that you deserve to live."

"You make it sound like a curse."

"Perhaps it is. There are worse things than death, and perhaps you will taste some of them. But I hope you will endure. I know little enough about this upheaval that has torn your country apart, and I know very few of your people. The result is that the ones I know seem to be symbols to me, you most of all."

"And what do I represent?"

"To me, you are the revolution. Impulsive, angry, vengeful, rushing righteously toward a destiny that even you cannot imagine. And I can hardly wish to see you stopped. You have earned at least a chance to see what you have done."

"Nonsense," said Madeleine. "I am nothing. I still have no power. If you want to save the revolution, you would do better to guard Robespierre, or even Andre."

"Robespierre seems only a schemer, and Andre is certainly a fool. I am more impressed by those like Madeleine Benet, who lament their lack of strength while they topple a throne. The men who seem to be your leaders would be nothing without you. Did they storm the Bastille, or even lead an attack on the estate of the Count de Corville?"

"Perhaps not," admitted Madeleine. "But I still cannot see myself as a symbol of anything. Next you will tell me that you see the Countess as a symbol of the old regime."

"It seems appropriate enough, since she is dead. And tomorrow your King will die. Does it mean nothing to you that you and your people have changed the course of the world?"

"It is what I have wanted for years, Sebastian, but to tell you the truth, I am hardly satisfied. I hope I shall be tomorrow when I see the King's head. But the truth is that I am still poor, still helpless, still a person of no importance. You tell me I control the fate of nations, but the fact is that I am a woman who is not allowed to leave her own bed. What have you done to Andre?"

"I would not touch him, I promise you."

Madeleine gasped. "Is it the King, then? Why are you keeping me here? Is there a plot to rescue him? Have we been betrayed, Sebastian?"

"Never fear, Madeleine. You know more of these affairs than I do, but it seems to me that you have won."

Obeying the gesture of the woman in the golden gown, Andre sat beside her on the marble bench. Had he been less intoxicated, he might have recognized her, but in all the time he had spent with Madeleine, he had never seen more than a distant glimpse of her illustrious mistress. And he was in no mood to inquire into the identity of his companion. She was a vision of the old world he had destroyed, not a victim of the new world he had created.

He felt himself shivering again, and knew that it was not only the cold that caused his limbs to tremble. He was afraid to speak, afraid to move, afraid to do anything that might drive away the woman at his side. He would not have been surprised to see her dissolve into the night, but he was shocked when he felt her cool hand stroke his cheek.

"Thank you for following me," she whispered. "When I saw you with that other woman, I thought you might have no time for me."

"I followed as soon as I saw you," said Andre. "No man could be mad enough to ignore such beauty."

The Countess inclined her graceful head modestly. "It is flattering to be noticed by a man with so much influence," she said.

"Me?" asked Andre, embarrassed by the compliment and by his clumsy response. "I am nobody."

"You are Andre Latour," she said, "a man of some renown."

"Then you know me?"

"And who does not? You have done much for France, and it has been noticed. This red ribbon I wear is a sign of my admiration for what you have achieved."

"It is a pretty thing, but not as pretty as the lady it adorns. You were wise to be so discreet. These women smeared with blood begin to sicken me."

"Death comes soon enough, Andre, and does not love men's mockery. The choker is enough to show that I know what death can do."

Andre stirred uneasily. "Why talk of death at all?"

"This is the night for it. This is the Ball of the Victims, and you and I have danced to its music."

"I have seen enough of it," Andre said. "Too many have died already, and far too many have rejoiced."

"Some deeds can only be paid in blood, Andre. How can you deny what you have done when you are disguised as a dead man?"

"It is the fashion, nothing more."

"And yet you are a handsome man beneath the paint. Were you obliged to disfigure yourself?"

"A man must succeed, or so I have been told. Yet I would give anything to undo what I have done and be what I was not long ago."

"Let me help you, Andre." Her cool white arms reached out and drew his head down to her bosom. "I have come to fulfill your dreams, even the ones you dare not acknowledge. I am here to set you free."

Andre felt his eyes grow wet with tears. "It is too late," he choked.

"Too late to go back," she whispered, "but never too late to go forward. We are much the same, you and I, and I know what you want. If you cannot shake off your guilt, then you must learn to revel in it. Embrace the death you fear, and you will find it sweet."

Andre raised his head. His eyes were wide. "Who are you?" he demanded.

"I have no name. I lost it long ago. I am only your dream, Andre."

Her pale lips brushed his eyes and closed them again as Andre embraced her desperately. His hands clawed at her naked shoulder as her teeth sank into his throat.

"No more blood," he moaned.

"The sun will rise soon," said Madeleine.

"And then you will be free of me again," Sebastian replied.

"Andre should have been back by now."

"He is drunk in a gutter."

"No, Sebastian. I know him too well. He always comes home. He always comes back to me."

"Even after what happened tonight?"

"That was nothing. We have been fighting for weeks, but the fool still loves me."

"And have you come to blows before?"

"I have bruises I could show you, and he could show you more if he were here."

"Is this the love you cherish?" Sebastian asked.

"No! This is not what I want. Nothing I have is what I want. But this is what I have, and it is mine. I will decide when it ends, not you. Not anyone! This is all the freedom I have, Sebastian, and if you have taken it away from me, then I will find a way to punish you."

"I have been punished enough. You cannot imagine what it cost me to be carried into your world, Madeleine. You cannot know the ecstasy I lost when a crazed old man solved the puzzle I was foolish enough to leave behind me three hundred years ago. You cannot dream of the universe I lost, where dreams were the only truth and freedom knew no bounds at all. But evidently the fates expect more of me. Can there be more suffering than what I have endured? I was a spirit, but now I am a beast of prey again. How do you think to punish me? Destroy this body, and perhaps you will be bringing me the liberty I seek. If I were sure, I would destroy myself. But what can you offer me more terrible than what I have?"

Madeleine's face turned grim. "I shall take from you whatever love you have," she promised.

"You have already taken much, if I have lost you. What has become of the courageous woman who stood in a dark street and offered me her blood?"

"She is with you, as she was then. Still a prisoner, Sebastian, still a victim. Still willing to offer much, but never willing to yield to force or treachery. What you have done to Andre will be done to you."

Sebastian turned away. "I tell you I have done nothing to him," he shouted.

"Then where is he?"

"He is coming up the stairs, I think."

"What? Can you hear him? Andre?"

"Is there anyone else you could expect at such an hour?"

"I'll murder him," said Madeleine. "How could he stay away so long?"

"I am amazed that he returned at all," Sebastian said.

"You must leave, Sebastian. It would not do for him to

find you here." For the first time in hours, Madeleine jumped up from her bed. She was nearly naked, her nightgown in disarray, her red hair streaming wildly, but she was past caring.

"I would not leave to please him," Sebastian said, "or even to please you, but the sky is turning gray. I have stayed past my time, Madeleine, and only for you. You will forget me now, but perhaps tomorrow you will realize what I have done, and how false your accusations were. I told you the truth, as far as I could see it."

"Have I wronged you, Sebastian? If I have, I will repay you. Come to me when you can. But go away! The sun will rise soon. The window!"

Madeleine scurried across the room and threw the casement open. Even she could hear the heavy footsteps on the stairs. Sebastian put his cold hand to her throat.

"You would have destroyed me," he said.

"I must be free," said Madeleine. "Do you want less, Sebastian?"

The pounding at the door distracted her, and when she turned back again Sebastian was gone.

The door burst open and Andre stood swaying on the threshold. Madeleine rushed across the room, but before she could reach him, Andre dropped to his knees. His face was green, and the lace at his throat was clotted with crimson. His wig, which Madeleine had claimed at the execution of the Count de Corville, had disappeared.

Andre slumped over on his side before she reached him, but the hoarse, heavy breathing she heard as she leaned over him assured Madeleine that this night was no different than the rest. She pushed him into a corner, blew out the candle, and crawled back into bed, but she had to get up again to close the open window through which a cold breeze blew.

20

The Maze

ON THE next morning, standing under a cold, cloudy sky, Madeleine Benet watched the death of a king. Twenty thousand soldiers surrounded the guillotine where the executioner Sanson served his most illustrious client; thousands of citizens witnessed the event from a disappointing distance. The carriage rolled through the ranks of armed men, and Louis XVI emerged at the foot of the scaffold. Drums were beating as he mounted the steps. He paused for a moment to address the crowd, but Madeleine was so far away that she could hardly understand him. The only word she heard clearly was "innocent."

It was over far too soon for Madeleine. The King was carried into place, the blade slammed down, royal blood spattered over the guillotine, Sanson held up the head for an instant, and the troops began to disperse.

The crowd had been silent, almost solemn, and Madeleine found the whole affair strangely depressing. She moved forward with a few hundred others to dip a bit of cloth in the King's blood, but she could not bring herself to join the dance that began around the scaffold.

She wandered sullenly away from the Place de la Révolution, wondering if the day might have meant more to her if Andre was there to share it. But he was at home in a stupor, sleeping off the effects of the previous night's debauchery.

Not even this execution, which should have been the culmination of his work, had been enough to sober him or even make him stand. Now that she knew he was safe, that he had not fallen victim to whatever she had feared last night, Madeleine was more thoroughly displeased with her lover than ever before; she wondered if she could bear to see his face again.

Yet when she climbed the narrow stairs to their small rooms and saw what condition he was in, Madeleine rushed to his side. Apparently he had crawled from the floor to her bed while she was away, for he was sprawled among the twisted blankets. His whole body was shaking, and the sheets were damp with his sweat. The green and red paint that had covered his face and neck had never been washed off, but most of it had smeared onto the pillows.

She put a hand to his mottled forehead and pulled it away at once. She needed no time at all to realize that he was aflame with fever. Andre groaned at her touch. "You idiot," she muttered as she rose to dip a cloth in water. "It's winter now. You can't wander through the streets all night in a stupor without catching cold. What were you thinking of, Andre? Are you so anxious to die?"

She put the cold compress to his head and felt his big hand close over hers. "Cold," he said. "So cold, and so sharp."

Madeleine sat on the edge of the bed and wiped some of the green paint from his damp face while she tried to guess how sick he really was. He had always been so big and strong that she could hardly imagine him seriously ill. This seemed like a small mistake, the result of too much winter and wine, something that would pass soon and leave him as he had always been. It was impossible that anything could be seriously wrong with him, she thought, and as she did she realized that she still cared for him. Sebastian might not have planned Andre's death, as she had feared, but the vampire had kept her from her lover's side when she was most needed, and this fever was the result.

"Damn you, Sebastian," she said.

Andre looked up at her, his face so full of tenderness that Madeleine's heart jumped, but then his curly head twisted away. For an instant she wondered irrelevantly what had become of the wig he had worn, the one she had captured at the execution of the Count de Corville.

"Not you," Andre murmured as his face turned toward the wall. "Where is the golden woman?"

"What?" Madeleine knew he was delirious, that he might say anything, but still the words hurt her. She raised her hand to slap him, then kissed his hot cheek and rubbed the damp cloth over his brow. Andre's eyes shifted toward her.

"It's a puzzle," he said. "Too many turns, too many choices. A cold puzzle, and when it's finished, everything is white. But it's too dark now. Where are you?"

"I am here, Andre."

"Not you. You hate me. Where is she?"

"Who?" screamed Madeleine. "Who is she? Who are you talking about?" She shook Andre so fiercely that when he fell back she was afraid she might have killed him. She bent over him, her red hair streaming down around his ghastly face.

"Dark," Andre murmured. "Twisted branches, twisted paths. An angel waiting in the middle of the maze, her skin as white as marble. An angel in gold."

Madeleine stiffened. She understood part of what he was saying; it was easy enough to guess that he had spent part of the last night wandering through the maze the Countess had constructed outside her house, but it was more difficult to know if the woman he spoke of was real or imaginary. In either case, her presence inside Andre's distorted mind was hardly flattering. Madeleine told herself that she should have been rid of this lout long ago, but even as she decided to forget him, she cradled his head in her arms.

Whatever he had done, she would see him strong again before she sent him away. And if he was not better by nightfall, she would summon a doctor. She wished she knew one. Neither Dr. Guillotin nor Dr. Louis seemed the kind of man she would choose to save a life.

The sun had dropped out of the cloudy, steel-colored sky only a few minutes ago, but Sebastian was beside her before the Countess de Corville had risen from her marble bed. As he opened the chest in the pale pavilion inside the maze, he saw the fluttering of long lashes as her dark eyes opened.

"You will destroy both of us," he said.

The Countess wrapped pale arms around his neck and allowed herself to be lifted up into the night. "How did you find me, Sebastian?" she asked.

"It was easy enough to guess when you appeared last night at the masked ball, and when you seemed so sure you would be able to seduce Andre Latour. You might have been anywhere, but this seemed the most likely place for you to hide, and clearly enough it is the one you have chosen. You are not safe here, Juliette."

"No? And who would think to look for me so close to home? Who even imagines that I exist at all?"

"Madeleine Benet," Sebastian said.

"She, above all others, is convinced that I am dead."

"That might have been true only a few hours ago, but you have betrayed yourself. If you had to take her man, at least you should have killed him in one night."

"What pleasure would there have been in that, Sebastian? She must be made to suffer!"

"But what do you expect her to think when he comes home with the marks of your teeth in his throat?"

The Countess smiled. "Perhaps she will think that you are responsible," she said.

"And would that please you?"

"It might. You are so cautious that you no longer entertain me. What good is a fiend with a conscience? Or even one who's careful? Madeleine will never find me."

"She found you before, and had you condemned to death."

"I had forgotten that. It seems so long ago."

"Remember, if you can. If your lust for blood overcomes your love for the life you have, then you will not survive. Madeleine knows something of magic, and that enabled her to find you not so long ago."

"But can she work her spells against me now?"

"I think not. We are no longer human, you and I. She has searched for my resting place without result. But it will take no sorcery to seek you out if Andre speaks to her."

"I told him to keep silent, Sebastian."

"Much good may it do you, Juliette. You risk destroying yourself for your revenge."

"Would you let her go unpunished?"

"It does not matter now. Are you blind? We are free of her, and free of all the intrigues this world demands. Forget her, Juliette. Forget all of it. How can you choose to wallow in the dust when I have shown you the stars?"

"You must wait a few days more, Sebastian. Andre is almost mine, and when he is we shall be rid of him forever. And rid of her. Be patient. I must settle with them before I can be yours."

Sebastian stepped away from her. "Is there no way I can persuade you to forget Madeleine?" he asked.

"Impossible."

"Then you must leave here at once, before this maze traps you as well as your victims. We must find you another resting place."

"That is impossible too, Sebastian. I must stay here. I am expecting a visitor this evening, and I cannot bring myself to disappoint him."

"Andre Latour?"

"Precisely, Sebastian. Will you stay and dine with me?"

"You will be happier alone, I think. I hope your night will be a pleasant one, for I fear it will be your last. If I had realized how weary of the world you were, I would have left you to the guillotine."

Sebastian turned on his heel and strode out of the room, but the Countess only smiled as the door closed behind him.

By nightfall Andre had recovered enough to sit up in bed and take some of the broth that Madeleine was feeding him, but after a few mouthfuls he snatched the spoon away from her and threw it to the floor.

"Must I be fed like an infant?" he demanded testily. "Do I look so helpless to you?"

"A few hours ago I thought you were dying, but I suppose I should have known better. My luck has never been good."

Andre glared at her as he took the bowl from her hands and poured the steaming broth down his throat. "Don't be ridiculous," he said. "Dying! Nothing is further from my mind. I admit I felt a bit funny this morning, but what can you expect after the night I had?"

"You had a fever, and you were raving."

"I was drunk, that's all. Look at my hands. There's still paint on them from the masquerade."

"Isn't it enough that I nurse and feed you? Must I bathe you too?"

"I can do it myself," said Andre as he threw back the bedclothes.

"Andre! What are you doing? You can't get up, you're not well enough. You can't be!"

"I feel fine," Andre insisted as he stumbled across the room to the wash basin. "A little weak, but a decent meal and a few drinks will settle that." He splashed some water into his face and peered into the sliver of mirror hanging from the wall. "Where are my clothes?"

"You can't have them. You'll kill yourself if you go out in this condition. You're not strong enough."

"Strong enough to strangle you if you don't give me the rest of my clothes at once. I'll catch my death for sure if I go out with only a nightshirt." His hands and face still wet, he pushed Madeleine aside and snatched his coat from the back of a chair.

She stood in the center of the room, torn between fear and anger, while she watched Andre sit on the edge of the bed and pull on his boots. "Don't go, Andre," she said, but there was no tenderness in her voice.

"What would keep me here? The chance to spend the night with you?"

"I remember a time when nothing would have pleased you more," said Madeleine. She sat beside him and put her arms around his neck, trying to kiss him even as she felt him pull away. She had only a glimpse of his throat before he rose abruptly and gave her a sharp slap in the face.

"Leave me alone, will you?" Andre shouted. He stormed out of the room and slammed the door.

Madeleine was so furious that it took her a moment to remember what she had seen, but when she recalled the two red punctures on Andre's throat she hurried after him, screaming his name as she rushed down the narrow stairs until she reached the street below.

The night was black and bitter cold; the street was empty. Madeleine wasted a few seconds wondering which way to turn, then ran in the direction he was most likely to have taken, still calling to him frantically. There was no sign of Andre in the next street. She reversed direction and backtracked until she reached the house again. She stopped at a nearby tavern that Andre often frequented, even though she knew by now that he had not gone out for wine; he was nowhere in sight, and the proprietor insisted that Andre had not been there for days.

Madeleine wandered around Paris for several hours, her despair deepening as she realized how little hope she had of finding Andre. Even if she did, she was convinced that it would mean finding Sebastian as well, and Madeleine was hardly prepared to confront a vampire at the height of his powers. Weary and seething with frustration, Madeleine made her way home.

She dragged her body up the dark steps, but her mind was racing furiously. It seemed clear enough that Sebastian had attacked Andre, but she could hardly guess how he had done it, much less understand why. Had there been time in the few minutes she had been unconscious for Sebastian to carry her away from the masked ball and still stop to drink Andre's blood? It hardly seemed possible. Certainly he could not have bitten Andre's throat in full view of hundreds of dancers, and it was equally unlikely that Sebastian could have lured Andre outside. Still, Madeleine had reason to know how persuasive the vampire could be.

She opened the door to her room and looked inside, almost convinced that she would find Andre there snoring drunkenly, but nothing greeted her except darkness and silence. She stepped inside, groping for a candle, and was suddenly gripped by the fear that Sebastian might be waiting for her. She struck the flint with quivering fingers and looked apprehensively around the shabby room.

No one was there. Madeleine raised the candle and peered into every corner as if there might be a clue to her dilemma hiding somewhere, but the only unusual thing she saw was the soup bowl lying on the floor where Andre had dropped it; the sight of it made her unaccountably miserable. She sat at the table and rested her head on her arms, shocked to realize that her eyes were filling with tears.

Like a black wave rolling over her came the realization that she had achieved everything she hoped for and still she found her life intolerable. If anything, it was worse than ever before. Long ago she had decided that Andre had outworn his welcome, yet she found herself mourning him. The revolution had apparently triumphed, and only today she had seen the King die, but still she was dissatisfied. Not even the deaths of the Count and Countess de Corville had given her the pleasure she expected. Perhaps if the Countess had not died in prison, perhaps if she had been guillotined, if Madeleine had seen her head dripping blood, it might have been enough to make the struggle seem worthwhile. As it was, there was only the dark despair into which Madeleine dropped exhausted, her last waking moments haunted by the face of Don Sebastian.

The sun was high in the sky before she woke from a series of bewildering dreams. The images that flickered and vanished into the recesses of her mind were so bizarre that her first response was to reject them entirely in the expectation that her life would resume its ordinary pattern. But Andre Latour had not returned. And however much Madeleine tried to reassure herself, she could not shake off the conviction that the puzzling pictures in her nightmare were closer to the truth than the prosaically domestic scene around her. It was most reasonable to assume that Andre had merely wandered off, that the red spots she had seen on his throat were only specks of red paint, that Sebastian had nothing to do with his disappearance.

Try as she might, Madeleine could not bring herself to believe that Sebastian had taken Andre for his prey. Even though she had suspected him, his denials had been strangely convincing; he evidently knew something about a danger that might engulf Andre at the ball, but he could hardly have desired it, unless it had been to eliminate a rival for her favors, a motive which Madeleine found utterly implausible.

Yet what other explanation could there be? Was there another vampire in Paris? Madeleine strained to remember every word of Andre's raving, and in a flash the pieces of the puzzle became the pathways of a maze. The maze hid a small white building, and at its center was a golden woman.

"The Countess!" screamed Madeleine. She jumped up from her chair, grabbed a candlestick, and sent it smashing through the window. Her second scream was louder and higher than the first, but it was wordless, as was the icy wind that rushed through the broken glass to answer her inarticulate cry.

21

The Storm

MADELEINE HAD smashed almost everything she could put her hands on before a frigid calm descended on her. She never doubted her surmise that Sebastian had transformed the Countess de Corville into one of the living dead, and that it was she, hidden in the marble box in the pavilion at the center of the maze, who had stolen Andre's blood. The sky was gray and forbidding, but there were still hours of daylight left, time enough for what Madeleine must do.

She wasted a few minutes wondering if she had a cross or a holy medal, then stopped long enough to laugh hysterically at the idea. Such artifacts were hardly necessary for Madeleine Benet. She knew well enough how to deal with the witch.

A broom leaned against one corner of the kitchen, its handle a sturdy stick of seasoned wood more than an inch thick. Madeleine tried to break it over her knee but only succeeded in bruising herself. Still, the thought of its strength pleased her. She took a heavy butcher knife from the wall and began to hack away at the broomstick.

The work was surprisingly tedious, but she took grim satisfaction in every stroke of the blade. She cut her fingers more than once, but when she was done she had a wooden stake as long as her arm, one end carved roughly into a crude but menacingly sharp point. Madeleine stroked it happily, imagining the ease with which it would penetrate her enemy's soft skin. She hardly noticed the sounds she was making in her throat, and there was no one else to hear them. She put on her hooded cloak and went outside.

Already a few light flakes of snow were dropping to the ground, and a certain tension in the air told Madeleine to expect a blizzard. She might have hired a conveyance, but apparently André had taken all the money they had. Still, Madeleine held everything she needed in the hands hidden beneath her cloak: a small hammer and a pointed shaft of wood. The buffeting of the wind only served to exhilarate her, and more than one shopkeeper engaged in closing his shutters against the storm was startled by the eager smile of the red-haired woman who trudged past him through the falling snow.

If she gazed anxiously at the sky, it was only to determine the time of day, but she passed enough clocks to assure her that she would reach the maze before the sun set. Her feet turned numb as she trudged across the city, but Madeleine hardly noticed. Her only concern was that the gathering drifts of snow would impede her progress. The journey from her poor quarter to the suburbs where she had been a servant was a long one, but she never faltered. She was a woman with a mission.

The roads she traveled grew gradually emptier as she moved out of the densely populated depths of Paris into a realm where only the rich could dwell; in this cold January the area was all but deserted. She passed many familiar houses, all empty now, until finally, late in the afternoon, she stood before the walls that had once protected the Countess de Corville.

The gates that had been so well guarded two nights ago hung open now; revolutionary slogans had been painted on the high walls surrounding the house. Madeleine found a grim satisfaction in the signs of squalor and decay, yet some dim vestiges of pride caused her to deplore the vandalism. In the ideal world the estate would not have been destroyed; it would have been presented to her.

The wind wailed viciously in the open spaces behind the walls, driving her toward the shelter of the maze. She entered confidently; though it was long since she had wandered here, the intricacies of the twisting paths had been mastered years ago. The broken, leafless branches of the shrubbery provided a blockade against the growing storm, and for that much she was grateful. She would have been happier, however, if the terrain had been more familiar. The troops of gardeners had vanished at the first signs of revolt, leaving a menacingly uncultivated route in their wake. The paths were clogged with branches, and the rough growth of nature left a mystery where once there had been confidence. Before she had time to realize what had become of her, Madeleine Benet was lost.

Each time she turned, shrubbery clawed at her face. The dismally dark borders of the twisted mind that had constructed the maze reached out to punish Madeleine at every turn. Her feet dragged through the wet, heavy snow; her hands pushed at the ragged hedges. Yet she was too bent on vengeance to give way to panic. Instead she took the storm for an ally. Her wanderings left deep tracks in the drifting snow and made it possible for her to avoid walking the same path twice, so that inevitably she reached the center of the maze.

The marble pavilion still stood in the clearing, the white stone with its covering of snow looming up against the gray sky. Madeline wished she could see the sun, but had no doubt that she had at least an hour of daylight left, more than enough time for her to finally destroy the Countess de Corville.

Madeleine paused at the entrance, suddenly afraid that she would find the door locked. She had never even considered the possibility, and the thought that she might be thwarted at the last minute chilled her more than the blasts of wind that buffeted her face with icy crystals. She tugged at the handle desperately, and when she felt it give, she came close to collapsing with relief. The door creaked open and Madeleine stumbled into the anteroom.

The inlaid floor was thick with dust; cobwebs hung from the corners of the ceiling. As Madeleine closed the door carefully to shut out the howling blizzard, she was struck by the odor of the pavilion, in which stale, musty air mingled with the faint fragrance of old perfume. Her memory of the scent made Madeleine feel for the first time the powerful presence of the woman she had served for so many bitter days.

The boudoir of the Countess de Corville was almost dark, and there the spicy scent was even stronger. The room looked much the same as it had when Madeleine last saw the Countess there; the chairs, the dressing table, and the canopied bed were all in place, and so was the long, low marble chest built into the wall. Yet an air of decay loomed over everything. The curtains that hung over the bed and the windows were dusty and bedraggled; a spider scuttled across the floor. The once seductive pavilion looked more like that tomb it had become. Madeleine pulled the purple curtains back from the window, but the feeble gray light that sank through the dirty panes made the scene no less depressing.

She turned toward the marble chest, the thumping of her heart so strong that it was almost painful. She felt colder than she had outside in the snowstorm. The few steps to the other side of the room seemed to take forever, but Madeleine was there before she really wished to be. She kneeled beside the chest that had served Sebastian as a coffin, never doubting that the Countess was inside, yet almost hoping to be wrong. She put the wooden stake and the hammer beside her on the floor, took a deep breath, and raised the lid. The heavy slab of marble moved back ponderously. Madeleine closed her eyes as she pushed it open, but the odor of perfume from the open coffin told her what she would see inside. When the lid fell back against the wall, Madeleine had to move away before she could bring herself to look into the marble chest.

The Countess de Corville, dressed in a bright yellow gown, lay on her back with her hands neatly folded. Her golden hair was piled around her head like a pillow, and a narrow band of crimson encircled her throat. Her skin was as pale as the marble that held her, as pale as the snow that fell outside. There was no touch of color in her face except for the blood on her half-parted lips. Her eyes were closed.

"Damn you," whispered Madeleine. She reached into the coffin, clutched a handful of the long blond hair, and pulled furiously, dragging the Countess de Corville halfway out of the chest. The limp body flopped clumsily as Madeleine rolled it out onto the floor. The Countess fell face down, but Madeleine turned her over with a kick, then reached for the wooden stake. "This isn't enough for you," said Madeleine. "Nothing is enough."

On her knees, the hammer in her right hand and the sharp shaft of wood in her left, Madeleine found her fingers slippery with icy sweat, and trembling so violently that she could hardly hold the stake, which jumped erratically as it hovered over the heart of the Countess. Madeleine pressed the sharp point down toward the vampire's left breast and felt the tender flesh sink under its weight. She raised the hammer, gritting her teeth and holding her breath in an attempt to keep her hands from shaking. She struck the first blow.

The sharp crack of the hammer mingled with a hideously liquid sound, and a crimson fountain splashed into Madeleine's face as she heard the Countess scream. Madeleine shook the blood from her eyes and raised the hammer again. The Countess bit wildly at the air, her dark eyes blind with agony, her hands clawing at the stake as Madeleine drove it deeper into her heart.

The Countess rose, her fingers tearing at Madeleine's face, her blood spattering over both of them. Madeleine pushed her back down to the floor and struck again. The vampire's terrifying shriek subsided into a series of rattling gasps as she grasped the slippery shaft of wood and tried to pull it out. Her hands fell back, and as she writhed in spasms of pain and terror, Madeleine could hear the point of the stake scraping against the floor. She had pounded it right through the body of the Countess.

Madeleine rose and backed away, wiping her hands on her dress as she watched the woman she had hated for so long endure her second death. The Countess clutched at her breast again while dark blood gushed from her mouth, then gave a final shudder as she sank down into a pool of crimson.

Madeleine waited for a minute to make sure the Countess would not move again. Then she dropped the hammer. Its rattle as it hit the floor reverberated through Madeleine's mind like a gigantic cannonade. Her eyes grew dim as the sound turned into a deafening roar, and she collapsed into unconsciousness.

Madeleine woke to darkness, her face resting in something wet. She sat up, every inch of her body aching with cold, and as her eyes adjusted to her dim surroundings, she realized that a stream of clotting blood had trickled across the floor. She had been lying in it. She rose with a shudder and wrapped her cloak around her. She was leaning on a chair, trying to summon up the strength to leave, when she heard a small noise somewhere in the room. She gasped and stiffened, suddenly afraid to move. Her eyes turned toward the corpse of the Countess, but it lay perfectly still while the sound of rustling came again, followed by an ominous creak. The noises came from the direction of the curtained bed.

Madeleine stood paralyzed with horror while a pale hand emerged from behind the dark and dusty curtains. She tried to speak, but no words came.

A gigantic figure crawled out of the bed and struggled to its feet. It shuffled toward her, its head swaying from side to side, its arms outstretched. "Madeleine," it said.

"Andre!"

"I need you, Madeleine. You must help me. I am hungry, Madeleine."

She backed away mechanically, her mind numbed by an idea she could not bear to contemplate. Yet she knew that it was true. Andre's white face rose before her straining eyes, his gaping mouth revealing long teeth and twitching lips that tried to smile.

"Not you, Andre. You can't!"

His cold hands touched her face as Madeleine felt her back meet a wall, and as his head sank toward her throat she screamed.

The thunderous sound of shattering glass and ripping wood shocked Madeleine so much that she thought her heart had stopped, and over Andre's shoulder she saw the window break into hundreds of glittering fragments as something huge and dark invaded the pavilion. Andre whirled to confront the towering presence of Don Sebastian.

"She is mine," snarled Andre. "Find another place to feed."

Sebastian strode forward, followed by a blast of frozen wind that enveloped him in a cloud of shimmering snow. He looked down at the Countess, his face turning into a mask of rage.

"Which of you has done this?" he demanded.

"She has served her purpose," Andre sneered. "She has set me free." He leaped across the room like a beast of prey, his big hands reaching for Sebastian's throat, and the two of them crashed into the curtained bed.

For a moment Madeleine could see nothing but the wild agitation of the dark curtains, then Andre was hurled from the bed. He struck the wall with force enough to kill an ordinary man, but neither of the combatants was mortal. Andre was on his feet at once, his huge fist striking out as Sebastian lunged at him. The blow caught Sebastian on the side of his head and sent him staggering toward Madeleine, who ran from him toward the opposite end of the room. She hoped Sebastian would save her from Andre, but she had no wish to be left alone with either one of them. She would have run for the door, but she would have to pass them both to reach it, and it would have been worth her life to come too close to such snarling beasts.

Andre had both of his gigantic hands wrapped around Sebastian's face and was pulling so hard that he seemed determined to rip flesh from bone. Sebastian's fangs hacked viciously at Andre's fingers and when their grip loosened for an instant he twisted away, turning again to deliver a brutal kick to Andre's side. Madeleine heard a sound that could only have been the splintering of bone, but Andre's howl had more of rage than pain in it. He dodged Sebastian's next kick and rolled across the floor, coming to rest beside the body of the Countess. He grasped the stake embedded in her heart and gave a tremendous yank as he jumped up again.

Madeleine watched in sick dismay as the bloody corpse of the Countess was hauled up by the very weapon that had killed her. Andre swung the limp body around him, and as the stake pulled free, momentum sent the flailing figure of the Countess careening across the room toward Madeleine. She saw in a flash the slack, distorted face and the hideously gaping wound, but she had no time to move before the corpse collapsed on top of her. Madeleine fell shrieking into a corner, the dead arms of her victim wrapped around her, the clotted locks of long hair brushing her face.

Andre grinned ferociously as he gripped the stake like a spear and jabbed at Sebastian's chest. Sebastian squirmed out of range and hurled a chair at his attacker, but it smashed into Andre with no effect except to throw him off balance. Andre lunged again at once, but this time Sebastian caught the end of the stake in his right hand. Andre tried to pull it away, but Sebastian's grip was too powerful; the shaft of wood splintered into sawdust under the pressure of his undead fingers.

Madeleine struggled to be free of her repellent burden, but as she tried to push the dead woman away, she felt her hands sinking into something revoltingly soft and slick. A loathsome odor filled her nostrils as the Countess de Corville, too long out of the grave, dissolved into inevitable decay. Madeleine could only groan and crawl away from the collapsing mass of liquid flesh and brittle bone, but much of it clung to her.

Andre aimed another punch at Sebastian, but before it could land, his jaw fell open as his target faded away into a glowing mist. Madeleine crawled up a wall and turned in time to see Andre leap through the broken window and into the howling storm outside, his fingers grasping fruitlessly at a shifting pattern of green smoke.

Andre staggered through the blizzard, his huge head twisting from side to side, his howls of challenge lost in the roar of the wind. He shook his fist at the dark sky, then reeled backward as a gigantic black shape swooped down on wings as mighty as the wind.

The titantic black bat sank its claws into Andre's head and bore him screaming into the clouds.

Madeleine walked to the window like a woman in a trance, indifferent to the freezing blasts that seemed determined to drive her back. She looked up to see two gigantic monsters battle in the snow-filled sky. The vampire bats wheeled through the blizzard on enormous wings, buffeted by gales as they lunged with fang and claw. Great gouts of blood made scarlet splashes on the blue-white drifts of glistening snow as the uncanny creatures grappled and parted, their struggle obscured by blinding gusts of cold, white wind.

The two vampires dropped earthward in a flurry of tortured twisting, caught in each other's grip. Brittle branches snapped as the monsters plummeted past a frozen tree and crashed to the ground in an explosion of powdered snow. Madeleine realized numbly that she had no way of knowing which of the two might be Sebastian, but when she saw them rise again she knew, for one of the monsters had become a man.

Andre Latour thrashed wildly in a white drift, his arms and legs struggling against the storm, the fangs of an immense bat buried in his throat. The thing dragged Andre toward the pavilion like a dog worrying a bone, until Madeleine thought she could hear Andre's whimpers above the wailing of the wind. Andre's face was caked with snow and ice, and his curly hair had turned dead white. His mouth twitched feebly while whatever blood remained in him was drawn away; his features seemed to collapse inward, leaving nothing but a pale parchment clinging to a hollow skull. Andre had been drained completely dry; there was nothing left of him but skin and bone.

Madeleine turned away, and when she looked again Sebastian stood before her. Her mind was shattered, but she heard her voice ask him a question.

"Why did you save me, Sebastian?"

"Are you safe, then?" His smile was as bitter as the cold.

"Did you come for me, or for the Countess?"

"Neither. I came here to die." His eyes, which had always been so dark, glowed like white-hot coals. Madeleine could not bear to look at them.

"What do you mean?" she asked.

"The blood, Madeleine. The blood of a vampire. It is forbidden." He held out his hands, and she saw to her astonishment that the skin was turning clear as glass. Every vein and artery, each muscle and bone, glowed through the transparent flesh.

"Poison?" gasped Madeleine.

"More than poison, and more than death. It is the light!"

Beams of pure radiance streamed from the sockets of his eyes, and Sebastian's features turned to crystal. His face and hands shone with a light of blinding brilliance, and his clothing began to smoke.

Madeleine covered her eyes and turned away just before the final devastating flash. Still, minutes passed before she could see clearly again, and her life was not long enough to help her forget the ghastly sound of something shattering, or the mingled notes of triumph and terror in Sebastian's final cry.

Madeleine fled toward the maze. She wandered there for hours, the victim of the drifting snow and her own approaching madness; each turn she took seemed to bring her back again to the white pavilion, where she was greeted again and again by the liquid horror that had been the Countess de Corville, and by the desiccated husk that was once Andre Latour.

Yet of Don Sebastian de Villanueva there was no trace at all.

22

Asylum

THE NEXT morning, civilian patrols discovered a young woman with red hair wandering through the streets of Paris. Her clothing was splashed with blood, and she was not able to give an account of herself. In fact, she appeared to have been struck dumb. She was taken into custody, and after due deliberation the authorities ordered her committed to Charenton Asylum.

Several years later, she was joined there by the Marquis de Sade. The turmoil in France had permitted him to rise for a time to the position of magistrate. As a judge, however, the former Marquis proved disappointing to his radical colleagues. He was too merciful; he even refused the opportunity to prosecute the mother-in-law whose machinations had kept him imprisoned for over a decade. He fell from power, failed as a playwright, and was soon reduced to poverty. Finally he was judged to be insane after his arrest as the author of two obscene books, *Justine* and *Juliette*.

The director of the asylum granted de Sade permission to stage his plays with the inmates as his actors, reasoning that such activity would be therapeutic, and the silent woman with red hair appeared in all de Sade's productions until his death in 1814.

The speechless actress survived the author of her greatest roles only briefly, and both of them were buried in the asylum's cemetery. Her name was never discovered.

Dr. Guillotin died in the same year. He nearly became a victim of the device that bore his name, but Robespierre was overthrown and lost his own head in time to save Guillotin's. He retired from public life at the age of seventy-six, still protesting the fact that his name had been bestowed on the invention he had inspired. He died peacefully at home, burdened with years and blessed with a dubious immortality.